A COLD DAY IN HELL

*The Spring Creek Encounters,
the Cedar Creek Fight
with Sitting Bull's Sioux, and the
Dull Knife Battle, November 25, 1876*

Terry C. Johnston

BANTAM BOOKS

NEW YORK • TORONTO • LONDON • SYDNEY • AUCKLAND

A COLD DAY IN HELL

A Bantam Book / February 1996

ISBN 0-553-29976-X

Published simultaneously in the United States and Canada

Bantam Books are published by Bantam Books, a division of Bantam
Doubleday Dell Publishing Group, Inc. Its trademark, consisting of the
words "Bantam Books" and the portrayal of a rooster, is Registered in
U.S. Patent and Trademark Office and in other countries. Marca Reg-
istrada. Bantam Books, 1540 Broadway, New York, New York 10036.

PRINTED IN THE UNITED STATES OF AMERICA

OPM   10 9 8 7 6 5 4 3 2 1

1.75

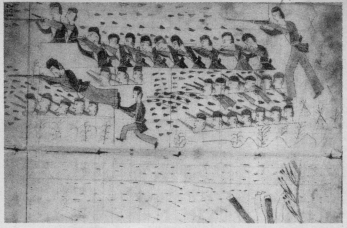

Top: Last Bull "Ledger": Facing soldiers at Powder River Fight *(Courtesy American Museum of Natural History)*
Middle: Colonel Ranald S. Mackenzie in the mid-1870s *(Courtesy University of Oklahoma Western History Collections)*
Bottom: High Bull "Victory Roster": Little Sun striking two Shoshone; roster captured from Sgt. Brown, 7th U.S. Cavalry, at the Little Bighorn *(Courtesy National Museum of the American Indian, Smithsonian Institution)*

with admiration and appreciation
I dedicate this novel to
Ken and Cheri Graves
of the Red Fork Ranch,
and to
Mike Freidel
of Vermillion, South Dakota,
who all three graciously opened up their
hearts and their homes and allowed me to spend
the better part of a day moving across the
historic Dull Knife Battlefield
as few have since that dramatic battle:
from horseback.

Cast
of
Characters

Seamus Donegan   Samantha Donegan

Military

Lieutenant General Philip H. Sheridan—Division of the Missouri
Brigadier General George C. Crook—Department of the Platte
Colonel William B. Hazen—commanding Sixth U.S. Infantry, Fort Buford, D.T.
Colonel Nelson A. Miles—commanding Fifth U.S. Infantry, Tongue River Cantonment, M.T.
Colonel Ranald S. Mackenzie—Fourth U.S. Cavalry, commanding cavalry wing, Powder River Expedition (brevet BRIGADIER GENERAL)
Colonel Richard I. Dodge—Twenty-third Infantry, commanding infantry wing, Powder River Expedition
Lieutenant Colonel Elwell S. Otis—Twenty-second U.S. Infantry (brevet BRIGADIER GENERAL)
Lieutenant Colonel William P. Carlin—commandant at Standing Rock Sioux Reservation, D.T., Seventeenth U.S. Infantry
Lieutenant Colonel Joseph Whistler—Fifth U.S. Infantry
Major George A. Gordon—Fifth U.S. Cavalry (Camp Robinson) (brevet COLONEL)

Major Caleb H. Carlton—Third U.S. Cavalry, commanding at Fort Fetterman (brevet COLONEL)

Major Edwin F. Townsend—Commanding Officer, Fort Laramie, W.T. (brevet COLONEL)

Captain Andrew S. Burt—H Company, Ninth U.S. Infantry

Captain Charles W. Miner—G Company, Twenty-second U.S. Infantry

Captain Malcolm McArthur—C Company, Seventeenth U.S. Infantry

Captain Louis H. Sanger—G Company, Seventeenth U.S. Infantry (brevet MAJOR)

Captain Mott Hooton—H Company, Twenty-second U.S. Infantry

Captain Augustus Randall—Quartermaster, Fifth U.S. Infantry, Tongue River Cantonment, M.T.

Captain Wyllys Lyman—I Company, Fifth U.S. Infantry

Captain James S. Casey—A Company, Fifth U.S. Infantry (brevet MAJOR)

Captain Andrew S. Bennett—B Company, Fifth U.S. Infantry

Captain Edmond Butler—C Company, Fifth U.S. Infantry

Captain Simon Snyder—F Company, Fifth U.S. Infantry

Captain Clarence B. Mauck—Fourth U.S. Cavalry (brevet MAJOR)

Captain Alfred B. Taylor—Troop L., Fifth U.S. Cavalry

Captain George M. ("Black Jack") Randall—Chief of Scouts, Powder River Campaign Twenty-third Infantry (brevet MAJOR)

Captain John Lee—D Troop, Fourth U.S. Cavalry

Captain Wirt Davis—F Troop, Fourth U.S. Cavalry

Captain William C. Hemphill—I Troop, Fourth U.S. Cavalry

Captain Henry W. Wessels—H Troop, Third U.S. Cavalry

Captain Gerald Russell—K Troop, Third U.S. Cavalry

Captain John M. Hamilton—H Troop, Fifth U.S. Cavalry

Captain James "Teddy" Egan—K Troop, Second U.S. Cavalry

Captain J. B. Campbell—Fourth U.S. Artillery battalion commander (brevet MAJOR)

Captain John V. Furey—quartermaster, Powder River Expedition

Captain Edwin Pollock—Ninth U.S. Infantry, commander of Reno Cantonment (brevet MAJOR)

First Lieutenant John Bourke—Acting Assistant Adjutant General for Expedition

First Lieutenant Walter S. Schuyler—aide-de-camp to General Crook

First Lieutenant Oskaloosa M. Smith—H Company, Twenty-second U.S. Infantry (Battalion Adjutant)

First Lieutenant William Conway—H Company, Twenty-second U.S. Infantry

First Lieutenant Benjamin C. Lockwood—G Company, Twenty-second U.S. Infantry

First Lieutenant Mason Carter—K Company, Fifth U.S. Infantry (brevet CAPTAIN)

First Lieutenant Theodore F. Forbes—G Company, Fifth U.S. Infantry

First Lieutenant Robert McDonald—D Company, Fifth U.S. Infantry

First Lieutenant William Philo Clark—I Troop, Second Cavalry, aide-de-camp to Brigadier General Crook

First Lieutenant Henry W. Lawton—Fourth U.S. Cavalry, campaign Quartermaster for the cavalry (brevet CAPTAIN)

First Lieutenant Charles M. Callahan—B Troop, Fourth U.S. Cavalry

First Lieutenant John A. McKinney—M Troop, Fourth U.S. Cavalry

First Lieutenant Oscar Elting—Troop K, Third U.S. Cavalry (acting agent at Red Cloud Agency after 31 June)

First Lieutenant Charles Rockwell—Fifth U.S. Cavalry, expedition commissary officer

Second Lieutenant Alfred C. Sharpe—Company H, Twenty-second U.S. Infantry

Second Lieutenant William H. Kell—Company K, Twenty-second U.S. Infantry

Second Lieutenant James D. Nickerson—C Company, Seventeenth U.S. Infantry

Second Lieutenant Frank S. Hinkle—Fifth U.S. Infantry

Second Lieutenant Hobart K. Bailey—Fifth U.S. Infantry, aide-de-camp to Colonel Miles

Second Lieutenant James Worden Pope—E Company, Fifth U.S. Infantry

Second Lieutenant David Q. Rousseau—H Company, Fifth U.S. Infantry

Second Lieutenant William H. S. Bowen—Fifth U.S. Infantry

Second Lieutenant James H. Whitten—Fifth U.S. Infantry

Second Lieutenant Joseph H. Dorst—Fourth U.S. Cavalry, Regimental Adjutant

Second Lieutenant J. W. Martin—B Troop, Fourth U.S. Cavalry

Second Lieutenant J. Wesley Rosenquest—M Troop, Fourth U.S. Cavalry

Second Lieutenant Harrison G. Otis—M Troop, Fourth U.S. Cavalry

Second Lieutenant Homer W. Wheeler—G Troop, Fifth U.S. Cavalry

Second Lieutenant Hayden Delaney—Ninth U.S. Infantry

Lieutenant Henry Allison—Second U.S. Cavalry

Lieutenant O. L. Wieting—Twenty-third Infantry

First Sergeant Thomas H. Forsyth—M Troop, Fourth U.S. Cavalry

First Sergeant James Turpin—L Troop, Fifth U.S. Cavalry

First Sergeant James S. McClellan—H Troop, Third U.S. Cavalry

Sergeant Patrick Kelly—F Company, Twenty-second U.S. Infantry

Sergeant William Hathaway—H Company, Twenty-second U.S. Infantry

Sergeant Frank Murray—M Troop, Fourth U.S. Cavalry

Sergeant Joseph Sudsberger—M Troop, Fourth U.S. Cavalry

†Sergeant Robert W. McPhelan—E Company, Fifth U.S. Infantry

Corporal William J. Linn—M Troop, Fourth U.S. Cavalry

†Private John Geyer—I Company, Fifth U.S. Infantry

Private William Earl Smith—Fourth U.S. Cavalry, expedition orderly to Colonel Ranald S. Mackenzie

Private Edward Wilson—F Troop, Fourth U.S. Cavalry

Private Thomas Ryan—M Troop, Fourth U.S. Cavalry

Private Jonathan Kline—G Troop, Fifth U.S. Cavalry

Trumpeter Richard Hicks—K Troop, Fourth U.S. Cavalry

Charles T. Gibson—Acting Assistant Surgeon, Glendive Cantonment

Joseph R. Gibson—chief medical officer, Powder River Expedition

L.A. LaGarde—army surgeon, Powder River Expedition

Marshall W. Wood—assistant army surgeon, Powder River Expedition

Civilian

Elizabeth Burt

Martha Luhn

Nettie Capron

Maynard Collins—trader at Fort Laramie

Johnny Bruguier ("Big Leggings")

John B. Sharpe—wagon-master, Powder River Expedition
Tom Moore—pack-master of the Powder River Expedition mule
    train
Jerry Roche—reporter, New York *Herald*

Army Scouts

Frank Grouard ("The Grabber")
Billy Hunter—half-breed guide with the Pawnee Battalion
Billy Garnett—interpreter with the Powder River Expedition
Robert Jackson—Glendive Cantonment
William Jackson—Tongue River Cantonment
Luther Sage "Yellowstone" Kelly—Tongue River Cantonment
Victor Smith—Glendive Cantonment
Billy Cross—Tongue River Cantonment
Joe Culbertson—interpreter, scout with Miles
Todd Randall—squawman with Sioux wife among Red Cloud's
    people
George Boyd—Tongue River Cantonment
John "Liver-Eating" Johnston—Tongue River Cantonment
Tom LeForge—Tongue River Cantonment
Major Frank North—commanding, Pawnee Battlion
Captain Luther North—second in command, Pawnee Battlion
Lieutenant S. E. Cushing—Pawnee Battalion
Tom Cosgrove—commanding Shoshone battalion
Yancy Eckles—second in command, Shoshone battalion
Baptiste Pourier ("Big Bat")
Bill Rowland ("Long Knife")—Cheyenne squawman, interpreter
    for Powder River Expedition
"Old" Bill Hamilton—scout on Powder River Expedition

Lakota

White Bull	Sitting Bull
One Horn	Gall
Long Feather	Bear's Face
No Neck	Red Skirt
High Bear	Jumping Bull
Fire-What-Man	Bull Eagle
Black Eagle	Rising Sun
Small Bear	Standing Bear
Spotted Elk	Red Cloud
Pretty Bear	Yellow Eagle
John Sans Arc	Red Shirt

Lakota (cont.)

Jackass   Three Bears
Feathers on the Head   Spotted Tail

Arikara/Ree

Bear Plume   White Antelope

Cheyenne

"Tse-tsehese-staeste"
"Those Who Are Hearted Alike"

Crow Split Nose   Last Bull
Sits in the Night   Morning Star
Little Wolf   Old Bear
Young Two Moon   Beaver Claws
Wolf Tooth   Brave Bear
Wooden Leg   Left Handed Wolf
Beaver Dam   Gypsum
Hail   Crow Necklace
High Wolf   Brave Wolf
Black White Man   Working Man
Buffalo Calf Woman   Braided Locks
Black Hairy Dog   Coal Bear
Box Elder   Medicine Top
Spotted Blackbird   Wrapped Hair
Yellow Eagle   Turtle Road
Medicine Bear   Long Jaw

at ambush ravine:

Curly   Little Hawk
Strange Owl   Bull Hump
Bobtail Horse   Little Shield
Two Bull   High Bull
Burns Red in the Sun   Walking Calf
Hawk's Visit   Four Sacred Spirits
Old Bull   Antelope
Buffalo Chief   Two Bulls
Wooden Nose   Charging Bear
Tall Sioux   Dog
White Frog

with Little Wolf at mouth of the ravine:

White Frog	Two Bulls
Bald-Faced Bull	Walking Whirlwind
Comes Together	Yellow Nose
White Horse	Big Horse
Little Horse	Beaver Heart
Big Head	Walks Last
White Buffalo	Young Turkey Leg
Sitting Bear	Fox
Stops in a Hurry	

Cheyenne scouts and in-laws with Bill Rowland:

Colonel Hard Robe	Roan Bear
Little Fish	Old Crow
Cut Nose	Satchel/Wolf Satchel
Hard Robe	Bird
Blown Away	

Pawnee

Ralph Weeks	Frank White
Peter Headman ("Boy Chief"/*Pe-isk-le-shar*)	
Rus Roberts	

Shoshone

Dick Washakie	Anzi

Arapaho

Sharp Nose	Old Eagle
Six Feathers	Little Fork
White Horse	William Friday—interpreter

Casualties

Spring Creek Encounter:

Private John Donahoe—G Company, Twenty-second U.S. Infantry (wounded)

Sergeant Robert Anderson—G Company, Twenty-second U.S. Infantry (wounded)

Private Francis Marriaggi—G Company, Seventeenth U.S. Infantry (wounded)

Cedar Creek Encounter:
Private John Geyer—I Company, Fifth U.S. Infantry (wounded)
Sergeant Robert W. Phelan—E Company, Fifth U.S. Infantry

Dull Knife Battle:
*First Lieutenant John A. McKinney—M Troop, Fourth U.S. Cavalry
*Corporal Patrick F. Ryan—D Troop, Fourth U.S. Cavalry
*Private John Sullivan—B Troop, Fourth U.S. Cavalry (only soldier scalped in the battle)
*Private James Baird—D Troop, Fourth U.S. Cavalry (only soldier buried on battlefield)
*Private Alexander Keller—E Troop, Fourth U.S. Cavalry
*Private John Menges—H Troop, Fifth U.S. Cavalry
*Private Alexander McFarland—L Troop, Fifth U.S. Cavalry (died on November 28 of his wounds)
†First Sergeant Thomas H. Forsyth—M Troop, Fourth U.S. Cavalry
†Sergeant James Cunningham—H Troop, Third U.S. Cavalry
†Private Philip Holden—H Troop, Third U.S. Cavalry
†Private George Talmadge—H Troop, Third U.S. Cavalry

---

*dead
†wounded

The fact of the case is the operations of Generals Terry and Crook will not bear criticism, and my only thought has been to let them sleep. I approved what was done, for the sake of the troops, but in doing so, I was not approving much, as you know.

—Lieutenant General Philip H. Sheridan (to General Wm. T. Sherman)

The [Battle of Cedar Creek] was no more bloody or decisive than the fight with Otis a week earlier, but it afforded Miles the chance to maneuver an entire regiment and laid the groundwork for much self-congratulation.

—Robert M. Utley
The Lance and the Shield

The encounter [at Cedar Creek] between the colonel [Miles] and chief [Sitting Bull] is one of the most striking episodes in the Indian Wars. It is as replete with imperious demands and arrogant challenges to combat as any knightly tale . . .

—Fairfax Downey
Indian Fighting Army

Neither the wild tribes, nor the Government Indian Scouts ever adopted any of the white soldiers' tactics. They thought their own much better.

—Captain Luther H. North
Pawnee Battalion

The noble red man is not a fool. He is a cunning no-mad, who hates civilization, and knows how to get all out of it that pleases him—whiskey, tobacco, rations and blankets, idleness in peace and a rattling fight whenever he is ready for it. And when he is beaten he returns to the arms of his guardians on the reservation, bringing his store of white scalps with him as pleasing memorials of the good time he had.

It is time to stop all that. The continent is getting too crowded.

—Editorial
New York *Herald*

This expedition was one of the best equipped that ever started on an Indian campaign ... [The Cheyenne] were foemen worthy of Mackenzie's or anybody else's steel. The battle which ensued was in some respects one of the most terrible in Western history, and in its results exemplified, as few others have done, the horrible character of war.
—Cyrus Townsend Brady
Indian Fights and Fighters

Never again would Northern Cheyenne material culture reach the heights of richness and splendor that the people knew before that bitter day in the Big Horns.
—Peter J. Powell
Sweet Medicine

Foreword

At the beginning of some chapters and some scenes, you will read the very same news stories devoured by the officers' wives and the civilians employed at army posts or those living in adjacent frontier settlements—just what Samantha Donegan herself read—stories taken from the front page of the daily newspapers that arrived as much as a week or more late, that delay due to the wilderness distances to be traveled by freight carriers.

Copied verbatim, word for word, from the headlines and graphic accounts of the day, remember as you read that these newspaper stories were the only news available for those people who had a most personal stake in the army's last great campaign—those people who had tearfully watched a loved one march off to war that autumn of the Great Sioux War of 1876.

By starting some chapters and scenes with an article taken right out of the day's international, national, and regional headlines, I hope that you will be struck with the immediacy of each day's front page as you finish reading that day's news—just as Samantha Donegan would have been from her relative safety at Fort Laramie. But, unlike her and the rest of those left behind who would have to live out the days and weeks in apprehension and fear because the frontier was often terrifyingly bereft of reliable news, you will then find yourself thrust back into the historical action of an army once more marching into the teeth of a high plains winter—this time to finish what it had begun nine months before in the trampled snow along the Powder River.

Success, or failure . . . one thing was certain. It was destined to be another cold day in hell.

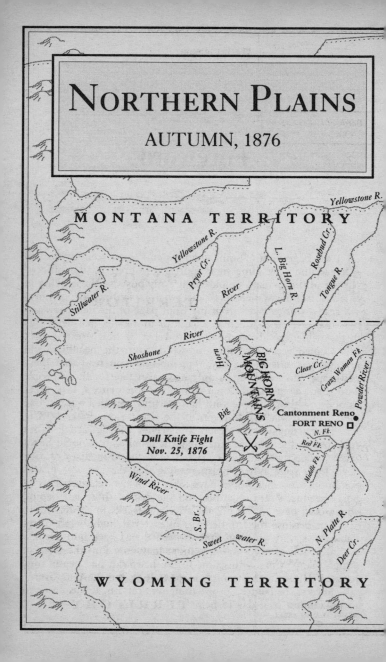

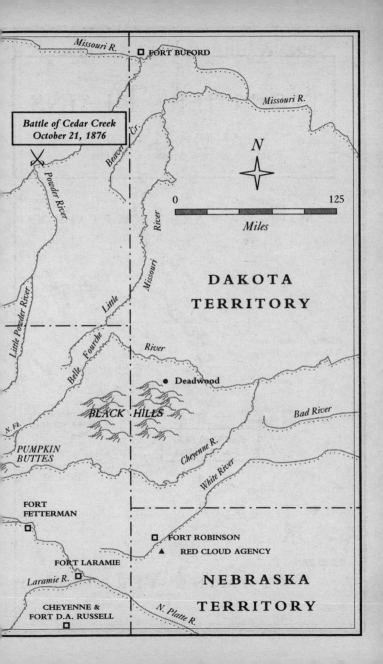

Battle of Cedar Creek
October 21, 1876

Missouri R. □ FORT BUFORD

Missouri R.

Beaver Cr.

Powder River

N

0   125
Miles

Little Powder River

Belle Fourche

Missouri

River

Little

DAKOTA

TERRITORY

River

● Deadwood

BLACK HILLS

Bad River

N. Fk.

PUMPKIN
BUTTES

Cheyenne R.

White River

FORT
FETTERMAN
□

□ FORT ROBINSON
▲ RED CLOUD AGENCY

FORT LARAMIE
□

Laramie R.

NEBRASKA

CHEYENNE &
FORT D.A. RUSSELL
□

N. Platte R.

TERRITORY

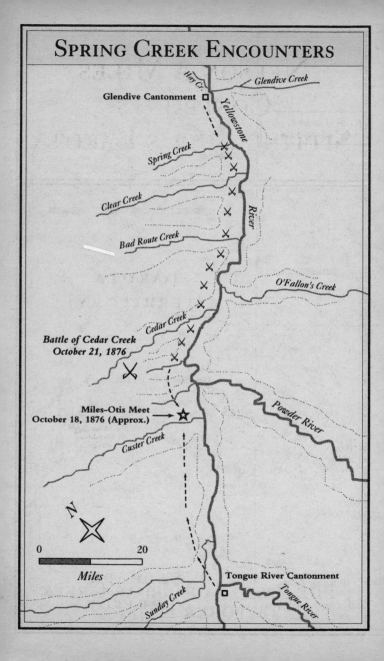

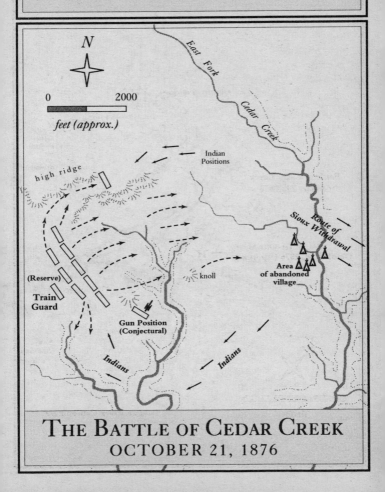

NELSON A MILES CONFRONTS SITTING BULL'S LAKOTA

N

0 — 2000

feet (approx.)

East Fork

Cedar Creek

high ridge

Indian Positions

Route of Sioux Withdrawal

Area of abandoned village

knoll

(Reserve)

Train Guard

Gun Position (Conjectural)

Indians

Indians

THE BATTLE OF CEDAR CREEK
OCTOBER 21, 1876

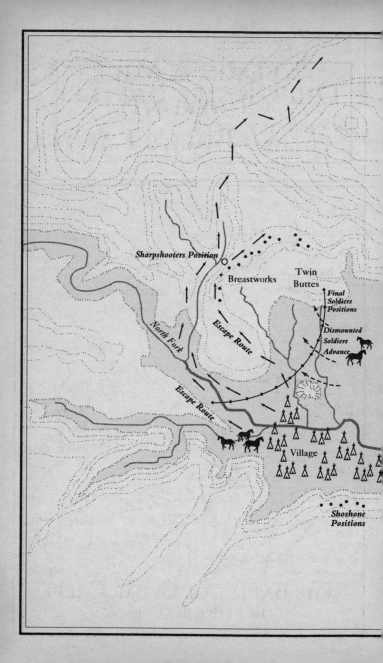

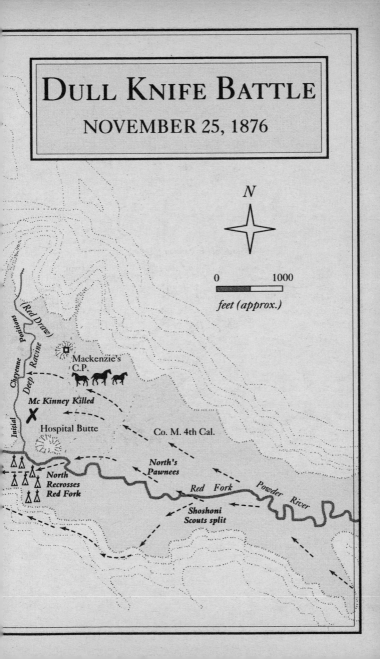

DULL KNIFE BATTLE

NOVEMBER 25, 1876

N

0   1000

feet (approx.)

Cheyenne positions

(Red Draw)

Deep Ravine

Mackenzie's C.P.

Mc Kinney Killed

Initial

Hospital Butte

Co. M. 4th Cal.

North's Pawnees

North Recrosses Red Fork

Red Fork

Powder River

Shoshoni Scouts split

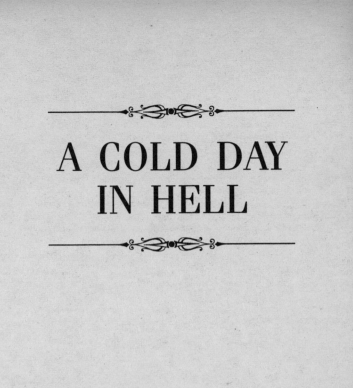

A COLD DAY
IN HELL

Prologue

6 October, 1876

"So when does Sheridan say he wants you riding off for Camp Robinson to keep an eye on Red Cloud's camp?" asked Seamus Donegan, his gray eyes reflecting the pulsing gleam of that dim-red glow of his pipe bowl as he drew smoke through the stem, those eyes then flicking another anxious look at the building fondly called Old Bedlam by those stationed here at Fort Laramie.

"He's give me till the morning," Frank Grouard answered. Then cleared his throat before he continued in that way of a person about to address a grave matter. "Seems worrying is a man's part in all of this birthing business, Irishman. 'Specially when it's his first."

The tall man with the thick crop of beard only nodded, sipping from his clay mug of whiskey, frosty streamers rising from his nostrils in the hoary cold of that night. The anxious father-to-be and the half-breed scout had stepped outside the sutler's saloon to catch a breath of the cold, dry autumn air. "Aye. But it makes it no easier: I wish there were something I could do other'n this bleeming wait and this god-blame-med worrying."

Close by, a woman's rising scream raised the hackles on the back of Frank's own neck. He watched that eerie sound cause Donegan to sputter, drawing down on that last swallow, his gray eyes registering grave concern as he gazed with concentration and smoky intensity on the building right next door.

Pushing some of his long brown hair back over his shoulder, Seamus murmured, "Maybe there's something I could be doing—"

"Come inside with me, Irishman," Grouard suggested, gently tugging at Donegan's elbow. "That's what you can do. She's got all the help in the world right now."

"Dear Mither of God," Seamus whispered as he turned toward the doorway with Grouard, gazing one last time over his shoulder at Old Bedlam where his wife lay—giving birth to their first born.

"C'mon," Grouard urged again. "They're all mothers with her, every last one of 'em. Ain't nothing to it—women's been giving birth this same way ever since the start of time."

His bloodshot eyes found the half-breed's as they turned the corner of the mud-walled building and stepped into the half circle of greasy yellow light splashing from the open doorway at that moment held open by John Bourke.

"Looks like I showed up at just the right moment," the thirty-year-old Lieutenant called out, bowing graciously low at the waist and motioning the two civilian scouts inside. "We just got word over at Townsend's that your wife is about to deliver." He saluted some soldiers as the men shuffled past him into the warm, bright, lamplit interior of Sutler Collins's watering hole. "From the look on your face, I figure you could use another drink. Can I buy you one, Seamus?" He pounded the Irishman on the back as the three snaked through the tables toward the bar in the low-roofed saloon that sat beside the sutler's trading room.

"I oughtta be doing something other'n drinking," Donegan grumped as Bourke motioned the barkeep to bring them all a mug of apple beer.

"Can't say as any of us ever get good at this, Irishman," announced Andrew Burt as he moved toward the trio at the bar. "Lord knows I've had enough of this waiting myself. But Elizabeth's there with your woman, and there's three others besides, Seamus. Things'll be fine now. Only a matter of nature taking its own sweet time."

"See there, Irishman," Frank replied as cheerfully as he could, not knowing a damned thing about this birthing matter. "The good cap'n here speaks from experience. No need to worry. Time like this, what a woman needs is other women to help out what was always meant to be a natural thing anyway."

"Grouard's right," Bourke said. "Just look at you, man— those hands of yours, the way they're shaking. That lip of yours, how it's trembling. Why, if you poked your nose in there, you'd do nothing but flux things up real good!"

"Wouldn't he now?" Grouard cheered, grabbing the Irishman by the nape of the neck and shaking him affectionately. "Seamus is a good man to have along on a scout, or creeping past a Lakota camp—but he'd be a goddamned bull in the parlor around a birthin' woman!"

As they all laughed, Captain Burt said, "Why don't you three come join Captain Wessels and me yonder at our table?" He motioned to the far corner where Henry W. Wessels of the Third Cavalry waved them over. "Seamus can keep his eye on the door, where Elizabeth will be sure to send word once Seamus has become a father."

"A f-father," Donegan repeated as the others ushered him stumble-footed toward the far table where Wessels, Lieutenant Walter S. Schuyler, and two other officers sat sipping at their whiskey or savoring their apple beer, a shipment come up from Cheyenne just that afternoon.

John Bourke settled into one of the ladder-back chairs, worn down to a warm, yellowed pine, then declared, "Frank—I want to hear about your race with Captain Jack."

"Yes!" cried Schuyler, like Bourke, an aide-de-camp to General George C. Crook. He hoisted his glass of pale whiskey into the air. "I've heard tell bits and pieces of the tale—but not a chunk of it from the horse's mouth."

Bourke tugged Donegan down onto a half-log bench beside him and turned to tell Grouard, "Start back to when the general gave you the dispatches you were to carry to the nearest telegraph."

Frank set his mug of beer down, savoring the sweet tang of it at the back of his tongue as he swiped foam from his mustache and gathered his thoughts. "Seems now like it was forever ago."

"I know what you mean," Donegan agreed with a glance at the door.

Bourke put his arm around the Irishman's shoulder, saying, "We haven't been back here but a few days now, Seamus. G'won, Frank—while our father-to-be is waiting for his grand news—tell us the story of your race with Crawford from the Black Hills."

"You want me to start back when I rode off from the command?" Grouard asked.

"Yes. Back to when the general gave you his dispatches he wanted put on the wire to Sheridan," Burt added.

Clearing his throat, Grouard stared at the low ceiling a mo-

ment to recapture the chronology of that contest of wills and
stamina he had waged against young Jack Crawford. "I was with
Colonel Mills when that run for it started."

"In Whitewood City, right?" Wessels asked.

"Right. Gone there with Lieutenant Bubb of Commissary
for supplies while the general brung up the rest to the Belle
Fourche. Folks in Whitewood treated us good when we got there
that night way after dark. With dawn Mills would start out to
buy up near every bite those hungry soldiers could eat. Before I
went off to find a place to sleep, I told Crawford for him to be
on hand come daylight—so he could go with Bubb to help out
loading supplies and hauling it all back to Crook's men. 'You're
to stay with the command,' I told him. 'What're you off to do?'
Jack asked me. 'I've got the general's telegrams to get through,'
I says."

"Did you know he was buffaloing you then?" Donegan
asked, then turned anxiously on his bench as a pair of soldiers
bolted into the saloon and hurried to the bar.

"No," Frank answered. "But I had my suspicions: just the
way he was acting—trying to go off on his own two times when
we was in Whitewood Canyon. But, damn, if Colonel Mills
wouldn't let him slip away from us! Then after we got down to
Crook City, Captain Jack said he was going off to sleep at a
friend's camp. Made sense to me—I didn't suspect a thing.
Crawford's been around the Hills for a long time, so I thought
nothing more of it when he told me that he'd be back come the
break of day."

"But you didn't see him in Whitewood that morning, did
you?" Bourke inquired.

With a shrug Grouard replied, "At the time it didn't make
no never-mind if I didn't see him. Wasn't looking for him, I
s'pose. All I done was splash some water on my face afore I
headed out to find some breakfast. Only one thing on my mind
back then: getting to Deadwood with the general's dispatches."
He patted the front of his shirt.

"Were you carrying news for any of them correspondents?"
Schuyler asked.

"Three of 'em."

Bourke said, "Bet them three each paid you good to get
their stories on the wire before any of the rest, right?"

With a sly grin the swarthy half-breed answered, "Let's just
say those fellas agreed to make a hard ride well worth my while."

Laughter rose all around that table, then Burt said, "So, I suppose you're buying tonight, eh, Frank?"

As the rest laughed again, Wessels asked, "I know that road as good as any man outside of Teddy Egan. So tell me: where'd you finally find out Crawford was gone on ahead?"

"Down at Deadwood, it was," Grouard answered. "I had them reporters' money to trade in my broke-down army horse and get me a good mount when I reached a livery at Deadwood. So when I went in the stable, what you s'pose I saw?"

Andy Burt replied, "I heard tell you spotted Crawford's mule tied up there!"

"Damn right I did," Frank said with a scowl. "Asked the stable man where it come from, who brung it there."

"He tell you?" Bourke asked.

"Not at first. Looked right suspicious about it—like he'd been warned to lie through his teeth, most-like. Finally he owned up to that mule coming in about five that morning. So I asked him where the man was come riding that mule into town."

"But he'd left already, hadn't he?" Bourke asked.

Frank nodded. "On a goddamned horse the livery man sold him. Making tracks for Custer City without so much as a minute's wait."

"That was the first idea you had Crawford was carrying dispatches for Davenport?" Donegan asked as he set his mug down on the table.

"By that time I was getting real angry, so the livery man owned up to that too. Jack been bragging high and low how he got his five hunnert dollars to get Davenport's story on the wire ahead of Crook's official report."

Bourke said, "And here you had just galloped off from Crook thinking you had all the dispatches from every reporter with the column."

"Including that snake-oil drummer Davenport," Grouard replied. "What that son of a bitch had done to make out like everything was on the up and up, he give me a copy of what he already sneaked over to Crawford—when he give Captain Jack orders to get his story to the telegraph twelve hours before Crook's official report."

"That son of a bitch wanted an exclusive," Bourke growled. "Damn his copper-backed hide! Davenport's made it plain all summer long that he's had a big bone to pick with the general—but to go behind Crook's back the way he did like this!"

"Army business, that's what Crawford was fooling with!" Burt exclaimed angrily.

Grouard held up his hands for silence, quieting the rest. "In the end, Davenport got his due, fellas."

"That's right," Donegan added, glancing at those around the table. "We heard tell he's down in Cheyenne City this very night, sicker'n a dog."

Wessels roared, "Served Davenport right—that puffed-up son of a bitch. Glad you whipped Crawford in the race!"

"Didn't look like it was going to come out that way at first," Frank explained dramatically. "General's plan was for me to hire another man in Deadwood to get Crook's dispatches through. But when I found out Crawford had the jump on Crook the way he did—there was only one thing for me to do."

"You gotta hand it to Crawford, Frank," Donegan said with no little admiration. "He took off through some rugged country thick with Injins in the blackest part of night—them Sioux been raiding all around there."

Schuyler agreed eagerly. "Just two days before, we heard a war party had jumped a fella no more'n two hundred yards from the main street in Crook City itself!"

Bourke leaned in, eager expectation lighting his face. "But if anyone was going to overtake Captain Jack, it could only be you, Grouard!"

"I told that liveryman to lemme have the best horse he had—but he said his best horse went with Crawford. So I grabbed up that bastard by the front of his coat and told him he better bring up the next-best horse or he'd be bleeding out of more holes than he figured possible."

"You get yourself a good horse?" Burt asked.

"Yep. I ended up riding that horse into the ground too," Frank replied. "But before I left, I told the stable man to get that animal bellied up on oats and saddled. I'd be back, just as soon as I had a local fella, Mart Gibbens, take me over to the bank and fetch me five hunnert dollars on the general's authorization order." He patted his breast pocket, then leaned back in his chair as he took another swig on his beer.

Wessels asked, "You got your money, right?"

With a nod Grouard continued. "Climbed into the saddle, tugged my hat down tight, and asked Gibbens what time it was. He told me it was ten-thirty. I didn't say another word. Instead I leaned down low against that horse's ear, whispering to him that I wanted all the bottom he had—then whipped that son of a big buck right down Deadwood's main street to beat the band that bright morning. Figuring then and there it was going to be one ugly ride to reach the telegraph at Fort Laramie—two hunnert miles off as the crow flies."

Grouard went on to enthrall his listeners as he worked into his story as a man would work up a thick, soapy lather conditioning his saddle or bridle. Explaining that Crawford already had a good jump on him—what with leaving Crook City that evening of 12 September while Grouard slept—Frank said he soon realized there should be soldiers at two places on the Black Hills Road between Deadwood and Laramie. One place or the other he figured he might convince an officer to send a fresh courier on with Crook's messages.

"So how far that first horse get you?" Donegan asked.

"Figure it was something on the order of twenty-five miles," Frank said as Bourke gathered up the empty mugs with a clatter after setting down some full ones. "Damn if he didn't give out about five hunnert yards from a road ranch. Packed my saddle and all in by foot from there."

"So did you buy a horse from the ranchkeeper?" Bourke inquired.

With a shrug of no little importance, Grouard replied, "There was three horses out front, all tied up when I walked in there. Looked 'em all over before I decided on the likeliest one. Was starting to throw my saddle on him when the ranch man comes out hollering, asking me what the hell I thought I was doing."

"He have a gun pulled on you?"

"No, didn't have a gun on him what I could see—but I figured there had to be at least one gun inside pointed my way. Tried to tell the fella I was riding dispatches for General Crook, even pulled out my orders to show him—then tightened the cinch on the horse, asking him how much he wanted for the gelding. Man said he wouldn't sell it, but he did want to do what he could for Crook and his soldiers—so he told me to give him fifteen dollars for the use, then see that the horse got back to him."

Burt asked, "Did you get that horse back to the man?"

After another swig of the warm beer, Frank said, "That'un dropped dead under me too. By the time I reached the next road ranch."

"Sweet Mither of God! How many horses you kill on that race?" Donegan asked, his eyes bouncing back to the doorway.

"Killed three of 'em. And the other three I used up so bad, they ain't worth a damn no more," Frank grumbled sourly. "Damn shameful thing to do to good horseflesh too. Goddamn that Crawford anyway."

"What was he doing at this time?" Bourke asked.

"S'pose he was staying just ahead of me ... leastwise through those first four horses I gone and run into the ground."

"When did you finally catch up to him?" Wessels asked.

"First I had to knock a big German off his horse," Frank boasted.

Walter Schuyler clapped with excitement. "By damn! Tell us about that part!"

"Seems that next-to-last horse I rode was all but done in. For as far as I could see ahead of me, wasn't a ranch in that piece of country. Horse under me was in a bad way, about to give out when I spotted a rider coming around the hill toward me on the road. I got down right there while he was coming up on me, pulled my saddle off, and let my horse go just before the rider reached me. I grabbed hold of his bridle and told him I wanted his horse. He was a big-boned German, that one was, likely could come close to making two of me—but he didn't have a gun on him that I could see."

"Did he make trouble for you?"

Frank nodded with a dour chuckle. "I reached right up under his leg, loosing the cinch as he goes to squalling—telling me I can't have his goddamned horse and cussing me two ways of Sunday. Told him I had to have it, and why. 'Bout then I needed him off the horse so I could set my saddle on—so I pulled him right off into the road. He started for me, so I finally had to pull my belt gun and hold it on him. All the time I was putting my saddle on, I was telling him I'd pay him for the animal. But he kept on telling me he wasn't going to sell him. Over and over he said I'd hang for horse stealing. So I told him I'd hire the goddamned horse out. How much did he want—but he'd none of that neither."

Andy Burt asked, "You end up just riding off?"

"Was near to it when he saw that I was about to," Frank replied. "Told him one last time he had that last chance to get his money before I was gone. Guess he figured that was that, so he said he'd sell for eighty dollars. I throwed him his money right there in the middle of that Laramie Road and kicked that horse in the ribs. It took off something smart."

"Eighty dollars for a horse?" Burt exclaimed.

"So did you end up with a eighty-dollar horse?" Seamus inquired.

Frank smiled. "That was no eighty-dollar horse, Irishman. Worth much more'n that. I'll tell you, boys: that was the best bargain I ever made for a horse. Son of a bitch had more bottom in him than any horse I can remember," he said with undisguised admiration.

"So when did you catch up with Crawford?" Wessels asked.

"Less'n five miles after I got on top of that German's horse," Grouard answered. "Come up on Captain Jack pretty quick then. His horse was all but winded."

"What'd you say to him?" Bourke asked.

"First thing: I asked him if he remembered his orders to stay with Lieutenant Bubb. He looked sheepish at that, but all he said was he had dispatches to get through for the New York *Herald*."

"That when you left him behind?" Donegan asked.

"Yep, but not before I told him he was no longer a army scout—from the moment he abandoned the column and disobeyed orders. I kept on with that German's horse, reaching Custer City twenty minutes before three o'clock that day."

Donegan whistled, looking around the table. "How far is that? Anyone know?"

Bourke shook his head and shrugged like the rest, while Wessels answered, "Just over a hundred miles."

"In four hours and ten minutes?" Bourke exclaimed, his voice rising in surprise. "You bloody well did ride those horses into the ground, Grouard!"

"Damn near did my own self in too," Frank added. "Had to be taken off that last horse when I reached Custer City. Couldn't get off on my own."

Burt asked, "What become of Crawford after you left him behind?"

"He limped on in on that crippled-up horse," Frank said. "Found me having my supper that evening. We come to an understanding that we'd start the race again the next morning."

"You figured you could trust him?" Bourke asked. "What with Davenport wagging all that money out in front of his nose?"

A wry smile came across Grouard's face. "You think I figured to let that son of a bitch burn me twice, Lieutenant? Hell no, I didn't believe a word of his song. But he didn't trust me neither. Fact was, he come to my room that night—checking to see if I'd gone and got the sneak on him after dark."

Donegan squinted one eye in appraising the half-breed. "Listen, you goddamned half-blood—I know you good enough to know you wasn't about to eat supper and lay your head down in no bed if there was a chance Crawford was about to get the jump on you through the night. So what'd you do?"

Smiling, Grouard replied, "To make sure of him not running off on me again—I sat tight and finished my supper before I went down the street to find me a good man there in town I could trust to carry a note to Captain Egan—"

"Teddy Egan?" Donegan asked.

Grouard nodded. "The same what led your charge on that village in the Powder River last winter. Told Egan that I needed one of his men to get the dispatches on through, and then had that fella ride off with 'em on a fresh horse down to Egan's camp at Red Canyon—a good forty miles off. Sent Crook's note on with the man too. Then I wrote me a letter to Crook, telling him what all I'd done before I went off to find me a empty bed. After Crawford come and shook me up, I didn't wake up for the next three days."

"Three days?" Wessels exclaimed. "What became of Crawford?"

With a shrug Grouard said, "I hear he got up and pulled out at nine the next morning. Seeing how I slept in, he likely figured he had the jump on me. Got to Red Canyon midafternoon, where Egan broke the bad news to him. Told Crawford he just as well ought to spend the night because he wasn't about to overtake those couriers by that time."

"That was the fifteenth—which means he didn't reach Laramie ahead of Egan's courier," Bourke declared.

"So how was it that Davenport's dispatch got on the wire before Crook's?" Schuyler asked.

"Crawford got to the key shack at Hat Creek about eight o'clock the night of the fifteenth," Burt replied, "but the line was down."

"Line was still down when I went through there," Frank disclosed.

Bourke shook his head, beginning to ask, "If the line was down—"

Burt interrupted, saying, "When Crawford came through there, the operator told him that the wire should be back up by the next morning. Now, I've heard enough of the story to know that Captain Jack had him a second copy of Davenport's story that he left right there with the key operator, with instructions to put the story on the line as soon as there was current."

"Where the devil'd he get that second copy?" Donegan asked.

The table fell silent. Slowly, man by man, Grouard felt all the eyes turn on him, expecting an answer. "He got it from me," he groaned.

"From *you*?" Bourke roared.

"I was so damned angry with him there in Custer City that I handed him that copy of Davenport's story that son of a bitch Davenport give me back at the Belle Fourche and told him I wasn't carrying it no more."

"So when the line was repaired, that's how Davenport's dispatch got on the wire before Egan's courier could reach here," Wessels said. "And in the meantime, Crawford himself kept on pushing for Laramie. The next key shack was up at Sage Creek, just forty-eight miles beyond Hat Creek, and that's where Crawford must've found out the line was up and working by that time. The operator there told him Davenport's story was already on the wire ahead of all the others."

Donegan sat his mug down with a clunk, wagging his head. "Damn the bloody hell of it—so that's how Davenport's story got out ahead of Crook's dispatches to Sheridan."

"But only part of Davenport's story," said Andy Burt.

"What do you mean, only *part* of it?" Donegan asked as Grouard rocked forward on his elbows.

"When the Hat Creek operator paused in the middle of Davenport's story for a moment, the operator at Laramie broke in and took over possession of the wire with Crook's official dispatches," Burt explained. "Still, with the jump Crawford had there at Hat Creek key station, Davenport's story got wired east a good five hours ahead of all the rest of those other newspapermen."

Bourke asked, "What'd Crawford get for his trouble?"

"It sure wasn't that five hunnert Davenport promised him," Grouard grumped.

Donegan grumped over his whiskey, "Davenport's the sort so tight he squeaks when he walks. I'll wager he gave Captain Jack no more'n a shinplaster or two."

Wessels explained, "I heard he got only two hundred dollars since he wasn't the first to Laramie and only part of the story got out before Crook's report."

"Where's Crawford now?" Schuyler asked.

"He laid over here a day," Burt answered. "Then he doubled back for the Hills."

"Let's drink to Frank Grouard!" Bourke cheered, raising his mug of beer.

The half-breed watched a sudden bright twinkle gleam in the lieutenant's eyes as the officer tapped Donegan on the shoulder and pointed out the window.

"Who's that?" Seamus asked, squinting through the smoke-smudged windowpanes.

"That?" Andy Burt replied. "That happens to be Lieutenant Capron's wife, Seamus. The woman who tonight is helping my Elizabeth deliver your child."

"Ch-child?"

Donegan and the rest suddenly whirled about on their seats in that next instant as Nettie Capron swirled into the room, a blast of autumn cold clinging to her long dress, a shawl clutched tightly about her shoulders. Burt stood immediately, signaling the woman through that smoky atmosphere. The rest of the men stood gallantly as she came to a stop at the table.

"Mr. Donegan?" Nettie Capron said softly.

"Y-yes?" he replied, his face sagging a bit as his knees began to turn to water.

"The captain's . . . Elizabeth Burt sent me to fetch you."

"And?" Andy Burt asked, his voice rising. "Is Seamus a father?"

"No, not yet—but soon," she answered, then turned to the Irishman once more. "Could you come . . . now? Your wife is . . . she's having a struggle of it. And, sh-she's asking for you."

Chapter 1

7 October 1876

If he lived forever, Seamus Donegan was dead certain he would never forget this night.

At first the women fluttering around Samantha had tried to convince him in hushed tones that he should stay no more than a few moments with his wife. Reassure her, console her—then go back to the saloon—just as a man was supposed to do when a woman's time came.

"S-stay with me," Sam begged in a harsh whisper as he came to the side of that tiny bed where she lay, her back propped up, the thin grayed sheet draped over her knees like sister mountain peaks covered with dirty snow. She held one hand out for him to grasp as he went to his knee beside the bed.

Almost immediately he watched the rise of another contraction show on her face, and suddenly the others squeezed forward once again: two on the far side of the bed, one at Donegan's shoulder. All of them muttering instructions to Sam, reminders about breathing, about not pushing.

"Where's the goddamned surgeon?" he looked up to ask them as Sam fell back against those tiny pillows and folded-up comforter they had braced behind her.

Elizabeth Burt was the one to answer. "We'll call him if we need him, Mr. Donegan."

He rose shakily from his knee. It hurt like hell down on that hardwood floor. As quickly he felt a flush of shame for thinking of that when Sam's hurt must be so much the worse. He squeezed her slick hand between his two rough, callused paws and said as quietly, as politely, as he could, "Looks to me we n-need him."

"No, no," Martha Luhn said. "Everything's going just fine."

"F-fine?" Donegan stammered, gazing back down at Samantha, who stared up at him, transfixed and steady, licking her dry lips with the tip of her tongue.

"Truth is, that surgeon wouldn't be a bit of help to us," Nettie Capron replied. "That man might know how to set a broken bone, or patch up a bullet hole, or what to do if you had an Indian's arrow sticking out of your back ... but he sure as the Psalms doesn't know near as much about what's going on with your wife as we do."

"Get me some water there, Seamus," Sam pleaded in all but a desert-dry whisper, diverting his attention from the scolding he was getting from the lieutenant's wife.

Elizabeth Burt leaned over Sam as Seamus turned to find some water, explaining, "You can only have a little, Samantha. Like we've been giving you all along. Remember—only a little."

"I want Seamus to give it to me," Sam said with a weary nod.

At the side of the bed stood the unsteady washstand where a china cup with its handle broken off sat next to a tinned pitcher. He filled the cup halfway before slipping a hand beneath his wife's neck and head, gently propping her up as he raised the cup to her lips. Sam took tiny sips with her parched lips and that pink tongue, a half dozen of them before her eyes rolled away from him and she started to pant.

Beside him Nettie Capron pushed Seamus back as Samantha gripped the bedsheet in both hands and started to groan. Her legs trembled beneath that grayed sheet.

He felt so damned helpless as the three women hovered close, attending his wife, while he could do nothing to take the pain, this excruciating travail, from her. In helplessness at her misery, he gasped, "I ... I must get the post surgeon—"

"No, you won't trouble him with this," Elizabeth Burt corrected more sternly this time. "You best trust *me* in this: that man doesn't know half of what any one of us knows about delivering your wife of this child, Mr. Donegan. Now—I'm warning you—don't you dare get in the way, or we'll have to ask you to leave. And that means the end to bothering us with any more of that fool talk about the post surgeon."

"Get in the way?" he squeaked. "She ... Sam asked for me—"

Elizabeth Burt moved down the opposite side of the bed, where she squatted on the edge of the tick, raising the sheet slightly so that she could peer beneath it without exposing Sam's legs. Donegan thought that most strange—wondering how these women figured he had put Sam with child if he hadn't seen her legs, indeed every last delicious inch of her! The woman's eyes came up to look at the others, then rested on his.

"It won't be long now," she explained, grim-lipped, as her eyes gazed down at the woman in labor. "Samantha—this child of yours is about ready to make its entrance into the world."

"S-seamus."

He turned and went down on his knee again at her side, stroking the back of one of her sweaty hands. From the nearby washstand he retrieved a damp, folded towel and dabbed at the pearling beads of sweat that glimmered on her brow and cheeks.

"Give me a kiss, p-please," she gasped as if her throat was raw.

Leaning down, he brushed her cheek with his mouth self-consciously. Good manners and upbringing allowed that a man might lightly kiss his wife there while in public.

"No," Sam declared, tapping her dry lips with one finger. "Kiss me here."

The Irishman swallowed hard, his eyes darting to the other women before he leaned over Sam once more and laid his mouth on hers. He felt the press of her hand at the back of his head, preventing him from pulling away.

She held his face close, whispering, "I wanted the ... the feel of your l-l-l-lips—"

Then she wrenched her hands down and was gripping the sheets once more, gritting her teeth and growling as the next contraction welled over her.

"That's good! That's good, Samantha!" Elizabeth exclaimed, observing the progress there between Sam's legs.

"Bear down. Go on and bear down, Samantha," instructed Martha Luhn as she pressed up at Seamus's elbow, taking the towel from his hand and dabbing it against the hollow at the base of Sam's throat where the sweat had pooled.

He stepped back a step in that crush of women and their dutiful purpose. Then another step, for the first time noticing how drenched she was with this labor. Sam's face flushed with her exertion ... oh, how it stood out against the white of that loose camisole, damp, plastered to the skin across her chest and her arms as if she had just been caught out in a summer thundershower. It appeared these women had taken off her most everything else she had been wearing earlier that evening for dinner with Mackenzie ... most all of it: dress and petticoats and bloomers—then draped that sheet over her legs as they began this long, agonizing process.

He suddenly wondered what time it was—feeling guilty for not knowing how long he had been down at the saloon. Drinking, sharing stories with other men, while these women had been up here with Sam.

She was his wife. He should have been here all along.

He watched as Sam gasped, then went back to panting, almost like a dog, her head bobbing in rhythm each time she exhaled in those short, rough gusts of wind. Drawing her knees up as far as she could just as the others reminded her to do in their calming voices, assisting Sam as she struggled in lowering her head as far as she could, as if she were cramping up. Sam began a low shriek—

To him the room felt suddenly very, very warm. Then he remembered he still had on his worn canvas and blanket mackinaw, sooted and smudged with the smoke of many fires, slick with wear and tattered at the elbows and wrists from long years' wilderness service.

He pulled his arms from it, one at a time, and dropped it carelessly in a far corner.

"Oh, no—Mr. Donegan," Nettie Capron said. "You put your coat back on. I'm afraid you can't stay."

"S-stay!" Samantha contradicted.

Martha Luhn turned to Sam, quietly declaring, "No. It's much, much better that he's not here."

"Why?" Sam asked in exhaustion as her head fell back against the pillows and comforter.

"Yeah," Donegan agreed, taking a shaky step back toward the bed as Sam held her hand out to him again. "Why not?"

The women looked at one another for a moment while Sam laid her wet hand in his two big paws, imploring him with those red-rimmed eyes of hers. She said quietly, "C'mere—let me hold you—"

He settled to one knee again there at the side of the bed just in time to have her clench one of her hands around one of his instead of the sheet with the sudden terrible avalanche of the contraction. Seamus sensed the blood squeezed out of the hand, felt the bones grind together as if another, more powerful man had his own callused paw caught in the grip of a vise. In a moment his hand began to tingle with its own pain, just before Sam collapsed back against the comforter and pillows, panting, her tongue lolling.

"It's not long now," Elizabeth cheered, her eyes flicking up to Seamus suddenly, then back down to her work between Sam's legs.

"What . . . what can I do to help?" he asked them, his eyes touching each one.

Nettie answered after glancing at the others. "You can stay right there at her side. Help your wife through each contraction, Mr. Donegan. Talk to her, talk her through each one."

"T-talk . . . talk her through—"

"Do you still love me?" Sam interrupted, bringing her free hand alongside his cheek, turning his face so that he looked down at her.

He gazed back down at her face, studying her at last—finding her hair plastered to her brow, at her temples, soaking at the back of her neck where she had tied it back with a ribbon upon returning to this room after their walk down to the cottonwood grove by the river.

"L-love you? Of course I do," Seamus answered. He slipped one of his hands free, brushing her cheek with his rough fingertips as she smiled up at him through glistening eyes. "I'll always love you, Samantha."

He watched her eyes widen with the coming contraction, her tongue darting out to flick over her lips with a little moisture, sweeping over the droplets of salty sweat that poured from her flesh. Again he daubed her brow and cheeks as she squeezed his hand through the coming and leaving of that circle of pain.

"Do . . . do you really love me?" she panted as she collapsed against the pillows. "Love me even tonight?"

He shifted beside the bed, leaning his face more closely over hers as he whispered, "I love you more tonight than I have ever loved you."

Sensing his eyes filling, Seamus drew back a little, blinked, and swiped at them with that damp towel. When he looked back down at her, he could see that Sam was weeping.

"Are you all right?" he begged, worried and anxious.

She forced a smile with the coming of the next contraction, tears suddenly gushing from the corners of her eyes. "I've n-never been b-better—"

The last word rushed out in a shriek as she clamped down on his hand and doubled up with the pain—panting, grunting, low and feral. The three midwives squeezed in around Samantha.

"That's it!" Elizabeth cried. "It's here! Your baby's here!"

With a jerk he looked down at Mrs. Burt, hoping for some sign of the child. Dear Mither of God—he prayed—protect them both at this moment!

"I see its head," Elizabeth went on. "Such hair. So much hair!"

Sam fell back, her legs—indeed, her whole body—quaking with great, volcanic shudders. Back and forth he looked, his eyes moving between Samantha and Elizabeth Burt.

"The head is here," the woman cried out, shifting her position between Sam's legs now, climbing up on the bed herself to kneel between the knees and shoving the sheet out of the way so that it tumbled down upon Samantha's great, round tummy. She glanced at Seamus quickly—as if to explain that duty must now dispense with propriety.

He nodded and looked away obediently, though he wanted so much to watch this child come forth. So much to watch its entrance into this world. Instead he turned back to kiss Sam on the forehead quickly at the moment she began to quiver with a new contraction, then began to growl as she hadn't before.

"Yes, Sam!" Martha Luhn prodded. "Give it all you've got now!"

Nettie Capron urged, "Push, Sam! Push!"

She had her fingernails digging into the palm of his hand so deeply, he didn't know if the dampness he felt was sweat or blood. It didn't matter. And then he glanced at Elizabeth Burt, saw her hovering close above Sam's belly.

"Again!" Elizabeth ordered. "Push harder now, Sam. It's here! Dear God—your beautiful baby's here!"

At Samantha's other shoulder Nettie Capron coaxed, "One

more good push and the baby will be out. Come, now. Give us one more good push."

"P-p-push!" Sam gasped, straining, her face flush.

"That's it!" Martha Luhn cheered.

Then Seamus turned quickly, saw the head already cradled in Mrs. Burt's hands. At that very moment the child burst into a hair-raising squall. With the child's cry Sam suddenly released the pressure she had on his hand and let out a great sigh. Seamus looked down as she collapsed back against the pillows, panting openmouthed like never before, her eyes clenched shut, tears streaming from their corners. It seemed everything had suddenly gone out of her. He felt queasy in that moment, afraid like never before that she might not have the strength to see this through. All these hours of labor. And now it must surely be early morning ... after all that work.

"It's a boy!"

He jerked around, wide-eyed as a mule on a narrow trail, staring at what Elizabeth Burt cradled in her arms. Seeing that dark glob of hair plastered against the strange little creature's head, its face all pinched and red, streaked with white lather and gobbed with blood. Mrs. Burt shifted the child in her forearms there between Sam's knees as Nettie Capron came to the side of the bed with a small blanket draped over her arms to receive the child.

"A b-boy?" Sam asked, trying to lift herself up to see, then tearing her eyes from the child for but a moment as they flicked into Seamus's—as if asking for his approval.

"Boy?" he repeated, his lips barely moving, practically no sound escaping from his lips.

"You're a father, Mr. Donegan!" Elizabeth Burt congratulated as she laid the newborn across Mrs. Capron's arms, then went back to work between Sam's legs, milking the umbilical cord toward the child. That done, the women tied a wrap of sewing thread around and around the cord two inches from the infant's body, then knotted it off.

In amazement at it all, Seamus watched Martha Luhn snip the purple cord with a pair of scissors.

Only then did Nettie Capron straighten, shuffle back the tiny blanket from the face, and scoot down the side of the bed to lay the bundle within Sam's arms.

"Is he ...," Samantha started to ask.

"Is he all right?" Elizabeth Burt repeated, still at work there between the knees. "Of course he is, Sam. He's just fine. Got all the right equipment, if that's what you mean. All his fingers and toes. Everything else. Just one thing."

"W-what?" Seamus asked in a gasp, twisting about suddenly, frightened at the sound of that.

The child began to squall, high-pitched and rhythmic, like nothing he had ever heard before. Now he was worried. Truly worried.

"Don't know what his folks are going to do," Elizabeth said gravely, but a smile betrayed her face, eyes twinkling, "seeing how he's come out about as homely as his father."

With a reassuring gush all three midwives chuckled at that and went back to their duties at the foot of the bed as Seamus bent low, helping Sam tug the blanket back from the child's face all the more.

"Lemme have a look, Sam," he whispered as he planted another kiss on her lips glistening with her tears.

He straightened slightly and began to slowly peel back the folds of the blanket. Beneath it lay the red, squealing, wriggling child—all arms and legs and mouth. The child clenched his eyes in that crimson face as he bellowed in protest.

"It's a boy, Sam," he cried, sensing his own tears begin to sting his eyes.

"Yes!" Elizabeth Burt exclaimed with genuine joy as she gathered more of the bloody sheets into her arms and passed them on to Nettie Capron. "Just listen to the set of lungs this'un has! My, my—never have I ever heard such caterwauling!"

Seamus repeated over and over, almost unbelieving how beautiful such a tiny creature could be, "A boy, Sam. A b-boy!"

Tears welled from his eyes now, his lower lip quivering as it never had before, even as it had in those last few minutes of bachelorhood before he stepped beneath that sheltering oak tree in Sharp Grover's yard near the Texas panhandle country, prepared to take this woman to his side forevermore.

She asked him, "You approve, Seamus?"

"Oh, yes—yes! A girl, a boy," he answered in a rush, leaning over to kiss the tiny infant's wrinkled forehead, gently brushing that thick crop of hair with his lips. "Anything—long as you both made it through, Sam."

"We made it through," she whimpered wearily beneath him, her eyes thickly pooling with tears, her lips smiling as she cried in joy. "We both made it through just fine."

"He's beautiful," Seamus explained as he glanced up at the

three midwives. "Don't you think he's just about the most beautiful thing you've ever seen?"

"Yes, he certainly is at that, Mr. Donegan," Elizabeth Burt said, still at work there at the foot of the bed. "And if I know anything about his father, Sam: I'll bet that little one is going to be a real hellion before you know it!"

Chapter 2

Canapekasna Wi
Moon When the Leaves Fall

S itting Bull's Hunkpapa called him "Big Leggings."
Among the white man he carried the name Johnny
Bruguier.

And ever since the last days of summer Johnny had been
running from the whites. They wanted to hang him for murder.

In the crisp chill of autumn Bruguier stirred the fire before
him at the center of the huge lodge he shared with Sitting Bull's
family. The old man and everyone else still slept this morning,
exhausted from yesterday's crossing of the Elk River.*

But Johnny could not sleep. It had been like this nearly every night since he'd fled the Standing Rock Agency.† Each time
he closed his eyes the nightmares returned to haunt him. He
awoke in a sweat. Afraid to close his eyes, afraid of those awful
dreams, he instead sat up and tended the fire through much of
the night, thinking. Brooding on all manner of things. Mostly on
the white men who would hang him. And hating his mother for
hooking up with a drunken white trader at the agency more than
two decades ago.

Life had been tough for a half-breed at Standing Rock. So
many times while he was growing up had he felt pushed outside
the Hunkpapa band. At the same time the whites closed their

*Yellowstone River, Montana Territory.
†On the Cheyenne River, Dakota Territory.

arms and cloaked their hearts to him. He damned his mother for choosing to bed down with a white man, damned her for ever giving birth to him. Damned himself especially now, for the way things had turned out at Standing Rock.

Because of his two bloods, Johnny was brought up knowing both languages. His mother knew some English, more than enough to cuss like the agency employees and the white teamsters who came and went. Likewise, his French-Canadian father knew enough Lakota to sweet-talk the agency Sioux out of most everything they owned, in trade for a handful of blue glass beads or a tin cup of whiskey, which the man had buried among his stores of treasures.

Able to speak both tongues, but feeling at home in neither world, Bruguier had reluctantly attempted to make a home for himself there at Standing Rock for the last few winters. He was one of the agent's three interpreters—at least that had been his life until he'd rubbed up against the wrong white man.

The one with the eyes so cold, he figured the man was already one of the "walking dead." No emotion had shown in those icy eyes, until a young woman had walked into the trader's store one late December afternoon. On such winter days most of the agency employees sat by the iron stove, whittling, telling stories, sharpening knives, drinking if they had pay coming on account.

This morning Johnny could feel the sweet tang of winter coming again to the high plains. The sharp teeth of winter were closing in upon them. His fire felt especially good this morning before the sun rose, as he remembered last winter. Remembered the woman. And the one with the walking dead eyes.

To the white men it would have been nothing more than an argument over a woman. Those things happened in that world. Among the Lakota, it had been a matter of the young woman's honor. How the white man had shamed her and defiled her when she'd nervously walked into the trader's store with her grandmother that cold winter afternoon almost a year gone now. No one else was going to tell the white man to take his hand off the woman's arm. No one else was going to tell the man he should not have cuffed the old woman aside when she'd cried out, trying to remove the white man's claws from her granddaughter's arm.

No one, that is, except Johnny Bruguier.

As he looked back now, he thought how things had a way of sweeping him up and carrying him along before he knew it.

Like a spring torrent of winter runoff rushing between two narrow creekbanks. He had his own knife at work on a piece of ash, carving a new stem for an uncle's pipe. How the old men loved to spend much time with their pipes and telling stories this season of the year. When the bad words and the loud talk started, Johnny already had his knife out. When the white man pulled his knife, everything hurried by in a blur.

He remembered the girl being flung aside, landing in a heap atop her old grandmother. He remembered the size of that white man's knife as he lunged for Johnny. And the last thing Bruguier was ever able to recall was the look in those walking dead eyes as the two men grappled. Those eyes no longer seeming dead at all, but lit with a bright, cold fire—such hate Johnny had never before seen.

Nor had he ever thought he would see so much blood pour out of a man. Something inside Bruguier had told him to put out the fire in those eyes, but Johnny did not know how he'd accomplished that, for he could remember nothing more until he was standing over the white man thrashing on the floor, bleeding from a dozen or more serious wounds, the floor beneath him slicking with dark puddles of blood and a greasy coil of gut. Too much blood, he had told himself. Too much for any man to lose and still live.

The white man died at Johnny's feet, his thrashing stopped, rolling onto his back to stare up at Bruguier with those walking dead eyes. But now he would no longer walk. And the fire was gone from them as they gazed blankly at the half-breed who had killed a white man before so many witnesses.

How the trader had started hollering, reaching under a counter for his big two-shoot gun. How Johnny had looked at the others, both Lakota and half-breed there in the store, sensing instantly that they would not dare tell the truth about what had happened. Afraid. Cowed. So shamed by their need for the moldy flour and rancid pig meat that they would not tell the truth.

Johnny fled Standing Rock on a stolen horse. And had been running ever since.

First to Bear Butte to find solace and help for his troubled spirit among the religious places he had heard so much about. Not that he had never been religious—certainly not like his father's Catholicism. Nor had he paid much attention to the beliefs of his mother's people. But he had remembered enough to know about Bear Butte, enough to feel the place call out to him.

For most of that hard winter he had clung close to the slopes of Bear Butte, hunting, sleeping, keeping an eye out in those early days for any from Standing Rock who might follow him. Only with the waning of winter did he finally relent and allow himself to believe no one would come for him.

So he wandered south to the Black Hills, that country the white man's government wanted back from the warrior bands so all white men could come and dig for the yellow rocks that made them hungry for whiskey and whores. It was no problem finding work in those settlements just beginning to dot the Black Hills: unloading wagons brought up from the rail depot at Sidney, Nebraska; helping build sluice boxes; cleaning up after all the puking white men in those great saloons covered with tent canvas, closed-in places that smelled of urine, sweat, and the desecration of that sacred land. There was work enough for any man willing to work. Johnny worked.

Until that summer afternoon he was tapped on the shoulder by his white employer. Bruguier straightened over his mop and slop bucket.

"You know anythin' 'bout this?" With a crackle the man noisily unfolded a stiffened parchment with a likeness of Johnny printed on it in black ink. Words, too.

"What's this?" Bruguier had asked.

"Says you're wanted, mister."

"For what?"

"Murder. You kill someone?"

His eyes must have given him up when he looked away, unable to look the white man in the face.

"Tell you what, mister," the white man continued, "you best be on your way and now. These here posters is going up all over town. They'll be up all over the hills afore the sun sets tomorrow. Likely you'll be as easy for others to spot, just as easy to catch. Then some miner's court decide to hang you."

To this day Johnny remembered clear as sunrise how that white man with dirt caked down in those deep wrinkles on his face and the wattle of his neck had pantomimed a rope dropping over his head, tightened, then strangled at the end of that noose. As calmly as he could, Johnny had nodded and set his mop against the wall. Then turned away, not once looking over his shoulder.

He stole another horse that day, the biggest one of those tied at the side of the saloon. Not one of the horses out front at the rail, but back in the shadows, an animal with a blaze face and two front stockings. It looked strong enough to carry him fast and far. But the best thing that made Johnny decide on the horse was what was tied behind the saddle: a thick blanket roll, wrapped in an oiled slicker, along with those two saddlebags stuffed to their limit. Plain to see that horse and rigging were ready for the trail.

Bruguier kicked the animal into a gallop as soon as he put the last tent behind him, heading west toward the setting sun. East and north meant trouble. That's where the white men were, with their pictures and their stories of murder, the nightmare of their hanging ropes that choked off the only chance his spirit could fly out of his mouth when he breathed his last. No man must die that way.

The only direction for him lay to the south and west. There was damned little of the white man north of the Platte or south of the Yellowstone, clear to the Big Horn Mountains. Especially that summer after the Lakota and Cheyenne had whipped the pony soldiers something fierce in two big fights. He set off to find sanctuary among his mother's people—that, or this journey would be his suicide.

Beside his fire that first summer night after fleeing the white man's settlements, Johnny unfurled the oiled rain poncho and rolled out the blankets inside their bedroll, a long canvas sack. Within he found a pair of well-worn batwing chaps.

"A cow-boy," he murmured to himself as he stood to hold the chaps against his hips, admiring the way they fluttered as he pranced around the fire ring—just the way the long fringe on Lakota leggings fluttered with a man's every step.

The next morning he put on the weathered chaps, running his hands over the dark oiled color of the leather. He had worn them ever since. Had them on that early morning he caught sight of the smoke rising from many fires beyond the low range of hills in the distance. By the time he reached the top of a far knoll, the smoke had dissipated and the village was already in motion for the day, slowly making its way north by west—back toward the Owl River.* Bruguier cautiously followed them all day, watchful of outriders protecting the massive line of march, all those women and children and travois, which would have stirred up a lot of dust had it not been for the season of the rains. By the time the procession went into camp, Johnny had them figured for Lakota. One band or another—but Lakota for

---

*The Moreau River, Dakota Territory.

sure. How he wanted to taste the words on his tongue once more, and forget the white man's language for the rest of his days.

Riding down from the slope slowly, he saw several of the young warriors turn and notice him while lodgepoles were being set in their proper order, lodge covers being unfurled over the first. Johnny kicked that big American horse in its flanks and rolled into an easy gallop. With a burst of noise and a flourish of the hat he ripped from his head, Bruguier shot past the warriors coming out to challenge him—dashing straight into the camp, knowing enough to aim for the center of the great village. Dead in the middle of the two horns of the crescent, he would find the chief's lodge. There he should be safe—despite the fact that he was dressed in white man's clothes. Despite the whole summer of bloody warfare against the white man.

Already he could see that he could not make it to the center of camp. Suddenly there were too many horsemen forming up, galloping to meet him. His way was blocked.

In panic, his eyes shot over the nearby lodges being raised. But ahead, close at hand, there was a big one. Well painted with dream symbols. A tripod stood outside with many scalps hanging from it. This man must surely be a war chief. Besides, it was one of the few already erected and close at hand.

Outside the big lodge he dismounted before his horse even stopped, and ducked within the lodge door without ceremony. Outside the children screeched in their high voices, the women shouting to their men that a white man had just invaded their camp, a lone white man. But inside the lodge all remained eerily quiet.

Before him the middle-aged warrior looked Johnny over carefully. The wrinkled, copper-skinned woman said nothing at all, but went back to laying out the buffalo robes and blankets while her husband eventually went on loading his pipe.

"Welcome," the warrior said finally as he raised a twig from the fire he had started with flint and steel.

When Johnny answered in Lakota, "Thank you," no surprise seemed to register on the warrior's face.

"Sit. We will have something to eat soon. Would you like to smoke with me?"

Bruguier answered, "Yes—"

But there would be no smoking, not just yet, for at that moment a wide-shouldered warrior burst through the open doorway and stood to his full height within the lodge, towering over the old warrior and his sudden guest.

"White Bull!" the young warrior cried, gesturing aggressively at Bruguier.

"You are welcome too, One Horn," White Bull said, gesturing for the warrior to sit. "Even though you left your manners outside this afternoon."

The young man sputtered angrily, "Is this man a friend?"

White Bull pulled on the pipe stem, drawing smoke into his mouth and lungs for several moments, then exhaled it and regarded the smoke that he cupped in a hand and dragged over the top of his head in a sacred fashion. "He is in my lodge. And we will eat soon. You are welcome to stay and eat with us."

"Sitting Bull wants to know," the young warrior spat. "If he is your friend, then the Bull wants you to bring this visitor to his lodge. But if he is not your friend, then Sitting Bull says we can kill him."

White Bull's eyes dropped to look at Bruguier. For a long time he seemed to study the swarthy-skinned intruder wearing the clothes of a white man. After interminably long minutes, he looked back at One Horn.

"We will go to Sitting Bull's lodge ... together."

"S-sitting Bull?" Johnny asked in a croak. "The same Sitting Bull who crushed the soldiers at the Greasy Grass?"

"Yes," White Bull said. "Come, now. We will go see my uncle."

Plunging through the long, jostling gauntlet of angry, oath-spitting warriors and keening, screeching women and old men, White Bull and Bruguier followed One Horn, who wore a provocative headdress with its single buffalo horn jutting from the wearer's forehead. While the trip did not require that many steps, it nonetheless seemed like an eternity to Johnny. These people screamed to take his scalp, his hide removed one torturous inch at a time. They wanted him to suffer horribly. That much he understood in their Lakota harangue.

Soon he could see the end of that gauntlet—the big unpainted lodge had its bottom rolled up some five feet all around its entire circumference so that the cool breeze could penetrate the interior. Perhaps so that onlookers could watch Sitting Bull's conference with this sudden intruder to this camp of Miniconjou and Sans Arc who had joined the great chief's Hunkpapa in their summer wanderings between the two armies—one army north, one army south.

"This one is your friend, White Bull?" the chief asked when all were seated.

"No, he is my guest."

"How is he your guest?" a very old man demanded from the far side of the fire.

"He came to my lodge," White Bull answered. "Therefore, he is my guest."

Sitting Bull looked at the intruder. "What is your name?"

"Johnny Bruguier."

Even though he said his white-man name, and spoke it in English, it caused the chiefs and advisers to mutter among themselves ... for the intruder must surely have understood Sitting Bull's question spoken in Lakota.

The Bull asked, "You speak our language too?"

"Yes. It is the language of my mother."

With a nod Sitting Bull replied, "This is why you speak our tongue as good as a Sioux."

"I am a Sioux," Johnny replied.

"You are a half-blood," growled another old man across the fire. "You are neither white, nor Indian. So you are not a Lakota. This one is like the Grabber! You remember him, Sitting Bull—the Grabber who leads the soldiers down on our villages."

One Horn pointed his finger angrily at Bruguier. "I say we kill this one!"

There arose an instant and loud agreement from many of those squeezed together at the lodgepoles, pressing in a great circle surrounding the Bull's conference. The chief regarded White Bull's guest, then stared at the small fire, considering. Again he regarded the intruder once more while the crowd fell to utter silence.

"Well," Sitting Bull finally said in a loud voice filled with an awesome command all by itself, "if you are going to kill this man, then kill him. But if you are not—then give him a drink of water. Give him something to eat. And give him a pipe of peace to smoke with us."

So it was that from the crowd immediately appeared a canteen that was passed hand-to-hand to Johnny. Bruguier pulled the cork chain from the tin container wrapped in wool and stamped with the initials U S. A bowl of dried meat was set before him, and Sitting Bull motioned for him to eat as the chief went about putting the redstone bowl onto his short pipe stem and loaded it with tobacco.

"Do you have a Lakota name?"

"My mother had no brothers to name me at Standing Rock, and my father's people are white from far to the north. I have no Lakota name."

Sitting Bull smiled and his eyes flashed over at White Bull. "This guest of yours, what shall we name him, nephew?"

For a moment the middle-aged warrior studied Johnny, then motioned for him to stand, there beside the fire, for all to see. Only then did he turn back to Sitting Bull. "Do you see what I will name him?"

"The way this half-blood dresses?"

White Bull nodded. "Look at his big leggings."

A smile crept over Sitting Bull's face as he stuffed a twist of dried grass into the flames to light his pipe. "Yes—this is good. Half-blood, you are now called *Big Leggings*."

Bruguier had gazed down at his wide, floppy batwing chaps and saw how appropriate the name was. Johnny smiled. White Bull motioned for him to sit and eat.

Bruguier settled again, repeating his new name in Lakota. "Big Leggings."

Now this morning in the cold of early autumn Johnny again thought back fondly on that first day among these people, as a guest welcomed in White Bull's and Sitting Bull's lodges. Their welcome had helped to drive away most of his fear of the white man's strangling rope. As the days became weeks, and the weeks became months, Johnny Bruguier thought less and less on what he had left behind in the white man's mining settlements. Too, he thought less and less in the white man's tongue.

Earlier this autumn Bruguier had taken up arms against the soldiers when Three Stars Crook had attacked American Horse's band of Miniconjou camped on Rabbit Lip Creek at the Slim Buttes. No matter that there were more soldiers than warriors from the surrounding villages, Three Stars had retreated, run away to the south, fleeing Lakota land.

Many believed there would be peace now as the Lakota wandered north by west, back toward the Elk River while the air turned cold and the first snows lanced out of the sky. Winter was coming, and they must hunt the buffalo once more to make meat in preparation for the time of great cold. The herds were gathering north of the Elk River.

But so were the soldiers, scouts had reported.

Sitting Bull vowed his people would stay out of the way of the soldiers if they could. But in this same camp Gall still mourned the loss of his wives and children at the fight along the

Greasy Grass. In a flux of rage the fierce war chief said the soldiers would drive the buffalo away and make it a very hard winter for their people. He wanted to lead the warriors down on the soldiers soon and drive them off the Elk River for good.

Still, Sitting Bull said they would wait. And see how the hunting went. So far they had not had much success. Which made for a restless anger growing among the people.

That cold morning a day after they had crossed to the north side of the Elk River, Johnny was one of the few in camp awake to hear the distant call shouted by the scouts returning from the hills.

"Soldiers!"

Bruguier swept up his big blanket coat and mittens, pulling that big floppy hat down on his head, and jabbed his way out of White Bull's lodge into the cold autumn air.

"Soldier wagons!" came the cry as the scouts swept into camp.

Already men were bursting from their lodges, weapons in hand, singing out to one another in excitement and blood oaths.

"Soldier wagons in the valley beyond the eastern hills! Many mules! Food, blankets, and *guns!*"

Then Gall was among them, raising his soldier carbine high overhead, shrieking that now was the time to finish what the white man had started.

"Come! Let us make war again!" he cried.

They answered him with hundreds of throats.

"Come!" Gall bellowed for all to hear. "Let us finish what we started on the Greasy Grass!"

Chapter 3

11 October 1876

"We're ready to roll, Captain," said the lieutenant, who sported a thick and jaunty mustache as he saluted his superior officer.

They both sat on horseback at the head of a jagged column of ninety-four wagons that fall morning as the horizon to the east was only then beginning to pale. Light enough to make out the rutted road to Tongue River.

"Very good, Lieutenant," Charles W. Miner replied to the battalion adjutant. "Let's be off."

First Lieutenant Oskaloosa M. Smith reined about and raised an arm in the air, shouting out his order. "For-rad ... *harch!*"

In a pair of long columns of twos and stretched down either side of the wagon train, four companies of foot soldiers set off under the bellowed echoes of their noncoms. Civilian teamsters slapped long lengths of well-soaped leather down onto the backs of those six-mule teams harnessed to these wagons filled to the gunnels with freight bound away for the army's cantonment at the mouth of the Tongue River. It was there Colonel Nelson A. Miles's Fifth Infantry had been throwing up log huts against the coming of what boded to be a very severe and hoary high plains winter.

Ever since August, in fact ... when General Alfred H. Terry had turned Miles back to the Yellowstone with his regiment—there to build a winter cantonment under the orders specified by

Lieutenant General Philip H. Sheridan. There to prevent the hostiles of Sitting Bull and Crazy Horse from crossing the Yellowstone, from there having a straight shot of it into Canada. Very plainly the colonel chomped at the bit to be the one who would turn back the Sioux, perhaps even to capture the very chiefs who had mauled and butchered Custer's regiment.

"Here we will be a stone rolled squarely into the hostiles' garden," Miles was fond of saying as summer waned and slid headlong into autumn.

The days gradually shortened as Terry and Crook lumbered about in search of the Sioux. And then the soldier chief called the Red Beard found a band of them camped beside the Slim Buttes. Yet in the end, Crook's men—infantry and cavalry alike—had barely survived getting the hell out of Sioux country, down to eating their horses.

Somewhere out there Sitting Bull and Crazy Horse still wandered about with their war camps filled with souvenirs from the fight along the Little Bighorn.

"It won't be Crook who gets a crack at them now," Miles had told his officers. "Terry's scampered back to Lincoln for the winter. And Crook's gone lame with that horsemeat march. He's headed back to Laramie with his tail stuck between his legs."

By autumn the free-flowing creeks were down to a trickle, no longer carrying a rush of water through this fickle country to the Yellowstone. And with the great river growing more shallow with every day, the steamer captains could no longer urge their paddle wheels clear up to the mouth of the Tongue, where Miles was building his base of operations for the winter. Instead, the pilots could navigate no farther than the mouth of Glendive Creek, a full 110 miles downstream from the Tongue. It was there that Miles had six companies of the Twenty-second Infantry go into camp, guarding the supplies off-loaded from the steamers, soldiers to act as escort for those wagon trains bound up the Yellowstone Valley before winter closed its fist upon this high land.

In the last few weeks two companies of the Seventeenth Infantry had also arrived on a supply steamer. But they were both small companies—no more than thirty-five men each, which made for long days of weary tedium in their escort duties, what with at least three trips to the Tongue River and back each month. As well as keeping an eye out for the Indians rumor hinted were headed for the Yellowstone.

But since August, Smith and the rest hadn't seen so much

as a feather, not so much as a warrior along the skyline. Except for the cold and their boring rations, and that grueling work off-loading the steamers and loading the wagons . . . it was pretty tame duty. Then a few days back they had received intelligence from their scouts that some six hundred lodges of hostiles were south of the Yellowstone and moving north. With any luck the Sioux would be more interested in hunting buffalo than in making a nuisance of themselves.

They had pulled those ninety-four freight wagons and an ambulance away from the Glendive Cantonment just past ten-thirty A.M. yesterday. It hadn't been long before Smith had noticed the first of the columns of white smoke far in their front beyond the hills. Instantly he recalled how Captain Miner had told his small cadre of officers about his uneasiness, at their breakfast fire when others complained that things had been too quiet.

"Those Sioux might even intend to intercept us."

By the time Smith had reined about and rode back that two hundred yards to the front of the column with his sergeant, most of the soldiers and civilians had already sighted the shafts of signal smoke. Refusing to halt for no reason, Miner kept them moving for the time being as the men grumbled among themselves and the wagons creaked with the cold trace chains jangling in sharp bursts of metallic chatter in the dry air.

Beneath a brilliant autumn sun things remained quiet throughout the afternoon, despite those ominous signal fires ahead of their line of march. Near five o'clock yesterday the column went into camp at Spring Creek,* at a place the soldiers and teamsters had come to call Fourteen-mile Camp. By firelight Captain Miner wrote in his official journal for the day:

> The camp is in the bed of a creek, and commanded by hills at short range on all sides but the south, where it is open toward the Yellowstone River. There is a good deal of brush, and some timber along the banks of the creek. The corrals were made as compactly as possible for the night, and secured with ropes; the companies were camped close to them, two on each side; thirty-six men and four noncommissioned officers were detailed for guard; two reserves were

---

*Present-day Sand Creek.

formed and placed on the flanks not protected by the companies.

"With all that smoke, them savages surely must be telling someone about us coming," First Lieutenant Benjamin C. Lockwood had said as night had come down on the 160 men of Miner's command.

"Then that means they're not strong enough to chance hitting us," First Lieutenant William Conway replied confidently.

"Those fires just means they're calling for more warriors," Second Lieutenant William H. Kell advised. "We best cover some ground tomorrow."

Just past eleven o'clock last night the entire camp was put on alert by a single rifle shot. Smith joined other officers rushing into the dark toward the ring of pickets Miner had thrown out around the wagon camp and the grazing mules.

"I's the one fired that shot, sir!" a soldier admitted from the inky blackness of that night.

"What for, soldier?" Miner prodded as the man stepped closer.

"Saw a figure—took it to be a Injun, sir. Give him the challenge word, and he skedaddled off like I'd painted his ass with turpentine. I give a shot to either drop 'im, or speed 'im on his way."

Miner rotated the pickets an hour later at midnight and the men had settled back in their bedrolls.

Near three-thirty a brief rattle of gunfire brought Smith and the rest out of their blankets. Shot after shot was fired into camp from a distant bluff. As the rounds whistled overhead or smacked into the earth around him, the lieutenant could make out the bright, flaring muzzle flashes of the enemy guns as all the men were formed up, put on alert, ready for action. Here and there in camp a spent bullet whacked against the side of a wagon or clanged against a cast-iron kettle. Because of the distance, Miner declined to engage the warriors in a long-range duel. Instead, he kept his men ready for any try the warriors might make for the herd. It wasn't long before Smith realized the warriors did indeed have the herd in mind: most of the shots were landing in and among the corral, wounding some of the mules, scattering many others that pulled up their picket pins and broke their sidelines.

After no more than an hour the firing died off—without the soldiers firing a shot. Orders were passed along that a cold breakfast was scheduled for later that morning: no fires to be kindled that would backlight the soldiers and thereby provide easy targets for any of the skulking redskins. Only water from their canteens and hardtack. Nothing more than that as the men struck their tents and reloaded their wagons.

And with the first graying of the horizon that Wednesday morning, the wagon master brought the worst news.

"How many did you say?" Miner squealed in dismay.

"Fifty-seven mules, Cap'n," the civilian repeated. "Likely run off by the Injuns when they went to shooting into camp last night."

The nervous teamsters anxiously hitched up what mules they had left to pull the freight, down to five-mule hitches on more than half the wagons. The sun hadn't yet put in its debut when Miner ordered the march, assigning Captain Malcom McArthur's C Company of the Seventeenth Infantry to act as rearguard. Their column had no more than strung itself out, jangling little more than a mile, when McArthur's men came under attack by a war party concealed in a ravine no more than two hundred yards to their left. From there, concealed by thick brush and stunted cedar, the warriors laid down a galling fire on the soldiers as the column ground to an immediate halt.

Within moments more than two hundred warriors broke over the brow of the nearby foothills rising between last night's campsite and the Yellowstone River east of that bivouac.

McArthur and Second Lieutenant James D. Nickerson immediately formed up their little company and led them out bravely, making a countercharge on the attackers. Smith watched those foot soldiers go, all bellow and bluster, shouting their lungs out as they dashed across the uneven ground toward the hillside where the firing died off as the warriors scampered up the far slope, pursuing the enemy across a rising piece of ground until the Indians eventually disappeared over a nearby bluff.

"That should cool their heels!" Miner cheered, setting the column back to its march as Company H of the Twenty-second went up to support McArthur's men in their countercharge.

But the wagons moved no more than eighty rods when the front of the column came under attack, this time from a brushy ravine on the right flank. Miner ordered another brief halt and across the next half hour the officers ordered out a squad here, or a squad there, engaging the enemy in long-range firing with their own infantry's "Long Toms." Yet Miner got the skittish civilian teamsters to move the train through it all—despite the fact that a gaggle of warriors swarmed in behind the column and darted back and forth over the campsite the soldiers had just abandoned.

"Looking for anything of value," Miner surmised as they kept on pushing west toward the Tongue River.

By the time an hour had passed, those warriors on their back-trail were inching closer to put increasing pressure on their rear guard. All the while, more knots of warriors were making themselves known along both flanks of the march, firing at the wagons, the mules, and the long columns of infantry strung out on either side of the rutted trail. Here and there a mule was hit, calling out in its dying with an ear-splitting bray. The team was immediately ordered out of column as other wagons moved around and the procession continued while the teamsters and soldiers descended on the wagon to cut the dead and dying mules out of harness, then urged the remaining members of the team back into line during this slow-moving, deadly game of leapfrog. Despite the losses and their snail's pace, as the morning waned and became afternoon, Miner refused to stop.

"That would mean us having to square the wagons and fort up, just for the sake of a short stop," he grumbled. "No—we'll keep pushing for Clear Creek, something on the order of eight miles. Go pass the word that the men have permission to eat while we're on the march."

The autumn sun hadn't fallen far from midsky when three of the lieutenants loped to the head of the column and presented their case to an increasingly anxious Captain Miner.

"There's more of 'em than we can handle come dark, Captain," Lieutenant Nickerson said.

Miner growled, "How many do you figure we're facing?"

After glancing at the others, Lieutenant William Conway replied, "Five, maybe as many as six hundred warriors, sir."

The captain seemed to shudder at that, then stoically said, "Their numbers won't make much difference come dark. I'm certain they'll break off their attack by dusk."

"Even so, Captain—we may not have enough of the mules left by morning to push on for Tongue River," Smith observed.

"Then what?" Miner growled, turning on the lieutenant.

"I figure we'll be forced to fort up and take 'em on till General Miles figures out we aren't coming."

"How long could that be, gentlemen?" Miner asked. "Worst case, that is."

They muttered and chewed on it. Then Smith broke the stalemate.

"Longer than we have ammunition, sir."

Miner was nettled, the crow's-feet at his eyes deeper than normal. "What are you proposing, then?"

"Turn about and countermarch, sir," Lieutenant Kell suggested.

"Back for Glendive?"

"Yes, Captain," Smith agreed. "I suggest we do it while we've got ammunition to make that countermarch. We get bogged down by forting up—they'll keep us holed up till we run out of ammunition. I say let's get back to Glendive while we can."

"But we're expected at Tongue River with these supplies," Miner grumbled within his five-day-old beard. "Those supplies don't get there—"

"Sir, begging your pardon for the interruption," Smith pressed on. "We fort up, run out of ammunition, and get overrun, we lose these supplies to them Sioux ... meaning they'll never get to the Tongue River troops anyway. But if we break off here and skedaddle back to our cantonment, I figure we can convince Colonel Otis to beef up our escort and make another go of it."

"How much of the stock have we lost?" the captain demanded gruffly.

Benjamin Lockwood answered, "They've run off with more than sixty-some mules already ... and wounded that many more, sir."

Miner cogitated on that for some time as his officers stood in silence. All around them the noncoms kept the men firing by squads—for the most part able to keep the swarming warriors at a safe distance from the column. The Sioux were clearly showing a healthy respect for those Long Toms, darting in here and there, but scampering out of range just in time as a squad came forward, dropped to a knee to aim, and fired. On one side then the other, at their front then at their rear, the enemy horsemen were making things more than ticklish for Miner's escort. The situation was growing downright scary.

"We get bogged down here, we're pretty well cut off here, wouldn't you say, gentlemen?" the captain asked.

"Yes, sir," Smith agreed. "So what's it to be, Captain?"

He slapped his glove against his dusty sky-blue pants and straightened. "Give the order, men—we're turning about for

Glendive. And, for God's sake: let's try not to let those red bastards kill any more of these blessed mules!"

Gazing into the face of her sleeping child, Samantha hadn't believed anything could be quite so beautiful.

Four days old he was. Despite the sleeplessness, despite the tenderness and outright pain in her breasts, the hot shards of torment she felt down below where she had torn giving birth—no matter any of it now. She was completely in awe at the miracle of that baby.

What she and Seamus had created together. Truly a gift from God.

It was so hard to believe, still so much like a dream: the long, agonizing labor; the explosive delivery; the joy in seeing the tears streak her husband's face; the sheer and utter happiness in holding the squalling child for the first time, listening to his little cry of protest.

Oh, how he had taken to her breast that cold morning as Elizabeth Burt had shooed Seamus from the room.

"You go off now and get yourself a whiskey and a cigar. And buy one for my captain, too, won't you?"

Then Elizabeth set about instructing Sam on the art of breast-feeding—how to hold the child just so, place the nipple against his lips and cheek to excite the sucking reflex, and then to relax. Just relax and enjoy such exquisite closeness. Oh, how the little one took to that! Surely, she had thought so many times since as the babe suckled, this was his father's child! So in love with a woman's bountiful anatomy were they both.

The babe lay beside her on the bed this late afternoon. The sun would soon set beyond Old Bedlam and the evening gun would roar down on the parade. She was weary from the trips up and down the steps, laundering the diapering cloths. Never had she believed it possible that such disgusting stuff could come out of so beautiful a creature!

Seamus helped as much as he could, often being the one to carry her work downstairs for her to the room where together they would boil the water and do the wash. Each evening he would carry the little child downstairs in his huge arms, clutched so lovingly against his great body, smiling to beat the band as they warmed water in a kettle on the woodstove, preparing the babe's daily bath. In their time together Seamus had shown her much tenderness with his big, hardened hands—those same hands carefully, lovingly lathering the infant in that washbasin they had set in the middle of that small table right beside the warmth of the woodstove.

"What will we name him?" Samantha had asked him that first morning while they gave their son his very first bath.

"I thought that was best left up to the women in the family," Seamus had replied, lifting the wriggling child from the water as she draped a towel around its rosy body.

"Not in my family, we're not," Sam had declared. "In this family, boys will be named by their fathers."

"Then I will have to give it some thought."

"You do that, Seamus Donegan," she told him as she pressed against him, the child held between them in that embrace. "You give good thought to this matter of naming your firstborn son. For this may well be one of the most important things you'll ever do in life."

He had bent to kiss the top of the babe's head, then bent to brush his lips against hers. Then he said, "Yes, one of the most important things I'll ever do in this young fellow's life."

She heard him on the stairs now. There was no other sound like his boots clattering up those steps, what with their high, two-inch leather heels so they would not slip through a stirrup, a bit of a shelf on the back of the heel to support a spur, and with stovepipes almost tall enough to reach his knees—yes, he had explained the usefulness of it all to her many times. But right now those boot heels announced his return from that conference he and a few others were called to have with Mackenzie and Crook.

It was not until late that night as they lay in the darkness, with the babe nestled snuggly in the hand-me-down cradle set right against Sam's side of the bed, that she lay against Seamus's chest and knew he was not sleeping.

In the blackness of their tiny room, she asked him in a whisper, "What's keeping you from sleep?"

Moments passed before he spoke. "I don't know what to do. Before . . . before the babe arrived, I was damned sure that I wouldn't ever go marching off to make war again."

She felt him shudder, not knowing if it was from fear, or from a sob. Then Sam suggested, "Mackenzie asked you to ride with him again."

"Yes. He's kept after me, he has."

"And this time you didn't tell him no."

"Not exactly, Sam. But—I said I'd tell him in the morning."

"Seamus, my love: it took me some time before I came to

really understand who you were as a man. The sort of husband you'd make. And now the sort of father you will be to our son. I know you will have no peace in yourself if you don't go off to do what it is that you need to do."

"Peace," he repeated that word in a whisper in the dark. "I look at our son. I hold him in my arms. I gaze into his little face as he lies in my lap. And I grow scared."

"Why are you scared?" she asked, nestling her head in his neck.

"Because I'm afraid that unless I go with Mackenzie, unless I keep going until this terrible matter is done, once and for all—there will be no peace for our son."

"You do have a job to do, Seamus," she eventually said, feeling the sting of tears come to her eyes. "Part of that job is being here with me when you can to be a husband. Part of that job will be helping me to raise our new son. And a very important part of your job right now is finishing what you have begun."

For a long, long time he did not answer her. And when he did, Seamus quietly said, "Thank you for understanding my fear, Sam. And for understanding that I'm the sort of man who must go and look my fear in the eye."

"Go do this for us, Seamus. Go do this for your son."

"Yes," he answered with a long, rattling sigh. "It's about time that we finished what we started ten long years ago."

Chapter 4

14–15 October 1876

Telegraphic

Gen. Merritt Marching Into Indian Land

THE INDIANS

Merritt on a scout—Bad Indians Still Raiding.

CHEYENNE, October 13.—General Merritt left Custer City with 500 men on a scout to-day. Their destination is not positively known but it is surmised to be the Bell Fourche Fork of the Cheyenne river. The remainder of the command is still at Custer. The party of Indians who killed Monroe near Fort Laramie a few days since also raided the ranch of Nick Jones on the old Red Cloud road, stealing twenty-five horses. Monroe's body was pierced by eight bullets.

Captain Miner's wagon train limped back to the Glendive supply depot after nine P.M. on the evening of 11 October, having hacked their way through the massing warriors, fighting for nearly every foot until the Sioux were certain the train was retreating to the east along Clear Creek. The warriors broke off their attack as the soldiers rumbled along a trail crossing higher ground, thereby giving the soldiers a commanding view of the surrounding countryside as darkness approached.

After allowing the mules and those four infantry companies two days to recoup their strength, Lieutenant Colonel Elwell S. Otis of the Twenty-second Infantry determined this time to set out himself to deliver those much-needed supplies to the Tongue River cantonment. On the afternoon of the thirteenth he informed his troops that with the addition of one more company to bolster their strength, they would be moving out come morning—at which point forty-one of the civilian teamsters buckled under and stated flatly that they were not about to ride back into the breech.

Like many of the other officers, Second Lieutenant Alfred C. Sharpe figured Otis's soldiers would be all the better for not having those mule-whackers along.

"So be it," Otis declared, nonplussed, when the civilians bowed their backs and refused to go. "We'll do with what we have for teamsters and fill the rest of the wagon seats with soldiers. I'm determined to go through to Tongue River this time . . . even if fighting takes us there."

Not only did they have the addition of G Company, Seventeenth Infantry, under Major Louis H. Sanger, this time they would haul three Gatling guns along with the wagon train.

That afternoon Otis dispatched a courier to ride off with news of the attack on Miner's train as well as the renewed attempt to reach Tongue River, that report bound for Colonel William B. Hazen, commanding the Sixth U.S. Infantry at Fort Buford.

At midmorning on the fourteenth Otis's eleven officers and 185 men departed Glendive cantonment, putting a scant ten miles behind them before going into bivouac for the night. Dusk had deepened, and many of the soldiers were preparing to turn in, when just past eight P.M. a shot was fired from one of the pickets, alarming the camp.

"I'll lay you odds we had a man blast away at another Injun ghost," growled Lieutenant Oskaloosa Smith as he trotted up beside Sharpe as they headed toward the disturbance.

"Like it was on your trip out, eh?" Sharpe replied.

Damn near a repeat, it turned out to be. Except for the fact that this time the picket reported spotting two horsemen when he offered his challenge—swearing to the officers on his mother's grave he had hit one of them—although a hastily formed search party found nothing in the dark. Camp settled down and the rest of the night passed uneventfully. It wasn't until first light when one of the outlying pickets brought within the lines a crippled pony he had spotted hobbling among some stunted cedar along the creek bottom.

"Injun pony," Alfred Sharpe observed as the officers looked the wounded animal over.

A pad saddle was lashed around its middle with a single surcingle. Several blankets were tied behind the saddle. It wore a single rawhide rein, as well as a picket rope trailing behind the animal.

"I'll bet that pony threw off the bloody savage and he had to fetch himself a ride with the other red bastard," one of the men surmised.

Otis pulled on his gloves and looked into the sky at the emerging sun. "Time we got under way, gentlemen. Mr. Smith, see that this animal is put out of its misery."

Just before seven A.M. on that bright, clear Sunday morning, the fifteenth of October, they resumed their journey. The drivers formed up the wagons into four long lines to make their way across the rolling, broken ground as the soldiers went into position to form a square surrounding the train. In the rotation of the march, Lieutenant Sharpe's company that day drew duty as the advance guard for the column. When his foot soldiers stepped out in lively fashion, making good time just in front of the first wagon and the rest of the escort, the lieutenant began to recall Sunday mornings he had enjoyed back east.

Peaceful Sabbath, he ruminated as the frosty air began to warm, sensing some contentment flood over him with those fond memories. How pleasant it would be back in the States today, he thought: to hear the church bells ringing and to see the good people coming into church. He almost imagined he could hear the sweet tones of the organ, the choir raising their voices in song with the old hymns, and that oft-repeated proscription of the preacher from Sharpe's youth, "The Lord is in His holy temple; let all the earth keep silence before him—"

The rattle of rifle fire cruelly shattered his reverie into a thousand tinkling pieces like the falling of broken glass. Officers shouted orders while most of the men bellowed oaths. Mules brayed and bucked in their harnesses. Timbers creaked and wagon tongues groaned as teamsters and green soldiers fought to control the unruly, frightened animals hitched to those ninety-four wagons. Immediately in their front the two point men, half-breed scout Robert Jackson and Sergeant Patrick Kelly, were whipping their horses back to the column, laying low in the saddle, bullets sailing over their heads as a band of horsemen suddenly appeared behind them, racing in hot pursuit. The hat flew from Sergeant Kelly's head in the mad chase. Immediately a warrior reined around and dismounted, picking up the spoils and planting the hat atop his braided scalp lock and feathers while the rest of the horsemen drew up and halted just inside rifle range, taunting Sharpe's soldiers as hundreds more made their show along the nearby bluffs, hollering and screaming like devils incarnate.

"Sergeant!" Alfred Sharpe bellowed.

"Sir!"

"Left front into line!" he called out the order.

"All right, you young sappies!" the sergeant growled as he whirled on his heel. "You heard the good lieutenant yer own selves now! Left front into *line!*"

Jackson and Kelly dusted to a halt among Sharpe's company and dismounted hurriedly. The swarthy half-breed scout collapsed to the round, ripped off one of his moccasins and held it to the sky for all to see, poking a finger through a new bullet hole. Sergeant Kelly inspected the track of a bullet that had ripped the thick shoulder of his dark-blue wool coat, the torn cloth now fluttering in the breeze.

Otis reined up on horseback immediately behind his forward company. "Mr. Sharpe—detach with ten men and deploy to that hill on your right! The rest of your company will move forward under Mr. Conway, putting pressure on those bastards holding that bluff. Drive them from it, Mr. Conway—is that understood?"

William Conway saluted anxiously. "Yes, sir!"

As Conway formed up the rest of H Company, Sharpe counted off his ten and jogged to the right, slowed by the steepness of the slope of that hill where they would have a commanding field of fire against the bluff where the enemy horsemen swarmed. While Otis kept the train moving and the rest of the foot soldiers came up double-time to bring their Long Toms to bear on the Sioux, the warriors began to fall back as bullets landed among them. Still they persisted, swarming on this flank or that, moving like a stream of quicksilver where they thought the soldiers weakest. As soon as that position along the rumbling wagon train was bolstered, the horsemen would dart off to put pressure on a new position while the wagons slowly punched safely through the defile and made the gradual climb up to the top of the rolling prairie.

"This is Sitting Bull's bunch, men!" the lieutenant colonel reminded them from horseback, first here, then there, above his men—making one fine target of himself. "These are the devils who butchered Custer! We have them! By Jehovah—we have them now!"

For more than an hour the long-range skirmishing dragged on as Otis kept his civilian and soldier teamsters urging their mules with every crack of the whip, hauling those wagons along the road as they inched closer and closer to the Yellowstone River. Behind them and in front, more and more Sioux boiled like an anthill before the coming of a thunderstorm.

"Lookee yonder, Colonel! We got some folks coming in!"

At the cry from one of Sharpe's men, the lieutenant and Otis whirled, spotting the three men sprinting on foot, headed directly for the soldier line from the nearby timber that bordered the north bank of the Yellowstone.

"Hold your men at ready, Mr. Sharpe," Otis ordered.

"Why—them's soldiers!" someone shouted.

"Bluecoats—sure enough," Sharpe replied with a wag of his head. "But look there at the rest of them Indians riding lickety-split to cut 'em off, Colonel."

Right behind the sprinting trio came a mass of warriors spurring their little ponies like angry hornets.

"Lay down some covering fire, by God!" Otis screeched. "Don't let those red sonsabitches cut those men off!"

Sharpe hurried H Company into position on the prairie, squad by squad stepping forward to use their far-reaching weapons most effectively. Here and there among the Sioux, riders fell back, but others kept on racing for the three men on foot. Suddenly, at just the right range, the last of the Sioux skidded to a halt and gave up the chase as the trio kept running for their lives until they reached the front of H Company. As they lunged among the soldier lines, gasping and grunting for wind, it was plain as paint to see they were Indians dressed in soldier clothes.

"Don't shoot!" Sharpe ordered his men, then he turned on the three. "Get your goddamned hands up!"

A dozen men had their rifles pointed at the trio as the three bent at the waist, weak-kneed from their spring, sucking in air as if every breath might be their last. Their eyes were wide, staring round at all the muzzles pointed their way.

"C-c-cap'n Miner here?" one of the trio huffed breathlessly in a thick, half-breed English.

"Yes, he's with us," Otis replied. "I'm Colonel Otis. Who the hell are you?"

"Otis? You the soldier chief from Glendive?" the swarthy man gasped, glancing at the other two with him. "We come from Miles." He pointed to the other two, both of them clearly Indians, then put his two hands to his head to make wolf ears—the plains sign for scout. "His scouts. Miles send us find Miner and wagons."

"This is it, mister."

The scout looked over his shoulder at the swirling Sioux. "Miles, he want us find wagons. We ain't seen wagons for so long."

"Yes, goddammit," Otis growled. "I understand we are overdue. But, by Jehovah, we're getting there. When did the three of you leave Tongue River?"

The dark-skinned scout watched momentarily as Robert Jackson came up beside Otis. "Four of us come from Tongue River. Hello, big brother," he called out, stepping forward with his arms held wide.

"Brother?" Otis asked, dismayed as the two embraced. "Is this your brother, Jackson?"

The two brown-skinned men embraced, pounding one another on the back; then Robert turned back to Otis and said, "This is my little brother, William. Miles send me to help you, and keep William to help him."

"You have water, brother?" asked William Jackson with a pasty tongue.

"Get these men some water," Otis ordered, then turned back to the two half-breeds and the Indian scouts. "You were saying you started off from the Tongue with four of you. And tell me how you came to be afoot."

"We started off with four horses from Miles to look for this train. Miner late with wagons—Miles start to worry days ago. Near sundown yesterday we run onto a big war party. Made a running fight of it. One of my Rees—White Antelope—he was knocked from his horse while we run from the war party. But Bear Plume here was able to get him on the back of his own horse, to protect his body from the enemy. We get White Antelope into cover down by the river, yonder."

"Down west of here?" Robert Jackson asked, pointing toward the distant Yellowstone.

"Yes," William replied. "We hide in the willow back a good ways. All our horses killed or wounded in holding the Lakota back. At sun going down yesterday we set the two wounded horses free to fool the enemy—and then after dark we make off toward the mouth of Clear Creek. The Lakota never found us all night we stay back in the brush. We hear shooting last night, off to the east."

"You must mean when some of these bastards tried to jump our picket lines," Sharpe said.

"We stick to the brush all night. We wait," Jackson continued. "Your fight start today, we hear the guns. Still we wait till we see soldiers."

"So you got a man dead?" Otis asked.

William Jackson nodded gravely, "Bleed a lot and die yesterday. Gone now."

"Where'd you leave his body? The Sioux get him?"

"No," William said, turning to point as he answered, "Carried him all the way down in the brush, beside that tall cottonwood." Some sadness crossed his face as he turned back to the lieutenant colonel and added, "Bear Plume wants to bury their friend."

"By all means," Otis replied knowingly, his eyes shifting to watch the long-range scrap between his men and the swirling horsemen.

True to his word, the colonel ordered Sharpe's H Company to push on toward the far copse of trees along the Yellowstone where Otis stopped the wagon train, set out skirmishers, and effectively held the Sioux at bay while he had a detail bury the dead Arikara scout before pressing on.

"Let's get this wagon train to Tongue River!" he finally cried, setting Sharpe's company out in the advance once more.

Hour after hour the rolling fight raged on as Otis kept his civilian and soldier teamsters grinding along, whipping mules ahead of their heavy wagons. In and out, back and forth the Sioux swarmed, shrieking, screeching—never drawing close enough to use their bows but firing their rifles instead, showing a healthy respect for those long-range guns of the infantry. Minute by minute it seemed the enemy horsemen were reinforced—new warriors arriving at the scene until there was an estimated force of some seven to eight hundred Sioux facing the beleaguered, outnumbered soldier column.

Desperate to punch his way through, Otis used every trick up his sleeve: with every Sioux charge, he ordered a countercharge by one company or another while the wagons continued on at a slow but steady pace. One after another he ordered out the various squads and companies, each unit skirmishing with the enemy horsemen before being recalled while another company was dispatched into the fray at a different position along the line of march.

As steady as was their progress, by two o'clock that afternoon Otis's column had made no more than six miles since morning, virtually fighting tooth and nail for every yard beneath the high autumn sun that caused the men to sweat despite the season.

"Looks like they don't intend to budge from that bluff to our front, Colonel," Sharpe cried out to Otis.

For a long moment the train commander appraised their situation. Just ahead of him lay the narrow valley of Clear Creek, the stream having cut itself to the bottom of a narrow gorge some two hundred feet deep. On the far side of the rocky ravine at least two hundred Sioux held a commanding position—awaiting the soldiers. The wagon train came to a clattering halt.

"We can't make that crossing," Lieutenant Kell complained.

"We must, sir," Sharpe argued, turning to study Otis's face—hoping to find some resolve there. "We must make the crossing, Colonel."

"Or?"

"Or we've been defeated and we'll never resupply Tongue River again."

Otis turned on Sharpe, bellowing loudly, "Absolutely correct, Mr. Sharpe! Gentlemen—those fiends will not turn us back. It's up to you. Do you understand?"

Sharpe saluted smartly and said, "Requesting that you position one of the Gatlings to lay down a covering fire for my men, Colonel."

"Dandy idea, Lieutenant!"

Within minutes the field piece was rolled into position and a crew set to rake the far side of the valley where the Indians waited while Sharpe quickly formed up his men and led them off on the double, rushing to secure the crossing. Just as they reached Clear Creek, with the bullets kicking up spouts of dirt around them, Sharpe's sergeant Hathaway grunted, falling to his knees beside the lieutenant.

"I'm hit, sir!" and he threw a hand to his breast as he collapsed to the ground.

In that moment Sharpe watched the sergeant pull his hand away and inspect himself. There was no blood, no bullet hole, but there at his knee lay the spent bullet that had whacked him on the chest. Yet in the space of that few heartbeats, the warriors on the far side of the stream got their range and began to lay in a galling fire on the gallant men of H Company.

"Into the stream! Now, men—be lively!" Sharpe called out, knowing if he did not keep them moving now, they would waver, fall back, and they would never secure the crossing.

Waving his service revolver in the air with one arm, he tugged his sergeant back to his feet; then together they raced to the creekbank, leading the soldiers through the skimpy brush and into the shallow water. To the far side they splashed, shooting and bellowing as the warriors on the far bluff yelped and screeched in dismay.

"Fire by volleys!" Sharpe ordered on the far bank. "First squad! Forrard . . . ," waiting for them to kneel, then, "aim—fire!"

The first six slogged forward, drenched above their knees, shivering in the cold autumn wind that knifed down the sharp ravine, immediately went to their knees, and fired on command.

"Second squad!"

A second set of six moved through the ranks of the first.

"Aim!"

Kneeling immediately, throwing their long rifles against their shoulders, cheeks to the stocks, eyes along the barrels.

"Fire!"

One after another Sharpe had the rifle squads leapfrogging forward, slowly purchasing a few more yards of ground on that far bank with each volley, inching their way up the slope to the rocks where the warriors held on, firing down on them.

"We can take the hill!" Sharpe shouted as the enemy fire began to taper off. "Now, men! On the double: *charge!*"

Like fiends themselves, H Company sprinted and skidded, slipped and clawed their way up the slope toward the Sioux. Some cursed, others screamed, and most silently went about their reloading, shell after shell after shell, foot by foot pushing back the enemy.

Atop the bluff now they could see that the last of the warriors had set fire to the tall tinder-dry grass. The flames leaped and crackled beneath each strong gust of wind, driving layers of stifling smoke down on the soldiers as they clambered up the rocky slope.

Near the top, Sharpe turned to look behind him for but a moment, and in that moment saw Otis himself leading the first of the wagons out of the stream and up the trail. By damn! H Company had secured the crossing. Wagon by wagon, the teamsters and soldiers were stopping in the shallow creek to water the stock as they reached the stream. Beside each wagon soldiers quickly refilled the water barrels before more teams pushed on down into the creek bottom. Two or three wagons at a time now rumbled up to the west bank of Clear Creek—which meant that now the warriors might swarm in on all sides of H Company and the supply train.

What made things all the more frightening for the lieutenant was that with the smoke and the fires, the noise and the way the battle rolled here, then there—for the life of him it seemed even more warriors were coming to reinforce the horsemen all the time.

Behind them Lieutenant Kell's K Company closed the file as the last wagons reached the creek and began taking on water before crossing—when suddenly more than a hundred warriors roared down on them from behind, yipping and firing on that little band of soldiers just moving into the water from the east bank. When Kell sent word to Otis that his men were running low on ammunition, the lieutenant colonel ordered down another thousand rounds and a few reinforcements.

About the same time that ammunition was reaching K Company, the last of the wagons began pulling farther and farther away across the stream. For a few minutes it appeared Kell's men would be cut off and surrounded by the hostiles—sure to be overwhelmed. Time and again the horsemen surged forward, sweeping past and dropping to the far side of their ponies, firing beneath the animals' necks before clattering away, hooves churning up clods of prairie. Charge after charge after charge—

"Major Sanger!" Otis screamed above the noise of wagons and men, mules and Sioux. "Take your men and break through to K Company. Bring them up to rejoin the column!"

Answering with only a salute, Sanger got his G Company off at a lope to reinforce Kell's besieged troops barely holding up the rear of the column. By now the Sioux had fired the tall dried grass on both flanks of the column on the west bank and to the rear, where they began to withdraw with Sanger's reinforcement of Kell's soldiers.

The air burned their lungs as they struggled to close up with the wagons. Men coughed, dropped to their knees as they were robbed of breath, sucking desperately at the air as black flecks of smoldering grass littered the sky all around them like July fireflies.

"Keep those goddamned wagons moving!" Otis yelled far to the front, prodding his drivers. "We stop here—we're all done for!"

Inch by inch, foot by foot, the mules and wagons formed up by fours once more having reached that high ground. Together with what was left of the escort not fighting in their front or to their rear, they ground their way along the rutted Tongue River Road.

They came to a jangling halt, men bellowing and the mules noisily fighting their harness—for out of the north and east swarmed a reinforced party of yelping horsemen.

"Keep those goddamned wagons moving!" Otis hollered, weaving in and among the leaders atop one of the five horses left for his men at Glendive Cantonment.

When things appeared their worst, the warriors on the right flank suddenly broke off their attack and boiled to the front of the column, where some of the horsemen crossed and reinforced their numbers, suddenly putting extreme pressure on the left side while the rest remained to stubbornly harass the front of the train. It was there the first wagons slowed even more until the entire line was all but stopped.

In heartbeats Otis lumbered up to his advance guard, ordering, "Mr. Sharpe—detach Mr. Conway with a squad of ten men and keep the way cleared!"

With Lieutenant Conway and his soldiers off to punch their way against the warriors at their front, Sharpe remained with the rest of his H.Company as well as G Company to hold back the extreme pressure of those warriors reinforced on their left flank. It took the better part of an hour before the wagons were once more able to move down the road. By that time the smoke became even more suffocating from the grass fires that raged around them on all sides—some of the wagons and mule teams forced to frantically dash through the leaping flames, men hollering in panic and mules braying in fear ... when within moments the winds shifted around from the west and for the most part raised that thick, choking pall—preventing the gray, stinging blanket from completely swallowing the movement of the soldier column.

Someone cried out on Sharpe's far right. He whirled to watch a soldier from G Company spin to the ground, clutching his knee. The man's bunkie was on him in an instant, ripping off

his belt and tightening it above the wound. It wasn't but a minute before Surgeon Charles T. Gibson was there to lend a hand.

At that very moment Sharpe realized just how cut off they
were: on all sides the rolling prairie lay blackened, smoldering, a
great gray shroud blotting out the midafternoon sun hung like a
red ball above them in the autumn sky. It reminded the lieutenant of the waste Napoleon had laid to the steppes of Russia in his
disastrous retreat more than half a century before. Then he
chided himself—to think that his little struggle was of any consequence compared to the great European campaigns he had
studied at the Academy.

Then almost immediately he decided theirs was a worthy
struggle. While Napoleon battled against a civilized enemy—
Otis's column found itself surrounded by a fiendish enemy who
fought not only with bullets, but with smoke and fire and dev-
ilish noise. In addition, they each struggled privately against the
twin demons of a soldier's nightmare: hunger and thirst.

From this high ground they had struggled so hard to reach
and to hold against terrible odds, the lieutenant now dared look
back at the narrow valley where the Indians swarmed against the
rear guard. Now the Sioux held the valley behind them. The enemy had possession of water and wood while the soldiers had
only what they hurriedly had taken on in crossing the creek. To
attempt to run that gauntlet back to the creek for water would
be nothing short of sheer suicide.

Up here on the high ground there was little to no firewood.
What there had been was now all but burned to ash as every
footstep and every hoof raised the stifling black dust into the air.
As a biting wind came up, the sun continued its rapid fall, closing on the far horizon.

Out there to the west . . . where Miles and his Fifth Infantry
knew nothing of their predicament.

Chapter 5

15 October 1876

"We are not done yet, brother," William Jackson said as he sat down beside Robert at the small fire they had dug into the prairie so that its low flames would not show.

There wasn't much wood to speak of in that cold bivouac the soldier column made on a broad depression that dominated the high ground that night. But at least they had plenty of food to eat—if a man could call hard bread and pig meat real food. And water. At least they had taken on enough water to see to the mules, enough for each man to refill his canteen for the night.

William's stomach rumbled. He stared at the tiny fire and remembered the meals his mother had set before them when they had been boys on the high Missouri: the boiled buffalo boss ribs, pemmican sweetened with chokecherries, stewed *pommes blanche*, and his favorite—dried camas. It made his mouth water, made his stomach feel all the more pinched to think on such feasting. Here at least, he told himself, they were warm.

The Jackson brothers and Bear Plume had scoured the scorched campground, pulling up the twisted branches and limbs of the scrub oak and cedar with their hands, gathering the charred wood within the flaps of their coats while the nameless Ree scout used his belt knife to dig a fire hole in the blackened earth. Now the four of them sat huddled around the low flames, talking in whispers.

From the best estimation of the soldiers, Otis's column had made all of fifteen miles during their day-long running fight before making camp at five o'clock, close to sundown. The Lakota continued to flit around on all sides of the soldiers as the wagons were formed into a large corral, and shots were exchanged between pickets and the daring horsemen until darkness fell just past seven P.M. From time to time one of the infantrymen made his shot count, so that by the time night sank over that bivouac, Otis's men could claim to have knocked at least half a dozen warriors from their ponies.

No soldiers had been killed during the day's skirmishing, but three men had been slightly wounded by spent bullets—the infantry's Long Toms had simply held the Lakota too far out of range to make effective use of their charges and whirling attacks. These foot-sloggers had, by and large, kept the maddening dash of those hundreds of horsemen at bay, holding them back at least a thousand yards, just beyond the range of their Springfield rifles. Otis had begun this journey with ten thousand rounds for his rifles. This evening his men reported they were down to less than half of that. Many miles yet to go, and surrounded by the enemy who outnumbered them as many as four to one.

"Tomorrow come," Robert agreed. "That will be a new day for Sitting Bull."

"Sitting Bull?" Bear Plume asked, recognizing the sound of the Lakota shaman's name in English.

"Yes," William answered as he held his hands over the glowing fire pit to warm them with the other men. "These are Sitting Bull's warriors. They cross the Yellowstone. Come to hunt all these buffalo we see after leaving Tongue River. Good hunting—always means lots of Lakota around."

Bear Plume grunted and fell silent.

Occasionally they would hear the clink of a tin cup against a rifle barrel, or the bray of a mule, a gust of muffled laughter, or the sneeze of some man down with a cold. It was that season of the year on the high plains. Even for men who spent most of their lives outdoors. With warm, sunny days and the sort of nights that could chill a man to his narrow—most folks out here simply put up with a seasonal cough or sniffle.

Tonight Otis's men were all on alert, out there in the rifle pits the soldiers had hastily dug on a perimeter five hundred yards out from the corral where they huddled, quiet and sleepless, watchful through the cold autumn night.

As the high plains awaited the coming of another winter.

William Jackson had seen twenty-one winters since his Blackfoot mother had given birth to him at Fort Benton, far, far up the Missouri River at the head of navigation, just downstream from the Great Falls. At that time the American Fur Company was in the buffalo-robe trade with the western tribes. He had to do no more than close his eyes these days to remember the great adobe and picket walls, the two-story buildings enclosed within—a great place to be a child.

His grandfather, Hugh Monroe, had been an employee of the great Hudson's Bay Company, first coming to its Mountain Fort on the Saskatchewan in 1816, where he married Fox Woman, daughter of a Blackfoot chief. He held the position of post hunter, and together they had two sons and two daughters. One of them, Amelia, would marry Thomas Jackson, the member of an old Virginia family who had joined American Fur in 1835. Unlike the rest of the company employees who followed the custom of marrying Pikuni women, a tribe of the Blackfoot Confederacy, Thomas had fallen in love with Amelia.

Robert was their firstborn. Two years later William came along. They were inseparable. What a life they shared! As children they learned the three languages spoken at the fort: English, French Creole, and Pikuni. The Blackfoot tongue dominated most trade talk. By the time the boys were six or seven, they could speak all three languages with equal ease. In addition, on those long winter nights huddled before their fires in the fort's quarters, father Thomas had taken pains to teach his two sons to read and write.

"You will learn never to shame the noble blood that runs in your veins," he instructed his boys. "Your mother comes from Pikuni royalty. And my own family goes back a long, long way in the Old Dominion."

Every year with the summer steamer their father made sure he brought up toys and games and storybooks from the company's offices in St. Louis. As boyhood slowly passed away, the boys learned to ride and shoot, use a knife and tomahawk from their mother's people. Such training was vital, for any man who carried Indian blood in his veins, the northern Rockies meant he would have friends, and he would suffer enemies. In their youth William and Robert narrowly escaped an Assiniboine war party. Not long afterward the first settlers came and threw up their log huts in the shadow of Fort Benton.

"That marks the beginning of the end for us!" grandfather cried, shaking a fist at the newcomers.

"What does this mean?" young William had asked, frightened.

"It means the whites are invading our country," the old white-head explained angrily. "They will build a town, right here! They will begin to swarm all over our plains and along the foot of our mountains. They will kill off our meat animals, trap out our fur animals. My young ones—they are the kind that will desolate our country with their cattle and make beggars of us!"

Occasionally the boys would go out for days and camp with "woodhawks"—those men who, at great risk to their lives, would cut the immense cords of wood they sold to river steamboats plying the northern rivers each summer. During those seasons of their lives, not a year went by without raids by the Northern Cheyenne or Lakota—taking the lives of many of these daring, hearty woodhawks who would move their camp every day, eat supper around a fire, then always float downstream a mile or so before making a fireless camp for the night.

In the early spring the ice began to break up in those northern rivers. Every day they watched the passing carcasses of buffalo, some of the beasts becoming lodged at the upper end of the islands or pinned against piles of driftwood. Some were creatures that had drowned, having broken through the river's icy crust the previous winter. Even more had been captured by the quicksands, slowly sinking to their death. Buzzards and magpies, coyotes and wolves, even grizzlies feasted upon such rich carrion tangled with the trash-wood snarled along the banks each spring.

Together with their father and others, the Jackson boys had trapped the Milk, Deep Creek, the Judith, and the Musselshell both spring and fall, returning to the post for the winter. By the time they were in their teens, American soldiers had begun to occupy the old fort, making their presence known among the tribes of the northern plains. One by one a long line of stores, hotels, and saloons went up nearby, almost overnight, after gold was discovered in the nearby country. Their father decided it was time to move downriver, away from the goldfields.

At Fort Buford, Thomas became a clerk for Charles Larpenteur's Northwest Company. Here they traded with the Yanktonais and some of the Lakota bands. The Sioux bands were a haughty, standoffish people who wanted nothing to do with the Jackson boys. Yet there were a few Arikara who camped near the fort. In fact, William and Robert became best friends with an older boy who was, like them, a half-breed. While his father was Sioux, his mother was Arikara—the two of them had married years before when the two tribes were enjoying a rare period of peace between them. With the coming of the white man, hostilities resumed between the tribes, so the woman returned to her own people and taught her son the Arikara's hatred of the Lakota.

This night at his tiny fire, with the cold stars like pinpricks in the black curtain overhead, William remembered his good friend, the Arikara named Bloody Knife. Remembered how for three summers he boasted of being Custer's favorite scout. So this night William thought on how Bloody Knife had died with Custer at the hands of his father's people—the Lakota—there in the valley of the Greasy Grass. Killed not that many months ago by these same warriors who followed Sitting Bull north in search of the buffalo herds.

Bloody Knife had been a good friend, warning them almost from that first day about the Lakota—how the Lakota made enemies all too easily and would never get along with the white man. From him and other Rees, the brothers learned the Arikara language that summer of 1871.

Two summers later at Fort Buford they learned that the railroad would be coming west.

"This will be the beginning of a real war," Bloody Knife had warned them. "The Lakota, the Cheyenne—now they will do everything they can to keep the white man out of their last buffalo ground."

No matter, both Robert and William were eager to become army scouts. When they told their parents they had enlisted, Thomas frowned and bellowed that he would not have it.

"Thomas," their mother intervened in that gentle way of hers, "the wild blood that is in these boys—the blood of Hugh Monroe and his fighting Scotch ancestors, the blood of many generations of Pikuni warriors—that blood cannot be denied. They are warriors. They must follow their hearts."

"Well, then," Thomas replied after some thought, "you always have your way."

Tonight William fondly remembered that afternoon three years before. How they had left their quarters with their father so that he could give his blessing before the post commander. He remembered how his mother's voice had risen plaintively as soon as they left the room: that high-pitched, mournful song, calling on the spirits, calling on the power of the Ancient Coyote, the sacred helper to watch over her sons as they rode into battle. As they chose to face death.

That summer they went downriver on a steamer for the first time with Bloody Knife and other Ree scouts. At Fort Lincoln they joined Custer's cavalry and the men who were mapping the route for the new railroad that would follow the Yellowstone west. The Sioux found them, harassed them time and again that summer before the soldiers finally turned back. William knew it would not be the last time he would face and fight Lakota warriors.

Nor would Custer shrink from returning—to fight them again, and eventually fall at the Greasy Grass.

Then the next summer—1874—the Jackson boys joined Custer once more, this time on a scout into the Black Hills.

Bloody Knife told them, "You know this is sacred ground to the Lakota. They watch us every day, wanting our scalps, but we are too strong for them. They will wait—and one day they will be too strong for Custer."

William remembered the look on Bloody Knife's face, remembered how they knew it would come to pass one day: this big fight when many of the scouts, and many soldiers, would be killed. And Custer would fall.

The past spring as the Jackson boys prepared to leave Fort Abraham Lincoln with General Alfred Terry's column, bound for the Sioux country, Bloody Knife came to speak to the Arikara.

"I have just come from a talk with the Long Hair Custer. He says that his woman is terribly low of heart, and that the women of the other officers are also. So when we leave in the morning, Long Hair wants us to parade past the fort, to show the women that we are many and strong, to quiet their fears. We, my friends—we Indian scouts—are to lead this parade. It is truly a great honor."

As Bloody Knife and Charlie Reynolds led them away from the fort the next morning, the Ree women sang a sad song that chilled William's heart. Tonight he remembered the day he rode into the valley of the Greasy Grass with Reno's men. He watched as Bloody Knife and Charlie Reynolds fell to the Lakota. He would always remember how the scouts had warned Long Hair that the Sioux were too many.

Tonight William wondered if there were too many for them to fight tomorrow.

Johnny Bruguier stared into the darkness and tried to imagine how those soldiers felt—knowing they were surrounded by more than the night. He wondered if any of them had been with Reno's men months ago: surrounded, bleeding, chewed up, and thirsty as they waited for the rising of the summer's sun. If there were any of Reno's men with these soldiers, their hearts would be small and frightened this dark night.

Knowing that the warriors of Sitting Bull and Gall had them encircled once more.

Out of the darkness, where the fire's light did not reach, emerged a warrior who came up to touch Johnny on the shoulder.

"The Bull wants to speak with you," the man said quietly before he pointed off in a certain direction and sat down at Johnny's fire, joining the other men, who talked in low tones of the day's fighting.

Bruguier rose and went briefly to stroke the neck of his pony. The bay was a gift from Sitting Bull, who had named it Hohe Horse. In return Johnny had given the chief a Winchester rifle.

As he set off, he knew where he would find Sitting Bull and the rest of the war chiefs. But what would they want of him, Johnny wondered as he moved through the darkness, between patches of firelight where the hundreds of warriors sat through the night, waiting for the coming of the sun when they could renew their attack on the soldiers' wagon train. Why had they called him?

If they ask me to help them figure out the heart of these soldiers, what am I to say?

Surely these Lakota can see the soldiers are not about to give in, to turn back the way the others did five days before. When Sitting Bull had led the bands across the Elk River a day before discovering that first train of soldier wagons, they had been looking for buffalo. The herds were great, and the beasts were fat. It was to be a good hunt—allowing the women to put away more than enough meat to last the winter as they did their best to avoid the white man.

"You have come, Big Leggings," said the Bull as he motioned for Johnny to come join the group ringing the cheery fire where women passed pots of coffee among them all. The great chief's most important advisers were all there in their blankets and robes: No Neck, Bull Eagle, Red Skirt, and Pretty Bear.

"What does Sitting Bull want of me this cold night?"

"Sit. Have some coffee to warm you. Then we will talk."

Bruguier took his cup of coffee, holding it beneath his chin to feel the steam, enjoying the warmth of it between his two hands. He took a sip, then asked, "How is White Bull's wound?"

"A soldier bullet tore through his left arm this afternoon before the fighting ended. The bones are broken and may not heal right. But already as the sun was falling—he talks of wanting to fight the soldiers again tomorrow."

"There are many in this camp who want to continue the fight tomorrow."

Sitting Bull looked pensive as he replied, "More fighting, is it? All we wanted was to be left alone. When it came time to cross to the north bank of the Elk River, our scouts told us soldiers were huddled in their camp to the east of us,* and that the Bear Coat had his soldiers building their log lodges west of us.† It was the right thing to cross between them to reach this country so rich in buffalo."

Around them, many of the elders and old warriors grunted in approbation of the Bull's words.

Then the chief continued, saying, "After we put meat away for the coming time of cold and took many hides for the women to work through the winter moons, we always go north to the white man's Fort Peck where we can trade with the Yanktonais Lakota and the Red River métis."

"For more guns and bullets, yes," Johnny agreed.

Sitting Bull sucked on his lower lip a few moments, staring at the fire before he said, "These soldiers are in our country. We try to stay away from them, but they come to our country, Big Leggings. We want only our country and to be left alone—but the soldiers come and trouble us in our hunting, trouble us in what our people have done for many, many winters on this buffalo ground. So it was that Gall and our warriors attacked the wagon train and drove it back the day after we crossed the Elk River. So it was that we again attacked the next wagon train yesterday."

Johnny wagged his head, saying, "I don't understand why the soldiers haven't turned back as they did the last time we shot their mules and made things hard on them. We have them outnumbered. Maybe it is the far-shooting soldier guns."

The chief glanced across the fire at the war chief who had lost two wives and three of his children in Reno's attack on the Greasy Grass that past summer. "My friend's heart still burns to kill more soldiers."

"It always will burn," Gall replied. "I don't think there is

---

*Lieutenant Colonel Elwell S. Otis at the Glendive Cantonment, Montana Territory.
†Colonel Nelson A. Miles at the Tongue River Cantonment, Montana Territory.

enough soldier blood to quench how my heart burns with hate for them."

Sitting Bull nodded, looking back at Johnny to say, "At dawn Gall wants to lead his warriors against the wagon soldiers once again."

With concern, Johnny's eyes flicked at Gall for an instant before he asked of Sitting Bull, "And what if our warriors cannot stop the wagons tomorrow?"

Sitting Bull continued to stare at the fire some more before he finally looked up at Johnny. "It might soon be time for you to talk to these soldiers who refuse to turn back from our buffalo country."

Chapter 6

16 October 1876

Telegraphic

Redskin Raids and Murders in Wyoming

THE INDIANS

Redskins Raiding in Wyoming.

CHEYENNE, October 14.—Last night two head of horses were stolen from a camp near Custer. A detachment of soldiers followed the trail and found the animals in possession of two Mexicans and whites, who resisted arrest and both were killed.

The Indians drove into the station a wood party working seven miles from Sage Creek. A number of Indians are reported as having left this agency at noon to-day and twelve horses were stolen by them from McIlvain's ranch near the Chugwater. Parker, with a detachment of the Second Cavalry, who arrived at the last named place to-night, came in contact with a large body of Indians at 12 to-day, ten miles from Hunton's ranch on the head of Richard Creek, and a fight ensued. Private Tasker was killed and left on the field. The Indians have about 1,000 head of stock and are heading for Buger's Ferry.

William Jackson stirred restlessly within his blankets before first light. It was the coldest time of the day, and he could tell the fire at their feet had all but gone out. With the buffalo robe pulled over his head, he half listened as the muffled sounds told him Robert had kicked his way out of his bedroll and was stomping around, stirring embers and punching life back into the tiny pit fire. William finally stuck his head out and peered into the coming of dawn, blinking at his brother.

The eldest said, "Tomorrow—you start the morning fire."

He was nodding to Robert . . . at the very moment the first gunshot awakened the rest of the camp. All around them officers bawled orders and men scurried cold and stiff-legged toward the perimeter pickets. Swearing and stomping life into their feet, teamsters rolled out from under the wagons and scrambled for their weapons. But in those scant few moments it became plain to see the camp was not being attacked by waves of horsemen. Instead, the threat proved to be nothing more than a few distant warriors gathered atop the far hills pitching long-range shots at the soldiers in the gray light of that autumn dawn.

Otis got them moving about with the morning routine as he rotated the guard one last time, bringing in the last watch to have their cold breakfast of salt pork and hard bread, washed down with what they had taken in yesterday afternoon in crossing Clear Creek. Watering the mules cost the men a good piece of that early morning, dipping the oiled-canvas nose bags into the kegs, forced to laboriously water each of the hundreds of animals one at a time. Just past seven A.M. Otis formed them up, putting the wagons in four long columns that would rumble along between the infantry escort, then slowly marched away from that scorched campsite.

Across the next anxious hour the Lakota kept their distance in the van of the wagon train, and far on either flank—watching. Sitting atop their restive ponies in the early cold. Watching. Occasionally firing a random shot at the soldiers now and then. Always watching as the wagons jostled and creaked, heading west along the Tongue River Road.

"Maybe they've learned their lesson," Otis thought to boast to the men around him after they had been on the trail for more than two hours.

"Perhaps, Colonel," agreed Lieutenant Oskaloosa M. Smith. "We unhorsed our share yesterday."

"Maybe they want to talk instead of fighting," William suggested, pointing into the gray distance.

Around him the soldiers grew quiet. Upon suddenly spotting the lone, far rider who reined up atop the low rise in their front, Otis threw up his arm. Down the column went the order to halt as everyone grew all the more wary. On either side of them sat hundreds of warriors. But in their front, only the lone horseman.

As William watched, the warrior slipped from his pony, dropping the single rein to the ground. At the end of one arm he waved what looked to be a white cloth back and forth over his head, then knelt, taking a long wooden stake from the belt that held the blanket around his waist. It appeared as if the warrior hammered the stake into the ground, then tied the white cloth to it before taking up his rein again and vaulting back atop his pony. There on the crest of the hill, the Indian circled three times, then kicked the pony into a gallop, disappearing on the far side of the slope.

"What you make of that, Jackson?" Otis asked, turning to his scout.

"Like I said: I think they want to talk."

The lieutenant colonel straightened, squinted at that hilltop where the white flag fluttered from that tall stake, then said, "All right. Have your brother go up there. Let's just see what Sitting Bull has to say for himself."

As much as he had wanted to go fetch that message himself, William realized Robert was Otis's scout. Sitting there with the rest of the headquarters group as his brother trotted forward, alone and wary, William studied either flank, back and forth, for some sign of betrayal. Something to confirm his unspoken fear that this was some kind of trap. In the distance he watched as Robert reached the crest of the far hill, circled the stake twice as he peered this way and that into the far valley of Cedar Creek, then leaned off the side of his horse to rip the stake out of the ground.

After untying the white cloth from the stake, Robert sat motionless for a moment, then hammered heels into the horse's flanks and set off at a gallop on the return trip. He skidded up before the lieutenant colonel, handing over the message.

From what William could see, there were English letters put together to make English words on that scrap of white cloth no bigger than a bandanna.

"What's it say, Colonel?" Lieutenant Smith asked. "Is it meant to be a message for us?"

"It most certainly is meant for me," Otis replied gruffly,

snapping out the cloth he held in his gloves. "Here, you read it aloud to the rest."

Smith took the cloth, then said:

> "YELLOWSTONE.
> I want to know what you are doing traveling on this road. You scare all the buffalo away. I want to hunt on the place. I want you to turn back from here. If you don't I will fight you again. I want you to leave what you have got here, and turn back from here.
> I am your friend,
> SITTING BULL.
> I mean all the rations you have got and some powder. Wish you would write as soon as you can."

"By gonnies!" Lieutenant William Kell exclaimed. "We've been fighting Sitting Bull!"

"Yes," Otis sighed, his eyes taking on a faraway look as he regarded the distant hill in their front, then gazing again at the stoic, motionless Indians on their left flank. "The same bastard who wiped out Custer's men."

Lieutenant Smith cleared his throat and asked, "Are we going to leave the son of a bitch powder and rations—like he asked for?"

"No, Mr. Smith," Otis replied acidly. "The only thing I'll leave him is the bullets we'll use to kill more of his warriors if he stands between us and Tongue River here on out."

At that point the lieutenant colonel took the cloth back from his adjutant and stuffed it inside the front of his coat. "Jackson," he said, looking at Robert once more, "I want you to ride back up there. Show them you have some word from me to deliver to Sitting Bull—and get it across to him in no uncertain terms that I'm taking this train on through to the Tongue River. Tell him that if they wish to stand in our way, I will be most pleased to accommodate them with a fight. In fact, I'll bloody well fight them for every goddamned foot if I have to. You understand all that?"

"Perfectly," Robert answered, his eyes darting to William before he reined his horse about and kicked it away, moving at a lope back to the far hill.

Otis turned in the saddle, looking down at the other officers who were without horses and said, "Let's get the word passed back: we're back on the march, gentlemen."

They pressed on as Jackson delivered the soldiers' reply to a single Lakota scout, then turned and galloped back to the wagon train. It became plain that the soldiers were not turning back. The warrior horsemen had not liked Otis's response to their demand: they were massing for another assault on the column.

But the attack didn't come until much later, when the van of the train reached Bad Route Creek and went about gathering deadfall and squaw wood the men shoved into the possum bellies beneath every one of the wagons. Too, the soldiers allowed the thirsty mules to drink their fill as the stream bottom was churned by hundred of hooves in the slow crossing protected by outflung skirmishers who held back the warriors swirling here, then there, probing for some weakness in the lines.

In little more than an hour the last wagons had crossed Bad Route Creek and the column was again on its way, despite the long-range sniping from the surrounding hillsides. They had covered little more than seven miles since leaving last night's camp.

"Looks like they want to talk to us again," Lieutenant Smith called out, pointing to the south.

From the direction of the Yellowstone appeared two horsemen. While one wore a white bandanna tied over his black braids, the other carried a white flag tied to a short staff he held high for all to see. Having appeared out of the southwest, the pair halted about halfway between the mounted warriors and the soldier escort.

"Shall we bring them on in, Colonel?" William Jackson inquired.

"By all means—let's see what else Sitting Bull has on his mind."

William walked on foot some two hundred yards before he stopped, signaling that it was safe for the horsemen to come on into range of the soldiers' big guns. As the two came to a halt before him, Jackson could see they were Lakota, all right. But upon talking in sign, he was surprised to learn they were not emissaries from Sitting Bull's roamers.

Telling the pair to follow him, that they would be safe even though there had been skirmishing all morning long, Jackson led the two horsemen back to see Otis.

"Colonel," he said as the riders came to a halt behind him among the headquarters group at the van of the train, "this is Long Feather and Bear's Face."

"They bring word from Sitting Bull?"

"No, not exactly. They come from the Hunkpapa bands at Standing Rock. But they came through Sitting Bull's camp this morning—before coming on through the warrior lines to get word to you."

"They're from Standing Rock Agency?" repeated Lieutenant Smith.

Jackson nodded. "Agent down that way sent them out to look up Sitting Bull—try convincing him to surrender and come on in for his people's good."

"Before we kill 'em all is what he should tell 'em," grumbled Lieutenant William Conway.

"They're carrying written messages for you too," Jackson added, signaling the pair.

"Hand them over, by all means," Otis replied with no small excitement.

The dispatches were from Lieutenant Colonel William P. Carlin, commandant at the Standing Rock Reservation, requesting Sitting Bull to surrender and move his people back to the agency.

When Otis looked up from the handwritten letters, William Jackson said, "They do have a message from Sitting Bull for you, Colonel."

"What's the Custer-killer want to tell me now?"

"Sitting Bull wants to meet with you," Jackson explained. "But only outside the lines."

"I won't even consider it," Otis replied hastily. "I will meet with Sitting Bull inside soldier lines. Nothing more shall I grant them."

Jackson translated and made sign with his hands, then sent the two Hunkpapa off with the soldier chief's gruff reply while Otis gave the order for the wagons to resume their march.

In less than an hour the two Standing Rock messengers were spotted coming back, joined this time by three more mounted warriors. With most of the headquarters group, Otis advanced a short distance, going out to meet them as the column continued its slow, relentless march toward Tongue River.

Anxiously the lieutenant colonel asked as the horsemen came to a stop before the soldiers, "Is one of those Sitting Bull?"

Jackson studied them all, especially the one with the stern face who held back behind the others, dressed in the shabby clothes of mourning. Then he wagged his head in resignation, saying, "I'm not sure—don't think so. Maybe he didn't trust coming here himself."

Grinding his teeth on that disappointment, Otis finally said, "Find out what news they bring from the son of a bitch anyway."

"They have nothing new to tell you, Colonel," William said after a few minutes, translating what the two of the new horsemen had to say to Otis's previous counterproposal. "This one called No Neck still wants to know why we are in this country, scaring off their buffalo."

"Is that the whole caboodle, Jackson?" Otis snapped. "Sitting Bull shows no willingness to come in and parley with us himself?"

For some reason Jackson was again compelled to study the stone-faced warrior who stayed in the rear, then finally answered, "Seems he don't want to show, Colonel. The Lakota keep saying they want you to stop killing and running off their game. For the trouble you've caused 'em—they tell me they want us to give them bullets and food."

"The only bullets they'll get—"

Jackson threw up a hand to interrupt Otis, "No Neck and Red Skirt say they're all weary of fighting. Ever since last spring—all they've been doing is fighting the soldiers."

Lieutenant Smith cheered, "By God—if they're tired, we've all but got them about whipped!"

Otis placed a hand on the lieutenant's arm, angrily saying, "Jackson—you tell these red bastards they won't get any powder and lead from me: tell them they've wasted enough ammunition shooting at us the last two days to last them a long damned time."

"Listen, they're tired and they want peace," Jackson emphasized, feeling a sense of weariness come over him, too, as he looked once more at the older warrior in the shabby buckskins who had not added a word to the parley.

"Peace, is it?" Otis scoffed haughtily. "When they go into the agencies, then we'll all have peace."

"You want me to tell them what your terms are?" Jackson asked.

Thinking better of it, Otis shook his head. "No. Just tell them I don't have the authority to negotiate with them on peace. I can't offer, nor can I accept, terms of surrender. On the other hand, they should follow us to Tongue River, where they can talk with Colonel Miles. He's the one who can negotiate with them."

When Jackson had translated, the emissaries' faces became grave. "Colonel, they don't think much of the idea of going to Tongue River with us. They don't figure they'll be safe there, or on the way."

"Assure them that nothing untoward will occur to jeopardize their safety."

In reply, Sitting Bull's messengers told Otis they would stay with their original plans to go north to the Missouri, where they would trade at Fort Peck—then journey back to talk to the Bear Coat at Tongue River. For a few minutes the trio sat quiet, watching the white men in silence.

Jackson finally said, "They want something of a sign from you, Colonel."

"A sign?"

"Some show of good faith," William explained.

"Yes. Of course," the officer replied, then turned to Smith. "Lieutenant, see that some food is placed over there on that slope for the warriors to see as a sign of my good faith."

"Food, colonel?"

"Certainly. Two sides of bacon and three boxes of that hard bread."

"Three boxes—yes, sir."

"I think one hundred fifty pounds of hardtack is sufficient," Otis replied, looking back at Jackson. "Lieutenant Kell, let's get this wagon train moving to Tongue River!"

William watched the Standing Rock Hunkpapa step aside with Sitting Bull's trio of lieutenants as the wagon train jangled back into motion, leaving the five sullen warriors behind with their gifts of bacon and hard bread.

As a disgusted Elwell S. Otis pulled his wagon train away, the masses of Sioux horsemen hung farther and farther to the rear of the slow-moving column, then eventually disappeared altogether. Throughout the rest of that Monday afternoon, the sixteenth, the column sighted increasing numbers of buffalo and small herds of antelope north of their line of march. With every new mile they put behind them before sundown, William Jackson came to understand all the more why the Lakota were willing to fight to hold on to the rich bounty of these high Montana plains.

By nightfall he knew with a bedrock certainty that Otis's officers were fooling themselves.

Not for a moment did he believe Sitting Bull would give up

so easily—backing off, perhaps eventually coming in to talk with Miles at Tongue River.

Not for a moment did Jackson think Sitting Bull would stop anywhere short of driving the Bear Coat's soldiers right out of the Yellowstone country.

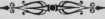

Chapter 7

17 October 1876

FOREIGN

The War in Servia

LONDON, October 16.—The *Times* publishes the text of the note in which Turkey offered the six months' armistice ... *Times'* Paris correspondent points to the fact that this is the first time Russia has clearly sided with Servia and Montenegro, and advising them to reject the propositions.

"See there, Seamus Donegan," post trader Collins retorted, stabbing a bony finger against the front page of Denver's Rocky Mountain *News* with a rustle of newsprint. "We aren't the only ones with war falling down about our heads, now are we?"

The gray-eyed Irishman dragged the pipe from his mouth, regarding it as he blew a stream of smoke toward the ceiling, then took a sip of Collins's heady coffee the sutler kept hot in a shiny pot atop that iron stove warming his trading post there at Fort Laramie.

"But don't you see? At least there's talk of peace in the world's other wars," Donegan reminded those men gathered there this early-winter morning.

They could only agree with him grudgingly.

Outside the air sparkled with hoar frost. Almost too cold to snow. But in there, squatting around the stove with their pipes and their tins of steaming coffee, these men—civilian and soldier alike—basked in the glow of male fellowship and camaraderie. This was exactly what Seamus had been seeking when he'd crept from the tiny upstairs room at the peep o' day—leaving behind Sam and their son, both of them asleep: Sam's head deep within the valley of a goose-down pillow, the babe still latched on to mother's breast. It had been a long haul of it—both worried, frazzled mother and bawling child up and down for most all the night. Then as the first gray fingers of dawn began to creep out of the east, they both fell asleep at long last. And Seamus crept out, quietly pulled the door to, and creaked down the noisy stairs into the cold of that mid-October morning.

"I'll bet their war is a big'un," Collins continued enthusiastically as he pried open the stove door and tossed in some more split kindling. "All cannon and cavalry!"

Donegan gazed out the window frosted with the pattern of the coming cold, caressing the new Winchester repeater he had just purchased from Collins with an oiled rag. "Aye, and in the bloody meantime, trader—right here ours is just a nasty little war, ain't it all? Nothing more'n a man here ... a poor sojur there."

THE INDIANS

News from Standing Rock.

ST PAUL, October 16.—A *Pioneer Press* special from Bismarck says the Indians at Standing Rock signed the treaty relinquishing the Black Hills on Wednesday. The treaty was so far modified as not to insist on their removal to the Indian Territory. The troops intended for the expedition to go in camp tomorrow, and will probably leave about Wednesday. General Sturgis is en route to join his regiment and will probably command the expedition, unless Terry goes in person.

With the half-breed tracker riding at his side, Luther Sage Kelly probed east across Sunday Creek north of the Yellowstone, the river that had given him his nickname. Out of the eight-foot-high willows and icy bogs where the horses had slow going, yanking one hoof after another out of the sucking mud, they slowly clambered to higher ground. In that moonless darkness,

Kelly knew the soldiers would be crossing farther upstream: where the banks were corduroyed for supply wagons from Glendive and the bottom wasn't such a maze of sinkholes as it was here.

Miles's infantry could afford to take the time to stay with the Tongue River Road right now—but Yellowstone Kelly could not. He had the colonel's orders to feel ahead of the column: to see if the Indians might have made their crossing of the river; and, perhaps even more important, to find out just what the hell had happened to that supply train long overdue from Glendive Cantonment.

Otis's wagons were long overdue. With rumors that the Sioux were closing on the south bank of the Yellowstone, in all likelihood intent on crossing to the north, it did not bode well for any supply train that might happen upon a massed war party. Luther, along with fellow scouts Victor Smith, an old friend, and half-breed Billy Cross, had accompanied Lieutenant Frank S. Hinkle and six soldiers on a dangerous scout to the upper reaches of the Tongue and Mizpah Creek, hoping to find the Indian encampment rumored to be in the area. They found nothing. Which could only mean the Sioux had to be farther to the east.

All the more worrisome, the party of Arikara trackers Kelly had sent out with William Jackson more than two days back hadn't returned. Miles feared they had been discovered by a hostile war party and rubbed out.

So at two-thirty this cold Tuesday morning Miles had the entire Tongue River encampment up to receive fourteen days' rations. Leaving behind two companies of the Twenty-second U.S. Infantry to protect their cantonment, in that first inky seep of dawn the colonel was ferrying his ordinance rifle and ten full companies of his Fifth Infantry to the north side of the Yellowstone. By eleven-thirty A.M. the other 10 scouts, 15 officers, and 434 soldiers formed up and moved into the cold gray light beneath the low clouds scudding along the Glendive Road.

"Not since the government's operations against the Mormons in fifty-seven has the Fifth marched as a regiment," Miles had said with undisguised pride earlier that morning as he'd stood on the north bank of the Yellowstone with Kelly, watching his men ferry over twelve at a time. Then the officer sighed, saying, "There's trouble out there, and Otis is right in the thick of it. I can smell it."

"We'll find out soon enough, General," Luther replied, slipping his boot into a stirrup. "We'll be back when I've got something to report."

This was to be Kelly's twenty-eighth winter—born in the village of Geneva, right in the heart of the Finger Lake region of central New York State, long before made famous by the notorious Red Jacket of the Iroquois Confederation. Many were the times over the years that Luther would claim as an ancestor none other than Hannah Dustin, the courageous backwoods woman who'd been captured by hostiles and conveyed north through the formidable wilderness, eventually making her miraculous and daring escape during the French and Indian War.

He pulled his hat down now, nodding to Miles, and reined his horse around to the east, kicking it in the flanks.

A hell of a lot of water had passed beneath his boots since that day long ago when he had stood gape-mouthed, watching the line of young drummer boys—every last one of them decked out in patriotic bunting festooned with rosettes made from red, white, and blue cloth—marching at the vanguard of the column of volunteers who were stepping off to make war on the rebellious South. Because he was only fifteen when his mother finally consented to his enlistment near the end of the war, Luther had to lie to recruiters about his age. And, in his youthful ignorance as well as exuberant zeal, promptly made the mistake of joining the regular army instead of the New York volunteers.

Before he knew it, he had taken his oath to the Tenth U.S. Infantry for a three-year hitch.

After some duty guarding Confederate prisoners, Kelly's unit was finally ordered to Fort Ripley on the upper reaches of the Mississippi River. After a few months his company was sent on to Fort Wadsworth, near Big Stone Lake in the Dakota Territory. By the spring of sixty-seven Kelly's company was ordered to establish Fort Ransome—a small station at the forks of the Cheyenne River, near Bear's Den Hill, far to the north near the Canadian line. It was the first time Luther had ever seen a buffalo.

"How 'bout it, Kelly?" his sergeant prodded him one of those last nights before his hitch would draw to a close. "You game to sign up for another?"

The handsome Luther smiled, showing his big, bright teeth. "No, sir, Sergeant. Now, don't misunderstand me, sir: there's nothing finer for a young fellow than a three-year term in the United States Army, for it teaches him method, manliness, physical welfare, and obedience to authority. But, in all truthfulness, Sergeant—one enlistment is quite enough—"

"Quite enough?" roared the old file.

"Yes, sir," Kelly replied steadfastly, "unless that man has decided to make soldiering his profession."

The sergeant looked upon the young man gravely. "And you won't?"

With a gesture Luther had waved an arm out there to the prairies and the mountains that fine spring day in 1868. "No, sir—I'll be saying good-bye to soldier life. There's too damn much I want to see right out there as a free man."

Back in St. Paul briefly to cash his last pay voucher, Luther quickly turned his face once more to the west, pointing his nose for the Canadian settlement of Fort Garry on his way toward the wild, open country that lay at the headwaters of the Missouri River. By the time he'd reached the Canadian settlements along the Red River, Kelly had run onto several miners escaping north out of Montana. Despite their warnings about roaming war parties on the American side of the line, Luther journeyed on— youth's bravado running hot in his veins.

At the crossing of the Assiniboine River he ran into some métis with their Red River carts, making their way to the buffalo country. He accepted their invitation to throw in with them. It wasn't long before he adopted much of their colorful dress, including the hooded capote constructed from a thick blue Hudson's Bay blanket. With a red sash to hold it closed about him, Kelly felt all the more the part of a high prairie prince.

While moseying south and west with the half-breed traders, he had a chance meeting with a band of Hunkpapa warriors led by Sitting Bull. When the haughty Lakota inquired who the lone white man was among them, the métis said he was their American friend—therefore under their protection. Although they stomped about a bit and made a fierce show of it, Sitting Bull and his Hunkpapa soon departed.

In those weeks before he parted ways with the half-breed métis, Luther hunted buffalo, helping the men shoot and skin their kills, watching the women dry strips of the meat, which they eventually put up into rawhide sacks as pemmican they would use in trade at the many wilderness posts dotting that formidable land. Then came the day the old man led him to a nearby rise and pointed into the beckoning distance.

"This is where your adventure continues," the wrinkled métis said, pointing.

"That means we are to part," Kelly replied sadly.

"There lies the country you seek. Look out for the Sioux, boy."

Moving south, Kelly reached Fort Berthold, where he met the Gerard brothers who were the post traders. The story went that the Gerards had acquired their initial capital after a party of Montana miners, descending the river in a small bateau with their gold, was attacked by a war party and killed. Having no knowledge of gold, the Indians had emptied the sacks into the boat, which they set adrift, later to be discovered downstream by the fortunate brothers. From Fred Gerard, Luther had purchased a Henry carbine and a supply of cartridges. Just this past summer Fred had been employed as an interpreter and tracker with Custer's column, assigned to Reno's battalion when the Lakota had badly mauled the Seventh Cavalry.

From Berthold, Luther trekked upriver on foot, hungry for adventure. Along the way he bumped into a party of wandering Mandan, out to hunt buffalo. From them he learned how to prepare *boudins*, chopped meat and marrow fat cooked within a casing of a buffalo's intestine. Later, when he found a little steady employment as a mail carrier between Forts Berthold and Stevenson—journeys on which he would take volumes of Poe, Shakespeare, Scott, and other classical authors into the wilderness for his own entertainment—Kelly met the noted Arikara tracker, Bloody Knife.

By the time Luther's hair had grown to his shoulders and his mustache had become all the shaggier, he had killed his first Lakota: two warriors intent on lifting his white scalp and robbing him of his Henry. Around Fort Peck, indeed all along the Upper Missouri, the story of that fateful encounter was told and retold by his friend Bloody Knife and other Arikara scouts who found work from time to time for the army.

It was while Kelly made some occasional money as a woodhawk, supplying the few upriver steamboats with fuel, that he was asked to guide for Colonel George A. Forsyth, come to map and explore the Yellowstone as a member of General Sheridan's Chicago staff on Captain Grant Marsh's *Far West*. From Fort Buford at the mouth of the Yellowstone, the party pushed past Glendive Creek and on to the mouth of the Powder before turning back. Back at Buford, Luther bid the soldiers farewell, then turned back into the country of the Milk, the Judith, and particularly the hunters' paradise of the Musselshell River, where he cut wood, trapped occasionally, and hunted wolf pelts until late this past spring when it seemed that wandering Sioux war parties became even more troublesome than normal.

In the Judith basin he had been following wolf sign among the tracks of a small migrating buffalo herd, for those winter-thick pelts brought five dollars American at the nearby posts. From there Luther moseyed farther south toward the Yellowstone that summer, picking the wild strawberries as they came into season until he reached the country near Pompey's Pillar. Upon those spectacular heights he looked down into the far river valley and caught sight of the white tents of an army camp lining a green bottomland near a bend in the sparkling river. From there to the mouth of the Bighorn, Kelly was rarely ever out of sight of soldiers or supply trains as General Terry prepared to pursue Sitting Bull and General Crook made ready to pursue Crazy Horse into the Black Hills.

Too many folks, Luther had groaned. Seemed the army was destined to stir up more trouble for itself. Kelly turned away to make his way up the river when he soon ran onto some Montana miners who were easing down the Yellowstone, having heard of the army's preparations to pursue the Indians who had massacred Custer. It was the following day when he was out hunting that he found himself confronted by a large cinnamon bear he dropped with his needle gun. Because the hide was very poor at that late-summer season, Kelly took only some back fat to use as gun oil, along with one of the big forepaws and all the claws.

On down the north bank of the Yellowstone, Kelly tramped with the mining party until they reached a sprawling military camp erected about a mile above the mouth of the Tongue River. There they crossed to the south side on a crude ferry the soldiers operated, finding the camp nearly deserted. Quartermaster Randall explained that most of the men were either out working the timber in the hills for their huts, or they were out on routine patrols of the nearby country.

"By the Land of Goshen!" Randall gushed as his eyes suddenly locked on that dark object suspended from the horn of Kelly's saddle and stepped forward to have himself a better look. "What in God's name is that?"

Luther untied the rawhide whangs from the saddle horn and handed it over to the captain. "Just the paw of a cinnamon I killed the other day."

"Never have I seen anything so huge!" Randall said admiringly of the paw over a foot long without the claws. "You shot this by yourself?"

"I did," Kelly replied. "But it wasn't my first. I've been out here for nearly eight years already—"

Randall interrupted eagerly, "You know this country, do you?"

"A good deal of it, yes."

The captain hefted the heavy bear's paw and declared, "The general will want to see you."

"The general?" Kelly asked. "Who's the general?"

"Why, Nelson A. Miles. He's curious to learn all that he can about this country."

At that moment the mischievous thought had struck Luther. He instructed the quartermaster, "There, Captain—take that paw to General Miles for me. Tell him it is my calling card."

In the next few moments Randall had the paw in the hands of his own orderly, on its way to the tent of Colonel Nelson A. Miles, commander of the Fifth U.S. Infantry, whose job it was to erect winter quarters there at the Tongue River, as well as patrol the Yellowstone and prevent Sitting Bull's Sioux from crossing north of the river, fleeing on to Canada.

Late that afternoon and into the evening, the intrigued Miles questioned Kelly in great detail about the country north of the river, indeed, all the way to the British line; seeking knowledge of it for a field of operations against the hostiles. During their talk Kelly told the colonel about his three-year hitch in the regular army, having seen some of his service in the Dakota Territory.

"As much as I know about a lot of this country, the stretch of ground just north of the Tongue River here is known only to the Sioux and maybe some Cheyenne," Luther explained. "Back in sixty-eight when I came to this country, it was already given over to the tribes by treaty. Not a man do I know who has come to this country and lived to tell his story."

"As I suspected, Kelly," Miles replied soberly. "But you know something of what's downriver?"

"I was there three summers back, with Grant Marsh and General Forsyth."

"You don't say?" the colonel asked approvingly. "We're here with orders to make a fall and winter campaign of it, Kelly."

Luther watched Miles sip at his coffee, then said, "Captain Randall filled me in with all that he could, General."

Miles rose from his canvas stool and got to his feet, one of the few men who stood as tall as Luther Kelly. "What say you to employment as a government scout?"

For a moment he hesitated. "When I'm not scouting for you, am I free to hunt for myself?"

Miles stroked the bear's paw. "By all means!"

Luther saluted. "Then I suppose you've got yourself a scout, General."

"You're not regular army anymore, Kelly," Miles replied, holding out his big hand. They shook. "Now you're chief scout for the District of the Yellowstone."

In those blackest hours just before dawn this cold autumn morning, with Miles and his soldiers coming along somewhere behind them, Luther and Billy Cross ran across a recent Indian camp. While the ashes in the many fire pits had grown cold, the ground beneath was nonetheless still warm.

"Perhaps no more than a day now," Luther said quietly.

"Cheyenne camp here too," the half-breed added, pointing to the small patch of ground cleared in an orderly circle. "Lakota always pitch lodges here and there, where they want. But this circle open to the east . . . it show some Cheyenne come with Sitting Bull too."

Since the two of them were so far ahead of the column by that time, Luther decided they could rest for an hour back in the brush. After awaking, they were up and in the saddle again as the sun peeked over the bare horizon blanketed with nothing but brown and yellowed grasses. For all their hunting, Luther and Billy didn't see a wagon or a war pony, either one, all that long, dusty day.

At sundown they made their own fireless camp and rolled up in their blankets as the temperature began to drop. Somewhere behind them the soldiers would be making their bivouac, Luther ruminated as he fell into a fitful, uneasy sleep.

At twilight that night, in fact, Miles finally halted the men so they could make coffee, their first real stop since leaving Tongue River that morning. After the choking dust kicked up by all those hooves and bootees, the quiet of the high plains night settled around them with a cold grip as the men huddled around a hundred tiny fires. But there would be little rest until he knew what had happened to Otis's supply train. In half an hour the colonel had the regiment up and moving once more.

Miles was anxious, straining to know what lay out there in the unknown. Sensing perhaps his date with Sitting Bull, and destiny.

The Glendive Road led the regiment into the moonless black of that night, probing across the broken, rugged ground until the colonel finally stopped them at one A.M. They had been at it over twenty hours already.

"The men can rest here for a few hours," Miles told his weary officers. "As soon as there's enough light to march, we'll be pushing on."

The Fifth Infantry had just put thirty hard Montana miles behind them.

Chapter 8

18–20 October 1876

**Late from the Indian Raids
in Wyoming.**

THE INDIANS

Troublous Times in Wyoming.

CHEYENNE, October 17.—The body of Private Fasker of K company, Second cavalry, was brought into Hunton's ranch yesterday. It was not mutilated but was stripped of all clothing. In the fight Messers. McIlvain and McFalan, of China Rock, each had a horse shot under them, and the latter received a slight flesh wound in the right shoulder. The Indians were armed with Sharp's improved rifles, caliber 40, a number of shells being brought in by Sergeant Parker. H. D. Lilly, who came into camp from the cattle round-up, reports twenty head of horses stolen by Indians from Searight's ranch last night, and Ashenfelter, a ranch-man who started from Georges' ranch yesterday for Searight's, has not arrived, and it is supposed he has been killed. A large band of Indians are believed to be in the mountains, and more raids are hourly looked for in this direction. A party is now organizing to go in search for Ashenfelter. A train just in to the telegraph camp near Custer reports seeing Indians between that

place and Red Canyon. The line will reach Custer tomorrow night.

Nelson Miles did not roust his weary command until dawn and
did not have them marching northeast out of their miserable
bivouac until nine A.M. With what scouts he had along reporting
no sighting of hostiles, the colonel dispatched some of his soldiers
in small hunting parties, hoping to discover some of the numerous
buffalo in that country.

Having already covered some sixteen miles that day, just
past midafternoon the advance called out that the wagon train
had been spotted in the distance. Within minutes Miles was eagerly shaking hands with Lieutenant Colonel Elwell S. Otis when
they met on the east bank of Custer Creek, some five miles upstream from the Yellowstone.

Together they went into bivouac for the night on the banks
of Cherry Creek, just as the sun fell late in the afternoon. While
the combined columns raided the willow bogs for firewood or
collected dried buffalo chips to heat up their coffee and supper,
Miles held a conference with the weary commander of the
Glendive Cantonment.

After Otis gave a full report on his running fight with Sitting Bull's warriors, Miles ordered him to proceed on with the
supply train to Tongue River the next morning, while the Fifth
took up the pursuit of the Hunkpapa.

"We're strong enough to punish them," Nelson vowed
before his officers. "By Jupiter, we'll make them pay this
time."

Well after dark, Nelson trudged through camp to find the
unit placed in charge of his single piece of artillery. Dismantled,
the Rodman gun had covered the last two days strapped on the
backs of a pair of mules. Those Napoleon guns assigned to the
regiment he had simply deemed far too bulky and immobile for
campaigning in rugged Indian country such as this.

He spent a few minutes visiting his nephew George and
his company before deciding he would take a few minutes that
evening to write more to Mary—perhaps to detail for her his
frustrations in hearing so much about Sitting Bull's Hunkpapa, knowing they were somewhere close along the Yellowstone,
but not yet having caught a single glimpse of that elusive chief
of the winter roamers who had wiped out Custer's five companies.

"Where are you, you red bastard?" he whispered as he

turned back toward his bivouac, really nothing more than a gum poncho tied over some willow branches where his bedroll had been thrown out. "I know you're out there, you wily son of a bitch. My Kelly will find you, then I'll snare you once and for all. And trust me: when I do catch up to you, I won't make the same mistakes Custer did, not by a long shot."

Nelson held strong opinions on everything, especially this Army of the West. To him it seemed that no other commander had taken the trouble to analyze their situation out there on the frontier when it came to fighting horse-mounted warriors. Most commanders truthfully didn't have the spirit it would take to defeat the hostiles. And those few who might have the gumption to make a fight of it simply lacked one or more of the other necessary traits to pull off the victory they were needing so very badly.

"Alfred Terry," he murmured as he settled atop his blankets and his dog-robber brought over a steaming cup of coffee.

"Sir?"

"Oh . . . nothing," Miles replied. "Just thinking to myself."

Indeed. General Alfred Terry, commanding the Department of the Dakotas, seemed the best of the lot for all intents and purposes. Yet even he had no experience in fighting Indians. Besides, he was the sort of man who time and again fell under the sway of subordinates with stronger personalities—too much influenced by the likes of the brash George Armstrong Custer and that dullard John Gibbon.

He took out paper and fitted his pen with a new nib, hoping it would not be so cold that the ink would freeze. He much preferred to write Mary with a pen instead of pencil. This night he again told his wife of his frustrations with her uncle at the War Department. Why William Tecumseh Sherman refused to turn the whole matter over to him was beyond Nelson. Then he realized he was starting to seethe more and more these days— like a dog snarling at the end of a long chain. So he wrote Mary that perhaps he should resign from the army, just as he had considered doing last summer—that, rather than endure another long, tedious, and poorly executed circus like the fiasco Terry and Crook had made of the summer's campaign.

He fell asleep over his writing tablet that night, his pen in one hand, that small cabinet photo of his wife in the other.

The cold that Friday morning, the twentieth, was even more brutal than it had been. As he stomped circulation back into his feet and legs, Nelson took all the more satisfaction with his foresight in equipping the men for what this country could dish out in the way of weather.

"Both officers and men profited by the experience they had been through in the winter campaigns in the Indian Territory," he had written in his journal weeks ago, "and applied themselves zealously to their equipment in every possible way."

In addition to the army-issue woolen clothing every man wore, Miles's soldiers cut up their woolen blankets to craft themselves heavy underclothing, as well as fashioning masks that covered the entire head, leaving three openings for the eyes and mouth. With those masks on, it was all but impossible to tell one man from the other, to tell private from colonel.

Since coming to the Tongue in early September, Nelson had seen to it that every steamboat shipment included what the men would wear once the weather changed: the thick buffalo-hide shoes commonly called arctics, as well as the thick horsehide gloves with long gauntlets made to slip over the wide cuffs on their buffalo-hide coats. Many of the men also cut up grain sacks they used to wrap around their stockings for an extra layer of thick warmth.

After a breakfast of coffee and tack, the Fifth moved out, marching north by east beneath an overcast and threatening sky. It wasn't long before those officers at the van of the march spotted the first warriors as the Sioux horsemen bristled along the skyline of a distant hill. Mile after mile, hour by hour, more warriors appeared in advance of the march as Miles kept his regiment moving, the men murmuring, wary, and watchful.

"Great Jupiter!" he exclaimed to those in his headquarters group. "Those must be from Sitting Bull's village."

By the time the colonel called a brief halt near midmorning, there were hundreds of warriors on horseback and on foot, arrayed atop the bare hills and windswept ridges directly in the regiment's front.

"Gentlemen," Miles told his officers, "let's deploy the Fifth."

"Battle front, General?" asked Wyllys Lyman.

"By all means, Captain. Battle front . . . and move out—ready to skirmish."

Again the Fifth Infantry moved out, this time arrayed in battle formation: making a wide front, company by company, with reserves immediately in their rear, yard by yard advancing toward the enemy, who slowly fell back, the Sioux maintaining the same respectful distance from those far-reaching Springfield rifles.

It was just past eleven when Nelson sighted two riders bearing a white flag leave a large body of horsemen on a nearby bluff and move toward the soldier column. They halted a hundred yards out, their grimy towel tied to a long willow branch snapping in the gusts of raw, cruel wind that kicked up dust from every hoof and boot.

With four of his officers Miles rode out to meet the pair with interpreter and scout Joe Culbertson, half-breed son of fur trader Alexander Culbertson.

"Their names are Long Feather and Bear's Face," the scout declared after some conversation with the two emissaries. "They come from Standing Rock, sent by the soldier chief there. The two of 'em say they've already talked to the soldier chief in charge of the wagons that headed this way."

"I'm glad we've got Otis behind us now and on his way to the Tongue," Miles grumbled. "If these two aren't part of that bunch that attacked the supply train—what the hell are they doing here in this piece of country?"

"Say they come to tell Sitting Bull's people to come in to the agency."

Miles waved an arm slowly in an arc across the hills and bluffs. "Then these are Sitting Bull's warriors? The same men who defeated Custer?"

Culbertson nodded. "S'pose that's the make on it. These two say Sitting Bull wants to talk to the soldier chief."

"Wants to talk, does he?"

"Bear's Face says Sitting Bull wants to talk to you about surrendering his Hunkpapa."

That sudden bit of surprising news jerked Nelson Miles up in the saddle as surely as a rope around his shoulders would have. "Wait just a minute—you sure you've got all their sign talk right, Culbertson?"

The half-breed's dark eyes flared with resentment. "Maybe you trust one of your soldiers better than me, eh?"

Miles watched the scout rein his horse around, kick it in the flanks, and lope back to the soldier lines. Then he turned to his aide-de-camp. "Mr. Bailey, I want you to go with these two."

"Yes, sir," responded Second Lieutenant Hobart K. Bailey. "I'll find out what I can about the status of Sitting Bull's surrender, General."

It was the better part of the next hour before Bailey finally returned.

"There's a half-blood with 'em, General," the lieutenant disclosed with no small excitement. "Named Brug-gair."

"He's the one you talked with?" Miles inquired.

"Bruguier was our interpreter for the little chat we had."

"What'd you find out?"

"Sitting Bull wants to meet the bear-coat leader."

"Bear coat?" Then Nelson glanced down at his own appearance. As tall as he was, draped within the buffalo coat, with its bear-fur trim at both collar and cuffs, along with his tall stovepipe boots and fur cap, perhaps he did look somewhat like a bear.

He dispatched Bailey back with his demands as to the number of warriors Sitting Bull would bring with him into that no-man's land where Miles agreed to meet the enigmatic Hunkpapa leader.

Before he advanced from the south, the colonel gave his staff orders for the deployment of the regiment along the crests of the nearby hills, positioning the Fifth to face the hundreds of mounted warriors, intending that they guard against treachery. All too well he remembered the tragic fate of General E.R.S. Canby out in the Modocs' Lava Beds five years before.* At the same time he placed Captain Wyllys Lyman's I Company to support the Rodman ordinance rifle Miles wanted positioned on a ridge north of the line of march where it could be trained on the hostiles. Then he moved First Lieutenant Mason Carter's K Company into position on the high ground to the south and threw out a strong line of skirmishers directly to the rear of the open ground where he would hold his council with Sitting Bull.

Accompanied by Lieutenant Bailey, three mounted enlisted men, and two mounted color bearers, as well as scout Robert Jackson, the colonel advanced some four hundred yards toward the designated site, then halted, waiting while Bailey and the rest of the party covered the last hundred windswept yards. It took the better part of another hour as Bailey and Johnny Bruguier held more protracted talks before a dozen unarmed Sioux finally dismounted and moved forward on foot from the north. They were followed at a prudent distance by more than twenty warriors who stayed atop their ponies, tails and manes tossing in the

*April 11, 1873—*Devil's Backbone*, Vol. 5, The Plainsmen Series.

cold breeze. Thirty yards out, the dozen Hunkpapa on foot stopped in the brilliant but brutally frigid sunshine streaming through the dispersing clouds.

"They want us to dismount, General," Bailey explained after he and the half-breed flung their voices back and forth across the distance.

As Nelson was considering whether or not to accept that request, five warriors moved away from the others, crossing half the distance to the soldiers before they spread buffalo robes and blankets upon the autumn-dried grass. They promptly sat, ready to parley.

"Which one is the chief?"

Bailey pointed to the one seated in the middle of the others as the more than two dozen Sioux horsemen milled anxiously some thirty yards farther away. Nelson suspiciously regarded those mounted Hunkpapa—every one of them armed with a Springfield carbine, Henry or Winchester repeater, a few with older model Spencer carbines. After a moment his eyes were drawn back to study his long-sought adversary. Sitting Bull wore only buckskin leggings, breechclout, and fur-lined moccasins. He wore no feathers, much less any sort of headdress, to signify his high office or his standing among the Hunkpapa people. Impassive, he sat clutching only a buffalo robe tightly around his shoulders.

Miles swallowed quickly with some growing excitement, then looked over his own entourage, saying, "Let's go see what Sitting Bull has to say about his surrender."

As the soldiers approached, the Hunkpapa chief waved an arm, signaling one of the horsemen forward. The rider came up, dropped a buffalo robe to the ground in front of his tribesmen, then reined about and returned to the rear with the others still mounted on their ponies. When two of the warriors with Sitting Bull quickly spread the robe on the prairie, the chief gestured to have Miles take a seat there before him.

Miles shook his head. "Bailey, tell them I think it better that we don't get quite so close."

But before the lieutenant could translate, the dark-skinned warrior seated at the chief's left hand was already whispering in Sitting Bull's ear.

"Who's that?"

"The one I told you about. Half-breed. Name's Brug-gair, something like that."

"He speaks their tongue well, eh?" Miles asked.

"Does a good job with ours too," Bailey replied.

"All right, if you fellas have your pistols ready under your coats," the colonel finally said as he trudged forward again, "let's see what these unsavory characters have to say for themselves."

Chapter 9

20 October 1876

**Russia Ready for an Advance
on Turkey**

**Austria, France and Germany
Remain Neutral**

**Indians Still Raiding Settlers
In Wyoming**

THE INDIANS

More Raiding up North.

CHEYENNE, October 18.—Almost every hour
brings news of new depredations by Indians upon
ranchmen located west and north of the Chug. On
Sunday last Coffey & Cunney's train, near Laramie
Peak, was run down to Kent's, on Laramie River. A
saddle blanket and vest belonging to a man named
Sullivan, of the independent volunteers, was found
near that place, and he is probably killed. Frank
Sprague was attacked on his ranch at the old mill near
Laramie Peak. He fought the Indians during a whole
day, killing two, but they burned his hay and ranch
and ran off all his stock. He escaped barefooted to
O'Leary's ranch on Richard Creek before the Indians
fired the bushes in which he had been concealed. Kerr,

who arrived at the Chug to-day, saw an Indian camp within two miles of Searight's ranch and men and ammunition left here on his order to-day. A large body of Indians encamped at the head of the North Laramie, distant from Fort Laramie forty miles. A party of volunteers who went in search of Aspenfelter and the mail carrier from Laramie city, who was due at the Chug Monday, returned to-night to that place having discovered no trace of the missing men.

As soon as the soldier chief in the big coat came up and stood by the robe, Johnny Bruguier said, "Soldier chief, Sitting Bull want you to sit while you talk with him."

"No," Miles said stiffly, his jaw jutting. "I think better of it. I'll just stand while we parley."

Glancing at the Hunkpapa chief a moment, seeing the strain of confusion in Sitting Bull's eyes, Johnny tried again. "If you want to make war, then stand. If you come to talk peace with these Lakota—then you must sit."

For several moments Nelson Miles deliberated on that, his eyes looking from the interpreter, to the seated chiefs, to the line of mounted warriors to their rear. Then back to the buffalo robe offered him. At last the wary officer turned and mumbled something to his men, then advanced a few more feet so that he could kneel on the buffalo robe.

"You will not sit to talk?" Johnny asked.

"I will kneel here," Miles grumbled, clearly vexed. "Now—get on with what Sitting Bull wants to tell me."

Johnny stepped over so he could sit directly between Sitting Bull and the colonel. The chief reached beneath his robe to pull out a pipe, which Sitting Bull lit by taking a smoldering coal from a small gourd his nephew, White Bull, produced from a pouch he carried over his shoulder. White Bull sat at the chief's left hand, while the Brule named High Bear sat on the chief's right, along with Jumping Bull, a Hunkpapa, and Fire-What-Man, a Sans Arc.

This ceremonial smoking and passing the pipe around the circle took much time. Johnny did not smoke. Instead, he watched the faces of those surrounding him in that small circle, both white and red. It had been many months since he had been so vividly reminded how he was a man-in-between. In his veins coursed white blood, and red too. But he was far from truly belonging in either world. While the Hunkpapa had accepted him, he had to admit he shamelessly enjoyed the raucous life of the bawdy frontier towns all the more. He was truly caught in between, one foot snared in either world, able to make a home for himself in neither.

As he looked now at Sitting Bull's face, for some reason the chief appeared older—the furrow between his brows, those deep clefts running down from the corners of his sharp nose. But mostly the sadness in his eyes. Yes, sadness. For many, many days now the chief had been in mourning. The loss of his child kicked in the head by a mule. Eating nothing, Sitting Bull had fasted, smeared cold ashes on his flesh, slept but little, and wore only his poorest of clothing. At first glance he looked anything but a great visionary and undisputed leader of the Lakota.

But behind those sad eyes burned the smoldering fires of stoic resolve to see his people through this whole struggle with the white man.

Already the Bull had seen many things through, ever since he had first become a warrior of wide repute more than a decade before, a warrior whose name was known not just to his Hunkpapa band, but to the whites as well as the other wandering bands of Lakota. He was one of the few among the many who steadfastly refused to have anything to do with the white man— choosing to avoid him at all costs if possible. And when it was not possible ... well, Johnny too had heard the mining camp talk of the Custer "massacre." That, and the campfire tales wherein the Lakota warriors related their coups and told their battle stories.

Strange, Bruguier thought, that this medicine man was called the chief of all the hostiles by the whites, when he was merely a visionary who possessed the ability to bring together the various Lakota peoples into a cohesive force. He was not a war chief—more so a savvy politician who drew strong people to his cause.

Yes, Johnny decided, Sitting Bull was careful not to let his face show much of anything as he sat in council, just as he did sitting here for the first time with a soldier leader since the great war had begun last winter along the ice-clogged Powder River. Clearly the Hunkpapa leader was a man who deliberated on a matter for some time before coming to his decision.

When the pipe had finished its rounds of the small circle and Sitting Bull held it once again, the Hunkpapa chief spoke. "I point the stem of my pipe to the Great Spirit. He thinks nothing bad of His people. I believe that He is near us and looking down upon us. We are agreeing to keep the peace and smoke this pipe together with you. The Great Spirit is a witness to this peace, but I am afraid you will break it, Bear Coat. My people, when they make an agreement, shake hands and exchange presents. What have you brought with you? My people expect presents in token of this friendship."

Johnny translated the soldier chief's demand for Sitting Bull, "Presents? You ask for gifts when your people have stolen everything you can get your hands on and butchered every white man who comes into this country? No presents. To have peace, you must first give back the mules your warriors stole from my wagon trains and promise you will never attack my wagons again."

The Bull's dark face was impassive, not registering the slightest show of emotion as he replied, "Tell the Bear Coat I will return the mules when he returns the buffalo his soldiers and wagons have scared off."

The officer's eyes visibly narrowed at that rebuke. He asked, "Does this mean Sitting Bull will not return what he has stolen?"

But instead of answering the question directly, Sitting Bull asked another through Johnny: "Why are your soldiers here?"

"I am here because these warriors attacked my wagons when your Indians should have been back at their agency."

Johnny wagged his head, working to get the question phrased just so. "No, soldier chief—why aren't the soldiers staying in their log lodges for the winter and leaving the Lakota be, as the soldiers have always done? Instead, the soldiers went to attack the Cheyenne last winter on the Powder. And now Sitting Bull wants to know why you come to his country to attack his villages. Winter is a time of peace."

"Yes, peace." The soldier's cold eyes flicked from the Hunkpapa to the half-breed. "That's exactly what we should be talking about. My lieutenant here said you told him Sitting Bull wants to talk about surrender."

Bruguier translated for the chief, then turned back to Miles. "There will be no talk of surrender today. Sitting Bull want to know why the army is here in Lakota country. Why are the soldiers here, scaring away our buffalo, building their log forts, chasing after our villages of women and children?"

"We are here because you are here," the soldier replied testily, beginning to show some exasperation as he shifted to another knee. "If Sitting Bull and all his people would go home to their agency, we would have no need of chasing after your villages. We would have peace."

"This is our country. This is our home. You are the stranger here. Sitting Bull wants you to take your soldiers and go back where you came from."

For a few moments Miles ruminated on what to say next. "This was once your home. True. But long, long ago. No longer are you free to roam it at will. Now you must return to your agency and surrender."

"Surrender?" Bruguier asked after Sitting Bull asked the question angrily. "Again you talk of surrender?"

"Yes," Miles repeated. "You told my man the chief said he was ready to surrender. I can offer you no terms but complete surrender: turning over your weapons and your ponies, then moving on to your agency at Standing Rock—"

"Surrender?" Johnny asked again, trying hard to control his voice, feeling the tension suddenly grow very taut in that small circle. He flicked a glance at the eyes of the Old-Man Chiefs as they tried to make sense of why he was not translating what Miles had said. "Sitting Bull has not talked of surrender."

"W-wait a goddamned minute here," Miles stammered, his face turning crimson, his eyes glowering slightly as they shot over to one of his soldiers. "But you told my aide that Sitting Bull wanted to discuss terms of surrender."

With a wag of his head, Johnny said, "No. Your soldier misunderstand. I told him all of these Old-Man Chiefs wanted to be left alone by the army. Some of them wanted to surrender and go back to their agency for the winter if the army was going to make hunting the buffalo hard to do. They would go in. But Sitting Bull? No. No. He has never said he would surrender to you. Not to any white army soldier chief. No, never."

For a few minutes the crisp autumn air seemed all the more charged with an unspoken electricity as Miles ground his teeth together, staring at each of the Lakota in turn, but reserving his hardest glare for the impassive Sitting Bull and his translator.

"Tell Sitting Bull we are not leaving this country," the soldier finally said, his voice even and moderate despite the anger flaring in his eyes. "We are here to protect the roads and the rivers. We will protect white commerce and white settlement. I repeat: the Sioux must return to their agency."

"Sitting Bull says he has never been to an agency," Johnny translated. "He cannot go back to where he has never been."

"Goddammit! You tell him it doesn't matter that he's never been to Standing Rock. That's where his Hunkpapa belong, and that's where he's going."

"Sitting Bull will not go where he does not want to go."

Miles fumed a moment, then said, "He can go voluntarily, on his own—you explain that to him. Or I can drive him home, like I can drive buffalo out of this valley, on to the next, and on to the next."

"We will go the next valley, Sitting Bull says. You cannot kill off all the buffalo, and you cannot kill off all the Lakota. You go away and leave us alone. Take your soldiers away from the log lodges at Tongue River. Take all the soldiers away from the big fort at the mouth of Elk River."*

"I have my orders from your grandfather in Washington City: I am to see that you go back on your reservation."

Johnny translated, then turned to ask Sitting Bull's question, "And if we do not go back to this Standing Rock Agency?"

"Those who do not go will be followed, hounded and harried . . . and perhaps even killed by the soldiers who are coming."

"There are no soldiers coming. Only you," Bruguier replied.

"It is winter. Wait until spring. Come spring, there will be more than before. Many more."

"We killed many of your soldiers this summer. The army did not drive us off of our hunting grounds. You will not drive us out next year."

"Tell Sitting Bull there are more soldiers coming. And more settlers. More white men than there are blades of grass on this prairie, more than there will be stars in the sky tonight."

For a few minutes Sitting Bull thought on those words, then stated, "I want only to be left alone. To live as my grandfather lived. I desire only to hunt buffalo. I want to do some trading—mostly to trade for ammunition for my guns so that I can hunt the buffalo. If you take your soldiers . . . all your soldiers out of our country and never return, we will leave you and your soldiers alone."

Miles wagged his head in frustration, glancing at the restless warriors on their ponies milling about less than fifty yards behind their chiefs. "You must go in to your agency or there will be war."

*Fort Buford, Dakota Territory.

"We have had fighting with your soldiers for many years already."

"Sitting Bull will not go in to Standing Rock voluntarily?"

Johnny finally shook his head, saying, "Sitting Bull says the Great Mystery above made him a free Indian. He did not make Sitting Bull an agency Indian."

"Tell the chief he must return to the agency, for the good of his people."

"Sitting Bull says he does not need to go to the agency for anything. All he needs is here in Lakota country. Plenty of buffalo—"

"Yes," Miles interrupted curtly. "I know Sitting Bull and his people intend to move north to hunt buffalo on the Big Dry River. Then go on to Fort Peck to trade for guns and ammunition so they can keep making war on white men coming into this land."

As Johnny translated that statement, Sitting Bull's impassive face suddenly came alive with rage. The chief demanded, "How does the soldier chief know where I want to take my people? How does he know we are going to the fort to trade with the métis? Who has spoken of this to the soldier chief?"

Evidently the loud, bellicose tone of Sitting Bull's voice spurred some activity among the mounted, armed warriors waiting behind the council. They stirred, brandishing their weapons openly, beginning to inch their way toward the conference.

"You better tell those men to stay back," Miles warned sharply, pointing over Sitting Bull's shoulder.

Now there was restlessness among the few soldiers with Miles as Johnny turned to look over his shoulder. Most of the mounted warriors were easing up on the conference, converging from two sides.

"Watch for treachery, men," Miles ordered in a low, clipped voice.

Putting up his hands, Bruguier first spoke in English, suddenly very frightened that events would spill out of control. "There's no danger here! There's no danger!"

Then he turned to Sitting Bull to explain why the soldiers were becoming anxious and afraid, keeping their hands near the fronts of their open coats.

"The soldiers will have guns under their coats," Johnny warned.

Sitting Bull glowered at Miles. "I come without a weapon to

talk to the Bear Coat chief. But he brings a gun to talk with me! Does he want to kill me?"

"No, I don't think he wants to kill you," Bruguier replied, trying his best to soothe, to calm the tension.

"Why does he bring his guns here?"

"I think he is afraid of the young warriors who come too close, showing their weapons."

"They hold their guns in plain view, openly," Sitting Bull protested. "Is this not honorable of a man? It is not an honorable thing to sneak a gun under one's coat as these soldiers have done. Maybe I should kill this Bear Coat who is not so honorable a man. Do you think I should kill him now, Big Leggings?"

Bruguier gulped, his face turning to Miles. He said, "Soldier chief—"

"You tell Sitting Bull that I am Colonel Nelson A. Miles, Fifth U.S.—"

"Shuddup and listen," Johnny interrupted. "Sitting Bull just asked me if I figured he ought to kill you his own self."

The soldier chief's eyes narrowed into slits. "S-sitting Bull said . . . said he ought to kill me?"

Johnny tried hard to overhear the whispers of those old men who huddled their heads close to Sitting Bull, snarling angry advice to the chief, whispering their denunciations of the chief's talk about killing the Bear Coat.

Bruguier started, "He asked me that—"

Miles interrupted, "Get those goddamned warriors back! *Now!*"

"Sitting Bull asked me if I thought he should kill you, but the others . . . they talked him out of killing you today."

"Tell those horsemen to get back, or by Jupiter there will be blood on this ground today!" Miles snapped.

Johnny translated for Sitting Bull, and at long last the chief turned to wave the horsemen back to where they had been waiting when the conference began.

"See there?" Bruguier asked nervously, hoping the fuse had been taken out of the powder keg. "There is no danger now."

"You tell Sitting Bull that even I entertained the idea of killing him by my own hand here today too. But I—Nelson A. Miles—knew it was not an honorable thing to do under a flag of truce. You tell him that. That I am an honorable man. Had I killed him here, and my men shot the rest of you—the whole civilized world would have denounced the act as barbaric."

"Sitting Bull does not think the white man truly wants peace with the Hunkpapa," Johnny said on behalf of the chief.

"I told you: I am an honorable man."

"But do you want peace with Sitting Bull?"

"Yes," Miles answered. "But to have peace, I want Sitting Bull and his people to go to the agency where they can live in peace with the white man."

"You are a soldier," Johnny translated. "Like Sitting Bull's warriors. He does not believe you are a man of peace. You have come to make war on his villages, on his women and his children."

"No," the soldier chief said quietly. "I want peace as much as Sitting Bull wants peace."

More whispering hissed among the Lakota warriors at Johnny's knee. As he watched and listened, he could see Sitting Bull stiffen with resolve. As much as the others might be trying their best to talk him into making some peaceful arrangement with the soldier chief, the Hunkpapa leader once more became resistant. His eyes went cold and his face became impassive for a long time as he listened and considered the words of the others. At long last he held up his hand, signaling the others that now he wished to speak.

"Big Leggings," he said, his eyes boring into the half-breed's, "tell the Bear Coat that my people do not intend to surrender. We will never go to the agency. I am born a free Indian and will die a free Indian. The soldiers will never change that. I will use my last breath to see that my people continue hunting buffalo and antelope in this country. You tell this soldier chief that we will continue to trade at the forts when we want to trade with the white man. Otherwise, the Hunkpapa want nothing to do with the white people. And you tell this soldier that we want his word of honor that he will take all the soldiers from our country—never to return!"

Licking his lips nervously, Bruguier began his translation, seeking the words that would show the fire of Sitting Bull's oration, but not so much heat that it would be like slap across the soldier chief's face. Even though the Hunkpapa chief might want that, there still existed a very real chance for tragedy and treachery in this small council held in the middle of this great buffalo prairie.

In the end Johnny translated as best he could the full force of Sitting Bull's declaration, the full impact of Sitting Bull's deadly warning.

Miles stiffened only slightly with the rebuke, his face becoming set like stone as he listened to Johnny haltingly translate all the thoughts in the chief's stern oration. Then the colonel considered his reply a few minutes before saying, "If Sitting Bull wants to continue hunting for this final season—to put meat up for this last winter his people are to hunt buffalo—I can understand. But in return for my allowing the Hunkpapa to continue their last hunt, Sitting Bull must leave these three men with me as hostages."

"H-hostages?" Johnny repeated, scrambling to figure out what he was going to say to the chiefs as a lone warrior dismounted behind the council, shifted his blanket tightly about himself, and moved toward the ring of men squatted on the prairie.

"That's what I said," Miles snapped, watching the approach of that lone warrior. "These hostages will guarantee me that Sitting Bull will keep his word."

The dark, chertlike eyes of all the Lakota leaders glowed with sudden hatred when Johnny translated the soldier chief's demand.

"No," Bruguier said when Miles repeated his demand for hostages.

"Sitting Bull says no?"

From the corner of his eye Bruguier saw the lone warrior kneel behind Sitting Bull, carefully parting his blanket so that he could slip a rifle from it. He slid the weapon beneath the buffalo robe the Hunkpapa chief had pulled about him, then rose slowly and moved back to rejoin the other horsemen as they continued to mill about, inching their ponies closer and closer.

Johnny declared, "The chief says he will never turn over his friends to the soldiers to keep while his people hunt. This is their land. These are their buffalo. You and your soldiers are not welcome here."

"Those warriors!" Miles suddenly growled, rising from his knee and stuffing his hand inside the flaps of his coat. "Tell them to get back—Now!"

Eyes wide with apprehension, Bruguier translated the soldier chief's warning as more and more of the chiefs began to chatter excitedly as soon as Miles got to his feet. Almost as one, the rest of the soldiers all put their hands beneath their coats.

Furious, Miles said, "You send all these warriors away. Only the chiefs can stay. Only the men who were here when we began the talk. Tell them that! Tell them right now before there is bloodshed!"

Sitting Bull remained cross-legged on the ground, his face refusing to register the tensions simmering around him. Yet in his eyes smoldered the anger Johnny could not fail to recognize.

The chief said, "Tell the Bear Coat soldier that these are my people and I will not send them away. I want the soldiers to leave my country now, leave it for all time."

As he listened to Bruguier's translation, Miles shifted his hat on his head nervously. Then, pulling his hand from inside his coat, he slapped his gloved hands down on his thighs and replied stiffly, "That's just about it, then." He slowly turned rubbing his knees from having sat so long on the cold ground.

"Where is the white chief going?" Bruguier asked, confused.

"Clearly—there is no more use in our talking," Miles replied over his shoulder as the other soldiers began to move off with him, all very wary and watchful. "We've been at this for many hours. Back and forth, with no good result. You tell Sitting Bull that we can continue our talk tomorrow."

After asking the Hunkpapa chief for a response, Johnny said, "Sitting Bull says he will talk with you tomorrow."

"Good," Miles declared with a gush of finality. "I think it would be wise of you to tell Sitting Bull to consider his remarks overnight. Best for him to think on the sad consequences if he chooses to continue making war."

By this time the sun had fallen halfway to the horizon from midsky. The day was rapidly growing old as Sitting Bull and the rest got to their feet, took up their blankets and robes, and turned away while Mile's escort strode back to the soldier lines. When the soldiers turned about and began to march west, back toward Cedar Creek, most of those mounted warriors who had remained close during the parley chose to follow the soldiers at a distance. Along the crest of the nearby ridges the horsemen slowly shadowed the blue column, flanking the soldiers as they countermarched nearly five miles and eventually went into camp for the night.

"Are the soldiers leaving us be?" asked Black Eagle that night as all the Lakota leaders held an angry council.

"No," declared Rising Sun. "They marched away in that direction so they could be in a better position to charge us when we move north, following the buffalo on our way to Fort Peck."

"Yes," Sitting Bull agreed as the council fell quiet. "My heart cannot believe the soldiers are leaving our country as we told them to do. They are not to be trusted."

"Perhaps we should consider going in to the agency when this hunt is over," suggested Small Bear.

"The reservation holds nothing for me," Sitting Bull said. "Only unhappiness and empty bellies. Here ... here in the buffalo country is where our men hunt and our women cure the hides that shelter us. We can never do that living at the white man's agency."

For a long time that night the leaders argued back and forth on what to do until one of the camp police, the *akicita*, came in to report that a few of their ponies had broken away, and in going after them some of the young men had discovered that their camp was being watched by many soldiers who had secreted themselves in the surrounding hills and bluffs.

"We must attack those soldiers at early light!" screamed an infuriated Standing Bear.

Other voices took up the call. "These soldiers mean to make war on us!"

Still more urged caution, restraint—reminding the council that their camp no longer possessed the great numbers that had overwhelmed and crushed the soldiers at the Greasy Grass back in the summer moon.

Suddenly Gall arose and waited while the assembly fell to a hush. He looked at Sitting Bull a moment, then said, "If we do not attack first, as Crazy Horse did to Three Stars on the Rosebud, then we can expect the soldiers to attack us."

Johnny Bruguier turned to watch Sitting Bull's face. The great Hunkpapa visionary nodded once, nodded slowly, his hand signaling his war chief to continue.

"If we can count on the white man to do anything, we can depend upon him to do what is most dishonorable," Gall explained. "When the soldier chief says he has come to talk of peace, it is only to make our senses dull, so that we roll over with our bellies to the sky."

Now Gall's voice rose an octave, sending a chill down the half-breed's spine as this barrel-chested, iron-eyed man who had lost so many loved ones to soldiers at the Greasy Grass now laid down his warning to the leaders of that great village.

"Come tomorrow," he barely whispered in the awful hush of

that huge council lodge, "when the soldiers come to attack our women and children ... it will be their blood left to soak into this ground."

"Remember the Rosebud!" one of the younger warriors suddenly cried out from the fringe of the crowd.

"Remember the Greasy Grass!" Gall shrieked, his face contorted in rage, flecks of spittle on his lips.

Remember the Greasy Grass!

Chapter 10

21 October 1876

**An Official Report on South
Carolina Troubles.**

**Why and How the Colored
Troops Fought Nobly**

South Carolina

**A History of the Late Troubles Near
Charleston.**

"**Y**ou fellas got to listen to this!" exclaimed trader Collins that chilly morning inside his store at Fort Laramie. "There's been a heap of trouble down in the South."

Seamus watched Collins smooth out the newspaper with both hands atop the counter cluttered with a shipment of soaps and lilac water directly up from Denver by way of Cheyenne City.

"What's it say?" asked John Bourke.

"This here's the official report of R. M. Wallace, United States marshal for South Carolina, addressed to Attorney General Taft—a letter read in the meeting of Grant's cabinet a couple days back. He writes

'SIR: I have delayed giving you a report of the recent unfortunate political riot at a place near the town of Clinsey, near this city, until I could get a correct statement of facts. It's one of the legitimate results of the intimidation policy on the Mississippi plan adopted by the democratic party in opening their campaign for the purpose of breaking down the majority in this state. The first meeting in this country at which the democrats put their shot gun policy in practice, took place over a month ago, on Cooper River ... The republicans had called a meeting and the democrats of this city chartered a steamboat and took one hundred and fifty well armed men to the meeting ... and demanded that they should have the time for their speeches. The republicans did not relish this kind of peaceful political discussion, but the request was backed up by one hundred and fifty Winchester repeating rifles in the hands of men who know how to use them.' "

Walter S. Schuyler broke in, asking, "Had to be them god-damned Johnny Rebs stirring up the trouble—right, Seamus?"

"Those sentiments go back a long time now, Lieutenant," Donegan replied to General Crook's aide. "It's been many a year since I faced reb guns. All in the past now."

Trader Collins cleared his throat to resnag everyone's attention and proceeded with his reading of the news story plastered across the front page of Denver's Rocky Mountain *News*.

"... The democrats carried a large force from the city to every meeting, who irritated the republicans by their violent denunciation of their leaders and their party. The meeting at the brick church was called by the republicans ... many of them being suspicious of the democrats carried such guns as each man had at his home—muskets—but no militia men went there with state arms and ammunition, as the democrats claim; and the best evidence of that fact is that all the dead were shot with buckshot and not with rifle balls."

"Jesus H. Christ!" Bourke roared. "You mean the democrats and republicans are shooting at each other down there in the South now?"

"Bound to happen," declared Captain Wirt Davis, a Virginia-born officer who had nonetheless thrown in with the Union in 1861. He wagged his head with grim resignation.

Captain John Lee, another officer in Mackenzie's Fourth, agreed. "Like my friend Wirt, here—I am a Tennessee man who loathes the sort of coward who hides behind a bedsheet bringing terror and lynching to my native land. But sooner or later this sort of trouble was bound to happen down there somewhere."

Collins bent over his paper and pressed on with the story.

"When the colored republicans arrived at the place of meeting, their leading men told them that they were violating the agreement by coming armed, and that they must deposit their arms at some place away from the grounds. The colored men complied with the request ... and some guns ... were placed in an old dilapidated building some fifty yards from the stand ... About one hundred and fifty democrats accompanied their speakers from the city, and soon appeared at the meeting. Soon after W. J. McKennely, colored, commenced, a commotion was observed ... next to the dilapidated building and McKennely jumped off the stand and said: 'There are white men in that house; they have the guns, and are going to shoot.' The colored men raised a shout, 'The democrats have seized our guns!' and made a rush for the other guns. The white men who had secretly slipped into the house and seized the guns then fired, and the first shot killed an old colored man about seventy years old. . . .

"The colored men returned with their guns very soon and attacked the party. They commenced a general fire on the democrats, who were generally armed with pistols. . . . Six white men were killed and one colored. Several whites were wounded ... and it is not known how many negroes were hurt."

"Begging Captain Lee's pardon—but it sounds to me like they're still fighting that war down there," Schuyler observed.

"Maybe that's as good a reason as any to be out here," John Lee replied as he set his steaming cup of coffee down with a clunk upon the table. "Eh, Mr. Donegan?"

With a wag of his head, Seamus replied, "All this hoopla and upset and bloodshed. I'm bloody well beginning to wonder if there really is anyplace safe for a man to raise his family in peace—or if the whole bleeming country's gone crazy!"

"Irishman!"

Donegan turned toward the doorway as the old sergeant burst in, his caped wool coat a'swirl with some of the snow falling outside. It seemed the soldier brought all of that wilderness cold in with him.

"Sergeant?"

"Cap'n Wirt," the sergeant said, coming to an abrupt halt and saluting. "Cap'n Lee, sir. Didn't know you was here."

Wirt asked, "What is it, Sergeant Forsyth?"

"The general, Cap'n. He sent me to fetch up the Irishman here."

"We're heading back to Camp Robinson already?" Lee asked.

"Yes, sir, Cap'n."

Outside on the parade, a bugle rasped through the wintry notes of "Boots and Saddles." As its stirring call faded over Fort Laramie, First Sergeant Thomas H. Forsyth leaned close to Donegan and whispered, "Best get a move on and say your good-byes to the missus."

Rising slowly, Seamus watched the two cavalry captains hurry out the door as he moved toward the frosted windowpane to gaze out at the bustle of activity on the parade ground. "Sheridan and Crook must really be in a hurry to get their hands on those Sioux guns and ponies, eh?"

"Mackenzie said to tell you you've got a quarter of an hour," the bearded veteran replied with a wink as he turned away, a knowing smile gleaming above his faded chevrons. "Use every minute wisely."

THE INDIANS

Movements on the Missouri

St. PAUL, October 20.—A *Pioneer Press* Bismarck special says that General Sturgis with eight companies of cavalry and three of infantry and a section of artillery moved south to-day on the east side of the Missouri, and General Terry with four companies moved south on the west side. Nobody knows where they are going. Whitney and others have arrived from the Black Hills bringing the body of Mr. Dodge, killed by Indians in April. Major Smith has arrived from Tongue River and says the Indians killed the herd of government animals near Glendive.

* * *

Just past dawn on 21 October, William Jackson moved out of the Fifth Infantry's bivouac with Luther Kelly and most of the other scouts, ordered to probe north along Cedar Creek, throwing outriders along both flanks as the soldiers formed up and began their march that chilly Saturday. At the rear, D Company was assigned to escort the regiment's supply train.

Miles intended to have his men out in front of the hostiles, blocking their way if Sitting Bull decided to make a sudden dash for the Canadian border.

It was nearing midmorning beneath a cold autumn sun when Jackson and Kelly cautiously reached the crest of a hill on their bellies in advance of the soldiers, scanning the distance for sign of the Sioux.

"They're making a run for it," Kelly said with some grim resignation.

"Just like Miles figured they would," Jackson replied as they both watched the distant village dismantling and setting out—the first of the laden travois and their vast pony herd protectively encircled by a great ring of hundreds of warriors. Horsemen milled about through the bare tripods as throngs of people went about their work like it was a fevered anthill.

Then Jackson added, "But, look. Instead of heading north—I'll be damned if they're going south by east."

"What strikes me is that the village is a lot bigger than we thought at first," Yellowstone Kelly observed.

"What do you make it? Three, maybe four thousand of 'em?"

The white chief of scouts nodded behind his field glasses. "Could be as many as a thousand warriors."

"Want me to go tell Miles?" William asked.

Luther Kelly pulled the field glasses from his face as he twisted around to look over his shoulder. "Yeah, you head out. I'll be along straightaway."

Jackson started to slide backward on his belly when Kelly put out his arm and stopped him there in that tall, dead, brittle grass rising out of the cold, cold ground as a nervous wind came up.

"See that ground, yonder there?" Kelly declared, pointing. "Tell the general they're headed into the next valley. Tell him I figure we can catch them if he comes up quick—on the double. Most of the village is still tearing down."

WASHINGTON

Terry After the Indians.

WASHINGTON, October 20.—Advices have been received at the war department that General Terry will immediately leave Fort Abraham Lincoln in pursuit of the hostile savages.

About the time his scouts came tearing back to tell him that the village was fleeing to the southeast, Miles spotted a dozen warriors dippling the crest of a ridge far in their front.

"They'll cover the retreat of their village, General!" Captain James S. Casey said.

"Damn right they will, Major," Miles replied, using Casey's brevet rank. "Let's get ready for action! Battle front, by companies! Bring up that goddamned train and alert Lieutenant Mc-Donald that his D Company may soon have his hands full protecting it on the rear! Now, by bloody damn! I don't want Sitting Bull slipping out of my hands!"

Ten companies of infantry moved out of column and formed up in a matter of moments, their Long Toms, formerly carried at port, now carried at the ready as their sergeants bawled orders and moved them toward the rising ground in their front—where more horsemen appeared against the cold pale-blue skyline. Four of the companies marched along each side of the trail that Nelson A. Miles blazed for them, leading them forward into action. While D Company brought up the rear behind the supply wagons, Captain Simon Snyder and his F Company provided support for the Rodman gun.

They covered no more than three miles when the colonel reached a spot where the ground continued to rise toward that rough country where Cedar Creek flows to the south off the divide separating the Yellowstone drainage from that of the Missouri River. Here he almost gasped at the savage beauty of the ground that lay before him—a tapestry of sharp escarpments and rounded knolls, hills, and wind-sculpted buttes stretching away to the north, east, and south as far as his eye could reach.

There in the foreground Nelson Miles saw more Indians than he had ever witnessed in one gathering—far, far more than he had laid eyes on even the day before.

"Got you, Sitting Bull," he whispered as he reined his horse about in position and signaled his adjutant. "I knew you couldn't get away from me."

Miles deployed his forces for their attack—or for the very real possibility that those warriors down there, who would be protecting their families, their homes, would attack first.

To that knoll where he sat atop his horse at the extreme right flank of his troops, Miles ordered the gun crew under Captain Snyder to establish an emplacement for their field piece. At the same time he sent Captain James S. Casey and A Company off to the far left flank, to temporarily hold the ground at the foot of the high ridges where more horsemen were beginning to swirl.

There in his front appeared more than two dozen riders emerging from the bristling mass of horsemen. One of the twelve held a white flag overhead. The party continued to advance toward Miles and his headquarters group as if the soldiers presented no danger, until the two sides were intermingled.

"The chief doesn't like that gun staring down on their women and children," William Jackson explained as the dozen came to a halt before Miles and the tension tangibly rose.

Miles recognized Sitting Bull among the group but was surprised to see that this morning the chief hung back, his buffalo robe draped over his head so that his face was hardly visible.

"Tell the chief I positioned my artillery there because I don't trust his warriors," Nelson replied. "It's there to protect my men. And you tell him: if he speaks honorably, he and his people have nothing to fear from our cannon."

Jackson started to interpret as best he could with sign when the half-breed translator from the day before came loping up on horseback. He came to a halt beside the chief. Only now did Sitting Bull allow the buffalo robe to slip back from his head, clutching it around his shoulders. Again this day he refused to wear feathers or adornment, and definitely none of the war regalia displayed by the others who moved about on the soldiers' front.

"Sitting Bull wants to talk with you again," the half-breed announced as his small pony pranced between the two leaders.

"You're the one who did all the talking for the chief yesterday," Miles said sourly. "You're named Bur-gaire?"

"Bruguier. Johnny's my first name."

"And you'd be a half-blood?"

The swarthy interpreter smiled. "How'd you guess, soldier chief?"

Leaning back stiffly, Miles replied, "So what's Sitting Bull got to say for the fact that we were supposed to talk this morning, but instead—I find him running off."

The half-breed shrugged. "This village moves all the time."

"Not when we agreed we would talk this morning," Nelson answered, his eyes flicking back and forth across the faces of those chiefs nearest him. As well he kept an eye on the movements of the village and the warriors swarming across the open ground between the soldiers and the Hunkpapa camp. They held their weapons high, screamed out oaths, and kicked their ponies savagely into short sprints, giving the animals their second wind.

"Sitting Bull says you did not keep your word, soldier," Bruguier declared. "Your soldiers sneaked around our village last night. And you made your camp where you would be right on our trail when we started marching north."

"That's why Sitting Bull is heading south now?"

When the half-breed had listened to the chief's answer, he said, "Your soldiers scare away all the buffalo up that way. So he will take his people to hunt buffalo somewhere else."

"I think it wise for Sitting Bull to talk with me some more."

It was a few moments before the half-breed turned away from the Hunkpapa chief, addressing Miles. "The chief says maybe-so it is a good idea to talk some more with you. He says you did not hear him too good yesterday."

"Maybe we will both hear each other good today," Nelson responded, his eyes moving past the nearby warriors, down the sloping ground of the dry ravines in their front, back up the far side. "There," he said, pointing. "That knoll right up there. Tell Sitting Bull we'll meet there to talk."

At the crest of that flat-topped promontory minutes later, Nelson waited with several of his officers and a few scouts while Sitting Bull and some twelve Sioux briefly conferred, then walked abreast up to the conference site in a broad line. Accompanying the chief today was White Bull, as well as many new faces who had not taken part in yesterday's long and protracted discussions: Black Eagle, Gall, John Sans Arc, Rising Sun, Small Bear, Red Skirt, the Miniconjou chief Bull Eagle, Standing Bear, Spotted Elk, Pretty Bear, and Yellow Eagle. As the delegation reached the top of the knoll, Miles signaled his adjutant and a color bearer to bring forward a pair of buffalo robes the soldiers quickly spread on the ground. It pleased the colonel to read the look of surprise that crossed Sitting Bull's face as Nelson seized the initiative in these subtleties of diplomacy.

It brought him even greater satisfaction when the Hunkpapa chief refused to sit on the offered robe, much as Nelson had done the day before.

The half-breed translated for Sitting Bull: "Yesterday I spread a robe for you to sit on and you refused. I shall have to refuse now to sit on your robe."

Despite the chief's steadfast refusal, within moments the other Lakota took their seats on the ground with Miles and his men leaving Sitting Bull to stand alone. For a few uneasy minutes he paced behind the others, embarrassed before this auspicious assembly, his face clearly showing the anger boiling beneath the surface, then finally took a seat and pulled his robe tightly about him as the wind stiffened on that high ground.

From the robe Sitting Bull once again pulled his pipe, filled, and lit it, saying his prayer through Bruguier, "Have mercy upon your people, Great Mystery. Allow nothing to be said here on either side but the truth. See into our hearts and make us do what is right. If any man who smokes this pipe with me today fails to keep his promises, I hope that he may not live to walk upon the ground—but that he may lay down and die."

With those solemn formalities out of the way, what talk Miles and Sitting Bull shared was little more than a rewarming of what both sides had had to say the day before. Try as he might, Miles could not find a better way to tell Sitting Bull that his people would have to come in to surrender, or bring suffering down upon their heads.

The Hunkpapa would never go in to Standing Rock. This was their country and here they would stay. What the white man could do to repay the Lakota for running off the buffalo would be to build a trading post closer to these hunting grounds.

"Tell Sitting Bull that his people can come in to the trading post we will have at Tongue River," Miles declared.

Bruguier replied, "The chief says his people will go to Fort Peck to trade, as they always do."

Inside, Nelson burned with resentment. Why, he had even offered to trade with this red-skinned criminal. . . . Maybe it was true what a lot of the old frontiersmen believed—like that scout Luther Kelly had hired to come along. The one named John Johnston. Old weathered plainsmen the likes of him believed the only thing an Injun understood was force. Nothing more than sheer might, and blood.

Just as they had done yesterday, warriors came and went while the discussion dragged on. But this time Nelson was prepared for their nerve-racking shenanigans. His orders called for a soldier to step up from the forward lines every time one of the Sioux advanced. When that warrior moved back, the soldier was to withdraw in kind. Hour by hour the numbers around the council waxed and waned, constantly shifting—more warriors and soldiers on the periphery, then fewer once more.

It was a time of unmitigated tension during which Nelson realized that the accidental discharge of a weapon on either side might well spell disaster for all in confusion between the two lines.

As the morning grew old, it became abundantly clear to Miles that instead of softening his position, Sitting Bull was growing more adamant in his refusal to budge in the slightest. Just as clear was the fact that a few of the other chiefs appeared ready to bend to reason, especially the Miniconjou chiefs Bull Eagle and Red Skirt. Even John Sans Arc provisionally agreed to give himself over to the soldiers as a hostage as a means of guaranteeing his band's good-faith compliance in returning to the agency. But it was just their bending which seemed to put all the more steel in Sitting Bull's backbone that cold autumn day.

Bruguier waited patiently, listening as Sitting Bull talked a long time, nodding occasionally to show he understood the Hunkpapa's words, then finally sought to translate all that had been dropped into his lap.

"The chief says that the whites hate Indians. And the Indian hates the white man. This is Indian country, so the Hunkpapa will not leave it. They mean to stay here for all time and live upon the buffalo—the way the Lakota people have lived from the time Wakan Tanka put them here, way before the white man ever came. Wakan Tanka gave the Lakota these buffalo plains to wander."

After a moment of reflection, Nelson replied, "Tell Sitting Bull he would be foolish to refuse to go in to his agency when to refuse will mean that the army will harry and harass his people, and many of them will die. There will be no time for the hunt this winter. My scouts will find your villages. My soldiers will attack those villages. Tell Sitting Bull that he must go in to Standing Rock or his people will be whipped."

As the half-blood interpreted, Nelson could see how his words stung the Hunkpapa leader. Fire glistened in the defiant chief's eyes as he glared stoically at Miles.

Finally Bruguier turned to say, "Sitting Bull says if you mean to make war on him, then make your war now. He does not want to live like those who hang around the forts waiting for the white man's handouts. Spotted Tail and even Red Cloud. Red Cloud!" and the translator laughed. "The war chief who drove the soldiers from the Bozeman Road! Now he is nothing but another old-woman chief who does not have teeth enough to eat buffalo meat. Only the white man's pig meat."

Miles wagged his head, saying, "Sitting Bull would rather his people die in war than live in peace at their agency?"

Nodding, the interpreter explained, "Sitting Bull says it is better for him and his people to fight and die than to be trapped at the agency and starve as those agency bands are starving."

Good Lord, Nelson thought. But try he must—as an officer and a civilized gentleman—if only this one last time. No one would ever fault Nelson Miles for not putting his back into every task. Long ago in his youth when he had decided he would become a professional soldier, no one had ever warned him he would also have to practice diplomacy.

"Tell Sitting Bull that it is unfair of him to answer for the old ones, the little children in that camp, and those who are too sick to last out the cold of this coming winter as the soldiers chase them down."

When Miles's words were translated, Sitting Bull's jaw jutted resolutely, cords of muscle throbbing in his thick neck.

"The chief says the white man is a liar and not to be trusted," Bruguier translated. "The white man has made many, many treaties with the Lakota . . . and the white man has turned around and broken every one of them. It's the only thing the white man can be counted on doing."

"I will give you *my* word—"

The half-blood interrupted with a snarl, "In the treaty with Red Cloud, the Black Hills were given to the Lakota for all time, but now the white man comes to take them back."

Lord knows he had tried, Nelson ruminated as he sat there—stung with having his own personal honor questioned—watching how some of the other dark faces showed disappointment, some showed fear, while Sitting Bull's remained a plate of cold anger.

"So be it," Miles finally said when Bruguier was done with Sitting Bull's long harangue. "You tell the chief that he has fifteen minutes to decide if he will accept my terms for unconditional surrender . . . or prepare for battle. And if it's a fight he wants—the whites will keep bringing more and more soldiers into this country until the Sioux are no more."

The half-breed's eyes flinched at that, quickly flicking toward the soldiers' positions, yet he turned and attempted to translate this concept of war beginning in a quarter of an hour—something unfathomable to the Hunkpapa mind.

His thin lips a pressed, colorless line, Sitting Bull exploded to his feet, jerking his buffalo robe about himself as he spat out his words. "So—the Bear Coat has me trapped? You bring me here, an honorable warrior—and tell me you make war on me *now*?"

Miles looked back and forth between Sitting Bull and the translator as the chief pointed to the dirty white flag that one of his men held at the end of a long coup stick.

For the chief, Bruguier interpreted, "This is the flag an honorable warrior respects. I believed we were safe with this flag over our heads when we come to talk today. You said your soldiers would not fire on us."

"We will not fire on you," Miles snapped.

"Those will be the first of your words I pray I can believe," Sitting Bull growled. He shot Miles one last glare and turned on his heel.

As Miles watched Sitting Bull hurry off, the chief began signaling to the horsemen, shouting his warning to the numerous clusters of armed warriors scattered across the hillsides. They burst into motion, waving, crying out, singing their songs at the top of their lungs.

In the silence the other chiefs watched the Hunkpapa mystic descend the far side of the knoll before they too slowly rose, murmuring among themselves, some shaking their heads, eyes filled with dread.

Nelson flushed with resolve. There was no turning back now. Before him was the man who had crushed Custer. This was the moment. This was his place.

"Mr. Bailey!" Miles turned slightly to call out to his aide-de-camp as he rose from that one stiffened knee. "Prepare the units for battle!"

Chapter 11

21 October 1876

Tears came to Samantha's eyes as she watched how her husband's big, roughened hands became such soft and gentle things he would slip beneath the sleeping child, raising the boy into his huge arms where he held the infant against his chest one last time here before Seamus would have to go.

Days ago Elizabeth Burt had come up with a crate from somewhere—likely due to her pull with the post quartermaster, Sam figured—and it was that crate she had padded with scraps of shawls and old blankets, fashioning a crude crib where the fitful newborn slept.

Elizabeth said it was colic. Nothing to worry one's self about, Sam was assured. And then Martha Luhn showed her all she knew about ridding the little one's gastric system of those awful bubbles that tied a newborn up in knots and made the babe cry out in such fitful pain. How to roll the child back and forth on his mother's knee to work the fit out of his system.

But for now the babe was sleeping as Seamus held the boy, gazed down into that tiny face in the midst of all that wrap of swaddling. Her husband placed one callused finger along the boy's cheek, stroking it softly, then nudged back that unruly lock of fine hair that swept down the child's brow.

The bugle cried again from the parade. And it made Sam's heart lurch with sudden fear.

He somehow seemed to know of her apprehension. Seamus always seemed to know.

This time he turned to her as the last notes floated off in the cold air of that morning. And came to sit on the side of the bed, nestling the babe down in her arms. Then he brushed her cheek as he had done the boy's. Smearing her tears, pulling her chin up so that she had to look into his face.

"I'll be back in a few days, sweet one," he said softly as the racket of more than three dozen men about to march became all the louder outside. Downstairs, voices rose, boot heels clattered on the landing, the door banged open, and it seemed as if a regiment of men were stomping off the porch, having themselves a gay time of it as they bid farewell to those who were to be left behind.

"I know," she got the two words out, realizing she would free nothing more because of the stinging ball suddenly clogging her throat.

"I was here to see our son born, Sam," he reminded softly as he leaned forward, laying his lips barely against hers with a brush of his breath behind the words. Then he moved his mouth slightly, pressing it against her ear to whisper.

"And I'll be back to name him—before a week is out."

The soldiers were facing at least two-to-one odds. No one could figure for sure just how many fighting men there were in that village being dismantled below. There were too many of them, swirling about like an anthill you'd kick with your boot toe just to see them swarming.

Again and again Kelly's mind kept returning to one fact: they were preparing to fight the warriors of Sitting Bull. And Gall. Crow King and the others. The ones who had crushed Custer's Seventh.

Yellowstone Kelly hoped Miles had some plan to strike first, to strike hard—before those Lakota swept up this rising ground as they had at the Greasy Grass. But Miles did nothing of the kind. Instead, for the quarter of an hour he had given Sitting Bull, the colonel steadfastly held his men in readiness, every soldier watching the frantic village below as the lodge covers came down, the travois were packed. All the while along the high ridge to their left more and more horsemen gathered, milling about and in turn watching the motionless soldiers. On the far side of the ravine on their right more warriors came and went noisily, whipping their ponies for their second wind.

"Gentlemen!" Miles's voice rang out, catching nearly everyone by surprise as he stuffed his turnip watch back into the pocket of his buffalo-hide coat. "Something more than talk is now required of us! The time has come to fight: battle front—forward!"

. Half a hundred other voices were suddenly raised in staccato as the companies were ordered to quickly disperse into battle array across a wide front. As the colonel himself moved toward that clear, open ground, he ordered some of his units to the left, intent on gaining those treeless ridges and knolls—determined to refuse the enemy their advantage. To the right he threw out another company as his men in the center moved warily into the breech. Yard by yard. Now two hundred. Then five hundred. Up one gentle slope and down another. A thousand yards now as the warriors screamed and beckoned, whipping their horses around in wild circles, stirring dust into the chilling air.

"General!" Luther cried out, reining his horse up beside the officer in a tight crescent. "Near as I can figure, they're drawing your men on and on."

"For what purpose, Kelly?"

"Only thing I can think of is to get your boys down in them ravines yonder while they hold the high ground," Kelly replied. "Maybe to tie your outfits up—"

"And make another massacre of it," Miles interrupted grimly, regarding the distance. "Like they butchered Custer at the Little Bighorn."

"Bailey!" The colonel waved over a courier and gave the soldier orders he wanted delivered to the units on each flank—to keep in sight of their center and immediately withdraw toward the rest of the command if threatened with overwhelming numbers—before it was too late.

"What do you suppose that half-blood son of a bitch wants?" John Johnston growled inside his graying red beard. He shifted the old Sharps across the horn of his saddle and pointed as the other scouts and some of the officers turned to watch that swale below the crest of the nearby knoll.

Down on the bottom ground loped Johnny Bruguier and two warriors, one of them carrying that dirty, tattered towel tormented in the cruel wind as they approached the soldier lines.

"Bear Coat Chief," Bruguier shouted as he raised his right hand and came to a halt some yards from Miles. His eyes were nervous. "Sitting Bull wants to know why your soldiers are following his women and children."

Miles tugged his heavy coat beneath his thighs as the wind

came up, then replied, "Since it doesn't look as if the chief is going to accept my offer for terms of surrender—I must consider
his fleeing to be an act of hostility."

"General!"

They all turned to find an officer pointing.

"They're massing on the ridge, General!" another officer
cried out, pointing as well to the north.

"Clear the bastards off the brow of that ridge!" Miles
shouted. "Give Major Casey's A Company the order to clear it
now!"

As they watched Casey's soldiers trot off from the left flank
at double time, shouts erupted from the right flank. Kelly turned
with the rest, spotting the sixty to seventy warriors bristling
along the high ground as if they had appeared out of nowhere.

"Send K Company to move those horsemen off our front!"
Miles bellowed. "Mr. Carter will see to driving them away."

The fast response of Lieutenant Mason Carter's foot soldiers
succeeded in preventing the warriors from sweeping around the
flanks of the column now dressed left and right in battle-front
and moving forward at a steady crawl. While horsemen remained
on both left and right ends of Miles's line, it was the center that
most concerned Kelly. That's where most of the warriors stood
waiting—as if in anticipation of their comrades sweeping around
the sides of the soldier formation, drawing the soldiers' attention, when those in the center would plunge like a huge dagger
right into the heart of the Bear Coat's troops.

"How far can your gun reach, General?" Kelly asked, gesturing toward Captain Snyder's company surrounding the knoll
where the Rodman gun—an 1861 model artillery ordnance
rifle—had been rolled into position and unlimbered for action.

"Not nearly the distance to the village," Miles replied. "But
we'll scare hell out of 'em anyway once we unload on those
horsemen covering the retreat."

Down into the first ravine Miles followed his forward
troops as the warriors boiled along their flanks and in their
front, shouting, singing, brandishing their weapons. But as yet
no shot had been fired.

The smell of something out of place on the cold wind
caught Luther's attention. There, at the far ends of the ravine,
some warriors had slipped in among the treeless brush and were
busy igniting it with firebrands.

He yelled, waving at Miles. "General!"

"I see 'em, goddammit!" Miles hollered, then cried out his

orders for a detail from the center to break off, to clear the ends of the ravine where the Hunkpapa sought to fire the grass and brush—all the better to obscure their escape, but even more frightening, perhaps veiling the very real possibility of a counterattack.

As the Fifth Infantry pressed on to the east, slowly, yard by yard, the warriors in the center thinned out, most of them flowing left and right, bolstering the horsemen troubling the soldiers on either flank. Those left in the center pranced their ponies in tight circles, yelling and brandishing their weapons, some of the warriors dropping off this side or that of their mounts. A few turning to slap their bare rumps at the white men.

"What you make of it, Kelly?" Miles asked anxiously as the wind cut up the draw onto the high ground, blowing dust against their cold faces with a gritty anger.

"Those who aren't busy saying we're women are giving those ponies their second wind. Looks to me they're going to make a fight of it."

The colonel gestured his arm across three points of the compass, asking, "How many you figure we're facing?"

"As many as a thousand, General," Kelly replied. "Depending on who they leave behind to fight with that village moving off. But it ain't just the men. Some of the women every bit as bad as the warriors."

"What's the best you make of it?" Miles hissed.

"Eight hundred," Kelly confessed.

Miles's eyes narrowed into a furrow of concern. "At least two to one."

Luther warned, "Just be mindful they don't flank us, one side or the other."

"Two to one, is it? Sounds like it's time to even up the odds," Miles said. He turned on his heel and stomped away, sending a courier up to Snyder on the high knoll. In a matter of seconds the captain's men set off the first round, both the belch of the Rodman and its booming impact on the far slope echoing and reechoing across the narrow valley.

From all sides the soldiers cheered that small volcanic spurt of dust raised in the distance. Now they were going to get in their licks! No more would they take what the Hunkpapa were dishing out without returning blow for blow.

On the right flank three dozen or more horsemen kicked their ponies into action as the Rodman spewed a second shell whistling through the icy blue air. Racing around the far right end of the line, the warriors were clearly intent on circling back of the knoll, where they could surprise Snyder's men and put the big two-shoot gun out of commission.

"Damn them anyway," Miles grumbled, seeing the horsemen start their flanking maneuver. He grabbed his aide's arm, ordering, "Bailey—get Pope's E Company over there on the double and keep those bastards turned in. Make sure he understands he can't let those Sioux flank the end of our line—whatever Pope does!"

"Pope's a good man?" Kelly asked.

Miles nodded. "Came west in sixty-nine. Made a fine marker of himself in our seventy-four, seventy-five campaign on the southern plains. He's the man for this job, I tell you."

Second Lieutenant David Q. Rousseau trotted up, breathless. He saluted. "General, sir—request permission to assist Major Casey in clearing that ridge for good." He pointed to the far left flank, where ever more warriors boiled, shouting, firing down on Casey's position.

"If you do gain that high ground," Miles responded, his eyes afire, "you'll have the key to the battle."

"Exactly, sir."

Miles stepped back and saluted. "Very good, Mr. Rousseau. Flank left of Major Casey and pitch into them. Have at them! We'll be watching to see if you need support. Have at them, I say!"

Minutes later, as the lieutenant led his H Company single file up the precipitous slopes of that sharp ridge on the left in the midst of stinging clouds of smoke from all the burning brush and grass, Miles finally reacted to the continued annoyance of the warriors on their right flank. At this time he dispatched Lieutenant Carter's K Company in support of Captain Lyman's I Company in driving off the horsemen once and for all from the slope leading out of the brush-clogged ravine where most of his soldiers were beginning to cross beneath the pall of gray-and-brown smoke boiling up from the autumn-cured buffalo grass set to smoldering by the screeching hordes.

"You'll have their village in no time now, General!" shouted the colonel's aide, Hobart Bailey.

"What's bloody left of it," Miles grumbled, his eyes narrowing on the all but abandoned Sioux camp. The only occupants now were knots of warriors covering the retreat of the last women and ponies they sent scurrying over the hillsides out of harm's way.

"I figured Sitting Bull was bound to put up a hell of a fight this day," Miles observed minutes later as he came to a stop beside Kelly. By now most of the battlefield lay shrouded with dense, roiling clumps of acrid smoke. "The way they're running—it's hard to imagine this is the same bunch that mauled Custer's Seventh."

Luther shook his head. "Sitting Bull ain't a fighting chief, General. My money says it's Gall leading this fight. He's the one lost a couple of wives and his children in Reno's charge at the Little Bighorn."

"Which means Gall will fight like the devil to protect that village now," Miles replied.

"I figure Gall thirsts to spill some more soldier blood to atone for the death of his family."

Miles turned slowly to regard his chief of scouts. For a moment the colonel's eyes slitted; then he asked, "Sounds like you agree with that red bastard."

Kelly shrugged. "Maybe I do. Maybe I don't. You're the family man, General." And he reined his horse away without another word.

It didn't take a plainsman like Luther Kelly to see how the Lakota warriors were maneuvering across the broken landscape in hopes of tying up the soldiers. This was perfect ground for a thousand horsemen to gain tactical superiority against the attacking walk-a-heaps. The main body of the hostiles held the prominent high ground on the north, east, and south. To get to the enemy, Miles would have to commit his forces to plunging into the deep, sharp-sided ravines that now lay between them.

As the infantry struggled forward through the pall of choking smoke, the center of the Hunkpapa line fell back, pulling the soldiers ever onward . . . hoping to entangle their disordered formations in the brushy, turkey-track coulees where the warriors massing along either side and to the rear of the line of march would pour in on the confused and frightened troops.

With every yard marched, Miles's formation began to string itself out, began to grow more ragged as his men crossed the rugged, uneven ground beneath and through the thick curtains of wind-tortured smoke and flame. No longer was it a solid, straight formation—but instead became a dark, wavy line snaking up and down across the tortured plain like a writhing serpent until the troops dropped down into the East Fork of Cedar Creek.

Here, for a feverish quarter of an hour, the Sioux struggled valiantly to hold back Miles's troops. It was here that a warrior swept in, screaming at the top of his lungs and firing his repeater. One of the shots dropped Private John Geyer of I Company, wounding him severely. But in the end the powerful and long-reaching Springfield rifles seized the day against the lighter Henrys, Winchesters, and what Springfield carbines the Hunkpapa had captured at the Little Bighorn.

Gall's warriors began to fall back.

On the far right side of the disjointed skirmishers companies K and I were the first to reach the outskirts of what had been Sitting Bull's village. Here and there in the midafternoon light still stood the bare skeletons of dismantled lodges, stripped and robbed of their buffalo-hide and canvas covers, yet within each circle of poles sat piles of robes and blankets, parfleches and scattered clothing dropped in haste. The Lakota had not taken all that much in their precipitous flight. Kettles, saddles, and untanned hides lay clustered about still-smoldering breakfast fires. All of that, and the tons of dried meat, back fat and newly ripened buffaloberries the women had been making into pemmican, storing this precious commodity against the cold of the coming winter.

Once Lieutenant Pope's E Company had driven the horsemen from the high ground on the right flank, Miles sent Kelly with word for them to press on and continue their sweep around to the rear, thereby reinforcing the train guard since the enemy horsemen were swelling in numbers as they continued to sweep the horns of both flanks, still threatening to encircle the command.

The noise was deafening: what with the bawling officers, the shouts of men thrust into battle in the midst of the stinging smoke and cinders, the screeching, crying warriors, the high-pitched protests of the wounded animals, and the continuous throaty thump of the Rodman from the lone knoll. All that cacophony of hell swirling and eddying around them as the wind rose and fell, rose and fell, rawhiding their cold faces.

On his feet and rallying his men of E Company to turn and face a rush of horsemen suddenly bursting out of hidden coulee, Sergeant Robert W. McPhelan was spun around, collapsing to his knees with an audible grunt. Pulling his hand away from his chest, he stared at the glistening red syrup, his eyes blinking dumbly as three of his men slowly eased him on his back.

McPhelan fought them, struggling to stay upright, protesting, "Don't . . . don't put me down—"

"We ain't gonna leave you, Sarge," one of his men snapped, heaving his weight against the officer. "You gotta let us plug that hole in you, goddammit!"

Suddenly Pope was above them. "Form a hollow square!" he bawled against the din of those booming Springfields, the crack of the Winchester repeaters from the encircling warriors. "Goddammit—form a square and hold those bastards off!"

Then Pope was kneeling over McPhelan in the next moment, his hand on the old sergeant's shoulder. "You gonna be all right, gunny?"

The red-rimmed, smoke-ravaged eyes were tearing in gratitude. "Ain't nothing but a flesh wound, sir."

Pope's eyes glistened too. "That's good, 'cause I'd hate to lose you, I would. We still got work to finish here."

"L-looks like we can hold 'em off, Lieutenant," McPhelan whispered. "Just keep the boys in their square—and we'll make the devil dance a different tune."

Gesturing with a nod up at Yellowstone Kelly, the lieutenant said, "The scout here brought word from the general: Miles wants us to drive off the last of the warriors around those watering holes right over yonder and hold on to 'em for the night."

McPhelan coughed, then said with a rasp, "We get the sons of bitches drove off—have some of the boys drag me over to them water holes and bring me my rifle. I can still shoot with the best of 'em if they come at us again, sir." He coughed a loose, fluid-filled rasp. "I'd like me a drink, in a real bad way."

Patting the sergeant's shoulder, Pope replied quietly, "Damn right you can have that drink of water." He signaled to have a canteen brought to him. "And your rifle too. God, am I proud to have you fighting on my side, Sergeant."

With E Company holding its own and the water holes securely in their grasp at the rear of the column, Miles continued to pursue the hostiles until sundown, then turned about and led the rest of the command back to the ridge Lieutenant Rousseau's H Company had cleared of hostiles. Here on the high ground that commanded a view of the entire countryside the order was given to bivouac for the coming night.

During the day the tenor of battle had constantly reminded the soldiers that these were the warriors who had mutilated the Custer dead. But the gallant Fifth had fought hard since first light, scratching their way after the fleeing Sioux across more than eighteen miles of uneven, rugged ground, through smoke and flames. Now, as night came down, the weary, blackened, cinder-smudged men found their spirits raised.

They had held off odds of two, perhaps three, to one ... and survived against the best Sitting Bull and Gall could throw at them. No longer would anyone boast that the Sioux were invincible.

"From what I can make of the various reports," Miles said, raising his head from his concentration over his field desk strewn with papers as twilight oozed light from the sky, "there were at least half a dozen Sioux casualties."

"Hard to tell," Kelly said with a shrug, then sipped more of his coffee nearby. "The way they always drag off their wounded. Could've been more."

For a moment the colonel pressed his full lips together thoughtfully. "Their biggest loss isn't in the casualties—is it, Kelly?"

Luther wagged his head. "No, General. You hurt 'em worse by getting your hands on everything they had to leave behind."

"Not just getting my hands on it," Miles replied, staring down at the ruins of the abandoned village, "but in destroying it. Among the captured herd we found some of the Seventh Cavalry horses. Damn well used up, they are—no more than skin and bones now."

"Doesn't surprise me a wit, General," Kelly replied. He stuffed a hand inside his coat, patting among his vest pockets for a cheroot, maybe even some chew. Something to enjoy with his coffee. "You decided if you're marching back to Tongue River in the morning?"

Miles looked up at Kelly, stared hard for a moment as if his scout had gone crazy, then shook his head. "No, by God—I plan on following Sitting Bull all the way to Canada if I have to!"

Chapter 12

22–23 October 1876

**General Sitting Bull Ready
to be Rationed.**

Red Cloud and His Braves on the Rampage.

**Indications that Crook will
Settle Their Case**

THE INDIANS

**Sitting Bull Wants to Winter at
Some Agency.**

WASHINGTON, October 21.—The following telegram was received at the Indian Bureau this morning: Fort Peck, Montana, Oct. 13, via Boseman—To the Commissioner of Indian Affairs, Washington:— Messengers from Sitting Bull's camp report that the entire hostile camp has crossed the Yellowstone at the mouth of the Big Horn, en route for this place. They claim to want peace. What course shall I pursue toward them?

[signed]   THOS. T. MITCHELL
Indian Agent.

After consultation with Gen. Sherman instructions were telegraphed to Agent Mitchell as follows: In form Sitting Bull that the only condition of peace is his surrender, when he will be treated as a prisoner of war. Issue no rations, except after such surrender and when fully satisfied that the Indians can be held at the agency. The military will cooperate as far as possible.

[signed]   S. A. GALPEN
                                      Acting Commissioner.

Through that long, cold night the grass fires glowed like flickering, crimson patches across the prairie below as Nelson Miles moved back and forth through his command like a man possessed.

The Sioux shouted and called out on all sides of their bivouac. Occasionally one of the pickets fired a shot or two at some noise, at a shadow, at one of the ghostly forms flitting in and out and around the abandoned village, intent on salvaging what they could from the army's destruction.

At long last the eastern sky showed signs of resigning itself to day. Miles had his men awakened, guard rotated, and coffee put over what fires the men could keep lit with the meager supply of wood they scrounged after the Sioux had set the prairie ablaze the previous day. As soon as it was light enough for the command to move across the uneven ground, the colonel gave the order to form up and moved out that Sunday, 22 October.

Almost immediately two dozen warriors appeared along the high ground beyond the decimated village, backlit with the rose of sunrise. They swept far to the right, heading for the rear of the march where Pope's E Company easily drove them away from the supply wagons. Then it grew eerily quiet as the Fifth continued its march into the coming of sunrise. After the deafening racket and din of yesterday's fight, the utter stillness of this morning lay like a heavy, suffocating cloak upon each and every wary man.

The scouts led them east along the clearly marked Sioux trail. Easy enough to follow the travois scars on the prairie. That, and the wisps of smoke from the fires the hostiles set all along their flight. Stifling curtains of thinning gray obscured the rising sun, turning it a pale-orange button as the soldiers plodded on across the blackened prairie where ash rose up to clog their nostrils, sting their eyes, choke their every breath.

As much as his brain told him the enemy had fled on through the night to put as much ground between them as possible, Nelson's heart nonetheless hoped that for some reason they didn't have as much of a jump on his command as he might otherwise fear. All along the wide, hoof-pocked trail the scouts and forward units came across abandoned lodgepoles and camp utensils, refuse abandoned along with a few lame ponies and mules—even more possessions taken from the bodies of Custer's dead.

Personal things, the sort almost every soldier carried: photographs from family and loved ones, ledgers and journals, gauntlets and hats, a watch or blood-smeared blue tunic.

"They're heading east, General," Luther Kelly reported that midmorning as he reined up, bringing his mount around in a tight circle, having just returned from a scouting foray with Billy Cross and Vic Smith.

"No sign of them angling off to the north?" Miles inquired anxiously. No matter what—he had to keep himself between Sitting Bull and that border.

Kelly shook his head. "They're hurrying for Bad Route Creek, east of here."

By midafternoon the rising wind gave such muscle to the smoldering prairie fires on both flanks of his march that Miles ordered a halt as the men choked and sputtered helplessly, a wall of flame advancing right for them. Into the fury of that blanket of smoke and ash the colonel sent out two companies to start backfires before the entire command was finally able to continue its wearying pursuit.

It wasn't long before the warriors figured out the soldiers had countered their strategy. More than three hundred horsemen suddenly bristled from the hilltops, spilling over the crests in a shouting, screaming, boiling mass, aiming straight for the plodding foot soldiers.

Platoon by platoon was ordered to strengthen both flanks as sergeants bellowed out their orders for the men to drop to their knees, aim, and fire before the next squad was brought up into position while the first reloaded. Above the steady, deep booming of those big Springfields, Miles made out the discordant rattle of the smaller weapons and the old muskets the Sioux were using to harass their march. A long-distance battle, and a slow crawl they made of it, throughout the agonizing hours that Sunday afternoon.

Marching in a hollow square, with four companies of skirmishers thrown out in front spaced five paces apart, two companies on each side and two at the rear, and with one final company bringing up the rear of the supply train and another supporting the Rodman gun, they made eighteen miles before the sun sank out of the clear, cold sky and the warriors disappeared.

The land breathed a sigh of relief as the men made their bivouac and lit their fires. Stars winked into sight. The night grew colder than any gone before.

Come the morning of the twenty-third, Miles put them to the march in that same magnificent formation, up and down the broken country in a hollow square. But this day they saw no Sioux, reaching the Yellowstone late in the afternoon nearly opposite the mouth of Cabin Creek. His exhausted men had put another twenty-eight miles under the soles of their boots that day—more than forty-two miles from their initial engagement with the Sioux at Cedar Creek.

Nelson stood watching Kelly and four other scouts head back his way, urging their mounts back to the north bank of the river. Miles had ordered the five of them to cross the Yellowstone to determine the depth of the ford. In midriver Luther Kelly eased out of the saddle and settled his boots into the river that had christened him for life. While he stomped around in the coming dusk, checking out the sands of the shifting bottom, Vic Smith probed on over toward the south bank. In the distance smoke hung in the air from the enemy's fires.

How Miles wanted to cross now as the Sioux were making camp there on the south side of the Yellowstone. If only to be sure Sitting Bull was really settling in for the night, praying the chief would not pull a rabbit on him and suddenly turn back north, recross the Yellowstone, and make a dash for Canada. That was Nelson's deepest, most unspoken fear as Luther Kelly splashed up the bank, into the cottonwoods, and dismounted near him.

"They're across, by God," the scout said, dripping from his waist down, shuddering with cold as the wind came up at twilight.

"And still moving south?"

Kelly looked over at Smith, who nodded; then Kelly said, "By all accounts, General."

"How deep is it?"

Kelly gazed down at his britches. "I'm wet to the waist. No deeper than that. Your men can make it in fine order."

'You don't think those Sioux will try to shake us and recross tonight?"

With that easy shrug of his, the mild-mannered Kelly regarded the south bank a bit, sniffled, then looked back at Nelson to say, "They're every bit as tired as your men are, General Miles. Maybe even more tired. I can't see 'em doing anything but stopping for a few hours—stopping to feed their children, bandage their wounded, and shiver out this goddamned cold night until they can start running again."

Miles felt himself bristle with resentment. "Sounds to me like you don't agree with my giving chase?"

There was the scout's quick, disarming smile, and Kelly said, "Nothing of the kind, General. Not many men would have the bottom you and this outfit have to herd those Sioux the way we've done. Pushed 'em real hard."

"Because of it, I just might succeed in forcing their surrender," Miles replied, finding himself becoming a bit testy not only by the extended chase, which had so far netted him nothing more than track soup, but by the scout's easygoing attitude as well.

"I don't doubt you'll get someone to surrender before this is done," Kelly said. "If it ain't the Sioux, it may damn well be your own men."

For a moment he stared at the scout's face; then Kelly cracked a smile, his eyes crow-footing at their corners.

Finally Miles smiled along with him "Damn you, Kelly," he said. "A laugh or two's good for the soul when a man's done himself proud."

"It's been a good chase, General," the scout answered, taking up his rein and beginning to lead his horse away with the other scouts. "We'll catch Sitting Bull yet."

Monday. Some time after midnight. Twenty-three October. Damned cold too, here beside the frozen fog rising off Chadron Creek.

Keep the talk at a minimum were the orders. And no smoking.

Just after dark, Mackenzie led his command away from Camp Robinson and into the cold, clear winter night—more stars overhead than Seamus could recall seeing since last winter on the Powder River.

Since arriving on the central plains last August, the Fourth Cavalry had been quartered in three temporary cantonments: Camp Canby, the original Sioux Expedition cavalry camp; Camp Custer; and Camp of the Second Battalion. Earlier in the month, while Mackenzie was gone to Laramie conferring with Crook on the coming seizures of Sioux arms, his regiment had been reinforced by some 309 new recruits shipped in from Jefferson Barracks near St. Louis, bringing the companies up to full strength. Besides drilling three times a day with and without their mounts, the men of the Fourth Cavalry had been kept busy cutting, hauling, and trimming logs for their crude log barracks, mess halls, and storage rooms.

Last night, with each man packing one day's rations and all of them in light marching order, Mackenzie had moved his troops away under the cover of darkness because the colonel did not want to be spotted by any agency tattletale who might scurry off to Red Cloud's or Red Leaf's and Swift Bear's camps, letting the cat slip out of the bag.

— A few hours back Mackenzie had briefly stopped his command at a predetermined rendezvous, where they awaited some riders who were to join up: the North brothers, Lieutenant S. E. Cushing, and forty-eight hardened trackers of their Pawnee Battalion, hurried north from the Sidney Barracks where they had been carried west, horses and all, along the Union Pacific line.

"By the Mither of God! I ain't seen you since that summer with Carr!" Seamus growled happily in a harsh whisper at the two civilian brothers there in the dark as they waited while some of the Norths' Pawnee probed ahead into the darkness.

Following the rendezvous, Mackenzie's march was resumed across that hard, frozen ground, at a trot or at a gallop as the rugged land allowed, until early in the morning when the scouts reached the point where the trail leading north from the agency split: one branch leading to Red Cloud's band, the other to Red Leaf's Brule camp only a handful of miles away. It was there that Mackenzie deployed his command: sending M Company of his Fourth Cavalry along with the two troops assigned him from Wesley Merritt's Fifth Cavalry to follow Captain Luther North and some of the Pawnee in the direction of Red Leaf's village, that entire force under the command of Major George A. Gordon.

The remaining five troops of the Fourth followed Mackenzie as Major Frank North and the rest of the Pawnee scouts led them on through the darkness toward Red Cloud's camp.

"That hot July of sixty-nine. Has it been that long?" Frank North replied now, also in a whisper. Mackenzie demanded that none of his surprise be spoiled.

"Summit Springs, it were," Donegan replied, tugging at his

collar, pulling his big-brimmed hat down as he tried to turtle his head into his shoulders. The wind was coming up.

"We had us a grand chase that year, didn't we?" North asked.

"I rode with Carr this summer."

"Don't say," North said, then stared off into the darkness. "He was a good soldier."

"By damn if he wasn't that bloody hot day when we caught ol' Tall Bull napping," Seamus replied.*

"Bet you four to one we've got Red Cloud and the rest napping this time too."

"We'll know soon enough," the Irishman responded as they watched some of the Pawnee emerge out of the dark.

They sat for close to an hour, waiting for some of the Indian trackers to return. The men were allowed to dismount and huddle out of the wind, but smoking and talk were forbidden. No telling if the Sioux would have camp guards out patrolling.

It seemed like an eternity until the order came to move out once more, marching a few more miles until Mackenzie halted his five troops and the Pawnee Battalion, saying they would wait right there until there was light enough to see the front sights on their carbines. Then they would send the scouts to seize the pony herd while they charged into the village.

So for now those three hundred men waited in the dark and the cold, knowing they had that unsuspecting Sioux camp in their noose.

While the government continued to press the "friendlies" to sell away the Black Hills as a condition for receiving their annuities of food, blankets, and ammunition, Sheridan nonetheless demanded that those same agency Indians were dismounted and disarmed. No two ways about it. If the winter roamers who were still out making trouble would ever be resupplied with ammunition and weapons to press on with their war, those supplies would have to come from the "friendlies" who had stayed behind at the reservations. To make sure Sitting Bull, Crazy Horse, and the rest were cut off from all such aid, Sheridan ordered Crook into action against the agency bands.

The little Irish general was positive that the hostiles could never have defeated Custer without aid from the agency Sioux. He expressed his steadfast belief in this position to William Tecumseh Sherman:

---

* *Black Sun*, Vol. 4, The Plainsmen Series.

Our duty will be to occupy the game country and make it dangerous and when they are obliged from constant harassing and hunger to come in and surrender we can then dismount, disarm and punish them at the Agencies as was done with the Southern Indians in the last campaign.

Phil Sheridan had a staunch ally in Ranald Slidell Mackenzie. He too believed that the hostilities would all be over by the spring of 1877, provided that the hostiles were corralled and the "friendlies" forced to surrender their arms and ponies, the animals then sold on the open market and the funds thus acquired used to purchase cattle for the agency bands. Never disguised as an attempt to civilize the Sioux into becoming gentleman farmers, Sheridan's plan was unashamedly to deny all mobility to the horse-mounted Lakota warriors.

Years before on the Staked Plain of West Texas, Seamus had come to admire Mackenzie's patient even-handedness in pursuing his relentless war on the Comanche.* Yet, in many subtle ways, it was a different, a changed Mackenzie who last August marched eight companies of his Fourth Cavalry north to join in this grand Sioux campaign. Many times over dinner, or in officers' meetings, in those off-the-cuff comments expressed to his cadre of scouts, the colonel made it exceedingly clear in so many subtle ways that he was no longer the same man: no more would he believe anything an Indian told him, nor could he believe that an Indian would honor his own word to a white man.

➤ According to Mackenzie all this rumination and discourse over selling the Black Hills back to the government was nothing more than a waste of time—it was plain to see that the Indians had stalled the protracted negotiations at the agencies while their free-roaming brethren pursued their own hostile intentions in secret.

Like Sheridan, Mackenzie now believed the time for talk had come and gone with absolutely no lasting result.

For the colonel, one thing had grown more clear across the last five years in campaign after campaign against the hostiles— whether they were Kwahadi, Southern Cheyenne, or Red Cloud's Sioux, what the Indian understood better than talk was *force*— might of arms, a cost in blood. He made no secret of the fact

---

*Dying Thunder, Vol. 7, The Plainsmen Series.

that he believed that the presence of the peace commissioners "unsettles the minds of these Indians."

Upon his return to Camp Robinson, where more than 982 cavalry, infantry, and artillery soldiers had been marshaled to dismount the Sioux, he had wired Crook his recommendation that his command should indeed proceed with the capture of the two villages:

> I do not think any of the principal bands will move in unless there is some strong power brought to bear to cause them to be obedient.

It was a sentiment shared by Sherman, Sheridan, and Crook.

Because the army had been receiving reports that three major camps would be wintering in the Powder River country—one band under Crazy Horse, another of Sans Arc, and a third of Northern Cheyenne—for weeks now Mackenzie made himself a nettlesome burr under Crook's saddle, irritating the commanding general with dispatches from Camp Robinson, the likes of which:

> A great many Indians have I think gone north quite recently and I wish that you would either come here or order me to get them together.

In the end Crook gave in and called Mackenzie to Laramie to plan this swift, decisive action against the agency Sioux.

Because he was certain the "friendlies" were harboring renegades responsible for raids off the reservation and would never cooperate with the Indian Bureau's civilian authorities, Mackenzie had long espoused that the agency should be sealed off and that all communication with the resident bands be prohibited except through the military. It was a recommendation wholeheartedly agreed to by Sherman on down.

The Fourth Cavalry was now free to clamp down with whatever means were necessary.

Then, while Mackenzie was conferring with Crook at Fort Laramie for his march over to this northwestern corner of Nebraska bent on unhorsing and disarming the bands—a time consumed in requesting Winchester magazine arms for his men, a request the quartermaster corps never approved—the jumpy agent suddenly telegraphed his growing anxiety when those two troublesome bands under Red Cloud and Red Leaf just up and moved some twenty-five miles away from the agency, camping in the vicinity of Chadron Creek.

When Major George A. Gordon of the Fifth Cavalry, the commander at Camp Robinson, ordered the bands back, the stubborn chiefs turned a deaf ear to the soldier chief. From the rebellious camps there was even some grumbling talk of war, which made Crook fear the bands were preparing to flee north in whole or in part. Unknowingly, the Indians had just handed Sheridan, Crook, and Mackenzie the ideal raison d'être for the coming action. Now the Fourth could move.

Only problem was that, to Donegan's way of thinking, the government and the army were in cahoots once more to make the tribes out to be the villains—just as they had schemed to do almost a year before when they had ordered the wandering bands back to their reservations or suffer military action. Once more the white officials were dealing with the tribes using two faces: on the one hand, Washington had dispatched its blue-ribbon commission to treat with the reservation Sioux to sell the Black Hills; while the other hand was dispatching army units to impoverish those very same reservation bands.

This morning's action against Red Cloud's and Red Leaf's runaways had been specifically designed by Sheridan, Crook, and Mackenzie to cripple, if not geld, that peace commission.

As well as designed to strengthen the military's hand before Crook's army marched north into the teeth of winter to capture Crazy Horse once and for all.

Chapter 13

23 October 1876

Trouble at Red Cloud Agency;

CHEYENNE, October 21.—Advices from Red Cloud Agency on the 20th are as follows: Immediately after the commissioners left the agency, recently, the Indians moved and camped about twenty-five miles away, sending in only squaws and a few bucks on issue days to draw rations. They were so far away that no information could be had as to their movements and doings, and doubtless many of them were off on raiding and plundering expeditions. Word was sent to them by Captain Smith, acting United States Indian agent, to come into the agency. To this they paid no attention. Meanwhile General Crook and several of his staff arrived there, and word was immediately sent to these Indians that no more rations would be issued till they came into the agency where they belonged and remained. Yesterday was issue day and very few Indians were present. Red Cloud was present, but none of his band, and he refused to receive rations. The ultimatum sent them will not be receded from in the smallest degree, and unless it is complied with trouble is anticipated. Lieutenant Chase, with 1,000 cavalry, left Fort Russell yesterday to intercept the raiding parties operating in the vicinity of the Chug.

He heard a dog barking, snarling, growling somewhere at the south side of camp, where the pony herd was grazing.

It was black in Red Cloud's lodge. But looking up to the junction of the eighteen poles, the Oglalla chief could see the paling of the sky. Dawn would come soon. Perhaps the dog had nosed some wild animal out early to find its breakfast.

Then a second dog took up the warning, and quickly a third. Suddenly dogs were barking throughout camp.

Throwing his robes aside as his wife sat up beside him, her eyes wide with fear, Red Cloud yanked on the furry buffalo-hide winter moccasins and wrapped a blanket around his shoulders. At the doorway he grabbed a belt of cartridges and looped it over his shoulder, then took into his hand the cold iron of the Winchester repeater that stood ready against a frosty pole.

By the time he ducked his head from the canvas cover and stood upon the old snow that crackled beneath his feet, many of the men in the village were emerging with their weapons. Dogs raced here, then there, as the forms emerged out of the frosty mist hanging like shreds of old, dingy canvas among the leafless trees bordering Chadron Creek.

Men on horseback! Most of them the Scalped Heads—Pawnee. Long had they been wolves for the soldiers.

Behind the Scalped Heads came mounted soldiers, their horses snorting great jets of steam from their nostrils, bobbing their heads, pawing the ground, eyes saucering with fright as the white men fought to maintain control of their animals there among the foreign smells of the village.

A cold rock in his belly told Red Cloud that the Oglalla's ponies were already in the hands of these Pawnee.

Somewhere among the ring of blue, bundled white soldiers on horseback a voice cried out, answered by more voices barking their *wasichu* words. The horsemen came to an immediate halt. Everywhere Red Cloud looked, from side to side, turning slowly to gaze behind him, the village was ringed with these silent sentries on their restive, snorting, frost-wreathed horses. Like filmy, disembodied ghosts taking shape out of the coming of day.

Then a voice barked more *wasichu* words and three men emerged from the soldiers' noose. One was a soldier. And the other white man Red Cloud knew as Todd Randall—a squaw man with a Lakota wife. The third, clearly a half-blood. The soldier said something, and the dark-skinned one nodded before he shouted to the camp in Lakota.

"You will surrender your camp! You will give over all your

ponies to the soldiers. And then your men must give up every gun your people have in this village."

Red Cloud swallowed hard, hearing the muttering of so many brave men nearby—his friends and relations—as his mind feverishly grappled with what to do now that they were surrounded.

Around him he heard the mad rustle as some of the women scurried into the brush with the children. White men shouted, growling like wolves, forcing the women and children back as their big American horses advanced out of the shreds of frozen fog.

Finally, the chief took a step closer to the half-blood and asked, "If I do not surrender our camp?"

Atop his pawing pony the half-blood shrugged, and without a word he made a slight gesture that was likely lost on even the white man beside him.

"I see," Red Cloud finally replied. "These soldiers and their wolves will murder our women and children, will butcher the old ones in my village."

"It is a good thing you understand."

"Ah," the chief answered, still grappling with it, his finger still inside the trigger guard of his repeater, arguing with himself on whether to fight and die where he stood, or whether to listen to what this half-blood said about giving over all their ponies and guns.

"Well?" the half-blood snapped impatiently.

With reluctance Red Cloud wagged his head. "If I surrender to these soldiers—what do they offer me in return?"

"Nothing."

"N-nothing?" he stuttered, feeling the severe chill slip beneath the folds of his blanket for the first time since he had emerged from the warm robes and his wife's body.

With another shrug of one shoulder, the half-blood scout and interpreter replied, "Perhaps not *nothing* . . . at least your people will have your lives in return."

"I know him!" one of the warriors suddenly growled as he came to stand behind Red Cloud, pointing at the half-blood. "He is a liar and his scalp should be mine!"

"Quiet!" the chief ordered. "It matters not if this half-blood is a liar, for we do not have to trust to his words. With our own eyes we can see he brings many, many of his friends to kill us if we don't do as he tells us."

The interpreter gestured with a thumb over his shoulder

and said, "Then I can tell the soldier chief that your people will lay down their weapons and turn over their ponies?"

Red Cloud looked left, then right, and behind him once more as if to remind himself that the entire village was ringed with horsemen, their weapons drawn. With a crushing resignation he turned back to the half-blood and nodded. "Yes. Tell your soldier chief his warriors do not need to kill women and children this morning, nor do they need to trample our old ones with the hooves of their horses before the sun rises. We are at peace with the white man—"

"Then tell these others," the half-blood demanded as he shifted in the saddle uneasily. "Tell them to drop their guns."

To his warriors Red Cloud shouted his command, explaining that they had no chance to make a fight of it, that they must think of protecting their families rather than spilling their blood on this ground. This, perhaps, was the hardest to say to his friends—most of whom had remained with him for many a winter.

Together they had risen up out of hiding in the snow and swarmed over the Hundred in the Hand near the Pine Fort.*

Together they had fought a day-long battle against the soldiers and their medicine guns the following summer.†

And together they had driven the soldiers from their thieves' road cutting through the Lakota hunting ground for what was to be all time.

But the white man had eventually returned to take back his promise, to take back the Black Hills too. Red Cloud's Bad Face band had little left them now that they lived on this reservation at the largess of the white agent.

Now this morning the white man and his Indian friends were there to take the last of what the Oglalla had—their ponies and their weapons.

As most of the cartridge belts and rifles clattered onto the frozen ground, the half-blood sneered and said, "It is good, old-woman chief. Once you were strong—but now you give up like a woman."

"What . . . what are you called?" Red Cloud demanded in a

---

*Fetterman Massacre, Fort Phil Kearny, Dakota Territory, *Sioux Dawn*, Vol. 1, The Plainsmen Series.

†Wagonbox Fight, Fort Phil Kearny, Dakota Territory, *Red Cloud's Revenge*, Vol. 2, The Plainsmen Series.

loud, clear voice that hung in the sharp, cold air above them all, halos formed with every syllable from his lips.

"Me?" asked the half-blood. "I am called Grabber by your people."

"Yes. I thought so," Red Cloud said sadly as he bowed his head and closed his eyes to more than the sting of the cold.

"Then you know of me, old-woman chief?"

Red Cloud opened his eyes and said with what strength there remained in his tired body, "You are the one who turned your back on Sitting Bull and Crazy Horse. And now you bring these soldiers here to take what little my people have left."

To Donegan's way of thinking, Red Cloud sure had picked one hell of a bad time to assert his independence, even if all the old chief had sought to accomplish was to move his people away from the agency to avoid what he could of the hostilities clearly looming on the horizon.

Once he had the Oglalla men under the muzzles of his guns, Mackenzie ordered the women in camp to be about taking down their lodges and packing up their few earthly goods for the trip back to the agency. But no matter that Frank Grouard translated the soldier chief's order into their Lakota tongue, the women in that village refused to obey.

"Goddammit!" Mackenzie roared. "If they don't comply, you tell them I'll put this whole place to the torch. Then they won't have a thing to drag back to the agency!"

Clutching the cold brass receiver of the new Winchester, Donegan watched as Grouard's words fell here and there among the sad-eyed, motionless women like slaps with a braided rawhide quirt. Still, they stoically stared at the soldier chief, refusing to budge.

"Are they daring me, Grouard?" demanded Mackenzie, his face flushing with anger.

"Can't say, General," Frank replied, scratching in his beard and extracting a louse he cracked between two fingernails and pitched aside.

"Tell them they have five minutes to begin complying or I'll start burning."

"I'll tell 'em if you want me to," Grouard said. "But these are people who don't have no idea of what a minute is, five minutes, or a hull goddamned day."

"Jesus Christ!" snapped the exasperated officer all but under his breath. "Mr. Dorst," he called his adjutant forward. "Call up

Captain Lee's men. Tell him to start with that lodge ... right over there."

"Yes, sir, General!" cried Second Lieutenant Joseph H. Dorst.

D Troop came forward from that circle surrounding Red Cloud's camp beside Chadron Creek. For a moment things grew very tense as the warriors grumbled angrily when a trio of the soldiers pulled back door coverings and invaded their homes, re-emerging with firebrands they held aloft, flames sputtering, crackling in the dim gray light of an icy dawn. As the warriors shuffled and stirred over the weapons lying at their feet, the rest of Lee's company held their carbines on the anxious Oglalla, who glared back at the soldiers with deadly hate.

Captain John Lee barked, repeating his order. The trio turned to the three nearest lodges and went about attempting to set the frozen buffalo hides and frosted canvas on fire.

Women shrieked, their tongues trilling in a call to their men. Weary and weakened old men began to keen death songs and stamp around on arthritic legs in tiny circles. Here, then there, a young man began singing his war song—strong and clear, faces turned in prayer toward the morning sky.

The hair rose on Seamus's neck to hear the men call for the mysteries to intervene, to hear so many women crying pitiably, to feel the babbling squall of frightened children and babies scrape down his backbone—reminding him he too was now a father.

Mackenzie's men sat atop their mounts like stone griffins, watching as a lone woman rushed forward, with her bare hands attempting to beat out the first flames licking up the side of her lodge. Two of the soldiers lunged over her, pulling the screaming woman back with great effort, dragging her legs through the snow as she collapsed, sobbing and wailing, tearing at her hair.

Here and there among the camp one of North's Pawnee burst from a lodge with a great and gleeful gush of chatter, holding a captured trophy aloft for all his comrades to see.

The flinty eyes of the Oglalla chief registered only hate. Never before in Red Cloud's life had he been talked to by a white man in the stern matter in which Mackenzie had addressed him. He was, after all, the chief who had brought the army to its knees in the two years preceding 1868 when the government finally cried uncle and gave up the Bozeman Road. Up until the dawning of this day, the white soldiers and treaty-talkers had all negotiated with Red Cloud.

But dealing with this Bad Hand Kenzie was something altogether different, Seamus brooded. Instead of any pretense at diplomacy, the colonel told Red Cloud the way things would be, and that was that. Never before had the infamous Oglalla chief been made to feel he was in the presence of his superiors—until now.

At long last the chief spoke again, this time not to Grouard. But to his own people. Although the Irishman did not understand Red Cloud's tongue, it was plain that his voice rang strong, confident, filled with uncompromising pride. And when the Oglalla leader had finished, his people visibly seemed to sag collectively before turning as one, returning to their lodges where they went about doing what they had been ordered by the soldier chief.

In the process Mackenzie's men counted over 120 men of fighting age among some 240 of Red Cloud's people in that village, yet from those warriors they confiscated no more than fifty serviceable rifles. Outside camp the Pawnee finished rounding up 755 ponies after firing a few shots over the head of one brave herder, a young boy who attempted to save a bunch of the horses by driving them off. While the soldiers allowed the women to select enough of those captured ponies to drag their travois for the return trip to the agency, only the old and the infirm, those too young or simply too feeble, were allowed ponies to ride on the journey. The rest were forced to walk on the fringes of their travois animals, completely surrounded by a slow-moving procession of soldiers dressed in their long, thick blue-wool caped coats.

A few miles down the trail Mackenzie rendezvoused with Major Gordon's battalion come from capturing the Brule camp of Red Leaf, chief of the Wazhazha Lakota for more than ten summers. Together the two villages accounted for more than three hundred lodges and some four hundred people being driven in under the muzzle of those army rifles.

Red Cloud himself likely suffered the heaviest personal loss: four family lodges, in addition to seven prized horses and one light wagon—gifts presented him during his recent visit to see the Great Father in Washington City. Clearly the old chief was coming to learn that what the Great Father gave, the Great Father could take away.

At sundown that Monday, Mackenzie determined that he would again divide his forces. After a brief halt Major Gordon was given charge of a battalion of four companies who would hurry on to Camp Robinson with the captured men of fighting age. Meanwhile, the colonel's battalion would follow at a slower pace, escorting the women, children, and the infirm, intending to reach their destination by the following noon.

Gordon's sad cavalcade returned to Red Cloud Agency a little after eleven P.M. beneath a lowering sky which threatened snow. While the warriors were immediately housed in a large warehouse building, Red Cloud and Red Leaf were both escorted to the guardhouse, there to be held until Crook would determine their status as prisoners of war.

The troopers hadn't eaten a meal or had a cup of hot coffee in more than twenty-four hours, and their horses had been pushed close to their endurance in completing last night's lightning march and the return journey—a round trip of just over fifty miles.

Yet those troopers, a full half of which were raw, green recruits, had succeeded in capturing the two villages—without a single casualty.

"Now," Mackenzie declared to his scouts and those officers riding near the van of their march back to Camp Robinson with the women and children, "all we need to do is bring in Crazy Horse!"

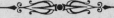

Chapter 14

25–26 October 1876

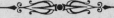

**General Crook Rounds up Red
Cloud & Co.**

**Disarms Them, and Puts
Spotted Tail in Command.**

WYOMING

Important Indian Movement.

CHEYENNE, October 24.—Gen. Crook being satisfied that Red Cloud and Red Leaf's bands of Sioux were about to depart with a view of joining the hostiles in the north, they having refused to comply with the orders to come into the agency to receive rations, stubbornly remaining in camp on Shadron Creek, from whence it is known that they were communicating with the northern Indians and receiving into their camps such as come in, he, without awaiting the arrival of Gen. Merritt's troops, determined on disarming them, and at daylight on the morning of the 23d Gen. McKenzie, with eight companies of the Fourth Cavalry, one battalion of which was commanded by Major Gordon, and another by Captain Mauck, successfully surrounded these two bands consisting of 3,000 lodges, and captured bucks, squaws and ponies without firing a shot. They were marched into the

agency after having been disarmed and dismounted.
Spotted Tail, who has evinced an unswerving loyalty to
the whites, was made head chief and Red Cloud deposed. Spotted Tail and Little Wound have agreed to
furnish Gen. Crook with all the warriors he may need
to co-operate with him in the coming campaign, which
will be inaugurated at once. Gen. Crook feels that a
great object has been attained in this last movement
and that we shall now know our enemies from our
friends.

"The Bear Coat Chief wants to talk to you again," Johnny told
the despairing Sitting Bull seated alone at his small fire after
the half-breed had dismounted near the Lakota leader's lodge.

For the last two days Bruguier had been away from the
Hunkpapa band, hanging back with the other chiefs when the
village split apart during the chase.

"It is good. Let him talk to the others. I have nothing more
to say to a soldier chief who will not listen."

Sitting Bull was isolated now. Unlike the other chiefs, he
alone had chosen to keep on running, to keep on fighting, putting the feet of his people on that hard path the day the soldiers
harried their big village right up to the banks of the Yellowstone.
While Gall, Red Skirt, Small Bear, and Bull Eagle decided to
cross the river, beginning to talk of surrender, of heading in to
the agencies, of giving up the fight they had been waging since
spring, the Hunkpapa leader instead turned his people north to
escape the Bear Coat and the army who came trudging along behind him.

Johnny had wrapped up his blanket and robe, riding off to
follow the trail of the Bull and his thirty lodges while the soldiers
continued their pursuit of the big village. Perhaps for some it
was better to talk than to fight those long-reaching rifles and that
big gun the Bear Coat's troops had used to drive the Lakota people south across the Yellowstone.

Four days ago Johnny had fought bravely in attempting to
hold the soldiers at bay while the village retreated. Even Sitting
Bull's nephew White Bull had been injured, shot through the elbow, his arm wrapped in a crude sling the past few days. And in
their retreat the chiefs had argued more and more on what path
to take—to surrender, or to stay on the free road.

It must surely hurt the old chief, Johnny brooded, now that

even White Bull had elected to stay with Red Skirt's Miniconjou and the rest.

But for Sitting Bull there was but one path. Once more he vowed he would never give up, even if it meant running north to the land of the Grandmother. Even if it meant he had to live on the scrawny flesh of prairie dogs.

As the sun came down and the wind came up, Johnny Bruguier gazed around him at the miserable camp of those who had elected to stay with Sitting Bull two days ago when the villages splintered. Those fortunate enough to get their lodges down before the soldiers invaded their camp had been taking in all of the very old and the very young they could, while the rest made do under bowers of blankets and robes, anything at all that would turn the frost of another night of running from the relentless pursuit of Bear Coat.

The morning after Gall, Red Skirt, and the others had crossed to the south side of the Elk River, Sitting Bull sent Johnny back to learn what would become of them once the soldiers pressed their advantage. By luck Bruguier had happened onto a dozen of the village's young men who themselves had recrossed the river to keep an eye on the soldiers: to see if the Bear Coat Chief would cross the river with his men, or simply retreat west to his post at the Tongue River. But in a run of more bad luck, the scouting party was spotted by a group of the Corn Indians,* who were the eyes and ears for Bear Coat's soldiers. They and many of the white scouts immediately gave chase after Johnny's group, making for a noisy running fight of it. On their escape back to the Yellowstone ford, a handful of the Lakota horsemen spotted a lone herder gone out to kill some of the stray Hunkpapa ponies unable to keep up with the fleeing herd. It was a funny thing to watch the squat, bearded white man clamber bareback atop his mule and flog it back toward the soldier lines, yelping and screeching at the top of his lungs as the young warriors closed in on him.

Within moments some of the walk-a-heaps came bustling out to the rescue, and soon more of the soldiers made that long-reaching big gun talk—throwing one of its charges so that it exploded right in front of the Hunkpapa horsemen chasing the solitary herder. It wasn't hard for Johnny to convince them it was time to turn back for the river and make their escape.

Not one of those young warriors liked turning his back on

---

*Ree, or Arikara, scouts.

the rescue detail, hoping as they were for some spoils if not to count coup. But it was plain that they were clearly outnumbered—every bit as plain was the fact that the Bear Coat was intent on following the wounded village. With the others Johnny forded the Elk River, intent on warning Gall and the others, and to learn what he could for Sitting Bull.

Such a sad thing to carry in one's heart, Johnny had thought: to know that the white man had once again succeeded in dividing Indian against Indian.

In the last seven suns the walk-a-heap wagon soldiers had succeeded in so much more: they had all but broken Sitting Bull's reputation as the only Indian strong enough to hold together a powerful confederation; twice they had beaten the finest Hunkpapa warriors Gall had rallied to harass the wagon road between the soldier posts on Elk River; in the end they denied the entire body of those fractured Lakota bands the robes, blankets, and meat vital to survival with the imminent approach of another high-plains winter.

And through his use of a little talk coupled with a headlong pursuit, now the Bear Coat had succeeded in splintering even more those confederated tribes clustered around the mystic visionary who brought about the utter and complete destruction of the soldiers at the Greasy Grass.

Then the wavering chiefs had had another parley with the soldier named Miles yesterday afternoon on the south side of the river. Johnny had been called to interpret the demands of Gall, Red Skirt, Bull Eagle, Small Bear, and the rest; the soldiers must leave the Indians alone, for the bands promised they would go into the agency after hunting buffalo for meat enough to see them through the winter. As well the soldiers must return to the Tongue River post and not cross to the north of the Yellowstone anymore, because they would disturb the buffalo the Lakota depended upon. Was it not plain enough to see that many of the people were destitute and in need of both food and blankets—made poor by the soldiers' capricious attack on their village at Cedar Creek?

"The U.S. Army will go wherever it wants to go," the Bear Coat replied to Gall's long list of demands. "If your young men take offense at that—then we will be happy to oblige them with a fight. Otherwise, you headmen are to make sure your people comply with the orders of the government to go into your agencies and stay there."

Bull Eagle held firm on the needs of his people, saying, "We must hunt the buffalo so that our people will have something to eat when the Cold Maker comes, when the snow is deep, when our men cannot hunt."

"Yes," Small Bear agreed. "But we are not the only ones who will go hungry, soldier chief. If your walk-a-heaps continue to chase our villages, come the cold and the snow, your soldiers will not have hunted the meat you need to last the winter."

With some difficulty Bear Coat tried to explain, "My soldiers do not need to hunt the buffalo to survive. You must explain this to the chiefs, half-breed," Miles told Bruguier. "Explain to these men that our supplies for the winter have already reached my Glendive depot. Tell them I have provisions enough to chase their villages right on through the winter if need be . . . a long, hard winter while their young men are unable to hunt, and their children's bellies cry out in hunger."

Black Hills Gold

CHEYENNE. October 24.—C. V. Gardner, of Deadwood, reports that the Black Hills Mining Co.'s quartz mill commenced operations on the 16th inst. On the following day they ran through seven tons of ore from the Hidden Treasure, which cleaned up $5,000. Gulch mining is still in operation and the quartz mines show better results every day.

"Where the blue-ball blazes did Sitting Bull slip off to?"

Luther Kelly watched the face of the half-breed called Big Leggings as he tried to explain to an angry Nelson A. Miles where the great Hunkpapa chief had gone.

It was at that meeting between the Sioux leaders and Nelson A. Miles on the twenty-fifth that the chiefs first admitted that Sitting Bull had managed to elude the soldiers, splintering off with no more than thirty lodges, crossing Bad Route Creek to sneak away down the north bank of the Yellowstone while the soldiers were in hot pursuit of the greater part of that fleeing village.

"Is he running for Canada?" Miles demanded angrily.

"No," the half-blood replied. "He wants only to hunt buffalo in that country close by the Missouri."

While the chiefs themselves had asked for the conference, it frustrated the colonel that they had still not seen the light. Gall stood adamantly against surrendering, wanting the soldiers gone from his country. And while Pretty Bear and the others were not as stone-faced as Gall, neither were they ready to surrender. The best that they offered was to talk some more the following day. Which suited Miles just fine. He sent his wagons on east to cover the twenty-four miles to the Glendive Cantonment for supplies.

Before the conference resumed on Thursday, the supply train was already back, carrying enough rations to permit Miles to continue his chase another twenty days. The arrival of those wagons would prove to be the straw that broke the Sioux will to resist.

Again Red Skirt and the other Miniconjou chiefs said their people lacked clothing and their horses were poor, but that they eventually intended upon going in to the agencies.

"Look upon my wagons," Miles told the Sioux. "You will see I can follow you wherever you go."

Kelly watched the dark eyes of the headmen in council with Miles, studied their faces as they regarded the wagons filled with boxes and barrels and kegs of supplies, while their people cried out in hunger, suffered with the cold as the season advanced and the creeks rimed with ice.

"I think you just may have them this time, General," Luther said quietly to the colonel.

Miles spoke out of the corner of his mouth in a whisper, "But—goddammit—I'm afraid that if I'm forced to escort this bunch all the way over to the Cheyenne River Agency, I can't turn about and pursue Sitting Bull."

The colonel's adjutant, Hobart Bailey, suggested, "General, what of returning the village to Tongue River with some of the men for an escort while the rest of us keep after Sitting Bull?"

Miles considered that only a short time before saying, "It won't work. We have limited supplies at our Tongue River Cantonment and this village would tax us beyond our resources. No. Instead I think I may have a plan that will accomplish all I want to accomplish with these chiefs, and still allow me to go after the biggest fish of them all."

So it was that Miles ended up proposing that the Indians give their vow to turn themselves in to their agents at Cheyenne River. In addition, five of the chiefs would volunteer to stay behind with Miles, those men to be delivered to an army prison in St. Paul, Minnesota, as a means of guaranteeing the surrender of their people.

"I will provide rations for your people to make the trek to your reservation. And I will allow you thirty-five days to make the trip. In addition, I agree to give you five additional days to stay where you are now presently camped to hunt buffalo."

For a long time the chiefs talked among themselves, then finally Red Skirt stood to present himself before Miles.

"I will go with the Bear Coat, to show the goodwill of my people."

One by one the others rose in turn. The older White Bull, a Miniconjou and father of Small Bear. Foolish Thunder, Black Eagle, and Rising Sun, all three Sans Arc. At the same time, Bull Eagle and Small Bear agreed to be responsible for getting their people to the reservation on time. In this, more of the headmen vowed they would not fail: Tall Bull, Yellow Eagle, Two Elk, Foolish Bear, Spotted Elk, and Poor Bear. Better than two thousand Miniconjou, Sans Arc, and Hunkpapa, accounting for some three hundred lodges, had surrendered without the Fifth Infantry firing another shot.

That night of the twenty-fifth Miles had much in which to rejoice as he finished a letter to Mary, apologizing for not having written her sooner, blaming the delay on the rigors of the campaign, declaring that one mistake on his part might cause a massacre the sort of which had overwhelmed his friend Custer. Sleep had been coming fitfully, he reminded her, but boasted that the rigors of the chase had caused him to lose a few pounds.

Next, the colonel wrote a letter to Mary's uncle, William Tecumseh Sherman, complaining about what he saw as conspiracy within the army against his interests. Because he had seen firsthand that the Sioux were running short on ammunition and staples, Miles wrote, "I believe we can wear them down." Then he wheedled for more cavalry, blaming his own lack of it on the wastefulness of Crook's past and present campaigning, saying his lack of horse soldiers was all that stood in the way between him and his victory over Sitting Bull—"It is not easy for infantry to catch them, although I believe we can whip them every time."

Last on his list of correspondence was a dispatch to General Alfred H. Terry:

> I consider this the beginning of the end. [The Indians] are very suspicious, and of course [are] afraid that some terrible punishment will be inflicted upon them. . . . While we have fought and routed these people, and driven them away from their ancient homes, I cannot but feel regret that they are compelled to sub-

mit to starvation, for I fear they will be reduced to that condition as were the southern tribes in 1874.

"What of Sitting Bull, General?" asked Captain Wyllys Lyman.

After a moment of reflection that dark night as icy points of snow lanced down from a lowering sky, Nelson A. Miles sighed. "Yes. Sitting Bull. He's still out there waiting for me, isn't he?"

Captain Edmond Butler inquired, "Will we go after him now?"

"We'll march the command back to Tongue River, recoup, then set out again—yes. By all means," Miles replied. "Although my nemesis is still out there, roaming free ... I have accomplished one thing I set out to do. I have succeeded in dividing the enemy against itself, whittling away at my enemy's forces where I can find and engage them."

"That's more than the other columns have been able to accomplish in this country," declared Andrew S. Bennett.

"We won't name names here, Captain Bennett," Miles replied, flatly waving off that comment pointed at both Terry and Crook. "From the reports of their disgraceful failures of late, I judge that the nation sooner or later will understand the difference between doing something and doing nothing."

Luther Kelly refilled his coffee tin, then asked, "Will we fight on into the winter, General?"

Miles turned to regard his chief of scouts. "You'll have a job for as long as Sitting Bull and Crazy Horse are free, Mr. Kelly. I will endeavor to keep the tribes divided and take them in detail. Never more will the hostiles band together. Make no mistake about it—I consider what we have done to be the beginning of the end for their people."

Chapter 15

Late October–4 November 1876

**Ann Eliza to Get Her Alimony
at Last.**

UTAH

Ann Eliza Gets Her Money.

SALT LAKE, October 25.—This morning, the ten days having expired which had been allowed Brigham Young in which to pay alimony to Anna Eliza, his nineteenth wife, and it not having been paid, Brigham appeared in court before Judge Shaffer, who ordered that A. K. Smith be appointed as special commissioner without bonds and ordered to seize property, sell the same and pay the sum required with costs, and special authority to be issued to the commissioner under the seal of the court; and it was further ordered that the defendant be discharged. The amount due as alimony up to the present time is about $4,000.

"**N**ot long after we got back to Camp Robinson, Crook had himself an audience with the chiefs and other headmen," Seamus said, speaking in a soft voice so that he would not wake the child who lay asleep in the crook of his father's shoulder. Samantha watched her husband step slowly across the tiny room, using what floor there was to pace back and forth as his son slept, nestled within his father's arms while she sat propped up in the rope-and-tick bed, watching them both, her knees drawn up where she rested her chin.

From the moment Crook's command had returned to Fort Laramie, Seamus had been with them both constantly, forgoing most of his nocturnal visits to the sutler's saloon, choosing not to join the other scouts and soldiers in their noisy camaraderie in these last few days before embarking on Crook's Powder River Expedition. Instead, to Sam it seemed that her husband hungered only for the companionship of his family across what hours and days were left him before Mackenzie's Fourth would plunge north into the winter wilderness, the spear point of George Crook's desperate last-chance campaign to find and capture Crazy Horse.

"Soon enough I'll have only male voices around my ears," he had tried to explain when she asked him why he hovered close, why he didn't wander over to Collins's saloon.

Again he had tried to explain the life of an army on the march: only the bray of mules and the snort of horses, the squeak of frozen saddle and the jingle of frosted bit—to touch, instead of loved ones, only the memories of these two most important people in his world, alone and trying desperately to keep himself warm with those memories as a second winter campaign swallowed him whole.*

"If Crook captured the Sioux chiefs," Samantha began now as she watched him pace with the child, "why would he even bother to talk with them at all?"

Shifting the infant from his shoulder, Donegan laid his little son across his left arm and adjusted the tiny blanket around the boy's head and face as he said, "What he had to say to that gathering of chiefs was most important, Sam. You see, Crook had the power—then and there, plain as paint before all the headmen and once-mighty warriors—to remove Red Cloud from his throne."

"Red Cloud? You mean the same chief who commanded all those warriors you fought in that northern country ten years ago ... the same chief who you told me drove the army out in sixty-eight? You're telling me Crook's made sure he is no longer chief of the Sioux?"

With a slight shrug Seamus nodded. "For all that it matters

---

* *Blood Song*, Vol. 8, The Plainsmen Series.

to the Injins staying close to their agency. Crook told them all he was determined to punish Red Cloud for running off from the reservation, for making his camp a place where warriors could come and go from the Powder River country. And then Crook capped the ball when he announced he was making Spotted Tail chief of all the Sioux."

"Spotted Tail—isn't he the one whose daughter died and is buried near this post?"

"The same chief," Donegan answered. "Long ago, as his daughter was dying, she made him promise her two things: that he would place her scaffold near the white man's Laramie fort, and that he would remain faithful to the white man's wishes. Spotted Tail never broke the promise he made to her."

"What of the other bands you say have been restless at the agency?"

"The Cheyenne and the Arapaho sat in on the conference with Crook. The general figured it would help to impress upon them his power to punish, as well as his power to reward. Crook finished his council by telling the bands what he expected of them from here on out."

"I imagine he demanded they all stay at home and become farmers," Sam replied with a sneer, then winked at her husband when he went to scowling at her. "Really, Seamus—I can no more see any of those redskins digging at the ground than I can see you living the rest of your natural years as a sodbuster."

Finally he grinned at her, then turned at the corner of the room and started back toward the bed with slow steps as he gently rocked the sleeping infant troubled this evening with another bout of colic. "Crook told the chiefs that the government was feeding their people, putting clothes on their backs—so the government and its army was damn well entitled to the tribes' loyalties. But what's the government got for all the flour and rifles, bacon and bullets? I'll tell you: Sioux warriors and all the rest have been acting like murderers and thieves off the reservation, then fleeing back to take refuge on the agency. Now it was time, Crook told them, to show their friendship with more than empty words. From now on the chiefs are going to be held accountable for the actions of their young men."

"Sounds like Crook enjoyed playing the part of a stern father to them."

Seamus smiled. "I damn well know he relished the role— telling the chiefs and headmen that if they did not toe the line this time, they would soon rue the day they acted so foolishly. He told them that if they all came in and began their lives as stock raisers, their troubles would end at once."

"But what of the others you've told me about, Seamus?" she asked. "The ones like Crazy Horse and Sitting Bull? The ones who have never come in?"

"Crook told the chiefs he was going after the last of the hostiles, those holdouts still roaming the wild country. He vowed the army would find them and drive them in."

"And those they can't drive in?" she asked dolefully.

"Yes," he nodded, gazing down at his son. "Crook told those chiefs that the army would wipe out all those who failed to come in. And he said he would do it with the help of the young men he had just rounded up and brought back to the agency. That's when Crook made it plain he was counting on the chiefs to convince their warriors to become scouts for him in the coming campaign."

"When you got back, I remember your saying Crook would be taking hundreds of mercenaries north with the column to help him find the hostiles still with Crazy Horse and Sitting Bull."

"From Spotted Tail's and Little Wound's bands Crook has enlisted a small army of Sioux and Cheyenne who will be going after their own kind," Donegan replied with a doleful wag of his head. "Hard to believe that so many would volunteer to hunt down their own kind still out there in the wild country ... especially two of the warriors we captured from American Horse's village at Slim Buttes in September.* But they were the first to sign up."

"There'll be some good come of them going along, Seamus," she said quietly. "Of that I'm certain."

He gazed down into the red face of that sleeping infant, saying, "I certainly hope so, love."

"All the good we do will one day be victorious," Sam explained, hopeful his coming and going would one day be at an end. "At long last we are finally treating the friendly Indians better than we have cajoled and coddled the stubborn ones who mean us no goodwill."

"Ah, how right you are, pretty one!" he answered. "Too long the agents have been cowed by the belligerent chiefs and haughty warriors, trying to win over the hostiles with gifts and pleadings,

---

* *Trumpet on the Land*, Vol. 10, The Plainsmen Series.

while the agency bands have been neglected as they come close to starving, given only thin blankets with the arrival of every winter."

"What did Crook have done with all those ponies Mackenzie captured?"

"The North brothers and their Pawnee are bringing them over—likely should get here tomorrow. The stronger ones the quartermaster will turn into remounts for the campaign."

"I pray to God you won't have to eat another horse as long as you're with Crook's army."

"My pretty—somewhere south of Slim Buttes, I vowed I'd only sit on a horse from now on—swearing on my mother's grave that I'd never again take a bite out of one!"

She laughed softly in that way of hers that made his heart leap an extra beat, ever since that first night he had laid eyes on her down in the panhandle of Texas. Looking down at the infant now, he saw so much of the boy's mother in the child's face—the kindness, the openness to expressing a wide tapestry of emotions, a ruddy glow that could come only from an earnest spirit.

Seamus continued, "After seeing to the quartermaster's needs, Crook will give the scouts their pick of the rest. And what's left will be sold on the market for what they'll bring."

"You said they were all a pretty sorry lot."

"Aye, Sam—they've already had a tough go of it this fall—and the real weather hasn't even poked its head over the hills to the north."

"And the guns? What about all the weapons Mackenzie's men took from the Sioux?"

"They've been put under lock in a warehouse at Camp Robinson. Crook's not sure yet what he'll do with all the guns: whether he'll come up with a value for them and pay the Indians, or give them back to the Indians who prove they can remain our allies against the hostiles in the Powder River country."

She pulled the blankets up under her chin. "Weapons were taken from all the tribes?"

"No. Red Cloud's Bad Face band was surprised to find out that the Arapahos and the Cut-off Sioux of Spotted Tail were allowed to keep their guns."

"It wasn't the first surprise Crook's given them," Sam added. "And I sure hope it won't be the last."

"Listen to you," Seamus marveled. "Talking just like a soldier's wife."

"Well, I am, aren't I?"

He grinned at her. "I suppose you are at that, Sam." Then his eyes came back to rest on the infant cradled across his left arm as Samantha struck a lucifer and lit the solitary oil lamp in the darkening room as twilight began to fade. "The more I've thought about things ever since riding with Mackenzie into those camps, I find myself in agreement with what Crook wrote to Sheridan after he had his meeting with the chiefs at Camp Robinson."

"What did the general say to Sheridan?"

"That old Red Beard said he feels that Mackenzie's success is the first gleam of daylight we have had in this whole business. So now we must get about the matter of putting to rest what's left of the hostile bands."

Disarming the Indians at Standing Rock.

THE INDIANS

Latest from Standing Rock.

ST. PAUL, October 26.—The *Pioneer Press* has a special from Bismarck which says: "General Terry was still at Standing Rock last evening. He had succeeded in disarming and gathering in the ponies of all the Indians at the agency, but he believed the Indians have most of their arms, as they had a day's warning and only about two hundred stands have been found, including shot guns and revolvers. A large number of ponies will yet be brought in and about six hundred have already been surrendered. The Indians seem to take kindly to the removal as they come to understand it, but some were at first disposed to resist. General Terry informed them that the property would be sold and the proceeds invested in cattle and such things as would be most useful for them. None outside of General Terry and those immediately connected with him have any idea as to where he will go next, whether to Cheyenne or to strike the hostiles.

*   *   *

Now that the government had stolen back the Black Hills, all that remained undone was this nasty business of trespassers.

There were those back east and among the political pundits who said all that was needed was a campaign to herd the winter roamers back onto their shrinking reservations. At the same time, there was also a hue and cry that what was still needed most of all was a crushing defeat for the enemy—a loss so devastating that the hostile bands would have no choice but to return to their agencies in abject humiliation. After Powder River, after the Rosebud, and especially after the burning ignominy of the Little Bighorn, what many in the army wanted most of all as October waned was to whip the enemy holdouts—whip them soundly, whip them once and for all.

The summer campaign that hadn't fizzled out until autumn was underway had been decidedly indecisive. Although the winter roamers had been hit and their confidence wounded, nonetheless Sitting Bull, Crazy Horse, and the other holdouts remained free and unpunished. There had been but one solution when Sheridan called Crook and Mackenzie to Laramie in September: a winter campaign. Once again the army would attempt to fashion the cold into an ally.

So it was that upon his return to Fort Laramie, George Crook went about putting the finishing touches to prepare for what he was now calling the Powder River Expedition. For the most part, the trials of 1876 had all but used up the forces of the Second, Third, and Fifth cavalries. In their place the general now outfitted six troops of Mackenzie's Fourth. With new mounts and a healthy sprinkling of fresh recruits popularly known in the press as "Custer's Avengers," Crook also called into service four companies of the Third and Fifth—a total of 28 officers and 790 horse soldiers.

Colonel Richard I. Dodge was placed in charge of 33 officers over some 646 infantry and artillery troops (who would be fighting as riflemen). Tom Moore and 65 packers would once more lead their famous pack train north, again attempting to keep tight rein on more than 400 obstinate mules, which would carry the cavalry's supplies once Mackenzie cut loose from the main column for the attack. In addition, more than 200 teamsters were in charge of a train of 7 ambulances and 168 wagons, which would transport the column's supplies north to the Reno Cantonment on the Powder River. From there Crook planned on striking out, swift and hard, once his scouts learned the where-abouts of Crazy Horse.

This time into the field the old Red Beard would utilize mercenaries from six tribes: 48 Pawnee riding under the North brothers; 151 Sioux, some 90 Cheyenne, and Arapaho, all of whom had joined up after the Red Cloud confiscation; and in the last month Crook had sent a wire to the Wind River Reservation hoping to again convince chief Washakie to send his Shoshone and allied Bannock warriors. In just the last week word telegraphed from Camp Brown assured Crook that Tom Cosgrove and his eager warriors would meet the column on the march.

Besides, Crook had already dispatched Captain George M. "Black Jack" Randall north along the west side of the Big Horn Mountains to again convince the Crow they should enlist in the army's struggle. Reports had it that the tribe would be sending two hundred of their best warriors to rendezvous with the expedition at or near the Reno Cantonment, if not by the time Crook reached Pumpkin Buttes.

In all, there would soon be nearly twenty-two hundred men marching north to stalk Crazy Horse.

"You've no business bringing him out into this cold," Seamus scolded Samantha, halting her at the bottom landing there at the front door of Old Bedlam. Outside on the parade, all was a ruckus of men and horses, wagons and mules. "I can say my farewells to you both right here—inside, where it isn't so bloody cold."

She looked up at his face with those eyes of hers and said, "If this truly is a son of yours, Seamus Donegan, then he'd best be getting used to this unearthly cold right here and now."

For a moment he studied the fiery intensity in her big, bold eyes and decided he was not about to talk her out of venturing onto the porch or the parade with the rest of the wives. "All right, then—cover him up best you can. The wind's kicked up this morning, Sam." Then, as she pulled the layers of swaddling and blankets over the infant's face, Seamus tugged at her shawl, bringing the long folds up on her head, tucking it all beneath her chin in a fat knot.

"There, now," she whispered up to him, her cheeks already rouged with the cold blustering in through the open door, "don't we two look a sight?"

"Never been a prettier mother."

"Perhaps your own, Seamus," she replied quietly as she took his elbow, the babe cradled across her right arm.

He stopped just outside the doorway as officers barked their commands, sergeants bawled out their orders, mules brayed, and horses strained at their wagon hitches, rattling trace chains with the strident squeak of cold axles and hubs.

"Prepare to mount!"

Gazing down into her face, he felt his eyes begin to mist. "My mother would have loved to meet you, Samantha Donegan."

Gazing at the carefully wrapped child, Sam said, "And to hold her grandson too."

Swiftly he brought her into him, yet gently, ever so gently, as he clutched them both to his bosom, the babe there between them, sheltered in their warmth from the wind and the brutal cold, sensing the tears spill down his cheeks.

"Mount!"

Cherishing this last moment between them, the last time he might hold these precious pieces of his heart for weeks to come. No more than a few weeks, he had promised her in the last days together—pained each time he remembered just how often he had been forced to break that very same vow.

Stirrups groaned as weight came down upon them. Saddles squeaked and horses snorted. The entire parade a fog of cold frost.

"You must go," she whispered, her voice muffled against the bulk of his blanket and canvas coat.

Blinking his eyes, Seamus looked over the parade, seeing how Dodge already had his infantry well away on their march, followed by the artillery caissons and all those wagons rumbling two by two down to the big iron bridge that would carry them across the North Platte. Only now were the cavalry wheeling about into column, company, by company, by company. Always were they the last in the line of march, and the first into the action. By the luck of the march, horse soldiers were the ones chosen to eat every other man's dust—and the first thrown against the enemy, the first to spill their blood.

Somewhere miles ahead already were Crook and his headquarters group, likely following the North brothers and their Pawnee trackers. It suited Seamus just fine that he would ride back here with Mackenzie's Fourth and the rest of the scouts, most of them Sioux, Cheyenne, and Arapaho, some of whom were beating on hand drums, all singing in their own tongue to the cold dawn sky.

Prayers.

Dear Father in Heaven, did he ever feel like praying right then.

She pulled her damp face from his coat slightly, looking up at his bearded chin. "You'll do nothing foolish this time out, Seamus Donegan."

"I've done nothing so foolish in my youth that got me killed—"

She grabbed some curls resting upon his shoulder, whispering, "Though many's tried to raise that beautiful hair of yours."

"But now that I've grown older, I find I'm one to do less and less that's so daring and foolish."

That too might be a vow hard for him to keep.

"It's just two days to Fetterman, Seamus. Promise you'll write us from there."

"As I always do."

"But this time write a letter to your son."

"And you will read it to him for me?"

"Over and over again, I'll read it to him," Sam answered, pressing her face back into the mass of him when the wind kicked up a skiff of old snow across the icy porch. People were cheering, crying out, young children leaping across the parade as they banged away on pots and pans while the cavalry strung itself out at long last and the rear guard was finally in motion. She sobbed, "I will read it . . . like his father was singing a lullaby to him every night."

With one finger he pushed back the shawl's hood slightly and smelled deeply of her hair this last time. The tears coming freely now, he could almost feel them freezing on his cheeks, in the burr of his beard. He wanted so to remember this scent of her across all those cold days and freezing nights yet to come.

"This will be swift and sure—I'll be home soon."

"And when you do, Seamus—you promised to bring home a name for your son."

"Aye," he whispered, his lips against her ear now. "We'll name him when I return from . . . from—"

"From Hell."

"I'll be home soon, Sam"—he barely got the words out. "Soon . . ."

Then he gently parted the blanket and gazed one last moment at the infant, bending slightly so that he could softly plant a kiss on the boy's forehead. In the next moment Seamus raised his face to her, laid his mouth against her full lips moistened with the gush of her tears, then suddenly, brutally, tore himself away from them.

From family. From what clutched most tightly at his heart. Gone to plunge back into the maw of Hell once more.

Chapter 16

Freezing Moon
1876

The Official Report.

CHICAGO, October 26—The following telegram was received at the military headquarters to-day:

STANDING ROCK, October 25.—*To Lieutenant General P. H. Sheridan, Chicago:*—Colonel Sturgis left Lincoln on the 20th, and Major Reno on the 21st. Each arrived here on the afternoon of the 22d, and Sturgis immediately commenced dismounting and disarming the Indians at Two Bears Canoe, on the left bank, and Lieutenant Colonel Carlin, with his own and Arendez force, dismounted and disarmed them at both camps this side. Owing partially to the fact that before I arrived at Lincoln, word was sent to the Indians here (it is believed by Mrs. Galpin) that we were coming and our purpose was stated, but principally, I believe, that some time since, owing to the failure of grass here the animals were sent to grazing places many miles away, comparatively only a few horses were found. The next morning I called the chiefs together and demanded the surrender of their horses and arms, telling them that unless they complied their rations would be stopped; also telling them that whatever might be realized from the sale of property taken would be invested in stock for them. They have quietly submitted, and have sent out to bring in the animals and some have already arrived. We now have in our possession about 700. More are arriving rapidly, and I expect to double this number, as I have kept the whole force here till now for the effect it produces. I shall start Sturgis tomorrow morning for Cheyenne, leaving Reno till Carlin completes the work here. Only a few arms have yet to be found or surrendered, but I think our results are satisfactory and not a shot was fired. Of course no surprise can now be expected. At Cheyenne the desired effect will be produced by the same means as those employed here.

[signed]   ALFRED H. TERRY
Brigadier General

More than almost anything, he loved the smell of firesmoke on the cold morning air.

But then, he told himself, perhaps that was because he was getting to be an old man.

Young men loved most their fighting, loved their ponies, loved their women too. Oh, how a young man loved coupling with a young woman!

But as a man grew older, he found other things to occupy his thoughts, other matters to consume his days. As he put winters behind him, Morning Star had come to learn life was not all fighting and coupling. There was the silence of the mornings, that first smell of woodsmoke on the breeze, the murmur of a stream beneath a thin coating of ice.

He wrapped the blanket more tightly about his shoulders as he moved through the leafless cottonwood toward the creekbank to relieve himself. A pair of magpies jabbered nearby, noisy above the racks of red meat drying for the winter. A dog appeared suddenly, snapping and barking at the black-and-white thieves, setting them to wing. Too bad, he thought—for the dogs would get very little of that meat they protected, while the magpies would get much, much more by brazen theft.

Moving his breechclout aside, his hand brushed the knife he carried in a sheath at his waist. And Morning Star chuckled. Long, long ago some of the Lakota had begun to call him Dull Knife—because Morning Star's own brother claimed Morning Star never had a sharp knife. It did not matter, he had decided many a winter ago. Some men lived by a sharp knife, while others lived by sharp wits.

The first cold had come. Then the land had warmed again, as it always did before this freezing moon. But now the weather had turned cold once more, and cold it would stay until spring, when buds burst forth on the willow and the cottonwood leafed. So, so much had happened since last spring.

For last winter's time of cold, Morning Star's people had remained at Red Cloud Agency. As he looked back, it seemed the summer sun had barely warmed the land before they had heard the reports of that first big fight with the soldiers on the Roseberry River.*

Then, no more than a few suns after that victory, word drifted in to the agencies of another, even greater fight. It was then Morning Star and the other Old-Man Chiefs decided they could no longer contain the eagerness of their people. They must go north, to join that great village living life in the old way—no more to settle for the white man's flour and pig meat, his parchment-thin blankets that fell apart with the first hard rain.

What a celebration that had been, all those lodges and the People—starting north to join the others who had twice defeated the soldiers sent out to herd those winter roamers back to the reservations.

Then of an early morning, near a tributary of the Red Paint River,† the young warriors riding out in front of their great procession were attacked by a group of soldiers. Yellow Hair was killed by the long-hair scout called Cody, and the rest of the cavalcade whirled about on their heels, hurrying back toward the agency as many, many soldiers gave chase, nipping at their heels. Fortunate it was that they made it across the boundaries to the White Water Reservation‡ with the women and children, with all the old ones who had been singing of once more seeing life as they had once known it. Now there was sadness, and weeping, and in Yellow Hair's lodge there was no fire for many nights.

The next time they sought to slip away to the north, Morning Star's people were much more careful. They did not boast among the layabouts that they were leaving. Those layabouts were satisfied to take the white man's droppings and betray the People to the white man. To think that the layabouts even sold

---

* Cheyenne term for Rosebud Creek.
† Mini Pusa, South Fork of the Cheyenne River.
‡ Red Cloud Agency.

Noaha-vose, the Sacred Mountain, to the white man! It was not the white man's, and it was not the layabouts', to sell. It belonged to all of *Ma-heo-o's* children.

So that next time Morning Star's people sneaked off the agency in small groups, leaving at different times, going in many different directions before they met up once more far to the north.

Then at last there was singing. The young and the old—oh, there was much singing. His people, the *Ohmeseheso*, were on their journey back to their hunting ground, no more to return to the reservation.

They finally reached the northern country not long after the great village had begun breaking up. Too many camp circles, too many bellies to feed, and too many ponies to graze. Turning their faces into the wind, the People left the *Ho-ohomo-eo-o*, the Lakota bands, to go their own way. For a time, the Crazy Horse people stayed close, many times camping in the same valley, hunting the same ridge, the wolves from both tribes keeping their eyes searching for the soldiers everyone was sure would come. Eventually. The soldiers always came.

Now that Morning Star's lodges had rejoined the People, three of the Old-Man Chiefs were present. It was good to see Little Wolf again—for he had many stories to tell about the soldier attack on Old Bear's camp along the Powder River during the Dusty Moon of last winter. And it made Morning Star's old heart swell to bursting the first time he saw the Sacred Hat lodge that Coal Bear erected at the middle of every camping site.

The All Father had sent *Esevone*, the Sacred Buffalo Hat, as well as the Sacred Sun Dance, to the People through the Great Prophet Erect Horns. *Esevone* was the living, life-affirming channel of *Ma-heo-o's* greatest blessings upon all the People. But especially did she bless the women of the tribe. The rest of that summer had been a time of feasting and good hunting, of celebration and dancing. Babies were born, and the old ones closed their eyes to begin their journey to *Seana*, the Place of the Dead beyond the Star Road. Everyone's heart was filled, and all were sure it was to be a time of rebirth.

The fourth Old-Man Chief, Black Moccasin, and Two Moons's band remained with the *Hotohkesoneo-o*, the Little Star People, who called themselves the Oglalla, throughout the warm months, preferring to camp with the Crazy Horse people. This was a good thing, for all of the *Ohmeseheso* had long been close to the Hunkpatila. To the village of Crazy Horse the survivors of the Powder River fight had trudged through deep snows, finding open arms, warm lodges, robes, and blankets after the soldiers drove Old Bear's people into the wilderness.

Then, as the summer wore on, Morning Star's people moved slowly down the Powder River, eventually reaching the Elk River. It was there they discovered some bags of corn left by the soldiers who rode up and down the river on the smoking houses that walked on water.* Many of the People ate some of that corn, fed some to their ponies, then poured most of it out on the ground so they could take the bags with them when they marched back up the Powder. Far, almost to the forks of the Powder, they went before journeying over to the Tongue, from there to the upper Roseberry, then finally hunted along the upper branches of the Little Sheep River.† Antelope and elk, deer and turkey, and the hides were good! The ponies grew fat on the tall grass. Best of all, the soldiers were far to the east, chasing about on old Lakota trails.

Truly, it was a time of many blessings!

With the coming of the Cool Moon when the People had wandered back toward the Elk River, fear of the soldiers faded even further from their hearts.

Then came a report that the pony soldiers of Three Stars had killed many people in Iron Plume's village of Lakota camped on the far side of *Noaha-vose*, beside the Thin Buttes.‡ Although that meant the soldiers were far, far to the east, there was again that fear the white man was raiding, burning, and destroying. So the three Old-Man Chiefs directed that the village move south once more, toward the country of the Upper Powder.

They journeyed up Pole Creek over the White Mountains,** intent on finding buffalo and antelope in the land of the *Sosone-eo-o*, the Shoshone—to make meat and cure hides for the coming winter. Their journey was far from disappointing. By the time they recrossed the mountains to the east, the high places were beginning to freeze, the leaves on the trembling trees were turning gold, and the air had grown cool. As the days shortened, more and more lodges drifted in, fleeing the White Water Agency with rumors that the soldiers would one day be coming to steal their guns and their ponies. Leaders like Standing Elk, Black

---

* River steamboats.
† Little Bighorn River.
‡ *Trumpet on the Land*, Vol. 10, the Plainsmen Series.
** Bighorn Mountains.

Bear, and even Turkey Leg, partially paralyzed by accidentally sitting upon *Esevone's* horn. The newcomers said the white man had stopped giving out rations, slowly starving the People on the reservation, threatening to force them south to Indian Territory.

Bravely, Standing Elk had told the government men, "You speak to me about another land, a country far away from this. I think you should not have mentioned this to me at all. My grandfathers and relations have lived here always."

No matter that so many came to join that autumn. They did not want for anything. *Ma-heo-o* had blessed Morning Star's people with plenty and with peace.

Here in the country of the Upper Powder they would be safe this winter, far from the soldiers to the south, far from the soldiers on Elk River, far from the soldiers to the east.

Here they would be safe.

THE INDIANS

Return of the Sioux Commission.

CHICAGO, October 27.—A telegram from the Yankton agency says the steamer C. K. Peck passed down at noon to-day, with the Sioux peace commissioners on board. They report that their mission has been satisfactory and successful. They held councils at all the agencies on the upper Missouri, and the treaty was signed by all the head chiefs of the different bands. The commission, at the request of the Indians, struck out the sections proposing to remove them to the Indian territory. The Indians accepted all the other propositions without objection.

"I suppose they're still counting, for what it matters to us," John Bourke grumbled.

Seamus looked up from his meal of bacon and biscuits, everything smothered in white gravy. "Counting what, Johnny?"

"The votes," Crook's adjutant replied with that tone a man took when he expected everyone else to know already what the devil he was talking about.

So Seamus went back to eating his late breakfast. Although he had missed morning mess because he was attending to the matter of reshoeing the big bay he was riding north, the army cooks liked the big Irishman's ready smile and his quickness with a kind word—so it wasn't hard to get a hearty breakfast rustled up and set before him in nothing flat.

"You know, the goddamned votes," Bourke repeated. "The votes for president."

Around a slab of bacon Donegan mumbled, "Right, Johnny—the votes. I suppose that's supposed to be the most important thing in our whole world right now."

"By bloody damn, it is!" Bourke all but shrieked. "It's been one of the toughest campaigns ever held. But then, you being from Ireland, I suppose it wouldn't matter to you?"

"Not matter to me?" Seamus growled indignantly with a mouth full of food, fire in his eye. "I left the land of me birth because me mither sent me away from County Kilkenny," slipping back into a peaty Irish brogue the way he did when he grew angry. "But I've damn well stayed here in America—John Bourke—because this is me adopted home. So don't ye go getting off so high-and-mighty with me, Lieutenant!"

"Easy, Seamus!" Bourke hushed, holding up both his hands in front of him as if he expected Donegan to make a grab for him at any moment. "I'm . . . I'm sorry!"

"Damn well you should be," the Irishman grumped, then drank down the last of his lukewarm coffee. "I'm as American as any man of ye now. Lived here in this country longer'n I lived in Eire, I have. So go and stuff that up your ballot box, John Bourke."

"Someone has been stuffing the ballot boxes, Seamus," Bourke said. "Both Tilden and Hayes are claiming victory in the swing states of Florida, Louisiana, and the Carolinas."

"How can they both claim victory? Ain't it a democratic election?"

With a slight shrug Bourke said, "I suppose the count is so close. This morning on the wire, word had it that General Augur—who commands the Department of the Gulf—is taking infantry and artillery units with him to Florida because of all the threats of bloodshed."

"I damn well thought we already fought one war of American against American!" Seamus howled.

"Things aren't settled down South—won't be for a long time," Bourke replied. "The news that our troops are being sent in is about as bad as news of hostilities with a foreign nation. This could be even worse, because internecine wars always have a rich infusion of religious fanaticism to them."

"Mind what I say, Johnny: more men been put to the sword in the name of one religion over the other, than for all the bleeming politics in the world," Seamus declared solemnly.

"Aye, Seamus," Bourke said. "Severe as our coming experiences in the Indian country may be, they will be more welcome that a campaign in the sunny lands of the South having to fight against our own misguided people."

"Is the coffee burned yet?" a voice called out behind them.

Seamus turned to look over his shoulder at the civilian entering Fetterman's mess hall, dusting the flakes of frozen snow from his fur hat.

"It ain't bad for beggars like us, Frank. They just brewed me a fresh pot. Come—have you a cup."

"Lieutenant Bourke," Frank North acknowledged the officer as he came to the table, "the general asked me to fetch you up. Says he's wanting you to bring up one of the Sioux leaders from the scouts' camp down across the river. To have a chat with him about all the complaining the Sioux have been doing."

An hour later Seamus and Bourke had returned with Three Bears and a few other ranking warriors eager to have an audience with Three Stars Crook. As the Sioux settled onto the floor in the tiny, drafty office, Crook dragged a chair around the side of the desk and set it directly in front of his guests. Then he glanced at his interpreters and asked, "What's Three Bears got on his mind?"

The general's question was translated. Getting to his feet and readjusting his blanket about his shoulders, the Sioux leader began to speak slowly, pausing now and then while the interpreters hurried to catch up.

"Before leaving Red Cloud Agency, I told the agent I wanted him to give our people their regular allowance of rations while we were gone on this scout. I am talking now for all our families left back to Red Cloud Agency. I want the beeves turned out the same as they ever were while we are away.

"I have three things to say and that's all. When that delegation gets back from the Indian Territory, I want it to wait for me and not go to Washington until we can start together. I don't want them to start before that time. As soon as we get through with this business out here, we can work together, and that's the reason I want them to wait for me. Sometimes I may want to ask for something, and whenever I do, I want Three Stars to agree to it. When we travel together, we ought to work together as one.

"A great many of our men back at the agency have guns but

no ammunition. I want to have a message sent to both those stores at the agency to have them sell ammunition for a couple of days, because the hostile Indians will come down there and raise trouble with our people while we are away. I want you to write this letter right away about my words, because if my young people don't cry for food while I am away, I'll like you all the better when I go back.

"The Pawnees have a great herd of horses here; we want half to drive along."

"Is that all?" Crook replied, his eyes moving from Three Bears to the interpreter, then back to the Sioux.

"Yes," answered the translator.

"All right. There'll be a fair division made of the horses."

Jutting his chin, acceptance brightening his face, Three Bears continued, "I want you to put in your letter we got one half of those horses back. And when you send us out on a scout, we want to work our own way."

The general nodded. "That's it, exactly."

"If a man wants to live in this world, he has got to do right and keep his ears straight," Three Bears continued. "Then he gets along without trouble. We are going to listen to you after this and do what you tell us. If we get any money for our country that you want us to sell back to you, we don't want it taken away from us. I want the Great Father to hear me when I call for oxen, wagons, and sheep—and when they are given to me, I don't want the agent to keep them for me in his corrals. I can keep them myself."

"I have no problem with that," Crook replied. "I'll see that it is done."

"It is good that we can work together, Three Stars," the Sioux leader said as he motioned the other warriors to rise.

"Yes, it is good," Crook replied. "Now, what say we go see about catching Crazy Horse?"

When the Indians had filed from the room, crossing the parade to follow the wide wagon road that would take them down the bluffs to the mouth of La Prele Creek, where they would cross on the ferry to the cavalry camp on the north bank, Crook watched them disappear in the swirls of ground snow.

"That son of a bitch was more savvy than savage, wasn't he, fellas?"

"Certainly was," Bourke agreed, coming up to stand at the window beside the general.

"Nothing wrong with keeping the welfare of his people always first," Seamus declared as he stepped to the door.

Bourke added, "I get the feeling Three Bears is going to play his enlistment as a scout for all the political and economic ends he can get out of it."

With his hand on the big iron hasp, Donegan asked, "You can't blame him, can you, Johnny?"

"No, we can't," Crook answered emphatically. "I'll see that he gets all he wants, just as long as he damn well sees that I get Crazy Horse."

Chapter 17

10–14 November 1876

General Miles Attacks and Defeats Sitting Bull.

The Insolent Savage to be Punished After All.

THE INDIANS.

Sitting Bull Attacked and Defeated by General Miles

BISMARCK, October 31.—General Miles had a successful fight after an unsuccessful council with Sitting Bull, on the 22d, on Cedar Creek, killing and wounding a number of Indians, his own loss being two wounded. He chased the Indians about sixty miles, when they divided, one portion going toward the agencies, and Sitting Bull toward Fort Peck, General Miles following. General Hazen has gone to Peck with four companies of infantry and rations for General Miles. Sitting Bull crossed the river below Peck on the 24th, and had sent word to the agent that he was coming in, and would be friendly, but wanted ammunition.

"Major, this horse belongs to me," Frank North addressed First Lieutenant William Philo Clark by his brevet rank as the civilian angrily wrenched the horsehair lead rope looped around the neck of a dark bay pony from the hands of the war chief leading the Sioux auxiliaries.

"It can't be," Clark replied indignantly. "Isn't this one of the horses taken from Red Cloud's band?"

Seamus Donegan nodded in agreement as he watched the cloud pass over the face of the war chief called Three Bears, then said to Clark, "In this case, you're both right, Clark. That's the horse Crook told Frank he could pick out of the ponies we confiscated out of Red Cloud's herd. Some of the Sioux scouts claim it's supposed to be just about the fastest thing on four legs."

"Damn well it has been," Frank growled in admiration as he fingered the horsehair rope nervously.

Just two days after the general's conference with Three Bears and the Sioux headmen there at Fort Fetterman, one of the Pawnee scouts had come tearing into the battalion's camp reporting that a dozen of the Sioux mercenaries had just come riding into the herd, dropped a rope around Frank's horse, and ridden off with it in tow. Outmanned and undergunned, the lone Pawnee horse guard had hightailed it straight to Frank North with the news. North promptly dispatched one of his riders to track down Lieutenant Clark, who, along with John Bourke, served General Crook as aide-de-camp, and demand that the young officer bring the horse to North's bivouac.

In less than an hour Clark showed up with Three Bears, the war chief pulling the lead rope wrapped around the neck of the pony in question.

Clark's eyes narrowed as he looked from Donegan to North, saying, "General Crook ordered that the horses captured from the Red Cloud and Red Leaf herds are to be used as a reserve. Three Bears's pony has given out, so I told him he could select a new one—"

"So he wants this one, don't he?" Luther North interrupted.

"He does," Clark snapped.

"Well, you just tell Three Bears that he can't have him," Frank added. "He's already called for."

"We got seventy extra horses," Luther attempted to explain to the perplexed lieutenant, "all of 'em given to the Pawnee as extra stock when ours give out. You can have Three Bears pick something to ride from among them."

"But this was a Sioux horse to begin with," Clark said after Three Bears seethed a moment in his own tongue, the Sioux leader's dark eyes fiery as he watched more and more of his traditional enemies, the Pawnee, gather nearby to listen in on the argument.

"Major Clark—I suggest you check with Crook before you go off half-cocked," Seamus said.

Clark whirled on Donegan. "A civilian such as yourself has nothing to say about this—"

"I damn well do have something to say if I see a man stealing a horse from a friend of mine!" Seamus snapped.

"The horse in question belonged to Three Bears to begin with!"

"That horse hasn't belonged to Three Bears since Mackenzie captured Red Cloud's herd!" Frank bellowed.

Clark wagged his head adamantly, pointing to the horse and saying, "I think for the sake of relations among our scouts that you could see your way clear to choose another—"

"The hell I will!" Frank shouted.

Clark's knuckles had turned white gripping his reins, in stark contrast to the red rising in his face. In an attempt to control the harsh anger in his voice, his words came out clipped and staccato. "If that's the way you want it, I will see the general about this, right now."

"You do that," Frank replied, seething, "and I'll be right behind you to see him too."

As soon as Clark and Three Bears reined their horses about, Frank called out for one of his Pawnee sergeants, telling the scout to have the dark bay saddled.

Luther grabbed hold of Frank's arm, saying, "If you'll wait for me to get saddled up too, I'll go with you."

"Count me in too, Frank," Seamus added. "I've got my horse saddled right over there."

The elder North turned to gaze across the river at the naked bluff on the south side where sat the fort's whitewashed buildings splayed against a pale winter sky. "All right. A few more minutes won't matter—go get ready, Lute. Thanks ... thanks, fellas."

The Pawnee sent to saddle up Luther's mount hadn't returned when one of Tom Moore's teamsters came plodding up atop one of the balky mules, hollering out in great excitement.

"Major North! Major North!" he bellowed as he brought his mule to a clattering halt and bolted from its bare back. "Had to come tell you."

"Tell me what?"

"Gloree! But you got them Sioux on the warpath!" he spat,

breathing heavily. "They say they're coming over here right now to clean out your Pawnee!"

"Goddamn their turncoat hides!" North snarled as he whipped about on his heel, shouting to this man and that, hurling orders for the entire battalion to take up their arms and make ready to defend their lives and their property against their ancient and mortal enemies.

"I knew better," Donegan said, all but under his breath.

"Knew better about what?" Luther asked as he trotted up.

"Crook should've knowed better than to try mixing Pawnee and Sioux in the same scouting party."

"The mortal truth, that is. Too much blood been spilled between 'em already," Frank North added sourly. "I figured Crook would know."

"It was bound to come to this," Seamus said with a doleful wag of his head as he slipped one of his revolvers out of its holster and confirmed that the cylinder was fully loaded. "They been enemies too bleeming long."

"You have our men wait here, Luther," Frank instructed his brother. "We'll head up to the fort."

"On that pony?" Donegan asked.

"Damn right—on *my* pony," Frank responded gruffly. "I'll get this settled with the general, once and for all—or the Pawnee battalion are going home."

"I'll have the men stay here and keep watch over the herd and our camp," Luther volunteered, waving one of his sergeants over. "I figure they can hold their own against the Sioux without us."

"Even though those Lakota outnumber the Pawnee more'n two to one," Donegan replied, "your boys ought to make a good stand of it."

The three civilians leaped into the saddle and loped away, heading toward the ferry. Problem was, between the Pawnee bivouac and the riverbank lay the Sioux camp. As the three riders came in sight of the Sioux mercenaries, Seamus could see that most of them had gathered in a large knot around Three Bears as he harangued them.

"Damn, but that one's a red preacher if he's anything at all!" Donegan muttered. "If he ain't sermonizing to Crook about this or about that, he's preaching to his warriors about you and that pony!"

Just as the trio approached the group, the Sioux all fell silent, staring with undisguised anger at the white men. Frank tapped the pony with a spur. Being a high-spirited animal, the pony began to dance and cavort as the three passed by the Sioux warriors. At the same time, Frank spontaneously began singing the Pawnee war song—well known to many of the older Lakota warriors.

Luther promptly joined in. At which time Seamus switched the reins to his left hand, positioning his right near the butt of the revolver he wore cocked over his left hip.

Not another word was spoken. Not one of the Sioux moved anything but their eyes as they watched the three white men pass by, two of them singing that song of their mortal enemy.

Atop the bluff at the fort, Frank spotted Clark and demanded the lieutenant accompany him to find Crook.

"I'm told the general's over in the sutler's store," Clark said. "Purchasing the last of his personal items for the march."

North said, "Suppose you go tell him we want to see him about this pony business."

"Yes," Clark seethed as he began to stomp off. "I'll do just that."

Donegan waited with Frank and Luther as Clark went into the sutler's shack and returned with Crook.

"General—there stands the pony in question," the lieutenant explained. "Per your instructions regarding the mounting of our auxiliaries—after your meeting with the Sioux scouts—I took Three Bears to the herd across the river and allowed him to select a new mount because his was played out."

"So explain how this altercation with Major North came about." Crook said, his eyes flicking from Frank to Luther, then back to the lieutenant.

Clark replied, "Major North refused to let Three Bears have the horse the chief picked out and took him back from the Indian."

"I see," Crook muttered, clearly nettled that he had to be dragged into what he saw as a trivial matter.

"Wait a minute, General," Frank said, stepping forward. "I didn't *refuse* that Sioux a horse. That's where your lieutenant here is wrong."

The lieutenant edged forward, saying, "I am not wrong!"

"Mr. Clark," Crook snapped. "You will wait until I ask you to speak. Go ahead, Major."

Frank said, "The horse the Sioux picked was the one you yourself allowed me to choose for myself back at Fort Laramie, General."

Rubbing his nose thoughtfully for a brief moment, Crook cleared his throat and turned on his aide. "Mr. Clark, it is clear to me that you should have gone to the Norths' camp before you took the Sioux chief to the herd to select a replacement mount. That way the major could have shown you which horses we were holding to remount the Sioux for the campaign."

"With the general's permission," the lieutenant protested, "I think the matter of this pony being returned to Three Bears should be given more weight—"

"Permission denied, Mr. Clark," Crook snapped angrily. "This is a horse I gave to Major North. None of the horses given out to the Pawnee will be returned to the Sioux. Is that understood?"

Clark nodded, abjectly humiliated. "Perfectly, sir."

"I will not have it said that George Crook gave ... then took away. Is that understood as well, Lieutenant?"

"Yes, sir. Absolutely understood."

Donegan almost felt sorry for Clark, if it hadn't been for the fact that the lieutenant had thrown in with the wrong side in a dispute over right and wrong.

North graciously suggested, "General—I have an idea, with your approval, of course."

"I'm listening."

"I have forty extra horses that you gave to my men after the roundup and capture. They will probably be all the extras we shall need on this campaign—so I'll be glad to turn all the others over to the Sioux scouts. Why not have them take all the rest of the horses that were kept out as extras?"

Crook's eyes brightened once more. "A splendid proposal, Major." He turned to Clark. "You'll see that you pass word on to our Sioux auxiliaries, Lieutenant?"

Clark grumbled, "Yes, General."

"Perhaps that will soothe their ruffled feathers."

"War feathers, General," Seamus corrected.

"Quite so, Irishman. Quite so," Crook replied.

"General, if I may," Frank North said, "while we're here, I'd like to address this matter of something the lieutenant said to me: that he was planning on having command of all the Indian scouts."

Clark hurriedly added, "That is what you told me, General—"

But Crook interrupted the officer by raising his hand, saying, "I get the feeling you have a problem with that, Major North."

Frank explained. "Not really me, General. My men won't go for it. They've fought under me and Luther for so long, and now you'd put them under the command of a soldier who rode boldly into our herd beside an old enemy, the one called Three Bears, to take one of our horses? I don't think your plan's going to work."

"I believe I see," Crook brooded, tugging at one of the two long braids in his beard. Then quickly he looked up, pointing at Frank, "You go tell your battalion that they remain under your command and will take their orders from no one else but the commander of this expedition."

"Understood, General," Frank replied.

Crook wagged his head as he looked at a sullen Lieutenant Clark, then turned back to Frank North. "Still, my heart wishes the Sioux and your Pawnee could get along better. To be friends now that we're all soldiers together."

Frank rubbed a boot toe on the frozen ground, in the manner of a man looking for the right words to put on a difficult subject. "General—if I may—to force the Sioux and the Pawnee to become friends will be very difficult, for they have been bitterest enemies for many generations." North went on to briefly relate how long ago the Pawnee felt the pressure of the Lakota bands when the Sioux first moved onto the plains.

Crook said, "I see. So it would be fair to say the Pawnee and the Sioux have had themselves a blood feud for a long, long time."

"Now, General—if you wish to issue an order commanding the Pawnee to make up with their bitterest enemies," North said, "I will do all in my power to have it obeyed."

After a moment more of reflection, Crook replied, "No, I don't wish to force them to be friendly against their will. Still, if they were friendly, I believe it would be better for all concerned, and this expedition."

"Well, I'll talk to my Pawnee about it and hear what they have to say," Frank said. "We'll head back to camp now and cut out those seventy head—the extra ponies the lieutenant here can turn over to the Sioux."

The task was done before twilight. Yet, as predicted, the matter appeared far from over, at least from the word brought to the North's camp that night by Todd Randall, the same white scout who was married to a Sioux woman at the Red Cloud

Agency and had been instrumental in helping the Pawnee trackers locate Red Cloud's village the night before the guns and ponies were captured.

"Just figured you ought to know to keep an eye locked on
your horses, fellas," Randall said. "Maybe best to keep 'em close
to your beds."

North asked, "Why's that, friend?"

"The Sioux say they're gonna get both them ponies you
brothers picked outta their herd. Kill 'em somewhere up the
trail."

Sitting Bull's Scalp in Danger
up North.

DAKOTA

The Fight with Sitting Bull

CHICAGO, November 1.—The official report of
the battle between Sitting Bull, Pretty Deer, Bull Eagle,
John Sausarie, Standing Bear, and White Bear, on Cedar Creek, the general results of which were given in a
Bismarck dispatch last night, states that a number of
Indians are known to have been killed and five
wounded. The report concludes: "I believe this matter
can be closed now by vigorous work, but some cavalry
is indispensible."

"Goddamn you, Soul!' the big sergeant major bawled at the
young private. "Be a little lively around here! We're pulling out,
by God!"

William Earl Smith swallowed, saluted, and stood stiffly until his superior had passed down that row of dog tents coming
down like fluffs of goose down upon the dirty snow. It had been
snowing off and on for two days now, and colder than anything
Smith had experienced back east.

Once Stephen Walsh was on out of hearing range there in
the cavalry camp below Fort Fetterman, Smith let out a gush of
air he had been holding during the cruel tongue-lashing.

"Great, big, overgrown Irishman," he muttered under his
breath, wondering if he had done the wrong thing by accepting
this assignment to become one of Mackenzie's five orderlies for
the Powder River Expedition.

He liked the general—why, Mackenzie had even offered

Smith a drink from his own personal flask the colonel kept buried somewhere inside that big caped wool coat of his. But that sergeant major who ran roughshod over all of Mackenzie's orderlies? Now, that was as close to genuine loathing as William Earl Smith had ever come.

Why, that damned mick made fun of the way Smith ate, the way he sat in the saddle, even how the private spoke. What with the way the orderlies were cursed and treated by the commissioned officers too, especially the tyrannical Captain Clarence Mauck, who more than once had threatened to make William Earl walk the whole campaign . . . how Earl dreamed of stepping right up to those arrogant stuffed shirts and poking one of them in the nose for good measure.

"Goddamn you, Soul—but it takes you longer to dress than a whole company!" Smith began to mimic the sergeant major's gruff and peaty brogue. "Smith this . . . and Smith that," he grumbled under his breath as he turned to finish packing his haversack. "Wished I was born with another name sometimes."

A few days back, when Walsh was bawling for him, the sergeant's abuse had finally got to the private and Smith had made the mistake of answering in kind, "What the hell do you want?"

Suddenly the sergeant had been towering there at Smith's tent flaps, his big meaty paws jammed down on his hips, his eyes like twelve-hour coals, spitting mad. "If you ever talk to me that way again—I'll tie you up by the thumbs!"

Earl had seen men tied up by their thumbs for hours at a time, their arms stretched high over their heads, their toes barely scraping the ground, held only by their thumbs to a stout wooden bar overhead.

Too, since joining the Fourth, he had heard reports of soldiers being placed in a big hole in the ground, so deep they had to climb down on a ladder. Or men lashed in a crouch around a stout piece of fence post then gagged for hours. Once Smith had seen that punishment—the soldiers who suffered it unable to move their cramped and tortured muscles once they were released.

On their march north to Fetterman a pair of soldiers had made the mistake of being slow to salute Mackenzie and addressing their commander too informally. That evening in bivouac the colonel promptly had Sergeant Walsh see that the two offenders stood in one place for an hour and a half, unable to move in that frigid weather except for saluting a tree stump for their transgression. A day later a few men in one company were late in relieving others on guard. Mackenzie sentenced those guilty to carry the hundredweight sacks of grain for their horses up and down across a mile of the rugged terrain as their punishment.

God must surely damn this army for putting some men over others, William Earl thought as he angrily jammed his supply of rations into the tiny haversack he would carry north.

Two days back, when the temperature had started to fall through the bottom of the surgeons' thermometers, one of Mackenzie's other orderlies—Private Edward Wilson—had gone up to the fort, invited to join Lieutenant Henry Lawton, quartermaster for the expedition's cavalry wing, as the two of them intended to drain the better part of a whiskey bottle at the sutler's saloon. As both were in no condition to walk back to their camp situated on the north side of the river, they climbed atop their horses and headed back in the dark and the blowing snow. Somewhere along the wagon road leading down the bluff to the ferry, Wilson's horse got away from him, prompting Lawton's horse to gallop off wildly too. As a furious lieutenant came up alongside the orderly, he yanked out his pistol and swung it across Wilson's face, knocking the private off his horse and unconscious with one blow. Sometime during the night Wilson came to, finding himself half-frozen, wet, and bleeding in the icy mud beside the North Platte. With the help of camp guards, he struggled back to his tent, where he passed out again before the sky grew light.

Although Mackenzie gave Lawton a stern dressing-down for striking a soldier, the colonel did nothing more in the way of punishment. As much as Smith had admired Mackenzie before, to him it seemed the man was really no different from all the other officers who either abused their men, or allowed the abuse by other officers to go on without proper punishment.

"Don't you see? The colonel can't bust Lawton down and order him to stay at Fetterman," said another of Mackenzie's orderlies. "He needs the lieutenant too damned bad—"

"I don't give a damn," Smith argued in a hushed voice. "What Mackenzie needs is to show his soldiers that fair is fair."

Far up the bluff on Fort Fetterman's parade that Tuesday morning, the fourteenth of November, a trumpet blared its shrill cry of "Stable Call" on the cold, brittle air:

> *Oh, go to the stable,*
> *All you who are able,*

And give your poor horses
Some hay and some corn.

For if you don't do it,
The captain will know it,
And you'll catch the devil
As sure as you're born.

"Ain't it the truth, Soul!" Smith groaned, mimicking again the big Irish sergeant's brogue. "Ain't it the truth!"

The cavalry and Indian scouts had been camped down there, already across the North Platte, with a toehold at the edge of enemy territory. Every one of the six days they waited there after marching north from Laramie, the sky had seemed to lower that much more, spitting cruel, sharp-edged ice crystals out of the belly of those clouds. While the cold Canadian winds came sweeping out of the north, the troops sat out their boredom.

Each having a winter campaign of his own under his belt, both Crook and Mackenzie understood the importance of equipping their men properly for the task at hand. Sheridan had promised them that the men of the Powder River Expedition would want for nothing. For once that was a promise kept.

Back at Laramie they had taken on their heavy underclothing, fur caps, wool gloves—since Crook was most unsatisfied with the poor quality of the horsehide gauntlets used on the March campaign—in addition to the normal issue of wool leggings, arctic overshoes or felt liners for their boots, along with two blankets apiece. That winter equipage would get a true test, for in the last two days the temperature had not once risen above zero.

There was an A-tent assigned to every four men. The soldiers pitched these so that two tents faced each other, a lightweight Sibley stove then placed in the narrow opening and the flaps of the two tents then pinned together to seal in the modest warmth. Outside each tent stood piles of sagebrush and greasewood stacked taller than the tents themselves. Some of the officers sported sealskin hats and long underwear made from perforated buckskin, pulling over it all a heavy overcoat with fur collars and cuffs.

Personal belongings were crated, marked, and left in the custody of the post quartermaster. Mackenzie had them down to fighting trim, ready to be off in as light a marching order as Crook could afford as they stared into the teeth of a brutal winter storm already working on its second wind. Each cavalry company would carry two hundred rounds of ammunition for each man, while in the wagons were freighted an additional three hundred more per soldier.

Last night at nine P.M. Mackenzie had come back from a card game and a conference with Crook and infantry commander Dodge. All evening it had been trying to snow, when the sky suddenly cleared and the bottom went out of the thermometers.

"We're going at dawn," Mackenzie announced to his orderlies as he stomped up through the fresh snow. "See that the company commanders are informed."

Then the mercurial colonel disappeared into his tent for the rest of what was left of that horrid night.

Chapter 18

14–18 November 1876

**Bloody Fight Between Sho-
shones and Sioux.**

THE INDIANS

**Sioux vs. Shoshones—A Village of the
Latter Wiped Out.**

SALT LAKE, November 2.—A report from Camp
Stambaugh, Wyoming, says a village of fifty lodges of
Shoshones was attacked October 30, by a large Sioux
war party, estimated at 1,300 lodges, at Pointed Rock,
near the scene of Captain Bates' fight, July, 1874, and
about ninety miles from Camp Stambaugh. As far as
learned only one Shoshone escaped by the name of
Humpy, who was the Indian that saved the life of Captain Henry, in Crook's second fight this summer.

The last of Dodge's infantry was finally ferried across the
North Platte that Tuesday morning in the overloaded wagons
easing down the ice-coated banks, the teamsters doing their best
to dodge the floating ice that bobbed along the surface of the
swift and swirling river some fifty yards wide at the ford, each
cake of the ice thrown against the ferry's sideboards with a re-
sounding and forceful collision.

Even Richard I. Dodge had confided to his personal diary, "The river is my terror."

Almost as much as he wanted to keep his foot soldiers warm and dry, the colonel had itched to get a leap on the younger Mackenzie—but already the cavalry was moving away into the sere hills streaked with snow. Dodge didn't have the last of his men across and on their way until 11:30 A.M. At stake each day in this unspoken race between foot and horse would be the best camping spots come sundown. Being second to get away from Fetterman put Dodge in a foul humor that would last for the next two days.

After days of intermittent snow, the sun was out that morning, hung in the sky like a pale, pewter glob behind the thin clouds. The temperature hovered at fourteen below zero.

To Seamus it didn't seem it could get any colder as he mounted up, tucked the tail of his long mackinaw about his legs, and set out with some of the other scouts, waving farewell to Kid Slaymaker and those of his whores still up after the expedition's last carouse before plunging into the Indian country.

A little west of north. Into the Powder River country searching out the Hunkpatila. The Crazy Horse people.

Donegan knew it was going to get a hell of a lot colder before he could once more hold Samantha in his arms. Before he would look into the face of his son and give the child a name.

Far in the advance he could see the dark column slowly snaking up what had become a familiar road that would lead them to old Fort Reno, like a writhing animal twisting across the white, endless landscape. On and on the bare hills and knolls and ridges lay tumbled against one another, each new one as devoid of brush and trees as the last, stretching into the gray horizon. For all any of them might know, Seamus thought as he pulled the wool muffler up to cover his mouth and nose, they could be marching across the austere, inhospitable surface of the moon.

Ahead of him and behind as well stretched Crook's Powder River Expedition, perhaps the best prepared and equipped force ever to plunge into this forbidding wilderness. Especially at this season. It made quite a sight: far out on each flank the hundreds of Indian auxiliaries, the neat column of infantry, ahead of them the wagon train and Tom Moore's four hundred mules, then the white scouts riding with Crook's headquarters group, and in the lead marched Mackenzie's cavalry.

As the day aged, the weather warmed too much to make for

good marching. The wind had piled the snow too deep at the sides of ridges and hillocks for easy passage, while the sun continued to relentlessly turn the snow to slush in open places, making for treacherous footing for the infantry following in the wake of all those wagons sliding this way and that as the drivers barked and cajoled, whipped and cursed their teams.

Dodge halted his infantry at the camping ground on Sage Creek after slogging eleven grueling miles. Mackenzie and the teamsters were obliged to push on another four miles before they could find sufficient water in Sage Creek for their animals—what there was had collected in ice-covered pools of brackish, soap-tinged water. As soon as the horses were unsaddled, the men spread out to scare up what they could of firewood. All they found was the smoky greasewood. Nor was there much in the way of grass for the animals. Fortunately, Crook had freighted both firewood and forage.

Shortly after taking up the march the morning of the fifteenth, some of the Pawnee discovered the tracks of three horses. Due to the condition of the ground, it proved difficult to determine if the animals wore iron shoes or not—so the trackers put their noses to the trail and took off at a lope.

"Can't help but think we're being watched by Crazy Horse's scouts," Crook mused that afternoon as they kept an eye on the horizon, watching for the return of those Pawnee.

In the afternoon two of the soldiers riding on the right flank were run in by four Indians, who gave the pair quite a fright with all their whooping and gunfire, but it wasn't until after the column made camp on the South Fork of the Cheyenne River, having put fifteen hard miles behind them, that the trackers returned to report that the trio of riders they had trailed all day had turned out to be white men.

"Miners, I'd wager," Seamus declared.

"More'n likely horse thieves," Dick Closter argued. The white-bearded packer spat a stream of brown tobacco juice out of the side of his mouth as he knelt to stir some beans in a blackened pot that steamed fragrantly, then smeared some of the brown dribble ever deeper into his snowy whiskers.

That night the entire command—cavalry, infantry, wagon and mule train, along with the Indian auxiliaries—all camped together for the first time, spread out along the Cheyenne where they could find enough room to graze the animals and throw down their bedrolls against the dropping temperatures as the stars winked into sight, the sheer and utter blackness of that clear winter sky sucking every last gesture of warmth from the heated breast of the earth.

Each night Seamus did as most of the others, bunking in with another man to share their blankets and body heat, after spreading their saddle blankets over "mattresses" fashioned from what dried grass and sagebrush they could gather to insulate them from the frozen ground.

At first light the column moved out again on the sixteenth, with Mackenzie's cavalry once more beating the fuming Dodge onto the trail the horses churned into a sodden mush for the foot-sloggers. Less than an hour after starting, all hands were halted and turned out to get the wagons and ambulances hauled up an especially bad stretch of the Reno Road, where the narrow iron tires skidded out of control on the icy prairie, unable to gain any purchase. Grunting and cursing side by side with the teams, muscling the laden wagons up a foot at a time by rope, the men finally reached the top of the long rise where they could at last gaze at the distant horizon, north by east at the hulking mounds of the Pumpkin Buttes. For the rest of the day most of the column was in plain sight of the rest of the outfit, even though it was strung out for at least five miles or more.

"Make no mistake about it," the old mule-whacker told Donegan that night at camp after another eighteen exhausting miles, "we're in Injun country now, sonny. How's your belly?"

"Just a touch of the bad water, Dick," Seamus replied. He lay by the fire, an arm slung over his eyes, feeling the rumble of that dysentery bubble through his system. "I'll be fine by morning."

Donegan wasn't alone. Almost half the command suffered diarrhea to one degree or another already, forced to drink from the mineral-laced streams. The horses fared no better, many of them suffering the same symptoms, which made for a messy stretch of trail for the infantry forced to plod along behind them.

Seamus slept fitfully that night as the sky closed down upon them, dreaming of holding Sam again, of clutching his son to his breast, smelling the babe's breath after it had suckled Sam's warm milk.

Dear God in heaven—make this a swift strike. Keep your hand at my shoulder as you have always done, I pray. For their sake . . . for their sake and not for mine.

That night of the sixteenth as William Earl Smith worked at the mess fire with two other orderlies, a courier rode in from Fetterman carrying parcels bursting with mail for the men. All those smoky, glowing fires fed with greasewood helped to hold back the gloom as men read one another their news from the States, greetings from loved ones back East, or clippings from newspapers many weeks old. Spirits ran high, despite the plummeting temperatures as the wind quartered out of the north, rank with the smell of snow in the air.

One man was far from buoyant at that campsite halfway to Reno Cantonment. Colonel Richard Irving Dodge figured he had taken just about all he could of the brash and arrogant Ranald Slidell Mackenzie, and stomped over to the cavalry camp to have matters settled once and for all.

After presenting himself at Mackenzie's tent, the colonels had themselves a good heart-to-heart—finding more in common than Dodge had supposed. The cavalry commander offered the infantry commander the use of two of his orderlies for the remainder of the march, besides suggesting they alternate days taking up the lead. In that way they would eliminate entirely the competition to be the first to arrive at the good camping grounds. Mackenzie's largess must have relaxed Dodge, for they soon began to confide in one another their common complaints about their superior.

"General Crook passes for a Sybarite," the high-fashioned and fastidious Dodge whined, "who is utterly contemptuous of anything like luxury or even comfort—yet he has the most luxurious surroundings considering the necessity for short allowance that I have ever seen taken to the field by a general officer."

"I suppose I'll have to agree with you," Mackenzie admitted, an officer who took pride in his uniform and the dashing figure he cut. "The way he dresses himself—you couldn't tell him from the lowliest man along."

"There is no doubt of Crook's courage, energy, will," Dodge continued, "but I am loath to say I begin to believe he is a humbug—who hopes to make his reputation by assuming qualities foreign to him. One thing is most certain. He is the very worst-mannered man I have ever seen in his position, though his ill manners seem to be the result rather of ignorance than of deliberate will. I believe him to be warm-hearted, but his estimate of a man will, I think, be discovered to be founded not on what a man can or will do for the service, but what he can or will do for Crook."

"He does have his own way about things, doesn't he?" Mackenzie observed wryly. "Far different is he from the man I served in the Shenandoah."

"Quite. Yes," Dodge snorted sourly. "I arrived here an hour before my men this afternoon to hunt up a good campsite and reported to the general for instructions. He sent me on my way to hunt for myself—all the choice spots already appropriated for his Indians and his mules."

"I've got the feeling those Indians and mules are Crook's favorite hobbies," Mackenzie observed. "Hobbies he plays with while we are about the business of making war on the hostiles."

"It disgusts me that those damned redskins wash the entrails from the beef carcasses in the creeks where our men are forced to drink somewhere downstream. He scarcely treats you and me with the dignity we deserve," Dodge grumped, "while he'll talk for hours with a stinking redskin or one of his dirty scouts."

By the time the two colonels shook hands and the infantry commander parted for his bivouac, it was clear to William Earl Smith, that unlettered former railroad brakeman from Peoria, that Dodge loathed the general while Mackenzie merely tolerated Crook until the time arrived for him to break off on his own with the cavalry. That very evening two men had forged a bond that would last out the waning of the Powder River Expedition.

Wind and icy snow returned to batter the command with the gray light of false dawn the morning of the seventeenth. Horses and mules stood facing south, their rumps and tails tucked into the freezing gale. Crook sent the wagons to the front of the march while the cavalry hung back in camp until nearly nine A.M. Fires were all but futile as the horse soldiers shivered and stomped about, finally allowed to break camp and set out on the road into the teeth of the growing fury.

Rather than flakes, the storm flung icy pellets at them, coating every man and beast with a layer of white, stinging the eyes and every patch of bare skin. Horses and mules plodded into the shifting winds, their muzzles straining forward with their task, barely able to breathe. Stout-hearted infantrymen struggled forward a foot at a time, hunched over, heads lowered as they covered mile after mile of that high, rolling mesa country. Somewhere past midday the command climbed to the top of the divide, where they finally looked down upon the Powder River Valley. Far to the northwest lay the Big Horn Mountains, all but their base hidden by the storm that failed to let up, icy flakes lancing down from a sky that continued to close in about the column with every passing hour, obscuring all but a frosty ring around the sun and creating that peculiar western phenomenon the frontiersmen referred to as a sun dog.

It was not until the late afternoon that the snow let up and the wind finally died, about the time Crook passed the order to make camp where the men could find room for their bedrolls and graze for the stock along the Dry Fork of the Powder. Some of Tom Moore's packers had reached the campsite an hour before the first of the column, reporting that they had flushed out a small party of Indians who had scurried off east toward Pumpkin Buttes. The weary, cold men had struggled through another twenty miles of high prairie.

Just after dark two ice-coated frontiersmen showed up at the cavalry bivouac with a trio of Shoshone warriors, asking for General Crook's camp. Mackenzie came out of his tent and introduced himself in a wreath of frost tinged orange by the nearby fire.

"Pleased to make your acquaintance, General Mackenzie," the taller of the pair replied as he dismounted and walked up to shake hands. "Name's Tom Cosgrove. This here's Texas Bob Eckles—but he goes by Yancy. We come to report in to Crook."

"You've brought in the Snakes, I take it."

"A hundred five of 'em, waiting up the road at Reno Cantonment for you," Cosgrove declared. "Every last one hankering to get in their licks on Crazy Horse just about as bad as any, I figure."

"The old chief Washakie with you again this time?"

"No," Cosgrove said, shaking his head. "Old man's got a fit of the rheumatiz pretty bad . . . ," and he rubbed his own gloves together. "We both figured it wouldn't do to have him out in this goddamn cold."

"No matter—the general will be pleased to know you're here," Mackenzie added. "Myself, I've heard tell a little of you, Cosgrove."

"Oh?" The squaw man stopped in his tracks and turned with renewed attention on Mackenzie.

"From a friend of yours who served me two years ago down in Texas."

"At the Palo Duro?" Cosgrove asked, his voice rising in excitement. "By damn, you must mean that big gray-eyed Irishman Donegan!"

"One and the same."

"Where would I find him?"

"Likely somewhere over by the packers, I hear," Mackenzie

offered. "Tell me, Mr. Cosgrove—is it true what I've heard about him and one of your Shoshone bucks standing over Guy Henry's body, guarding it with their lives at the Rosebud fight?"*

"If what you heard was that they stood back to back and shot at Sioux until their guns was empty—then they set to swinging those damned rifles like they was war clubs—cracking skulls and breaking bones, pitted agin Sioux bullets . . . then you heard right, Colonel."

Breaking camp at daylight on Saturday morning, the eighteenth, the column continued down the valley of the Dry Fork of the Powder through the austere, ocher countryside streaked and pocked with skiffs of icy snow beneath a graying sky. By midmorning, Mackenzie had clearly become impatient to reach Reno Cantonment. He turned to his orderly from Peoria, Illinois.

"Smith, come with me." Then kicked his horse into a lope.

Together the two jumped ahead of the column through the rest of that morning, anxious to cover the nineteen miles. By early afternoon they had reached the Powder River itself, stopping momentarily at the icy, hoof-pocked ford.

"This is gonna play hell on Crook's wagons," Mackenzie muttered, then urged his horse down the graded slope into the water.

Through the sluggish, ice-choked water the two riders pushed their mounts, up the north bank where they plodded slowly through the ruins of old Fort Reno: now nothing more than a jumble of charred timbers, abandoned caissons, and wagon running gears poking their black limbs out of the icy mantle of white.

Turning upstream, Mackenzie and Smith crossed the last three miles to reach the Reno Cantonment, established in mid-October as a supply base for the army's expeditions when Crook decided to press his advantage against the winter roamers. Situated on a low stream terrace some ten feet above the floodplain on the west bank of the Powder, the post sat nearly opposite the mouth of the Dry Fork in a big, gentle bend in the river. Here the soldiers could be close to water as they went about constructing their log and dugout structures on fairly level land.

Reno Cantonment also added a military presence here at the southern edge of those hunting grounds most fiercely defended by the Sioux and Cheyenne, while Nelson Miles's Tongue

---

*Reap the Whirlwind, Vol. 9, The Plainsmen Series.

River Cantonment established an undeniable presence at the northern edge of the traditional hostile territory. As far as the War Department saw the situation, it appeared they had the enemy surrounded and contained, if not corralled. All that was left was mopping things up.

A Pennsylvanian by birth, Captain Edwin Pollock of the Ninth Infantry had first joined the volunteers to fight the rebellion in the South, becoming regular army after the Civil War. An officer whom the carping Dodge characterized as "the most conceited ass that every existed. He thinks he can give advice to the Almighty and talks to General Crook and everybody else as if he tolerated them. . . ." Pollock commanded the army's new supply base on the Powder River, nothing more than fifteen log dugouts scraped out of the nearby embankments, along with a crude hospital and cavalry corrals—all of them the barest of shelter thrown up against the horrendous thunderstorms and the blinding blizzards that frequented that country. Nonetheless, here they were within sight of the Big Horn Mountains.

Earl Smith found the captain to be no different from most other officers—tolerable at best. Presenting themselves at the commanding officer's quarters, Mackenzie introduced himself and asked Pollock to recommend a site for the cavalry camp.

"About a mile below the fort," the captain replied, gesturing downstream. "There's level ground enough for your battalions, with a high embankment that will block most of the wind coming out of the north and west. Close by, your stock will find good grazing along the bottoms and up on the benches."

The first of the command reached the ford at midafternoon, the wagon train hoving into sight soon thereafter. But true to Mackenzie's fears, the teamsters had their worst struggle of the journey so far in getting those 168 wagons and 7 ambulances down the icy corduroy of the south bank, and across the soupy quagmire of the river bottom, where the half-frozen gumbo seized hold of the wheels and refused to let go.

The cold air turned an icy blue as the sun began to fall into the last quarter of the southwestern sky, soldiers and civilians alike cursing, whipping, flogging the animals, throwing their shoulders against those wagons, icy water swirling about their thighs as the men struggled to muscle the first freighters across. The process only grew steadily worse as the river bottom became all the more churned with hooves, wheels, and boots. At last Mackenzie organized his men together in relays, throwing ropes around the struggling teams and hauling each wagon across the Powder by sheer willpower alone.

As each wagon clattered up the north bank onto the flat ground, a cheer went up from the exhausted relay that would now get a few minutes of rest while another twenty men slid down the icy bank, locked their frozen hands around the inch-thick ropes, then set their feet in the rutted mud and laid their backs into the task at hand.

One by one by one, Crook's supplies crossed the murky Powder. From here on out, the expedition was firmly in this last great hunting ground of the Sioux and Cheyenne. Ten summers before, Red Cloud had warned the army that it would forfeit every soldier who crossed the Powder. But after a decade Red Cloud had become a toothless old lap dog, corralled at Camp Robinson.

Yet somewhere north of here lay the village of Crazy Horse.

From the way Smith saw Mackenzie staring into the distance that twilight, the colonel must have been trying to sense where he would find his elusive quarry—as he had done time and again chasing down the slippery Quanah Parker.*

Never before had the Fourth Cavalry marched so far north to fight an enemy. For Ranald Mackenzie the stakes had never been so high.

---

*Dying Thunder, Vol. 7, The Plainsmen Series.

Chapter 19

18–19 November 1876

"**D**on't you agree, Seamus?" John Bourke asked that Saturday evening at their fire near the packers' camp as icy shards of snow danced and pirouetted on a capricious wind about their bivouac. "That God is on the side of the heaviest battalions?"

"Sounds like a god-blamed army maxim." Donegan answered in turn.

"Napoleon," Bourke replied.

"But it sounds to me that if you have the heaviest battalions—the most men and secure supply lines—then you don't need to worry about God being on your side, Johnny."

"My point exactly!" Bourke cried with glee. "Here we are, within sight of the Big Horn Mountains once again, much better equipped than we were last March—ready, willing, and able to catch the Crazy Horse warrior bands laying low in their lodges to wait out the winter. While we have the men, the matériel, the supply lines to make that red bastard's capture a sure thing."

Behind them a voice called out, "Is that the Irishman's voice I hear?"

Out of the dark appeared the swarthy half-breed. It brought a smile to Donegan's face. "Last I heard of you at Laramie, Crook said you was taken terrible sick and the soldiers hauled your worthless carcass down to Cheyenne City in the back of a wagon."

Frank Grouard held out his hand to shake, but Seamus promptly pushed it aside and gave the scout a fierce embrace.

The half-breed pounded Donegan on the shoulder, saying, "There and then I figured I should go farther west, maybe back to Utah to get myself on the mend—but what do you know? On the train I laughed myself into a cure."

"You're pulling our legs!" Bourke declared, coming over to shake Grouard's hand.

"The honest truth," Grouard replied with a smile, holding a hand up in testament to the fact. "A good laugh will always cure what ails you."

Seamus asked, "So how'd you end up getting here?"

"Rode in with the paymaster from Fort Fetterman."

"Paymaster?" Bourke almost squealed in excitement. "Damn, but don't they always show up where a man has no place to spend his money!"

Grouard went on to explain, "You'd been two days gone from Fetterman when I was fixing to take off. So I offered to guide that paymaster in here, protecting all that mail and pay for all you soldiers."

"You made sure that paymaster reported in to the general so we can all have us a round of drinks, didn't you, Grouard?" Bourke cheered.

"Sure as hell did," Frank replied. "If I didn't, I figure there's a few hundred unpaid soldiers ready to stretch my neck with a rope!"

Is that Frank Grouard out there?" Crook stuck his head out the flaps of a nearby tent glowing with lamps, the small space filled not only with a map-strewn table, two cots, and a Sibley stove, but with Mackenzie and Dodge.

Grouard began moving that way, saying, "It is, General."

Mackenzie immediately pushed past Crook and held out his hand at the flaps. "Ranald Mackenzie. Commanding, Fourth Cavalry. I've heard a lot about you, Grouard."

"Good to meet you too, General."

"Well, Frank—what have you seen?" Mackenzie asked as he slipped a glove back on his right hand.

"Seen heaps."

Mackenzie scratched his chin. "So where are the reds?"

Gesturing with a slight toss of his head to the west, Grouard answered, "I make 'em over in the mountains."

As Donegan stood there watching the three expedition leaders, he once more noticed the stark contrasts between the men. While Crook seemed oblivious to his dress—wearing worn and dirty wool coats and fur caps naked of any insignia or badge of office, even to the point of carelessly tying up the long ends of his bushy red beard into a pair of braided points with twine—Mackenzie and Dodge, on the other hand, were the noble specimens of a cavalry or infantry officer: wearing their complete uniforms with pride.

"John," Crook said, turning to Bourke, "bring Three Bears to see us."

"Something up, General?"

Crook's eyes bounced over the small gathering of officers and civilizations at that fire outside his tent. "Yes. This time I've decided to keep Cosgrove's Shoshones as reserves and let the Indians most familiar with this ground do my scouting for me."

"Makes good sense," Grouard replied.

"I'm glad you agree," the general replied. "I've put Lieutenant Schuyler over the Snakes, to work with Cosgrove and Washakie's two sons who came along. But come on inside now, Frank. We've got some talking to do before I figure to send some of those Sioux scouts north to feel out where we go from here."

"Very good, General," Bourke replied, pulling on his wool gloves and stepping away. "I'll return shortly."

Well after moonset eight of the Red Cloud Agency Sioux and six of the Arapaho slipped quietly into the dark, rationed for four days, instructed to scout north by west toward the mountains.

By the time the expedition had reached Reno Cantonment, many of the Indian scouts had sorted out for themselves who were some of the more powerful soldiers. Clearly Crook, Mackenzie, and Dodge, along with those men nominally placed over the auxiliaries . . . but to the warriors' way of thinking, one of the soldier chiefs with the biggest medicine was Lieutenant Charles Rockwell, commissary officer for the Fourth Cavalry. After all, it was he who had unquestioned authority and control over such immense stores of the coveted bacon, sugar, and coffee! But try as they might to get Rockwell to trade items of clothing and beadwork for heaps of rations, the young lieutenant remained steadfast in his duty and played no favorites as he and his men kept a lock on the valuable foodstuffs.

With the arrival of the paymaster that night, a spontaneous celebration erupted among the cold men as there was at least a cramped log trading store close by the cantonment where the soldiers could fritter away their meager month's wages on the sutler's crude whiskey.

Dawn of the nineteenth found the sky lowering and a new

storm approaching out of the west over the mountains. As soon as the wind quartered out of the north, the temperature seemed to fall ever farther. While most men continued throwing away their pay on wild debauchery, a few in each outfit pooled their money and purchased tinned tomatoes, potatoes, and other delicacies, making for a brief change in their drab and monotonous diet. For miles up and down the Powder River, infantry soldiers and cavalry troopers, teamsters, packers, and scouts caroused noisily.

"If Crazy Horse had any doubt the army's coming after him," John Bourke said as half a hundred men hurried to watch a fistfight broken out a few yards away, "that red bastard will be able to hear this bunch all the way to the slopes of the Big Horns!"

Seamus chuckled, sipping at his steaming coffee. He was content and relaxed, lounging on his saddle blanket, his back against a downed cottonwood trunk, feet to the fire. "I know for damned certain this isn't where the devil was born, but from the sounds of it, Johnny—this seems like the place the devil was sure as hell raised up!"

The lieutenant stood, tossing the last dregs of his coffee onto the snowy ground as dusty flakes tumbled all about them. "You're coming over to the council?"

"Is it that time already?"

Stuffing his big turnip watch back inside his wool vest, Bourke replied, "Soon enough. I should try to be there before the warrior groups show up."

After taking another drink of his coffee, Donegan asked, "This council really has to do with the Sioux complaining to Crook?"

Nodding, the lieutenant said, "When the general had Three Bears come to his tent last night to enlist some warriors to go scout the foot of the mountains—the Sioux war chief seized the opportunity to complain to Crook that the Pawnee hadn't been treating them all that kindly."

"Kindly!" Donegan shrieked. "Mother of God, but they're blood enemies—by the saints! Back to their grandfather's grandfather!"

"C'mon, Irishman—this ought to prove interesting to watch."

Seamus stood, bringing his pint tin of coffee steaming in his hand. "How right you are, Johnny. Here I been thinking Crook was making himself a reputation as an Injin-fighter . . . and now he's got to go and play diplomat between his own bleeming Injins!"

Crook's primary purpose in holding this council with the leaders of his four hundred Indian auxiliaries was to have them eventually come to understand his ground rules for the fight that was sure to come.

While the Sioux had come to complain they were being snubbed by their traditional enemies, for the general there were clearly bigger fish to fry. Yet as the Pawnee showed up arrayed in their full uniforms, and the Shoshone arrived wearing their native dress mixed with some white man's clothing garnered over the decades of friendly relations, the Sioux and their allies came to the meeting in their war paint and scalp shirts. Frank North and Tom Cosgrove hurried to call the open provocation to the general's attention. John Bourke watched as Crook quickly dispensed with this matter of Indian dress by waving it off with a hand and going to seat himself near the center of the great crescent gathered just outside Captain Pollock's tiny quarters at Reno Cantonment.

When all had fallen quiet, the general told the Indians, "A new day has come to this land. You, as well as ourselves, are servants of the Great Father in Washington, and we all ought to dress in the uniform of the soldier, and for the time being we all ought to be brothers."

He waited while the first translations were begun, then continued. "I am here to tell you that your peoples must put aside differences from the past and remain friends with the other bands. We have a job to do, and I hired you to do it. It is most important that when an army goes into battle, we are all in that battle side by side, united in action. So—if you want to fight among yourselves—then you have no place with me. Decide now if you are here to be part of this army."

He let the many translations finish, the babble of at least eight different tongues rumbling around the crescent where the leaders sat and smoked in their blankets, considering the words of Three Stars. Then Crook continued.

"If, however, it is more important for you to complain and to attack your neighbor, I will take your guns and send you home on foot. You will not have a weapon, you will not have a pony. And you will be every bit as poor as I am going to make the followers of Crazy Horse."

Firelit copper faces set hard when those words went round

that council, words so harsh that Crook wanted to be certain there was no misunderstanding. "I will ask it again—is there any among you who want to complain about the others? Any among you who want to give up your weapons and ponies right now and turn back for your homes?"

This time many of the scout leaders were quicker to speak, rising to their feet to address Crook and the assembly. All turned to the general to announce that they understood the reason for his remarks, promising that they would put aside their petty differences and remain friends with the others for the sake of the war that was to come. It was particularly moving when Three Bears arose, signaled one of his young warriors to follow him, bringing along a prized pony. The two Lakota walked directly to stand before the Pawnee delegation.

He held his hand out to *Li-Heris-oo-la-shar*, one of the Pawnee sergeants, who was also known as Frank White. They shook, then Three Bears spoke, telling his old enemy and that council, "Brother, we want to be friends—and as a sign of my sincerity I give you this warhorse. From this day on, your fight is my fight."

White stood, unbuckling his prized revolver from his waist and handed it to the Sioux war chief. "I too wish to bury the past. We are friends now. We are both warriors, with a job to do. I will fight by your side. Your enemies will be my enemies, and my lodge will be your lodge."

As much as John Bourke had been around Indians in Crook's Arizona campaigns against Cochise, wherein the general had enticed one band of Apache to track down another band of Apache, the young lieutenant had never in his wildest dreams believed he would truly see these ancient enemies forging a lasting partnership to fight the last of the hostiles. Although the council took on a dreamlike air of friendly festivity, Crook was clearly pleased with how things had turned out.

After more speeches professing friendship were traded among the Pawnee, Sioux, Cheyenne, and Arapaho, as well as that scattering of Nez Perce, Bannock, and Ute warriors who had come over from the Wind River with Cosgrove's Shoshone, the general continued, waxing in a most uncustomary eloquence.

"All these vast plains, all these mountains and valleys will soon be filled with a pushing, hardworking population. The game will soon be exterminated. Domestic cattle will take its place. The Indian must make up his mind, and make it up now, to live like the white man and be at peace with him—or be wiped off the face of the earth. Peace is what the white man wants. But war is what the white man is prepared for."

Every few words, Crook halted briefly while the translators caught up in their many tongues.

"I want to impress upon you that rule by law is not tyranny. You will come to learn that people who obey the laws of their land are those who in turn have the greatest liberty. It is not the white man, but the Indian, who is afraid when he goes to sleep at night, afraid that he and his family might be murdered before morning by some prowling enemy."

John Bourke watched the way so many of the dark eyes furtively glanced at the other bands.

"You are receiving good pay as soldiers," Crook reminded them, "and so long as you behave yourselves, and so long as I can find work for you to do, you shall be my soldiers. But you must never spend your pay foolishly. Save every cent of it that you can to buy cows and broodmares. While you are sleeping, the calves and the colts will be growing—and someday you'll awake and find yourself a rich man. Then you'll be ashamed to call upon the Great Father for help. When you capture the enemy's herds in the coming fight, they will be divided among your peoples. They will be yours to keep. Use those captured horses wisely—not for war, but to make a living for your families."

Around that crescent many of the Indians grunted their approval.

Then Sharp Nose, leader of the Arapaho scouts, stood to speak. "I have waited a long time to meet all these people and make peace. We have been living a long time with the white man and have followed the white man's road and do what he says. I hope these other bands will do the same. We have all met here today to make peace, and I hope we'll remain at peace. And I hope that General Crook will take pity on us and help us. . . . I hold my hand up to the Great Spirit and swear I'll stick with General Crook as long as I'm with him. When this war is over and I get home, I want to live like a white man and have implements to work with. We have made peace with these people here today, and we'd like to have a letter sent home to let our people know about it."

More of the war chiefs and their leaders grunted in agreement or raised their voices to signal they were one with the soldier chief.

Frank White stood proudly in his dark-blue uniform, his face and shaved head savagely painted, large brass rings hung from the edges of his ears, feathers tied to his small, circular scalp lock tossing on the cold wind. Gesturing to Crook, the Pawnee scout said, "This is our head chief talking to us and asking us to be brothers. I hope the Great Spirit will smile on us. . . . The Pawnee have lived with the white men a long time and know how strong they are. Brothers, I don't think there is one of you can come out here today and say you have ever heard of the Pawnee killing a white man . . . I suppose you know the Pawnee are civilized. We plow, farm, and work the ground like white people."

He then turned to Crook, saying, "Father, it is so what the Arapaho said. We have all gone on this expedition to help you and hope it may be a successful one. . . . This is all I have to say. I am glad you have told us what you want done about the captured stock. The horses taken will help us to work our land."

At last Crook stood before them, bringing the assembly to silence as he collected his thoughts, scratching at a cheek, and finally said, "To bring this council to an end, I want you all to hear my words clearly. When we come upon a village of hostiles, you must make sure your men do not kill women and children. Any man of you who kills a woman or a child will be punished severely by my hand."

Bourke knew the general was laying down his order not so much out of some Anglo-American cultural trait as out of a carefully considered military strategy.

"When we do not kill the women and children—instead we capture them—we can use those women and children as hostages to lure in the men. The fighters. The warriors. It is not the Great Father's desire to kill the Indians if they will obey the laws of this land. On the other hand, we want to find the villages of our enemies, to force them to give up their ponies and guns so that in the future they will behave themselves."

After supper late that evening, Bourke sat with others at the fire outside Crook's headquarters tent. He said, "The war's over already."

"What makes you say so?" Donegan asked.

"Because the Indians we've been fighting are now our friends, and they're even friends with the Indians who have always been our friends."

"Perhaps you're right," the Irishman replied as he stared into the flames of that welcome fire as the temperature dropped like lead shot in a bucket of water. "What Crook accomplished today without firing a shot, what he did last month in capturing the ponies and the weapons—was more than we accomplished on the Powder River last March. Or on the Rosebud in June.* Or beneath the Slim Buttes last September."

Then Donegan held up his coffee tin. "More than a toast, I make this my prayer: that this goddamned war is as you say it is, Johnny. May our bloody little war truly be all but over."

---

*Reap the Whirlwind, Vol. 9, The Plainsmen Series.

Chapter 20

Freezing Moon
1876

A sliver of the old moon still hung in the sky this morning before the sun crept from its bed in the east. With sixty-eight winters behind him, an old man like Morning Star was up and stirring, out to relieve his bladder. It seemed the older he got, the more urgent was this morning mission.

Before too long would come the Big Freezing Moon. And the hard times would begin. As the autumn aged into winter, more and more agency people wandered in to join the great village while the men hunted for the meat the women would dry over smoky fires. Game had been plentiful on the west side of the White Mountains,* but here along the east slope the hunting had become hard. The men were forced to go farther, hunting great distances out onto the plains, among the tortuous tracks of coulees and ravines, the dry washes where the deer and antelope had taken shelter from cold winds. A man of the *Ohmeseheso* was duty-bound to provide for his family and the village. Survival of the People was more important than earning coups in war or stealing another tribe's ponies. As the white man tightened his noose around this great country and the game disappeared, Morning Star felt the pull on his inner spirit which all young men must also feel. Usually the snows brought elk and

---

*Big Horn Mountains.

deer down from the high places in these mountains touched this morning with a gentle pink as the sun poked up its head.

Perhaps something else had driven the animals away.

But he did not want to think about that. Morning Star stoically remained faithful in his belief that the Powers would protect the People for all time if they would only resist the white man's seduction, the white man's destruction.

Yes! Perhaps the Powers would truly guard the People this time, especially now that both sacred objects were here together in their great village.

Morning Star's people had camped along a small stream at the base of the White Mountains when Black Hairy Dog arrived from the Indian Territory far to the south. There was loud and joyous celebration in the village when the old warrior who had succeeded his dead father, Stone Forehead, as keeper of the *Maahotse*, the Sacred Medicine Arrows, rode in. Black Hairy Dog's wife rode on a second pony behind him, carrying the arrows in their kit-fox-skin quiver on her back—in that ancient, reverent way proscribed by Sweet Medicine.

In hurrying from that hot land to the south to reach the Powder River country, the warrior, who had seen fifty-three winters, and his wife had bumped into a wandering soldier patrol in the country off to the southeast, not long after making a wide circle around Red Cloud's agency. When the soldiers began their chase, the couple divided the arrows and galloped off in different directions. Days later on the upper reaches of the Powder River the two found one another with great rejoicing and happy tears. With the four arrows reunited, the couple continued their journey to search for the great village in the mountains.

At long last both Great Covenants of the People rested in their sacred lodges at the center of the camp crescent, the horns of the semicircle opening, like the lodge doors, toward *Noahavose*, their Sacred Mountain. From its high places flowed endless new life for the People, invigorating both the Sacred Buffalo Hat and the Sacred Medicine Arrows. Now Morning Star could dare to hope once more.

Up till now, everything else had been only prayer.

More than once he had confided to Little Wolf that the People should not associate so closely with their belligerent cousins, the Lakota. Though the scars had faded from his flesh, the deep wound to Morning Star's pride had never healed in ten long winters. When the soldier chief Carrington had wanted to talk to the *Ohmeseheso* leaders at the Pine Fort,* Morning Star had joined the other headmen in visiting the soldiers. That night, back in their camp a short distance from the fort, they were surrounded by a large band of Lakota warriors led by Man Afraid of His Horses and a youngster named Crazy Horse, Lakota warriors who beat Morning Star and the others with their bows— humiliating the old *Tse-Tsehese* chiefs for betraying their alliance by talking to the hated white man.

Ever since, Morning Star had been wary of the Lakota in general, and Crazy Horse in particular. Even Little Wolf, a just and courageous man, tended to distrust the Lakota more with every season this conflict dragged on and on. Unlike most of their people, Little Wolf had refused to learn the Lakota tongue, only one of the increasing symptoms of tension in the tribes' long alliance.

Morning Star turned upon hearing the shouts and cries from the far north side of camp. On his spindly old legs, the chief hurried with the others brought from their beds to see what had caused the disturbance. By the time he arrived, there were hundreds crowding in on the two Lakota riders who had been visiting the People and two days ago departed to rejoin their own people camped with Crazy Horse on the Sheep River† at the mouth of Box Elder Creek. Now the pair were telling and retelling their story as more and more men and women came up to join that excited throng.

"After sundown the day we left your village, we drew near what we thought was a camp of our people north of here. But something just did not feel right. We stopped short of the village and decided to investigate. Waiting until first light, we finally saw some people coming down to the river to swim. The closer we looked, the more we could tell it was not a Lakota camp."

"Who was it?" someone cried out from the crowd.

"Were they friends?"

"Were they our enemies?"

"They were Shoshone!" one of the Lakota shouted.

"Enemies!" a woman screeched.

"How many?"

The other Lakota answered, "Not many. We can kill them all!"

---

*Fort Phil Kearny, Dakota Territory—autumn, 1866.
†Big Horn River.

"Yes! Kill them all!" was the cry taken up by the young warriors.

In a matter of moments the whole village was abuzz with battle plans and preparation. The various leaders from the warrior societies quickly decided who among them would go to fight, and who would have to be left behind to guard the village while most of the fighting men were absent. Before the sun had climbed off the bare tops of the cottonwood trees, the war party galloped off. Women went about preparing for a great feast when the men would return.

The next day their victorious warriors came home, carrying the many scalps and fingers taken from the enemy dead, as well as the hands of twelve Shoshone babies killed in the fight where they left no survivors—bringing back a lone infant they would raise as one of their own people, taken from the breast of a brave Shoshone woman. But for that victory, the People had paid a heavy price.

Because of the battle casualties, the *Tse-Tsehese* moved camp down the foot of the mountains, and the village remained in muted mourning that first night. The following day at sunset they began their victory dance. It began snowing again, fat flakes falling so thick that they hissed into the great skunk, that huge bonfire the warrior societies built and lighted for the celebration. Each warrior's wife brought out the scalps her husband had taken while he recited his battle exploits—telling how the enemy had been packed and ready to move for the day when the warriors attacked; telling how the enemy ran, leaving all their goods and ponies and took to the hills where they could throw up some breastworks of rocks and brush; from there the Shoshone put up a hard fight—Little Shield, Walking Man, Young Spotted Wolf, and Twins were all seriously wounded in the fight, and the Shoshone killed nine *Tse-Tsehese* warriors in their desperate defense; the fighting raged until sundown, when the last of the enemy was killed. The dancing and feasting continued throughout the night as the stars whirled overhead.

And in the morning, Little Wolf, another of the Old-Man Chiefs, came to tell Morning Star that someone had stolen his ponies overnight while the camp was celebrating.

"Who could have done that?"

"Not the Shoshone," Little Wolf speculated.

"No, not them. The attack took care of them."

"I think the *Ooetaneo-o*, the Crow People. From the tracks I followed a ways, the thieves came from the north."

"Over the mountains?" Morning Star asked.

"Yes, I think so."

"Why would they steal only your ponies?"

Little Wolf wagged his head, as if attempting to sort it out. "Perhaps to lay a trap for one of us, a few of us—whoever will go after those ponies. Not the whole band."

"Are you going after your horses?"

"No," Little Wolf said, gesturing with his hands moving outward from his chest. "I give the ponies to the Crow People. I will not go after them."

Morning Star watched his old friend walk away. It was a strange feeling inside him now. For this was the only time in his long, long memory that the People allowed stolen ponies to go with the thieves without giving chase.

The village moved again that day, to the mouth of Striped Stick Creek on the Powder River. As the women raised the lodges and started the fires, many of the men rode down the Powder hunting for deer and antelope. In the evening when they returned they brought the news of finding many, many tracks of iron-shod American horses tramping through the snow and mud, finding the ruts cut by the white man's wagon wheels too—all of them moving north by west along the divide south of the Powder River.

"Surely they go to that small soldier camp beside the Powder," Little Wolf observed that night as the old men and war chiefs gathered to discuss what course of action to take.

"There are always wagons coming and going from that place where the soldiers live in their dirt lodges," Yellow Eagle said. He was one of the hunters who had seen the tracks for himself. "This was not the same. Too many wagons. Too many horses and walk-a-heaps."

Last Bull growled, "They are coming to look for us!"

"We do not know that yet," Morning Star quieted the alarmist.

"We should find out," Little Wolf decided.

And the rest agreed. They decided to select four wolves to investigate what the tracks truly meant. The Old-Man Chiefs instructed the two Servant Chiefs to handpick certain young men with specific talents to go on this important mission. The Servant Chiefs went first to the lodge of Hail. There they took the young man by the arms and brought him to the Council Lodge. Again they went out and returned with Crow Necklace, one of the most respected Crazy Dog little chiefs. Again they went out and brought back Young Two Moon. Finally they returned to the Council Lodge with the last of the sacred four, High Wolf.

When the wolves were seated in a line before the old chiefs, Morning Star explained, "We have selected you four because we know we can depend upon you to go out and follow the trail Yellow Eagle and the others discovered to the south. When you find the trail, stay with it. Do not leave it until you learn who made the tracks, and where they are going. Why they are in this country."

Then Little Wolf said, "Perhaps the trail will meet another party somewhere. As Morning Star has said, we are depending upon you to find out the answers to all our questions and to return with what we must know. Now, go catch up your strongest ponies, but return to this lodge before you set out on your journey."

When the four had returned with their horses, weapons, blankets, and coats, the chiefs led them through the village in a long procession behind the Old-Man Crier who sang out, "Behold! I come with four young men for whom we will look in the days to come. For whom our ears will listen in the days to come. They are going out to look for the tracks of those who have sneaked into our country. This sacred four will return here when they have news of these enemies!"

The four companies drawn from units of the Fourth, Ninth, and Twenty-third infantries to man Reno Cantonment certainly enjoyed their visitors and did all they could to join in on the revelry those first two days after Crook's men were paid and all hell broke loose. The carouse allowed Pollock's men a brief respite from the ongoing construction expanding the warehouses, cavalry corrals, teamster shed, blacksmith shack, and the company mess kitchens, each one built of logs "half-above-ground."

During the night of the nineteenth three shots were fired in the raucous camp, leading Colonel Dodge to call upon General Crook to have the sutler's saloon closed. Dodge came back to the infantry camp grumbling and cursing the general: Crook had refused because he was a personal friend of the trader, and together they were partners in an Oregon sheep ranch.

So rowdy was the nonstop celebration that Dodge himself went to appeal to Pollock, asking that the cantonment commander close down the trader's saloon. Little did the officers know that the sutler was in cahoots with another civilian who had set up an awning over his peddler's cart some distance upstream in a copse of cottonwood, where many of the horse soldiers had been going to cut and peel the cottonwood bark to feed to their mounts as the snowstorm continued into the night.

More shots were fired in the cavalry camp by drunken soldiers after moonrise. Investigating, some of Dodge's officers discovered the whiskey peddler, confiscated his goods, and knocked in the tops of the kegs with their rifle butts, spilling all that heady saddle varnish across the frozen ground.

Still, they were too late for one of the Fifth Cavalry troopers who had already stumbled away from the scene by himself, down to the icy bank, where he tripped and fell into the Powder River. Soaked to the gills, he belly-crawled onto the muddy bank, exhausted and unable to move any farther. At sunrise his bunkie awoke and went looking for the missing trooper, finding him dead in the frozen mud beside the river. His company scratched a hole out of the unforgiving, icy ground and laid their comrade to rest late that afternoon of the twentieth as the howling gales of wind-driven snow began to taper off, there to sleep through eternity beneath the flaky sod of Indian country.

That afternoon a party of thirty-four starving Montana miners stumbled into the cantonment. Just days before, the blizzard had caught them out and unprepared. For better than forty-eight hours they had trudged on through the jaw of the storm, the mighty winds at their backs, pushing them farther and farther south. Perhaps remembering how well some Montana prospectors had served him so ably at the Battle of the Rosebud, Crook graciously supplied the hungry civilians with some of Quartermaster John V. Furey's rations, blankets, and tents for shelter.

Throughout the night of the twentieth the gusty winds continued to bully the land with snow flurries, keeping most of the men huddled close to their wind-whipped fires. Nonetheless, Crook's auxiliaries were far from deterred in expressing their new friendship for one another—holding mutual feasts, dancing, and serenades far into the night.

Snow lay drifted against the sides of the tents when the sun finally peeked over the ridges to the east on Tuesday morning, the twenty-first of November. Mackenzie had his cavalry battalions up early, breaking camp and saddling up to move another mile downstream so the horses could find more grazing where the wind had blown patches of ground clear. Seamus hung back with the packers near the teamsters' camp. To him, all that packing up and moving no more than a mile seemed work for work's sake. Just like the army way of things. And that made it something the Irishman loathed.

"Seamus! Seamus!"

Donegan turned to find old Dick Closter lumbering up from the latrines dug north of camp. "What's up, mule skinner?"

"They're back!"

"Who's back?"

Closter turned, his white beard brilliant against his smoke-tanned face. "Them Injun scouts Crook sent out! They're back!"

"Good to hear," Donegan grumbled, and tucked the muffler higher around his ears. "Maybe now the general will find out where we need to go—"

"I'll lay you ten to one the general's Injuns know where to find Crazy Horse!"

That got the Irishman's attention. He bolted to his feet. "Where's those scouts now, by damned?"

"Yonder," Closter said, pointing. "They was heading for Crook's camp, taking their prisoner to show him off to the general."

Chapter 21

Freezing Moon
1876

Snow fell off and on throughout the first three days Young Two Moon and the others pushed southeast toward the course of the Powder River. From time to time the clouds parted and they would see patches of startling blue, but the broken sky did not last for long. Again and again the heavens darkened, lowered, then spat sharp, icy flakes in a swirl around the scouts and their ponies.

They shivered as they rode ever onward. They shivered each night they made camp and lit their small fire, sat around the low flames, talking in quiet voices, and one by one tried to sleep while the ponies stood nearby, rump-tucked to the north wind. The four grew colder as the journey grew longer.

The third day they pushed past Warbonnet Ridge—which they named because the three trees that grew upon it made the prominence resemble a warrior's feathered bonnet from a distance—then on to House Ridge, which they named because at its top sat a large boulder that resembled a white man's house. It was there the four turned their faces into the cold wind, urging their ponies north by east toward the Powder River at last. Once they neared the divide that would take them into the Powder River Valley, the young scouts put more distance between themselves, spreading apart in a broad front, moving slowly, slowly, studying the frozen ground, the icy mud in every coulee, the tracked-up snow in every bottom, searching for tracks.

By the time the sun set that third day, the Cheyenne warriors reached a wagon road that appeared to take them down to the river itself. The storm had returned on the back of a ferocious wind, making it difficult to see left or right, up or down in the dark.

Hail stopped them on the road after a short distance. "Now I believe we can take this road and follow it down across Powder River, until it reaches the top of those three bald buttes, and stay there till morning; from there in the daylight we can see much country."

With only nods of agreement, the other three followed Hail, the oldest among them. Upon reaching the buttes, they moved in the lee of the tallest, halted, and let the ponies blow. After some time Hail spoke again.

"With this storm it is useless to climb this hill until it is near daylight."

Young Two Moon said, "You are right. We won't see anything, not even a fire's light in this weather."

High Wolf added, "Let's just stay down here out of the wind and try to keep warm until there is enough light to see come morning."

Together the four walked their ponies into the crevice between the tall butte and one next to it, keeping their ponies close at hand for the warmth the weary animals put off. Young Two Moon dozed fitfully, unable to really sleep, each time awaking with his muscles cramped from the cold ground. His belly growled for food, but he did not really hunger for the dried meat they had brought along in the small parfleches. The cold and the hunger were merely trials that an honorable young man had to suffer for what good his people expected of him.

He was nudged and only then realized he had finally fallen asleep near first light.

Hail said, "Now we must climb this hill and be ready when day comes to look over the ridge up and down Powder River Valley."

Bellying to the top, the four immediately made out the firesmoke hanging in a layer low in the supercold air, off in the middistance along a bend in the river. As the light slowly brightened, the scouts gradually made out the whiteness of the soldier tents against the stark and spidery blackness of the leafless willow and cottonwood. When the graying light ballooned a bit more, Young Two Moon saw some of the white soldiers along with some Indians dressed in soldier uniforms and some Indians wearing their own native clothing all turning their horses loose to graze the snowy ground. One group led their herd to the base of the bluff where the scouts watched, leaving the ponies and returning to their fires. Another group of Indians drove their ponies across the icy river to graze on the far side of the Powder. And still a third group of soldier scouts returned to the herd beneath the tall bluff, climbed a distance up the side, and sat down to watch the ponies.

Because of those enemy herders, the four wolves dared not speak to one another, nor could they move without alerting those soldier scouts watching over their animals. They could only lie flat and motionless, mouthing their silent words to one another as the day became brighter and the river bottom came alive with men, wagons, mules, and horses.

Crow Necklace, the youngest among them, wanted action, whispering, "Let's go down there, make our charge, and drive off some of those horses."

"No," Hail scolded between his chattering teeth.

"We can steal those horses," Crow Necklace persisted. "It will be easy, and we can return to our families with something to show for this cold journey!"

"No," Hail snapped, his eyes watching the soldier scouts below them on the slope. "If we do as you suggest, we might not ever make it home to our families."

"Hail is right," Young Two Moon asserted. "Look, Crow Necklace—the snow is deep. There are many people down there. They could overtake and capture us. Look, see how far it is now to the foot of the mountains where our village lies. Our ponies are tired from the last three days. The enemy's horses are strong. And it is a long, level stretch of ground where we would have to run—we would not even make it into the breaks before they would catch us."

They lay on the frozen ground among the squat sage for most of that day,* afraid to move for attracting attention. Not until late in the afternoon as the sun pitched into the southwest did the soldiers and the soldiers' Indian scouts begin driving in all their horses for the night. Still the four wolves waited as the soldier fires began to glow, the dancing flames shimmering against the skeletal cottonwood trees and willow, the orange-

---

*21 November 1876.

titted flames reflected off the low, heavy clouds. How Young Two Moon yearned for some of that warmth for himself.

Long after dark they pushed themselves back from the brow of the hill and crept down toward the soldier camp, finding the horses all tied in long lines to picket ropes strung between the bare trees.

"I think we should leave our ponies here," Young Two Moon suggested. "Two of us should go in, and two of us should stay with the horses."

Hail nodded. "It is a good plan. If the soldiers or their scouts catch the two, then the others can mount up and escape in the dark."

"I will go," Young Two Moon said emphatically. "Who chooses to go with me?"

Eagerly Crow Necklace replied, "I will go with you!"

Turning to the younger man, Young Two Moon said, "This is good, for we may have ourselves a chance to get some soldier horses down there."

"High Wolf and I will wait for you here," Hail said. "Be careful."

Young Two Moon gripped Hail's wrist and looked into his friend's eyes. "If you hear guns, or we do not come back soon— mount up and ride like a snow wind back to our village. Tell my family that I died doing my duty for my people."

Hail grinned, saying, "You will be back. And you will be the one to tell the village of these soldiers yourself. Now, go. And we will rest here with the ponies until you return."

"That young Cheyenne they caught up on Clear Creek is named Beaver Dam," Frank Grouard told the white and half-breed scouts huddled by the fire late that Tuesday night, 21 November.

"Young and *stupid*!" snorted Baptiste Pourier.

Seamus Donegan shrugged. "Maybeso, Big Bat. But out in this weather, the way a man has to bundle himself up to keep out the cold—I couldn't tell one Injin from another. Can't blame the boy for making that mistake, I can't. G'won, Frank—tell us what Crook learned."

"Smart it was, for them Lakota and Arapaho scouts Crook sent out wasn't wearing a bit of soldier gear—being fifty miles off in enemy country," Grouard continued his story. "So this Beaver Dam come right up to them, figuring them to be a scouting or hunting party from Crazy Horse's village. They waited till the boy was in the middle of 'em—jabbering away about all the villages in the neighborhood, him answering all their questions and such—before they grabbed the boy, tied him up, and hurried him back here to the general."

"Means there must be Cheyenne in the country," Seamus said.

"Damn if there ain't a big bunch of 'em over on a branch of the Powder," Frank went on. "But that youngster claimed he come from a small village of only some five or six lodges. He told Crook that his people would get afraid if he didn't show up after he'd been out hunting—then they'd likely scamper off for Crazy Horse's camp."

"I'll bet that got Crook's attention!" Pourier said.

"Bloody well right," Donegan agreed. "Crook's been wanting to get eye to eye with Crazy Horse for the better part of a year now. Where's Beaver Dam's village, Frank?"

"Said it was up on the head of the Crazy Woman Fork."

"He tell Crook where the Crazy Horse band was camped now?"

Grouard nodded. "A long ways off from here. Clear up on the Rosebud, near where we had our little fight with him in June."

"That'll be a goddamned long march—it will, it will," Seamus muttered, stomping the deepening snow to shock some feeling back into a numbing foot. The cold was simply too much even for the double pair of socks he wore in the tall stovepipe boots he always bought two sizes too large. He feared he might lose some toes to the surgeon before this trip was over.

"So now Crook's give out orders to all the units: moving northwest toward the mountains as soon as it's light," Frank explained. "He wants this expedition to come back with a worthy trophy."

Big Bat cried, "Like Crazy Horse's scalp!"

"The whole outfit's moving in the morning?" Donegan asked.

"Yep, the whole shebang," Grouard replied. "At least for now."

"I figure Crook'll break off Mackenzie soon enough—once he's found the Crazy Horse village," Seamus added as the wind seemed to stiffen and the snowfall thickened. "Damn," he muttered again, stomping his feet. "Think I'll go do what some of the others is doing, fellas: taking this last chance to write down a few words to send back to Fetterman with one of Teddy Egan's couriers tomorrow. Too cold to sleep anyways."

After midnight Crook sent off a Second Cavalry courier to race the ninety miles back to Fetterman with his wire to Sheridan:

> Scouts returned to-day and reported that Cheyennes have crossed over to that other side of the Big Horn Mountains, and that Crazy Horse and his band are encamped on the Rosebud near where we had the fight with them last summer. We start out after his band to-morrow morning.

It was better that the two of them act as bold as they could. So Young Two Moon and Crow Necklace walked right along the string of horses on the picket lines, in among the soldiers and their tents as if they were two of the Indian scouts. Their bravado worked.

At the near edge of the camp a large fire blazed where many Shoshone and Arapaho scouts were busy cleaning weapons, drinking coffee, and playing several noisy games of "hand" on blankets and buffalo robes. There beside the fire a handful of their own people stood, singing Cheyenne war songs.

But they were not prisoners! Who were these Cheyenne in the soldier camp?

"I think that is Old Crow," Crow Necklace whispered right against Young Two Moon's ear. "And the other, he looks like a friend of my uncle's—named Satchel."

"I know of Satchel," Young Two Moon replied, his gall rising. "Now I realize why these *Tse-Tsehese* are here. This Satchel is a relative of Bill Rowland at the White River Agency."

"The white man married to one of our women?"

"Yes. That must be why they are here," Young Two Moon replied. "Bill Rowland brought them here to find our camp in the mountains. To capture our ponies and take away our guns—just like the soldiers are doing at the White River Agency."

"If these two are here with Bill Rowland," Crow Necklace said sadly, "then there must surely be more of our people here with them."

"I am ashamed for them," Young Two Moon said, a sour ball of disappointment thick in his throat. "We have come to this: the white man making some of our relatives hunt down the rest of our people."

After watching the singing and the games for a while, the pair moved on through the firelit darkness, walking below the soldier bivouac until they reached the camp where some Indians spoke a strange language.

"Who are these people?" Crow Necklace asked in a whisper.

For some time Young Two Moon stood and listened, studying the warriors who for the most part wore pieces of soldier uniforms. "I believe they must be the *Ho-nehe-taneo-o*, the Wolf People."*

"Many, many winters have they have scouted for the soldiers."

Looking about them in all directions, Young Two Moon grew frightened for the first time on this journey. The disappointment he had felt in finding *Tse-Tsehese* from the agency was now replaced by the beginning of fear for his people. He waited and did not lead Crow Necklace away from the camp of the Wolf People until the enemy had all gone to their war lodges made of blankets laid over bent willow branches, until the enemy's fires burned low. In all that time of waiting his fear slowly boiled into hatred—until he decided they must do something to injure these ancient enemies.

When the whole camp had grown very quiet, Young Two Moon led his friend toward the enemy's horses. They selected three of the nicest ponies the Wolf People had tied to a picket rope and cut them loose. Then the two started back across the length of the river bottom, skirting the camp to reach the spot where the other two scouts waited.

But in passing by the Arapaho camp, they found a fire still glowing cheerfully, around it a few Indians singing and eating, and a warrior frying cakes in a skillet. Beside the fire sat a large stack of cakes. The warm, luring fragrance was simply too much for Young Two Moon's empty stomach. It growled at him not to walk on by.

"I must get me some of those cakes from that man," he explained to Crow Necklace.

"I am hungry too. But what do we do with these horses?"

He thought a minute, trying to keep his stomach from speaking louder than his good sense. "We will let them go here. They should not wander far before we have eaten our fill."

They released their stolen ponies, then walked boldly toward the fire. Just as they reached the light, two soldiers rode up and shouted to the Arapaho in English.

"Stop your singing and keep your eyes open!"

_____

*Pawnee.

The soldiers rode off once the Arapaho fell silent. Grumbling, the Indians trudged off to their beds, disappearing within their makeshift war lodges. As the last Arapaho went to his blankets, the two Cheyenne scouts dashed in, scooping up a handful of the hot flour cakes, then cut loose three more ponies.

Crow Necklace claimed one, and Young Two Moon led the other two back to find their friends.

They found Hail and High Wolf curled up beneath their blankets, back to back—asleep. And discovered that their four Cheyenne ponies had wandered off.

"Hail, you come ride with me," Young Two Moon said. "Jump up behind me. High Wolf can ride a horse, and so can Crow Necklace."

They did their best to follow the tracks of the four horses and eventually found them, heading north by west, wending their way back home to the village.

Now they climbed onto the backs of their own war ponies, and leading their three captured animals, the four young scouts set off at a gallop into the cold and the dark.

They had news to tell Morning Star, Little Wolf, and the other chiefs.

The *ve-ho-e* soldiers were coming!

Chapter 22

22 November 1876

"A damned sad place to be at this hour."
Seamus turned at the voice, finding old Bill Rowland stopped a few yards behind him in the cold black seep of predawn. "A sad place to be any time of the day."

The scout waited a moment more, then moved up quietly to stand beside the Irishman. Married to a Cheyenne woman back at the Red Cloud Agency, Rowland already had proved his worth by translating for the auxiliaries Crook brought along to hunt down the hostile winter roamers. Now that the general was no longer chasing after Crazy Horse, but had instead heard tell of a large Cheyenne village somewhere close in the mountains, the Powder River Expedition might well find a man with Bill Rowland's talents highly valuable in very short order.

It wasn't snowing again, cold as it was, but every molecule of moisture in the air had frozen, making it hurt to breathe, the very air around him like icy grit against Donegan's skin as he slipped his hat back on his head.

"You know any of 'em?" Rowland asked, gesturing across the collection of grave sites at the outskirts of the old fort—now no more than a collection of charred stumps of construction timbers protruding like blackened, splintered bones poking from a gaping, rotted wound.

The Irishman shook his head, tugging his soft-crowned felt hat down upon his long hair that tossed in the harsh wind. "No. Not really, I didn't."

"Thought you might have," Rowland said. "The way you come up here . . . when none of them others could give a damn if—"

"Sojurs like them don't need reminding of dying when they're fixing to set off to fight," Seamus interrupted, then thought better of it. "I'm sorry. Didn't mean to snap your head off, Bill."

The older frontiersman shrugged it off. "Don't make no nevermind to me."

"You come to fetch me?" Seamus asked, refastening the top collar button on his blanket-lined canvas mackinaw.

"They're setting off. General wants us now."

For a few moments more Donegan continued to gaze reverently over the dozen busted, dry-split headboards, each one bearing a wind-scoured and unreadable name, a good share fallen beneath the deep snow but more leaning precariously at their last stations there in the flaky soil above the gallant roll call of those who had given their all to this high and forbidding land.

"Tell me—the Injins leave this place alone, don't they, Bill?"

"Yes," Rowland answered quietly as he reached his horse and rose off the ground. "Place like this is powerful big medicine to the Cheyenne. They'll go half a day around to keep out of the way of such a place."

"Smart," Seamus said as he took up the reins and stuffed a foot in a stirrup, rising to the saddle.

"For the Cheyenne?"

"For any man," Donegan replied. "Any man what does his best to keep out of death's way."

He nudged the big bay into motion beside Rowland, putting behind them the crumbling adobe walls that would not hide the rusting debris of iron stoves and broken wagon wheels, a solitary broken-down wagon box, and a half-burned artillery carriage for a mountain howitzer.

He was venturing back into this hostile wilderness, crossing the milk-pale Powder River as he had times before, again to put his body into the maw of this ten-year-old fight . . . come here again to this tiny plot of ground to think and pray alone, remembering many faces, knowing very few names of all those who had dreams and hopes and families. For those who had fallen on this consecrated ground, Donegan would always say his prayers as his mother had taught him—to go down upon one knee and to bow his head before the presence of something he could not begin to comprehend, but knew existed just the same.

Although he knew not how God ever allowed one man to set himself against another.

It warmed him this morning, as he and Rowland caught up to the head of the column, to think on his mother again, now especially because he was a parent. Not really having known his father, knowing instead his uncles, who stepped into the breach to try helping raise their sister's boys. Would Seamus's own son come to know the feel of his father's hand at his back when something frightened the youngster, that reassuring touch to let the child know his father was there? Would the boy come to love stroking, pulling, yanking on his father's beard in loving play? Oh, how he prayed he would have many, many more hours of holding that soft-skinned, sweet-breathed infant against his shoulder, singing the child to sleep with the low, vibrant words of ancient Gaelic melodies and the lowing rhythm of his heartbeat. How he wanted his son to know these things, and pass them on to his own children.

From a huge patch pocket in the mackinaw, Seamus pulled the small amber jar Ben Clark had given him last winter. With his teeth Donegan dragged off his thick mitten and stuffed it under an arm before putting the cork stopper between his teeth and taking it from the jar. Inside he always kept a good supply of bacon tallow. Dipping some on a finger, he lathered it all around his cracked, oozing lips and the inside of his cracked and inflamed nostrils. How it stung! His flesh cried out as he laid on a thick coating of the sticky fat, then licked the fingertip clean, put the jar away in that big pocket, and quickly pulled on his wool mitten.

All the while wondering if any man knew where his grave was going to be. Deciding the not knowing didn't matter when a man's time finally arrived.

After an hour on the trail north from the Powder the order came, "Dismount!"

They were going to save what they could of the horses' strength—especially now that Crook had some idea of where a village was and Mackenzie's cavalry must be ready.

The soldiers in those eleven troops made no attempt to come out of the saddle as one. This was not parade drill, nor retiring the colors. A few hundred cold, bone-weary men who were anxious for action, ordered to walk beside their mounts for the next half hour until they would be ordered back into the saddle. Such walking by the troopers saved some reservoir of strength in the animals, besides helping the men stay warmer with the exertion as they trudged through the ankle-deep snow beneath the scummy clouds that lowered off the Big Horns.

Away to the northeast herds of buffalo dotted the prairie in black patches against the bleak white landscape, grazing in sight for the rest of the afternoon. Up and down throughout the remainder of the march they cut a swath through the stretch of monochrome and desolate country that took them ever nearer the foot of the Big Horn Mountains. That bitterly cold twenty-second day of November Crook had them cover all of twenty-eight miles of tortuous, bleak prairie travel before making camp on the banks of the Crazy Woman Fork. Common legend held that the creek earned its name from a crazed woman who had lived by herself on its banks for many years before dying about 1850. However, the English equivalent of "crazy" never had translated to mean true madness as much as it signified sexual promiscuity. It was likely the woman had been cast out of her village for her lascivious activity—a theory much more fitting the Cheyenne belief in the value of a woman's virtue.

Cloud Peak rose in the distance, just under a hundred miles off, its helmet at times peeking from the top of the wispy white clouds that brushed across the painfully blue sky . . . before it began to snow again.

Through sandy ravines and across cactus-covered hillsides the expedition plodded on until late afternoon. As the last of Wagon Master John B. Sharpe's teamsters were jangling in, the pickets to the northwest spotted a solitary rider appear atop a knoll carrying a white flag. Crook sent out a party to bring in the horseman.

Seamus joined the small crowd who gathered to listen as Frank Grouard interpreted.

"Says his name is Sitting Bear. From what I can tell, he's come up from the Red Cloud Agency—sent by the soldier chief down there to talk the warrior bands into surrendering and coming back to the reservation," Frank explained. "Not far north of here he says he ran into those five lodges the Cheyenne boy come from."

"Are they running?" Crook asked.

"Going north, just like that Cheyenne boy figured they would."

Crook mumbled his great disappointment under his breath.

Grouard continued. "Sitting Bear talked to 'em. but they wasn't about to turn around and head into the agency now. They're scared—and hightailing it for Crazy Horse's bunch."

"To warn them?" Crook squeaked.

"You can count on it," Frank replied. "That pretty much ruins your surprise on Crazy Horse, don't it?"

Crook's eyes narrowed as he gazed at the broad smile on Grouard's face. "What the hell's so funny to you, half-breed? I thought you wanted Crazy Horse as much as me."

"Oh, I guess I do, General," Grouard said. "But there ain't a chance of us catching him now, is there?"

"Not if those Cheyenne are going to warn his Oglalla." Crook stood pulling at one end of his beard, then another.

"How'd you like some good news from this here Sitting Bear fella?" Frank spilled it.

The general cracked a smile. "Why, you devious bastard! That's why you're smiling. But—if Crazy Horse is going to slip away before I can get there, what good news could you possibly have for me?"

"How about a village of Cheyenne dropping in your lap?"

"Cheyenne, you say?" Crook asked, taking a step closer.

"The biggest damned village the Cheyenne had together in a long, long time," Frank exclaimed. "Sitting Bear's been there—claims that village got more Cheyenne in it than they had when they camped alongside the Lakota and Custer marched down on 'em all at the Greasy Grass."

Crook whirled about, pounding a clenched fist into his open left palm, a fire igniting his eyes. "Bourke! Goddammit, Bourke—move! Get me Mackenzie! Get Mackenzie here on the double!"

Just before sunrise Crook sent out a large party of his Indian allies—each man selected for his expert knowledge of the surrounding countryside—to follow the Crazy Woman upstream into the mountains, searching for any sign of the enemy village estimated to be no more than forty-five miles away. With the scouts went a small command of soldiers under First Lieutenant Henry W. Lawton, Quartermaster of Mackenzie's Fourth, charged with preparing the stream and ravine crossings for the attack march.

As soon as there was enough light to work that morning of the twenty-third, the packers and the cavalry set about the task of unloading Sharpe's wagons and packing all the rations and ammunition that would soon be hoisted onto the backs of Tom Moore's mules. While Mackenzie's cavalry would soon strike out to follow the trail the scouts had taken into the mountains that morning, Crook himself had decided to remain behind with Teddy Egan's K Troop of the Second Cavalry which would be engaged as provost guard at headquarters and employed as couriers, along with Dodge's infantry and artillery and any men on sick call, all of them charged with protecting Captain Furey's wagon train, which would remain corralled right where it was until such time as Mackenzie called them up for support.

That morning Mackenzie grew bitterly disgusted with the glee shown by those soldiers who were to be left behind at the Crazy Woman.

At the same time, he was clearly worried. Like the general, Ranald Mackenzie feared most that the enemy would surrender without a fight. As John Bourke had put it during last night's officers' meeting, "A fight is desirable to atone and compensate for our trials, hardships, and dangers for more than eight months."

By midafternoon that Thursday, the spearhead of Crook's winter campaign was ready.

"Stand to *horse!*"

In the cold blue air lying low in the valley of the Crazy Woman, officers called out the order to the anxious troopers. Company noncoms had made sure every man had two blankets, one of which he draped over the back of his horse to protect the animal from the intense cold. The other was to be rolled behind the saddle.

"Prepare to *mount!*"

Sergeants echoed the command up and down the company rows of tents and picket lines.

"*Mount!*"

Those horse soldiers settling down upon those God-uncomfortable McClellan saddles would not be taking their tents and Sibley stoves along from here on out. Only those two thin blankets, along with a shelter half or the protection of each man's heavy wool coat, would have to do until they rejoined the wagon train. To dispense with some of the other baggage, Mackenzie ordered his officers to mess with their companies.

Eleven hundred men—as many as a third of which were Indian scouts—trudged away into the growing gloom of that winter afternoon carrying three days' rations in their packs and another seven on the mules bringing up the rear. Each man had on his person twenty-four rounds of pistol ammunition and in his saddle packs one hundred rounds for his seven-pound, forty-one inch, .45/70 Springfield carbine.

Mackenzie loped to the lead and set the pace himself out in front of the guidons and his colorful regimental standard, the top of the pole bearing the battle ribbons his own Fourth Cavalry had won in a legion of contests against the Kickapoo, Lipan, Kiowa, and Comanche across the southern plains.

Here at the age of thirty-six, Ranald Slidell would at last pit himself against the best of the northern tribes.

It was to be Three Finger Kenzie's last Indian fight.

The village migrated while Young Two Moon and the other wolves had been out discovering what all those tracks on Powder River meant.

By the time the four returned, the People had moved to a beautiful canyon at the southern end of the Big Horn Mountains, rimmed with high, striated red-rock walls, through the heart of which flowed a branch of the Powder River itself. The *Ohmeseheso* had entered the valley by the southern trail, one of only three or four narrow entrances to this canyon that afforded good protection from the cold arctic blasts known to batter the plains at this season. In addition, a small spring near the southern end of the canyon by and large kept the stream free of ice even at the coldest of temperatures. For the most part the valley lay flat, but near the southwest corner the floor became snarled by rounded knolls, upvaulted escarpments of brick-red rock, scarred by deep ravines, hidden cutbanks, and jagged cliffs. On either side of the stream grew a profusion of willow and box elder, and only a scattering of the sheltering, leafless cottonwood. It was here along the Red Fork of the Powder that the People raised their lodges, each spiral of poles lifting a gray streamer of smoke to the cold heavens of that morning as the four scouts gazed down upon the valley from the heights.

"We have time to save our village," Crow Necklace gasped in the cold air, relieved to find all still peaceful.

"Let's hurry down to give the warning!" High Wolf said, then wheeled his pony about and led the other scouts down the narrow game trail toward the end of the valley.

The four howled like wolves as they approached the camp. Instantly men, women, and children burst from the lodges, quietly murmuring as the scouts slowly led them through the long, narrow campsite to the lodges of the Sacred Powers. There the four Old-Man Chiefs awaited their return, standing silently as the sun finally made its way over the eastern rim of the high valley.

"You have discovered what the tracks mean?" Morning Star asked as the crowd hushed.

"Soldiers," Young Two Moon answered.

The talk around them grew louder, like a rumble of a mighty river beneath a thick layer of ice.

"What of these soldiers?" Little Wolf asked. "Where are they going?"

"They could be going anywhere!" Last Bull interrupted. "They could be searching for Crazy Horse! They cannot know we are hidden here inside these mountains!"

"Perhaps you are right," Morning Star said, his face grave, as if he wanted to believe.

"No," young Crow Necklace said recklessly, challenging his elders, stunning the crowd by his disagreement with the powerful war chief of the Kit Fox Society, Last Bull. "They will be coming here."

Last Bull whirled on the young scout, stepping right up to his pony and glaring at Crow Necklace. "How are you so sure?" he snarled.

"Only what we saw," was the answer.

"And what we heard," said Young Two Moon, feeling desperate to protect Crow Necklace.

"What you heard?" Little Wolf asked, moving up beside the ponies.

"In that soldier camp we saw many, many Indians," Young Two Moon explained.

"No!" many of the people protested in disbelief.

"Captives?" asked Morning Star.

"No," the young scout answered. "They were soldiers. Four different tongues did we hear in that camp while we stole ponies and ate their food."

"What enemies of ours are these that come to help the soldiers in our own country?" Little Wolf demanded, his eyes narrowing.

Perhaps the old chief was remembering how the soldiers had attacked that sleeping camp on the Powder River last winter,

Young Two Moon thought as he began to answer, "Pawnee, Shoshone, yes—our old enemies. But ... but Arapaho ... and ... and *Tse-Tsehese* too."

"Cheyenne!"

"Yes," Young Two Moon said. "If those soldiers and all their Indians reach our camp ... I think there will be a big fight here."

Chapter 23

24 November 1876

"Who was this California Joe you talk about, Lute?" Seamus asked the younger North brother.

"A scout and guide for many a year on the central and southern plains. He knew a friend of yours—Bill Hickok. Joe scouted with Jim Bridger too."

"I met Bridger myself a long time ago, up in this country—at Fort Phil Kearny," Seamus replied.* "And now Hickok's dead."

"Few weeks back when I saw Joe in Nebraska, he told me he was in Deadwood at the time Hickok was killed."

"Murdered," Donegan snorted angrily.

"Joe said he and some others in the Black Hills made it clear what they thought of that gang of gamblers they figured put up that young'un to shoot Wild Bill in the back of the head."

"And now you say Joe's been shot too?" Seamus asked.
Frank nodded.

Then Luther added, "A soldier caught up with us at Laramie and told us Joe was shot in the back."

"Ambushed," Frank growled.

"Out in this country, you go and make somebody mad," Seamus replied quietly as they rubbed their hands together and stomped their feet to stimulate circulation as the surgeon's ther-

---

*Sioux Dawn, Vol. 1, The Plainsmen Series.

mometer hovered close to thirty-five below at that coldest hour of the day, "you best be watching your back and sleeping with only one eye closed."

This morning Mackenzie allowed none of the command the luxury of a small greasewood fire where they could heat coffee in the darkness before dawn, expected to eat their rations of salt pork and hardtack cold, washing it down with nothing warmer than the mineral-laced water in their canteens.

They had marched some twelve miles up the Crazy Woman yesterday afternoon, not stopping until they reached the mouth of Beaver Creek, a small tributary that flowed in from the south. The ground had been soggy earlier in the day but began to re-freeze as soon as the sun tumbled from the sky. What firewood the men could scare up simply didn't go around, so most of the soldiers had turned to hunting for sage and buffalo chips. At least there was plenty of water and some good patches of wind-blown grass for grazing the mounts.

Lieutenant Lawton's work detail had pushed themselves to the limit, straining with pick and ax to prepare the frozen ground at every creek crossing for the main command that had followed in their wake. Progress had been slow, this patch of country slashed with many ravines, coulees, and sharp-sided washes that, come spring, winter would fill with spring's foaming torrent. The sides of every crevice had to be chipped away so the horses and mules could pick their way down, then claw back up again.

Before picketing his bay last night, Seamus had carefully inspected each hoof and leg, smearing tallow and liniment into the scrapes and wounds caused by the icy crust on the snow. Next he had followed his nightly campaign ritual. With his cold, cramped hands Donegan ripped what he could of the brittle, frozen bunchgrass from the hard, flaky ground before he pulled back the single army blanket he kept over the horse's back, from withers to tail root. After he brushed the animal carefully with the clumps of bunchgrass, the Irishman replaced the blanket so the animal could retain as much of its own warmth as possible. A horse soldier always cared for his mount as if it were his best friend on the campaign trail—for a horse soldier never knew when his life might truly depend upon the care he had given to that best friend.

How he wished again this morning that Teddy Egan were along for this cold winter's attack—remembering the singular courage the captain showed one and all when they had charged into the enemy village beside the frozen Powder River.* Thinking on old comrades now that they were within striking distance of the enemy.

So tightly strung were every man's nerves that when one of the pickets thrown out during the afternoon stop came loping back across the sage, hollering out his warning, everyone went into position to meet the enemy attack.

"They're coming! The Injuns is coming!"

But almost as quickly the older hands at the front of the column realized the danger was minimal from that handful of Indian scouts who backtracked at near a gallop to rejoin Mackenzie's cavalry. The five brought the exciting news that they had located the village. Two of the seven, they explained—Red Shirt and Jackass—had volunteered to remain behind in the icy rocks above the village through the cold of the coming night, watching the Cheyenne camp while their companions returned to hurry the soldiers along the trail. Already the temperature was continuing to plummet.

"How many lodges?" Mackenzie wanted to know from his translators as soon as one of his aides was sent down the column to explain that they were not under attack.

"Not sure. Say there's heap ponies, though. I figure from all they tell me about the size of the herd—maybe two hundred lodges at the outside."

Seamus watched the Indian fighter's eyes narrow in that way Mackenzie appeared to calculate the odds.

"With at least three warriors of fighting age for every lodge," the colonel replied, "I've got them right where I want them." He pointed west, toward the brow of a wide ridge. "We'll go into hiding there, beneath that overhanging ledge of rocks where the men and animals can rest ... then push on as soon as the sun has fallen—as soon as we can be assured no spies know we're coming. Tell the troop commanders to use that time to fix up their companies for the night march we're going to make of this. I plan on attacking at dawn."

"We must break camp at once!" Black Hairy Dog had cried when the four young scouts brought their report of soldiers marching in their direction.

*Blood Song, Vol. 8, The Plainsmen Series.

While the Keeper of *Maahotse* spoke of his fear, everyone remained quiet, respectful, reverent—for he was Sweet Medicine's successor. As the chosen protector of the Sacred Arrows, Black Hairy Dog was one of the two men who owned the People, who held the People in the palm of his right hand.

Morning Star thought, if any man here has the right to speak for *all* of us at a crucial time such as this, it is Black Hairy Dog.

There arose murmuring assent among Coal Bear, Keeper of the Sacred Buffalo Hat, Morning Star, and the other Old-Man Chiefs. It looked as if all four would agree to put the village on the move out of this valley before the soldiers and their Indian scouts could find them there.

Since it was a meeting of the chiefs of the Council of Forty-four, no warrior-society headmen were allowed to speak. Only during the grave emergency during the Fat Horse Moon, when the soldiers marched down upon the great Lakota encampment beside the Greasy Grass, had the war chiefs been permitted to speak among the council chiefs. Unless the Old-Man Chiefs again gave such permission, the warrior-society headmen were to obey protocol and keep their opinions to themselves.

But instead—

"No!" Last Bull shouted, shoving some of the older warriors aside to thrust his heavy body into the small ring of those six older men who were deciding upon the fate of the village.

Many of those men and all of the women who had gathered that afternoon to hear these important deliberations clapped their hands over their mouths in astonishment.

Last Bull, leader of the Kit Fox Warrior Society, stomped about haughtily, his red face a chiseled portrait of anger. "We will stay here and fight!"

The Sacred Arrow Priest said, "You have no right to speak—"

The war chief whirled on Black Hairy Dog, his fury barely contained. The older Keeper of the Arrows inched back a step, cowed by the bulk, the fury, of Last Bull.

"These soldiers have chased the People since last winter!"

From the fringes of the crowd arose the first excited response from the chief's warrior society—yipping like kit foxes with the smell of prey in their nostrils. That approval brought a smile of immense satisfaction to the war chief's face as he continued.

"Fighting alongside the Lakota, we have defeated the *ve-ho-e* soldiers once," Last Bull continued haranguing the crowd now, ignoring the six older chiefs who sat around the small circle where he stood, gesturing wildly. "Despite that defeat—the white man has proved how stupid he is in continuing to haunt the backtrail of our village, to harass and harry our people!"

As Morning Star watched the edges of the crowd, it seemed more and more of the Kit Foxes stepped to the fore, made bold by the strong words of their leader.

Last Bull growled, "We must not allow the white soldiers to chase us from place to place to place! No more!"

Now the young warriors were becoming worked up. Some were humming their war songs, some chanting rhythmically, others outwardly shrieking like snarling wolves in battle.

"If we do not fight them here," Last Bull shouted, "then we will have to fight them somewhere."

Lowering his head, Morning Star peered furtively at the other five chiefs, each of them as saddened, as chastened, as he. His eyes drooped to his lap.

"We will fight them here!" Last Bull screamed, trembling with emotion. "My warriors—to you falls the duty of assuring that no one leaves this village!"

Shocked by that, the old chiefs gazed up, their faces carved with terror. Struck silent were they—perhaps more scared of Last Bull and his warriors than they were of the soldiers advancing on their village.

"Yes! Be sure to stop anyone who attempts to flee. Cut their cinches! Slash their lodges! Break their poles and smash their kettles! Some of you, begin to bring in wood—much, much wood. We will build us a big, big fire and bring out the drum we captured from our enemy for a dance tomorrow night."

Last Bull threw out his chest like a puffing sage cock, his face drawn into a sneer.

"And the rest of you, now go among the People and collect the young girls who we will hold prisoner to keep the families here while we dance! To keep everyone here while the soldiers march down into our trap!"

The following day at sunrise Box Elder sought out Morning Star. The old man had seen more than eighty winters come and go, and was now all but blind. Yet no man would doubt the sacred power of Box Elder's visions.

"This morning, as always, I sat facing the east, my face feel-

ing the first warmth of the sun's rising," the old man explained
after Morning Star had assisted him inside the chief's lodge and
seated him beside the warm fire.

"Yes, go on."

Box Elder continued. "As I sat staring at that holiest of directions, I saw a mighty vision of soldiers and their Indian scouts
riding toward our camp, moving out of the rising sun into this
valley."

Morning Star swallowed, hesitating to ask for any more rev-
elations from so powerful a mystic. "These soldiers—"

"The soldiers and the Indian scouts charged through our
camp and killed many of our people."

He could see that Box Elder's rheumy old eyes were tearing
now.

The ancient one said, "Now I must go and find my son,
Medicine Top, who will call for the camp crier."

"Yes," Morning Star agreed, rising beside the old visionary.
"Bring the crier to me so that I can tell him to alert the families
that this camp will be attacked early tomorrow morning."

Quickly the chief bent to sweep up one of his warmest blankets before he reached the lodge door, where Box Elder cried out,
his face lifted slightly toward the smoke flaps, his cloudy eyes unable to see anything but his fateful vision.

"You must have the women and children go to the ridges
and bluffs, into the high cliffs surrounding our camp," Box Elder
explained. "There they must raise up breastworks. There they
should stay in hiding. Then they will be saved. See that our people do this—or we will all die."

By the time the sun had poked its head over the eastern rim
of the valley that morning, the camp crier had spread the word
and the village pulsated with activity. Ponies were being brought
in, the first lodges were being unpinned, stakes torn from the
frozen ground, buffalo robes rolled up around important family
treasures that would be loaded upon the travois.

While this was happening, Brave Wolf and a handful of
other older warriors had gone into the sloping crevices of the
ground west and north of the village to locate some places where
the women and children could pile up rocks for breastworks—
just as Box Elder's vision had commanded of them. The People
could abandon the village for the night and stay in the surrounding hills, where they would be safe.

"You must leave your lodges standing!" the camp crier instructed the People when he learned that the village was being dismantled. "Do not take down your lodges! The soldiers must believe we are still in our beds when they come! Leave your lodges standing!"

The plan might work, Morning Star believed. If the soldiers believed the village deserted, they might not go in search of the women and children in the hills. But if they did, then the warriors could then fight a holding action while their families fled.

Now the camp's attention turned instead to taking warm clothing, robes, and blankets with them into the hills. There were many newborns, infants, and young children. They would need to be protected from the painful, life-robbing cold that night as they waited for the white man to come sneaking in upon them.

But before any of the women could herd their children into the hills, the Kit Fox Society crier loped through camp, shrilly calling out that Last Bull's warriors would prevent anyone from leaving the village—just as the angry war chief had commanded yesterday.

"Forget what the old chiefs have told you," the crier announced. "The Kit Foxes will protect you and drive the soldiers away after our great victory is won! Look around you: our warriors now control camp—not those old men who have grown as frightened as old women! No one will be allowed to leave. It is the decree of Last Bull!"

Some families waited for the crier to pass them by, then resumed their preparations to flee into the hills. But the rider came through camp a second time, shouting that anyone who disobeyed Last Bull's orders to stay put would be punished. Suddenly there was the Kit Fox chief himself, darting through the sprawling village on his war pony, brandishing a long rawhide and elk-antler quirt he swore to use on anyone he caught attempting to leave. Beside him rode Wrapped Hair, second chief of the Kit Fox Society.

Together they waded into a small group of those who were throwing robes onto their ponies.

"Cut their cinches!" Last Bull demanded.

From the crowd around them burst half a dozen warriors tearing their knives from their belts. Boldly they hurled the men and women aside, slashing at the cinches holding travois to the ponies' backs, cutting saddles from the ponies' girths, freeing rawhide strips tying up blankets and buffalo robes.

"No one will leave!" Last Bull screamed, his lips flecked with spittle, his eyes spiderwebbed with red.

Wrapped Hair echoed his shrill defiance of the village chiefs. "Tonight all the People will dance to celebrate our victory over the Snake—and tomorrow at dawn we will have our victory over the soldiers!"

Chapter 24

24–25 November 1876

L eaving Tom Moore's pack train behind, with a single company for escort and orders to follow after a wait of two more
hours, the Indian scouts led Mackenzie's command away from
Beaver Creek as the sun set behind the Big Horns, while the land
was becoming nothing more than a dimly lit, rumpled white
bedsheet pocked with the darker heads of sage and the faint trace
of willow-lined ravines snaking darkly among the drifts of white.
From time to time the column would pass a buffalo skull lying
akimbo, half-in and half-out of a skiff of crusted snow. Tracks of
an occasional coyote or deer or antelope crisscrossed the rippled,
wind-sculpted icing smeared over the rumbling land they
climbed and fell with throughout that twenty-fourth of November.

As the command dismounted for the first of some twenty
times, each man walking single file and leading his mount so
they could squeeze themselves through a narrow ravine into the
impenetrable bulk of the mountains, the soldiers coughed,
sneezed, grumbled, and cursed—but the troopers and their allies
had been ordered to enforce a strict silence, for a column moving into position for the attack, unaware that it has already been
discovered by the Cheyenne, is not allowed the luxury of a great
deal of noise.

Everything that could be tied down had to be kept from
causing racket. Although they were ordered not to smoke, not to
light a match for their pipes, many consoled themselves with

their favorite briar anyway. By and large the officers turned away without scolding—knowing that for these men forced to endure this subzero march, a bowl of Kentucky burley could be a small but meaningful pleasure.

From time to time orders were whispered back down the column for the troops to reform in columns of twos, but soon came another command for the men to proceed in single-file through the winding, narrow passages they encountered. As the column strung itself out for more than five miles on such occasions, the men were required to stop and wait at times for more than half an hour before they could move on. While many impatiently waited out the backed-up muddle, some of the older hands dismounted and slept right where they hit the ground, reins tied around their wrists. Other men merely dozed in the saddle despite the plunging temperatures. More and more it was proving to be slow going with all the delays, with the rise and the fall of the trail—considering they already had the scent of their quarry in their nostrils and should have been closing in for the kill.

The ranks grew all the more quiet as the darkness swelled around them like an inky, purple bruise until the ground finally smoothed, growing less rugged after they had pierced the outer wall of the mountainside. On the far side of the high peaks above them the sun sank beyond like death's own grave as soldiers and scouts alike followed the Arapaho Sharp Nose's trail out of the narrow gorge where they had been strung out for more than half a dozen miles, those eleven hundred men inching along in the coming dusk one at a time as the land began to lead them up, up from the plain into the darkest recesses that would ultimately draw them into the veritable heart of the Big Horn Mountains. No longer were they in the land of the curious prairie dog that would stick its head up from a hole for a peek and a protest at the passing beasts before ducking back into the warmth and darkness of its protective burrow while the frozen men and animals plodded past.

Here the cliffs and towering monuments of stone closed in around them on both sides, seeming to slam shut on their rear too—forbidding any retreat.

In the west the sky had turned from rose to purple to indigo, lowering as they pushed on through the glittering, frozen darkness, feeling their way step by icebound step in their heaving climb to over thirty-five hundred feet among the juniper, stunted jack pine, and cedar. Every man, horse, and mule of them stumbling, slipping, sliding sideways on icy patches where the sun hadn't penetrated between the narrow battlements of wind-eroded red rock.

Every now and then at a particularly difficult ravine an order came back for the column to "close up, close up!" Each time those at the head of a company would report to the troop in their advance that they had successfully made the crossing; the last man of that troop calling out to the company behind them in the dark, bringing them on with nothing more than the encouragement of that voice coming out of the gloom of that oppressive, frozen darkness.

And with every narrow stream or creek they were forced to cross, the cold, frightened horses splashed the icy water onto their riders, drenching the troopers, leaving every man frozen to his marrow, every animal shuddering in uncontrollable spasms.

Throughout their long night march the overanxious allies hurried past the slow-plodding soldiers on right flank or left, darting by singly or in pairs, all of them urging their ponies faster than the troopers pushed their big cavalry horses—until every one of the scouts had coagulated at the front of the march.

Ready to strike.

As the moonless winter night squeezed down, a man here and there fell out to await the tail of the column—those few who precariously clung to their saddles, careening side to side as if they were about to retch, stricken with that strange and sudden malady known as altitude sickness, perhaps numbed by the endless cold, even those few in any battle-ready regiment who are always taken with a sudden case of unquenchable fear.

From time to time in the coallike blackness it tried to snow. None of them could really see it snowing, able only to feel the frozen crystals sting the bare, exposed, and stiffened parchment of their cheeks and noses as the wind tossed and gusted through each narrow defile while the column drew closer.

Closer.

Again and again the forward scouts whirled back to Mackenzie and his staff through that long, cold night—urging the soldiers to press on, faster, ever faster . . . morning was coming and the village was near. Impatient were the auxiliaries all to be in position before first light. On and on the scouts prodded the white men to hurry. Morning would soon be upon them. The time for attack.

"Better that we let our Indians feel their way ahead as far

as they want to," Mackenzie muttered to those around him sometime late that night. "Some itch tells me there may well be a trap laid for us up there, the way those scouts are leading us through these narrow canyons. Perhaps the Cheyenne have a surprise waiting for us."

But as much as they feared it, as ready as they were for it, as closely as the soldiers watched the rising tumble of rock around them—there came no ambush.

So dark and cold and suffocating was the night that Seamus began to believe they were the only creatures stirring in this part of the world. So small and insignificant did he feel here at the bottom of each gorge, beneath a sky so black that it seemed to go on forever, sucking every hint of warmth right out of the earth.

Donegan could not remember ever seeing as many stars as this back east in Boston Towne. Even away from the cities and the streetlights—never could the sky be as brilliantly flecked, for only here was the air so dry. He licked his fevered lips and remembered the amber jar stuffed in his pocket. Once more he dabbed the cold dribble from his inflamed nostrils with the huge bandanna that hung around his neck, then swabbed more of the tallow over the end of his nose, into the wide, oozy cracks on his lower lip.

Would they ever get into position to make their charge and begin the attack before daylight?

Or would they find they had to lay to another day in some pocket away from the village and not be able to have their fight until the twenty-sixth?

He fretted at their snail's pace, knowing most of the others must be every bit as anxious as he was to get on with the fight. Now that they were there, now that it was cold enough to freeze the balls off a brass office monkey, there simply was nothing that could warm a man up like a fight for his life. A good blood-throbbing scrap of it.

How he wanted to get this over and done with, then home to both of them.

I'll figure out the boy's name on the trip back, he promised himself again. Time enough to do that, Seamus. Get this fight out of the way—and you can name your son.

Near two o'clock the column squeezed itself again through a narrowing crimson defile the scouts from Red Cloud's agency called "Sioux Pass." For more than five miles the column snaked through the tall, rocky canyon, the immense walls of which were stippled with stunted trees. Directly above them glittered no more than a long angular strip of star-studded sky. Ahead in the distance hung the silver-blue quarter of a moon, quickly falling into the west after its own brief ride across the heavens.

"Eight more miles," came the whispered word back from the Indian trackers leading them through the darkness.

Eight miles below the valley where the scouts claimed Mackenzie's soldiers would find the Cheyenne village, they struck the Red Fork of the Powder River. Out of that bleak, early-morning darkness two horsemen approached the head of the column. They proved to be Red Shirt and Jackass, the two Sioux scouts who had stayed behind to keep an eye on the village. It was plain to see that their ponies were done in: Jackass's animal stumbled about with its weary rider and eventually fell. Both men jabbered excitedly about seeing many ponies and even counting a few lodges in the dark. During the brief halt the pair was fed hardtack and cold bacon, then told to rejoin their fellow warriors as the column pressed on into the darkness.

Hoar frost from every nostril and mouth hung like a thickening blanket over the entire serpentine column eventually slithering itself out of the rocky gorge, emerging upon a patch of smoother, more open ground some half-mile wide by three miles in length, which the Sioux had long ago named the "Race Course." Behind them to the east, the first telltale narrow thread of gray light stretched atop the distant horizon.

How close were they now?

While Seamus and the head of the march spread out there where the narrow ravine widened beside the nearby stream tumbling over its icy bed, its faint echo splashing off the canyon walls, the rest of the column came to a halt behind him. The men quieted their animals without instruction from their officers. And listened.

They needed no prodding, for all could hear the distant, throbbing, man-made reverberation wending its way up to them from afar.

"That's a goddamned drum!" whispered Billy Garnett, Sioux interpreter with the expedition.

"Hell if it ain't!" said Billy Hunter, half-breed guide serving the North's Pawnee battalion.

"Shush!" someone ordered nearby.

You could almost feel them hold their breath—eleven hundred of them now. So damned quiet a man could make out the snort of a horse halfway down the entire length of the column, maybe even hear the fart of one of Tom Moore's mules at the very end of the entire procession.

"Rowland!" Mackenzie called out to his headquarters group.

"I'm here," the squaw man replied, inching his horse forward.

"Bring some of your Cheyenne," the colonel ordered. "Have them take us ahead to where we might get us a look at the village."

Rowland gestured to Roan Bear, Cut Nose, and Little Fish, three of those who sat their ponies behind him. Wordlessly the trio led off as the squaw man and Mackenzie followed until all five were swallowed by the leafless willow choking a bend in the valley ahead.

Now the nearly four hundred Indian allies visibly became restless, muttering and restive, barely able to contain their primal excitement. Most of them took this moment to pull off to one side or another, leaping from their ponies. Donegan had seen the whole process many times before, yet it never ceased to make his heart leap in anticipation—to watch these Indians go about their toilet, pulling out paints and grease, bringing forth feathers and amulets, those stuffed birds and animal skins they would tie in their hair, smearing their braids with white earth or hanging empty brass cartridges in their black tresses, every last one of them mumbling to the spirits and invoking his private war medicine now that they were within earshot of the enemy.

Now that every last one of them knew they would not have to wait out another day.

This was the morning of the attack.

There were Northern Cheyenne in there. While the various Lakota bands might eventually be whipped in detail and driven back to the agencies—the Northern Cheyenne were known to fight to the last man.

As Sharp Nose rode among the Red Cloud scouts, whispering low, signing with his quick hands, the scouts dropped to the ground, adjusting their reins and pad saddles.

Behind Donegan the soldiers were now ordered out of their McClellans, instructed that here they would tighten cinches, check the loads in their .45-caliber single-action Colt revolvers with the seven-and-a-half-inch barrels. Make sure they had handy the hundred rounds of ammunition each of them carried for his .45/70 Springfield carbine.

The Indians went among one another, talking low, touching hands, pounding one another on the shoulders, making low cries of the wolf or some other creature which would provide its spiritual protection now that they stood on the brink of battle.

Donegan knew they were reminding one another that this would be a glorious day—perhaps a great day to die. Knowing that these Northern Cheyenne would put up a fight truly worthy of a warrior's reputation.

He fingered the buckle on his bridle, then nervously loosened both pistols in their holsters, checking next the lever and trigger action on the Model '73 Winchester, and finally allowed himself to turn, looking up the darkened canyon whence came that low, steady hammer of a great war drum. The enemy was awake. And perhaps they were ready for the attack.

As he stood beneath the halo of frost steaming from the bay's nostrils, Seamus thought of Samantha and the boy. Hoping she would not worry, praying she would talk to the child about his father every day, just as he had pledged her to do while he was gone from them both.

Then he thought on his mother, his eyes drawn up to the sides of the canyon that rose before them. Thoughts of Uncle Ian far to the west in that Oregon country—how he raised family and stock and crops, his feet buried in the rich soil, the sort of man a woman could clearly count on.

Then as his eyes climbed even farther, ascending from the ridgetop into that icy blue pricked with countless stars, his thoughts naturally turned to Uncle Liam. And Seamus began to weep, silent tears spilling from his eyes, freezing on his cheeks, icing in the mat of winter's beard.

Somehow sensing that man was with him at this very minute, in this forbidding land—at his shoulder once more, now that the fighting was at hand.

Last night as the sun began to lengthen shadows at the upper end of the valley, Last Bull's warriors organized the men of the village to drag in dry timber from the surrounding area. They stood the huge trunks on end to form a conical "skunk," into the center of which they then stuffed smaller kindling wood. As the light disappeared from the sky, the Kit Fox Society ignited their bonfire while others dragged up the huge drum they had captured from the Shoshone village. Six men could sit around it without crowding, each of them singing and beating time for the dancers.

At the quivering fringe of the firelight some of the mothers protectively hovered beside their daughters. Other mothers tied lengths of rawhide or braided horsehair from their daughter's belt to another until five or six of them were joined together in this fashion. It was their hope that such a precaution would prevent the young Kit Fox warriors from dashing up to snatch one of the young women and pirate her away when the celebration became heady with passion. By and large most of the mothers did not stray far from the dancing circle, staying in sight of their daughters, hoping to protect them from Last Bull's strutting warriors.

And strut they did.

They came through the village, herding everyone toward the huge dance arena. And when the hundreds were gathered and the drum began to throb, the cocky warriors went among the crowd, commanding all to dance or be beaten with bows—a degrading humiliation. Only the most courageous refused to dance to the Kit Foxes' victory over the Shoshone.

Men like Brave Wolf, who had taken a vow as a Contrary. Even Last Bull did not molest such a crazy, wanting-to-die warrior. It was gratifying to Morning Star to find that Brave Wolf and a handful of other young Contraries kept moving in and out of camp to the east in their lonely vigil—their keen senses on edge for the soldiers they expected to come from that direction. Up among the huge boulders along the sides of the canyon they rode, listening for any sound, watching for the glint of a rifle barrel or bridle in the winter moonlight.

Then the moon fell in the southwest and only the stars lit the sky with a cold blue light. Brave Wolf and the others returned to camp, reporting in to the three Old-Man Chiefs. What starlight fell from the sky was not enough to help them see an enemy far away in that rugged country.

The singing and dancing continued as the People grew more and more weary, and the Kit Foxes worked themselves into a frenzy of war lust.

Sometime after the moon had fallen, Sits in the Night went to check on his ponies he had driven down below the village to graze. As he was approaching the open glade where he had left them Sits in the Night saw someone driving the ponies off to the east. His heart in his throat, he reined about immediately and raced back to the village. There he told his story to the camp crier, who immediately went through those gathered at the dance to tell the story of someone stealing the horses.

"I got there in time to see people driving off my ponies. I could see them whipping my ponies. I could hear the blows as they struck my animals. I think the soldiers have come—for farther down from there I heard a rumbling noise!"

"Aiyee!" screeched several people in terror.

Many held their hands over their mouths, their eyes wide as silver conchos, afraid that Box Elder's vision was coming to pass.

The crier declared, "We had better look to making breastworks! The soldiers are nearly upon us!"

Crow Split Nose—chief of the *Himo-we-yuhk-is*, the Crooked Lances, and second in command of the Elk Society only to Little Wolf—stepped forward to bravely declare, "I think it would be a good idea for the women and children to tear down the lodges and take them up to that cutbank to the west where there is a good place to throw up breastworks. They should do this at once."

Emboldened by the news of strangers around their camp and the courageous words of those who would defy Last Bull's Kit Foxes, many of the families turned away at this time and once more prepared to take blankets and robes and special treasures into the surrounding hills to safety.

But as quickly the brazen chief and Wrapped Hair appeared in their midst, screaming for their warriors, sending the bold young men here and there—ordering them to whip anyone who attempted to leave the village. If simply cutting cinches would not work, the Kit Foxes were to beat their own people with their bows.

"No one will leave this village tonight!"

Wrapped Hair agreed, raising his voice in the martial call. "We will stay up all night and dance—then defeat the soldiers come morning!"

Last Bull whirled on Crow Split Nose with a cruel sneer, spiting out his words, "Why are you so afraid of the *ve-ho-e* soldiers, Crow Split Nose? You will not be the only man killed if we are attacked!"

"I do not care for myself," the Elk Society leader replied stoically. "I care only for the women and children who will be killed because of your foolishness. I want to get them up where they will be safe when the bullets fly about our heads. We must leave only men in camp."

"Yes—there will be men in camp!" Last Bull roared.

"Good," Crow Split Nose said, his eyes gleaming with fury. "Come morning you will know what is to happen to our people. Wait until morning, Last Bull—and your fate will be at your door!"

Laughing off that challenge, the war chief of the Kit Foxes turned to his warriors and once more commanded them to scatter, staying on guard to see that no one fled camp. Once more he waved his arms and the drum began, the songs rising into the cold night air as the hundreds of feet pounded the frozen earth.

It filled Morning Star's heart with sadness as he watched his own three sons join the dancing.

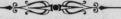

Chapter 25

25 November 1876

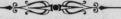

At long last the final company was "up," closing the file, those last soldiers joining the rest in that gently sloping patch of ground before the entire command once more fell silent between the hulking shoulders of that canyon they would be plunging into momentarily.

They had covered more than twenty-five miles in darkness to stand here on the threshold of attack, listening to the distant voice of that war drum.

Then Mackenzie returned with Rowland and the Cheyenne scouts, coming alive, the colonel animated suddenly—officers old and young clustered around him. He raised himself in his stirrups as his staff came to a halt, fanning out in a crescent around their leader.

"From what our scouts tell us, the Cheyenne are having war dances in at least four locations in that village. Rowland's men spotted at least three pony herds, and the lodges are pitched on both sides of the creek. Seems they tell me that with all the noise and activity going on, we can advance up the canyon some distance before we would be in danger of alerting the village," the colonel told the hushed gathering in low tones. "We'll get into position, conceal the column, and begin the attack at daylight."

He then went on to order up the companies he believed were most ready to spearhead the first assault into the village, ordering the North brothers to lead their battle-eager Pawnee into the breech in advance of any soldiers—punching through the village and on to secure the Cheyenne pony herd should there be the slightest chance of an enemy ambush.

Then he gave the order of the attack, company by company.

And concluded his terse, clipped instructions by saying, "Gentlemen, inform your battalions of their deployment. I hope to capture the village in a pincers: between one arm formed by the Shoshone and Pawnee, and the other arm by our troops. If all units do as I have ordered, we should surround the village completely, shutting off all chance for the hostiles to escape. With that in mind, remind your men of General Crook's admonition—that we must do our best to assure the enemy's capture, especially the lives of the women and children. Spare all noncombatants as we seal off the village."

Mackenzie arose in the stirrups once more, tugging at the brim of his big black slouch hat, preparing to tear it from his head dramatically. "This is what we've prepared for. Let it be us who go and end this war, here and now."

"It must ache like hell," Seamus had been speaking in low tones to the lieutenant beside him.

John Bourke was roughly kneading one hand with the other, both of them securely wrapped inside their heavy wool mittens. "Damn, it does."

"The cold will bother it for the rest of your life, aye?"

"Ever since last winter at the Powder."

"When you stuffed you hand down through that hole in the ice and plunged it into the freezing water," Donegan commented. "You gonna be all right to handle a gun with it?"

Bourke tried out a feeble grin in the gray light ballooning behind them as the walls ahead of them echoed the distant drum upvalley, where they watched Mackenzie, Rowland, and the Cheyenne scouts returning, emerging suddenly out of the mouth of the valley. "I can still hold a pistol as good as any man, Irishman. And pull the damned trigger when I have to."

"Just promise you'll stick close to me, Johnny," Seamus suggested. "I'd like to have a man of your caliber at my back."

The grin became a warm smile. "We have had our backsides hung over a few fires together, haven't we, Seamus?"

He smiled back at the officer. "And a lot more to come too."

"And now the Cheyenne."

"This? Why this morning is just another day at the office for you desk-jockey sojurs!"

"Damn you," Bourke replied with a grin, then said, "Look at that, will you?"

Seamus turned, finding the morning star brightening the sky behind them in the east. "It's a good omen, Johnny."

"Damn right, it—"

Then they both jerked up, finding Mackenzie standing frozen in the stirrups as the entire force of Indian allies fell mute—their medicine songs stopped in midphrase—a hush fallen over the whole of Mackenzie's column. Stunned into silence as they began to realize that the big drum had been stilled. No longer did they hear any of the fragments of primal songs reverberating down the canyon.

Suddenly many of the weary troopers were coming off the icy ground, leaping to their feet, having lain down next to their horses to sleep, reins tied at their wrists, so exhausted they paid no heed to the deep snow and the subzero temperatures.

Then all was a noisy blur as the men began knocking the white fluff from their coats with tiny billows while the captains and sergeants and corporals hurried through the litany of forming up their units.

In that next instant one of the Sioux scouts kicked his pony savagely, pounding his heels into its flanks, bumping into Donegan's bay as the Indian shot past the stunned Irishman. Everyone else suddenly speechless with this bold and idiotic act.

"Who the hell is that?" someone cried from the headquarters group.

"Scraper!" Frank Grouard hollered angrily.

"Get that son of a bitch back!" Mackenzie ordered, pulling his revolver and yanking back on the hammer as if he were prepared to knock the brash Sioux out of the saddle himself.

In a flurry of feathers and greasy blankets, rifles held high, two more Sioux scouts dashed past, ordered by Three Bears to head off the young man's daring solo assault on the village.

"Dumb son of a bitch," Bourke murmured. "Eager to get in the first coup."

"Or get himself a name for being the first one to die fighting in the village!" Donegan replied.

"He was just arguing with Three Bears," Grouard explained as he moved up. "Mad he didn't get his sergeant's stripes. So I figure he wants first strike."

Everything was close to pandemonium as the troops finished dressing their formation, every last man pitching himself into the saddle with great urgency of a sudden, horses sensing what was to come. The allies pressed in upon the colonel and his headquarters bunch—eager to be off to join those three who had disappeared through the tall willows and around a sharp right-hand bend to the valley's throat.

"Lieutenant Dorst—it's time to order the charge!" Mackenzie bellowed above his group, again rising in the stirrups, finally ripping the floppy-brimmed hat from his head and waving it enthusiastically as his adjutant pranced up on his mount. Then the colonel turned to Crook's aide. "Captain Bourke—would you care to take the order for our charge back to Major Gordon and his battalion?"

"I'd be honored, General!" Bourke replied, twisting his horse about in a tight circle and giving it his heel to race back across that patch of open ground.

Mackenzie was then waving his hat, emphatically signaling. "Major North! Now! In with your Pawnee battalion!"

Those forty-eight allies had stripped off coat and saddle, down to the barest battle dress, maintaining enough of their uniforms so that the soldiers would recognize them in the din, confusion and fear of the fight now about to open in all its color and splendor, the crushing weight of its blood and its terror.

"Major Cosgrove!" Mackenzie hollered as the North brothers galloped off, shouting their orders, the Pawnee sergeants twisting about on the bare backs of their ponies to pass on the commands to each troop of the battalion as an excited babble of many different tongues rose over the command. "You and Lieutenant Schuyler—in with the Shoshone! Take and hold that high ground on our left flank! In with you, *now*!"

Brave Wolf did not join in the dancing last night.

The Contrary warrior and a few of his friends successfully eluded the Fox Soldiers who were charged with preventing anyone from leaving camp . . . but slipping out was easy, for it seemed Last Bull's warriors had celebration on their minds. Women and dancing. Women and laughter. *Women.*

It was easy for Brave Wolf and his friends to sneak from camp, thread their way through the leafless brush, and climb the plateau north of the village where one or more of them kept a vigil throughout those frigid hours among the rimrocks. Expecting the soldiers to approach the camp sometime during the night and attack once dawn had arrived.

In the cold light the flames from the huge bonfire were eventually allowed to fall, and at last the Fox soldiers allowed the

People to stumble off to their beds. So weary were they from dancing nonstop across the night.

An old man looked up from his bed and asked his son, "You have been up in the rocks?"

Brave Wolf nodded in answering his father as he ducked into his family's lodge. "Yes. We saw nothing. Some of us heard a rumble, in the east. But . . . we saw nothing."

"They are coming," his father declared, his eyes wide with anxiety.

Brave Wolf glanced at his mother, looking at them both, a blanket pulled up to cover most of her well-seamed face, only her frightened eyes showing like radiant pools in the dim light. His two wives and his children were already soundly asleep in their robes and blankets.

"What do you want me to do, Father?"

"Do not take off your moccasins," the old man instructed. "Take nothing off . . . so you will be ready when the soldiers come here."

"My mother is ready?" Brave Wolf asked.

"We did not take off our clothes," his father replied. "None of us—not your wives and children—so we will be ready to run to the cliffs when the shooting starts."

Swallowing with growing apprehension, Brave Wolf settled on his haunches before the dead fire his father was beginning to rekindle with shaking hands. "I told you, Father: we saw nothing. No sign of the soldiers—"

"You remember Box Elder's vision?"

Brave Wolf nodded.

His father continued, "I believe the power of that man's medicine. All the times Box Elder told our people some event was about to occur, it came true. I believe he is right when he told the village he saw soldiers attacking us here."

"All right, Father," Brave Wolf said as he crawled over to his blankets and robes. "I too will sleep with my clothes on—so I will be ready when the soldiers come."

Around Seamus and Bourke crowded the Sioux, Arapaho, and the Cheyenne scouts under Lieutenant William Philo Clark and Second Lieutenant Hayden Delaney, their ponies prancing, sidestepping smartly—every man wound as tight as the mainspring in a two-dollar watch.

Mackenzie's big chestnut was among them in the next moment. "Mr. Clark! Mr. Delaney—as ordered, you will lead your battalion up the center and into the village!" The colonel's eyes fell on Donegan as men yelled and horses grunted. "You— Irishman! Watch that pretty head of hair!"

"Aye, Colonel! Hep-haw!" And they were all off like the rush of a wave crashing upon the shore, him and his bay carried away at the front of those Indians, who suddenly freed their wildest screams and screeches all around him.

He was part of it, this rising of his gorge, this swelling of the animal within him. And then Seamus was bellowing along with the Indians, his throat raw with the cold, the muscles in his neck bulging as his horse tore down into the willow with the rest thundering all about him.

The cold along his cheeks stung every bit as much as the whiplash of those eight-foot-tall bare willow branches slapping, clawing, snatching at him and the others as they threaded their way across a little feeder stream, up the other side, the horses slipping on the icy ground, slashing the far bank with their hooves, a few of the ponies going down—the cries of their riders swallowed over with the rest of the clamor. Men left to climb back out of the frozen mud and boggy marsh, to remount and follow in the wake of those who clung to their wide-eyed, frost-snorting mounts like hellions thrust right out of the maw of Hades and flung headlong into this new dawn.

Right through the narrowing neck of the canyon where the riders could race four abreast now and on into the widening valley where the lieutenants shouted and Cosgrove bellowed— leading their Shoshone to the left, their ponies scratching for a hold on the red-rocked side of the slope they began to ascend, one horse at a time, climbing, climbing to reach that high ground where they could seize a commanding field of fire over the village.

Now the Pawnee were beginning to cross to the far side of the creek to the south of the canyon. Slowed, their ponies cautious, as they slipped and fought for footing again on the ice-rimmed banks, most of the animals hurtling into the water—legs flailing in the air as they came down into the shockingly cold creek—rising with a struggle to leap across the stream with their riders and vault to the far side, sprays like cock's combs roostering into the gray light of that bloody dawn, the first crimson light of day smeared recklessly on the tops of the high red bluffs above them all. The Pawnee screeched and cried out, exhorting one another, brandishing their carbines, many of them clamping the reins in their teeth as they splashed one another in that mad race to be the first in among the lodges ... to be the first in to claim the finest of those Cheyenne ponies.

Among them one lone Pawnee shaman blew on a wooden pipe, its high-pitched notes rising with a waver above the hammer of hooves and the grunts of the horses, the cracking of ice and the snapping of bare willow limbs against legs and saddles and muscled pony flanks. A sound not unlike the wet, steamy whistle of the boats in Boston Towne's harbor, these notes the man blew as they raced along—a strange, eerie war song that lifted the guard hairs on the back of the Irishman's neck. Made that huge scar across the great width of his back tingle once more with alarm.

He had been swept up in half a hundred charges during the Civil War, riding stirrup to stirrup with brave men only heartbeats away from death, their bodies shredded by grapeshot and canister erupting in their midst. Seamus had been wounded before—hit not by shrapnel from Johnny Reb cannons, but hit instead by bone from the comrade riding to the left or right as their gallant troop set out behind the colors and banners and battle streamers for the enemy lines.

But nothing had ever stirred in him the feeling of being so carried away, of being so ultimately helpless against the powerful thrust of this moment in time, the way this charge reached down inside him and yanked him up by the balls. His heart rose to his throat, raw as it was—then he realized he was screaming at the top of his lungs with the rest of the copper-skinned scouts.

It surprised him when the first shots cracked the cold, brittle blue air of that valley morning yet to be touched by the faintest intrusion of the winter sun.

"Bet that's one of them sonsabitches shooting off his gun at a herder boy!" Grouard growled beside him. "Get 'em some Cheyenne ponies!"

"Don't make me no never-mind, Frank," Seamus said. "The bleeming ball's been opened, which means you and me are up for the first dance!"

Maybe it was one of the Cheyenne in the village who heard the first thunder of the hooves, Donegan thought as the big bay surged beneath him, all muscle and foaming fear ... perhaps a warrior snatching up his weapon and bursting into that frozen morning, standing naked to confront that trio of Sioux scouts.

No matter now: the whole bloody village was brought to life with battle cries and thunderous echoes from each side of the canyon—up ahead children screaming and women crying out, the old wailing as they stumbled into the gray light of that terrible morn.

This dawning of a cold day in hell.

Warriors sweeping up weapons and cartridge belts, quivers and bows, hurriedly tying their war medicine at their loose hair or dropping the cords of pendants around their necks. Taking time for little else—this sudden attack did not allow them the leisure to paint, time to dress, the luxury of fleeing with blankets and robes. Instead these warrior would thrust their naked, shivering bodies between the first of the soldier scouts and their families. Protecting, defending. Laying down their lives.

And then Seamus realized what it was that was dragging its razorlike claws across the inside or his belly: he suddenly sensed how it must be to protect those you love, to defend your home, to stand and face the assault at all costs. Somewhere inside he sensed as he had never before sensed just how these Cheyenne warriors would fight this day—from lodge to lodge, rock to rock, yard by yard ... and it scared Seamus down to the marrow of him.

Now Gordon's soldiers were pressing hot upon the scouts' tails, Mauck's battalion coming hard behind them: a mad cacophony of men bellowing orders on the run above the deafening tumult of sound laid back upon sound within the re-repeating echoes quaking within that canyon—not a single mount slowing as the soldiers fanned out, sweeping into a broad front behind Donegan and those savage mercenaries Mackenzie brought there to destroy the Cheyenne.

As if they had suddenly emerged from the narrowing maw of a cannon, immediately before them lay the narrow plain—the enemy village no more than three quarters of a mile ahead. Behind him troopers whooped and hollered. Indian scouts cried out anew with their medicine songs. And every heel hammered unmercifully into the ribs and flanks and bellies of their heaving mounts.

Somewhere far behind him and to his right, where Mackenzie's headquarters group would be, a lone bugle stuttered out the notes of the charge. Again and again it echoed back on itself from the terrible blood-tinged red walls.

As if any of these men had to be told, Donegan mulled to himself as he clamped tight and low to his animal. As if any of them had to be told they were to hurl themselves into the goddamned thick of it.

Ahead in that dusky darkness of a night graying into morn

Seamus made out the first faraway muzzle flashes. The sharp cracks of carbines stuttered a heartbeat later. Then the big drum suddenly throbbed again, this time not with the steady, rhythmic beat that had signaled last night's revelry. Now it was beaten frantically, a call of alarm hammered out upon its taut surface, warning and awakening even the heaviest of dark-skinned sleepers.

At that moment Seamus watched the North brothers turn their battalion off the narrow terrace that ran along the mountain to their left and plunge their mounts down into the boggy creek bottom to make a recrossing. For what godforsaken reason, he could not figure out. While the Pawnee ponies jammed up in the the miry ground, slowed to all but a stop as they struggled up to their bellies in the muddy swamp, Seamus and the other scouts rumbled past.

Then in the growing clamor of gunfire and wailing women, Seamus turned—suddenly hearing the eerie croon of that Pawnee's sacred flute again in the noisy cacophony of gunfire and screaming voices, surprised to find the first of the North scouts freed from the boggy ground, all of them laid out along their ponies' necks, racing with total abandon once more toward the heart of the village, which for the most part lay along the south bank of the creek as it flowed to the east out of the canyon.

A few gunshots rattled behind him—among the Pawnee.

They must have run onto a herder out alone back there, Seamus thought as his horse swept across the grass slickened with icy frost toward the first of the deserted lodges erected in the starkly beautiful amphitheater, the walls rising above them five hundred feet in places, a thousand feet in others. In numberless icy brooks and freshets, waters tumbled down into a maze of shallow ravines, each one slashing the valley floor in its race to feed its waters to the Red Fork, each crevice thereby marked with the telltale path of willow and box elder.

As the lodges loomed closer, his nose came alive.

Woodsmoke and green hides laid out for fleshing, roasting meat and animal fat to be mixed for pemmican with last autumn's cherries, the odor of fresh dung and the scent of unmitigated fear. Donegan had smelled all these before—as far back as the summer of sixty-nine and the destruction of Tall Bull's village at Summit Springs.*

On to the Comanche and Kiowa and Cheyenne camps hud-

---

*Black Sun, Vol. 4, The Plainsmen Series.

dled at the bottom of Palo Duro Canyon, which rose majestically above the smoke-blackened lodges in just the way this valley rose above these lodges he and the rest of the scouts found themselves among of a sudden.

In the middistance the flashes of the enemy guns became a steady, pulsing light as the Cheyenne warriors fired, retreated to another lodge, turned and fired once more as they sought to stem the overwhelming tide ... then hoped for nothing more than to protect the retreat of their families.

To his right Seamus could see that down the northern edge of the elongated valley ran a low plateau for something on the order of a mile. Ahead beyond the village the canyon itself disintegrated into a series of upvaults and deep ravines, flat-topped hills and snakelike gulleys where he could barely make out the black flit of bodies against the growing light of that cold day. Swarming into every recess in that rocky red sandstone maze— the Cheyenne were making good their escape among those rugged slopes that tumbled one upon another into the high white mountainsides just now touched with the rose of the sun's rising this cold, cold day.

It reminded Seamus of the color of blood daubed, spilled, smeared upon the snow.

The way the warriors had fled to the steep sides of the canyon, there likely to take cover and train their fire down upon the village, Donegan realized Mackenzie's dawn attack already had the makings of one damned cold day in hell.

Chapter 26

Big Freezing Moon
1876

He could not see if it was light yet, for he had been many, many winters without the power of sight. But behind his eyes where the sun never shined, Box Elder nonetheless knew. In his mind he could see what was about to happen as clearly as he had seen with his eyes as a young man.

In his dream he heard the thunder of the hooves before he heard it with his ears. Beneath him he felt them coming.

And he sat up.

"Bring me the Sacred Wheel Lance!" he cried, his voice thin and reedy with so much singing and praying among the rocks in the hills last night as the celebration had gone on at Last Bull's big fire.

Now his throat was sore, and it hurt so to use it.

His young nephew, the son of a son of a friend who wanted the boy to apprentice to the great shaman of the *Ohmeseheso*, quickly snatched up the ten-foot-long lance at the end of which hung the round rawhide-braided wheel that was Box Elder's special medicine—given him by the earth spirits so many, many summers ago when he had first begun to use his powerful gifts.

One of those gifts he had used time and again was the power to see what was to happen in some time yet to come.

He had seen the soldiers and their friendly Indians coming.

And now they were here!

Young Medicine Bear helped the frail old man throw back his blankets and the heavy robes and get to his feet.

"Put the long shirt over my head—hurry!"

The youth dropped the long, fire-smoked elk-hide shirt over the gray head, the four long legs of the animal almost brushing the floor of the shaman's lodge. Besides that heavy shirt, Box Elder wore no more than a breechclout.

"My buffalo moccasins. Hurry—we must go!"

One at a time Medicine Bear shoved them on the old man's bony, veiny feet, then rose to help Box Elder shuffle to the door and step out into the bitter cold.

"The sun is not at the top of the ridge?" the old one asked, unable to feel its warmth on his face as he emerged from the cold lodge.

"No—"

"Box Elder!"

He turned at the sound of the voice crying out his name. Already screams floated like shards of ice from the lower end of the camp. "Curly? Is it you?"

Then the warrior grabbed Box Elder's thin arm. "It is I, old friend. Come—we must hurry into the hills with your Sacred Wheel Lance."

"What of Coal Bear?" Box Elder asked, his voice high and filled with dread.

"He already has *Esevone** wrapped in its bundle, and I see they are coming this way," Curly explained.

"Box Elder!" he heard Coal Bear, the Keeper of the Sacred Hat, call out to him.

"You have *Esevone?*" the old man asked, wishing his eyes could see, for his ears were already telling him of many guns beginning to explode at the far end of the valley.

"It is on my wife's back."

"She is with you? And you have *Nimhoyoh?*"†

"I do, in my hands—here, feel it now, for we must go quickly!"

Box Elder reached for Coal Bear's wrist, his fingers working down to the hand that held the round cherrywood stick about the length of a man's arm. Suspended from the stick was a crude rectangle of buffalo rawhide, the edges of which were perforated, then braided with a long strand of rawhide. From the three sides

---

*The Sacred Buffalo Hat.
†The Sacred Turner.

of *Nimhoyoh* hung many long buffalo tails, tied to the rawhide shield like scalp locks.

"Hurry, old friend!" Coal Bear repeated.

Laying a hand on Coal Bear's arm, Box Elder started to move off. "All of us go together. I will flee with you and *Esevone*! Give the Turner to Medicine Bear so that he might carry it above him on his pony to turn away the soldier bullets!"

Coal Bear gave the heavy object to the young apprentice. "And we must let the woman walk ahead of us," Coal Bear turned to instruct the other two men with them. "She carries the Sacred Hat and we must not walk too close to her."

The blind shaman nodded, saying, "I think we should walk a little to the right and behind her, my friend."

Other warriors appeared like shards of black ice through that cold mist slinking among the lodges, mist that hugged the ground with its bitter, bone-chilling cold. Peeling off to the left and right in a tight crescent behind the woman, Coal Bear and Box Elder, those determined men, formed a protective guard as Coal Bear's wife walked toward the hills as slowly as if she were merely carrying the sacred object to another camp.

While they moved along, Box Elder held his Sacred Wheel Lance over his head so that the whole group would have its protection from the soldier bullets. First in one hand, then in the other, back and forth he switched it as his thin, bony arms grew tired holding the long lance in the air so that its power could rain down upon them all . . . but he would not let any of the younger men carry it. Nor did he falter in this duty to his people.

The Sacred Wheel Lance would make them all invisible so the soldiers and their terrible Indian scouts would not see them fleeing with *Esevone*.

Cries of the dying and screams of the frightened, thunder of hoofbeats and hammer of footsteps, rushed past their little party like a spring torrent cascading from these very mountains, bullets snapping branches and slapping the frozen lodges—but none of it gave Box Elder's group any concern.

All around them the People ran and the enemy raced.

It was as if Box Elder and the rest were not there.

The hard, icy, compacted snow whined beneath his winter moccasins made of the thick buffalo hide with the fur turned in as Young Two Moon plodded across its silvery surface beneath the last of the night's starshine. Day was coming.

And with the dawn, so too would come the soldiers.

He believed it not in his mind, but knew it in his belly. With a certainty he had experienced few times in his young life.

Although he was a Kit Fox—and duty bound to obey and serve last Bull—Young Two Moon had seen the soldiers with his own eyes, even walked among them and joined the soldiers' many Indian scouts at their fires as they spoke in the Shoshone* Pawnee, Ute† and Bannock, even Lakota and Cheyenne tongues! Such a force of pony soldiers and their many, many wolves were not out in this country, surely not out marching in this mind-numbing cold, on a lark.

But that's just what it seemed to be: a lark for Last Bull and the rest of his Kit Fox Soldiers, who enjoyed themselves far too much bullying the entire camp so that no one could flee to the breastworks, escape to safety, prepare to defend the village.

But Young Two Moon was an honorable warrior. Sadly, reluctantly—he took his place with his warrior society and kept everyone in the camp dancing and singing.

By the time he wearily reached his family's lodge at dawn, it seemed everyone had already gone to sleep, so exhausted were they from that night-long dance, around and around and around the drum when instead the young men should have had fighting on their minds. Not young women.

It was dark in the lodge. And cold here too. He let his eyes adjust to the dim light as he squatted near his parents' bed at the back of the lodge. And struggled for a moment more before he knew he had to speak what he had been fighting all night.

"Father."

He waited a moment.

"Father?"

"What do you want?" Beaver Claws grumbled with fatigue.

"I want my family to get up and dress. *Now.*"

The man rolled toward his son, pulling the buffalo robe back from his face. When he spoke, his words became frost in the gray light of dawn-coming. "You want us to get dressed? We just came here to sleep! Be quiet and go to bed."

"Please, father. Get the family up and dressed and come with me," Young Two Moon pleaded, then turned slightly, hearing the rustle of blankets, finding his father's second wife rising to an elbow to listen at the side of the lodge.

---

*Sosone-eo-o.
†*Mo-ohtavaha-taneo*, "Black People."

"The soldiers?" the older man asked.

"Yes. It will be soon," he replied, his voice thinned by urgency. "Please hurry! The day is nearly here! We must go to the far end of the canyon, climb into the rocks where you will be safe!"

"All right," Beaver Claws answered in a louder voice, then patted the woman beside him on the rump as he sat up, the blankets and robes falling from his bare chest. "Everyone! Get up! Get dressed! This young warrior believes the soldiers are coming—and I choose to believe him . . . because he has seen the enemy with his own eyes!"

Black Hairy Dog was not used to such cold as this.

For generations beyond count his people had ranged the southern plains. But now that the white man had rounded up the many clans and forced them onto the reservation in the southern country,* he had fled north with the Sacred Arrows once his father, Stone Forehead, had died.

Now the powerful objects were Black Hairy Dog's responsibility. On his aging shoulders rested so much of the fate of his people. He was one to trust the visions of the old ones much more than he trusted the preening talk of the war chiefs.

There had been much strutting last night as the People gathered around the great, roaring skunk and danced shoulder to shoulder, sliding their feet a step at a time, the throbbing circle moving right to left, following the path of the sun.

Last Bull's brash young men, drunk with their sudden power, swayed in the dance, singing out to boast of their war coups over the Shoshone. One of them held aloft the withered hand and arm of an enemy woman. Another cavorted about with a bag filled with the right hands of twelve Shoshone babies. Another, called High Wolf, proudly displayed his necklace of dried fingers. Flitting overhead in the fire's light wagged some thirty fresh scalps tied at the ends of the long poles as the Kit Fox warriors and their wives sashayed in and out of the grand circle.

When the People warmed to the celebration, the older trophies came out. A warrior swirled into their midst wearing the fringed buckskin jacket he had taken from the body of the man he had killed in the terrible fighting at the north end of the hill above the Greasy Grass River. Another proudly sported the black

---

*Darlington Agency for the Southern Cheyenne, Indian Territory.

hat emblazoned with the chevrons of a cavalry sergeant. Instead of a heavy blanket, another warrior pranced about in his soldier-blue caped mackintosh.

All around them voices sang and whooped until they were hoarse. And danced until their legs could barely move in those moments just before sunrise when the drum fell silent and the loudmouthed Kit Fox Soldiers told everyone to be off to bed.

"No soldiers are coming! Do not believe the Elk Scrapers—they are frightened old women! No soldiers are coming!"

So Black Hairy Dog laid his weary bones down in his robes and tried to sleep, but could not. Unable to shake the feeling deep in his marrow that for days had convinced him the village must be moved . . . time and again he remembered how nearly forty winters before a warrior society among his southern people had beaten the Keeper of the Medicine Arrows with their bows for publicly opposing them.

Again it was the power of the Arrows' intangible medicine pitted against the might of angry and prideful young men.

He pulled his clothes back on, then clutched a robe around his shoulders as he went to the nearby brush where he had tied his ponies to keep them close. Knowing in his heart that the soldiers were coming. The soldiers always came.

Black Hairy Dog began to drive the ponies up the south-eastern slope of the canyon, away from the village, when he heard the first yell break the cold, misty silence on the floor of the canyon.

Then heard that first shot.

And from that far end of the village he heard that first Cheyenne cry out as a woman spilled onto the bloody snow trampled beneath the onslaught.

"The soldiers are here!" Black Hairy Dog screamed, turning in the deep snow, tripping and falling—then picking himself back up to stumble down toward the village. "Hurry! Hurry! The soldiers are here!"

Damned funny, Seamus thought as the horse lurched beneath him, then fell back into its ground-eating stride.

For the life of him he couldn't figure out why the first of the Cheyenne warriors appearing out of the cold mist were firing at the heights south of the village. They weren't acting as if they realized the soldiers and their scouts were all but upon them. Instead, the warriors fired and dodged, dropped to one knee and fired, aiming at the Shoshone that Cosgrove and Schuyler had raced to the high ground. Up there Seamus could see the Snake dismounting, horses being led back from the edge of the cliff where the scouts plopped onto their bellies and began to pour some harassing fire down among the Cheyenne lodges.

Not far away, on Donegan's right, he watched some of the Sioux and Cheyenne scouts peel off for the village, leaving Mackenzie and his headquarters group suddenly exposed. A moment later a Cheyenne warrior leaped to his feet atop the low plateau on the north edge of the valley, leveling a rifle at the soldier chief.

Seamus no more got his mouth open to shout a warning than the colonel's orderlies all fired their pistols into the warrior. He was pitched back, spinning about, rifle tumbling out of his grasp as he disappeared into the brush, Mackenzie and his orderlies thundering on past.

To Donegan's left Frank and Luther North led their Pawnee among the first lodges, which were pitched at the end of the camp near the mouth of a dry creek clogged with leafless underbrush and stunted alder. From their left, near the opening of that ravine, a blanketed form sprang up directly in front of Lute North, who whirled his carbine down at the target and fired at almost the same instant that Frank pulled the trigger on his carbine. The shock of both bullets at that range catapulted the Cheyenne warrior off his feet, back into the brush as the horsemen raced on by.

Behind them the Pawnee yelped their approval and praise for making that first kill, *"Ki-de-de-de! Ki-de-de-de!"*

Singing out, the coatless battalion pushed on for the village, hoping for plunder, ready to fight hand to hand for enemy scalps as they plunged through the camp, intending to meet Mackenzie's soldiers on the far side and thereby seal off all chance for the Cheyenne to escape. But the delay caused by their recrossing the creek to join Mackenzie minutes before now doomed the colonel's plan of attack to frustration, if not ultimately to failure.

Already Donegan could make out the dark forms of the Cheyenne spilling from the west end of village far ahead, making for the high ground like coveys of quail flushed from the protective undergrowth.

"Dammit," he muttered, realizing that with the Cheyennes' flight, this was bound to turn into a long struggle of it. The warriors would quit fighting only if Mackenzie's men were able to capture the women and children.

As Seamus reined up at the downstream fringe of the lodge

circle, he turned the bay around, then wheeled the horse around again, searching out a target for the long-barreled .45-caliber Colt's revolver. North of him across the flat ground he saw Mackenzie and those outfits at the head of the charge slow—

A bullet hissed by.

Then a second snarled past his left ear, splitting it painfully.

"God-damn!" he bellowed between clenched teeth. As many times as he had been seriously wounded, still, nothing he had experienced had ever hurt with so much raw-edged torment as that wound to his ear as the cold breeze made every nerve come alive in the ragged laceration.

Jamming his pistol back into its holster over his left hip, Seamus tore off his gloves and yanked at the knot in the greasy bandanna tied at his neck. Ripping off his hat, Donegan quickly whirled the bandanna around several times to make a long bandage he quickly lashed around his head. When it was tied, he pulled on his hat and again hauled out the pistol just as his horse snorted and sidestepped.

Losing his balance with the animal's sudden move, Donegan spotted the approaching warrior from the corner of his eye as he was pitched from the saddle into the snow.

The lone Cheyenne skidded to a stop, kicking up a slow-rising rooster tail of fine snow with his feet as he brought a repeating carbine to his bare shoulder.

Rolling onto his belly as he landed with a cascade of snow, Seamus stretched out his arm, turned on his side, and squeezed the trigger. Sensing the jolt of the pistol in his paw, he continued his tumble sideways while drawing the hammer back with his thumb a second time.

He felt a bullet whine past him. Too damn close.

Rolling up onto his knees, Seamus brought the pistol's front blade to that spot where his instinct told him Indian had been . . . and pulled the trigger again. He watched the slug slam into the warrior's chest, knocking the Cheyenne off his feet. Spilling backward into the half foot of trampled snow, he skidded on his back a few feet before coming to a stop, arms and legs crooked and unmoving.

The amphitheater around Seamus thundered with the deafening rattle of hooves, shouts of men close at hand, and distant screams of the women bursting out of the far end of the village.

He dragged his legs under him and rose to his feet, dusted some of the snow off his front with that seven-and-a-half-inch pistol barrel, then turned at the hammer of hoofbeats bearing down upon him.

Past him on both sides burst more of the Sioux and Cheyenne scouts, led by Three Bears, streaming into the heart of the village.

Turning, Donegan whistled to the bay, then swept his hat out of snow, shoving it down so hard on the bandanna and flesh wound that it made him wince. Snagging the saddle horn in both gloved hands with the pistol between them, he vaulted atop the horse without using the stirrup and slammed the small rowels of his spurs into the animal's muscular flanks. It bolted off, straining to catch the scouts plunging into the mass of hide-and-canvas lodges.

Ahead of him the Sioux and Cheyenne advance was slowing, some men dismounting in a noisy, shouting whirl as the fighting became hotter. Less than a hundred yards away Cheyenne warriors were retreating one lodge at a time, fighting hard even in the face of the enemy horsemen.

Off to Donegan's left the pony ridden by the Sioux chief Three Bears reared, wheeled, and shuddered, becoming unmanageable in the midst of all those singing bullets and shrill voices, wing-bone whistles and lead slapping into the frozen lodge covers. After a great leap while it bowed its back, the pony suddenly tore from side to side crazily, then bolted straight for a cluster of lodges where the rifle fire from a knot of Cheyenne was the hottest.

Almost as fast as the pony bolted away, another Sioux named Feathers on the Head recognized the trouble Three Bears faced. Slamming his quirt down on his own pony's flanks, he bent low along the withers to avoid the enemy's bullets. He was all of thirty feet behind Three Bears when the war chief's horse wheeled to the left, leaped down the creekbank and up the far side, into the other part of the village still firmly held by the Cheyenne—only to halt suddenly in a spray of snow, go stiff-legged, and keel over, spilling its rider against a drying rack loaded with meat, and into the side of a canvas lodge.

Feathers on the Head was across the embankment and among the enemy lodges before a dazed Three Bears even had his legs under him. The horseman held out a foot and extending a hand as he wheeled his pony about, putting himself and his animal between the Cheyenne and his war chief, grunting as he pulled Three Bears up behind him.

It was a pretty, pretty show, Seamus decided, watching the

two of them spin about in the next heartbeat, all four of their legs kicking the pony into a gallop to speed them out of that devil's den of whining lead.

Something warned him, something so airy and ethereal— yet with enough substance that he thought he recognized it as Sam's voice in his ear, crying out. Seamus jerked around, certain he would find her there, the voice had been that real. Instead, at seventy yards he saw them coming, ten, perhaps a dozen of them: bare-breasted warriors yelling as they raced toward him.

In that next breath Donegan realized he was alone.

With the whine of a bullet passing by his cheek, the Irishman collapsed along the neck of the bay and slapped the long end of the reins down its front shoulder, feeling it explode into motion beneath him. The animal leaped back out of the brush, across the icy stream, where it slipped twice before clawing its way up the cutbank to the north side of the Red Fork, hooves cutting into the crusty snow as lead followed man and horse across the flat toward Mackenzie and his bunch now that the other companies were just emerging along the north side of the canyon.

The cold, icy fingers of frozen mist were only then beginning to lift from the willow-clogged bottom ground.

Why everyone believed Hades was hot, Seamus figured he would never understand. As far as he was concerned, this morning had all the makings of hell itself.

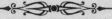

Chapter 27

Big Freezing Moon
1876

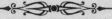

The power of *Maahotse* must protect the People!

As he raced back to his Sacred Arrow Lodge from the hillside, raising the alarm, Black Hairy Dog found his woman already taking the *Maahotse* bundle from its tripod where the Arrows hung at that singular place of honor in the lodge. When he burst into the lodge, his woman turned toward him with a start, carefully cradling the Arrows in their kit-fox quiver. Around it she had wrapped a layer of thick buffalo rawhide.

"I will follow you," she said to her husband as she laid the bundle across his arms.

"Together we will protect them," he said as her fingers brushed the back of his hand lovingly. "Just as these Arrows have protected our people far back into the time beyond memory."

Outside the lodge a group of men and boys had already gathered by the time Black Hairy Dog ducked through the door into the swirling, freezing mist that clung about their ankles. Most wore a shirt, or a vest of wool or buffalo hide, yet none wore leggings. On every face was the grim mask of determination. They had come there to protect the second of those two sacred objects of the *Ohmeseheso*.

"We must go to the hills," the Arrow Priest told them, slowly stepping into the small gathering without another word, parting them like a boulder thrown down in the middle of a narrow creek, the group closing in behind Black Hairy Dog's woman.

He knew he must take the Sacred Arrows to a hill overlooking the upper end of the village, leading that small procession of those who would protect him and the *Maahotse* as the terrible clamor grew at the far end of the village: gunshots, hoofbeats, the cries of enemy Indians, and the shrill blasts of the soldier horns.

Only then, from the heights overlooking the battle, could Black Hairy Dog rain the terrible unseen power of the Arrows down upon the enemy . . . and those *Tse-Tsehese* scouts who had come to help the soldiers against their own people.

"Dammit!" Ranald S. Mackenzie hollered, shrill as could be above the tumult as he slowed the orderlies and aides around him.

From what he could now see off to his left front, the Pawnee hadn't got into the village quick enough to shut the back door on the damned Cheyenne. They were streaming out of the far end of the lodges, fanning across that flat ground taking them toward the deep gulch and the rocky slopes at the western end of the valley.

That had been the whole purpose of sending those damned North brothers in at the head of the charge with their Pawnee! That, and making sure he didn't get his soldiers snared in a trap.

With the way the first of his troops had failed to form up into position during their charge, he had ordered the Norths to recross to the north side of the stream. In that way Ranald felt he had those additional horsemen close by—

Suddenly the air around him erupted with pistol fire. He spun in the saddle at the crack. Nearly every one of his orderlies had their revolvers barking, smoke curling up from the muzzles of the long-barrels, smoke whipped away on the brutally cold breeze. He spun to the other side in the saddle—spotting the Cheyenne warrior who had popped up nearly under their horses' bellies as they had passed by. The near naked body flopped back into the thick brush, quivered a moment, then lay still.

Now we're in the thick of it.

To the right his eyes quickly bounced over the slopes above him along that low plateau stretching a mile or so against the north side of the valley.

They could be anywhere in those rocks and brush. They'll fight us like that—one at a time from behind a tree, a clump of willow, down at the edge of a ravine. Dammit, it's going to be a dirty job to clean them out and mop this thing up now that the whole goddamned village is scattering.

"Smith!"

He watched the young orderly nudge his horse closer.

"Yessir, General?"

"Get back there as fast as you can ride." Mackenzie spat his words out with Gatling-gun speed. "Tell those company commanders to hurry their outfits through that neck and get across the creek! Got that?"

"Yessir!"

"Wait, Smith—I want those troops here and into the fight faster than on the double! Can you get that across to them!"

"Yessir!"

"Dismissed—now *go!*"

Smith hunched forward as his legs pummeled the ribs of his mount, all the while savagely sawing the reins of his horse to the side—nearly twisting the animal back on itself before it bolted away like the spring in a child's jack-in-the-box toy when the lid came flying back.

"General!" hollered Edward Wilson.

Mackenzie turned again, expecting to find another sniper along the hillside, but instead found some of his orderlies pointing in the same direction Private Wilson indicated.

"Bastards are making for that herd, aren't they?" the colonel growled.

Damn! For starters they hadn't sealed off the village, so now they would have to make a long and messy fight of it. And now it looked as if those damned Pawnee had got themselves bogged down in the village with those scouts from the Red Cloud Agency—which meant none of them were rounding up the enemy's herds.

Which just might mean some of the Cheyenne would be free to scurry after the herds themselves and drive them off before Mackenzie's force could capture them.

If the Cheyenne got those ponies into that broken ground at the far end of the valley, there was little his men could do to get them back, short of suicide. He had to keep those warriors— maybe two dozen or more from what he could count through his field glasses before the eyepieces fogged up against his face—had to keep every last one of them from reaching that big herd grazing up toward the bench to the west.

"Lieutenant McKinney!"

"General!" The handsome twenty-nine-year-old officer came up and skidded his horse to a halt, swapping his pistol to his left hand and saluted.

"My compliments," Mackenzie said, once more proud of this young officer he had taken under his wing since his graduation from the U.S. Military Academy in seventy-one. "You see those reds yonder?" the colonel continued. "The ones hurrying to get their hands on that pony herd?"

The Tennessee-born McKinney squinted in the misty gray of that dawn. "Yes, I see them, General."

"Can you see more of the enemy has taken up position behind that far hill down to the left of the herd?"

"Yes—I can make them out too."

"I want you to take your men—"

"K Troop, yessir!" McKinney interrupted enthusiastically.

"Take your men and drive a wedge between those sonsabitches running on foot for those ponies yonder. Drive them off, keep them from getting the herd. Then turn your attention on those bastards setting up shop along the top of the knoll there," Mackenzie said, grinding his teeth in frustration at possibly losing that herd to the enemy. "When you've got those warriors tied down on the knoll, take some of your men to wrangle that herd the enemy is attempting to recapture and get them headed back this way! Do you understand your orders?"

"Yes, sir—I think I do."

"I've given you a handful, Lieutenant," the colonel repeated with the affection he felt for McKinney evident.

"Yes, General!"

He watched the officer start to turn his horse away, then yell at McKinney's back, "Lieutenant!" The officer reined up suddenly and turned, his face eager, expectant, a great smile cut across its lower half. "Lieutenant McKinney—this is your day to shine!"

"Yes, General!" McKinney cried out loudly. "Thank you! Thank you, sir!"

"For a goddamned brevet!" Mackenzie reminded with a flourish and a smile, flinging his fist in the air as the officer wheeled about to dash back to his men.

"Yes, sir!"

"Carpe diem, Lieutenant! Seize the day, by God! Seize the day!"

*   *   *

Box Elder and Coal Bear walked a respectful distance behind the Buffalo Hat Woman, while Medicine Bear rode behind them all on a skittish pony, holding aloft *Nimhoyoh*, waving the thick hide of the Sacred Turner and its long black buffalo tails back and forth to ward off the enemy's bullets that kicked up snow and dirt from the ground at their feet, sticks and splinters from the trees all about them.

"We have a long way to go," young Medicine Bear called out, his voice filled with strain.

Distance mattered little to Box Elder. He could not see near nor far anyway. "We will get there. The powerful medicine in the Sacred Wheel I hold has made us invisible to the enemy—and the power in *Nimhoyoh* you carry turns away all the bullets flying around us. Do not be afraid!"

But the young man's words were true: they did have a long way to go. Barely out of the village, the party was progressing all too slowly. From off to their right arose the thunder of many, many hoofbeats. Only iron-shod American horses made such noise on frozen ground.

"I see a dry creekbed—not far!" Coal Bear announced, his voice raspy with apprehension.

"We will make it there safely," Box Elder replied confidently.

After reaching the mouth of the shallow ravine, the Buffalo Hat Woman led them up its twisting course as the ravine became deeper, until it intersected with the narrow canyon west of the village. Far up the sides of the canyon the women and children were climbing to the top, where the first arrivals were already digging rocks out of the side of the slope to stack one upon the other, forming breastworks for what they knew was coming: an all-out siege.

"Father!" a man's voice called out from among the noisy din of many crying, wailing, cursing women.

"Is it you, Medicine Top?"

"Yes, father," and the middle-aged warrior was at his father's side, touching Box Elder's arm.

"Your wife and daughter?"

"I brought them here," Medicine Top answered. "They are safe. Now I return to the village to fight."

A new voice called out, "Medicine Top!"

"Spotted Blackbird!" the son sang out. "Is your family safe?"

"My mother and sisters are all here now. Come with me back into the village to fight these Wolf People."*

"Wait," Box Elder said to restrain them, turning his face out of the sharp wind that stung his wrinkled cheeks as it fiercely drove the particles of old snow against his bare flesh. "Look back toward the village, into the valley. Is there a low hill where I might go to look down upon all that takes place?"

For a moment the old man waited on Medicine Top; then the young man answered.

"Yes. I see it. A rounded hill."

He gripped his son's arm tightly. "How far?"

"Not far."

"Take me there," his voice pleaded at the same time it demanded.

Spotted Blackbird protested. "We should be fighting the soldiers and their scouts in the village before they destroy all that we have!"

"No," Medicine Top argued, laying a hand atop the old man's. "I will stay with my father for now."

"Spotted Blackbird—you both will take me to the hill," Box Elder said. "From there I will show you how our medicine fights the soldiers just as powerfully as our bullets and guns."

"Irishman!"

"General!" Seamus called out in reply as he reined up near Mackenzie and his aides.

"You've been to the village?"

"Barely. Fighting off snipers."

"How goes the fight?"

"The Pawnee are having a time of it, what with the struggle the Cheyenne are making of it—determined to hold on to their village," Donegan huffed, twisting in the saddle to point behind him at the high ridge to the south of the camp. "But up there Cosgrove and Schuyler have the Snakes laying down a pretty heavy fire among those lodges. Making things hot for what warriors are still in there."

"There—that's the bunch that worries me," Mackenzie said, pointing his gauntleted arm to the southwest.

"Along the brow of that hill?" Seamus asked, squinting into the growing light reflected off the bright and crusty snow.

*The Pawnee.

"They're covering the retreat of their women, and harassing our men already in among the lodges, securing the village."

"But from the looks of things," Donegan replied, seeing the troopers formed up and beginning to move out, "you'll have that under control in short time."

"That's McKinney's troop—they're going to have a field day of it!" the colonel said enthusiastically.

"May I join them?"

"By all means, Irishman," Mackenzie answered. "Get your licks in before there's nothing more than some mopping up—by all means!"

"General!" Seamus whooped, his adrenaline bubbling as he saluted before wheeling away at a gallop.

He had covered most of that gently rolling, level ground, easing the bay into a full-out gallop to reach the tail roots of the last of McKinney's men racing forward in a tight column of fours, pistols drawn up, elbows bent, at the ready—when he saw the lieutenant suddenly rise in his stirrups, waving, reining to the side at the sudden appearance of that lip of a dark scar slashed across the white prairie.

At the next moment those first four troopers behind McKinney immediately sawed to the right, two dozen—maybe as many as thirty—Cheyenne warriors sprang out of the ground directly in front of the soldiers.

Right out of the bloody ground!

For that instant Donegan's mind grappled with it, knowing the enemy must have hidden themselves down in that twenty-foot-deep ravine so well that the soldiers were powerless to see the enemy until they were right upon them.

As the second group of four struggled to wheel right, they jammed into McKinney's first four as the shots exploded into them, point-blank.

His breath frozen in his chest, Donegan watched the muzzles of those Cheyenne rifles spit bright-orange jets of flame, illuminating the dawn mist, gray gun smoke wisping up from the lip of that ravine to congeal over the warriors' heads as they fired more shots into the confused ranks.

Then the rest of McKinney's troopers were all thrust together: many of M Troop's horses suddenly reared at the gunshots and the Cheyenne's cries, fighting their riders who twisted on their reins. The mounts corkscrewed about on their hind legs, pitching backward wildly with forelegs slashing the air, hurtling their riders off to the side as the sound of those deadly volleys rumbled across the flat ground toward the north slope.

As Seamus leaped off his horse, dragging the Winchester over the saddle with him, he watched McKinney's horse go down in a twisted heap, flinging its rider off toward the edge of the ravine. While the Irishman crouched forward on his knees, he fired, then chambered another cartridge.

Beyond him the young captain struggled valiantly to one elbow atop that snow quickly turning crimson beneath him, spitting blood as he stared for a moment down at the glove he slowly took away from one of his half-dozen wounds, finding it slicked with red, then collapsed beside the animal wheezing its last.

The muzzles from those countless Indian rifles puffed with red flames again as most of the other horses struggled up on their legs, tearing off in panic and terror to the four winds, their hooves throwing up clods of frozen snow behind them. One by one McKinney's fallen got to hands and knees, some able to do no more than claw themselves away on their bellies.

Then Seamus became aware of the distant roar of more gunfire coming from that nearby knoll, where more warriors lay now, all those guns trained down at these fallen soldiers like ducks in a tiny backwoods pond. Beneath the rattle and echo of near and distant gunfire, on the cold wind floated the cries of the wounded and the dying.

He chambered and fired into the teeth of those screaming Cheyenne bristling along the rim of the ravine.

Five of McKinney's troopers moved, some better than the others, as most of those not hit circled and milled. In their midst Second Lieutenant Harrison G. Otis attempted to regain control and order over M Troop. Most had all they could handle struggling against their balky horses, at the same time attempting to fire their pistols down at the side of that ravine where the Cheyenne had waited, and waited ... until the last moment—then burst up to shoot point-blank, all but under the bellies of the big American horses.

Two of the soldiers did not move, sprawled on the snow like some dark insects squashed there, their legs and arms akimbo. Just a few yards back from them the first of the mortally wounded horses were collapsing at last, one already flopping down, and the second going to its knees, then keeling over to its side, where all four legs thrashed until there was no movement in that air so quickly stinking of death, and blood, and the acrid smell of burned black powder.

That stench of burning sulfur reminded the Irishman of Hell ... the cries of both the Cheyenne and the wounded troopers convincing Seamus that this was Hades itself.

Another man lay beneath his dying horse, its big, muscular neck struggling time and again to lift its heavy head until it finally collapsed. The soldier was McKinney's bugler, Hicks, bleeding badly and with his legs pinned, bright crimson gushing from his mouth each time he called out in a hoarse voice for the others not to abandon him, for someone to free him before the Cheyenne would rush out to get him.

Try as Otis did to rally the remnants of McKinney's shredded command, M Troop milled, yelling at one another, some of them ready to bolt, some sitting numbly in their saddles, most ready to obey Otis's orders and stand their ground, although frightened to the core by the sudden, devastating shock of it. The young lieutenant suddenly ducked; a bullet spun his big black hat completely around on his head and pitched it to the snowy ground.

That was enough for two.

A pair of the soldiers suddenly wheeled about and put heels to their horses, breaking away in a wild retreat, making straight for the Irishman as he crabbed up on hands and knees. Behind the two, it was clear four more were ready to scatter in wild disorder.

Seamus stood suddenly, leveling his rifle at them, his hands shaking—sensing that gravity of pointing his weapon at white men, soldiers, comrades in arms ... as the first two soldiers drew close.

"Halt!" he bellowed, watching their wide eyes grow even wider, realizing these were youngsters likely never before tested in battle—green as recruits could come. "You can't retreat!"

"Just who the hell are you?" one of them demanded as both soldiers reined up, pitching up clods of icy snow.

"I'm the one gonna shoot you if you don't turn back to help!" he bellowed, eyes narrowing as he now saw the wounded trumpeter twist his body beneath the horse so he could position himself to shoot over the animal's quivering body at the Cheyenne crawling out of the ravine less than ten yards away from where the bugler lay trapped and stranded.

Of a sudden behind Seamus arose a clatter of hooves hammering the frozen ground, men's voices raised in unintelligible panic and battle lust. Donegan twisted about, reluctant to take his eyes off the two soldiers ready to run in retreat but suddenly frozen by the sight of that something behind the Irishman.

A troop of cavalry was racing headlong for them, both flanks spreading out left and right, moments before ordered out of a walk into a rolling gallop across a broad front. At Ranald Mackenzie's excited order, Captain John M. Hamilton was the first to lead the men of his H Troop, Fifth U.S. Cavalry, to the rescue.

More gunfire exploded back near the far head of the deep ravine—off to his right—drawing Donegan's attention. Another H Troop, these men from the Third U.S. Cavalry under Captain Henry W. Wessels, Jr., suddenly found themselves in the thick of it as they too dashed up under orders to support McKinney's butchered company on the extreme right side of the line. Now they became the big targets on those tall American horses.

Wessels's men began dismounting in ragged confusion and a rush of adrenaline as more Cheyenne warriors flooded over the lip of the ravine, continuing to lay down a galling fire among the arriving soldiers. Some of Wessels's horses escaped, yanking free of their riders and bolting to the rear, while a few horse-holders managed to grab hold of reins or bridles, clumsily snapping on the throatlatches to pull the unruly, frightened animals out of the action while the rest of H Troop inched forward, fighting on foot.

Close and dirty.

As Wessels's men hurried to the right, up toward the northern end of that jagged ravine so they could cut off the advance of the Cheyenne snipers, Seamus turned back to the coming thunder, finding Hamilton's mounted company was almost upon them.

"Get out of our way!" one of McKinney's terrified soldiers screeched, digging his brass spurs into his horse's belly as he shot past the Irishman.

Donegan leveled the rifle, then lowered it from his shoulder.

"I'll . . . I'll go back . . . with you," the other young soldier coughed the words out with a struggle, swallowing down his fear, no less terrified than the coward who already had his back to them and was tearing off at an angle away from the wide front of riders coming at a gallop to the rescue.

"Then get down here and fight on foot, sojur!" he cried as the massed front neared.

He watched McKinney's man wheel out of the saddle and

slap his horse on the rear flank—sending it off with a clatter as he joined Donegan to sprint headlong back into the breach while the first of that battlefront Hamilton had arrayed finally reached the bloody battleground where McKinney's soldiers lay dead and dying, all but swallowed by the warriors sweeping over them to count coup and claim the soldier weapons.

Hamilton's men were but moments from finding out they had just pitched into what would be the toughest fighting of that cold day.

Chapter 28

Big Freezing Moon
1876

"**G**et your guns!"

At the terror in that warning cry, Morning Star jerked up with a start, clawing for his leggings, kicking his feet out of the blankets and heavy robes.

"The camp is being attacked!"

Now he realized it was Black Hairy Dog's voice, crying out from the hillside at the upper end of camp.

"The soldiers are here! Get your guns! *Get your guns!*"

The enemy was swarming everywhere the moment he poked his head from the long opening he slashed in the back of his lodge with a butcher knife, pushing his wives and a nephew into the shockingly cold air. Guns boomed, their echoes reverberating from the red sandstone walls towering over the sleeping lodges.

War whoops cracked the frosty air on all sides. The shrill call of wing-bone whistles cried with the off-key notes of a flute. Then he saw them through the frozen mist.

Wolf People!

Bullets smacked into the lodge where he stood.

Morning Star whirled to find more soldiers' scouts high upon the red, snowy ridge that rose high over the south side of their camp. Fire spat from the muzzles of their many, many guns. But those were not Wolf People. Instead they wore their hair like Snake—a tribe friendly with the white man for a long, long time. They fired down on the village, some of their bullets even landing among the warriors covering the retreat on the west side of camp.

By now the Wolf People were already among the lodges, dashing in and out with screams of joy as they plundered the Cheyenne homes. These were old enemies too—so it was natural that they would join the soldiers in making war on Morning Star's peaceful *Ohmeseheso*.

Then he cocked his head slightly, listening carefully above the noisy din a moment as he watched his family flee from that slit in the back of his lodge. So painful to hear Lakota spoken by many of those scouts rushing to capture the village's ponies.

But what crushed Morning Star's spirit was to hear his own tongue spoken by some of the scouts. *Tse-Tsehese!* Cheyenne had come here to help the white man destroy this camp where both the four Sacred Arrows and the Sacred Buffalo Hat rested in peace and plenty. *Aiyeee!*

Past him and the other chiefs who stood protectively at the edge of camp flooded the last of the People now—most of them naked, bolting from their beds without robes and blankets, the men taking little but their weapons and cartridge belts, and the women dragging only their children into the cold and the snow. Many of these had slashed their way out of their lodges, plunging the blades of long knives through the backs of the frost-stiffened lodge skins or canvas lodge covers, frantically shoving their barefoot families out of the long slits into the bloody terror of that day-coming.

"Run! Run to the hills! Lie behind the rocks!" mothers cried at their little ones, men and women screamed at their aged relatives.

There in the breastworks the children were to stay until the parents could come to find them, until the strong could gather up the sick and the old—only then to continue their escape over the mountains to safety.

One group of five young women, including Buffalo Calf Woman—whose younger brother was blind—hurried clumsily past Morning Star, stumbling, collapsing together in a heap because they were all still tied together, just as they had been at the all-night dance of the Kit Foxes. Together they pulled one another to their feet, screaming in panic, starting away before the Old-Man Chief grabbed the last one in that line, jerking them all to a stop with one hand as his other snatched his dull-bladed knife from his belt. Quickly he raked the weapon against each thong binding the young women, one by one pushing them away toward the mouth of that narrow canyon running northwesterly from the edge of camp.

"Go!" he shouted. "Hurry!"

As he watched after them for that brief moment, he caught sight of his childhood friend, Little Wolf, standing there like a beacon fire a man would ignite atop a high and faraway point of land. Waving on the fleeing girls.

Just as the legends said Little Wolf had done last winter when the soldiers had attached Old Bear's camp on the Powder, the Sweet Medicine Chief of the *Ohmeseheso* again courageously stood his ground at the mouth of that maze of ravines which pocked the ground west of their camp, urging everyone past him to hurry in their flight, hollering his orders, urging speed as the men, women, and children darted from this direction and that into the deepening canyon where they would be safe from all but a full-scale assault.

It brought a mist to Morning Star's eyes as he looked upon Little Wolf, his old friend of many, many winters—standing there beneath the onslaught of the weapons fired by those Wolf People scouts penetrating the lower end of the village, standing his ground while the bullets fell about him, putting his flesh between those soldier guns and the lives of the People.

A chief's first responsibility.

Once the children and wrinkled ones were out of the village and on their way out of that network of ravines at the upper end of camp and into the deep and narrow canyon where the soldier bullets could not reach them, many of the women made their climb up the wall of that deep ravine and began to gather rocks at the lip of the canyon, erecting breastworks where they and their men would defend themselves to the death. For now the women sang their strong-heart songs as they worked, their voices rising like a prayer to give its power to their husbands and fathers, their brothers and uncles.

With their families out of camp, most of the warriors turned back to take up positions across the hillsides or at the crest of the knolls, where they flopped to their bellies on the snow and frozen ground, to fire down upon the advancing pony soldiers.

While none of the warriors at the lower end of the village had time to snatch up anything but their weapons as they urged their families to flee—some of those men choosing to make their stand there and then, dying on the bloodstained snow among the lodges—the men on the upper end of camp had enough frantic moments to catch up their horses, perhaps load a blanket or robe aboard them, and drive those ponies into the hills among that broken ground west of the village.

A few even whirled their ponies around and galloped back across the stream, singing out their war songs and exhorting one another to have courage once they spotted the first white soldiers approaching from the east at the foot of the hills along the north side of the valley. Although they had no hope of stemming the blue tide with their small numbers, nonetheless these young warriors raced toward those attackers, screaming and firing their weapons—if only to give the families a few more heartbeats to flee by laying down their own lives.

Some—rather than charging with the others—even dismounted and slapped their ponies on the rear to drive them off, each young warrior disappearing among the thick brush and undergrowth, from there to snipe at the white men as they came hurtling into the valley.

Morning Star's chest went cold as river ice with terror. He felt as if his heart had stopped—suddenly realizing one of his sons had pitched his family's lodge at the lower end of camp, where the enemy was thickest.

In the murky, misty darkness of that dawn, all Morning Star could see among the lodges and the trees were the startlingly bright muzzle flashes of the guns, hear only the crack-crack-crack of the weapons. A fierce fight was taking place . . . and the old chief knew, as any father would, that his child was offering up his life so that others might live another day.

The gunfire grew deafening on the far side of the village now. Bullets slapped the frozen lodge skins like hailstones, splintering the lodgepoles above his head. Morning Star's stomach rose into his throat: soldier scouts, Wolf People, were among the lodges on the south, seizing control of the village!

While those first soldiers appeared out of the north along the low plateau across the stream from the village, more than three-times-ten half-dressed warriors hurried on foot into the mouth of the deep ravine, all of them sprinting north at the bottom of the wide scar where the warriors would lie in wait to ambush some of the mounted soldiers if they came to attack the hills where the families fled for safety. At the same time a handful of warriors turned aside, dashing directly north across the open, rolling ground toward one of the pony herds.

The white man must not capture those horses!

The ponies were their wealth—what made waging war possible! What would allow the People to escape, to rebuild, to fight on!

Morning Star realized they must counterattack . . . about the time a group of soldiers against the north hills kicked their gray horses into a gallop and made a charge toward the low hill where Yellow Nose, who as a boy had been captured from the Black People,* commanded the many others who lay on their bellies firing their weapons at the Indian attackers pushing into the village.

Just as he was about to turn from the camp, he watched Yellow Eagle, Little Hawk, Strange Owl, Bobtail Horse, White Frog, Little Shield, and even Bull Hump—Morning Star's own son—as well as all the rest crouched in readiness . . . waiting . . . then suddenly spring out of the bowels of that ravine like hares popping out of their burrows, their rifles spitting fire and destruction into the faces of those charging soldiers—spilling horses, men crying out in shock and pain and death, some of the white men crawling, pleading for help, others not moving at all as the warriors unleashed a second volley, then a third into the backs of the confused, milling, retreating soldiers. Three warriors clambered up the steep wall of the ravine, onto the plain, shrieking as they leaped upon the *ve-ho-e* bodies to be the first to strike the dead enemy, then take the soldier weapons and cartridge belts.

Morning Star watched his son give the third strike to a soldier leader with the muzzle of his rifle. Then Bull Hump knelt beside the soldier's horse, cutting free the fat pouch tied behind the saddle. He raised it in triumph and screeched a victory cry.

"It is filled with many, many bullets!"

But then more soldiers were coming. Bull Hump and the others must have heard the hooves, the soldier guns, for they lunged back to the ravine . . . but instead of leaping to safety, Morning Star's son skidded to a stop, sliding to his knees in the trampled snow as he scooped up a revolver, crawling on all fours to pick another off the icy ground. Jamming both of them into his belt, he hobbled on to the lip of the ravine and pitched over as more soldiers charged up.

Shrill voices rang out behind Morning Star, filled with challenge.

---

* The Ute.

Below him at the upper end of the village, the last of Little Wolf's warriors now gathered to taunt the soldier scouts who had seized the ridge above the south side of the village—flinging their voices at the Snake, those ancient enemies: boasting to the scouts that only days before they had wiped out a Shoshone village, every man, woman, and child falling victim.

In the midst of that hail of bullets, Little Wolf and the others screamed their challenge to the Shoshone and boasted that in a time to come they would take revenge for this day's attack.

As soon as the left flank of those reinforcements began dismounting in a flurry among McKinney's survivors, Seamus got himself a good look at an insignia here and there.

This was the Fifth Cavalry. H Troop. As battle hardened a bunch as there ever was

"Thank God," he whispered, his eyes turning heavenward.

More bullets were again whistling among them. Those sharpshooters atop that knoll were spraying a galling fire into the horsemen arriving at the edge of that twenty-foot-deep ravine where the fallen horses and McKinney's men lay scattered upon the crusted snow.

"Halt!" came the shrill command behind Donegan and the wounded lieutenant's decimated troop.

There arose a cold clatter of metal and whining leather, scraping hooves and muttered oaths, as the entire command in battle front skidded to a stop.

Then an officer bawled, "Dissss-*mount!*"

The troopers leaped to the ground, yanking hard on their reins to turn horses about.

As Captain John M. Hamilton whirled toward the enemy, pistol held high, sergeants took up the cry, "Horse-holders to the rear!"

In a flurry every fourth soldier snatched the reins of three other horses, locking on the twenty-eight-inch throatlatches before wheeling about on his heel to drag his horses to the rear while the rest pushed forward on foot.

"Time's come you young'uns make sure you're loaded!" suggested an old file off to Donegan's right.

"L-loaded, sir, Sergeant!" some high voice squeaked.

Then Hamilton's boys were thrust into the thick of it.

Turning for one last look behind him at the plateau where he had galloped off from Mackenzie's group, Seamus spotted another company coming up on the double, dismounting right among H Troop's horse-holders, who were struggling away with their frightened, rearing mounts.

Now, with these numbers, at least they might just have a chance to cut their way out of things, Donegan thought as he dropped on one knee to take a steady shot—then immediately levered another cartridge into the breech and fired again as quickly as he could make that cold action work.

In the next instant he was back on his feet among the others, at least half of the soldiers advancing in a foragers' charge while the rest of Hamilton's company threw open the big trapdoors on their Springfield carbines and rammed home another of the fat, shiny sausages. Step by step, yard by yard, Hamilton expertly leapfrogged his men in two squads until Captain Wirt Davis's F Troop, Fourth Cavalry, reached the back of H Troop's line and infiltrated the skirmishing. Now both troops advanced together in a massed front as the Cheyenne on the tall bluff beyond the ravine laid their hottest fire in among the soldiers.

As the broad blue front inched forward across the bloodied snow, Seamus heard one man, then a second, cry out immediately as they were hit, both of them sprawling backward in the snow. The first went down noisily, thrashing and smearing the white, icy ground with a crimson stain, then lay still. The other collapsed to his knees, slowly settling backward as if he were merely sitting down to Sunday dinner without a complaint while his mouth moved soundlessly to form the word "Mother" and his blank eyes implored the cold blue sky above him

As the soldiers neared the edge of the ravine, the sun suddenly snapped over the ridge behind them, immediately flooding the snowy valley in an eye-stinging brilliance.

"By God," Donegan murmured under his breath as he jammed another half-dozen cartridges into the Winchester's receiver, his numb, clumsy fingers spilling a shell on the snow, "—the bastards have the sun in their eyes now!"

Some men grumbled curses all around him as they drew close to the enemy. A few men shouted commands as most struggled to reload with clumsy gloves and frozen hands—none of the platoons firing in ordered volleys now.

More warriors now at the edge of the ravine.

They were almost within spitting distance of the enemy. Still advancing on the Cheyenne. Foot by bloody foot. Another soldier cried out, and two men on either side of him knelt to grab the wounded one, turned and dragged him to the rear as he flailed his legs and screamed for immortal mercy, the front of his belly slicked with a dark stain.

"Damned gut wound," the Irishman whispered under his breath. A horrible way to die. A slow journey, one filled with teethgrinding agony.

So it was he suddenly remembered American Horse, how bravely the chief had died that night within the smoking ruin of his village at Slim Buttes.* Would this madness ever end?

But as quickly Seamus knew it would not. Could not. Not until the Indian was back on each miserable patch of ground the government laid out for him and called a reservation. Not until these brave men had all been stripped of weapons and ponies— stripped of their warriorhood.

It was plain that these at the ravine had chosen to die standing up, fighting to the end as they protected family and home. Such a man fought savagely, Seamus recalled. Because he had so much to lose . . . and at the same time had nothing more to lose.

Such an enemy fought much, much harder than any soldier far away from home would ever fight.

Off to the right and at the center of the line the soldiers made the first close-quarters contact with the Cheyenne in a sudden clash of shock and noise and voices, grunts and screams. Then as quickly the rest of them were in the maw of that hand-to-hand struggle. Suddenly so close the troopers could smell last night's supper on the breath of the warriors who flung their bodies against the two troops, close enough to smell the frozen grease on their hair. Close enough to smell the fear seeping from a man's pores.

He smelled no fear from the Cheyenne this day.

Just in front of Seamus one of McKinney's men flopped down onto his back, both his empty hands locked around the wrist of a warrior as the half-naked Cheyenne leaped onto him, a huge bear-jaw knife poised over his head. It was McKinney's sergeant, Thomas H. Forsyth.

Seamus turned at the hip, aimed at the warrior's head, point-blank, and squeezed the Winchester's trigger. Watched the Cheyenne's head snap away to the side in a bright spray of blood. Some of the crimson splattered upon that well-tanned face, which showed instant gratitude to him before the sergeant rolled out of the bloody snow.

Forsyth and another, Private Thomas Ryan, knelt over the

---

* *Trumpet on the Land*, Vol. 10, The Plainsmen Series.

body of their lieutenant, protecting McKinney as more warriors swarmed out of the deep ravine. Cartridge by cartridge they slammed beneath the trapdoors of their Springfields, daring to hold back the horde that screeched defiance and death.

"Deploy, goddammit!" the old sergeant bellowed again above the lieutenant's body. "Don't let them overrun us! Deploy as skirmishers! And *stand!*"

Then Donegan himself bawled a command above the clamor as he levered another cartridge into the breech and turned to meet the red onslaught, "Look the bastards in the eye, goddammit! Stand and look 'em in the eye!"

In the next breath Sergeant Frank Murray and Corporal William J. Linn were beside Ryan and Forsyth over the officer's body, standing, waving, hollering, rallying others who were still some twenty yards behind—exhorting every man of them to make a stand over their fallen comrades.

Lieutenant Otis darted here, then there, moving among the rest of the men as they knelt and went about their bloody, dirty work of it, ordering his soldiers of M Troop to lay down fire to cover the four who were protecting their commanding officer.

Linn pitched back, clutching at his hip, groaning as his legs thrashed in the snow and he scooted off in a bloody furrow, clawing the snow for his carbine. Another soldier knelt over him holding the wounded man down as he stretched for the Springfield.

Forsyth suddenly twisted to the side as he was reaching out to the wounded corporal—struck along the side of the head with a bullet that knocked off his hat, opening up a bloody flesh wound.

"We'll keep at 'em, Sarge!" Linn hollered in a pain-ridden gasp. Then he rolled over onto his side and dragged up his carbine, coolly slamming home another copper cartridge as he went on fighting despite the disabling wound.

Emboldened by the spirit of such brave men, Seamus inched forward, fired at a sudden appearance of more warriors breaking over the rim of the ravine, then crouched to reload. His scar prickled.

Whirling at the same moment he heard the whistle of the war club knifing through the freezing air. At the end of the club stood a tall, sinewy warrior whose eyes glittered with the fires of hate. Seamus started to lunge aside—

Grunting as the club's handle smacked across his left shoulder, the Irishman collapsed into the snow. Stars shot from his eyes as he sensed the startling cold smack his cheek; then he slowly realized a shadow blotted out the brilliant sunlight.

Pulling his '73 Model Colt and raking back the hammer in one motion, Donegan pointed it at the wide, screeching mouth above him ... as the pistol jerked in his left hand.

He quickly rolled aside onto the wounded shoulder and fired again from his back. A second time the warrior jerked as another bullet struck him ... then slowly the club pitched from his hands and he fell stiff-legged all but atop the Irishman.

Heaving the dead warrior off him, Donegan rose to one knee shakily. He swapped the pistol to his right hand, the whole left arm gone numb of a sudden, all but refusing to move. There on his knee he snapped the hammer back, aimed, and fired. Drew the hammer back again. Aimed at one of the warriors swarming over the nearby soldiers. Pulled the trigger. Watched the Cheyenne heave forward, clutching his armpit—as the Irishman yanked down on the hammer once more. Then fired as he pitched to his feet.

The screeching cries pulled him around as surely as if someone had him on a short length of rope. Up the bottom of the ravine bolted more warriors hurtling into the eye-to-eye combat, the first of them throwing themselves against the slick side of the coulee after firing a few shots at the soldiers, there to claw their way up through the icy snow to reach the heart of the battle itself.

In those few terrible minutes the ground lay littered with the refuse of that close and dirty fight: discarded weapons here and there among the bodies of the fallen warriors and the wounded soldiers.

Hamilton's men began to fall back against Davis's troopers beneath the ferocity of the warriors' attack as the Cheyenne cut and slashed and hacked their way into the blue ranks. Muscle strained against muscle until a knife or club, tomahawk or bullet, found its mark.

Then Donegan realized there was something wrong about the sound of those bullets whining in among the skirmish, most of them landing in the midst of the Cheyenne reinforcements clambering out of the ravine. The shots hadn't been fired from anywhere close—those bullets were instead fired from the far ridge ... where Cosgrove and Schuyler had their Shoshone scouts positioned.

As the allies walked their rounds into the melee, the Cheyenne turned, one by one, suddenly aware that they were drawing

fire from far away. Just as quickly as it seemed the weary, frightened soldiers were about to be overwhelmed and to die among
the bodies of McKinney's men, the tide of that skirmish shifted
dramatically. Precipitously. In the time it would take a man to
pass his hand over a candle.

Perhaps believing it to be something mysterious that bullets
were falling among them from the sky—at the very least a bad
omen—the warriors began shouting among themselves, falling
back, most of them tumbling back down the icy side of the ravine, picking themselves out of the disturbed snow at the bottom
and racing away from the soldiers.

Like the rest, Seamus fired the last shot in his revolver at the
backs of those warriors, then pulled his second pistol and cocked
it—aiming this time at the Cheyenne riflemen who still lay ensconced on the top of the nearby knoll, where they were doing
their best to hold a long-range duel with the Shoshone and put
short-range pressure on the soldiers arrayed all along the rim of
that ravine of death.

How his shoulder ached when he dared move it, but move
it he could. Only the cold made it hurt, he promised himself. It
would get better once he got warm. He cocked and fired again
at the distant targets as he recognized the approaching sound of
hoofbeats. At least two more companies were hurrying to the
rescue, a battalion made up of some Fifth and Third cavalry
troopers under Major G. A. Gordon. Puffs of pistol smoke rose
like gray tatters above the racing horsemen as they bore down on
the fleeing warriors, yelling, urging on their mounts as the soldiers wheeled left, following that path the ravine slashed across
the prairie. Perhaps to cut off the warriors' retreat.

As the heat of that close and dirty fighting passed, the cold
seemed to rush back in to take its place. Donegan turned, stepping back to join the others who knelt over the wounded.

Gazing to the northeast, Donegan realized Mackenzie had
committed all his troops. The colonel had himself no more reserves to pitch into the fray. Which meant ... if Hamilton and
Davis and Wessels hadn't got the job done by themselves—they
too would have likely been overrun.

"How many you figure we got?"

Seamus looked up suddenly, finding the young soldier who
had been with McKinney's company when they were ambushed,
the same young soldier who had been in full retreat before he
agreed to return to the fight.

Gazing toward the ravine, Seamus quickly counted the bodies the fleeing warriors were carrying off. "Ten. Maybeso it looks like it could be a dozen."

Around him a handful of the troopers were making sure what Cheyenne still lay on the battleground were dead. One, two shots or more as the blood lust flushed out of the young soldiers brought so close to death themselves.

"And at least eight up here they didn't get off with," Frank Grouard said as he came up to pound Donegan on the shoulder.

Shards of pain splintered up his neck and shot down his backbone. "Dammit, don't do that!"

"You hit?" the half-breed asked with worry on his face as a bullet whispered over their heads.

"No. Leastways I ain't been shot," Seamus replied. "Where the hell did you come from?"

"Up there with that captain's outfit at the head of the ravine," Frank replied, pointing his rifle toward the north side of the valley. "I hear his name is Wessels."

Turning to the youngster, Donegan said, "Twenty of 'em—we got at least twenty of 'em, Private."

"Yeah," the soldier whispered with a shudder. "Twenty."

Seamus studied his face a moment, then said, "You can bloody well be proud of that fight you just come through."

The young soldier glanced around quickly as the officers formed up platoons to lay down covering fire while a few others gathered up the dead and wounded, dragging them back out of range of those Cheyenne riflemen on the knoll.

"Things still feel a little hot here," Grouard said, cradling the Irishman's left wrist. "Let's go find you a surgeon—have him take a look at your shoulder."

Donegan shrugged him off. "Leave it be, dammit. Look at them others they're taking off—lot worse off'n me. There's more here for them sawbones to worry about than my bleeming shoulder."

Chapter 29

25 November 1876

The cold in her belly was far icier than the cold in that tiny room at the top of Old Bedlam.

Gripped with its sudden, startling, frightening presence, she awoke with a start in the dark, blinking ... and her arm habitually reached across that narrow bed for him. To assure herself of his presence, the warmth of his bulk—but that great abiding security of his nearness was not there.

Samantha sat up with a start. Her heart beat as if it would fly out of her chest, her breath catching in her throat like a ragged scrap of muslin snagged on a rusty strand of barbed wire. Streamers of frost gathered before her face. The small stove in the corner barely glowed at all.

Then she remembered the baby. Turned. Found him wrapped in his swaddling, beneath his old blanket so worn and soft with the years and washings beyond number. The blanket she had wrapped around herself as a child, then laid away in a cedar chest until it came time that she went to Texas to join sister Rebecca, knowing that in it one day she would wrap her own babies.

She touched his face gently. How warm he was, and at such peace when he slept. What with the colic and all, they both snatched nothing more than fevered bits of rest through these days and nights of waiting.

He was seven weeks old this morning.

Slowly laying her head down once more on the pillow, Samantha pulled the babe against her as he slept. Then drew him even closer to her breasts to feel the very warmth of him, his breath against the base of her neck in tiny puffs as the cold solidified in the pit of her the way the ice had formed along each bank of the creeks, each side straining day by day for the other as the cold deepened in these first weeks of winter.

Try as she might to shake that cold cake of river ice congealing within her, Samantha could not escape the feeling that she had awakened of a purpose: that something terrible had just happened to him, far to the north in Indian country.

Had he fallen in battle? Oh, God!

She squeezed her eyes shut to stop the tears, biting her lower lip so she would not cry out and wake the child. Seamus's son.

Had he been wounded? Was he lying somewhere in the snow, the frozen white turning red and mushy beneath him? Was he still alive—and thinking of her right at this moment? Is that why she awoke, because his soul was calling out to hers across all the miles?

Yes, she decided, and with a tiny yelp stifled deep within her throat, Samantha began to sob quietly in that dark room where the gray of dawn had just begun to intrude.

There drifted to her the muffled sounds of footsteps and stove doors opening as coals were stirred and fires stoked for the morning, concerns with coffee and breakfast—a woman's lot, this matter of waiting out another day while her man was off to war.

He was wounded. M-mortally, she convinced herself. That is why his spirit had reached out to her in these, his final minutes. There in the cold and the dark, upon the snow, perhaps fearing that the next footsteps he heard would be those of a painted warrior who would step over him—driving a war club down between his eyes, then slashing off his scalp.

At that moment in the dark and the cold, she felt his anguish as if it were her own—shuddering in the aloneness, she and the babe more alone at this moment than in all the days Seamus had been gone.

Colder now than she could ever remember being. Here her second winter at Laramie—knowing in the core of her that if he did not return whole to her ... that she would never again be warm, not for the rest of her life.

Near the mouth of the gulch where Bull Hump and the others had ambushed the pony soldiers, Yellow Eagle fell back during the fighting, his attention drawn by a small group of women and children who were trapped between the soldier scouts in the village and the soldiers being reinforced along the edge of the deep ravine.

"Yellow Eagle!" cried one of the old women, her arms extended to him, imploring. "Help us!"

He burst into a sprint, turning his back on the fighting, his lungs searing with the dry, extremely cold air. Bullets smacked into the snow around the group as they scurried a few feet in one direction, then back in the other, snow kicked up as the lead landed around them. They reminded him of a covey of small, frightened sage hens. He had to find a way out for them.

"Hurry, Yellow Eagle!" another woman called out.

In her arms she held a small child, one of its tiny feet clearly gone, a bloody pulp from the ankle down where the mother clamped with a hand to stop the bleeding.

This way and that he looked as he ran, searching, not knowing where he could lead them. There—beyond them across a dry wash was the wide mouth of another ravine. Perhaps . . .

Then he knew it would not work. The Wolf People scouts on the southern slope among the lodges would have a clear shot into the ravine. These women and children would all be dead before the cold sun climbed much farther in that achingly blue sky.

As he reached them, the women grabbed him, the children clustered at his bare legs, young and old alike whimpering at him like wild, frightened animals caught in a snare. Then he saw a way. Perhaps the only way.

"I will go first," he explained, laying his hand atop an old woman's head. Her cheeks were smeared with blood and frozen tears. "That way I can show you the way. Come with me now."

Without a word of protest the women herded the children before them, following the young warrior as he slipped back into the mouth of the ravine and quickly retraced a few of his steps.

It was there he stopped at the narrow entrance of another coulee.

"You will go in there," he instructed, his voice terse. "The head of the ravine runs out in the distance of an arrow shot away from here."

"Then where do we go?" one of the women pleaded, clutching at his bare arm.

"You will climb right up to the prairie," he told her, looking the woman straight in the eye. "And run the rest of the way to another coulee you will find at the back of that hill, where our warriors are firing down on the soldiers over by the deep ravine."

"But . . . but we will be running right out in the open!" an old woman cried.

"Yes! And right under those soldiers guns at the deep ravine!" another protested.

"If you do as I tell you," Yellow Eagle tried to calm them, "go one at a time—even the children—then the soldiers are not likely to see you. You will not draw their attention in that way. But you must go one at a time. Do you understand me?"

One of the old women nodded, then answered for all of them. "Yes."

"The second of you must not leave the head of this shallow ravine until the first has made it all the way to the back of that hill—where you will all be safe. From there you can make it into the canyon and up to the breastworks, where the others are singing the strong-heart songs to our warriors."

A small, frail woman pushed herself up between two younger women and clutched at the warrior's hand, gazing up into his face with watery, rheumy eyes. "I have no husband, and now my son is dead this day. But I will be the first to run as you say, Yellow Eagle. And when I reach the breastworks—I will sing the strong-heart songs for *you*!"

So it was that he took her bony hand and led her to the head of the ravine, and there helped her to the top.

"Now—run! Run like the rabbit!" he hollered at her as she took off in a lumbering gait, all too slow. "Run like the wolf was after you!"

Then the soldier guns exploded. He jerked around to look at the distant ravine, seeing the gray powder smoke lifting above the blue-clad soldiers. They had fired in volley—with a roar so loud, it made a sound like a riverbank caving in come the torrent of a spring runoff.

Holding his breath, he watched her reach the other shallow ravine behind the knoll, where she disappeared over the side. For a heartbeat he worried, ready to send the second person—this time a child, but keeping the youngster until . . .

There! He saw the ancient one wave back at them. And knew she was safe.

One by one by one he lifted them up the slick, icy side of the ravine, raising their frozen, bare feet as he heaved them onto the snowy prairie, where they began their dash to safety. Time and again the soldier guns exploded as a woman or a child zigzagged the way he told them, all the way to the shallow ravine where the ancient woman stood waving them on. Calling out for them to be brave in her frail, reedy voice.

Four of them fell, wounded by soldier bullets. But every one of them rose again as quickly, dragging a bleeding leg, or clutching a bloody arm that dripped a telltale path on the snow. Three times ten he helped out of that ravine. Three times ten would now live on.

The last one had reached the distant coulee, and Yellow Eagle had turned to find Little Wolf and one of the other Old-Man Chiefs . . . when he heard a high, wispy voice lift itself over that corner of their battlefield.

She had reached the breastworks. The ancient one with no men to sing for that day. No man, except for Yellow Eagle.

It was for him that now she sang the strong-heart songs.

Hoka hey! If this was to be Yellow Eagle's day . . . then it was a fine day to die!

With Medicine Top on one arm and Spotted Blackbird clutching the other, Box Elder made it to the slope of the low hill.

"Take me up, almost to the top, then both of you must turn back," the shaman instructed them.

"You will climb the rest of the way by yourself?"

"I must," Box Elder told them.

The last struggle was his alone in his darkness, knowing he had reached the top only when he felt the wind on his face once more and the ground falling away from beneath his moccasins on the far side.

Setting his feet, Box Elder spread his arms out for a moment—so good was it to feel the sun's coming warmth as it bathed the valley. Then he sat and pulled his small pipe and some tobacco from the pouch that he had carried away from his lodge and fit the bowl to stem. Packing pinches of tobacco into the bowl, he sang loud enough that his voice encircled the knoll for all the others to hear above the noise of the battle.

When he had the pipe ready, Box Elder got to his knees, raising the pipe overhead while he bowed—offering the pipe to *Ma-heo-o*, the All Spirit, and to the Sacred Persons . . . asking for their blessing on his people this terrible, bloody day.

Startled, he felt the pipe bowl grow warm in his hand, and he smelled pipe smoke on the wind.

Bringing the stem to his lips, the old man sucked—surprised to find that it was burning.

"Blessings, *Ma-heo-o!*" he sang out in a high, thin voice. "You have lit the pipe for me! Thank you!"

As he completed his fourth puff from the pipe, the first soldier bullet landed near his knee, striking one of the red sandstone rocks with a splatter of lead.

Box Elder next blew smoke toward the heavens.

Several more bullets whined past his head or collided with the ground at his knees.

The old shaman calmly blew his last puff at the earth—the mother of them all.

Now the soldier bullets were coming so close and with such frequency that he knew the white man must have spotted him atop this knoll.

Yet again he held the pipe up to the heavens at the end of his arms and prayed for his people's safety, not thinking about the soldier bullets at all.

Even though he had left the Sacred Wheel Lance below with his son and was no longer invisible, Box Elder knew no bullets would touch a holy man.

He kept on praying.

Already some of the soldier scouts were pounding victoriously on that big drum in the center of camp.

Little Wolf's heart bled a little more. It felt as cold as his bare legs, and surely laid upon the ground.

The enemy was in possession of their village ... beating that drum in victory even as the battle raged around the perimeter of the valley, the Wolf People scouts playing their flutes and whistles, the Shoshone firing from the ridge above him, and those Lakota who came to guide the soldiers—how it sickened his belly.

But what threatened to rob his spirit were the *Tse-Tsehese* scouts who had led the soldiers down upon their own people!

If he had the chance this day, Little Wolf vowed he would use all the strength in the Sacred Arrows and the Buffalo Hat to call down the wrath of the Everywhere Spirit upon those who not only turned their backs on their own people, but led the soldiers down upon this village to help in destroying the *Ohmeseheseo.*

With his own eyes Little Wolf had seen Old Crow—who was himself one of the Council of Forty-four Chiefs—among the

soldiers' scouts entering the village. With the pony soldiers as
well were Cut Nose, Little Fish, Hard Robe, Bird, Blown Away,
Wolf Satchel, and more ... most of them relatives of the one the
People called Long Knife, the squaw man known as William
Rowland among his own white people. These men were brothers
and uncles and nephews of the daughter of Old Frog, the woman
Rowland had married. Why, Old Frog had been a member of the
Council of Forty-four in the time before the great treaty at Horse
Creek.

And now these relatives had joined the white man in destroying their own people!

"Little Wolf!" one of his warriors cried in panic. "See!"

There at the mouth of the narrow canyon where he had
taken charge of the other men who were helping the women and
children to flee toward the mountainside and up to the breastworks, he turned to look. Little Wolf saw.

Through the last fringe of lodges advanced many pony soldiers; among the first of them to come out of those shrinking
shadows were a few Wolf People. Voices called out among them
and the horsemen stopped, the scouts too. All of them dismounted their big American horses, which were led away—back
into the abandoned village.

Then the enemy began their advance on the mouth of the
ravine and that high, narrow canyon where the helpless ones had
disappeared in fleeing to the breastworks. Where they now stood
behind their rocky fortifications and raised their strong-heart
songs over this western end of the battlefield.

"Behind the trees!" Little Wolf shouted to his men. "Take
cover behind the rocks—anywhere you can hide!"

"We cannot fight so many!" one of the faint-hearted
screeched.

"We must," Little Wolf growled, snatching hold of the man's
arm and shaking him as one might try shaking some sense into
a wayward child. "If we cannot hold the soldiers here—then all
will be lost."

"But they have the village!" another cried as the lead began
to snarl by them into the trees, slapping the bare, skeletal
branches. "We are lost!"

"Let them have the village!" he shouted them down. "But
we must not give up these hills. Never must we give up the hills
where our people take refuge!"

He whirled as the white voices grew louder—snapping off a

shot at the *ve-ho-e*. A soldier fell against those behind him, screaming as he clutched his chest.

As the other warriors took cover behind rocks or trees, down in the brush or behind a finger of land at the opening to the canyon, Little Wolf nonetheless stood his ground. Just as he always had. For he was an Old-Man Chief—and his first duty was to protect the People, even at the sacrifice of his life.

From moment to moment one of his companions cried out in pain, declaring they had been wounded in the leg, or the shoulder, perhaps an arm or hand. All the while the soldiers and their wolves continued to advance slowly, warily, for they did not know that they greatly outnumbered Little Wolf's pitifully small force protecting the mouth of the ravine as the women sang out above them.

So it was that the brave chief stood in the open that morning, doing his best to draw the enemy's fire, to taunt them, to make the soldiers angry as he sprinted back and forth before their massed front. Showing the other warriors just how poorly the soldiers and their allies shot their weapons.

Of a sudden he felt the sting at his back. The force of it bowling him over and over in the cold snow that shocked his bare legs. Lying there, breathing quick and shallow, Little Wolf put his hand to his lower back, brought it away with a thin film of red beginning to crystallize in the terrible cold. Then he pushed aside the short tail on his war shirt. An ugly, narrow finger of ooze was all it was. A flesh wound.

"*Hoka hey!*" he cried, leaping to his feet like a youngster a third of his years.

Little Wolf turned this way, then that so that his fellow warriors could see that he had not been seriously hurt.

A bullet whisked over the top of his shoulder—opening a painful furrow in the muscle atop his arm that hurt in the extreme cold, bloodying the shirt he wore.

"This is not our day to die, my friends!" he sang out, turning his back to the white men and their dogs who led the soldiers to this camp. "See me dance in the midst of their bullets!"

Others with him cried out with exultation, exposing themselves here and there, jumping out to take a shot, then falling back to reload and appear on the other side of the tree or rock or brush—their strategy causing the front rows of that massed assault to begin losing its stomach for fighting such daring warriors.

At times one or more of them were hit and bleeding, yet—like Little Wolf—they too suffered only minor wounds. At the mouth of the ravine they rallied around their chief, standing their ground to protect the ones who could not protect themselves.

After all, a man's blood coagulated very quickly in the cold of such a terrible day.

Donegan watched as Lieutenant McKinney clutched the front of the surgeon's coat with one of his bloody hands pale as the crusty snow beneath him—hoisting himself up slightly with the last shred of heroic strength that remained in his riddled body.

At least six bullets had struck the officer at the moment the Cheyenne rose out of that ravine and fired point-blank into the front of McKinney's charge.

"Dr. La ... LaGarde," the dying soldier gurgled, blood bubbling at his lips. "See that ... see my mother gets my ... my—"

Then McKinney went rigid for a moment and fell backward onto the blanket where the survivors of his company had laid him only minutes before.

The lieutenant and the others who fell at the edge of that bloody ravine had been hurried behind this low red butte, where the surgeons were establishing their temporary field hospital. There was far less danger of any more Cheyenne bullets falling among these men here at the base of this gentle slope among the brush as the sun continued to climb in that dazzling blue sky above.

"Is he ... is he dead?" one of the soldiers asked, snatching hold of the surgeon's coat sleeve.

LaGarde shrugged off the man's grip as he laid his head down on the bloodied chest. He listened intently, his eyes closed—then opened them to look up at the expectant faces closing in about him.

As the surgeon used two fingers to ease down McKinney's eyelids, he said, "The lieutenant's dead. From every one of these wounds ... hell, any one of which could have killed him on the spot, and all the goddamned loss of blood ... why—it's nothing short of a miracle that he lasted until you got him here."

A big soldier grabbed hold of LaGarde, dragging the surgeon to his feet there beside the body. "But you couldn't do a damned thing for him, could you?"

Donegan stepped in, putting his left hand on the soldier's thick arm. "Leave it go, Cawpril."

The man's eyes shot to Donegan's, filled with hurt as much as they were filled with rage. For a moment Seamus inched his right hand nearer to the butt of the pistol riding over his left hip.

Then the soldier sagged and looked back at LaGarde. "G'won now, damn you!" he snarled between his teeth as if he were trying his best to control his rage. "See what you and the rest of your cloth can do for the others."

Without a word, only the gesture of tugging down his coat to straighten it, LaGarde turned away and stepped over McKinney's body, ready to kneel beside one of the five other surgeons at work on the rest of the lieutenant's wounded.

"How 'bout looking at this one, Doc?" Frank Grouard asked, tapping on LaGarde's shoulder.

"What one?"

The half-breed pointed at Donegan.

"You're bleeding?" the surgeon asked, turning to the Irishman.

"No. Just my shoulder."

"You fall?" And LaGarde took hold of the Irishman's left arm in both hands, beginning to raise it gently.

"No—easy there!"

"What happened?"

"A war club."

"Back here across the shoulder blade?"

"I s'pose," Seamus replied, beginning to wince in pain as the arm came up even more under the surgeon's urging. "I don't know for sure: I wasn't really watching what was going on behind me—hold it! God-bleeming-damn!"

Releasing the arm slowly, LaGarde asked, "How far can you raise it on your own."

"Don't wanna raise it very far a't'all."

"Show me."

" 'Bout there," Donegan declared.

"Don't you think you ought'n keep him outta the fighting, Doc?" Grouard asked. "Just to keep a eye on it?"

"No way a few bruises gonna keep me outta this fight, you bloody half-breed!"

LaGarde shrugged. "You can see I've got lots of bleeding men here. Some of them gonna die soon too. So the two of you can go argue somewhere else for all I care."

"But what about his arm and shoulder?" Frank demanded.

"It isn't broken—if that's what you're asking," the surgeon replied and turned away.

Grouard quickly stepped in front of the retreating doctor. "But don't you think he should do something about it?"

"If he wants, he can tie it down. Wrap a bandage around his chest like this," and he pantomimed the arm being splinted against the left side of his rib cage.

Seamus said, "I'll be all right, Frank. Leave the man go to see to them others."

"You're about as mule-headed as a Lakota woman I once knowed," Grouard grumbled.

Donegan grinned as he took up his rifle and started back for their horses. "Bet I'm prettier'n she was too."

Frank stopped, cupping a hand underneath Donegan's bearded chin, turning the Irishman's face this way, then that before he replied, "You just might be at that, you ugly son of a bitch."

Seamus knocked the half-breed's hand away from his chin. "The hell you say. I'm just as pretty as the next man. C'mon, you horse-faced renegade—let's go see if Mackenzie's got something for us to do."

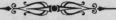

Chapter 30

Big Freezing Moon
1876

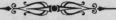

"Father!"

Box Elder turned slightly at the sound of Medicine Top's voice. He must be coming up the side of the slope, drawing closer. "I am asking for a blessing, my son!"

Then Medicine Top halted close to the summit of the hill, where the bullets still hit but with nowhere the frequency as they had. He reached out and touched his father. "I see a warrior along the ridgetop to your left."

Box Elder turned his face in that direction, as if he could himself see. "Who is it?"

"I think it is Long Jaw."

"Why do you tell me this?"

"He is drawing the soldier fire from you!"

"The soldiers are firing at him now?"

"Yes," Medicine Top explained. "Once he appeared, the soldiers stopped shooting at you, and now they are trying to kill Long Jaw."

"What is he doing?"

For a moment Medicine Top chuckled. "He is jumping around, back and forth on that ridge—making the soldiers look like fools for trying to hit him with all their bullets!"

From the hillside below him and from nearby where the women had gathered at the breastworks, into the sky now went the cheers and strong-heart songs of those who watched Long Jaw's bravery. And then a quick ripple of laughter.

"What does everyone find so amusing?" Box Elder asked, wanting to see the event through his son's eyes.

"A dog has joined Long Jaw now on the edge of the ridge—and they are both running back and forth. He yells down at the soldiers and then the dog barks at the white men. But as much as the *ve-ho-e* would like to hit the man or the dog—they are doing no good. Bullets are striking the ground everywhere around them."

Then there was an audible gasp from the spectators. Box Elder grew worried immediately. "Did the soldiers hit him?" he asked his son.

"No, father," Medicine Top replied after a long moment. "He just dropped out of sight behind a big rock."

As Long Jaw stood there behind the boulder, facing northwest to wave at them, the women renewed their buoyant strong-heart songs. Then he jumped back into the open, the dog at his heels once more, barking all the louder now as the man jogged back and forth, taunting the soldiers and their scouts.

"Long Jaw is back!"

"It is good," Box Elder said as he brought the pipe stem to his lips. "I must finish my prayer now."

As soon as Young Two Moon saw his family on their way into the narrow mouth of the deep canyon where they would climb to the rim to build breastworks, the warrior clamped his arms around his father and said farewell as they both leaped upon the bare backs of their ponies and rode off in different directions. Beaver Claws went to the south side of camp, where the Shoshone were firing down from a high ridge and the Wolf People were pushing in among the lodges in a fierce struggle. Young Two Moon urged his pony into a lope, guiding it right down through the middle of the village.

His long elk-hide shirt, his carbine and pistol, plus his two cartridge belts were all he wore over his breechclout and leggings. And before he left the family's lodge, he had taken a moment to open the rawhide container where he kept the warbonnet, its feathers protected. Smoothing each one with a deft motion of his hand, Young Two Moon had tied the bonnet onto his head before stepping into the bitter cold of that morning, the double trailer long enough to reach the ground.

At the east side of the village the firing became general,

growing heavy. Up ahead through the mist clinging in among the lodges he spotted his good friend.

"Crow Necklace!" he called out to the horseman whose pinto darted back and forth as he fired at the advancing enemy pushing into the village. "Crow Necklace!" he cried again as he kicked his own horse into a faster lope.

But Crow Necklace did not seem to hear, for he suddenly reined about and galloped toward the south side of the village.

Just then Young Two Moon had heard the staccato call of the soldier bugle—cold and brassy on the dawn air. He wheeled about and headed north—toward the bugle call, knowing there would be soldiers where he heard such a brassy horn play its fighting song. He leaped his horse down the bank into the creek, then up and onto the rolling plain just in time to see the gray horse troop charging forward across the flat ground. Another group of soldiers rode off to their right toward the head of a faraway ravine. And an even larger bunch of the pony soldiers spread out and came galloping toward him, toward the creek and the village standing on the far side of the narrow stream.

Skidding to a halt, Young Two Moon yanked savagely on the single buffalo-hair rein, spinning the horse around and turning his back to the oncoming enemy. He could hear the bullets pass him more than he could actually feel the air they split in their passing. Back across the stream he raced the pony, into the heart of the village, heading for the south side of camp—where the fighting had already grown intense.

"Young Two Moon!" Crow Necklace hollered, still atop his pinto, as he saw his friend emerge out of the rolling, frosty mist hugging the frozen ground.

Then, as Young Two Moon watched, his friend was slung sideways off his pony, blood smearing his belly.

Racing to Crow Necklace's side, Young Two Moon leaped to the ground, grabbing the young warrior's arm to wrap around his neck. Bullets sang around them like angry hornets. Young Two Moon struggled to rise with Crow Necklace, murmuring all the time to calm his friend and the pony until he succeeded in hoisting Crow Necklace over the back of the pinto. Then, scooping up the pinto's rein, Young Two Moon climbed atop his own horse and kicked it into motion—fleeing that furious close-quarters fighting with the Wolf People.

He sped with the body of his friend into the mouth of the narrow canyon where the women and children had gone, hoping to find someone to help him. Ahead of him a short distance ran five barefoot women, both young and old. He called out to them.

"Come back!"

After they stopped and finally seemed resigned to return to the young warrior, he told them, "My friend is hurt. Will you help him?"

"Is he a relative?" a woman asked, her eyes as frightened as the others.

"No. He is my friend."

A second woman spoke up as she looked into Crow Necklace's face. "This man is one of the scouts who found out that the soldiers were coming. Are you one too?"

"Yes, together we saw the soldiers and their scouts coming from the Powder."

"We will take him," the first woman said as she stepped forward and slipped the pinto's rein from Young Two Moon's hand. "If your friend is meant to live, he will live. You go and fight now."

The power of the People brought tears to Coal Bear's old eyes that bitterly cold morning. Not only did they have the strength of *Esevone*—the Sacred Buffalo Hat protecting them. Not only did they have the power of *Nimhoyoh*, which Medicine Bear continued to wave from side to side up there atop the breastworks. Not only did the *Tse-Tsehese* have the strange magic of Box Elder's Sacred Wheel Lance to make them invisible.

They had men like Long Jaw drawing the soldier and scout bullets away from Coal Bear and his woman as they hurried *Esevone* through the shallow ravine and onto another ridge. While they scrambled as quickly as their old legs would allow them, they again attracted the attention of soldier bullets. But as quickly as the snarling wasps began to strike the ground around them, up raced the boy called Medicine Bear on his pony, waving the Sacred Turner on the wand at the end of his arm with its sacred power to turn aside all harm from the old couple.

It was only in this way—from ridge to gully, from gully to bluff, and on to the next ravine—that Coal Bear and his woman finally made it to the deep canyon where the others had fled, where the women old and young clutched their children against them and together sang the songs their warriors needed to hear as they plunged into battle.

Foot by foot the old man climbed, stopping often to turn and reach down a hand to his woman, who would pass up the

Buffalo Hat; then she would climb on around him, and he would
pass the Sacred Hat up to her. Leapfrogging their way up the
steep side of that cliff, they made it to the top of the breastworks
where the others had gathered.

Many of the women trilled their tongues when they recognized it was Coal Bear—keeper of the Northern People's power.

There in the cruel wind that kicked up frozen, icy snow off
the ground around him, the old chief raised the sacred bundle
over his head, looked into the rising sun, and began singing.

His eyes closed, tears streaming down his cheeks.

"Hear me, *Ma-heo-o!* Save my people! If you must take
someone—take me, I pray you! But save my people!"

By the time Donegan and Grouard reached Mackenzie, the
colonel and his orderlies were more than halfway up the side of
a red sandstone spur that jutted from the north wall of the canyon onto the valley floor. From the heights Mackenzie could
monitor most of the battlefield, save only for what fierce fighting
was still raging at the south side of the village as the Pawnee and
Sioux punched their way through the camp yard by yard, lodge
by lodge.

The Cheyenne had fallen back foot by foot, covering the retreat of their families. And for the first time that morning as the
sun climbed fully above the eastern rim of the valley, it looked
as if the village was all but in control of Mackenzie's forces. The
colonel had deployed his battalions with deadly effectiveness.

Some of the companies hung back of the others to act as a
rear guard and to prevent the Cheyenne from slipping around
behind the soldiers' flanks.

Other units worked in concert with the Pawnee as well as
the Sioux and Cheyenne scouts to muscle their way into the village, plunging through it, where the fighting was tough against
the hardy horsemen and snipers who hid within the lodges, con-
testing every foot of ground.

Still more of the troopers hunkered down in a copse of
timber at the far western edge of the village, pinned there after
beginning an assault on the warriors who tenaciously held on to
the narrow mouth of a deep canyon where the women and children had escaped. Despite the fact that they were fighting against
great odds in that skirmish, the warriors put up a stern resis-
tance, firing from behind boulders and piles of rock, from behind this tree or that as they seemed to be constantly moving,
never giving the soldiers a stationary target.

And from that low hill just to the northeast of the village came bullets that rained down here and there—as warriors sought to harass the soldiers on three sides of that battlefield. As the moments dragged on, fewer and fewer of the Cheyenne remained atop that knoll, until there were only five.

Mackenzie pulled the field glasses from his eyes, squinting in the brilliant sunlight bouncing off the snow. "That handful are making a damned nuisance of themselves."

"They're almost in the middle of the fight now," commented Lieutenant Joseph H. Dorst. "They command quite a field of fire, General."

"I can see that!" Mackenzie snapped uncharacteristically at his regimental adjutant. Then he turned to the half-breed and the Irishman. "How about you two? Should we wipe that hilltop clear?"

"As long as those Cheyenne are up there making things hot for your sojurs," Seamus said, "none of us gonna be safe in that village."

"Just my thinking exactly," Mackenzie replied, wheeling about to pull Dorst close. "Take my compliments to Captain Taylor over there by the village. Tell him I need to clear that hilltop as soon as I can, and for him to form up a charge on the heights."

Dorst saluted, saying, "I'll leave in just a moment, General."

He slid from the saddle and threw up the stirrup fender so he could give a tug on the cinch. Finding it secure, the adjutant climbed back atop his horse, asking, "Am I to return here, sir?"

"By all means, Lieutenant. Report back as soon as practicable. And whatever you do—stay low on your ride. Until that hill is cleared, any courier crossing that open plain makes a sitting duck of himself."

Tugging down the brim of his hat, Dorst bade farewell to the headquarters group with a smile. "So—until I see your hairy mugs again!"

And he was off, lying back in the saddle a ways as his horse picked its way down the steep incline of the rock outcrop until he neared the bottom. There the wiry Dorst leaned forward and leaped his mount onto the rolling prairie, shooting off like a jockey spurring his blooded thoroughbred in a sudden burst of speed out of the starting gate. Lying low along the animal's withers, he slapped its front flanks with a side-to-side arch of his reins.

"General?"

They all turned to find interpreter Billy Garnett loping to a halt with the Sioux leader Three Bears.

"What is it?"

"I better tell you something now while I got the chance."

"Tell me what?" Mackenzie asked. His eyes flicked toward the Sioux chief impatiently.

"Three Bears says you gotta listen to his way of fighting—or all your men gonna fall like Custer's."

The colonel snorted. Some of his aides laughed outright. "Jesus H. Christ, Garnett!" Mackenzie scoffed. "Just look at the battlefield! Does it appear we're about to be overrun?"

Garnett's stoic face did not betray his belief in the words of Three Bears. He continued, "The Cheyenne are all driven out. Meaning they're all around us now. They got the hills, the high ground, General. Three Bears is dead set on telling you what he thinks you oughtta know."

"And what is that?"

"He says you gotta order your men to fight one by one. Not like soldiers anymore. Not like them what got killed with Custer—they hung together like soldiers. Officers kept 'em bunched up like sheep. You gotta tell your men to fight the Indians one on one, like these here Cheyenne are gonna do to us."

Mackenzie turned quickly to the Sioux chief. "Is that how these Cheyenne are going to fight me now, Three Bears?"

The Indian nodded, not requiring any translation.

"From bush to bush, is it? Fighting from rock to rock, man to man, eh?" Mackenzie asked. "I don't think so, gentlemen. In fact, you will soon see my battle plan prevail." Then he turned his back on Three Bears and Garnett as if dismissing them both, placing the field glasses to his eyes as he slowly perused the terrain below him.

"How do things look, General?" asked Major George Gordon, still seeming a bit anxious. "Do the Cheyenne have us surrounded, like they did Custer's outfit?"

"The day is won, gentlemen," Mackenzie reassured them as they all watched the bullets begin to kick up tiny cascades of snow around that lone horseman, Dorst, sprinting across that open ground below. "But we still have much to do before this victory is complete."

"Will we destroy the village and its contents, General?" asked Lieutenant Henry W. Lawton.

"Damn right I will," the colonel replied, then—noticing the dour expression on the two civilians' faces—Mackenzie asked,

"Don't you two think we should wipe the earth clear of all that this band of renegade Cheyenne ever owned?"

"I suppose that's what you're needing to do," Donegan said. "It's just that I can't shake the memory of what Reynolds did all too quickly last winter farther north on the Powder."

Mackenzie visibly bristled, his eyes glowering. "Damn you, Irishman! I'm no pompous desk straddler like Reynolds! And I've never been accused of an error in judgment. Now, you yourself were with me at the Palo Duro* when we impoverished the Kwahadi of Quanah Parker, then slaughtered their wealth in ponies. It was a total success. So that's exactly what we'll do here."

"As long as your men ain't freezing and you ask 'em to march on empty bellies," Grouard commented.

His eyes became cold fires as he glared at the half-breed. "Never have I asked more of any man than I was willing to sacrifice myself. I have my orders. General Crook expects me to finish the job here."

Donegan said, "That's right, General. Just like Reynolds was told to finish the job on the Powder."

"Listen, you son of a bitch," Mackenzie snapped with uncharacteristic alarm. "I don't know what's come over you, but maybe you don't remember just who the hell asked you to join in on this expedition."

"Hold on, General," Seamus began to apologize, his tone becoming softer. "Perhaps I was a bit out of the barracks with that talk about Reynolds. Sorry that what I said nettled you the way it did. No offense meant toward you. Damn, if I don't find myself running loose in the tongue department when I oughtta be keeping this bleeding mouth shut."

"It's all right," Mackenzie said, his face softening as well, the anger passed.

Donegan explained, "General, I for one should damn well know you're not the kind to go off and do something stupid . . . leaving your men without food or protection against the weather. I'm sorry, for I plainly spoke out of line."

"Apology accepted, Mr. Donegan." Then Mackenzie's smile was gone as he rose in the stirrups and brought the field glasses to his eyes. "Looks like Mr. Dorst is at the end of a pretty ride, gentlemen."

Seamus squinted across the dazzling shimmer reflecting off

the snow. Dorst was nearing the end of his race across the open no-man's-land hard to their left.

No longer was it a close and dirty scrap, hand-to-hand and mean. Now Mackenzie had himself what was shaping up to be a day-long battle to fight.

And the sun had barely lifted off the ridges to the east.

In their front at the center of the open ground, troopers under Hamilton and Hemphill were hunkered down, all but under the guns of the Cheyenne who had taken up protected positions among the rocks dippling the nearby heights.

Off to the far right at the northern spread of the valley, Wessels and Russell of the Third were holding their own far up at the head of that deadly ravine where McKinney's men had charged into the jaws of Hell.

And some minutes earlier Captain Alfred B. Taylor's battalion of L and G troops, Fifth U.S. Cavalry, had just set up a dismounted skirmish line where they began a long-range duel with those dogged and persistent warriors atop the low knoll on the far side of the deep ravine. That skirmishing began at the completion of a gallant charge into the lower end of the Cheyenne camp, where they slashed their way lengthwise through the long, narrow horseshoe crescent of lodges—driving before them the last snipers who burst from the far end of the camp.

Killing every warrior who would not be driven before them.

As he strode up and down the skirmish line behind his men, Taylor himself discovered the tattered hole in the wide, flapping lapel of his caped mackintosh: pierced by a Cheyenne bullet—right over his heart.

He licked his dry lips and shook his head, soundlessly uttering his prayer of thanks as he kept on moving up and down the line, cheering on his men in that hot little fight they were having of it.

"It's our day!" he cried in the bitter cold. "They're whipped and on the run now!"

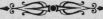

Chapter 31

25 November 1876

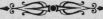

When the daring warrior appeared from behind the knoll atop his pinto, Second Lieutenant Homer W. Wheeler wasn't ready for the sight of such a man prancing his animal back and forth out there, clearly within range of their carbines, a man who taunted the soldiers and the Pawnee scouts as he exposed himself to their bullets with no more protection than a buffalo-hide shield on his left arm and a bonnet of eagle feathers on his head, its red wool trailer spilling over the pony's rump and all but brushing the snowy ground.

"Goddammit," Wheeler growled as his unit's bullets kicked up spouts of snow here and there around the pony's hooves. He turned to the trooper next to him, reaching for the soldier's Springfield. "Gimme your carbine! I'll take a crack at him!"

But try as he might—holding high on the chest, then raising his sight to the warbonnet, in addition to adjusting what he thought he should for windage—not a damn one of his shots hit their target as a small but growing crowd around him cheered for all of those taking a crack at the warrior, jeering the magically charmed Cheyenne horseman.

"Lookee there, Lieutenant!" one of the troopers yelled, pointing to their left among the brush that bordered the village.

Just then a warrior poked his head up, yelling something quickly before his head disappeared again within the thick clump of willow.

"All right, fellas," Wheeler declared. "Looks like we got us another good target to practice on. Let's see if any of you can hit that damned redskin!"

Immediately a half-dozen guns cracked into service, but in that momentary lull while the soldiers reloaded, the warrior's voice cried out—more shrilly this time, and plainly terrified.

"Pawnee!" a voice shrieked behind the Lieutenant.

Wheeler turned on his heel as a Pawnee scout came sprinting up to the skirmish line, terror on his face.

Gesturing wildly, the scout repeatedly shouted, "No shoot Pawnee!"

Standing to wave his arm, and shouting, Wheeler ordered the second platoon to hold their fire while he sorted things out. "That's one of your Pawnee in there?" he asked slowly of the scout, pointing at the brush. "In there?"

Without hesitation the scout nodded his head, pointing too. "Pawnee, him. Pawnee, me. Pawnee!" Then he turned away from the lieutenant and hollered to the distant clump of brush.

Like a frightened bird poking its head from a clump of ground cover, the warrior peered out. When both the Pawnee scout and Wheeler began to wave him on, the warrior finally leaped from his place of hiding, darting straight for the soldiers.

"Pawnee," the frightened scout said breathlessly as he reached the skirmish line, pounding himself on the chest. "See, Pawnee!" He grabbed hold of his long scalp lock, braided with three shiny conchos and the claws of a red hawk. "Pawnee!"

"Pawnee hair, yeah," Wheeler said, shaking his head and turning back to the rest of his men, who went back to their attempts at knocking that lone Cheyenne warrior off the back of his prancing, dancing pony.

Wheeler wasn't sure whose shot it was—there were so many guns going off together in a steady staccato—when the warbonnet began to tip to the side and the man under it slowly slipped from the pony's bare back into the snow, causing a small eruption of the trampled white flakes as he sprawled across the ground in a heap.

"I got him! I got him!" someone hollered, jubilant enough to leap to his feet and dance a quick jig.

"You stupid bunghole!" another challenged. "It was me!"

"Both of you—take yourselves a good look there!"

And from beyond the slope of that hill came another elaborately dressed warrior also displaying a great eagle-feather warbonnet, with a slightly oblong shield attached at his left elbow. His pony shot out to halt in a spray of snow between the soldier lines and the fallen Cheyenne, where its rider leaped off, knelt, and immediately swept the wounded warrior into his arms. Rising, he laid his comrade across the pony's withers, then leaped up behind the warrior and kicked the animal into motion.

At the crest of the hill other warriors stood cheering that act of bravery, raising their weapons and shields, bows and lances, raising their voices to the heavens above.

And down there at the timber, the soldiers went back to work. Some stood to aim at that retreating target. Others knelt, locking an elbow into the crook of a knee to steady their weapons. The rest plopped to their bellies in the frozen, icy snow, attempting to keep that front blade on a distant bobbing target.

Almost reaching the hillside . . . when the rescuer threw out his arms, his head pitching back as he twisted off the rear flank of the pony. The warrior he had rescued bounced along upon the horse's withers for a few more yards before tumbling off as well, cartwheeling along a skiff of wind-crusted snow.

"Two of the bastards!" a corporal muttered with a grim satisfaction. "Two for the price of one, I'd say!"

"Their medicine was bad today," Wheeler corrected. "That's all it was. Just a bad day for their medicine."

Then the lieutenant closed his eyes a moment.

And I pray mine will be stronger.

In that first hour of the battle the fighting had been hot and furious as the *Ohmeseheso* contested control of their village, countering the charges of the cavalry—hastily setting up an ambush here and there as they covered the retreat of their women and children.

But now that the sun had fully risen over that frozen valley to dispel the slinking mists from every last one of the cold places, dazzling the eyes with its painful brilliance reflecting off the snow, the battle was slowly becoming no more than a painful standoff.

The army had possession of the valley in a jagged line running from the twin buttes west of Mackenzie's observation point on the north, across and through the village to the southwest, where the Pawnee and Shoshone were ensconced up the slopes and at the top of the high ridges where they could fire down on the enemy. Any Cheyenne now left behind that blue line lay dead in the village abandoned by all to the dogs. Out of the cold shadows slunk the wild-eyed curs, creeping so low their bellies nearly brushed the snow, ears back and noses wary as each one went to sniff the freezing horse carcasses, the motionless bodies of the Cheyenne who hadn't broken from their lodges quickly enough.

A sniff, then a lick. Dead, yes. But not yet dead long enough to become carrion to these half-feral beasts.

On they loped, those wild dogs picking up the scent of the next odor. Then the next. And the next. The stench of death hung heavy over what had been their village.

Brave Wolf shivered. Not so much from cold as from fear. Down there in the village remained his sacred Thunder Bow. Last spring, when he had taken the vow of a Contrary, the bow had been blessed by the old shamans—never to be used in hunting, only in battle to protect the People. And it was never to go inside a lodge. So Brave Wolf always hung it outside his door, in the branches of a nearby tree. Where the Wolf People scouts now would find it, perhaps burn it when they destroyed the camp.

Worse yet: they would steal its magic from him!

Oh, how he felt hollow and cold, as if a shaft of frozen winter ice had been driven through the center of his chest. So sad, yet so afraid, he could not cry. At least not while they were fighting their way out of the west end of the village, each man scurrying from tree to tree, dodging from rock to rock, then working his way into the ravines and across the valley to the far side where he could huddle among the rocks on the northern slopes.

The soldiers were not all that lucky trying to pin down the warriors who used every cleft and shadow to their advantage in staying out of sight, where they could snipe at the *ve-ho-e* in the valley.

Below Brave Wolf some of the young men were talking excitedly, pointing, planning how they were going to sneak back in among the pony herd that was already captured—to steal it back from the soldiers and their Indian scouts. As he watched, the first two went to their bellies among the thick, leafless willow that stood taller than a man and crawled out of sight, like snakes making their creep upon an unwary prey.

"Help me, brother."

Brave Wolf turned at the sudden address from a clump of brush, thinking he recognized the voice. "Is that you, Braided Locks?"

"Here is my hand, brother," the wounded warrior said. "Pull me in there with you."

As he dragged his friend by the arm, Brave Wolf could see all the blood smeared across Braided Locks's belly. As the wounded warrior twisted over, he saw the exit wound in the small of the back.

"You are dying?" he asked, laying his friend in his lap.

Braided Locks rested his head upon Brave Wolf's thigh, his eyes clenched in pain, his breath short and ragged until his breathing came easier. "No. No, I am not dying, brother. This hurts too much to be dying."

"How long have you been shot?"

"It seems like all morning," Braided Locks replied, finally opening his eyes in the shadows of those rocks at their shoulders. "I was in the deep ravine below, with the others when the soldiers on horses charged us. Some of us were near the top of the ravine and fought the soldiers there, close enough to see their eyes. Just as the others did farther down the ravine—toward the village. They too fought close enough to see the soldier eyes."

"We lost many of our friends down there at the ravine."

"I know," Braided Locks said softly, his voice reverent with remembrance. "As I fought and fell, then crawled all the way up here to these rocks, the bullets struck around me so loud, I thought it was hailing. I thought I was crawling on bullets, there were so many."

Brave Wolf shuddered looking at that dark, purple pucker of a bullet hole. "I have only this to put on your wounds," he admitted, slashing two strips off the back of his long wool breechclot.

Braided Locks looked down at himself, regarded the bullet hole in his belly. "Thank you, brother. But it seems the cold is enough that I do not bleed anymore. See?"

He watched his friend's eyes slowly close and immediately became more frightened. "Are you dying?"

The warrior wagged his head slowly. "No. I am ... just so tired. Now that you are here with me ... I want nothing more than to sleep for a little while."

As it became painfully clear that his men were going to pay a hefty price for not sealing off the Cheyenne escape, Mackenzie sent First Lieutenant Henry W. Lawton across that dangerous no-man's-land with another order for his dismounted units.

Stop all firing except at close range, and then—only when sure of a target.

Across that snowy valley fell an eerie quiet, punctuated from time to time with a short burst of gunfire from both sides before the rifles and carbines fell silent once more. During the lull Mackenzie dismissed his orderly.

"I don't need you for a while. Get some rest and some food."

More tired than hungry, William Earl Smith led his horse back into the thick brush where a few other soldiers had hunkered down, tied off his horse, and made himself comfortable enough to doze in the cold shadows.

He awakened to find only one soldier still nearby. Smith inched over, figuring to nudge the man awake—but found the soldier dead, his mouth and eyes open. Shot through the head, right where he had been sitting. No more than an arm's length from William Earl.

A cold drop slid down his spine as he leaped to his feet, nearly collapsing as one leg refused to move—frozen. Tingling with the pricks of renewed feeling, Smith rubbed it hurriedly, then dragged the reluctant leg along, back to the brush where he had tied his horse.

Mounting up, he led it down into the boggy ground, where he eventually reached the streambank. There he pulled off his boot and plunged his leg—britches, stocking, and all—into the icy water, figuring that was sure to end the sharp pains he was suffering. After a bit he struggled back into the saddle and, dripping wet, endeavored to report back to Mackenzie. He was weaving back and forth atop his McClellan, finding it difficult to keep the frozen leg in its stirrup when he spotted the rest of the orderlies ahead, signaling him from the high, rocky observation point.

"Smith! You're wet! Where the hell have you been?" the colonel demanded as the private reached headquarters.

"Tending to my leg, General."

"You're wounded."

"Not rightly, I ain't, sir," Smith admitted. "After you let me go off to sleep, 'pears my leg never wanted to wake back up!"

"Go on down there and report in to the hospital the surgeons have established," Mackenzie ordered. "See if they can do something for you, then report back to me when you're in shape to sit a horse."

By the time Smith loped down to the hospital, he had decided against reporting to the surgeons. They had their hands busy enough with bullet wounds. Pushing on past the field hospital, the orderly found some of his old company settled in on a skirmish line and taking a moment to enjoy some well-deserved victuals.

"Is that Smith I see?" hollered one of them as the orderly came up.

"It is," he called out, grinning, happy to see his old comrades. "Is that tacks and bacon I see you wolfing down?"

"They sure as blazes are," cried another soldier, holding up his rations. "Sit yourself and eat up with us!"

"Where'd you come on to them vittles?"

"Don't you know? The pack train's in," the first soldier replied. "The general don't know?"

"I don't figger the general much cares to eat anyhow," Smith replied as he snatched up an offered tack and a small slab of fatty bacon. "Knowing him—Mackenzie won't give his belly no nevermind till he wins this fight."

When Young Two Moon had turned from the women who moved off, cradling the body of Crow Necklace, hurrying into the mouth of the ravine, he immediately headed for the warriors who lay upon the rounded knoll, firing their rifles at groups of soldiers near the fringe of the captured lodges.

Reaching them, he said, "Come with me into the village. We must see if anyone is left alive."

Only Brave Bear chose to leave the sniping from the hill with Young Two Moon. Together they mounted up and raced around the back of the knoll heading for the lodges, but suddenly turned away before reaching the camp circle. Already too many Wolf People were busy among the lodges—shooting, looting, slashing the hide-and-canvas covers, trampling the Cheyennes' sacred objects hung on those tripods erected in front of most of the dwellings.

When the two warriors galloped back for the hills, fired upon by the soldiers, the pair became separated and Brave Bear's horse was shot from under him, spilling its rider. Nevertheless, he managed to crawl unseen for some distance before he finally ran to safety behind some rocks where he carried on a long-range shooting match with the soldiers.

Under heavy fire, Young Two Moon whipped his pony to greater speed, dodging bullets and rocks, the animal slipping and nearly falling several times on the icy ground. By the time he made it to the base of the ridge where the women were singing their strong-heart songs behind the breastworks, the young warrior decided his horse was of no more use.

He let it go and chose another from among those few some of the herder boys had managed to drive into the ravines and hillsides at the moment of attack. Leaping onto its back and taking up the rein, Young Two Moon headed east along the north foot of the valley—hoping to find a good place to fight, seeking to find where the soldiers were holding more of the *Ohmeseheso* ponies.

Slipping around the northwest end of the canyon toward the twin red buttes just west of the deep ravine where many warriors had surprised some of the gray-horse soldiers, Young Two Moon halted, spotting a rider approaching some distance away, a horseman hugging the thick brush along the high plateau at the northern foot of the valley. As the man and horse drew closer, Young Two Moon could tell the rider was an Indian: he rode easily without a saddle, his feet and legs hanging free of stirrups. Nearer and nearer he came until Young Two Moon saw that it was the youngster called Beaver Dam, riding a cream-colored horse with a white mane and tail.

But . . . Beaver Dam had left the village many days before—traveling with a small band of the People who were heading north, seeking out the camp of Crazy Horse.

Could this be that he was back?

Young Two Moon grew concerned—because Beaver Dam was coming from the east, the same direction the soldiers had come. But even more damning: that cream-colored pony Beaver Dam was riding happened to be one of the ponies stolen from Sits in the Night by strangers during last night's dance!

Oh, how could this be?

With a pounding heart Young Two Moon knew there was only one way Beaver Dam could have got his hands on that horse. He was in league with the soldiers' Indians!

The young man had betrayed his people and their village.

As the horseman drew closer to Young Two Moon, Beaver Dam raised his arm in greeting, a smile coming to his face. Then the smile suddenly disappeared and the youngster froze at the very moment Young Two Moon heard ponies coming up behind him.

"Who is that?" a voice demanded behind Young Two Moon.

He looked over his shoulder and recognized the old warrior Gypsum and a handful more coming to a halt on the hill beside him, all of them watching the approaching rider.

Young Two Moon said, "It is Beaver Dam."

"Aiyeee!" Gypsum cried wildly. "Then he is the one who brought these soldiers here!"

In a flurry of hoofbeats, the half-dozen warriors kicked their ponies into motion and stopped only when they had the youngster surrounded, frightened, and at gunpoint, when Young Two Moon reached the tense scene.

"I am going to kill you myself!" Gypsum growled. "My sons were killed in the ravine by the soldiers you brought down upon our village. So now I will be the one to avenge their deaths!"

"No!" Beaver Dam shouted, his wet eyes like a frightened rabbit's caught in a snare. "I am not a scout for the soldiers. Many days ago I left Buffalo Bull Sitting Down's* camp to come home to my People after they had two fights with the soldiers and began marching north."

"So you're coming home now with the soldiers' scouts?" Gypsum demanded. "Planning to loot and plunder like the Wolf People?"

"No, I tell you," Beaver Dam's voice quaked. "On my way here I saw a party of Arapaho. When I got close, they looked like friends, so I went to their fire and ate their food. After they asked me all their questions about our village, only then I found out they were wolves for the blue soldiers. They pulled their guns and pointed them at me. They captured me."

Young Two Moon asked, "Did they take you to the big soldier camp?"

Beaver Dam nodded emphatically. "The soldiers tied me up tight, hit me, put guns to my head—here—and to my breast—here—trying to make me tell them more about our village. I saw you and Crow Necklace in the soldiers' camp . . . saw you steal the scouts' horses that night you walked through the soldier camp."

"Why didn't you call out to them?" Gypsum demanded. "Ask them to help you escape?"

"If I had, Young Two Moon and Crow Necklace would be dead—killed by the soldiers or their scouts. I could not betray them, so I kept my mouth closed and waited."

"Your story is very hard to believe," one of the others snorted.

Beaver Dam looked at the warrior. "We were a small group coming home from Buffalo Bull Sitting Down's country, and

*Sitting Bull, Hunkpapa Lakota leader.

when we spotted some people far off, they sent me to find out who those people were."

"And they were the Arapaho who captured you?"

"Yes!" Beaver Dam replied anxiously, then wagged his head dolefully. "Now I do not know where my people are." He looked up at Young Two Moon anxiously. "Are my relatives here?"

"No," he told young Beaver Dam. "Your people have not come here."

So the youngster said hopefully, "Perhaps when I did not come back, they turned around and headed back to Buffalo Bull Sitting Down's people."

"That is too far away," Young Two Moon said. "Wiser to seek out the Crazy Horse people."

"Perhaps," the youth considered. "White Bull is still with them."

"How is it you have this horse?" Gypsum asked angrily, his hands flexing as if he would jump the youngster at any moment. "It is not a soldier's American horse."

"I know this horse!" cried another of Gypsum's warriors. "It belongs to Sits in the Night! The enemy stole his horses last night during our dance!"

Gypsum edged his pony closer, grabbing Beaver Dam's rein. "Where did you get this horse?"

He swallowed hard, his voice tight with fear. "Once the soldiers began their attack this morning, the Arapaho let me go, saying that it was too late for me to spoil their surprise. They said to pick a horse from the captured herds. I knew this horse. It belongs to Sits in the Night, and I knew it is a strong one which can outrun most soldier horses. I picked it."

"You've had time to come up with a good story, little one," Gypsum snarled, then suddenly lunged for the youngster, knocking him off his pony.

Both of them toppled to the ground, grappling as other warriors leaped into the fray, attempting to pull Gypsum off Beaver Dam. Two men held the older warrior back as he swung for the youngster.

Left-handed Wolf said, "This young man has told his story, and it is not so long since he left us that he could have betrayed his people to the soldiers. I think you should let him be."

"No!" Gypsum snapped, lunging for the youngster although restrained by the others. "I must kill him! My sons are dead because of him!"

"This man did not kill your sons," Left-handed Wolf argued

as Gypsum struggled. "Listen! Hear those soldiers shooting? They have not stopped shooting at our people all morning long. Those soldiers and their Indians—they are the ones who killed your sons. Not this boy! If you want to fight, go fight the soldiers, Gypsum. Don't let me catch you fighting this boy now! He is one of our people—"

"He is not our people!"

"He is *Tse-Tsehese!*" Young Two Moon shouted, shoving his way into the tightening circle of angry men. "We have enough enemies among the soldiers and their scouts from the agency who betray us—we must not fight among ourselves."

"I will fight the soldiers," Gypsum growled, flinging his arms out wildly, knocking down one of those who held him. "But first I will kill this one who caused the soldiers to kill my sons in the ravine!"

Yanking up his long braided rawhide quirt, Left-handed Wolf pressed it hard against Gypsum's cheek as the others regained their hold on him. The cold wind tousled its ten thin strips of leather. "If you touch this youngster—I will come back to whip you myself!"

Gypsum's eyes narrowed. "So—you are turning your back on your people too?"

In a flash Left-handed Wolf raked the quirt down Gypsum's cheek, cocked his arm back, and snapped it forward, striking the warrior on the temple with the thick antler handle.

Gypsum's knees turned to water as he slowly sank between his two holders.

"Let that be a lesson to any of you!" Left-handed Wolf shouted. "We have enough enemies to fight out there, and there, and over there too. We must not make enemies of our strong-hearted people!" Then he turned to Beaver Dam. "Go yonder to the high ridge west of the village. You will find the women and our children there. Among our families you will be safe from soft-headed fools like Gypsum."

For a moment Beaver Dam glanced at Young Two Moon, as if seeking permission.

Young Two Moon nodded, telling the youngster, "Yes. Go ahead. You will be fine there. Help the women pile up rocks at the breastworks."

Without another word the young man leaped atop his cream-colored pony and hurried away to the west. In his wake Gypsum stood shakily, his angry eyes filled with tears of rage and loss.

"This day two sons have been taken from me, and I do not know where I can find my wife!" Then he shook off the two warriors holding his arms. "Tell me, Left-handed Wolf: how is it you find it so easy to know your friends from your enemies when they are both *Tse-Tsehese?*"

"No matter the color of his skin or how he wears his hair," the other warrior replied, "it is always easy to tell a friend from an enemy."

"No," Young Two Moon said sadly. "I do not think it is so easy anymore, Uncle. Even if they are *Tse-Tsehese*, I do not think it will ever again be easy to tell a friend from an enemy."

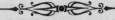

Chapter 32

25 November 1876

"I never would've been a man to put no money on it, Irishman," Frank Grouard declared with a wag of his head. "I'd figured all along them Lakota and Cheyenne scouts of Mackenzie's would've run off—had it figured they'd never stay put when the fighting got dirty. Just not the way of an Injun."

Down below them along the stream, among the willow, and in the midst of the uppermost fringe of lodges those scouts enlisted from Red Cloud's agency had taken their places: dutifully following the orders of the officers as they dug in for the long haul this fight was turning out to be.

"Ain't no man here knows better'n you, Frank," Seamus replied, "just what a warrior will do to earn himself a little coup and make off with a lot of plunder."

"Heap ponies!" Grouard roared, pounding his chest once with a fist as he played the role. "Me want heap ponies!"

"Shit," growled Baptiste Pourier with mock indignation, "if that's all you ever wanted—why, we could've quit this goddamned soldiering business long ago and be living fat and sleek with our women right about now!"

Against the far northern rimrocks some renewed gunfire rattled across the valley.

"How 'bout you, Seamus?" Grouard asked. "Now you got a family started—you gonna get straight in your head and quit this soldiering business?"

For a moment the Irishman stared at the side of the knoll

where the Cheyenne warriors milled about upon what ponies they still possessed or had managed to recapture during the morning. "Can't say for certain, fellas," he admitted. "Don't know how it is for you both. But looking back on my own life now—seems soldiering is about the only thing I ever done. Besides a good start on wenching and drinking as soon as I stood tall enough!"

All three snorted with laughter, then Donegan continued. "Soldiering is about all I've done . . . from the time I slick-talked myself into the Army of the Potomac because I wasn't near old enough. Been fighting ever since, it seems."

Donegan tried to cipher it, pulling number down from numbers—just the way the village priest had started to teach all the young boys to maul over their arithmetic—but none of it rightly made sense just then. For some reason he simply felt it was too damned long ago when he first took up fighting in the rebellion of the southern states. Could it really be closing on a quarter of a century of carrying arms?

"More'n . . . better'n twenty-some years now," he answered softly, in awe himself at the passage of time.

He had been a fighting man of one description or another for more than half his life. And what had he to show for it? Nothing at all like other men who owned a piece of ground—opening its breast every spring and pulling sustenance from it every fall. Men like his uncle Ian. Still others preferred a more tidy existence tending a shop or mercantile, even as a licensed sutler.

Yet there always seemed to be a few . . . footloose they were ofttimes called by the more rooted around them. No tilled plot of ground nor four walls and a roof would ever hold them. Men like that merry leprechaun of an uncle, Liam O'Roarke.

"So, tell me, Seamus—what the hell you fix on doing when we get these Injuns back to their agencies and the soldiers all go home?" Big Bat asked.

"Maybe I'll finally get to scratch around for a little gold, like I always intended," Donegan answered. "Don't think I'd make much of a farmer. Not no shopkeeper neither."

Grouard shaved off a sliver of army chaw and slipped it inside his cheek on the tip of his knife's blade, asking, "What if the damned gold's already dug up and took out of them Montana mountains by the time you get around to it?"

"S'pose the only thing to do then is to become a gentleman horse breeder."

"You don't say," Pourier marveled.

"If there's no wars to fight. And no gold to dig up neither," Seamus said with a casual shrug. "What else you 'spect a fella with my talents to find himself to d—"

"Well, I'll be gol-danged," Grouard suddenly grumbled, rolling onto his belly and jerking the field glasses to his eyes.

"Look at that, will you?" Donegan gazed onto the open plain with the rest, seeing the big warrior come prancing out of hiding atop the pretty gray horse.

For a moment something sour caught in his throat, just with that remembrance of the General—the beautiful animal he had taken from a Confederate officer in the Shenandoah Valley during those last battles of the war, the very same horse he brought west to Fort Phil Kearny in sixty-six, then made their last ride together on the plains of eastern Colorado in that scorching September of sixty-eight. Remembering now with a cold clutch at his heart how that big, gallant horse carried him to the sandy island in the middle of a nameless river with fifty other white scouts as more than seven hundred Cheyenne Dog Soldiers came charging down on them at dawn.[*]

Except for the black blaze on that war pony's face and a pair of white front stockings, this horse looked mighty similar.

"What you figure he's fixing to do?" a soldier hollered nearby.

"He's come to ask you to dance," Seamus answered even more loudly.

More than two dozen scouts and soldiers laughed. A few went about adjusting sights, screwing elbows down into the snow for a firmer rest, lying there over their rifle barrels calculating distance and wind and just how much lead to give that daring rider.

"You don't reckon he's fixing to lead the rest of 'em on a charge, do you?"

Donegan turned to the young soldier who had asked the question, saying, "No. That one's on his own. My money says he's out to prove he's got balls all by hisself."

"Five dollars to the man who empties that saddle!" a lieutenant yelled to the Irishman's left.

"Five dollars!" several men echoed in unison.

"And I'll put up another five dollars!" piped in another officer on the right.

"Ten dollars, boys!"

"Did you hear that? Ten do—"

The rest of the chatter was drowned out as the whole line unloaded with a deafening racket, boom and whistle. In amazement Seamus watched the contest lying there between Grouard and Pourier as army bullets sailed across the flat, kicking up spouts of snow around and beyond the horse's hooves. Despite the closeness of the rounds, the warrior kept his animal under control as it pranced first to one side, then back to the other. In the wind the Cheyenne's buffalo-horned warbonnet danced, each feather fluttering all the way down the long trailer that draped along one of his bare legs, ending just past his moccasins.

At his right elbow the warrior had strapped a large war shield painted with a starburst and adorned with scalp locks. In his left hand he clutched some sort of a club, at the end of which were two long elk-antler tines which he held over his head, waving the weapon as he yelled out to his enemy.

"You figure he's calling out a challenge—have one of us come out and fight him?" Donegan asked.

"If he's fool enough," Big Bat replied.

"Damn, but he's pretty," Seamus replied, enjoying the sheer spectacle of it—

—and in the next heartbeat watched the buffalo-horn headdress tip forward as the warrior pitched backward onto the flanks of the big horse. No longer under strict control, the animal suddenly reared and the warrior tumbled off, the club and shield still in his grip as he spilled into the snow.

Off tore the horse, making for the safety of the hill—its single rein flapping in the cold wind. The long, thick buffalo-hair lariat knotted around its neck played out in spastic jerks across the icy ground yard by yard until the warrior's body suddenly tumbled sideways, quickly straightened out, yanked across the ground as the pony dragged its owner bouncing back behind the Cheyenne lines.

"Shoot the horse!" an officer cried. "Shoot that goddamned sonofabitching horse!"

The entire line unloaded again almost as one, a great, ear-shattering volley. A few more considered shots followed.

No matter. The pony completed this last mission for its master. Horse and warrior gone from sight.

"I'm almost glad that horse got away with that Injin," Seamus said with no little admiration.

Nearby some of the soldiers turned and gave him the hardest looks before they went back to reloading.

"Looks to me there can't be no more real fighting," Grouard stated. "Not up close, no ways."

"That's right," Big Bat agreed. "Scary thing now is them warriors that's left are gonna do all they can to prove their bravery one way or t'other."

Sure enough, it wasn't long before a pair of half-naked Cheyenne warriors emerged from behind the rocks not more than fifty paces away, carrying no weapons to speak of. Instead, the two held buffalo skulls high over their heads as they advanced on the soldier lines, chanting, singing, crying out their medicine songs in discordant notes as the soldiers tried their best to drop the two.

Daring to get as close as twenty paces from the white man's position, the pair split apart, one wheeling left, the other right, both riders moving parallel to the side of the bluff where the soldiers continued to curse and reload and fire again and again at the two daring horsemen. Then the pair turned around slowly, moving back to rejoin one another and eventually retreating toward the knoll where the Cheyenne hung on with stoic desperation.

"Looks like we've just been cursed by them two, don't you think, Frank?" Bat asked.

"Wouldn't put it past 'em," Grouard replied. "Not one bit."

"Wait a minute!" Donegan cried. "Curse? What sort of curse you figure they put on us?"

"Don't know Cheyenne very good," Pourier said, shaking his head.

"Too far to hear good anyway," Grouard added.

Then Big Bat continued, "Way I seen Injuns do before—them two likely prayed for their spirits to take away our homes and families from us. Same as we done to them."

The duty of an Old-Man Chief was to protect his people, at all costs.

So Little Wolf would have stood against the soldiers and their Indian scouts alone if he'd had to. But that cold day other brave men had chosen to stand at his shoulder against the enemy. Together they suffered. But together they held back those who had come to harm their families hiding in the narrow ravine.

Were it not for the rifles and cartridges they had captured

from the soldiers at the Little Sheep River,* Little Wolf's courageous band likely would have been crushed. Instead, time and
again they humiliated the soldiers and their scouts with their
daring—fighting out in the open against the enemy, who took
cover behind every tree and rock, bush and boulder. With every
advance attempted by the enemy, Little Wolf and his men drove
back those who would make war on women and children.

Throughout that long morning, Bull Hump, one of Morning Star's sons, remained beside with the Sweet Medicine Chief.

Also steadfast was Walking Whirlwind, Little Wolf's own
son-in-law . . . until the warrior was hit by a soldier bullet and
never regained consciousness, dying at Little Wolf's feet while
the sun continued its climb to midsky.

High Bull—a hero of the fighting at the Little Sheep River,
who had captured one of the pony-soldier chief's roster books
during that great fight—also died defending the mouth of the
narrow canyon.

Burns Red in the Sun. Walking Calf. Hawk's Visit. Four Sacred Spirits. Old Bull. Antelope. All gave their lives that morning,
falling around their Sweet Medicine Chief like the brave men
that they were. With the death of each old friend, Little Wolf's
eyes clouded all the more with tears—still, he shot straight that
day, and not once did he cower from the fight despite the desperate odds against them.

Instead he fought and sang—reloading his rifle as he prayed.
Each time he asked for the Everywhere Spirit to make every one of
his bullets find a target, asked Ma-heo-o to use Little Wolf's simple
body to save the helpless ones he had vowed to protect.

Nearly every one of those who were not killed at the ravine
mouth that terrible morning were wounded. Scabby, one of Little
Wolf's old friends from the Southern Country, fell as several bullets pierced his body, and he had to be dragged back to where
the women could care for him. So too was Curly wounded. Bald-
Faced Bull, although he was hit with three bullets, continued to
fight as long as he could hold a rifle. Buffalo Chief was hit twice,
and—although he spat up blood from his chest wound—refused
to retreat as long as his eyes could see and he could point his
gun at the enemy.

Two Bulls and White Frog were both wounded more than
twice. Wooden Nose was shot through the neck and could not

*Little Bighorn River.

speak, for his throat filled up with blood—yet all three remained steadfast with their Sweet Medicine Chief.

Among their numbers only Charging Bear and Tall Sioux were not wounded in that desperate struggle at the mouth of the ravine as the shadows shifted and the sun crawled relentlessly toward midsky.

When the last of the women and old ones had clawed and scrambled their way to the breastworks, and their village was deserted of all but the dead, the wounded Little Wolf finally turned to his comrades.

"We can go now. Up the canyon to the ridge where our families wait."

"They have our village!" Bull Hump protested, his face smeared with blood and tears.

Little Wolf laid a hand on the shoulder of Morning Star's son. "Pay heed—for you are like a nephew to me, Bull Hump. Our fight is far from over—but we have many dead and many who will die from their wounds if we do not care for them now. It is time we disappear and choose another place and time to fight this enemy."

Try as the soldiers did to drive the Cheyenne warriors back into the recesses of the snowy, rocky heights surrounding the valley that morning, the enemy doggedly remained in range of the village.

Mackenzie could have inflicted more casualties among the warriors by pushing his advantage, ordering his men into the hills after the troublesome snipers. Which was sure to mean many, many more soldiers brought back to lie beneath blankets upon the cold ground there at the hospital knoll.

Instead the colonel chose to consolidate his grip on the village and inflict his punishment on the Cheyenne in a more dramatic and possibly far-reaching way. At the same time, he had to assure that his men did not waste their precious ammunition as the day wore on and the battle became a long-range duel. Using a dozen orderlies along with his aides Dorst and Lawton, as well as William P. Clark and even John G. Bourke, as couriers who raced back and forth alone across that dangerous half mile of no-man's-land where the Cheyenne marksmen did their best to kill rider or horse, Mackenzie sent strict orders to his units deployed in every corner of the valley that they were to conserve their resources at all costs.

For the moment it appeared the Cheyenne were doing no

different. All too readily did the warriors realize just how few cartridges they had snatched up to carry away from their lodges at the moment of attack. So what few shots they did aim at the soldiers were meant to garner the maximum demoralizing effect on the colonel's men.

At the same time, to Mackenzie's growing aggravation, not only had the Cheyenne apparently figured out the range of the Springfield carbines, but they appeared to be using their ammunition more wisely than his soldiers. Too, many of the warriors constantly slipped from crevice to rock, from rock to bush— moving into effective range, forcing the soldiers to keep their heads down, at times even luring some into giving chase up the sides of the hills and along the ridges, thereby bringing the white man into range of their guns.

Yet for the most part, as exasperating as the day was for Mackenzie, his soldiers reaped one small victory after another.

With his F Troop, Captain Wirt Davis laid plans to turn the tables on perhaps as many as a dozen warriors who had doggedly remained behind some rocks fronting a bluff, where the soldiers simply could not dislodge the enemy. Davis spread the word, then ordered his men to retreat on the double, turning and sprinting to the rear of a sudden. Sure enough, the eager warriors followed headlong, howling in victory, sure they were about to cut apart the rear of the soldier retreat when Davis's men suddenly leaped into a shallow ravine, turned, and fired a deadly volley into the onrushing Cheyenne.

Those warriors not killed or critically wounded as the gun smoke cleared quickly retreated in panic and dismay.

Another group of Cheyenne took shelter in a shallow cave among the rocks on the north side of the valley. From there they put up a valiant fight until all were killed by Wessels's company, who poured volley after volley into the dark recesses of the hillside.

At the rocks where Seamus had joined Grouard, Frank North, and a contingent of soldiers that morning, the warrior marksmen on the knoll were becoming all the more troublesome in forcing the surrounding white men to warily remain behind cover while from time to time more horsemen appeared on the open plain, each of them singing their war songs and shouting to the high ground, crying out to the Shoshone and Pawnee, to the Lakota and their brother Cheyenne—demanding the enemy to come out and do battle honorably; man to man.

And behind them all, on the distant ridge where they had

erected their breastworks, the women keened and the old men sang their strong-heart songs—a strange, eerie, discordant background to the occasional burst of rifle fire that echoed off the cold red heights. From those rocks the Cheyenne could not escape without endangering their women and children for the time being, nor could they be dislodged without inflicting serious casualties on Mackenzie's troops.

During the long-range sniping, a cavalryman disregarded orders to keep down and out of sight until the snipers could be ferreted out. Instead, he curiously raised his head and shoulders above the rock where he had taken cover and immediately earned a bullet through the jaw for his foolhardiness. Unconscious, he pitched forward against the side of the slope, head twisted in such a way that he drowned in his own blood as others watched helplessly.

Despite that one soldier's fate, a particularly obnoxious trooper from the Fifth Cavalry had begun to boast that no Cheyenne bullet would find him.

"Ain't a red-belly can hit me!" he bragged.

Goaded by his more cautious fellows, the soldier began to expose more and more of himself to the distant enemy as his bravado became all the heartier . . . until a bullet finally found him.

A stunned silence fell upon the soldiers as the wounded trooper collapsed.

"Yes . . . they can too, Cap'n," the trooper cried out in shock and pain as he stared down at his own blood. "Give 'em hell for me!"

As it turned out, his wound was but a slight one, and the soldier was soon back with his company at the skirmish line—this time showing a more healthy respect for the abilities of the enemy.

Throughout the rest of the morning and into the afternoon, the man's comrades good-naturedly gave the soldier no mercy as they continued to roar with laughter, lightening everyone's spirits as they repeatedly called out to one another in the midst of that terrible battle, "Yes, they can too!"

"Yes, they can too!"

Chapter 33

Big Freezing Moon
1876

After leaving his wife with the other women near the breast-works, Black Hairy Dog plunged into the dangerous and rugged landscape at the northwest rim of the valley. Together with a handful of other warriors, the Keeper of the Sacred Arrows climbed over and around rocks, slid down the steep sides of ravines, and then clambered back up the far side, again and again through every one of those thickly timbered wrinkles until he found the spot he knew *Ma-heo-o* had guided him to.

A level thumb of ground jutted out into the valley ever so slightly. Here Black Hairy Dog would bring the power of the *Maahotse* into the light of day and thereby save the People.

"Quickly!" he told those who had followed him. "Gather up the white 'man' sage for me."

Without a word of question or protest the others bent in search of not just any sage, but that pale variety considered both male and sacred by the *Tse-Tsehese*. As the warriors brought back their harvest, Black Hairy Dog had them spread the branches upon the ground at the very lip of that height of land extending out over the valley floor. Only then did he kneel beside that bed of white sage and reverently begin to open the bundle.

First he released the thick sheet of buffalo rawhide and set it aside. Next he untied the top of the kit-fox-skin quiver, reached inside, and pulled forth the first Arrow.

Some of the warriors gasped quietly, taking a step back, while two leaned in closer for a better look at this powerfully sacred object the Keeper laid upon the bed of sage—arrow point facing the enemy.

Black Hairy Dog reached in and pulled out a second Arrow he laid so that the fletching of the arrows touched, and its stone tip pointed toward the enemy, lying a few inches from the first point.

A third came into the light of day, then the fourth, until he had them all arrayed upon the bed of sacred sage, the power emanating from their points streaming across the entire valley where soldiers and their scouts battled the People from long distance.

"All of you," he told the others as he got to his feet. "Come here and stand on either side of me."

The warriors lined up to his left and right, facing the village the enemy had captured from them.

"Each of you do as I do—for we must release the power of these Arrows upon those who would do us harm, those who would take away our buffalo and our way of life."

Black Hairy Dog stamped the earth four times. The others did the same. Then he pawed the snowy ground with one foot, like a buffalo bull in the rut. The others copied him, each of them growling as he continued to bellow in challenge.

"Now, take your bows and pull on the strings—pointing your weapons at our enemies in our village."

Each of the warriors took their bows from the quivers at their backs and held them at arm's length, pulling the strings back and twanging them as if shooting invisible arrows into what had been the People's camp. Those who carried only rifles pointed the weapons at the village and pretended to shoot their firearms at the enemies.

Below that high point Black Hairy Dog could see some of the other warriors turn where they had been fighting—each of them drawn to the buffalo sounds and the magnetic pull of the shaman's powerful magic. They spotted the Arrow Keeper and the handful of helpers above them—and they realized the significance of this powerful ceremony.

His prayers to *Ma-heo-o* gave the warriors in the nearby ravines and on the faraway knoll a strong heart, renewing the resolve among those who were helping the last of the old and the sick to climb the steep sides of the rocky hills to reach the breastworks.

Eight winters before Black Hairy Dog's father, the powerful mystic known as Stone Forehead—later called Medicine Arrow after he became the Keeper of *Maahotse*—had used his power to place a curse upon the soldier chief called *Hiestzi*, the Yellow Hair* who was driving all the Southern People back to their miserable agency.

These Northern People knew well the power that rested in the Arrows, and in their Keeper.

As Black Hairy Dog and his companions continued to paw the earth and roar with the furor of the buffalo bull, the warriors below turned back to the fighting with renewed strength, knowing they now had the protection of the Everlasting.

Never would *Ma-heo-o* fail His people.

"General wants to know if you and your Pawnee will go shut up those red-bellies shooting from them rocks," the young orderly breathlessly asked the North brothers after he had raced across that three-eighths of a mile of open ground. "The sonsabitches are really making it hot on the hospital yonder."

Like the other civilians and five of the Pawnee sergeants, Seamus turned toward the low hill behind which the surgeons had set up their bloody shop. He squinted into the harsh, metallic glare of the bright winter sun ricocheting off the icy snow. Tiny forms hovered over the prostrate soldiers that lay in an irregular semicircle between the base of the hill and some clumps of leafless willow. The surgeons' stewards had started several fires—the smoke rising some ten feet before it disappeared on the strong wind that gusted and swirled, kicking up the snow on converging eddies that danced across the floor of the valley.

Like a persistent shred of cobweb that refused to tear itself loose of his memory, the stench of those Civil War field hospitals remained with Donegan. Not a single one of them he had run across really was any better than that stinking island out on the middle of the plains of Colorado Territory as more than half of Forsyth's fifty lay dead or wounded beneath the hot sun that continued to bake the carcasses of their horses and mules, each and every one of their animals shot in the head and brought down in a spray of horse piss, stagnant river-pool water, and gritty sand to form what breastworks they could hide behind for the charge they all knew was coming.†

---

*George Armstrong Custer, *Long Winter Gone*, Vol. 1, Son of The Plains Trilogy.
† *The Stalkers*, Vol. 3, The Plainsmen Series.

Whether it was in marching away from Pennsylvania's Gettysburg or down the length of Virginia's Shenandoah—those field hospitals all smelled the same. Long ago Donegan realized he never would cleanse his memory of that rank odor of blood and cauterized flesh, the sight and smell of those unattached arms and legs, bloodied hands and feet all piled obscenely high. Those wartime surgeons with their gum ponchos tied at their necks and around their waists—grim, humorless men splattered with the blood of more than a thousand soldiers, each one now become something less as men. Splattered with the blood of those they could save.

"Yeah," Seamus answered the courier before anyone else spoke up. "We'll go keep them Cheyenne from making it any tougher'n it has to be for your surgeons. Right, Frank?"

For a flicker of a moment the older North studied the Irishman's eyes, then looked at the young orderly. "Yeah. Go tell the general he can consider it done."

"I'm coming too, Frank," Luther said as he tugged his collar up around his ears.

"No, Lute—I got something for you and one of our boys to do while the rest of us are working our way up on those snipers," Frank explained.

Luther licked his cracked lips, the bottom one oozing blood that froze as it seeped into the dark whiskers bristling below his lower lip. "It damn well better be as much fun as you two are gonna have."

Frank winked at Donegan. "You can be sure of that, little brother. Take one man—your pick—and . . . you see them Cheyenne ponies yonder?"

"I sure as hell do," Luther answered as they all turned their attention to the herd still grazing beyond the northwest end of the deep ravine, some two or three hundred yards from the Cheyenne breastworks. "Must be a hundred or more of 'em."

"You remember when we was boys, Lute? How you was always the one to raise more hell than me?"

"Damn if I didn't."

"Well, it's time you went and raised some hell," Frank declared, clamping a hand on Luther's shoulder.

"Now, you and me both know some of them Arapaho scouts tried to run them horses off a while back and they couldn't get close enough. Then a bit later, some of Cosgrove's Shoshone boys tried too—but they had the same poor luck."

"And one of 'em was shot for all his trying," Donegan added, the beginnings of a grin wrinkling the corners of his red-flecked eyes. "Besides, your friend, Three Bears, and some of his boys gave it a shot too before they failed."

The elder North nodded, saying, "But none of them had the Irishman and me working with 'em at the same time."

Luther cocked his head slightly. "I'd like to give it a try, brother."

"No *try*," Frank replied stiffly. "If our boys try it, I'll expect them to bring in those horses—right?"

"What you got in mind, Frank?"

"I want you to take them ponies away from the Cheyenne. Just you and one more."

Luther shrugged. "Only two of us, eh? Tell me what your thinking is."

"All right—the two of you head down east, hugging the timber," Frank replied. "And when you hear the signal—Seamus and me firing steady-like right under them rocks—you go ride out across that open ground where those snipers been laying their shots all morning. Get over yonder fast as you can, whooping and hollering and waving your hat . . . and you wrangle them horses back this direction."

"Whoooeee!" Luther exclaimed, pounding the side of his fist against his big brother's chest. "Does sound like a fine chiveree of it!"

"And while you're having yourself a good time and drawing the attention of them snipers, little brother," Frank continued, "this big dumb Irish Mick and me are gonna take us a handful of our Pawnee—and we're gonna silence them guns once and for all."

"Well, shit, Frank—now I don't know just who's gonna have the most fun!"

"Get on with you," Frank declared. "Go pick a man and get yourselves ready."

"I know who I'll pick, brother—Boy Chief."

Donegan asked, "Wasn't he with us when we took Tall Bull's village in sixty-nine?"*

Luther nodded. "*Pe-isk-le-shar*. But a few years back he took the white man name of Pete Headman." Then Luther turned away, heading toward the saddled horses.

The older North took up the short reed pipe he carried

---

* *Black Sun*, Vol. 4, The Plainsmen Series.

around his neck and blew on it. The shrill call of that whistle brought up more than twenty of the Pawnee. From them he quickly picked five to accompany him and Donegan. When Frank had informed them of their mission, the five turned away to begin stripping for battle. Each one of them took off all they had left of army clothing, changing from boots to moccasins, but were sure to tie bandannas around their heads to look as unlike the Cheyenne as possible, since they would be plunging into that no-man's-land and thereby coming under the muzzles of half a thousand soldier guns.

Only an hour or so before, Frank North had ordered some thirty of his scouts to climb the far slope at the upper end of the camp in hopes of getting around and behind those Cheyenne fleeing into the breastworks. But to the cold, battle-jarred troopers, North's men looked too much like Cheyenne against the snowy heights. When the soldiers began firing into his Pawnee, the scouts had to retreat under cover, rock to rock, back to the village while Frank and Luther raged at some of Mackenzie's officers for their stupidity.

A half hour later as Seamus and the rest had circled east from the camp, Frank whispered, "Here's where I figure we've got to be right under 'em."

From the captured village he and Donegan had led the five Pawnee through the leafless thickets bordering the valley floor, heading east into the thickest of the willow bog on horseback, finally tying the animals at the bottom of that long, low plateau that jutted from the northern heights. From there the seven had crept on foot from rock to rock, ever so slowly, keeping an eye on both the distant snipers across the valley floor and on those snipers up above them in the rocks with the big guns trained on the field hospital.

"Lute oughtta be chomping at the bit by now," North said after he signaled the Pawnee to check their weapons and be ready to open fire.

"If you're ready—let's open the dance!" Donegan bawled.

Frank rolled out to his left, and the Irishman to his right, plopping onto their bellies to fire almost simultaneously. To one side or the other the Pawnee scouts darted, hoping to cause the most surprise and confusion in the Cheyenne marksmen. Hoping for a little fear as well.

The steady staccato of gunshots booming from that northern rim of the valley was Luther North's signal. With a whoop and a war yelp from the Pawnee sergeant, the pair kicked their heels into their horses and sprinted into the open—immediately drawing the fire of the warriors still on the rounded knoll, along with a few shots from those Cheyenne above Frank and Seamus.

As the handful of Pawnee pumped their bullets into that hole in the rocks where the enemy marksmen had set up shop, North and Donegan scrambled up onto their feet and hurried into another patch of scrub timber. Yard by yard they climbed the steep slope, ice and talus spilling away beneath their boots, making the footing treacherous.

A shadow crossed the snow in front of the Irishman.

One of the marksmen suddenly pitched out of a crack between two large rocks and slid twenty feet down the snowy slope, lying as still as the old snow where he was sprawled.

In that twenty-below-zero cold, bullets whistled past their heads, slapping the bare branches of the brush around them as the Cheyenne and the Pawnee traded war songs and hurled taunts at one another. A second Cheyenne was hit, pitching backward out of sight to the angry wails of his companions.

For a few long moments the gunfire from above fell silent . . . then some loose talus pitched down the slope toward the white men with a clatter.

Donegan dared stick out his head for a better look, finding at least six warriors fleeing up and across the slope toward the west.

"Lookee there! Those war dogs're skedaddling!" Frank cried out.

"By the saints if they're not!" Donegan cheered. "Whaaa-hooo!"

North took up the reed whistle and blew on it, a different call this time. As the handful of Pawnee turned their attention to their leader—Frank silently signaled them to pursue the Cheyenne.

"Just for good measure," North growled. "Make sure they're on the run, all the way home."

"Them Cheyenne can't go home," Donegan replied dolefully, looking out across the valley at the village. "Mackenzie's fixing to put the whole damn thing to the torch."

Frank sighed, watching the Pawnee scrambling up the talus and around the scrub brush after the warriors for a few moments. Then he blew on the whistle a last time, recalling his scouts. At first they seemed reluctant to return when they stopped, talking among themselves, arguing, perhaps—then ultimately turned back donwslope.

Down below on the valley floor Luther North and Boy Chief rode along the fringe of the captured herd, driving them along with yelps and grunts, waving saddle blankets in the air as shots rang out and bullets hissed over their heads. First one of the Cheyenne ponies dropped. Then a second pitched headlong into the snow. Finally a third and forth horse dropped before the two whooping wranglers raced the stolen ponies out of rifle range and across the creek into the village.

To the young warrior named Dog, Crow Split Nose was an uncle who had helped raise him, the sort of man each boy needed to teach him the ways of man and honor in battle. Chief of the *Himo-we-yuhk-is*, the Crooked Lances, Crow Split Nose had been an undisputed hero during the fight with the soldiers at Little Sheep River.*

As glorious as that summer battle had been, for Crow Split Nose today must surely have been a better day to die.

Camped at the upper end of the village, Dog had sought out his mentor when the first shots and shouts rang out in the valley. During those frantic heartbeats as the People poured from the lodges and warriors began to organize the retreat of their women and children, throwing up their solid line of defense squarely in the middle of the village where they would make their stand and give no ground—Dog found Crow Split Nose in the heart of the fighting.

Not only were the soldiers' scouts attacking from the eastern edge of the village, and the soldiers themselves riding in from the north rim of the valley, but there were some of the enemy firing from the edge of the ridge just to the south of the lodges. In those frightening moments Crow Split Nose's gallant band of warriors were holding ground against an enemy pouring bullets at them from three directions.

When the last of the little and old ones had been hurried to the west, Crow Split Nose turned to his fellow warriors and ordered that they begin their retreat at last, lodge by lodge, until they could find safety among the ravines at the upper end of camp. He declared he would be the last to withdraw from the enemy, then ordered the rest of his warrior society to fall back.

*Little Bighorn River.

For his bravery, Crow Split Nose fell beneath at least two Snake bullets fired from the ridge over their heads.

Dog watched it happen, sensing almost as much pain as if the bullet had torn through his own gut. When he started back for Crow Split Nose, two older warriors had to drag Dog from the field into the mouth of a narrow, twisting ravine.

"We must get his body!" Dog had yelled at them. "We are Crooked Lances!"

Eventually he convinced them, although they would be coming under the same murderous fire that had just killed the chief of the *Himo-we-yuhk-is.*

When Dog and some of the others dashed in to attempt the rescue, the enemy's fire was hot all about them. So concentrated was it that when they attempted to drag the body away, three of them were wounded and they had to give up. For the moment Dog had to content himself by covering his uncle with a burial blanket.

"Those Indians will scalp him and butcher his body," Dog growled once he and the others had reached the safety of the ravine. "We cannot leave our chief to the enemy!"

"It is no use," one of the voices protested.

"For you, perhaps," Dog protested, no longer a young man—feeling the power of his People this terrible day. "For me, I must die trying. As I would die trying to rescue any one of you, my brother Crooked Lances." He scooted forward, picking up a flat red stone.

"I will come," said one as he crabbed forward to join the youthful warrior.

Another inched up on hands and knees, crouching by Dog. "I will come too."

Across the stream they dashed again, only three of them this time, zigzagging as they ran through the willow and up onto the flat beneath the red ridge where the Shoshone began to call out their taunts and shoot down into their midst. Quickly Dog and another grabbed the dead man's arms while the third snatched up the burial blanket. Turning, grunting, dragging, weaving this way and that, the trio lumbered back to cover with the body as the bullets slapped the icy snow and zinged off the red rocks, rattling among the nearby lodges like hailstones.

Back at the mouth of the narrow ravine, all three were panting as the others congratulated them on their courage.

"We must remember this day," a young warrior said, gulping air.

Dog replied, "We will remember this day—and all Crooked Lances will remember where our chief fell."

"How will we remember?" asked another.

"I put a red stone on the spot, marked with the sign of Crow Split Nose. We will remember—for at that place a brave man died for his people."

Chapter 34

25 November 1876

"Sweet Mither of God," Seamus mumbled under his breath as he, the North brothers, and Frank Grouard recrossed the far eastern end of the snowy valley and entered the village after driving the Cheyenne snipers from the rocks.

More times than he cared to count he had set his feet down upon one battlefield or another, through all those battles serving with the Army of the Potomac and then Sheridan's Army of the Shenandoah, through ten long years of war between white and red, enduring this struggle between all that was wild and those who sought to tame all that was less than civilized.

Here at the opening of the lodge circle's horns, here at the eastern fringe of the village it was plain to see the Cheyenne had no chance to flee before the soldiers' scouts were upon them. Here most of the casualties fell beneath the hooves and the bullets of Mackenzie's onslaught. Here among their homes, their possessions, their families.

By the time Donegan reached the village after driving off the snipers, a handful of the canvas agency lodges had already been set afire by the Pawnee. The thick hide lodge covers would have to wait till the fires grew hotter. But for now, no more than a half-dozen agency lodges smoldered, their canvas hanging in blackened tatters to the charred spires of peeled lodgepole straining at the sky in a graceful spiral, oily smudges of destruction giving stench on the downwind.

The stiff wind was cruel that day. Despite the bright, bright sun. Seamus gathered the ends of his tall collar in one fist and held it over his nose and mouth as he rode slowly through the devastation, past the bodies of men and women already stripped and scalped by the scouts. Everything still too fresh, and the air far too cold for any decay.

Yet the stench of death clung to this place.

Dead cavalry horses and Indian ponies lay here and there, perhaps bunched near a spot where some fierce fighting took a great toll—those dark, stiff-legged lumps frozen on the hoof-churned snow. Some time ago the uninjured animals on both sides had been withdrawn, now protected back in the ravines, behind the snow-laced red ridges where the enemy's bullets could not find them.

"You there!"

His attention snagged, Seamus turned slightly, finding a young soldier hollering at a handful of Pawnee loosely surrounding the body of an old Cheyenne woman.

"Shit," Donegan grumbled, and reined his bay in the group's direction.

"I told you sonsabitches to leave the woman alone!" the frustrated picket cried out more in desperation and disgust than in anger.

The Pawnee held their rifles pointed at the ground for the most part, but they smiled at the soldier as if they could shoot him just as quickly and guiltlessly as they had the woman if he nettled them any further. Not a one of them spoke.

Donegan shouted, flinging his voice over his shoulder. "Frank! Major North!"

The older of the brothers signaled Grouard and Luther to follow Donegan.

Seamus came to a halt, crossed his wrists over the saddle horn, leaning forward so his right hand lay near his pistol. "Frank, you think you can get your boys to leave off the women and the old ones?"

Frank North bristled. "With my own eyes I've seen how the Pawnee have suffered at the hands of these people—"

"They ain't suffered a goddamned thing from that old woman!" Donegan snapped, about ready to pull the gun on those grinning Pawnee scouts.

The major's eyes glared a moment, then softened, and he turned away from the Irishman, saying something in Pawnee as he shooed them away with his arm. The scouts shot the young soldier and Donegan one last look of derision before they moved off among the plundered lodges.

"I told 'em," the soldier grumbled morosely, stepping up to the body sprawled on the bloody snow. "Told 'em I found her—in that lodge right there."

Seamus asked, "What's your name, son?"

"Private Butler," he answered, staring down at the woman's body. Between the bullet hole at close range and the crude scalping, there wasn't much humanly recognizable about the head. His hands shook as they squeezed his carbine. "S-second Cavalry. I told 'em to leave her be. Said I was coming back with something to tie 'er up with so's I could take 'er somewheres the general could talk to 'er a bit."

"I suppose she was armed?" Luther North asked.

Butler looked up at the younger brother. "If you're asking because you figure that's why your Pawnee killed her—the answer's no. The old woman wasn't armed when I found her hiding under a blanket and some robes. Shaking like a autumn leaf. She could barely walk when I dragged her to her feet."

"Yeah, lookit that legs of hers," Grouard replied, kneeling beside the corpse. "She's had trouble healing that old wound."

"Likely she got herself left behind," Frank North surmised.

"And shot before we could take her prisoner," the soldier growled.

"The army don't often take prisoners in a fight like this," Luther North boasted.

"That's plain as the nose on my face!" Butler snapped. "Look around you! Ain't a prisoner left in this hull goddamned village, is there?"

The elder North swiped the back of his glove across his cracked lips and said, "I suppose there isn't, soldier," then quickly nudged his horse in the ribs and moved past the private and the old woman's bloodied body. "C'mon, Grouard. Mackenzie wants you and me to put a count to these lodges before we start torching any more of 'em."

"You going with us?" Luther North asked Donegan.

"Naw. I'll stay around here for a while," Seamus replied, easing out of the saddle. For a moment he watched the three civilians inch through camp, counting aloud; then he walked the bay over to some willow, tying off the horse.

Turning, he stepped over to the back of a lodge where the canvas cover had been slashed open at the moment of attack. Parting the fold with his two hands, Seamus peered inside, his eyes adjusting to the dim light. An interior liner of undressed hides hung from a rope strung around the circumference of the lodge from pole to pole to provide more of a wind buffer and insulator. It too had been hacked through at the moment of escape. By the fire pit sat kettles of water and a skillet filled with dried meat. Rawhide parfleches and boxes hung from the liner rope or sat here and there against the liner itself atop the beds. Everything, including the rumpled blankets and buffalo robes, appeared as if the inhabitants might return at any moment.

Here one moment. Driven into the teeth of winter the next.

When he pulled his head from the slit and his eyes had adjusted to the startling sunlight, Donegan watched more of the Pawnee dragging plunder from nearby lodges. Piles of clothing, knives and axes, kitchenware, craftwork, and a few weapons were already being deposited on separate piles destined to be loaded upon the captured ponies and driven home to make a good many Pawnee wives very happy that they had allowed their husbands to go riding off to make war on the Cheyenne.

A high-pitched sudden scream rang out across the camp near the stream—louder and more grating on his soul than the intermittent din of battle. Then a pistol shot. And all fell quiet—except for the rattle of a far-off, long-range gun battle.

As he moved around the side of the lodge, Seamus saw a seventh pile of plunder the Pawnee were collecting. By far the smallest in size, it would nonetheless prove to be the most jarring of the spoils.

Stopping at the edge of the small mound, the Irishman knelt down, picking up the fringed sleeve of a buckskin jacket. He dragged it on out into the light; finding a small, bloody bullet hole in the back. Beneath the coat lay the bright red, white, and blue of a few of the Seventh Cavalry's regimental guidons. A motley collection of leather gloves and gauntlets, some clean, most greasy, dirty, and stained with blood. Soldiers' blouses and officers' coats—gold chevrons and bars and hash marks sewn up the cuff. Here and there a smashed felt or straw hat, even a few old kepis, all having seen their better day.

Besides, there were saddles and currycombs, memorandum books and tiny bundles of letters tied with twine or faded hair ribbons, numerous canteens and wallets still containing a few of the green-and-yellow army scrip the victorious warriors had no use for.

"Hey, mister—it's time to eat!" a soldier called out from a

nearby lodge. "Pack train's set up camp over yonder near the willows. By the butte where the wounded get took."

Seamus waved in thanks, then looked back down at the pile at his feet.

Something shiny in the reflected light caught his eye. Plunging his thick glove down into the pile, he pulled out a tarnished pocket watch with vest chain attached. Pressing the release, he opened the watch to find inside the cover a faded brown chromograph of an attractive older woman cracked and wrinkled with age. A cold drop of sweat tumbled down his spine.

Feeling the ghosts of Custer's dead at his shoulder.

Quickly snapping the watch shut, he stuffed it at the bottom of the pile once more and covered it up with those shirts once worn by the living. How strange he felt—here in this place of the dead Cheyenne, going through the effects left behind on this mortal plane by Custer's dead.

Seamus stood, disgusted with himself, ashamed. Like a damned grave robber. Like these goddamned Cheyenne. Just like those Lakota they had bumped into at the Slim Buttes.* All these souvenirs stripped from the soldier bodies left on that hill beside the Little Bighorn.

"Goddamned grave robbers!" he cursed under his breath, thinking about that watch and that woman. About the man who loved her and rode off with an army far, far from home.

Then that thought of the watch made him wonder what time of the day it was—thinking on what Sam and the boy were doing right then.

From the hang of the sun, it was likely past noon. Perhaps as much as two hours past. And in that moment he remembered how hungry he was.

He untied the bay and walked it east toward the commotion: men hollering and snapping like starved, gaunt dogs around that pack train. None of the drooping mules had been unloaded nor none of the escort's bone-weary horses unsaddled for almost twenty-four hours.

"Irishman! Over here!" Frank Grouard called out.

As he came up to the headquarters group, Seamus saw that Mackenzie had turned his complete attention to the swarthy half-breed and place a folded sheaf of paper in Grouard's glove.

Frank promptly loosened a button, shoved the papers inside his coat and wool blouse, then rebuttoned his buffalo-hide coat

---

*Trumpet on the Land, Vol. 10, The Plainsmen Series.

as the North brothers turned away and the Irishman came to a stop. "Donegan! I'll be carrying word to General Crook to bring up the infantry."

"Good for you, Frank. If you can carry word from the Black Hills to Laramie for Crook, I figure you're the best man we got for this job. Good luck, you ugly child."

Mackenzie turned as Donegan held out his hand and shook with Grouard. The colonel seemed to size Seamus up and down a moment, then said, "How would you like to give me a hand yourself, Mr. Donegan?"

"This about them words we had earlier?"

"That? Hell, no—that's all forgotten."

Donegan asked, "What you have planned?"

"I figured you'd like to help me see if we can put an end to this long-range sniping and get ourselves a truce worked out with the warriors in the hills."

"Yeah," he quickly answered. "I'd like to have the chance to do that. What's your thinking, General?"

"Go round up Rowland for me—that squaw man who can talk the enemy's language," Mackenzie said. "I first thought of using one of the scouts—but I'd always wonder if I was being told the white man's truth. So go fetch Rowland for me. Bring him here. I want the two of you to see about quieting things down and getting these folks to surrender before night falls."

Seamus glanced at the sun keeling over into the western quadrant. "We don't have all that much time, General."

"That's why I'm in the hurry I am, Mr. Donegan. If the warriors aren't going to surrender soon, then I want the infantry getting here on the double to force 'em out of the rocks tomorrow."

"And?"

"And," Mackenzie replied thoughtfully, "if the warriors will at least surrender their women and children to me for the night—then not one of the noncombatants needs to die from this inhuman cold."

From all that Young Two Moon could see, there were only five left on top of that rocky knoll. Before, there had been many, many more. But now so many had retreated as the soldiers had punched through the village and scattered the warriors in the rocks along the northern wall of the valley.

So only five remained. Cut off. And the soldiers were moving in.

Two, three, then four times the Cheyenne made futile attempts to reach the five courageous warriors who continued to make things hot on the soldiers and scouts scampering around in the upper end of the village.

"Do not worry about us!" they shouted down to their friends far away. "We sing our death songs and will take many of the enemy with us this day!"

It was clear they had given up. Almost like the suicide boys whom the elders had paraded through camp the night before the soldiers had attacked that great village nestled alongside the Little Sheep River. But these five were not suicide boys. These were seasoned, veteran warriors who had likely calculated the gamble of being caught where they were when they first went to the top of that hill. From there they would have had themselves a perfect view of the destruction of the gray-horse soldiers by the warriors in the ravine. On the brow of the hill he recognized White Horse, Long Jaw, and Little Horse. Young Two Moon did not know the others.

"Look!" a voice called out behind Young Two Moon. "See who is coming to fight!"

"Yellow Nose!" the cry went up among the warriors at the side of the slope leading up to the breastworks.

"Yellow Nose has come!" the women screamed above them, trilling their tongues and shrieking with renewed passion.

Yes, Yellow Nose—one of the most daring in the fight against the *ve-ho-e* soldiers at the Little Sheep River. Captured from the Black People* as a child, Yellow Nose had grown to become one of the most courageous warriors among the *Ohmese-heso.*

Somehow this morning he had rescued his feathered warbonnet, or perhaps he wore that of another man. It did not matter. How magnificent he looked atop the bare back of that pony, wearing only leggings and breechclot. No shirt nor moccasins as he moved the horse slowly through the crowd that clamored about him, touching his leg, calling out his name.

"Who will go with me?" he asked in a booming voice.

Immediately many hands shot into the air, their courage electrifying everyone within hearing.

"Bring your weapons and come with me!" Yellow Nose cried out, pointing the muzzle of his Winchester repeater at the

---

*The Ute.

knoll. "Some of my friends are in trouble and I must help them!"

By the time they were streaming across the rugged ground for that slope, Young Two Moon figured there must have been at least three-times-ten streaming out like a flight of geese from Yellow Nose, just as the rest of the long-necked flock veed from the point goose while they winged overhead in the first cold days before winter. Many of them wore bonnets and feathers, skins of wolf and badger and skunk—everyone shouting, raising his hoarse voice into the cold air to frighten the soldiers and give their hearts daring for this charge.

One, then two and three at a time . . . the guns began to fire around Young Two Moon and the rest. The five warriors on the hill looked over their shoulders and saw their friends coming. Three of them climbed to their knees, waving their rescuers on enthusiastically, whooping and pounding their chests with fists, others shaking their fists at the enemy scouts who yelped and howled in dismay when the five quickly retreated from the hilltop while their rescuers held the soldiers at bay.

At the base of the slope Yellow Nose whirled and pranced atop that pony, shouting at the enemy, calling out instructions to his warriors until it came time to run back to safety.

This time they had rescued the five. They had dared gamble with their lives for their friends.

And they had won.

Chapter 35

Big Freezing Moon
1876

Nearly naked, she had been standing resolutely with the other women, most of them older than her fifteen summers, among the rocks they had piled up along the top of the ridge at the upper end of camp.

Above what was left of their village, now that the soldiers and their Indian scouts had begun to set fire to all that the People possessed in their lives.

After singing so long in that terrible cold—here where none of them found any protection from the winter wind—her voice was all but gone. Her throat so raw, it gave her great pain just to draw in each breath, one after the other, much less to sing with all her might.

But this was what she was called upon to do. And Buffalo Calf Woman would sing the strong-heart songs as long as it would take. Vowing she would sing as long as her younger brother kept singing.

At dawn's first cry, that first gunshot, those first hoofbeats that had startled everyone at the upper end of camp, she and some of her friends had been talking in those moments after the drum had fallen silent and the dancers had dispersed, everyone going off to their beds. When the dancing had started the night before, Buffalo Calf Woman had been knotted to five others by her mother with lengths of rawhide so none of Last Bull's Kit Fox warriors could snatch them away.

At dawn they were still tied one to the others.

So with the coming of the soldiers and their terrifying scouts when the six of them had attempted to flee in six different directions—all of them had spilled onto the trampled snow as the hoofbeats and the war songs and the whistles and the snarling bullets drew closer and closer.

From somewhere an old woman appeared with her long and worn butcher knife. She slashed it down on one rawhide strand, up through the next, on and on until all six girls were freed to scatter as the enemy reached the top of the ridge south of camp—firing their rifles into the lodges.

To the door of her family's home Buffalo Calf Woman flew, finding the interior dark and empty, a kettle filled with water beside the coals of last night's fire, dried meat laid out, ready for boiling their breakfast.

"Flying Man!" she had cried in panic, her heart in her throat as she'd turned away from that abandoned lodge, women and children dashing past her, screaming, screeching, keening, and crying.

"Flying Man!" she hollered with fleeting hope through that upper end of camp until it was too late and two warriors had to drag her from the village before she was captured or killed by the enemy's scouts. There at the far edge of the village she had found her mother's body seeping a slush of blackening crimson onto the torn snow.

Yet it was no time for tears.

"I must find Flying Man!" she had tried to explain to the warriors who pulled her from the body. She was seeking her younger brother—the boy who was born with a dark blanket pulled over his eyes for all time.

Had he gotten out of the village in time? Had her mother taken him just so far and no farther in their flight? With her mother killed—what had become of Flying Man?

Reluctantly climbing the western ridge with the others, digging with her torn and bloody fingers at the rocks they pulled from the frozen ground, piling them one by one atop the other to erect breastworks—she kept looking for Flying Man. Kept asking each new arrival if they had seen her brother.

He would be frightened. Blind to the danger—able only to hear the terror in that village put on the run.

"Buffalo Calf Woman!"

Only faintly at first she had heard the voice, looking here and there until she heard it call out again—a little stronger this time. Then she found him, struggling up the long slope of the ridge, an old bent woman clutching his arm. The ancient one's back curved so far that she had to twist her head to the side to look at anything but the ground; nonetheless, the woman clung to the blind boy and helped his feet to see every step of their way together.

He sang out again, "Buffalo Calf Woman!"

"I am here, Flying Man!" she shrieked, pitching down the slope in a mad run, skidding to a stop on the icy snow, clutching him to her breast, her tears spilling as she next brought the old bent woman within her embrace.

"I was so scared after mother's hand was ripped from mine and then she would not answer me," Flying Man said quietly, tears from his unseeing eyes spilling on his cheeks. "But the old one here found me and told me I must be strong for her—to take her to safety with me."

Buffalo Calf Woman put out her hand and touched the wrinkled cheek of the old one, skin like the bark of a long-dead cottonwood. "You . . . you both were very brave."

"We must sing, young woman," the old, toothless mouth said with a raspy croak, the watery eyes blinking in the severe cold.

"Yes," Buffalo Calf Woman agreed as she took her brother on one arm, the old one grasping her other. "We will go now to the top where we will sing for our men."

All morning the three of them had been there together. The young boy, who raised his sightless eyes upon that valley where his people were fighting for their very existence. The old woman so bent with age and troubles and her many winters that she had to turn her head to fling her voice down to the warriors below them on the valley floor.

And Buffalo Calf Woman—not knowing where her father and older brothers were in the fierce struggle below.

Yet knowing her mother's spirit stood beside them now—her mother's voice giving them all its magic to sing the strongheart songs behind the tears.

This old fur trapper reminded Seamus of Bridger. Ol' Gabe. Big Throat. Jim Bridger.

For any man's purposes, Bill Rowland was indeed cut of the

very same cloth. A simple frontiersman who, like Bridger, had married an Indian woman and taken up with her people.

Donegan turned in the saddle and glanced over his shoulder at the high ridge behind them. Up there, south of the village, Tom Cosgrove and his friend, Yancy Eckles, both were squaw men among the Shoshone on the Wind River. But this Rowland had to be a hell of a lot older than those two Confederates. Been out here on the plains from the time of the buffalo-robe trade—when the tribes still dressed hides for the white man, before the time the hide men began to set about wiping out the herds.

The man must surely have grandchildren by now, Donegan thought as the two of them moved their horses cautiously out of the tall willow and headed west at the foot of the long plateau bordering the north wall of the valley.

"See what they've got on their minds, Rowland," Mackenzie had ordered. "Take some of your relatives with you and see if you can't convince these chiefs to call off their dogs."

"You want me to tell 'em you're fixing to call it quits, General?" Rowland had asked before he'd moved out with Donegan.

"No—I'm not calling off our attack. But you're to find out if these Cheyenne want to surrender any of their women and children, the old people too—before we destroy everything they own."

Rowland only nodded and turned away. His eyes brushed Donegan, watery they were. With a look in them that told Seamus the old frontiersman knew why Mackenzie was sending the Irishman with him.

That son of a bitch don't trust me, those eyes said. So I don't figure I got a damn reason in the world to trust you neither.

The four men Rowland quickly selected to accompany him regarded Seamus with those same eyes filled with wary distrust. Donegan knew that, unlike Three Bears's Sioux scouts, these men very well might have relatives among the people in this camp they had attacked at dawn. Such a thing naturally made a man suspicious, nervous, downright uneasylike when he had come to wreak destruction upon his kinfolk.

Every now and then a high-powered rifle roared and its echo rocked back and back and back from the canyon walls. But for the most part the battle had reached an uneasy lull with the sun heading quickly for the southwest. Already the shadows of the rocks and brush were lengthening below their horses' hooves.

"I figure we better go on foot from here," Rowland advised, then turned and spoke quickly to the others in Cheyenne.

They all dismounted and the youngest among them gathered up the leads to the horses, taking the animals back a few yards to the mouth of a narrow coulee, where he would ground-hobble them with their single horsehair rein lashed around one fore hoof, which would allow the horses to graze under his watchful eye.

As the old man moved out, Donegan signaled the others ahead. He preferred to have them all in front, where he could see them. If there was the slightest chance of monkeyshines, he didn't want one of these sonsabitches at his back. Not that any of these Cheyenne might know of an ambush, but, for all he knew, they could get themselves into a fierce skirmish and decide to turn the lone white man over to their relatives in the rocks as a way to save their own hides.

But hell, Rowland's a white man. I can't keep forgetting that.

Up ahead the scouts suddenly went to their knees behind Rowland. The old man was calling out to the hillside.

Then a voice cried down from the rocks above them and to the left.

Back and forth Rowland and one of the Cheyenne scouts hollered to the unseen warriors. Then the old frontiersman turned slightly in his crouch, motioning Donegan forward.

"They tell me their whole family's hungry and cold," Rowland explained as Seamus came to a rest beside him. "Those what ain't dead anyways."

"What's going on?" Donegan wondered after a long and uneasy silence.

" 'Pears to me they sent one of their bunch to fetch up one of the Old-Man Chiefs," Rowland replied.

"Old-Man Chiefs?"

"The real rulers of the tribe."

"Not the war chiefs?"

He shook his head. "Nope. One of them what decides how the rest of the band will fare."

A voice shouted down, echoing slightly from the snow-laced red boulders.

Rowland announced, "They just told us they see Morning Star coming."

"Morning Star?"

"White man calls him Dull Knife," Rowland explained, then

shrugged, saying, "You ought'n be glad he's a better man than he is a fighter."

"Bill Rowland!"

That deep voice cried the name with Cheyenne inflection.

"Don't let that fool you—he don't speak no American," Rowland declared. "He just knows how to say my name."

"I'm here!" the frontiersman shouted in Cheyenne.

"The rest are with me, Bill Rowland."

"Is that you, Morning Star?"

"Yes. At my side are Gray Head, Roman Nose—"

"Wait," Seamus growled with a temper. "We killed Roman Nose in the fall of sixty-eight. September, it were."

The older white man's brow furrowed gravely as he studied the Irishman. "You ... you were with Forsyth's ... his rangers at the fight on the fork of the Republican?"

"It's where I buried my uncle ... after Carpenter's buffalo soldiers come in to raise the siege," Seamus replied softly, feeling two of the others with Rowland devote their undivided attention to him. He felt the old pain well up within him. The empty hole inside—that nothingness which no one could fill—even now after all the years that Liam had been gone.

"Naw, Irishman. It ain't the same Roman Nose what got hisself killed trying to run Forsyth's men down." Slapping his glove against his thigh, the frontiersman said, "Dang, if I'd knowed—why, up there in them rocks is Turkey Leg."

"So? What's that mean to me?" Donegan watched Rowland purse his lips with a crestfallen look over his face.

"Hell—that's been too long," Rowland considered. "He isn't 'bout to remember you, is he?"

Donegan answered. "What's so all-fired important about talking to this Turkey Leg anyway?"

"He and Little Wolf—another of the chiefs with 'em right up there—they're the fighting chiefs of the hull bunch. They won't be ones to talk peace. Turkey Leg was a war chief back to the time they tried to rub out Forsyth's bunch."

Seamus dragged the back of his glove across his cracked, oozy lips, squinting into the sunlight's reflection off the snow. "Go 'head, Rowland. It don't matter if them war chiefs are up there. They might just listen. G'won and give this parley a try for the general."

Nodding in resignation, Rowland stood slowly, his arms high above his head. "I have no weapon in my hands. I stand here before you, to talk with you about what the soldier chief wants from you."

"He wants us all dead!"

Rowland whispered to Donegan, "That was Turkey Leg. He's an old, old man—been around since dirt."

"Got to be, by damned."

"And he's never met a white man he likes."

"Including you?" Donegan asked.

With the faintest of grins, Rowland admitted, "Well, maybe not every white man he's met. But that bugger's hated the color of our skin long before the Dog Soldiers' fight agin you'uns with Forsyth."

Rowland spoke again, back and forth, with the disembodied voices from the rocks above them, as did one of the Cheyenne scouts nestled near the old frontiersman. From the tone of the enemy's voices, Donegan could tell the chiefs were drawn tight as a cat-gut fiddle bow. Bone weary. Tested to the extreme. Cold and hungry. While that sort of deadly mix might well make most men all but give in to any talk of surrender, give in to talk of a warm fire and food for his belly . . . everything Seamus had ever heard about the Northern Cheyenne coupled with what he had himself learned at that Beecher Island* siege and from the Reynolds's fight at Powder River last winter,† these weren't the kind of men to count out, not by a long chalk.

"Little Wolf says their families are safe in the hills but they don't have many cartridges to fight us," Rowland struggled with some of the translation.

"But they ain't about to come in and take Mackenzie's offer to surrender, are they?"

With a doleful wag of his head, Rowland said, "He shouted to me, 'Rowland! Go on home now with the Lakotas and all your *Tse-Tsehese* from the White River Agency—you have no business here! We can whip these white soldiers alone . . . but we can't fight your Indians too!' "

Licking his oozy lower lip, Seamus said, "They'd likely give us a good fight of it without these Indian scouts—wouldn't they?"

Rowland nodded, then shrugged a shoulder. "Damn if they already haven't give us damn good fight, Irishman."

Donegan shuddered as the wind kicked up, driving some icy

---

* *The Stalkers*, Vol. 3, The Plainsmen Series.
† *The Blood Song*, Vol. 8, The Plainsmen Series.

snow crust against his cheek. "Don't look like you can talk 'em into sending down their women and children to go back to the reservation?"

"I'll try again—if'n you want."

"All you can do is try."

For a few minutes Rowland and the Cheyenne scout parleyed with the voices of the chiefs, until the old frontiersman turned suddenly, a fresh smile on his lips.

"Morning Star says he'll come down a ways and talk to me where I can see him."

"By the saints! Do it! Do it! See what you can do to change his mind."

The closest they ever came to laying eyes on that aging warrior was to see a man stand some twenty yards off near some rocks where he could quickly retreat if treachery threatened.

"Morning Star said he's lost his three sons today," Rowland explained as he whispered down to the Irishman.

A sudden pull seized Seamus's heart—as he remembered how it felt to hold his own son in his arms, there near his heart. Remembering how it felt to look down at that tiny face. How Morning Star must have experienced it with all three of his boys. And what despair the old chief must now suffer in losing them. Yet—there he stood, amazingly, as solid as a rock. Talking with a white man ... when the white soldiers had taken his children from him.

"Says he wants peace. Wants to surrender. He'll bring in the women and children himself ..." Then Rowland stopped. There were angry voices from above. "Wait ... but ... but the other chiefs won't let him surrender for them. They want to keep on fighting. Shit—there's Little Wolf with him now."

"Who's he?"

"The hard one—that's who," the old frontiersman answered. Then he listened to Little Wolf speak for a few minutes.

"What's he saying?"

He turned to tell Donegan, "Little Wolf says, 'You have killed and hurt a heap of our people today! So you may as well stay now and kill the rest of us!"

The Irishman instructed, "Tell him—tell all of them—that if they surrender, Mackenzie might leave them their lodges, their belongings, if they surrender and start back to the agency under escort."

Then Seamus watched the old man's eyes look away, staring across the valley with great regret.

Finally Rowland shook his head with sadness. "Look," he said.

When he did look, Donegan saw the oily spires of black smoke curling into that pitifully cold blue sky across the white valley beyond the leafless timber bordering the stream. And with that sight, so much hope went out of him too.

"They can see it . . . can't they?" Seamus asked.

"They seen it all along," Rowland stated. "Likely ever since we been talking."

Swallowing hard, Donegan said, "Ain't no wonder Morning Star can't talk 'em into surrendering. Not with their women and children, the old and sick ones, all of 'em watching their homes—everything—go up in smoke like that." The wind gusted cruelly where he knelt in the thick brush. He sniffled, dragged a glove beneath one eye as he turned back to gaze at Rowland. "I suppose there's nothing any of us can do now."

The frontiersman nodded once. "I figger there's nothing more for us to talk about."

Rowland tapped his young Cheyenne companion on the shoulder, and they were both beginning to scoot backward toward the protection of some rocks when Little Wolf stepped in front of Morning Star and called out to Rowland again.

Donegan whispered, "What's he say?"

The frontiersman listened until Little Wolf turned and disappeared. Morning Star slowly turning away into the rocks without another word, his shoulders sagging with a great weight.

"Little Wolf . . . he says some of his warriors—they gone for help. Gone for some Lakota up north. Big village, not far from here. Gone there for help."

"So they mean to keep on fighting?" Seamus asked. "Even if the coming night don't kill 'em?"

"Yeah," Rowland said as he came alongside the Irishman. "Little Wolf said they was gonna bring them Lakota back here and clean us out."

Chapter 36

Big Freezing Moon
1876

Two of Morning Star's sons were dead. The other could not be found.

Four of his grandchildren lay dead.

In all his sixty-eight winters, he had never seen such devastation and despair visited upon the *Ohmeseheso*.

Perhaps there was hope for that third son. Morning Star wanted so to hope, because at the moment of attack one of his friends, Black White Man, had managed to save his son, Working Man.

In the recent fight with the Shoshone, Working Man had been badly wounded: a rifle ball striking him in the buttock and exiting from the meat of his right thigh. His father and others had constructed a travois to haul the young warrior back to the village of his people after wiping out the enemy.

So it was that Working Man lay helpless in their lodge earlier that morning when the soldiers attacked. Black White Man had herded his wife from their lodge, thrusting her atop his war pony he kept picketed by the door.

"Wait for me here!" he ordered as he ducked into their lodge.

Then, as the bullets fell about the village like hailstones upon the canvas-and-hide covers, the father returned for his son. After slashing a tall opening in the back of their lodge, Black

White Man lifted the young warrior into his arms and carried him to the pony, hoisting him behind his mother.

"Ride to the breastworks!" he was shouting when Morning Star ran through camp on his old legs—driving all the people before him. He told his wife and son, "Go before the bullets find you!"

"You are not coming?" his wife shrieked.

"No. I stay to fight. Take our son to safety, now!"

Then Morning Star watched as Black White Man turned away to join first one group, then another, fiercely protecting the flight of all women and children.

A little later Morning Star caught sight of his friend again. This time Black White Man had been joined by Elk River and others who were on their way down a shallow ravine, on their way to recapture some of the ponies run off by the soldiers' Indian scouts. From time to time they disappeared from view among the winter-bare brush clogging the brow of the coulee ... so Morning Star had turned away to help others escape the village.

When his attention was yanked back with the great noise: the shouting of the angry soldiers, the thunder of the hooves on the cold, solid ground, and the yelling of the brave warriors who had leaped atop the bare backs and were escaping with some of their prized animals. An enemy bullet struck one of the boys with Black White Man in the neck, and he nearly fell. But almost as soon as the blood began to stream down the boy's chest, another warrior was there beside him so that he would not fall.

As the sun rose high that day, in that final desperate struggle before they lost their village to the enemy's scouts, Morning Star watched with Black White Man from the low ridge where together they saw the Wolf People scouts fight their way through the scattered cluster of lodges.

"There," Black White Man had said, gesturing to the side of the hill. "Those are some of my ponies the enemy will steal! I must get them!"

"You cannot—it is too dangerous!" Morning Star told his friend. "Those soldiers will see you—and train their guns on you."

"Look there!" Black White Man had said suddenly, pointing into the dazzling light of that sunny morning.

"I see!" Morning Star exclaimed, his heart rising in hope. Some of Little Wolf's warriors were crawling up on their bellies to the crest of the adjoining ridge. There they began to train their fire on the soldiers among the fringe of the village.

Black White Man got to his knees, slapping his friend on the back enthusiastically. "Because those *ve-ho-e* will be worried about the bullets—they will not worry about one lone warrior going in among the ponies! *Aiyeee!*"

And with that he bolted to his feet, dashing away from Morning Star, who watched, his heart in his throat, as the daring warrior reached his lodge pitched close to the stream. There he plunged into the midst of the frightened, rearing ponies he had picketed nearby, each of the frightened animals darting, lunging, pitching back and forth at the ends of their tethers.

One by one he cut them loose, then waved and shouted, "Hey! Hey! Hey!"

Running behind them, he drove his ponies toward the upper end of the village, into the narrow canyon behind the ridge where the women and children were singing with loud, clear voices at the breastworks.

As he was fleeing the village, Black White Man encountered a young boy who dashed from the doorway of a lodge to join him in his race to safety. While Morning Star watched, the enemy's bullets landed all around the two, warrior and boy, sometimes kicking up the trampled snow between their legs—but neither was hit.

Later, as the sun continued to slip into the southwest that long winter afternoon, Morning Star heard a lone warrior begin the steady, rhythmic work with his big gun, tucked somewhere among the rocks down the slope of the ridge where the women sang. With each shot came a deep boom, then its fainter echo—as the warrior placed his bullets in among those who were destroying the village. Burning everything that belonged to the *Ohmeseheso*. Bringing to a sudden, savage end their whole way of life.

When Morning Star went to talk with the white squaw man named "Long Knife" Rowland who had married the daughter of Old Frog, Little Wolf, Roman Nose, and Turkey Leg joined the sour-tongued Last Bull in refusing to surrender long enough to assure that the little ones, the sick, and the wounded would have a warm place beside fires in the valley while twilight descended and this brutal night fell around them like winter ice.

As many of his people as he had seen die this day, now he mourned most his relatives: sons and grandsons and nephews. Why some fathers like Black White Man were spared by the spirits, while others had to die in this fight, Morning Star did not understand.

Oh, *Ma-heo-o,* why?

Perhaps the Everywhere Spirit was punishing him for selfishly wanting his family to remain in this north country, their true home ... when the *ve-ho-e* demanded they move to that hot southern land.

Oh, *Ma-heo-o,* spare us this terrible day!

How many times before had he learned that in all things concerning the white man—there was simply too high a price to pay.

By now it was plain to Colonel Mackenzie and everyone else around him that the Northern Cheyenne were not about to surrender.

Since it would be nothing short of suicide to attempt to dislodge the warriors from their fortifications in the hills, that work would be left to Dodge's infantry, being summoned up by the half-breed Grouard. In the meantime, Mackenzie's cavalry and Indian scouts would proceed with rounding up the enemy's ponies and turning to ash everything the Cheyenne possessed.

With the pack train finally reaching the valley and the units being fed in rotation after a night-long march and more than half a day of battle, the colonel got down to the business of not just defeating the Cheyenne, but decimating any hope Morning Star's people might ever have of again becoming a powerful people.

"We must end once and for all any thought these people might entertain of surviving off their reservation," the colonel instructed.

"Hear! Hear!" some of the officers shouted enthusiastically as they pitched into the destruction.

"Every blanket and buffalo robe, every last shred of clothing, every bit of shelter these people can put between themselves and the wrath of winter," Mackenzie instructed his officers as they set a torch to the village. "Those of you who fought with me on the southern plains know firsthand how vital it is to thoroughly destroy the enemy's ability to wage war in the future."

"Hurrah!" a chorus of officers cheered.

"We drove Quanah Parker's Comanche into that winter. So as you feed everything to the flames—think how much deadlier will be our destruction here on these northern plains."

William Earl Smith shuddered involuntarily.

Not that it was any colder than it had been a moment ago. The young brakeman from Illinois shook with the cold fire he saw blazing in the colonel's eyes as Mackenzie rallied his officers.

As icy as the weather had been for the past week, the surgeons were nonetheless already predicting that this night would see temperatures dropping further still. How they would know, Smith could not dare to figure out.

After all, this afternoon beneath a bright winter sun the mercury in the surgeons' thermometers had risen to a high of fourteen below—which meant it didn't have all that much to fall before it froze into a solid silver bead at the bottom of the bulbs . . . at thirty-nine below zero.

By the time Donegan returned to the village with Bill Rowland, the destruction of the Northern Cheyenne was well under way.

"Mackenzie sent North's Pawnee into the camp to get things started," John Bourke explained as he walked up while Seamus dismounted, tying his horse off beneath the rocks of the south ridge. "Major North told me that within minutes of starting their work, four of his battalion's horses had been hit by enemy fire and killed."

Nodding, Seamus said, "They're in the hills around us—and it will take too damned many good lives to blast them out." Bitterly, he gazed around at the cavalry-horse carcasses scattered here and there upon the trampled snow.

Bourke went on to explain that by keeping out of sight of those Cheyenne snipers while the sun was still hung in the sky, the Pawnee were able to go about their grisly work nonetheless, concealed behind the lodges they were plundering and burning.

Then the lieutenant said, "You all right, Irishman?"

He sighed. "Yes. Just that . . . the fighting don't ever get any easier, Johnny."

For some time Bourke didn't say anything; then he explained, "Just a while back Mackenzie told me that he most regrets losing McKinney."

"All of us can regret losing a good fighting man."

"Mackenzie seems especially . . . well, morose about it," Bourke continued. "In his private despair he said that he alone had recognized young McKinney's potential four years ago when the lieutenant had been what the general called a hard-drinking and irresponsible shavetail."

"He came out of the Academy and into Mackenzie's Fourth to get the green worn off, that it?"

With a nod Bourke said, "Sadly, the general told me he watched over McKinney and pushed him along until he could call McKinney one of the most gallant officers and honorable men that he's ever known."

"You and me both have seen a lot of good men fall in this struggle, Johnny," Seamus said, reflecting on all the faces, young and old, that passed through his mind.

"But some deaths a man takes harder than others," Bourke replied. "I don't know if Mackenzie's going to hold up, Seamus. As the afternoon has waned, so have the general's spirits. I feel his despair ... his gloom is deepening."

Nearby, the noisy, dirty work of complete and utter destruction continued. What the Pawnee had begun, soldiers now relished in completing. Captain Gerald Russell's K Troop, Third U.S. Cavalry, along with Captain Wirt Davis's F Troop of the Fourth, had been dispatched to get on with this matter before night descended upon the valley.

With camp axes and tomahawks found among the lodges, Russell's and Davis's soldiers had begun by cutting each canvas or buffalo-hide lodge cover from its graceful spiral of poles. Dozens of cold and brittle blades rang out as the thin poles were cut down, hacked into pieces, then fed to the roaring bonfires, where many of the detail warmed themselves momentarily before they plunged back into this ruinous business of total war.

Everything that could not be consumed to ash was broken: metal bits were smashed beneath rocks; holes were knocked in the bottoms of kettles, punched through canteens and pans and other utensils; all manner of ironware—including spades, picks, shovels, hammers, scissors, and all manner of knives—all of it broken before they were tossed into the fires.

Everything else was fed to the flames that grew hotter and higher as the sun slipped toward the west and the shadows lengthened like the talons of the long winter night itself.

In several unusually big lodges the soldiers found the inner walls ringed with countless saddles and woven bridles, along with war regalia hung from the liner ropes in these warrior-society gathering places.

From every family dwelling the Pawnee and troopers pulled clothing and craftwork. Into the flames went skin paunches, bladders, and rawhide parfleches stuffed with fat and marrow. Flames roared audibly over the distant, eerie keening of the

women courageously gathered at the breastworks. Nowhere in
the valley could a man escape that audible crackle produced by
the many immense fires, a roaring, gushing sound akin to some
monstrous appetite demanding more and more sustenance.

Early on it was clear the Pawnee and soldiers had failed to
uncover small kegs and cans of powder among the provisions
tossed upon the flames. In consequence, from time to time the
valley rocked with that occasional throb of explosion, men
shouting out warnings with each booming bark of sudden thunder, spewing a cascade of showering sparks that never failed to
scatter the nearby soldiers as burning lodgepoles rained down
like jackstraws until the roiling flames once again diminished
from their spectacular, fiery heights.

Near the edges of each warming bonfire, soldiers and scouts
clustered, some slowly feeding themselves and the flames from
the same hide satchels, ordered this night to burn what they
could not eat of the Cheyennes' winter meat. With muted pop,
crackle, and sizzle—the victors laid tons of buffalo meat to waste
as a hungry people watched from the hills.

Empty bellies, Seamus knew, seemed always to fill hearts
with hate.

"These are funeral pyres," Bourke declared proudly. "Great,
scalding, ruinous funeral pyres of what was once Cheyenne
glory."

"Johnny, I'm sure you remember what Reynolds destroyed,
and what he left behind in that Cheyenne village beside the Powder River last winter."

"I damn well do. Because of that vivid memory, I've reminded General Mackenzie that here the destruction must be
complete," Bourke explained as the two walked on. "We know
firsthand from our experience with these hostiles what can become of them if we don't completely destroy everything the enemy possesses."

Into the piles of plunder or the great, leaping bonfires went
the clatter of bottles filled with the white man's strychnine used
to poison wolves.

Joining unimaginable amounts of fixed ammunition and
loose—bullet molds, cartridge cases, and black powder.

Then an angry voice pricked Donegan's attention.

"I don't figger I oughtta pay for that saddle, Lieutenant!"

Close at hand a soldier stood his ground against young Homer Wheeler, commanding G Troop of the Fifth Cavalry.

"Easy, Private! As you were before you'll be disciplined! You know as well as the next man that a soldier loses his saddle and bridle—he's docked the pay!" Wheeler argued.

"But, sir! I had that goddamned horse shot out from under me," Private Kline declared. "You know your own self I was carrying a dispatch for the general, right across that open ground yonder—and the horse went down under me. The way them bullets were smacking all around, I wasn't about to hang on until I could somehow get that saddle off my own dead horse!"

"Very well," Wheeler replied in exasperation, looking up to see Bourke and Donegan approaching. "I'll make a note of it here in my memorandum book so you'll not be charged for lost equipment assigned you."

Kline stood rigid, snapped a salute, and said, "Thank you, Lieutenant."

"Report over there to our company at the foot of the hill and get yourself some food, soldier."

"Yes, sir!"

Wheeler watched the private go, then turned to Bourke and Donegan. "Lieutenant Bourke—good to see you. Why, you can't believe what we've been finding among the belongings pulled from the redskins' lodges."

Donegan followed the two lieutenants over to a pile of plunder lit by the last rose glow of the falling sun and by the leaping yellow flames nearby. Wheeler knelt, barely touching the human hair, then looked up at Donegan.

"Doesn't take a scout like you, mister," Wheeler said, "to see that these here scalps belonged to a pair of young girls—neither one of them older than ten years, I'd imagine. One blond. The fellow with Cosgrove, one named Eckles, he said the other's likely Shoshone."

"Cosgrove's bunch been down from the heights?" Donegan inquired, gazing for a moment at the high ridge south of camp.

With a nod Wheeler answered, "I'll say. And when they went among the lodges, a few of his boys found some Cheyenne souvenirs of a battle they fought with a band of Shoshone not long back."

The lieutenant went on to tell about what grisly trophies had been pulled from the lodges slated for destruction: a buckskin bag containing the right hands of twelve Shoshone babies; several of Tom Cosgrove's auxiliaries readily recognized the scalp of one of their herders killed at the outset of the Battle of the Rosebud, easily identifiable by the ornaments the departed youngster had worn in his hair; besides, there were at least thirty

Shoshone scalps taken in a recent battle; in addition, the Pawnee had come across a large pouch containing the right arm and hand of a Shoshone woman.

Something caught the Irishman's eye. "I'll be damned," Seamus said as he examined a cartridge belt he picked up from one of the blankets spread upon the snowy ground. "Look here, Johnny."

Bourke took the belt, studying a shiny silver plate that served as its buckle. "Little Wolf."

"You suppose it belongs to the Cheyenne war chief?"

Wheeler explained, "One of Wessel's men took it off a dead Indian he killed on the far side of the valley. The sergeant said it was hand-to-hand, over at the head of that deep ravine."

"You can believe him, Lieutenant," Seamus said. "On my dear mither's grave: that was some of the toughest fighting I've ever dragged myself out of."

Wheeler studied the Irishman's face a moment, then asked, "From the looks of that belt and buckle—you figure we got one of the chiefs, eh?"

Bourke wagged his head. "Could be—I know Little Wolf was one of the leaders who went back east to Washington City here lately."

Donegan said, "Mayhap he got this as a present from the President, Johnny."

Bourke wagged his head, "Or from some kindhearted official in the Indian Bureau." Throwing the belt down onto the blanket, the lieutenant grumbled. "The red bastard sure showed his gratitude in a strange way, didn't he?"

"Come with me," Wheeler suggested, leading the two away. "I've got a lot more to show you."

He stopped beside another pile of plunder.

"Was that a guidon?" Bourke asked, bending to feel the cloth.

"Damn right it was," Wheeler replied. "You can see who it once belonged to."

From that bloody silk swallowtail guidon of the Seventh Cavalry some industrious woman had fashioned herself a pillow stuffed with prairie grass and sage.

"You figure these belonged to a white man?" Bourke asked as he rose holding a crude, grisly necklace at the end of his outstretched arm.

"Badly mortified," Wheeler replied, "but—yes—looks like the fingers of many different white men to me."

Bourke asked, "Mind if I keep this?"

Wheeler shrugged, saying, "It was going into the fire anyway, Lieutenant."

"I know just where I can send this back east where folks will get a chance to see it in the museum," Bourke added as he toed aside some saddle blankets as if searching for something to put the finger necklace in for safekeeping. Suddenly he leaped back. "What the goddamned hell is that?"

Seamus bent to look at it, nudged with his toe, turning the object over and over. "Looks to me like it was once some man's ball-bag, Johnny."

Bourke shuddered at the thought, swallowing hard. "As much as I try my best to understand these people, they never cease to surprise me with their penchant for supreme savagery. I suppose I'd better take that for the museum too."

Donegan asked, "Not for your collection, Johnny?"

"Hell no, Irishman. I've got one of my own," and he cupped a hand beneath his own scrotum when he answered. "I'll keep it all with me until I can ship them back east."

Donegan snorted, saying, "Good idea. Having a reminder like that around just might help you take better care of your own balls."

From pile to pile Wheeler went on to lead the lieutenant and the scout, showing them many of the other remarkable souvenirs pulled from the Cheyenne lodges.

That taffeta-lined buckskin jacket recognized as having belonged to Tom Custer.

A hat bearing inside the headband the name of Sergeant William Allen, I Troop, Third U.S. Cavalry—killed at June's Battle of the Rosebud and buried in the creekbed with the other casualties.

"Did you know him, Johnny?" Donegan asked quietly.

"Not that well, but I could have picked him out of a crowd nonetheless," Bourke replied sourly as he carefully set the hat back atop a greasy blanket where other items lay for the viewing of all.

There were currycombs marked with troop initials and the Seventh Cavalry brand, as well as hairbrushes, some with men's initials crudely scratched into the wood.

Donegan leafed through a notebook that listed the best marksmen at every target practice held by Lieutenant Donald McIntosh, killed in Reno's retreat across the Little Bighorn and up to the heights.

Next he carefully thumbed page by page through a memorandum book. Its one-time owner, a Seventh Cavalry sergeant, had penciled in his last entry: "Left Rosebud June 25th." That page and many of the rest were embellished with drawings by an unknown Cheyenne warrior to illustrate his battle exploits and coups—one showing him lancing a cavalryman who clearly wore sergeant major's chevrons, on another page the warrior was seen killing a teamster, on the following page the Cheyenne was shown killing a wretched miner somewhere in the Black Hills, and across two facing pages of the book he adorned an illustration of himself escaping from Reno's barricade on the hill— represented by a round line of rifle fire, with saddled horses lying down inside—amid a hurricane of bullets. On other pages the Cheyenne represented himself as having been wounded once and his horse shot four times in that battle beside the Little Bighorn.

Bourke examined an officer's blue mackintosh cape for signs of ownership, but no name was found.

Likewise, a gold pencil case and a silver watch provided no clues as to who had been their previous owners.

On another Indian blanket the troopers had collected China plates, cups, and saucers.

"It's clear to me," John Bourke commented, "that contact with the white man has given these aboriginal people a profound taste for acquiring the finer things in life."

"I saw a few of these earlier today," Donegan said, holding up a wallet partially stuffed with greenbacks. He asked of Wheeler, "How many of these have you come across?"

"Enough to know that Custer's men hadn't had a chance to spend their pay before they were butchered—"

"Dear God," Bourke suddenly murmured softly there by the crackle of the fire as he handed Donegan an envelope.

Seamus turned it over, immediately recognizing it as a letter addressed to a woman back east, stamped and sealed by some soldier, ready for mailing.

"Look on any of these blankets," Wheeler commented. "You'll find even more. We've come across a lot of mail once addressed to members of the Seventh Cavalry, come from relatives and loved ones."

Among the beaded pouches and shields, the shirts and leggings adorned with quillwork, lay many faded, wrinkled chromos and cabinet photos of many a soldier's family members: parents, wives, children, and sweethearts all far away from these men gone off to war.

These small articles of personal value lay scattered among the many McClellan saddles, canteens, and nose bags all emblazoned with *7th*.

That twilight, as the sun began to sink beyond the southwestern hills, a bitter John Bourke flung a canteen down onto the blanket with a loud clatter, saying, "No man now in this valley with Mackenzie should dare think—after looking at all of this bloodied loot—that we aren't completely justified in such extreme punishment being meted out this very day to such a band of thieves and robbers."

"I'd daresay from the looks of it, Johnny," Donegan added, "surely some of these warriors have fought against the army in every encounter this year."

"By damn!" Bourke growled. "Not even a gunnysack must be spared the flames and left behind for these murderers!"

From the angry intensity of the soldiers' work, it was clear to the Irishman that all such reminders of dead soldiers fallen in battle to this warrior band during the months of what had become known as the Great Sioux War only increased the thoroughness with which Mackenzie's men went about destroying what had been the greatness of the Northern Cheyenne.

More than seven hundred Cheyenne ponies and horses, some of which had once belonged to the cavalry—their flanks plainly branded with *US* and *7*—had been captured and were now in the hands of the cavalry. Close to a hundred of the finest war ponies were claimed by the Norths' Pawnee and were already loaded with plunder hauled from the lodges by the time the first spire of oily black smoke had curled into the afternoon sky.

As an eerie background to the destruction, the Shoshone scouts continued beating on that huge drum found near the center of the horseshoe of lodges as twilight deepened into the gloom of winter's night. That same drum captured from their people, and now back in their hands once more, throbbing with the thunder of victory that reverberated from the hills where the conquered Cheyenne faced the coming dark and frightening cold.

One hundred seventy-three lodges once stood in the valley of the Red Fork of the Powder River.

Until that day the Northern Cheyenne had been a prosperous people, by far the wealthiest of warrior bands on the northern plains.

Never had so rich a prize fallen into the hands of the frontier army.

Still, Ranald Slidell Mackenzie had paid a price for his victory: McKinney and four troopers had been killed in the battle; a fifth had been felled by the sniper with the big gun hidden among the rocks.

As the canopy of blue turned to a deep indigo over their heads, Bourke asked, "You realize how fitting it is, don't you, Irishman?"

He turned to the lieutenant. "What's so fitting?"

"The date."

Turning away to regard the huge, leaping flames once more, Seamus struggled to sort it out, then replied, "I'm afraid I don't know what the date is, Johnny."

"It's the twenty-fifth, Irishman," Bourke said almost prayerfully as the darkness came down around them like an oozy wound.

Donegan's breath caught in his chest a moment; then he said, "I . . . I hadn't realized."

"Just think of it: five months—to the day, Seamus . . . since these Cheyenne bastards joined Sitting Bull's devils to wipe out Custer. Five months to the day."

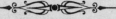

Chapter 37

25 November 1876

"You can damn well be glad it got dark before you showed up to beg a cup of coffee off us," Luther North said to the Irishman as he handed Seamus a steaming tin.

"I suppose you're right," Donegan replied, dragging his gloves from his fingers and welcoming the warmth into his hands. "Coffee does taste better when it gets as cold and dark as it will tonight."

"He didn't mean nothing about the bloody cold," Frank North corrected, walking up to join them.

"I was talking about that son of a bitch with the big gun up there in the hills," Luther added. "He's been right handy with that buffalo rifle he's got."

Seamus savored the warm track the coffee cut in coursing its way down before he said, "Good enough shot to pucker your ol' bunghole, eh?"

"Naw. He never come close enough to hit us," Frank explained.

And Luther snorted, "But that weren't for want of trying!"

Just as the sun had eased down on the southwestern rim of that canyon of the Red Fork, Frank and Luther North had given their Pawnee scouts permission to kindle their supper fires, having gone more than twenty-four hours forked in the saddle, under the guns of battle, and without a hot meal. With Mackenzie's troops now ringing the burning village in a horseshoe stretching from the north, to the east, and along the south to prevent the possibility of the enemy charging or sneaking in to regain their village, the Pawnee eventually went about making their camp for the night near the center of those Cheyenne lodges. Backlit there by many of the roaring bonfires, and clearly illuminated by their own cookfires, their shadowy forms provided some tempting targets for those snipers still moving about among the snowy slopes and rocky hillsides.

The warrior with that big buffalo gun who had taken up his station in the bluffs west of the Pawnee proved to be the greatest annoyance as he placed a bullet in their vicinity every few minutes, slowly walking his shots in by using the cookfire to gauge his distance. Time and again bullets flew into the area immediately around the fire where the scouts had cleared the ground of snow. Dirt or splinters of firewood splattered in their frying pans with every round. A little later as the darkness became all the deeper, a well-placed bullet did strike a frying pan in the fire, scattering ashes and dried buffalo meat over the Pawnee scout tending his meal close to the North brothers—causing all of them to jump.

After more than a half hour of sensing the sniper's bullets inching closer and closer to them, during which time the North brothers stoically returned again and again to sit on their log by the fire, placing their backs bravely to the west, eating their supper and having their coffee to show their scouts what little danger there was, they both suddenly leaped nearly out of their skins—

No sooner had a loose mule wandered contentedly up to their fire to stand some twenty feet to the east in front of them than another shot rang out and the lone animal set up a noisy screech, thrashing about in a crazed circle as it went down, legs kicking in those moments before it wheezed its last.

"Damn!" Luther had grumbled, determined to sit tight despite the danger. "You s'pose he was aiming to hit that mule?"

"Doubt it," Frank replied. "Figure that poor dumb creature just got in the way."

Luther added, "Means that fella's just about got our range."

Frank studied the sky a moment, then said, "Getting too dark to really see us."

"But he's got the fire," Luther replied. "Besides, Frank—you know he's probably using a hundred-twenty grain cartridge."

"S'pose you're right, Lute: a bullet like that'll sail right out there, by damn."

"And if that fella lowers his sights a little," Luther continued, "he could make us move, after all—"

The next shot perforated Frank's huge quart-sized tin cup filled with coffee where it sat on the log between the Norths.

Without waiting for the Cheyenne rifleman to place his shots any more accurately, Frank and Luther helped their scouts erect a breastwork constructed of the many bundles of dried meat not yet destroyed in the bonfires. It was behind this shelter at the far side of the Pawnee cookfire where Seamus had now found the brothers and their scouts lounging, their legs stretched out toward the merry fire, enjoying the last of their repast washed down with the wilderness elixir of army coffee, here in their nest of peace and relative safety.

"That sharpshooter took a few more shots at us," Frank explained as Donegan settled to his haunches nearby, cup in hand, "but he soon gave up."

"For some reason," Luther added, "we haven't heard a thing from him now for a while."

"I'll bet he's the one knocked a couple of the couriers out of their saddles this afternoon," Donegan declared.

"Eat your fill, Seamus," Frank suggested, rising to pass the Irishman a plate heaped with slices of the lean buffalo meat. "I'll be back shortly, Lute. Going to get the sergeants to post our guard for the night."

By the time Donegan had eaten his fill and had more than enough coffee to warm the cold knot of his belly, a dozen of the Pawnee scouts had returned from the east gap where they had dismounted that morning before dawn, unsaddling their horses and stripping off heavy coats for battle. Luther had sent the twelve back to fetch their saddles and blankets.

"Look here," Frank White said as he strode into the firelight. Behind him stood the eleven others, each one clutching the reins to his horse. Then the scout dramatically threw down a saddle at the feet of the North brothers, its cinch and straps freshly cut.

"What the devil is this?" Frank demanded, dragging over the saddle to inspect the butchered cinch.

"All like that," Peter Headman came up to explain. "All."

"They've been cut, Frank!" Luther screamed. "Those sons of bitches wanted that horse of yours so bad—now them goddamned Sioux gone and done this to our boys!"

"Hold on! Hold on a minute here," the elder North said, gripping Luther by the arm. "We don't rightly know who did this."

"Who had the chance?" Donegan wondered.

"Who?" Luther squealed with indignation. "We all know the Sioux and Cheyenne were behind us in the charge!"

Frank's eyes narrowed. "Ho-hold on, Luther, I know it looks like Three Bears and his bunch skulked back and done this ... but, dammit—I don't want to go blazing away half-cocked like that."

"You better get yourself ready for a row, big brother," Luther snapped, wrenching his arm away from Frank. "I'm going to report this crime to Mackenzie. By God—he'll have the Sioux replace these saddles for our men, or this is the last time our battalion will ever march on campaign!"

Seamus hung close to the fire to finish his pipe, then set out for the hospital about the time it began to snow again, lightly at first. He meandered northeast through the scattering of bonfires as the destruction continued, picking his way through the many cooking fires and smoldering heaps of ash still aglow with crimson coals.

From the groans and cries of those men in restless agony, it became all the easier to make out where the surgeons had set up their bloody business. There, some three hundred yards east of the ravine where the warriors had ambushed Lieutenant McKinney's troop, lay the bodies of the dead and the wounded. For a moment he stood planted in place, peering at the doctors and their stewards hunched over their work in the light of blazing fires and a pair of lamps one doctor had his assistants holding close above his work as he probed a deep back wound while the dying soldier was held down by three of his companions, groaning through teeth clamped on a bit of bloody rag.

Off to Donegan's left two soldiers suddenly appeared whole from the northwest out of the black of that night, stepping into the snowy firelight and coming to a halt by another surgeon at work retying a bloody bandage.

"Is our lieutenant here?" one of the pair asked.

The doctor said nothing, only pointing before he continued with knotting the cloth on the struggling soldier beneath him.

However, one of the stewards helping that physician asked, "You in the lieutenant's troop?"

"We are."

The steward shook his head. "He's dead."

"D-dead? We didn't know."

Now the doctor looked up. "Didn't know he was dead? I thought you said you were in his troop."

"We are . . . w-were," the soldier answered. "Got separated when the red-bellies pitched into us."

"He was killed and a bunch more wounded," the steward explained. "How come you didn't know they was all taken off the battlefield? You didn't run, did you?"

The two young soldiers looked at one another; then the first tried to explain. "No. We ain't no cowards. Got separated from the rest and had to hide when things got hot."

"Hide?" asked the doctor.

"All day," he replied. "Been waiting for it to get full dark afore we could come in. Up in them rocks we didn't know how bad it got for any of the rest of the boys. But we did know the lieutenant and the sergeant got hit afore we took cover up the side of that ravine."

Donegan wagged his head—remembering the fear he had swallowed down time and time again as a young soldier faced with those moments before making a charge, those terrifying heartbeats as the fighting, the scuffling, the cannonade began all around them. Perhaps the difference between a private and a sergeant had always been that the private was supposed to be scared. And in this army the sergeant was never allowed the luxury of fear.

"Irish . . . Irishman."

Seamus turned at the sound of the soft, croaking call. It took a moment for his eyes to adjust to the dim light.

The voice called again, "Over here."

He started toward the sound, in a few steps reaching the feet of McKinney's sergeant.

"Forsyth?"

"Yes."

"It is you," Seamus said as he squatted beside the wounded soldier and nodded to the young private who sat at the sergeant's head, holding a wool blanket over them both as the flakes came down.

Forsyth said, "Started to snow again, dammit."

For a moment he laid his wool glove on the sergeant's arm. "You're warm enough?"

"I'll be fine on that account. Others worse off."

"I seen they brought you in with the rest," Donegan said.

"Was pretty well et up with the pain by then," Forsyth replied. "Then the doc give me some laudanum and he went to work."

The young soldier added, "Damn bullets flying over our

heads all day—scaring the bejaysus outta every last one of these sawbone meat cutters, they have."

"How's it been for your cawpril over there?"

Forsyth turned slightly to glance at the big soldier who had stationed himself beside the blanket shroud laid out at the edge of the field hospital, both the corporal and the dead man slowly collecting ribbons of white as the snow began to fall more insistently. "He's been quiet. Been there all day for what I know. Ain't never left the cap'n's side."

"Good for him," Seamus said.

"Yes," agreed the young soldier as he shifted the blanket bower above him and Forsyth, "good for him. The lieutenant never had him a chance. The doc said he counted four bullets in him—any one of 'em s'posed to kill him right off."

"F-four bullets you say?" Forsyth asked.

"One gone through his chest. 'Nother one gone through his lower arm and ended up in his belly. Third one done the worst: shattered his backbone. And the last one hit him in the head—stayed right there in his brains 'thout coming out."

"Damn!" the sergeant whispered. "I'm sure thirsty, soldier."

"Yes, sir. Here," and he handed over a canteen.

Forsyth took himself a drink, then held it up for Donegan. "You thirsty, Irishman? Sure you are: ary a fighting man gets thirsty after doing his duty, don't you think?"

He took the canteen, hesitating because he was not really all that thirsty—when the sweetish fragrance of the corn mash whiskey drifted up to his nostrils. Seamus sniffed at the canteen.

"Gloree be, Sergeant Forsyth!" he exclaimed with quiet wonder, then tilted the canteen up slightly to let a little wash across the end of his tongue. "That tastes good enough for me to stay here and kill my thirst with you, it does, it does. But—a man in your state needs your thirst killer much more'n I do."

"You're sure you don't want none, are you?"

"Aye. I'm sure, and thankful too we had men like you on that line today." Donegan watched the sergeant's eyes soften. Wondering if it were the laudanum, or the whiskey, or maybe it was enduring all that pain that made them go soft and doelike right then.

"You won't drink any more of my whiskey," Forsyth said, "then you'll have to give me your hand before you go." They shook quickly. "Man like you, Irishman—you had no business coming on that charge with us. No reason on God's green earth to be at the edge of that ravine."

"I had every reason in the world," Donegan replied. "But the two most important reasons are waiting for me back at Laramie."

"Then see that you get yourself back to them whole," the sergeant ordered as he sagged a bit, jamming the cork back in the top of his canteen, his eyelids drooping. "You don't mind—think maybe I'll grab me a bit of shut-eye now."

"I'll look you up tomorrow," Donegan declared, patting the sergeant's arm before he got to his feet and moved away into the firelit snowy night.

As he walked back toward the creek, his mind snagged on how McKinney had clutched at Dr. LaGarde, speaking of his mother so far, far away with his dying breath.

Natural that Donegan's thoughts turned to his own mother now in heaven, still watching over her firstborn son come so far, far away to distant Amerikay.

Throughout the waning of the light that afternoon, Morning Star's people had scrounged through the snow to gather wood to kindle the fires one of the old men started with the flint-and-steel fire-striker he had carried from his lodge at the upper end of camp that morning. These were not big fires like the ones the soldiers below fed with all that the *Ohmeseheso* had once owned. Instead these were small by comparison as the wind came up along the ridgetops and the snow began to fall around them.

It weighed down his heart to think that some of his people would not last this cold, cold night despite the small fires where the strong ones rubbed the hands and feet, legs and arms of those who were too small or too sick or too old to warm themselves. Not only had he lost family and friends to the soldier bullets this day, but with the coming night, Morning Star realized he would lose a few more to the winter giant.

As a Council Chief, it was his station in life to worry about such things—to concern himself more with the fate of his people than with his own family, his own fortune. So it saddened Morning Star that he thought again of Old Crow, a longtime friend who had elected to stay at the White River Agency* last summer when Morning Star and the others had decided to return to the north country. Especially after the soldiers had turned them back

---

*Red Cloud Agency, Nebraska.

in the skirmish* with the soldiers near the Mini Pusa,† men like Old Crow had elected to stay behind.

So why was it, Morning Star asked, that Old Crow and other old friends of his then decided to join the soldiers in tracking down their own tribesmen? To side with the *ve-ho-e* in making war on their old friends, their own families?

How could the world have got so crazy that a man would turn his back on his own and join with the enemy?

Throughout the morning's battle several warriors came to Morning Star reporting that they had seen Old Crow and others—some relatives of the squaw man Rowland—all from the White River Agency, among the *Tse-Tsehese* scouts fighting on the side of the soldiers. This was so hard to believe!

But that afternoon Morning Star saw for himself.

A solitary horseman rode out from the enemy's side of the valley and approached the bluffs where the warriors continued to put up a strong fight and Black Hairy Dog was working his medicine with the Sacred Arrows. As the lone rider drew closer to the rocky hillside, Morning Star recognized his friend, despite the white man's heavy blue coat and the canvas britches.

"Old Crow!"

"It is me!" the soldier scout cried out.

"You best not come closer!"

The rider reined up. "I am here to tell you something."

A warrior in the rocks near Morning Star angrily hurled his voice at the horseman. "Tell us nothing but that you are coming to fight beside us against the soldiers."

"I must fight against you," Old Crow sadly admitted from the back of his skittish pony.

"Then perhaps we should kill you as we will kill the soldiers!"

Other warriors in the rocks shouted in derision too, but no one fired a shot at Old Crow. Killing one of their own would be so hard a thing to do.

Morning Star's voice rose above the others. "You have come here for a reason, my friend. Tell us."

The horseman patted the pockets of the dark wool coat he wore. "Although I am forced to fight against you—I am leaving a lot of ammunition for your guns on this hillside."

They watched him ease out of the saddle, lead his pony to

---

*Warbonnet Creek—17 July 1876.
†The South Fork of the Cheyenne River.

a rocky outcrop, then quickly empty his pockets. Then the Council Chief leaped back into the saddle, tightened his grip on the reins, and called out in parting.

"The old days are gone, Morning Star! We are watching the sun set on the old ways. Do not let the soldiers kill any more of your relatives. Bring them to the agency where we can live out the rest of our days together in peace, smoking the white man's tobacco."

Jamming the heels of his winter moccasins into the flanks of that pony, Old Crow reined about in a cascade of snow and bolted away, turning his back broad and inviting to the warriors among the rocks.

But no man fired his weapon at Old Crow. It simply would not be an honorable thing to raise a weapon against one's own people.

Even if that man no longer acted like one of the *Ohmeseheso*, but acted instead more like a white man . . . the hated *ve-ho-e* who brought destruction wherever his boot left a track.

Chapter 38

Big Freezing Moon
1876

Every throb of that drum was like a tiny stab at his heart—making pain for him in each of his six wounds. Little Wolf knew the Snake Indians would beat it right on through the bitterly cold night.

But for the tiny fires they had kindled here and there in the breastworks and among the rocky crags that shadowed the valley, it was very dark. The stars had been blotted out not long after the sun had turned the clouds a deep reddish purple. And then it began to snow.

The clouds hovered just over their heads, shrouding the tops of the mountains, as the chiefs and headmen of the People gathered in council to discuss what course they should take.

There wasn't much arguing—for their choice seemed clear. While there were those who spoke on behalf of the wounded, the sick, the old, and the little ones, who whimpered with the intense cold and their empty bellies, still no one chose to surrender to the soldiers in the valley. There was but one course to take, and that was for them to start away from the valley that very night, abandoning the camp where everything they owned had been destroyed.

How proud Little Wolf was that his people were still fierce and as full of fight as ever despite their devastating loss.

"I will remain behind, even if no others stay with me,"

Young Two Moon volunteered. "Tonight I will sneak down close to the village under the cloak of darkness and wait for the soldiers to leave tomorrow when I can go down to what piles of rubble and ash are left—to see what I can find for us to use."

"This is good," Little Wolf replied. "And we need others to follow the soldiers' trail as they leave the valley. To see where they are going now that we journey north."

"We must travel through the mountains for a long distance," advised Walking Whirlwind. "If we go onto the plains too quickly, the soldiers will find us there and we will never reach the Crazy Horse people."

Just as Old Bear's small band of *Tse-Tsehese* had done last winter following the fight on the Powder River in the Sore-Eye Moon, they would again seek out the Hunkpatila Oglalla band of Crazy Horse, said to be camped for the winter along the Tongue River.

Besides that drumming and the triumphant singing of the Shoshone scouts in the valley below, all around the chiefs women were keening softly, crying out with shrill and angry voices, mourning the dead, singing over the wounded as the old shamans shook their rattles, blew their prayers into each bloody, frozen bullet hole with four long puffs of air.

Brave, heroic men like Yellow Nose suffered in silence for the most part, asking only for sips of melted snow as they lay curled close to the small fires.

For all the pain they had caused his people, Little Wolf still would gladly take Old Crow's gift of soldier bullets—those boxes of the shiny cartridges left behind in the rocks below Morning Star and the others. Yes, Little Wolf was never so proud he did not use the white man's bullets to defend his people.

He wondered now how Old Crow slept, wondering if he slept at all—having turned against the *Ohmeseheso* even though he too was one of the Council of Forty-four. Perhaps the power of the *Maahotse* would indeed kill all those who had turned their backs on their own people.

For a long time that afternoon Black Hairy Dog had prayed over the Sacred Arrows he pulled from their fox-skin quiver. Many warriors and women eventually gathered around the priest, all joining in to stamp their feet and sing the songs that would put a curse on every one of those who fought on the side of the white man against their own people.

Then, slowly, with much respect, the Sacred Arrow Priest lifted the Arrows one by one from the white-sage bed he had made for them to overlook the valley, replacing them in the quiver. Then just past twilight Little Wolf sadly watched Black Hairy Dog place the *Maahotse* on his wife's back, and together with an escort of some eighteen families they began their retreat to the south. Big Horse, White Buffalo, Young Turkey Leg, and others were, after all, Southern People like Black Hairy Dog.

"We will stay east of the mountains as we go south," they told Little Wolf and the rest at their last council just before departing. "When we reach the foot of Hammer Mountain* we can then turn our faces south by east back to our agency.† Only then will I be sure the *Maahotse* are safe."

Esevone was safe as well. Some time ago Coal Bear and his woman had fled up the mountain with the Medicine Hat as men like Box Elder, with his Sacred Wheel Lance; Long Jaw, with his bullet-riddled red blanket cloak; and Medicine Bear, with the magic of the Turner, first used their powers to cloak the old couple with invisibility, then diverted the enemy's bullets. By sundown there were many who had poked their fingers through the countless holes shot in Long Jaw's cape, whispering in amazement that not one *ve-ho-e* bullet had penetrated his body.

Truly, the Everywhere Spirit had watched over His people this day. But they still faced the winter, and the wilderness, and the search for the Hunkpatila of Crazy Horse.

Little Wolf winced with the pain in his six wounds as he turned to look up the slope into the darkness at the faint points of red light glowing here and there. Beside one of those fires rested the Hat Bundle. With its power secure, the People just might survive the coming ordeal.

But at a terrible cost.

Then he shuddered to think how many were sure to die in the coming ordeal.

During his short nap in the midst of the long-range battle yesterday afternoon, William Earl Smith's leg had gone to sleep and a deep cold had seeped into the muscles. As the night wore on, the leg continued to hurt all the more, making any attempt he made at sleep fitful and sporadic. Between the leg and the cries of the wounded in the nearby field hospital, Smith didn't figure he had slept for more than an hour at a time all night long.

* Pike's Peak.
† Southern Cheyenne Indian Agency, Darlington, Indian Territory.

Each time he awoke, he came to with a start, slowly realizing where he was, listening to the groans of those in pain and the voices of those men on picket duty, or what soldiers were unable to sleep. And each time he came awake, the private always found Mackenzie pacing back and forth. At first he figured the colonel was attending to one matter or another, but Smith soon came to realize Mackenzie had instead slipped into some kind of deep depression.

William Earl liked the man, and it bothered him to find Mackenzie so sorely troubled. It even shook the young private to the core to have seen the colonel openly cry when he learned Lieutenant McKinney had been killed at the ravine.

The following morning Smith scribbled in his journal:

> I don't believe he slept at all that nite. His mind must of been troubled about some thing. I don't know what, for he is the bravest man I ever saw. He don't seem to think any more about bullets flying than I would about snowballs.

By dawn all of the killed and wounded soldiers had been brought in and accounted for, since it was generally believed the Cheyenne would resume the battle as soon as there was enough light for them to see their targets. Instead, the hilltops and rocky ridges were eerily silent as night bled into that Sunday, the twenty-sixth of November.

"It's just as well," Mackenzie murmured over his breakfast of black coffee as the sky grayed. "Last night in officers' conference I decided that even the infantry would pay too high a cost trying to dislodge the warriors from the rocks in these mountains. Sadly, I now realize we've already paid too high a price for this victory."

For a time Smith figured his commander might be morose simply because of losing so many casualties to the enemy, while at the same time during that officers' meeting last night Mackenzie could personally verify no more than twenty-five warriors killed from the many reports. To justify so many dead soldiers, he should have clearly killed many, many more Cheyenne.

"But those are only the bodies which fell into our hands, General," Wirt Davis had coaxed.

"How well we all know that the Indian drags off most of his comrades," said John Lee.

"Perhaps," answered a perplexed and clearly agitated

Mackenzie as his men went about settling on the official accounting of the enemy dead.

The Pawnee had taken six scalps. Two soldiers had taken another pair of scalps. Frank Grouard himself had lifted one scalp. While one lieutenant reported he had personally killed one warrior, Captain Davis stated his company had killed six to eight more. Then Cosgrove's Shoshone stated they had dropped four Cheyenne warriors. A one-eyed civilian scout claimed to have killed another warrior. And the combined Sioux and Arapaho scouts tallied another dozen enemy killed.

That cold, snowy morning as Mackenzie penned his official report, gray clouds hung low along the silvery mountaintops ringing the red valley. While the men stomped their cold feet and trudged about through six inches of new snow, enjoying their coffee around the cooking fires, Mackenzie sent out some of his Cheyenne and half-breed scouts to make contact again with the enemy—perhaps now to coax them into surrendering after the awful cold of last night.

But as much as the scouts called out to the hills in their native tongue, there was no answer but their echo. Cautiously they inched up the slopes toward the breastworks at the upper end of the valley, fully ready to encounter an ambush. Instead, the snow only became deeper, nearly covering all the tracks. The Cheyenne had been gone for some time.

Returning to the valley at midmorning, the scouts reported to Mackenzie what they had discovered. The numerous black rings of long-dead fires had been drifted over with new snow. Deep trails showed how the many had struggled single file up the rugged slopes for more than five miles into the mountains. The broad scoops of old snow told of many travois used to carry the dead and wounded warriors as the defeated Cheyenne disappeared into the wilderness. And they did not forget to mention the occasional patches of blood not yet covered by snow at the tops of the mountainsides.

But what spoke most eloquently were more than a half-dozen pony carcasses found here and there along the trail. Once the tribe's most prized possessions, those horses were now the Cheyenne's only food.

"You say they did what with the entrails?" Mackenzie asked the scouts for a clarification.

Interpreter Billy Garnett repeated, "It's what a Injun'll do, General. They'll shoot the pony and slit it open soon as it's dropped. They pull everything right out of the belly so the old ones getting froze up can stuff their hands and feet into the gut piles to keep from dying."

"Dear God in heaven!" Mackenzie gushed in a whisper. "How . . . how many of those fresh carcasses did you find?"

"At least six, General. But we turned back—likely more on over the top. We didn't dare get up that far. They had themselves a strong rear guard forted up and ready for us."

"The enemy's gone—you're sure?"

Garnett nodded, saying, " 'Cept them what's staying behind to keep a eye on your army."

"Yes," Mackenzie replied as if his mind were elsewhere. "Now that I have stripped them of their pony herds and destroyed everything they own . . . the enemy will want to know what more I'm up to. Yes, by all means: let them flee through these mountains if that's what they want. And for now, we'll let the forces of 'General Winter' deliver the final blow to the Cheyenne."

Late the night before, while the snow had fallen as thick as cottonwood fluffs drifting down from the low-slung clouds, Young Two Moon had stealthily crept toward the camp where the soldiers continued their destruction of their village. Far from the firelight that lent an eerie, otherworldly crimson glow to the bellies of those snow clouds, the young warrior waited, and watched, as the *ve-ho-e* cooked and ate, talked and slept.

It was long after that soldier camp grew quiet enough to hear the moans of their wounded that Young Two Moon suddenly remembered the few lodges that had been pitched some distance away from the main camp—across the creek and closer to the base of the red bluff where the soldiers had dragged all those who had fallen in battle.

There were no fires burning, no flames casting their glow upon the undersides of the clouds from that direction. Perhaps . . .

Alone, Young Two Moon slunk back up the slope of that western hill into the thick, soft, icy cold of that snow-cloud before he began traversing the hillside. It took him a long time to pick his way toward the site of those abandoned lodges, in and out of the shallow ravines, crossing from willow clump to willow clump in the darkness—stopping every few steps to listen to the sodden, silent night for the breathing, the boot sounds of any soldier-camp guard standing his rotation.

What a wonder! For some reason the Everywhere Spirit had

seen to it that these lodges had been spared. *Ma-heo-o* had not completely turned his face from his People!

Yet, despite the fact that the lodges were still standing, for the most part the white man's scouts had already plundered the dwellings. Growing less hopeful as he entered first one, then the second, Young Two Moon found only three old buffalo robes among them all—hides so poor and bare-rubbed that the enemy scouts had thought them all but useless.

Still, they had proved to be a valuable treasure to a people who had nothing.

As he had gathered up that third thin robe, someone downstream cried out sharply, in a language Young Two Moon did not understand. A shot was fired in the darkness—then a long rattle of gunfire was punctuated by shouting among the white men.

One of their camp guards must have thought he heard something, the young warrior brooded as he slipped away into the darkness.

Quickly he retraced his steps, dragging those three robes back up the mountainside to the first fire, where he helped wrap an old woman and two of her grandchildren within one of the robes. At the second and third fires up the slope, he watched the abandoned robes enwrap several little ones huddling together to share their mutual warmth. For the most part, the adults were too cold to utter any thanks as they crouched by the fires, rubbing bare hands together over the flames, kneading the frozen flesh of their naked feet, gazing up at the young warrior with eyes pooling with gratitude.

And at the edge of the dim light thrown out by each of those fires sat young mothers slowly rocking back and forth on their haunches as they softly keened their mournful death prayers. The first of the tiny infants had begun to die one by one—children so small and nowhere strong enough to survive the brutal cold of that long, terrible day now stretched into an endless winter night.

Other women murmured their death songs for fallen husbands and brothers and sons as they hacked off clumps of their hair, dragged knives and pieces of sharp red chert across their arms and down their legs, mutilating themselves again and again throughout that long, horrid night while the oozing blood froze until the ugly wounds were repeatedly reopened by the mourners.

Here and there in the shadows flickering on the frozen snow lay the wounded warriors, some with a peeled branch between their teeth, others grinding their pain into strands of wrapped rawhide or twisted fringe so these stoic ones would not cry out in their private agony.

Some of these would surely die this night.

The dead. Already there were three-times-ten on the battlefield, young and old warriors who had fallen too close to the soldier lines to recover their bodies. They would be scalped by the enemy's scouts.

But among these who had been brought to the fires in the breastworks and this mountainside, even more had died after Young Two Moon and the handful of others who would remain behind had crept back into the darkness of the ravines and coulees, slipping silently toward the soldier camp.

There the young warriors had waited in the first cold streaks of day-coming as the white man and his Indians finally saddled, formed up, and began their retreat from the valley.

The *ve-ho-e* having stripped a once-powerful and very proud people of everything . . . everything but their lives.

Chapter 39

26 November 1876

Early on the afternoon of the battle, Second Lieutenant Homer W. Wheeler had been ordered to take his men of G Troop, Fifth U.S. Cavalry, and establish a guard outpost on the heights south of camp where the Shoshone scouts had remained throughout the fight.

Some two hours later one of Mackenzie's orderlies had ridden up the narrow game trail to those heights.

"Lieutenant Wheeler?"

"That's me."

"The general commanding sends his compliments—"

"Forget the formality, soldier. What is it?"

"He requests to see you at once."

"My troop?"

"Sir, he said nothing about that. Just that he wants to see you."

Flinging himself into the saddle, Wheeler led the pink-faced private back down that winding, narrow path to the site on the south slope overlooking what that morning had been the Cheyenne village, where Colonel Ranald S. Mackenzie was overseeing the final mop-up of the enemy camp.

The young officer dismounted, handing his reins to the orderly, then stepped up, clicked his heels together, and saluted.

"General. Lieutenant Wheeler: G Troop, Fifth Cavalry. Reporting as ordered, sir."

"Mr. Wheeler. Very good," Mackenzie replied, returning the

salute as the muscles along one side of his jaw convulsed. "I have an important duty for you."

"Yes, sir. Anything to help."

The colonel nodded, turning away to look across the decimated camp where scouts and soldiers were busy at that moment dragging plunder from the lodges, stripping the lodgepoles of their hide-and-canvas covers. Wheeler stepped up at the tall Mackenzie's elbow to look down upon the scene.

"Do you see our hospital?"

"Yes, General."

"The surgeons certainly have had a time of it today."

"I can quite imagine, sir."

Now Mackenzie momentarily glanced at Wheeler. "Lieutenant—I'm placing you in charge of transporting our casualties back to our wagon camp on the Powder."

"Y-yes, General," he said, his shoulders snapping back proudly. "It is an honor, sir!"

"What will you require?"

His mind burned with adrenaline as it raced over what he needed. "Twenty men, General."

"Certainly."

"And as many packers as the mule train can spare to handle the animals."

"You have my authority."

"With the general's permission: can I inform you later just how many civilians I will require?"

"Yes, by all means. Now you must speak to the surgeons and see to things at the field hospital yourself."

"Yes, sir. I'll go there now, with your permission. Thank you."

"Very well, then," Mackenzie said quietly, almost too quietly to be heard above the commotion of the destruction being pursued downslope at their feet. "Do you have any further questions of your assignment?"

Wheeler turned on his heel, coming to attention, saluting smartly. "None at all, General. Thank you, sir. Thank you!"

Mackenzie saluted, murmured, "Good day, Lieutenant." Then the colonel wheeled about on his heel, his shoulders sagging as he returned to his headquarters group—looking more like a man who had just suffered a defeat than a man who had just claimed a major victory in this long and indecisive campaign.

For a few moments more, Wheeler stood there, rigid—

letting the personal triumph of it wash over him, enjoying this singular honor.

When he finally realized he must look a sight standing there by himself, staring from that outcrop of rocks at the village and the valley beyond, Wheeler quickly took his reins from the young orderly and remounted. Going to Tom Moore, he requested four packers at that time to lend a hand to the twenty troopers from his own company who could construct the travois they would need from the Cheyenne lodgepoles.

They had found it no easy task that late in the afternoon to scrounge up enough poles, rope, and robes or blankets for those travois. Most everything had been cut up and was in the process of being consigned to the leaping bonfires crackling throughout the village. Throughout the rest of that afternoon and on into the night, the two dozen men under Wheeler went through the grueling work of constructing thirty travois by firelight, using rope and strips of hide and canvas beneath those robes they had saved from destruction.

Because of the twenty-six enlisted men who had been wounded, as well as three more men so sick they could not ride in the saddle on their own, the surgeons reported to Wheeler that they would have no trouble filling those thirty travois. Dr. LaGarde and the others had decided to bury one of the six privates who had been killed there on the battlefield. Because his transport detail could not come up with material to construct more travois, Wheeler and the surgeons decided they would have to carry four of the dead unceremoniously slung over the backs of Tom Moore's mules.

As each of the travois was finished, it was immediately taken to the hospital, where it was placed in a slightly inclined position and another wounded soldier was gently lifted onto it. In that gray light of Sunday morning, 26 November, the last casualty was put to rest on his travois, joining all the rest who faced one another in two long rows on either side of a string of fires that had kept them from freezing throughout that frightful night.

A cold gust of wind slashed across Wheeler's face when he turned slowly, thinking he had heard Mackenzie's voice. The lieutenant shivered suddenly as he rose to greet the commander, his stomach growling hungrily, feeling the stupor of having gone without sleep for a second night.

"Lieutenant Wheeler."

"Yes, General. Good morning."

"Morning. Yes. Mr. Wheeler, I came to see how you were getting along. We'll be moving out before noon."

"I'll be ready."

"I see." Then the colonel pointed down to the end of the row of travois. "Why are your men standing there holding those travois and wounded?"

"I have only four packers, General," Wheeler said. "It takes two packers to lash up the travois to a mule. So some of my men are waiting with the wounded men who will be the next to have mules brought up for them."

"Your men can't get this done any quicker?"

In utter exhaustion he looked down at his boot caked with snow and ice. "No, General. My boys don't know a thing about a proper mule hitch. But if I had—"

"—more packers," Mackenzie interrupted, "you could hitch them all up at once. Is that correct?"

"Yes, sir. About the size of it, exactly."

The colonel turned to his regimental quartermaster as they started away. "Mr. Lawton—see that Wheeler gets the help he needs. Immediately. And then we'll leave him alone. He seems to know what he is about."

Wheeler watched Mackenzie's back for a moment more, his weary mind sliding here and there in unconnected thought . . . wondering if he would have time to grab a nap before they would be moving out.

Morning Star ached to the bone with fatigue and cold.

Through that long night he had kept moving from fire to fire with the others as his people trudged step by frozen step more than five miles into the mountains. As wounded as was his own heart with his personal loss, Morning Star did what he could to console the relatives of those warriors who had been killed, their bodies fallen into the enemy's hands.

Too, he sat for a time with each one of the mothers who had lost their infants to the incredible cold. And he joined those who were rubbing warmth back into the hands and feet of the old ones too frail and sick to move about and warm themselves.

Again and again he instructed this group or that to sacrifice one of their ponies not only for food they could roast over the tiny fires, but so that the old people could stuff their hands and feet among the warm organs and blood.

Still, the *Ohmeseheso* had suffered greatly that first night after the battle. Many of the old ones, the sick, the weakest—they had simply given up their spirits in the great cold, unable to keep the frightful temperature from their hearts.

Up ahead of him on the slope that gray-skinned morning as the sun blurred the eastern horizon to a narrow band of bloody red, a mother held the hand of one of her young children as they stumbled along, stiff-legged ... while in the other arm she carried the frozen body of her infant who had died while struggling to nurse at its mother's breast throughout the night.

How heavy his heart had become, for it seemed the very young and the very old were being ripped from the People. Perhaps all that would be left to his band would be those old enough to suffer the cold without dying, those young enough that the cold could not weaken their frail bodies.

All these winters of his life—through the battles and the migrations, in all that greatness and feasting, the women he had loved and the children who had sprung from his loins—so many winters that had flecked his hair with their snow ... his heart had never been so heavy.

And he had never been quite so cold.

Last night he had squatted at a fire beside his missing son, Bull Hump, and some of the other old warriors, talking quietly while the keening surrounded them and the groans of the wounded reminded them all that there would be more to die.

Softly, Bull Hump had said, "The only thing that saved the lives of any of us was the smoke from so many guns—smoke which hung so low in the ravines and gulches, smoke which clung to the mountainsides so that the soldiers could not see us clearly as we fought. Had there not been so much gun smoke—more of us would have fallen."

Now, as Morning Star reached the top of the icy, slippery slope and turned, the dry, cold air scratching his lungs with the torment of a porcupine-tail hairbrush, the chief gazed down through the bottom of the snow clouds at the valley below. Watching the last of his people struggling up the long slope through the timber, many crawling up hand over hand, barefoot, dragging tiny ones and the old with them through the depth of that new snow as they pushed ever onward into the soft underbelly of those clouds.

Up here where the smoke hung just beneath the clouds there clung the stench of death and destruction. Everything gone to ash and smoke. Those lodges of each warrior society exquisitely decorated with regalia, painted to record the exploits of their members, their finest deeds: a retelling of men and soldiers and horses pitched together in struggles from the past. A glorious past.

—Each man's most important clothing was gone in the smoke. Beautifully tanned hides, quilled and beaded—a warrior's holy clothes that he would wear into battle. Scalp locks and the medicine drawings on each shirt, the leggings, his fighting moccasins. The great spray and tumble of war eagle feathers worn by some, or the great provocation of the horned headdresses that adorned others.

But with the attack yesterday morning, there was no time to dress and paint while one said his prayers. Only a few at the upper end of camp had a moment to sweep up a sacred bonnet or a special amulet to give them strength in the coming fight. Their sacred war medicines, prayer bundles, all of it—everything except *Maahotse* and *Esevone*—was gone. What hadn't been burned had been carried off by the enemy's Indians.

Even the Sacred Corn, given by the Grandmother Earth to Sweet Medicine to feed his people at the beginning of time. How it had stabbed Morning Star's heart to watch the soldiers throw the last few ears of their Sacred Corn into the fire. No more would the People know freedom from want with it gone. Now—he knew—they would always be hungry.

The *Ohmeseheso* were running again.

So Morning Star wondered if it would not have been better to die the death of a warrior in yesterday's battle, along with his two sons and those grandchildren ... better that than to watch his people's greatness die at the bottom of those bloody footprints scattering up the silent, mourning mountainside.

In addition to the twenty-four soldiers and Indian scouts wounded in the battle, Lieutenant Homer Wheeler's detail was attending to one of the Shoshone who had suffered a terrible abdominal wound. Because of the poor prognosis for a man shot through the intestines, the army surgeons didn't hold out much hope for the scout named Anzi to survive long enough to reach the wagon camp. Since he was marked for death, the course of treatment was simply to make the patient as comfortable as possible and administer as much painkiller as was necessary.

For Anzi, Dr. LaGarde prescribed laudanum, a morphine derivative, and approved all the whiskey the Shoshone wanted. With such a combination coursing through his system, the warrior had somehow survived the night, lasting into the next morning while Mackenzie's cavalry prepared to leave the Cheyenne village behind.

But rather than slipping away, as the surgeons had predicted, the warrior instead began to insist upon more and more whiskey from his attendants through the long, cold night.

"Oh, John!" he would call out to one or another of the hospital stewards or Wheeler's escort detail. It mattered little what the soldiers' names were, because Anzi preferred to use that common expression many of the Shoshone gave when addressing any white man.

"What you want now, Anzi?" a soldier would ask.

"Oh, John! Heap sick! Whiskey! Whiskey!"

So all through that night and into the gray of dawn Wheeler's troopers poured whiskey down the mortally wounded scout, as well as sharing some with a few of the other critically injured soldiers like Private Alexander McFarland, who lapsed in and out of consciousness. But by midmorning, as the cavalry was preparing to embark, Wheeler had been forced to kneel at Anzi's side, explaining that there was no more whiskey for him, no officers' brandy, either.

"No whiskey, John?"

"No whiskey. No more. None."

Grim-lipped and resolute, the Shoshone slowly rolled to his side as if he were about to give up the ghost, when he dragged his legs beneath him and rose unsteadily between a pair of his fellow Shoshone, there at his side in a deathwatch.

"Where are you going?" Wheeler demanded, stunned as he called out to the Shoshone's back.

Over his shoulder the wounded scout replied, "Anzi go ride. Warrior always ride."

As tired as he was, Seamus Donegan nonetheless preferred to be one of the last out of the valley that Sunday afternoon. He hadn't snatched a bit of sleep for two nights now, what with the march of the twenty-fourth, then with the way the Shoshone scouts caterwauled all last night after the battle, mourning their tribesmen, women, and children recently killed by the Cheyenne of this very village.

Shortly past eleven A.M. Mackenzie gave the order, and the scouts began driving more than seven hundred captured ponies ahead of them through the bogs and the willow thickets, heading downstream.

Minutes later the men swung into position by columns of

fours where possible, pointing their noses south by east toward the gap they had entered in the cold, gray-belly light of dawn the day before. Seamus wondered if he had become more accustomed to the deep cold, or if the temperature might be moderating, actually allowing it to snow gently once more on the dark, serpentine column snaking its way across the pristine white that bordered the Red Fork of the Powder River.

As he and those who closed the file on the column entered the boggy willow thickets, Donegan turned in the saddle one last time to look back on what had been the Cheyenne camp. Among the wispy sheets of the wind-whipped, billowy snow, he thought he caught sight of three Cheyenne warriors reentering the village.

He reined up, curious. Alone now as the sounds of the column inched away from him, the Irishman watched the trio of warriors move slowly from one pile of ash and rubble to another until they finally collapsed as if all the spirit had been sucked right out of them. As he nudged his heels into the bay's flanks and moved out once more, Seamus listened to the distant, sodden wails of grief from those three warriors who sat in the ruins of their village, crying out in despair and utter pain, wailing with implacable grief.

Up ahead of him the men cursed and yelled, packers and soldiers alike, as they struggled with their mules and horses. The animals slipped and slid crossing every precipitous slope—skidding onto their haunches and braying in protest.

Meanwhile, Lieutenant Wheeler and his escort of two companies of the Third Cavalry quickly discovered it best to lower the travois with their wounded still attached by several ropes rather than careen down each treacherous hillside. The most dangerous slopes were the long ones, which required the soldiers to tie their lariats together as they had to lower each wounded man down more than two hundred feet, one at a time to men and mules waiting below. Once the ropes were untied from the travois, they were drawn back up the hill and another travois lashed in and lowered.

As the progress of the column was slowed, Seamus repeatedly caught up with Wheeler's escort. Each time he lent a hand where he could, joking with some of the wounded, touching the shoulder of others who were clearly in great pain. Always offering what comfort he might give.

"Aye, and that last drop was a daisy, Irishman," one old private snorted as his travois was tied up and made ready for another trip down the snowy slopes. "Why—I'll have you know I ain't had sech a pucker of a toboggan ride since I was in knee britches!"

For the journey two men were assigned to each of the mules carrying the dead, to make certain the cantankerous animals did not break away and possibly disfigure their departed comrades by colliding against rocks and deadfall. Four men were positioned around each of the wounded: one to lead the mule, two to dismount and heft the travois around difficult terrain, and a fourth to lead the four cavalry mounts. At every stream crossing, the soldiers and packers were forced to dismount and unhitch the travois—carrying the wounded across the icy, slippery rocks by hand and on foot. To assure that the wounded troopers were given the finest of attention, Wheeler had assigned one noncommissioned officer for every five travois.

Because of such care only one accident happened that entire first afternoon. At one of the many repeated crossings of the Red Fork the mule jerked the travois out of the hands of the litter handlers and dragged the wounded soldier on through the shallow creek. But because of the length of the poles and the inclined position of the soldier upon them, he wasn't soaked—only splashed by the skittish mule's hooves.

Yet it wasn't only those steep and narrow parts of the trail that made the day's journey so treacherous.

Late that afternoon Seamus had gone ahead to reach that smooth, undulating ground the Lakota and Cheyenne scouts had christened "Race Horse Canyon." To the rear arose yelps and curses, the clatter of hooves and squeak of leather. A wild-eyed mule careened its way with travois bounding and bouncing across the sage flats. Wheeling the bay quickly, the Irishman raced to catch up the runaway animal, slowing it until it turned with him and stopped—when Donegan immediately dismounted to lunge back to the wounded trooper still strapped in.

Breathlessly the Irishman asked, "You ... you all right, sojur?"

The hapless passenger caught his breath, blinking his eyes, then grinned gamely as he gazed up at Donegan to say, "Let her go, by damn! Whoooeee! If I had me some bells jingling, I'd think I was taking a sleigh ride back home!"

"Where are you wounded?"

"Hip, sir."

"You want me fetch up a surgeon to come see to you?"

The soldier shook his head bravely; then, as he shifted himself, his face clearly etched with pain, he said, "There's others hurt worse off'n me, mister. I'll fair up in a minute or two. Just let me catch my breath, will you? And you can put this gol-danged mule back in line with the other boys."

Donegan readjusted the thin blankets over the wounded man, tucking them in beneath the soldier's chin.

"All right, Private," he said quietly, feeling his eyes mist. "Let's you and me head for home."

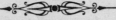

Chapter 40

26–27 November 1876

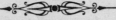

Throughout their march away from the Cheyenne village that
Sunday afternoon, Mackenzie's men came across the horse
tack, clothing, and superfluous equipage the cavalry had cast
aside in its hurried, cold-night march to reach the canyon of the
Red Fork, abandoned litter that spoke eloquently of a trooper's
privations and sacrifices in service to his unit.

Which only made Seamus dwell all the more on those men
who had suffered through the night with their wounds, given
whiskey and laudanum and kept as warm as possible. On their
shoulders more than any other the weight of battle had been
borne.

At least Mackenzie's sawbones could give them something
to ease their goddamned pain, Donegan thought as the procession wound in and around to the east. Too damned many good
men fated to die were all too often forced to die in pain.

He squeezed his eyes shut to stop the spill of tears and took
a deep, shocking breath of that cold wind. Thinking on
Samantha to ease some of the private torment in his heart,
thinking on the wee boy who would soon have a name.

Late in the afternoon of that first day's countermarch, a
cadre of Shoshone and Pawnee scouts rejoined the column after making a reconnaissance to learn more of the Cheyennes'
intentions. Back on the twenty-third they had departed
Crook's camp on the Crazy Woman Fork, sent north toward
the Bighorns. As it turned out, the fourteen scouts brought in

a few head of ponies, and a report of their own skirmish with the enemy.

"Seems they ran across what the Cheyenne have left of a pony herd," Frank North explained to Donegan as the two marched along with the slow column. "No more'n two hundred head at the most."

"But our scouts cut out almost half of them before the Cheyenne herders discovered what they were up to," Luther jumped into the conversation.

"And for their enthusiasm our boys nearly got themselves chewed up by those Cheyenne licking their battle wounds," Frank declared. "If the snow clouds hadn't rolled over about that time, our Pawnee and Cosgrove's Snakes would not be here to tell the story."

"They have any guess how many Cheyenne they saw?" Seamus asked.

Frank replied, "Could be as many as twelve hundred, maybe more."

Luther said, "But the good news is—from what our boys could see, the Cheyenne really are badly cut up, all but naked, without moccasins, blankets, or ammunition . . . dragging all their wounded through the mountains toward the headwaters of the Crazy Woman."

"They're headed for the Crazy Horse people," Seamus replied. "Just like they did after the Reynolds's debacle in March."

Frank stated, "That was right about the time the warrior bands started coming together for the spring and summer hunting seasons."

For the rest of the day rumors ran through the anxious command because of that nearby contact with the fleeing Cheyenne. Fears arose that Morning Star's warriors would be waiting to ambush the column somewhere along the trail. So frightened were some of the wounded that the colonel ordered his Indian scouts to the head of the command, where they stayed for the rest of the day in the event of a surprise attack. Indian would again be the first to bear the brunt of any ambush by Indian.

Just past sunset Mackenzie ordered a halt for the night on the far side of Willow Creek, which would lead them out of the mountains and back to the plains, where they could rendezvous with Crook and Dodge on the Crazy Woman Fork. The weary, cold cavalry had put twelve miles behind them by the time they kindled their fires and settled in among the snowdrifts for the long winter's night.

Tom Cosgrove waved the Irishman over to his fire. "Come. Sit. Have yourself a cup of my terrible coffee, you no-good, sonofabitchin' blue-belly."

Seamus took the tin from Yancy Eckles at their cheery fire. He asked the two, "You mind if I bunk in with you here?"

"Sure you don't mind the noise?" the short squaw man Eckles asked, throwing his thumb back to indicate the loud, uproarious scalp dance the Shoshone were holding nearby.

"No," Donegan said all too quietly. "The noise won't bother me near as much as the quiet would tonight."

"Sit yourself down, then," Cosgrove replied, stretching out his long frame. "My home is your home!"

"Truth be—I don't want to stay down there with the others where I was," Donegan replied, then sipped at the scalding coffee.

Eckles inquired, "With Wheeler's wounded train?"

Wagging his head, Seamus said, "It ain't the wounded. It's them dead ones."

With a snort Cosgrove threw a fist at Donegan's shoulder. "That's a pretty one! With all the dead men you've seen in all your goddamned wars—now you've gone and got yourself funny feelings about a few dead soldiers?"

For a moment Seamus stared into the fire. "They're frozen."

"We all are," Cosgrove replied casually.

"No. I mean really frozen, Tom," Donegan argued. "They froze near solid on the ride here this afternoon."

His eyes narrowing, Eckles asked. "Hanging over the backs of them mules?"

Nodding, Donegan said, "And when Wheeler's men took the bodies off the mules, they just set each dead man up to stand all on his own, bent over in a half hoop, posted on hands and boots."

Cosgrove trembled involuntarily. "Like they was bowed up?"

As the war cries and songs of the Shoshone reached another crescendo, Donegan only nodded, his cracked, bloody lips warming at the rim of the coffee tin and didn't say another word.

Finally Cosgrove stated quietly, "Sure, Irishman. We'll always make room for you here."

They drank their coffee in silence for some time, each of them listening to the noisy Shoshone celebration, until Eckles spoke.

"You figure Grouard got to Crook already?"

"Yeah," Seamus replied. "I'll wager the infantry're headed this way already."

"General?"

George Crook sat upright at the sound of the orderly's voice, rubbing at his gritty eyes. Damn, but it was dark. "Yes! Yes! What is it?"

He could see it was not yet light. Nothing more than the first seep of gray from outside, a gray that streamed through the canvas shelter half he had stretched out from the sidewall of one of Furey's freight wagons to keep the snow off his bed. Crook shifted on his mattress of blankets and sagebrush, hurriedly grabbing for the first boot in the dark.

"It's a courier, General."

His heart rose to his throat. "From Mackenzie?"

"Yes, sir."

"And?" he snapped, bursting to his feet and bolting out of the shelter half with one boot on and the other in his hand, both braids of his long red beard flung back over his shoulders.

The orderly fell back two steps, surprised by the general's sudden appearance. "Th-th-there's been a f-fight, sir."

"By Jove! That's exquisite news!" Then he noticed the courier at the fire, having just filled his cup. "So you're the one who rode in with this splendid report, Frank?"

The half-breed Grouard nodded, taking his first sip at the coffee sending curls of steam into the frosty light of predawn. "Cold as hell out there, General."

Dammit, he wanted answers—now. "Mackenzie . . . he won?"

Nodding, Grouard replied in that easy, slow way of his. "Not like Reynolds last winter. Not like that at all."

Crook did a quick little stamp with his feet, something on the order of a Phil Sheridan Irish jig, only then realizing he hadn't put his second boot on as he stomped down on the pounded snow with his thin stocking. "A victory, Frank?"

"Damn right, it's a victory, General. But the *Tse-Tsehese* are up in the rocks around their camp and the carbines can't bring 'em down. Mackenzie said to tell you he needs the Long Toms."

"Fix this man some breakfast," Crook ordered the men around the fire, grinning from ear to ear and waving his arms like a man possessed, getting all of his orderlies and dog-robbers moving at once. "And pour me a cup of the strongest coffee you've got. Wait right here, Frank—I'm going to grab my coat and hat . . . then go roust Dodge. When we're back, you're going to tell us all about Mackenzie's fight."

The commanding general of the Department of the Platte awakened Colonel Richard I. Dodge that cold dawn of the twenty-sixth, literally pulling the infantry commander from his trestle bed.

"Mackenzie sent back for your boys and their guns! He's got the whole lot of 'em on the run!"

"M-my guns?" Dodge said, shuddering as he pulled on his tall boots, blinking his eyes.

"Damn. Tucked away up there in the rocks, one of those blasted warriors is worth ten of my troopers," Crook growled, grinding his gloves together thoughtfully. "But your riflemen should more than even the odds for General Mackenzie."

Dodge stood, buttoning his long caped coat. "When shall we embark?"

"As soon as you've drawn two days' rations and issued every man one hundred rounds of ammunition."

The infantry commander stabbed his way out from the flaps of his canvas tent. "I'll return shortly, General—to report to you when we're ready to depart."

"Perhaps you misunderstood, General," Crook said to Dodge, watching the colonel freeze in the middle of his salute. "I am accompanying you on this forced march."

"Of . . . of course, General," Dodge finally replied with studied disappointment, and finished his salute.

It wasn't until close to noon that Dodge had his men dressed, fed, outfitted, and mustered into columns. By then the sky had lowered and the tops of the nearby Bighorns had once again disappeared among the gray, heavy clouds. Three inches of new snow had fallen atop the eight inches already on the ground from last night. And even more was dropping as the column of foot soldiers set out at a trudge, their faces pointed into a harsh west wind.

The snow eventually began to let up near sundown and the sky turned patchy overhead as the infantry pushed on into the coming of that winter night without halting. All afternoon they had repeatedly found Mackenzie's trail to be wide enough to accommodate only one foot soldier at a time, forcing their march to slow as it proceeded in single file up and down steep slopes, across slick-sided ravines and fording icy creeks.

As the darkness swelled around them, Crook hurried ahead with Grouard, thankful the new moon was some ten days old that night. From time to time it splayed the forbidding canyons of the Bighorns with a silvery light reflected off the brilliant tableau of the rugged landscape. Theirs became a two-color night as the black of scrub timber and huge stands of pine and fir contrasted sharply against the shimmering monotony of a whitewashed world.

Near eleven that night the general and the half-breed reached the valley of Willow Creek, a small tributary of the Powder River.

"How much farther, Frank?"

Grouard considered a moment, then answered, "A few hours. Not many. We're mighty close.

He sighed in disappointment. "Let's wait for the rest to come up." Crook said as he stepped down from the saddle.

"Hoping you were going to say some such, General."

"Get us a small fire going, will you, Frank?" Crook suggested. "I feel like making us some coffee."

"You're going to call a halt here?"

Crook stared back down the trail, then up toward the Bighorns. He had to resign himself to it. "We'll stay the night."

When Colonel Dodge's infantry came up, they were ordered to fall out by companies. Some built small fires, where they boiled coffee and ate their supper of cold bacon and frozen hard bread, while others simply collapsed where they were in the snowdrifts and sank into a sound, sound sleep without ceremony or any coaxing.

Oblivious to the cold.

At dawn on Monday, the twenty-seventh of November, after a restless night, Mackenzie's men were no less skittish about a possible hit-and-run attack by the Cheyenne than they had been the day before. The cruel, slashing mountain wind finally died and it again began to snow heavily.

Seamus ached to the marrow with the cold, thinking again on how warm he could be within the shelter of Samantha's arms.

Even before the column moved out at midmorning, some of the Indian scouts rode in from their dawn search of the country, reporting the presence of another large village of hostiles off to the west of Mackenzie's position. Strung out in single file and scattered as they were forced to cross that rugged piece of country, Donegan grew every bit as concerned as the soldiers: should the enemy jump them in the narrow canyons or crossing these deep ravines, Mackenzie's command would be in sad shape to withstand such an attack without suffering terrible casualties.

The new snow of the past two days made the narrow trail all the more slippery, forcing the horses to work all the harder for their footing. That day some of the weakest, poorly fed mounts gave out, were shot, and their carcasses abandoned along the banks of the eastbound Willow Creek. By late afternoon they had put no more than fourteen miles behind them when Mackenzie ordered the column to halt for the night on that feeder of the Powder River as the sky continued to snow.

At this time of the year, a few hours of daylight became all the more precious to an army on the march, Seamus ruminated. Then he brooded on Samantha, wondering if it was snowing down at Laramie. If she was warm. How it must feel to hold the boy.

From dawn till dusk that day, Mackenzie kept his Indian scouts ranging on all sides of their line of march, determined not to be surprised by the Cheyenne. In addition, for that night he ordered a double running guard posted around the camp and the herd as the sun sank beyond the white-draped mountains lit with a rosy spray of dying light. Up and down the banks of the creek tiny fires began to glow like red and yellow eyes in the black face of winter night as evening came down, men heating their coffee and salt pork, soaking their hardtack in the thick, sizzling grease that popped and crackled in the small skillets.

"Crook's camp can't be that far off," John Bourke commented as he flung his saddle down near Donegan's fire and settled atop it to hand over his empty tin cup. "Fill me, would you?"

"The infantry coming, are they?"

John nodded. "Mackenzie just got word from one of the Sioux scouts that they ran into the general and Dodge's boys going into camp a few miles east of us."

"We going to rendezvous tomorrow morning, I take it."

Bourke watched the black, steaming coffee hiss into his cup from the battered pot and shook his head. "No. Crook sent word back to Mackenzie that since our column has disengaged and doesn't need Dodge's outfit, since we're on the return march, he'll take those foot soldiers back to the Crazy Woman and await us at the supply camp."

"That must have been some forced march they made," Seamus replied.

"Thirty-five miles of it," Bourke declared, staring at the

flames. "Crook wrote Mackenzie a letter saying the rugged hike took its toll on Dodge's boys: many of them are crippled with cold and lack of sleep."

For the most part it was a quiet, subdued camp that night while the anxious soldiers continued to argue over the possibility that they could be attacked. It was the general consensus that with that morning's sighting of an enemy camp to the west, the Cheyenne had followed the cavalry's trail that afternoon and would likely jump the bivouac sometime before dawn.

Quiet too were Cosgrove's scouts. After two full nights of grieving and celebrating, even the subdued Shoshone did not wail and sing. By the time most of the weary troopers were crawling into their cold blankets, their feet toward the grease-wood fires they struggled to keep going for want of fuel, the valley of Willow Creek lay somber and quiet beneath the lifting clouds that played tag with a mercurial three-quarter moon.

Seamus had banked the fire for the first hour of fitful sleep and dragged his saddle blanket over him and John Bourke, releasing a long sigh as he tugged his collar up and the coyote-fur cap down over his ears ... when the wild, screeching shouts yanked him to his feet about the time the first volleys of gunfire cracked the serenity of the night.

"Goddamn!" Bourke shouted, rolling out and looking toward the head of the column's bivouac.

"I know, Johnny!" Donegan snapped as he snatched up his rifle. "I figured the h'athens would hit us from the rear!"

Bourke tugged down on his floppy slouch hat, saying, "Looks like they circled round to strike our front!"

While noncoms barked orders and officers dashed about to form up their units in the dark, every man kicking snow into the fire pits, the wounded cried out not to be abandoned, helpless and tied to their travois now that they were under attack. Many of the horses yanked and pitched against their picket pins driven into the frozen ground near every fire, or fought against the short length of rope that sidelined each mount.

More gunshots snapped the frigid blackness like cracks in the back of a mirror. Screams and bloodcurdling battle cries floated in from the Indian scouts' camp on downstream at the head of the march.

Bounding over the sage and zigzagging through the confused, frightened companies sprinted Donegan and Bourke, racing for the scene of the attack. By the time they reached the outskirts of the scouts' bivouac, Cosgrove, Eckles, and Lieutenant Delaney were seizing control of the situation.

Donegan skidded to a halt in his tracks, shaking his head. "A god-blamed buffalo shoot!"

"Mr. Cosgrove!" Bourke hollered in dismay.

"Yes, Lieutenant?" the civilian came trudging over at double time.

"What the hell's the meaning of your men shooting at buffalo at a time like this?"

Cosgrove glanced at Donegan first, saying, "Well, Lieutenant—"

Bourke interrupted angrily. "Don't you realize how downright skittish those soldiers are back there?"

"You don't under—"

"And you've gone and allowed your scouts to fire their weapons?"

"Hold on, Johnny," Seamus soothed. "What's going on, Tom?"

With a great shrug Cosgrove replied, "Them buffalo just moseyed on into our camp all on their own."

"Didn't know they grazed at night," Bourke commented. "I'm ... I'm sorry I jumped on you—"

"No problem, Lieutenant," Cosgrove replied. "If you fellas will excuse me—I've got to help get things settled back down."

"You do that, Tom," Donegan declared with a joyous roar. "And when you have all this noisy spill stuffed back into the bottle, what say you bring around a nice big buffalo-hump roast for me and my nervous lieutenant friend here?"

Bourke nodded and agreed, "I could do with some buffalo to eat, Tom. Doesn't look like we'll be going back to sleep anytime soon!"

Chapter 41

Big Freezing Moon
1876

THE INDIANS

Late News from Crook's Command—
All Well.

CHEYENNE, November 27.—General Crook's command reached Fort Reno November 14, in good condition, and was paid off by Major Stanton. The weather is severe but the troops are well prepared for a winter campaign. One hundred Snake and Shoshone Indians joined the command there, making nearly 400 Indian allies in all, and the total strength of the command 2,000. The hostile Indians, according to the best information, are scattered on both sides of the Big Horn mountains, and a campaign on each side may be necessary before completing the work. Meantime Crazy Horse, with about 4,000 lodges, is on the Rosebud, near the scene of the June fight, for which point a cavalry command left under General McKenzie, and would have to march about six days before reaching it. The cavalry are in excellent condition, and if this movement is successful the heaviest work of the winter would have been accomplished.

*O*h, *Father of All Things! You see into the heart of all men. We*
thank you for sparing so many of us that we may flee to re-
build our people. Watch over all who you have chosen to carry on.
Keep our feet on the road you would have us walk.

And help us to see that in death, there is also rebirth.

Little Wolf opened his eyes to the rising sun as it came up
far, far away across the frozen white plains.

He stared, his arms outstretched, clad only in his leggings
and breechclout, crude and stiffened pieces of green horsehide
tied around his feet in place of the beautiful war moccasins he
had lost in the fires that had destroyed nearly everything his
family owned. Bare-chested, shivering with the fierce cold of that
dawn, fighting down the pain in each of his six wounds, the
Sweet Medicine Chief breathed his silent prayers, then knelt to
fill the small pipe he took from the bag he snatched up in his
lodge the morning of the attack.

Slow to move in the cold, slow to move with those wounds
he had suffered from soldier bullets, perhaps wounds caused him
by the *Tse-Tsehese* scouts who had come with the soldiers, Little
Wolf lit the pipe from a smoldering coal he had laid among the
white sage at his feet in the center of a patch of bare ground he
had kicked free of the drifted snow moments ago.

To the four winds and to the spirits that watched from both
earth and sky, he gave thanks for the deliverance of the People.

Then Little Wolf thanked the Everywhere Spirit for the deliverance of the People's greatest treasures: *Maahotse* was safely
on their way south with Black Hairy Dog and a small escort
of warriors; *Esevone* hung in a bundle strapped on the back of
Coal Bear's woman back in the shadows and the ravines of the
mountainside where Lodgepole Creek* issued from its canyon,
rushing onto the rugged plain.

Standing in silence some twenty feet behind the Sweet Medicine Chief, the old, blind prophet, Box Elder, turned his own
wrinkled face toward the warmth of the coming sun. It made
Little Wolf's tears fall and freeze in tracks on his bronzed cheeks
when he turned to look a moment at the ancient one. Standing
so stoic, brave, steadfast there . . . sightlessly standing guard over
Little Wolf with his veiny, deformed hands gripping tightly the
tall staff from which hung the Sacred Wheel Lance. Behind the
old man another ten feet stood Medicine Bear, the young ap-

---

*Present-day Clear Creek.

prentice who held the Turner, its buffalo tails dancing upon each gust of wind.

With the power of those objects, the two men protected Little Wolf as the Sweet Medicine Chief said his prayers for the People. Asking the Everywhere Spirit to protect His people one more day as they moved out of the fastness of the mountains, trudging northeast toward the plains where they hoped to find the Crazy Horse people.

He prayed no more infants would be asked to die of the endless, horrid cold. The first night nine had given over their spirits. Then three more last night.

This morning there were faces missing from the fires built along the spine of these White Mountains. Old, wrinkled faces—ones who had seen so much greatness, now witness to so much devastation. Few of the old ones had the strength to last out this grueling march, most preferring to step aside and let the others pass, there to find a place where they could sit among the rocks, beneath the branches of the great sheltering trees.

And there to wait for death to come on the wings of Winter Man's hoary cold.

Today, just as they had done from that first night of flight, the able-bodied warriors would go ahead of the march until they were almost out of sight. There the young men would gather wood and kindle a new fire with a coal carried from one of the old fires where the People sat waiting, trying to warm themselves. When that new fire blazed, sending its shimmering waves of heat into the cold of that vast mountain wilderness, a lone warrior would ride back to signal the others to come ahead. The many would reluctantly rise, setting off toward the distant blaze, where they would again sit and rest while a new fire was kindled farther down the trail toward the Hunkpatila of Crazy Horse.

They were leaving a trail chopped with the footprints of the old and the small ones, footprints spotted with blood. As well as a trail of pony carcasses. A few times each day a horse would be slaughtered for food to feed the many cold, empty bellies. As the warm green hide was stripped off to be wrapped around cold children, or cut into crude boots to protect frozen feet, some of the half-dead old ones stumbled over to stuff their own hands and feet into the warm gut piles steaming in the terrible cold. Just enough warmth to allow them to trudge on, on through the wilderness to find the Oglalla wintering on the Tongue.

One of his old friends, White Frog, had been wounded four times in the battle as he drew bullets to himself protecting the women and children. Although he stumbled with the agony of his wounds and oftentimes fell in the snow, White Frog nonetheless struggled to be one of the first who led the others from fire to fire, cheering them on.

Behind White Frog proudly walked Comes Together, White Frog's woman, clutching their infant son beneath her hide dress, sharing what warmth she had with the tiny, sick child.*

"*Ma-heo-o!*" Little Wolf called out as loudly as he could with a hoarse throat. "Hear your people! We belong only to you! When you remain steadfast to us—not even the power of the *ve-ho-e* can ever destroy us!"

A generous portion of the meat butchered from those buffalo killed during last night's folly was distributed among the wounded that Homer Wheeler was escorting back to the wagon camp on the Crazy Woman. Those soldiers who could eat found themselves strengthened for the arduous journey that Tuesday, 28 November—their third day struggling through a mix of sand and deep snow icing the hilly country.

Well after sunrise the lieutenant's detail loaded the frozen dead onto the backs of the restive mules once more, preparing to move out with their ghoulish cargo. Then the travois were attached to the mules, each set of poles strapped to their aparejos pair by pair. The wounded had not been moved since sundown the day before, placed at that time in two rows, their feet to glowing fires, their travois pitched at an incline upon pack saddles for their comfort.

"Sir?"

Wheeler turned, finding one of his men coming up. "What is it, soldier? We're preparing to move out."

"I know, Lieutenant," the private answered, grave worry carved on his face. "It's . . . it's private McFarland, sir. He's . . . well—he's gone out of his mind."

"Out of his mind?"

"I don't think he'll make it through the day," the soldier replied. "He's in a real bad way."

Sighing, Wheeler said, "All right. See that you make him as comfortable and warm as you can. Then get him hitched up with the others. There's nothing we can do that the surgeons haven't already done for him."

"You mean . . . them surgeons say he's gonna die anyway?"

*Little Coyote—one day himself to become the Keeper of the Sacred Medicine Hat, *Esevone*.

"That's no concern of yours," Wheeler snapped impatiently. "You have a job to do for Private McFarland while he's still alive. So you go do it."

"Yes, sir." He saluted and turned away.

Already Homer could hear the chanting as the Indian scouts were the first to pull away from last night's bivouac. Throughout most of the last two days' march they sang over the few scalps Mackenzie had allowed them to take from the Cheyenne, holding the hair aloft at the end of long wands where the bloody trophies tossed in the fitful, icy wind.

Not long after they set off that morning, Wheeler spotted three Shoshone horsemen sitting motionless atop their ponies at the side of the trail. As he drew closer, the lieutenant recognized the greasy blanket coat the middle warrior wore. Homer halted before them. "Anzi," he said, not surprised to see the pain written across the Indian's face.

"Melican medicine man," the wounded warrior said, the mere sound of his words echoing the agony of his wound as he stoically remained hunched over in the saddle.

"Want to ride," said one of the other two riders in his broken English. He and his companion supported a wobbly Anzi between them.

"Ride?"

"There, Melican medicine man." Anzi pointed at the travois just then going past them.

"On one of the litters?" Wheeler asked in consternation. "You want to lay down in a travois?"

"Yes, yes, medicine man," Anzi gasped, seized with pain. "No whiskey—Anzi do no good."

"No whiskey, Anzi," Wheeler replied sourly. "And I'm afraid I don't have a litter for you either."

"No?" asked one of Anzi's companions.

"No," Wheeler repeated. "The one you got out of two days back is now carrying a sick soldier."

"Soldier sick as me?"

"No," the lieutenant admitted. "But you gave up your travois when you found out we had no more whiskey."

"Yes, whiskey. Whiskey good for Anzi."

"No travois, Anzi," Wheeler replied, beginning to feel his patience draining. "You'll make it."

"To Cluke wagon camp?"

"Yes. Hang on. You'll make it there. And—you'll find more whiskey there too."

"Whiskey. Anzi not die he got whiskey in belly with bullet."

With the remnants of a grin, Wheeler reined away and re-joined his hospital group as they plodded east away from the mountains.

An occasional snowflake lanced down from the intermittent clouds rolling off the Bighorns and onto the plains as Wheeler's men and mules plodded on in a ragged column, surrounded by their escort of two troops of cavalry. It wasn't long before they heard the dim reports echo back along the trail as soldiers began to shoot their played-out horses—daring not to leave them for the Cheyenne to capture. While the country was nowhere near as rugged as the mountain trail had been, that day's journey none-theless required the skill and hard work of Wheeler's crew in crossing every steep-sided ravine and ice-banked stream, easing their way down and back up every snowy slope.

"Lieutenant Wheeler, sir!"

Homer turned in the saddle, recognizing the young soldier riding up from that morning. The lieutenant halted and reined about, awaiting the man.

"Sir, it's McFarland," he said as he came to a stop before Wheeler.

"Is he dead?"

"All but, Lieutenant."

"C'mon," Wheeler said as he put heels to his weary, ill-fed horse, moving back along the column.

Private Alexander McFarland's attendants had pulled their patient, mule, and travois out of column and halted. Two of them had even removed their hats, holding them clutched at their chest as they stood over the soldier's body suspended in its blankets. The wind repeatedly tousled their hair into their red-rimmed eyes that bespoke of grief silently endured.

Leaping down from his saddle, Wheeler bent over the pri-vate, placing his ear over McFarland's nose and mouth. He heard nothing at first, but waited for something, anything. Then came a long, low death rattle deep within the dying man's chest.

"Sir?"

Without looking up at the soldier near his shoulder, Wheeler kept his ear over McFarland's face a moment more, then straight-ened. "We'll wait here a little longer, men."

"He ain't dead yet, sir?"

"Not . . . just yet."

It wasn't long before McFarland's heart finally beat its last. No breath wisping from his nostrils.

"All right," Wheeler said with resignation as he straightened his fur cap on his head. "Let's get the private wrapped up in a blanket and lashed with rope like the other dead men."

"Beg pardon, Lieutenant," grumped one of the escort, who stepped up to rest a gloved hand on the dead soldier's body. "Alexander . . . Private McFarland, he was a friend of mine, sir. What you got in mind for him, you go tying him up in a blanket like the other dead, sir?"

"Why, I'm fixing to put him on one of the mules," Wheeler explained, growing annoyed after so many days bare of sleep and warm food, filled only with bone-numbing work and spirit-robbing cold. "Like those others—"

"I beg you, Lieutenant," a second attendant pleaded as he came up. "McFarland don't deserve to be hunched over no goddamned mule's back to freeze like a croquet hoop, sir! Let us leave him be on the litter till we get back to—"

"But I need that litter, Private."

"Who you need it for?" demanded the first soldier suspiciously.

"For one of the scouts."

The second soldier prodded, "You mean one of the civilians was wounded?"

"No," Wheeler explained, growing more nettled as more and more of the column inched past them in the snow. "I mean one of the Shoshone."

"Take his litter away for a goddamned Injun?" a soldier cried.

Another shrieked, "Not even no white man?"

"As you were, soldiers!" Wheeler ordered. "I've made my decision. While I understand your friendship for McFarland, we also owe what we can to the scouts who put their lives on the line too."

"But you can't put my bunkie on no god-blamed mule!"

"Why not?"

" 'Cause he's . . . he's dead, sir!"

"Exactly, Private," Wheeler answered. "Don't take this wrong, but McFarland doesn't know the difference any longer. And I'll damn well do what I can to make one of our allies comfortable."

How he hated feeling their eyes between his shoulder blades as he turned, waving one of his noncoms over. "Sergeant, go up to the Shoshone detachment and locate the one called Anzi."

"Anzi, sir?"

"You'll remember him," Wheeler sighed. "He was the one drank most of the whiskey we had us the night after the battle."

"Yes, sir. I remember that one. For sure I do."

As the sergeant reined off into a lope, it started to snow again right overhead. Wheeler looked to the east where the sky was a patchwork of clouds and sunlight, blue and gray. But above the column it was beginning to snow again to beat the band. Big, thick, soft flakes that seemed to hiss through the brittle air as they tumbled from the lowering sky.

Behind Wheeler a voice grumbled, "That son of a bitch—"

Turning, throwing his shoulders back wearily, so tired he did not want a fight, the lieutenant declared, "I hope whoever spoke out of turn will be a man and own up to calling his superior a son of a bitch behind his back."

The eyes shot here and there until an older private admitted, "It was me, sir."

"You?"

"B-but I didn't mean you, Lieutenant," the older man apologized. "I was saying that Shoshone scout you call Anzi is the red-bellied son of a bitch. Him, sir: for taking McFarland's—"

"I see," Wheeler interrupted with a sigh, telling himself to be patient with these weary, half-frozen men. "Well, now—we all know that red-bellied Shoshone son of a bitch has lasted two days longer than our army surgeons said he would. So if he's what you say he is, soldier . . . at least he's one goddamned tough red-bellied son of a bitch."

George Crook had pushed Colonel Richard I. Dodge's doughboys to their limit, driving them some thirty-six miles in twelve hours that first day—a march of astonishing speed and endurance considering the temperature, the wind-driven snow, and the difficult terrain.

Just before ten A.M. yesterday, 27 November, five Indian couriers had reached Crook's bivouac as the infantry was preparing to continue its march west. From the scouts the general learned that Mackenzie had departed the battlefield and was headed his way, bearing his dead and wounded out of the mountains.

"It appears General Mackenzie no longer requires your services," Crook informed Dodge.

The glum infantry commander asked, "What now, General?"

Crook regarded the fuss-budget Dodge a moment longer, then replied, "Why, we countermarch to our wagons."

"Do you plan on reaching the crossing tonight, sir?"

"I most certainly do, Colonel. I most certainly do."

Late that Tuesday morning, the twenty-eighth, another trio of couriers rode into the Crazy Woman camp. They bore Mackenzie's official written report of the engagement. Barely able to contain his excitement, George Crook read and reread the first word the outside world knew of that dramatic and tragic confrontation in the valley of the Red Fork:

Sir: I have the honor to report that at about twelve o'clock AM, on the twenty fourth (24th) inst. while marching in a south westerly direction towards the Sioux Pass of the Big Horn Mountains I was met by five (5) of the seven (7) indian scouts who had been sent out the evening before who reported that they had discovered the main camp of the Cheyennes at a point in the mountains, about fifteen or twenty miles distant. Two of the seven (7) indians remaining to watch their camp, the command was halted near sunset and then moved toward the village intending to reach it at or before daylight, owing to the nature of the country, which was very rough and in some places difficult to pass with Cavalry. The command did not reach the village until about half an hour after daylight. The surprise was, however, almost complete. The approach to the village, the only practicable one, entered the lower end and the indians taking alarm took refuge in a network of very difficult ravines, beyond the upper end of the village, leaving it on foot and taking nothing but their arms with them. A brisk fight for about an hour ensued after which shooting was kept up until night. The village consisting of one hundred and seventy three (173) lodges and their entire contents were destroyed. About five hundred (500) ponies were taken & twenty-five (25) indians killed whose bodies fell into our hands. And from reports which I have no reason to doubt, I believe a much larger number were killed. Our loss was one (1) officer and five (5) men killed & twenty five (25) soldiers & one (1) Shoshone indian wounded. Fifteen (15) cavalry horses and four horses belonging to the indian scouts were killed. The com-

mand remained in the village during the night and
moved on to this point today. Lieut. McKinney, Fourth
(4th) Cavalry who was killed in this affair was one of
the most gallant officers and honorable men that I
have ever known.

> (signed) R.S. Mackenzie
> Colonel, commanding
> Fourth U.S. Cavalry

Immediately calling for Dodge, Crook showed the colonel
Mackenzie's report.

"He's done all that you asked of him, General," Dodge replied, returning the dispatch to Crook.

"Yes," the general said. "From the sounds of things, I think
the fighting is finally over."

"I certainly hope so, General."

Crook nodded, peering down at the maps littering his field
desk. "Perhaps now Crazy Horse will either surrender, or decamp
and go off to hide himself in the badlands."

"You seem much pleased with your success."

Crook's eyes narrowed as he regarded the prim Dodge, as if
the colonel were passing judgment on him. "I have every reason
to be pleased. I have marched hundreds of miles and fired hundreds of thousands of rounds, killing and wounding soldiers as
well as wasting an entire regiment of horses ... to be able to
stand here today—finally able to state that we have had a success!"

"Then, here's to Mackenzie, General!"

"By all means," Crook responded with gusto. "Here's to
Mackenzie!"

Chapter 42

28–30 November 1876

THE INDIANS

Crook Has Another Fight.

CHICAGO, November 27.—General Crook, under date of Camp Crazy Woman's Fork, November 18th, reports that Colonel Mackenzie of the Fourth cavalry, attacked the Cheyenne camp consisting of a hundred lodges, on the west fork of the Powder river, on the 15th instant, capturing villages and the greater portion of the Indian herd. The loss on both sides was thought to be considerable, but was indefinitely ascertained when the courier left. Lieutenant McKenny, of the Fourth Cavalry, was killed. The weather is represented as being very severe.

Near noon that Tuesday, the twenty-eighth, it began to snow again, whipped out of the north on a cruel and cutting wind as Mackenzie's column struggled east. By the time the command went into bivouac for the night after ten tortuous miles, the snow lay two feet deep on the level and the wind was consumed in laying up immense drifts.

As his troops were going into camp and dismounting, Mackenzie rode over to pay a call on his Indian allies. There among the scouts, Donegan watched the colonel tell of his gratitude for their service against Dull Knife's Cheyenne. For each of the two Sioux and two Arapaho scouts who were credited with discovering the enemy camp, Mackenzie declared that he was giving them four of the captured ponies of their choice. To the North brothers' battalion of forty-eight Pawnee scouts, he gave sixty ponies. For any acts of individual bravery under fire, Mackenzie donated an extra animal. And for all the rest, Mackenzie stated they would be allowed to choose one horse for themselves before they departed for their agencies.

Theirs was a shabby bivouac: hardly any wood to speak of for their supper fires, fires meant to keep at bay the marrow-robbing cold as the sun dropped out of sight and the temperature fell beyond human endurance. Because of their struggle for footing on the crusty snow, the trail-weary animals had little strength left to fight down through the icy drifts for what meager grass might be found. As the stars came out in those few patches of clear sky overhead, it was a quiet, melancholy camp of many men crowding around what few fires were kindled—surrounded by their herds of morose cavalry mounts, pack mules, and captured Cheyenne ponies.

For the past few days Seamus had become gravely concerned for the bay. Already its ribs were flung up beneath its heavy winter coat the way a brass head rail might poke its spindles beneath a bedsheet. If these big American horses did not get grain, and soon, the soldiers might just be limping back to the wagon camp afoot. He shuddered, remembering the horrors endured in their horse-meat march last September;* then recalled how he had struck a bargain with another horse during that ordeal—vowing that he would do everything he could not to allow it to go down, unable to get back up.

Man and animal alike hung their heads that night, all God's creatures struggling to keep from freezing during that tortured, sleepless night until dawn finally arrived. They had no wood left for breakfast fires. No coffee to boil anyway. Only hardtack and cold bacon, and what good water they might find in their canteens.

Still, every man knew they would reach Crook's wagon camp before nightfall. And that hope was enough to get these frontier warriors to their feet and pushing on at daylight. Another ten miles brought them into sight of the pickets Dodge had thrown out on the surrounding heights. The forward cavalry

---

* *Trumpet on the Land,* Vol. 10, The Plainsmen Series.

command hailed the infantry, and the word instantly shot back through the column like a bolt of summer lightning.

"I see 'em!" one man yelled at the head of that first troop. "The tents! The tents!"

Cheers and huzzahs went up as the weary, frozen men straightened in their saddles and joyfully slapped the trooper riding stirrup to stirrup beside them on the back. The warmth of those tents drew on them like iron filings to a lodestone as the hundreds of infantry fell out to watch the return of Mackenzie's victorious horse soldiers. Dodge's men cried out their congratulations, cheered, and tossed their hats in the air as the long column snaked over the hills and down to the banks of the Crazy Woman.

There was a lot to be thankful for. Many of the cavalry received mail that day, news of home and loved ones. There were even two letters from Samantha for him. More than hot food or a chance to get out of the wind beneath some heavy army canvas—simply to read her words, to touch those pages she had held in her hands days ago, to smell of those letters for the faintest breath of her fragrance . . . all of it warmed the Irishman as twilight fell.

That evening by the light of a fire kindled right outside a tent he shared with Frank Grouard and two others, Seamus sharpened his stub of a pencil with his folding knife and put it to paper. The weather was far too cold for him to dare writing her in ink, he told Sam, praying she would forgive him the inelegance of the lead pencil.

But after no more than the first three sentences, Donegan fell fast asleep over the borrowed field desk. And did not awaken until he caught himself shivering in the gray, seepy cold of dawn.

Finding himself among the raspy, throaty snores of rough and unlettered men, long-haired, bearded, and caked with the stench of horses . . . instead of awakening within the warm bosom of his little family.

For Young Two Moon there was nothing warm about the last two mornings. As they moved out of the mountains into the foothills, it snowed off and on throughout the day, and each night it grew so cold even he found it hard to move come the dawn.

Yet some of the young warriors had managed to locate some game. This, like the horse meat that had sustained them, the women would throw onto the glowing red bed of coals in the fires, as they had no cooking utensils. Using their belt knives, the men occasionally would turn over the strips and slabs of meat until they were properly roasted. The old folks and the little ones were always fed first. And with what was left, the women and warriors finally ate at every stop. Never was there anything left but hoof and hide.

Joining Yellow Eagle, Turtle Road, Beaver Heart and a few others, Young Two Moon had mounted some of the stronger ponies and left the main group behind as they skirted the foothills to the south. These young men intended to see once more where the soldiers were going, and possibly steal back some of their captured herd from the Indian scouts.

Early in the evening the warriors caught up with the soldier column after it had settled in for the winter night—fires glowing, men talking, many of the *ve-ho-e* attempting sleep beneath their blankets. Some distance beyond the head of the soldier march the warriors discovered the pony herd, this night watched over by the *Tse-Tsehese* men who were scouting for the soldiers.

On that subfreezing night, those guards had little idea they were watched by the ten warriors as the herders went to the mouth of a draw where they would be protected from the wind and built themselves a shelter from dried brush, bark, and grass. Inside, the herd guards built a fire. It was not long before Young Two Moon and the others—waiting silently in the snow and the cold—heard the snoring of the guards.

"Those ponies will remember our smell?" Yellow Eagle asked in a whisper.

"It does not matter. We move among them slowly," Young Two Moon asserted, "they will come to know our smell."

"Then we can take them home to our people," Turtle Road declared.

It was as Young Two Moon had said it would be. They went among the unguarded herd, stroking the ponies, breathing in the nostrils of some of the mares, then slipped horsehair ropes around the necks of ten ponies. These few the young warriors led up the long slope to the north. In the dark, silvery silence of that winter night, many of the herd followed obediently.

And once beyond the hilltop, Young Two Moon signaled the others.

"Now we ride!"

With quiet yips of excitement, the warriors leaped to the backs of the ponies they had brought to this place from the People's march and quickly got the herd of eight-times-ten moving into the snowy night.

"It is a blessing upon us!" Little Wolf cried out as the ten warriors returned just before dawn with the horses. "Now more of the old ones and the ones crippled with cold can ride."

They continued that day down Lodgepole Creek* all the way until the People reached the "Big Lake"† before following their scouts over the divide to the head of Crow Standing Creek,‡ where darkness caught them for a third cold night, forced to huddle out of the wind and snow, taking shelter down in the coulees and draws near the frozen streambank.

It was to this camp early in the morning that Big Head and Walks Last returned from their ride with five others back to the burned village in the Red Valley. They had gone back to search for any ponies that might have run off into the hills then wandered back to the People's camp once the soldiers deserted the canyon. None of the seven warriors brought in any horses.

The white man had taken them all.

THE INDIANS

Gen. Mackenzie's Fight—List of Casualties.

NEW YORK, November 29.—a dispatch dated in the field, November 25, via Fort Fetterman the 27th, gives the following additional particulars of General Mackenzie's fight on the 25th: The hostiles had been having a war dance all night, and were not taken by surprise by the attack which was made at sunrise. The village was located in a canyon running nearly north and south. It contained about 200 lodges, with perhaps five hundred warriors. General Mackenzie's fighting force numbered nearly one thousand men. Most of the enlisted Indians behaved well at the start but after the first heat of the charge very many of them relapsed into apparent indifference to everything except plundering the abandoned tepees of the Cheyennes, and trying to run off horses. About twenty Indians that can be counted were killed, and doubtless many more have

---

*What the white man today calls Clear Creek.
†Lake DeSmet.
‡Present-day Prairie Dog Creek.

fallen behind the rocks. About five or six of our forces have been killed. The following is a partial list of casualties: Killed—Lieutenant John A. McKinney, Fourth Cavalry; Corporal Ryan, Company D, and Private Keller, Company E. Wounded—Sergeant Thomas H. Forsyth, Corporal W. J. Lynn, Corporal W. H. Pool, Corporal Dan Cunningham, Jacob Schlafer, privates E. L. Burk, G. H. Stickney, J. E. Talmadge, August Streil, Issac Maguire, Charles Folsom, Joseph McMahon, Edward Fitzgerald, Alexander McFarland, George Kinney, Henry Holden, William B. Smith and David Stevens.

The fight in that red canyon would eventually claim one last victim—its daring cavalry commander.

But for now, ever since returning to the Crazy Woman camp, rumor had it Crook was going to return the troops to winter quarters. There'd be no more god-awful chasing around in the cold and the snow.

For Richard I. Dodge, it was just about the best news he had heard through this whole insufferable campaign.

Then at eleven A.M. that Thursday, 30 November, one of Crook's men came by to pay a courtesy on the colonel, informing Dodge that the general was dispatching twenty-five of the best men on the strongest horses to follow up the rumor that there was a large band of Cheyenne warriors in the neighborhood under a chief called White Antelope, ready to attack the wagon camp. Earlier that morning Crook had sent out Luther North and four Pawnee to push north through the deep snow to Clear Creek, where they were to look for sign of the fleeing village.

Then at noon what cavalry wasn't on guard duty turned out to solemnly commit five of their number to the frozen, rock-hard Wyoming ground. Between two long double lines of silent mounted men, the thirty pallbearers trudged with their blanket-wrapped corpses to the common grave. Nearby sat the sad-eyed spectators—Sioux, Cheyenne, Pawnee, Shoshone and the others—in all their wild finery as they witnessed this most final of the white man's rites.

All morning long soldiers had struggled in relays to force open the breast of the earth just enough to admit these five young soldiers. As the hundreds fell silent, two officers read from the Book of Common Prayer, then Crook said a few words over the grave. In the end seven guns were fired in three relays, the last sharp rattle disappearing over the windswept hills before a lone trooper took up the mournful notes of "Taps." As the quiet returned to the valley of the Crazy Woman, one of the men from the Third played a sad dirge on his tin fife, each plaintive note quickly carried off by the stiffening wind.

Lieutenant McKinney's body rested in the back of a freight wagon—to be returned east by way of wagon and rail, there to be buried among his people.

Yet for all the excitement of Mackenzie's return, and later the melancholy of the burial, for once there wasn't all that much for his infantry to do that afternoon but rotate the guard and watch the cavalry troops grain and water their horses, besides wolfing down their poor Thanksgiving dinner of fried bacon and flapjacks.

Clutching a cup of steaming coffee, Dodge returned to his tent and his diary, where he confided his first intimations of a troubled Ranald Mackenzie, who seemed to be plagued by second thoughts about the success of his Dull Knife fight.

> Altogether it has been a very successful affair. It might have been much more so had McKenzie possessed as much administrative and political sagacity as he has gallantry in the field. Still it is no time, nor is there any cause for grumbling. The affair stamps our campaign as a success even if nothing more is accomplished. I only regret that my portion of the command had no share or lot in the affair. All say that had the Doboys been there not an Indian would have escaped. If I had been allowed to go, we would have had a more complete story to tell.

Indeed, for much of last night and into today, Dodge found Mackenzie consumed with chastising himself for not pressing the warriors once the Cheyenne encapsulated themselves in the rocks. While both Crook and especially Dodge offered their words of encouragement, the cavalry commander nonetheless appeared to be snared in a deepening well of despair, delusion, and melancholia.

Dodge went on to pen in his diary:

> We found [Mackenzie] very downcast—bitterly reproaching himself for what he called his failure. He

talked more like a crazy man than the sane commander of a splendid body of Cavalry. He said to an officer that if he had courage enough he would blow his brains out. [The other officers present] went out soon, and Mac opened his heart to me. He is excessively sensitive. He said he had often done better with a third of the force at his command here—that he believed he degenerated as a soldier as he got older—that he regarded the whole thing as an utter failure. He even stated that he was sensitive lest someone might attribute cowardice to him—and much more of the same kind.

He was so worked up that he could hardly talk and had often to stop and collect himself. I bullied him and encouraged him all I could—told him that he was foolish and absurd to talk so, that we all regarded the affair as a grand success and that his record was too well known for anyone to attribute cowardice to him. I left him feeling much better, but he was in such a state that I thought it right to tell General Crook about it. The General was greatly worried and soon left my tent, I think to send for Mac and get him to play whist or something.

Those bitterly cold days in the wake of his fight on the Red Fork of the Powder River would mark the last campaign of Ranald Slidell Mackenzie ... as well as the beginning of his slow and agonizing mental disintegration.

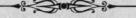

Chapter 43

Big Freezing Moon
1876

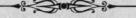

For many days now, more than two-times-ten by the count of notches on the stick in his belt pouch, Wooden Leg had been out hunting with a small party of other young warriors. The last they had seen of Morning Star's village, it was moving south slowly toward the Red Canyon of the White Mountains.* There Wooden Leg and the others expected to find their people camped a few days from now as the young men began turning about, slowly working their way back to their village.

That morning as the sun rose pale and heatless in a cold blue sky, Wooden Leg's party was moving upriver along the western bank of the Tongue River, slowly working the game trails before them as they eased along.

"Look!" one of those in front called out.

Quickly they all halted—putting hands to their brows, frost curling from their faces as they squinted into the distance.

"They are walking," Wooden Leg declared.

"A few ride," said Stops in a Hurry. "Why do they have only a few horses?"

"Yes. Who are these people?" Wooden Leg wondered aloud. "Why would they be so poor that they are not riding?"

"Indeed, they are very poor," commented Fox, another of

*The Big Horn Mountains.

their warriors. "You see they have few robes and no blankets to speak of."

"Let us go closer and take a good look," Wooden Leg suggested. "Then we might know if these are friends of the *Ohmeseheso* or if these are our enemies."

Quickly retreating down the slope into the long, wide ravine, the young hunters hurried their pack animals south by east in the direction of the strangers. Then, upon leaving their horses in a coulee, some of them went to the brow of a snowy hill to have themselves a closer look at the slow procession inching its way below like a dark worm wriggling against a white world.

The more he studied the people, the more confused he became. Few wore moccasins. Most had stiff, frozen pieces of raw hides lashed crudely around their feet. Some helped old women and men hobbling along between them. Small children rode in the arms of the women, or on the shoulders of the men. There were no travois. These strangers had nothing to carry from place to place!

"These . . ." Wooden Leg gulped in shame, feeling the burn of sadness sting his heart, "these are the poorest people I have ever known."

"Perhaps we should take them to our village," Fox suggested. "We are prosperous and we can share all we have with those who have nothing."

Then both of them heard the breath catch in the throat of Stops in a Hurry. He had the far-seeing eyes. And with them he stared at the strangers in shock.

Wooden Leg demanded, "What do you see?"

Painfully, Stops in a Hurry turned, his face gone pale with horror. "These are . . . are our people."

"Our p-people?"

"*Tse-Tsehese?*" asked Fox. "*Ohmeseheso?*"

To the rising despair of the young hunters, it was indeed their own people—their own families, their own relatives and friends who had been driven into this winter wilderness with little but those green horsehides frozen on their backs. The young men rushed back to the coulee, leaped atop their ponies, and kicked them into a lope.

When the hunters were still a long way off, the women started trilling their tongues in warning. At first the warriors escorting the sad procession hurried forward on cold, stiffened limbs—prepared to meet the attack. But in a few moments they realized the young horsemen had not come to attack them. The older warriors, the chiefs, began to call out.

And the young hunters answered to their names, quickly searching among the many for their loved ones and relatives. Women began to cry and old men began to weep. And it made Wooden Leg cry too, for here he looked over the three Old-Man Chiefs. And thanked *Ma-heo-o* that Coal Bear's woman still carried *Esevone* upon her back. Too, Medicine Bear helped the feeble prophet called Box Elder hobble forward, his bony hands still clutching his Scared Wheel Lance and the Turner over their heads.

While they might have no lodges and few weapons, while they no longer owned the finest in clothing and an ample supply of winter meat—the *Ohmeseheso* still had what mattered most. They had protected their most sacred objects. The People could rebuild!

"The soldiers and Wolf People came to our camp in the Red Canyon," the story was told to the young hunters in a gush of words and tears, both happy and sad.

"We were camped far up Powder River near where you left us," said another.

"Our women and children had to run away with only a few small packs."

Wooden Leg nodded bitterly with remembrance, then said, "Just as we did last winter far down on the Powder River."*

"This time the soldiers and their Indian scouts made sure they burned all our lodges and most of our horses were stolen. Many of our men, women, and children have been killed in the fight. Others have died of their battle wounds or have starved or frozen on our journey here."

And a woman shrieked, "One of my sisters and her boy were captured with two other women by the Wolf People!"

"Where are you going?" Wooden Leg asked.

Little Wolf looked away into the distance a moment, then back into the young warrior's face. "We are going there." He pointed north. "Down the Tongue River . . . to find the Hunkpatila people."

"Here," Wooden Leg replied as the other hunters came forward, "take our horses for those who cannot walk. We will cross the ice with you and go down the river until we find Crazy Horse. Last winter when the soldiers drove us out into the snow

---

*Blood Song, Vol. 8, The Plainsmen Series.

and cold, Crazy Horse welcomed us ... welcomed us as if we were his brothers."

Headqrs. Mil. Div. of the Mo.
Chicago, Dec. 1, 1876

Gen. W. T. Sherman
Washington:

The following telegram from General Crook, dated Crazy Woman's Fork, Wyoming Territory, November 28th, has just been received:

(signed) P. H. Sheridan
Lieutenant General

Before reaching General Mackenzie, I learned of the Indians' retreat, and that he was returning with his command; so I countermanded the foot troops to this place. I sent you Mackenzie's report of his operations against the Cheyennes. I cannot commend too highly his brilliant achievements and the great gallantry of the troops of his command. This will be a terrible blow to the hostiles, as those Cheyennes were not only the bravest warriors, but have been the head and front of most all the raids and deviltry committed in this part of the country.

(signed) George Crook
Brigadier General, U.S.A.
Commanding

The day before had been a damned forgettable Thanksgiving, Seamus brooded that next morning, the first of December. What with the burials of those dead soldiers, and the presence of that lone pine box Crook would have Lieutenant O. L. Wieting of the Twenty-third Infantry deliver by rail to McKinney's family back in Memphis, Tennessee. For the rest of the afternoon details of the Fourth Cavalry rode teams of horses back and forth over the mass grave, and that evening the men started fires over the site in hopes of betraying that sacred ground to both the enemy and any four-legged predators roaming this wilderness.

Donegan could not remember ever seeing Mackenzie nearly as melancholy. The colonel marched to the grave site with Crook and Dodge at the head of the procession, but while the others sang the hymns and bowed their heads in prayer, Mackenzie only stared into the distance, transfixed on the clouds mantled across the snowy mountains. The man looked numb, almost unaware of events around him, his face a mask to some private torment and despair.

Perhaps Mackenzie was dwelling on the same dark thoughts that tormented Donegan: more soldiers buried in more unmarked graves, those final resting places abandoned to the ages.

Come the end of this month a full decade will have passed, he thought that next morning as he huddled beside a greasewood fire and clutched his hands around a steamy tin of coffee. Ten full years since we buried Fetterman's dead inside Carrington's stockade.*

Ten long, long years of scooping holes out of this bloody wilderness where dead soldiers can sleep alone and forgotten for all of eternity.

That Friday, the first of December, a horse fell beneath a Fourth Cavalry sergeant, rolling over on the soldier, crushing him so that he died in agony within minutes, his lungs filling up with blood as he thrashed on the snow in the midst of his friends helpless to save him.

A quiet and somber camp again that night as Crook grew restive and anxious, awaiting Luther North and the Pawnee he had sent north to pick up the Cheyenne trail, hoping it would eventually lead him to Crazy Horse. Just past nightfall word began to circulate that they were to be ready to march back to Reno Cantonment at dawn.

On top of the twenty-eight miles of icy, windblown, snow-drifted prairie the command put behind them before reaching the north bank of the Powder that second day of December, the continued and extreme cold was taking the last bit of starch out of the horses. The temperature continued to slide down ever more rapidly as the sky cleared.

Early that Saturday evening two Cheyenne scouts came in from the Red Cloud Agency. To Crook they reported having learned that the Sioux war chief Lame Deer and a sizable war party was on its way from the Belle Fourche for the Little Powder.

Into the night wild speculation coursed its way through the column. Was it too much to hope that Crook would move them back to Fetterman and Laramie to retire the expedition? Or—as

---

*Sioux Dawn, Vol. 1, The Plainsmen Series.

some of the senior officers hinted—could the general really be contemplating another march to the Belle Fourche and the Black Hills in hopes of snagging himself another victory by cutting off Lame Deer's band?

The last of Mackenzie's command did not dismount on the banks of the Powder until well after dark, not eating until nine o'clock—for the first time since breakfast. And Furey's wagon train did not roll in until shortly after midnight.

At dawn on the third orders came down for the cavalry to mount fifty of the best men from each company on fifty of their strongest horses and be prepared to move out by nine. That Sunday morning chief medical officer Joseph R. Gibson turned over his wounded to Marshall W. Wood and some of his five surgeons, who would begin the southward trek with the casualties to Fort Fetterman the following day under the command of Major George A. Gordon.

With the rising of the cold buttermilk-yellow sun, Tom Cosgrove reported to Crook that his auxiliaries were anxious to be relieved of their duties and return home, certain from the trophies they had discovered in the Cheyenne camp that a disaster had befallen some band of their people.

"How soon do you wish to leave?" Crook asked.

Cosgrove turned slightly, gesturing with an arm as the Shoshone battalion mounted in the distance and began to move in his direction. "We're pulling out now," he explained in his Texas drawl.

"I see," Crook replied, his brow knitting in disappointment.

"With your permission, General—we'll be mustered out so that we can return to see to the safety of our homes and families."

"Yes, well," Crook muttered, cleared his throat, and blinked into the brilliant cold light lancing off the glittering snow. The Shoshone came to a halt in a long, colorful line behind Cosgrove and Eckles, knee to knee in silence as their horses pawed the icy snow and thick streamers of frost wreathed their muzzles. "Very well, Captain Cosgrove. Your men have served me well for many a campaign."

"We'll go where you need us, General."

"You always have," Crook replied, smiling bravely.

Twisting in his saddle, the civilian motioned forward Dick Washakie, the great chief's son. "Before we go, my men wanted to present you with a gift."

"A gift?"

Washakie brought his pony to a halt beside Crook, handing a ceremonial pipe down to the general who stood on foot.

Feathers fluttered from the long stem as Crook inspected it, then finally whispered, "This is ... quite a gift, Captain."

"And for Major Pollock," Cosgrove said as a second Shoshone came forward bearing his gift, "a war shirt."

Captain Edwin Pollock, commander of Reno Cantonment, stepped forward, his cheeks red with embarrassment as he took the buckskin shirt that had been painted black—the color of war—and decorated with scalp locks as well as yellow horsehair plumes. "Th-thank you. Thank all of these fine men," Pollock stammered.

"And especially for Lieutenant Schuyler," Cosgrove said, motioning a third warrior forward to lay his gift at the feet of the young officer who had commanded the Shoshone battalion atop the high ground the day of the battle, "this token of their regard for you as a war chief."

For a long moment Walter S. Schuyler was speechless as he picked up the bow case and quiver filled with iron-tipped arrows, as well as a saddle cover of beaded buckskin, a pair of beaded moccasins, and a war shield ringed with eagle feathers.

"General Crook," Cosgrove said with finality and a salute as his horse pranced backward of a sudden. "Till we meet on another war trail, on another battlefield."

Crook, Schuyler, Pollock, and the rest saluted as the two old Confederates snapped their arms down, reined right in silence, and kicked their ponies into a lope. At the end of the long, colorful line of Shoshone they signaled with their arms only, and as one all the warriors heeled smartly into a column of twos, their unshod ponies kicking up clods of icy snow, feathers bristling and scalp locks flying on the cold breeze as they climbed the far slope, crested the top, and began to fade into the distance.

Donegan somberly watched the old friends slowly disappear in the cold, sunlit distance of that snow-caked land, those brave men hurrying southwest toward the Wind River Mountains, sensing the remorse at that parting of men who have together borne the terrifying weight of battle and utter hardship.

For the rest of the morning while the command was packing up, the Irishman found his throat all but clogged with a sour ball of sentiment, his eyes close to betraying him as he thought on all those years he had watched friends fall in battles, or perhaps just as painful, watched friends ride off—perhaps never again to gallop stirrup to stirrup into the jaws of death.

"I figure you ought to know what the general's up to with this march, Johnny," Seamus declared later that day as he brought his horse into line beside Lieutenant Bourke's shortly after the column moved out up the Dry Fork of the Powder, headed south by east.

"Hell, this is as much a mystery to me as any man," Bourke replied with a shrug.

"Crook ain't said a thing to you where we're going or for why?"

With a shake of his head the lieutenant answered, "Only thing I know is that the general conferred with Mackenzie about making this march."

Seamus's eyes narrowed. "Mackenzie?"

"That's right. I was there when the two of them studied the general's maps."

"Looking for what?"

"Where best to make the crossing of that country between the Little Powder and the Belle Fourche."

"By the saints! That's back to that god-bleeming desert country we crossed last September!"

Nodding, Bourke replied, "About sixty miles worth of desert crossing, Seamus."

"No wood, no graze, and damn well no water to speak of!"

"Sixty miles of it," the lieutenant said. "But both Crook and Mackenzie figure the gamble is worth the test."

"To save some days?"

"Exactly. About ten days by the looks of things on the maps."

"Crook wants Crazy Horse even more'n I ever dreamed he could hunger to get his hands around that red savage's throat."

That day they put twenty miles under them before stopping for the night at Buffalo Springs on the Dry Fork. Then Crook kept them there—in camp and in the dark—for both the fourth and the fifth. As did many of the men during that interminable wait, Seamus wrote his loved ones.

Finally on the morning of the sixth Crook moved them out again, marching only seven miles in the wind-driven snow, where they found little water—what there was proved to be muddy and loaded with alkali salts—as well as finding they had no firewood. The command had all but emptied the wagons of forage for their animals, and there was little hope of any reaching Mackenzie's men from the south anytime soon, what with the severity of the recent storms likely blocking rail shipments to Medicine Bow Gap, the same horrid weather blocking wagon shipments from there north to Fort Fetterman on the North Platte.

The men huddled together as best they could through the night, suffering greatly, as did their horses, while winter continued to pummel the high plains. Just before dawn the surgeons reported that the mercury in their thermometers hovered at thirty below zero. Hundreds of men reported cases of frostbitten fingers, toes, noses, and ears at sick call upon awaking.

They packed up in light marching order in a severe snowstorm that morning of the seventh, ordered to make ready for the fifteen-mile march north by east that would take them to the Belle Fourche. Off in the shimmering, icy distance to the south stood the hulking monoliths of the Pumpkin Buttes, orange and ocher against the newly fallen snow. Only the leafless branches of cottonwood and willow marked each frozen water course winding its way down to the Belle Fourche. Few if any birds were seen roosting along the line of march, while far overhead the great longnecks honked, these last to hurry south in great undulating vees. For as far as the eye could see, the land lay beneath a solid sheet of white—more desolate, bare, and destitute of life than ever Seamus could have imagined it.

In camp late that night after the wagons had finally rolled in so the men could boil their coffee and prepare supper of what deer, elk, antelope, jackrabbits, and even a few porcupines they had managed to kill along the trail that day, a few soldiers grumbled their bitter recriminations about Crook, sharing their tales of how the general had punished another command and its horses three months earlier.

"Some say Crook figures to find Crazy Horse near Slim Buttes," Billy Garnett explained.

"Now, that's hard to believe," Seamus said. "Surely the general's smart enough to know those Lakota aren't still in this country, that they're gonna move on after all this time. That's better'n four months now!"

With a shrug Garnett replied, "Can't figure what Crook's thinking. Only know what we all know: the general's been wanting that red son of a bitch for the better part of a year now.

"Sweet Mither of God! Crook ain't gonna find Crazy Horse anywhere near them Slim Buttes or the Black Hills country."

"Shit!" Garnett scoffed with a grin. "So, mister know-it-all, why don't you tell me why in the hell Crook's gonna take us off in this direction if he doesn't expect to find Crazy Horse in this here country?"

But for the life of him ... Donegan couldn't come up with a single good answer.

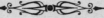

Chapter 44

8 December 1876

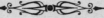

THE INDIANS

Mackenzie's Official Report—What Crook Says.

CHICAGO, December 1.—The official report of Colonel Mackenzie was received to-day. It states that about noon on the 24th, while marching in a southwesterly direction towards the South Pass of the Big Horn mountains, five advance scouts met him, reporting the main camp of Cheyennes about fifteen or twenty miles distant. About sunset the command began moving toward the hostiles, reaching the village after daylight, completely surprising the Indians, and compelling them to vacate the village suddenly, taking refuge in a ravine. After a brisk fight, lasting an hour and skirmishing until night, they capitulated. The entire village, having 173 lodges, was destroyed, 500 ponies captured, and 25 Indian bodies found. It is almost certain that a much larger number were killed. Five soldiers and one officer were killed on our side, and twenty-five wounded, besides one Shoshone scout belonging to the United States. Fifteen cavalry horses and four horses of the Indian scouts were killed. The command moved to the camp on Powder River, whence this report was made on the 26th instant. Lieutenant

McKinney, of the Fourth cavalry, who was killed, was
one of the most gallant officers and honorable of men.
General Crook, in transmitting the above report, says:
"I cannot commend too highly this brilliant achieve-
ment and gallantry of the troops. This will be a terrible
blow to the hostiles, as the Cheyennes were not only
the bravest warriors but have been the head and front
of most of the raids and deviltry committed in this
country."

What or who George Crook was relying upon for his information about where he would find the Crazy Horse people
was as much a mystery as anything in the world. Perhaps he was
doing no more than grasping at straws in his hope of finding his
archnemesis.

But for some reason the general clearly had grown satisfied
that the Oglalla warrior bands had now abandoned the country
of the Rosebud and Tongue River and were wandering east toward the country of the Little Missouri and the Moreau.

In explaining his intent to prolong the campaign, the general wrote Sheridan:

I shall endeavor to ascertain these points before leaving
here, so that in case they leave the Rosebud country, I
will not make that march as it would unfit the horses
of the command for any further service this winter,
and in case Crazy Horse has gone to Slim Buttes, I will
go there via the Black Hills.

"You see, Mr. Donegan," Crook explained in his tent that
night of 8 December along the frozen banks of the Belle Fourche,
"General Mackenzie and I have decided against pursuing the defeated and impoverished Northern Cheyenne."

Mackenzie himself cleared his throat, then stated, "Instead
we think better of marching the expedition down the Little Powder, where the general desires to establish a temporary base of
operations."

"Right in the heart of the country haunted by the Sioux and
Cheyenne hostiles!" Crook exclaimed, slamming a fist down into
his left palm. "Squarely in the country where our deadliest enemies clung tenaciously and have likely taken refuge from our two
columns."

"Two columns?" Donegan asked, perplexed.

"Ours to the south, and north of the enemy—General Miles and his Fifth Infantry."

"But they're all the way up yonder on the Yellowstone," the Irishman replied.

"Exactly," Crook said.

Mackenzie moved up to explain, "Don't you see—our intelligence tells us that the Crazy Horse hostiles are somewhere between us."

From the sound of things in that tent, Donegan decided Crook and Mackenzie had grown tired and frustrated of the past two weeks of teetering back and forth between bouts of sulking despair and fits of self-righteous exultation over the Red Fork fight. On the one hand, at times they brooded: with the escape of most of the Cheyenne, had it been no more than a hollow victory? But at other times the two commanders cheered themselves in thinking: by destroying all that meant wealth to that powerful warrior band, hadn't they in fact delivered a solid thumping to a steadfast enemy?

Then yesterday a courier had arrived from Fetterman, giving Crook real cause to rejoice: receiving a telegram from Sheridan, forwarded on from William Tecumseh Sherman, commander of the U.S. Army.

> Please convey to Generals Crook and Mackenzie my congratulations, and assure them that we appreciate highly the services of our brave officers and men who are now fighting savages in the most inhospitable regions of our continent. I hope their efforts this winter will result in perfect success and that our troops will hereafter be spared the necessity of these hard winter campaigns.

But in that same leather courier packet lay some less than happy news. In a short and apologetic dispatch from Major Caleb H. Carlton, commandant at Fetterman, Crook and Mackenzie learned that bureaucratic bungling had further delayed supplies in reaching the Sydney, Nebraska, depot, much less getting them to the Medicine Bow depot by rail where they were to be off-loaded into wagons and freighted up to Fetterman, on from there to the Powder River Expedition. Not only rations and ammunition for the men, but the desperately needed grain for all those horses and Tom Moore's mules.

"And with Crazy Horse's hostiles wintering somewhere between here," Crook said, jabbing a finger at the Belle Fourche River on the map below him where his own expedition sat in bivouac, "and General Miles up here on the Yellowstone," as Crook slid his finger across all that unknown hostile territory to the north of them that cold night, "I'm mad as hell that I can't go get him here in the heart of the winter."

"For no other reason than the delay in getting our supplies brought up to us," Mackenzie snapped.

"What . . . what does all this have to do with me?" Donegan asked, growing more confused by these two military commanders confiding their frustrations in him. "I'm afraid I don't under—"

"Look here," Crook said, tracing a finger in a small circle around that country to the north and west of their position on the Belle Fourche. "I had hoped to move over to the Little Powder, march down from there to the Powder itself, and upon reaching that stream send out our Indian scouts—the Sioux and the Cheyenne, who know this country so well."

"We had planned to lie in wait," Mackenzie explained, "until the scouts located the Crazy Horse village, and then we could go after them with our cavalry and pack train."

Crook cheered, "Just as Mackenzie's battalion did so splendidly against the Cheyenne!"

The Irishman wagged his head slightly, still not all that sure what they were trying to tell him. "Sounds like it will work. But why me . . . just where are you fitting me in with all of this?"

Seamus watched Crook glance at Mackenzie, then the map, and finally back to look at the Irishman.

"I have been forced to change my plans, don't you see? With no supplies for me to continue my march into the lower Powder country after the Crazy Horse hostiles—I am compelled to alter my thinking."

"Can't you just send out your scouts from here?"

Mackenzie answered, "We can. And we will, Donegan."

"You're . . . no," and he suddenly saw it as clear as a summer day, causing the hair to stir on the back of his neck, ". . . you're not figuring on me going with them scouts, are you? Them Lakota and Cheyenne?"

Crook said, "That's precisely what I've brought you here to propose."

"But—what about Frank? Grouard's been in that country. And he knows how to talk Lakota with them scouts."

"That's right," Crook replied quietly. "I could send Frank

Grouard—but he won't be going north, because he's going to carry some dispatches for me to the Black Hills communities."

Seamus said, "It seems like you oughtta send Frank out with the scouts, and me to the Black Hills."

Again Crook looked at Mackenzie before saying, "It's not just the fact of going out with the scouts, Mr. Donegan. There's ... something more."

"More?"

"Some ... task for which the army will pay a man handsomely. Should he decide to undertake the risk."

"What risk?"

Mackenzie stepped up, saying, "Bluntly speaking: there will come a time when you will leave behind the Cheyenne and Sioux scouts."

"L-leave 'em behind?" Then, with his sense of peril really itching, Seamus asked, "Just where in bloody hell would I be going to leave 'em behind?"

"North of here," Crook replied after a moment's pause. "On your way to the Yellowstone."

"Now, why in hell would I want to go back to that country for, says I?"

"Yes—I quite understand you've been there before," Crook said. "We all were last summer. Well, I need you to carry some important messages for me."

Donegan's eyes narrowed again. "Messages. To the Yellowstone."

Mackenzie and Crook nodded.

Donegan's suspicions were all but confirmed. "To the Tongue River Cantonment?"

"That's right," Crook stated. "I wish to communicate with General Miles."

"Miles is said to also have a supply depot at the mouth of Glendive Creek," Mackenzie said, rubbing a fingertip at a thin inked line on the map that joined the Yellowstone east of the Tongue.

Seamus studied the faint and meandering inked-in rivers and streams a moment. "No, General. Seems to me that Glendive Creek's too far east for a man to set his sights on going ... at least if he's coming from here on the Belle Fourche."

Looking up, he caught Crook giving Mackenzie a knowledgeable nod, something that showed great self-satisfaction.

The son of a bitch thinks he's got me, Seamus thought.

Then Donegan went on to explain, "Makes far more sense

for a man to head down the Powder to its mouth. No more east than that."

"Yes, yes, exactly," Crook replied. "The Powder's about half-way between Glendive depot and the mouth of the Tongue."

"Then you'll go?" Mackenzie asked.

"Wait a minute! I ain't said nothing like that," Donegan demurred, studying the map, all that unknown, dangerous country between here and there. "How far you figure the scouts will go with me?"

Shrugging, Crook said, "Perhaps as far as the mouth of the Little Powder, Mr. Donegan."

"I see," he considered, staring at the convergence of those two lines on the map—the thrill of it beginning to rise from the soles of his feet with the tingle of genuine danger. He looked up at them steadily. "Why me?"

Crook glanced away from Mackenzie, to the map, then into the Irishman's eyes. "The honest truth of it is that I thought you would want the money."

It almost made him bristle, to have these men think he could be bought. Instead, he asked, "Why did you figure that?"

Crook answered, "Because . . . because of your new family, Mr. Donegan."

"That's why I recommended *you*," Mackenzie said joyfully. "I told the general about your new son—how devoted a family man you are . . . and I thought—"

"So what is it you'll pay a fool for riding out on a fool's errand?"

With the smile of a man who had hooked his catch, Crook said, "I've figured out how many days it might take you to get there and back—"

"You better be figuring on me taking twice as long."

"But even if you moved only at night—"

Seamus interrupted Crook. "How much, General?"

Crook swallowed, stroking his long beard. "A hundred dollars."

"What?" he snorted, almost ready to laugh. "A hundred dollars is what you brought me here to offer? Wanting me to ride alone into that country and risk my hair for a hundred dollars!"

The commanding general straightened as if stung. "Then tell me—what is the journey worth to you?"

"Nothing is worth getting myself killed for," he said all too quietly, suddenly souring on the idea that had lit a spark in him.

Mackenzie asked, "Not even the chance to provide well for your wife and newborn son?"

"If I ain't alive to ever see 'em again . . ." Seamus muttered, then began to consider an option.

"Two hundred dollars," Crook suddenly blurted in that silence. "I can offer no more than that."

For a long moment Donegan closed his eyes, conjuring up in his mind the images he had carried with him of Samantha, and the boy he was still to name. Knowing he had brought her here to this wild north country from the Staked Plain of Texas in hopes of reaching the goldfields of Montana Territory—there to strike it rich, all the better to provide for her. And now there were two relying on him.

He licked his lips as he opened his eyes, staring down at the map that told a man too damned little about that country where roamed the wild hostile tribes. All there were across that expanse were far too few inked lines: river courses, a few streams. Nothing else of any use.

Donegan looked the general squarely in the eye. "You'll pay me two hundred dollars?"

"I said that, yes," Crook replied, a bit anxious. He laid his two palms down on the map, rocking forward slightly.

Mackenzie stepped closer to lay a hand on Donegan's shoulder. "My old friend, will you go?"

For a moment he stared deep into the colonel's eyes. Over the last two weeks he himself had seen in those eyes, on Mackenzie's face, the first flickers of madness, the first tattered shreds of severe depression; then as quickly he had watched those eyes clear of imbalance as the man suddenly became as lucid as any man could claim to be.

"I will go—"

"Good!" Crook exclaimed exuberantly, starting to reach for a small stack of foolscap.

"Wait," Donegan cautioned. "I'll go on two conditions."

"What are they?" Mackenzie inquired.

"The first is that you pay me the two hundred dollars before I begin my ride."

Mackenzie turned to Crook, asking, "Is that possible, General?"

Finally Crook nodded. "Anything is possible. Yes, Mr. Donegan—I can have that arranged. But why would you want to carry that much—"

"That's the second condition," Seamus interrupted.

"Yes?" Mackenzie asked, more curious than ever before.

"I'm not going to carry that money on me," Donegan replied. "I want you to issue my pay to me, but see that it is sent with your next courier to Fetterman, and on down to Laramie."

It was Mackenzie who asked, "To your wife?"

"No," he answered. "Not yet. Send it to Colonel Townsend—with my instructions that he is to hold it in secrecy for Samantha . . . to guard it safely until I send him word upon my return to this outfit that he can turn it over to my wife . . . or . . ."

"Or?" Crook asked.

"Or . . . Colonel Townsend can give it to my wife and son . . . when he informs them that I've been killed in the line of duty."

Epilogue

Big Freezing Moon
1876

THE INDIANS

Spotted Tail and His Band.

ST. JOSEPH, December 2.—Spotted Tail, now chief of the Sioux nation, and the ninety-six Sioux braves sent to examine the Indian territory, with a view to the removal of the Sioux nation there, passed through the city this afternoon homeward bound in charge of Col. A. G. Boone and Dr. J. W. Daniels, of the Sioux commission, and disbursing agent Major Howard. They have been five weeks from home. The St. Joe Herald's interview say the delegation took wagons at Wichita, 424 miles through the territory, to Muskogee, on the M.K.&T. road, driving twenty-five days. At Ockmulgee two chiefs of the Creek nation made speeches, and Spotted Tail replied. The Indians say nothing, being under bonds to those at home to say nothing until their return. The commissioners say they see the Indians are pleased with the country, and think, if the right men are sent to treat with them, the whole of the Spotted Tail and Red Cloud agencies, 2,000 in number, will move to the territory without trouble in the spring. The Indians liked their trip.

After meeting up with Wooden Leg's group of hunters, the People crossed the Tongue River* and continued down the low ocher benches along the east bank to the mouth of Otter Creek, where they made their cold camp that night.

As the sun came up the following day, Morning Star had the scouts lead the people north by east along Otter Creek into the rising hill country. Sleep and walk. Sleep and walk again. Day after terribly cold day.

Upon reaching the forks of Otter Creek the scouts took the weary, hungry people over the low divide to Box Elder Creek.† It was on this day that the weather turned milder than it had been in a long, long time. For many days now Wolf Tooth had been wearing his frozen coat. Ever since the time when the People had emerged from the mountains and the young hunters had killed the first buffalo, Wolf Tooth had been wearing what he had cut from the soft underbelly of the cow's hide. Slashing a hole for his head, he had draped the green hide over his naked body to stay warm. But long ago the cold air froze the skin solid, so stiff Wolf Tooth could not get himself out of the hide. Not until today—when at last the temperature rose enough that, with the help of two friends, the old warrior could struggle out of his heavy, icy prison.

At long last, eleven suns after the fight with the pony soldiers and their Indians, the advance scouts came galloping back, yipping in excitement, to the head of the march where Morning Star, Little Wolf, and the other chiefs came to a stop, new snow nearly reaching their knees.

"What is it?" Morning Star demanded of the three excited young men who came skidding to a halt nearby.

"Have you seen more soldiers?" Little Wolf asked.

"No!" one of the young scouts answered joyfully. "There! Beyond that hill! We have seen the Crazy Horse people!"

As word shot back through the cold stragglers, the old men began to sing once more the strong-heart songs, and the women trilled their tongues in joy. Once more *Ma-heo-o* had delivered His People from the hand of disaster.

Hurrying to the crest of that low hill where he could smell woodsmoke, Morning Star peered down, his limbs stiff and wooden with cold. Below, along a bend on the east side of Beaver

---

*Just above the site of present-day Ashland, Montana, on the Northern Cheyenne Reservation.
†Present-day Beaver Creek.

Creek, among the leafless cottonwoods where they would be sheltered from much of the winter's cruel wind, sat the lodges—smoke rising from their crowns of poles. Already there were a handful of young Oglalla warriors and sentries headed their way through the deep snow, and dark, antlike forms of the Lakota people emerged from their lodges below, coming out to see what had caused all the excitement among the camp guards.

—"Come, Morning Star," Little Wolf said quietly as he came alongside, tugging on his old friend's elbow. "Let us go tell Crazy Horse that the *ve-ho-e* soldiers have attacked us again."

For the longest time that afternoon the *Tse-Tsehese* leaders sat with Crazy Horse and the other Hunkpatila headmen, discussing Three Stars's attack on their Red Fork village—talking over the why, and considering just what the Oglalla could do for their close cousins, the *Ohmeseheso*. Just as the two bands had done last winter in the cold moons before deciding to go in search of Sitting Bull and his Hunkpapa.

But this time there was a different sound in the throat of Crazy Horse. This time he did not speak with the same voice as he had when the pony soldiers had attacked Old Bear's village beside the Powder last winter.

This time there was a hardness on the face of Crazy Horse. Nothing soft in the eyes of the Oglalla war chief.

"We have little," the Lakota leader explained icily to his people as well as the *Tse-Tsehese*. "After the soldiers chased us from camp to camp to camp since summer—forcing us to keep moving all the time—we do not have many hides to give you to replace your lodges. And we do not have enough meat to feed your people."

For a long time Morning Star was stunned into silence. Then he finally asked, "What can you give us?"

Wagging his head coldly, Crazy Horse said, "I do not have enough to feed my own people and you as well."

"What would you have us do?" Little Wolf asked angrily.

Drawing himself up, Crazy Horse said to his old comrades in war, "I will give you what my people can spare . . . for three days. But no more."

"Where will we find Sitting Bull?" Morning Star inquired.

"Yes," Little Wolf said, his face showing his cheer. "Sitting Bull will help us again. Tell us where we can find him!"

As the Oglalla leader's eyes crimped into resolute slits, he replied, "Sitting Bull is no longer in this country."

Morning Star asked, "Where can we find him?"

"You will not," the Lakota mystic answered. "For he is long gone from here."

"Where?" Little Wolf demanded sharply.

"North of the Elk River—and he is running away from the soldiers too ... racing for the land of the Grandmother."

THE INDIANS

General Crook's Splendid Campaign.

BUFFALO SPRINGS, WYOMING, December 3. —General Crook's whole force left Fort Reno this forenoon, his intention being to move down the Little Powder to its junction with the Powder, and there, forming a supply camp, operate against the hostiles as circumstances dictate. This point will be convenient for operations to Tongue River, Little Missouri or Bell Fourche. The latest information is that Sitting Bull has about 400 lodges and Crazy Horse about seventy, equivalent to a fighting force of 1,500 to 2,000. The command is rationed to about January 1st. Grouard, chief scout, is of the opinion that unless surprised the hostiles will not make a stand. The wounded of McKenzie's fight leave here to-morrow for Fetterman. General Crook's plan is to feed the Indians on powder.

Valley of the Belle Fourche
Wyoming Terr.

My Dearest Heart—

He got that much written on a small sheet of paper with the lead pencil he had borrowed from Bourke, then sat there in the darkness of that early morning. A Sunday. The tenth of December.

Outside the lieutenant's tent a few men stirred, mess cooks mostly, those already building up the fires to boil coffee and beginning to wrassle up breakfast for the various companies. But for the most part the troopers and their horses were quiet in the cold of this last hour before sunrise.

It looks to be we'll be here awhile. Crook's waiting for supplies to come up from Fetterman. We were supposed to have them before now, but someone else

ended up with them. So here the army sits. At least until the supplies come and Crook and Mackenzie can go
off on the march again.

He sipped at the coffee going cold in the tin cup at his elbow, then flung the lukewarm dregs at the foot of the canvas tent
flap where it would soon turn to ice.

How was he going to keep from telling her, without lying to
her?

But there wasn't a damn bit of good sense in telling her
what he would soon be about, where he was going, and what he
would be facing. No good sense at all. But, he reminded himself,
how to keep from saying anything without it being less than the
truth?

It promised to fair off this day. To warm above zero. And
the wind had yet to come up. Perhaps it was a good omen, this
day starting off so fair. They were about due, he thought. What
with all those cold days in hell they'd suffered already.

Don't fear that I'll grow bored here, Sam. Crook
and Mackenzie will see to that. They've got scouts going out in this direction or the other all the time.
Coming and going. And they plan on having me out
too. While we are waiting here for rations and grain for
the horses, the generals want to know what the Indians
are doing. Where Crazy Horse and Sitting Bull are
camped, or moving. So the Indian scouts are being
sent north toward the Yellowstone, into the Powder
River country. It's there the Indian scouts say Crazy
Horse and his warriors have gone.

In a matter of moments he would be mounting up with the
Indian scouts and they would be pointing their noses a little west
of north. As soon as he had wolfed down his breakfast, washing
it all down with some more of that scalding coffee.

He could hear the sound of horses being brought close. It
could be Three Bears and some of his men—the ones who would
accompany him half the way to the Yellowstone. At least to the
mouth of the Little Powder.

So at least I have something to do from day to
day. Able to saddle up and ride out rather than hang
about camp here with the soldiers, playing cards with

no money, fighting, sleeping, and otherwise getting on one another's backs. I'd rather be out on the back of a good, strong horse that doesn't talk back. Where it's quiet enough to hear my own thoughts.

Where I can think about you. And our boy.

I promised you I'd return soon, back to your arms. And once I'm back at your side, I promised I would be ready to name our first born. In the weeks since we parted, I have given thought to this matter, weighing my choices from your family and mine. And while I haven't yet decided, I am near to making a decision.

Just as I promised you—our son will have a name by the time I return to you both.

Shall we have him christened at that time? There with the chaplain at the Laramie post? I am certain that is what we should do as soon as we have given him his Christian name. To stand at your side, holding him in my arms as he is blessed, and we are blessed with him.

The cook just stuck his head in and told me my breakfast was out of the kettle and on the plate. It will freeze soon if I don't eat it right away. And I'm ready for another cup of his dreadful coffee. It will be light soon and time to go to work for the army. For Crook and Mackenzie and the Powder River Expedition. To mount up and ride out.

It gives my mind a lot of time to think, and my heart a lot of time to ache, Sam. Missing you both more than I ever dreamed I could miss anything or anyone. But we both know I have a job to do while I'm here. There aren't many things I have the talent to do. I am a simple man with big, clumsy hands and a half-slow brain, but I can do army work. If this is how God wills me to put the food on my family's table, to put the clothes on your backs and a roof over your heads, then so be it.

I will always do what God sets before me, to the best of my ability—for there are those who are counting on me to see my way through all trouble and travail thrown down in my path, for there are those who are counting on me to make my way back home to them. Soon.

Know that I will do all that is within my power to
be back beside you by Christmas, our son's first. If for
some reason the army keeps me here in this far north
country longer than that—I vow to do all I can to be
home shortly after the coming of the new year.

Keep me in your prayers, Sam. Hold our son close
morning and night for me too. Oh, that I could wrap
you both in my arms right now, it is so cold here. So
very, very cold here. For the love of God, please pray
for me—pray that God will hold me in his hand and
deliver me to you soon.

And remember what I've always told you. That
God watches over drunks, and fools, and poor army
wretches like me. I'm coming home soon, Sam. Watch
the skyline to the north. One day I'll be there, big as
life, come home to hold you both again.

Until then, hug yourselves for me. And tell my
son that his father loves him more than breath itself.
Know that I love and cherish you more, much, much
more than I do my own life.

                                                        Seamus

Afterword

As promised in the afterword of *Trumpet on the Land*, at the very beginning of *A Cold Day in Hell* I've taken the luxury of moseying back in time a bit toward the story we covered at the end of that earlier novel, by having Frank Grouard relate his little-known private horse race with the poet scout, "Captain" Jack Crawford who had likewise accompanied George Crook's army through Wyoming, Montana, and Dakota Territory.

I was able to draw this exciting and ofttimes silly tale not only from the memoirs left by Frank Grouard and Jack Crawford themselves, but from Captain Andrew S. Burt as well. From his account we learn that James Gordon Bennett, wealthy publisher of the New York *Herald*, not only paid Crawford the $500 promised him by the grouchy news correspondent Reuben Davenport, but another $225—in payment for "horses killed and expenses."

After speaking to General Sheridan at Laramie, Crawford returned to Custer City in the Black Hills, where he learned he had been discharged as a scout for slipping away without notice at Crook City. Quartermaster records, in fact, show that he was relieved of duty on 15 September. He may well have spent the month of October among his old haunts, enjoying his notoriety among the prospectors and merchants of the Black Hills.

But by the second week of November he was in Omaha, on his way to Philadelphia, where he joined up with Buffalo Bill's newly reinstated production of a western melodrama. In the next few months Crawford "discovered that his talents for entertaining extended beyond the glow of an evening campfire." After the successful spring season of 1877, he broke with Cody and formed his own theatrical company.

In the years to come we will find the Irish-born "poet scout" relating many of his exploits in the form of rhyme and verse before Chautauqua audiences and upon many other lecture platforms. But he will reemerge in the future, for he served as a scout during the Apache warfare in the Southwest, at the conclusion of which he established a ranch on the Rio Grande where Crawford would live until his death in 1917, living each day according to the personal philosophy he oft times recited:

> *I never like to see a man*
> *a 'rasslin' with the dumps,*
> *'cause in the game o' life*
> *he doesn't always catch the trumps;*
> *but I can always cotton to*
> *a free and easy cuss*
> *as takes his dose and thanks the Lord*
> *it wasn't any wuss.*

Lieutenant Colonel Elwell S. Otis's encounters with the Hunkpapa of Sitting Bull and Gall are little known, as contemporary accounts of the Spring Creek skirmishes are extremely rare. I owe a great debt of thanks to historian Jerome Greene for the landmark work done in two of his books, for digging up what scant information does exist in what was left by three of the participants. For the military story of the "Spring Creek encounters" I relied upon the writings of Oskaloosa M. Smith and Alfred C. Sharpe. The lone Indian account was recorded by Stanley Vestal from the mouth of Lazy White Bull (Joseph White Bull).

We have more to rely upon when it comes to the Cedar Creek councils between Miles and Sitting Bull, and their Battle of Cedar Creek—although it is far from being a "wealth of information." Not only did Miles leave an admirable record of his momentous talks with the Hunkpapa leader, but we again have White Bull's remembrances, along with those of Long Feather, Bear's Face, and Spotted Elk to give us an idea of what was going on in the Lakota camp during those crucial hours and heated deliberations.

Extremely critical, don't you see, for this was the first time a representative of the white man's government had met with a leader (if not *the* leader) of the Indian coalition that had for months checkmated, then trounced, the Army of the West. While Cyrus Townsend Brady's account erroneously has both parties

meeting for the protracted councils on horseback, the importance of the meetings rests in the fact that such a face-to-face
confrontation allowed Miles to see for himself "the condition
and temperament" of the bellicose Lakotas after months of fighting, months of being chased and harried by the soldiers.

In addition, and by no means less important, these dramatic conferences exhibited to the war chiefs the readiness of
Miles and his soldiers to bring the nomadic warrior bands to
bay, and eventually in to their reservations. Because they could
plainly see the Bear Coat's resolve, on 27 October over four hundred lodges of Miniconjou and Sans Arc surrendered—some two
thousand people. Since Miles had no way to feed that many additional mouths at the Tongue River, he took five of their chiefs
as hostages for the good performance of the rest of their people,
who promised to move in to their agency at Cheyenne River.

As it turned out, only some forty lodges ended up turning
themselves in at the reservation. The rest hightailed it up the valley of the Powder to join what would become a large winter village of the Crazy Horse people and the Northern Cheyenne—an
imposing gathering by any standard!

In the end that confrontation between Nelson Miles and the
warrior bands in the valley of Cedar Creek in Montana Territory
would set the stage for the colonel doggedly pursuing his winter
campaign against the enemy, a story we will tell in the next volume of the Plainsmen Series, *Wolf Mountain Moon*.

In late October at the same time Miles was chasing Sitting
Bull to the banks of the Yellowstone, and Crook sent Mackenzie
to capture the Red Cloud and Red Leaf camps, Colonel Samu-
el L. Sturgis and his wounded Seventh Cavalry had marched
away from Fort Lincoln to impose Phil Sheridan's sanctions at
the Standing Rock and Cheyenne River agencies. Sturgis and his
troopers seized more than two thousand ponies and assorted
weapons.

Few today know little of those military seizures on the reservations, wherein we see the army commanders once again per-
sisting in their pattern of marching against those they can punish
in a misguided belief that those agency bands were in fact supplying the nomadic hostiles with ponies, weapons, and warriors.
In his autumn offensive, Sheridan used more than five thousand
troops, those either directly involved or those who stood in reserve at the frontier posts should they be needed ... a full fifth
of the U.S. Army at that time!

Sheridan was proud to boast that, "For the first time, all the agencies ceased to be points of supply and re-enforcement for the hostile Indians; and henceforth the troops will have only to contend with the Indians hereditarily and persistently hostile."

The pony and weapon seizures went on into the following year as one small warrior band after another limped in to their agencies to surrender, even after both Crook and Terry were re-assigned.

But perhaps the real shame is that of all those ponies seized, the animals drew an average of only six dollars each in auction. Worse still was the fact that of the auction's receipts, not a dollar was ever used to purchase cattle for the agencies, as had been promised. In military archives those thousands of dollars have never been accounted for.

It was surprising to me to learn that Mackenzie's 1876 journey to that section of the Big Horn Mountains was not the first. Two years earlier in 1874 Captain Anson Mills of the Third Cavalry marched his Big Horn Expedition almost due north from Rawlins Station on the Union Pacific line, instead of starting out from Fort Fetterman to the southeast. In the fall of that year they had gone as far north as practicable before turning east, eventually reaching the rim of what is today called Fraker Mountain, which overlooks the valley where the Dull Knife Battle would take place. Because there was no way down for their horses and pack mules, Mills's men were compelled to backtrack several miles until they could find a better way into the valley of the Red Fork. The expedition eventually did pass directly over the site in making their way downstream, exiting the canyon to the east through the same gap Mackenzie's troops would use in approaching the Cheyenne village.

To better impress upon the reader just how steep and forbidding is the terrain at the upper end of the valley where Morning Star's people took refuge, built breastworks, and eventually struggled in their nighttime winter climb out of the valley through what is today called Fraker Pass, let me quote that observer who accompanied Captain Mills in 1874:

> The situation on the western end of the battlefield area, as I remember it from 1874, . . . is that of mountains, pure and simple—not "Bad Lands," as understood by frontiersmen.

I am particularly indebted to the labors of historian Sherry L. Smith in recounting the journal of her relative, William

Earl Smith—a private who served as one of Mackenzie's orderlies during this critical campaign. Through him we have one of those rare firsthand glimpses into not only the day-to-day weather and human interest of the campaign trail, but a very microscopic look at the relations between soldier and officer in the frontier army.

She states:

> The relationships among enlisted men, non-commissioned officers, and commissioned officers— [were] relationships characterized at times by affection, at others by brutality. The army caste system is vividly revealed in Smith's description of the expedition's daily life. He is acutely aware of a system that allows officers to abuse soldiers verbally and physically with few restraints ... Smith's account (as well as those of his military superiors) undermine the notion of a purposeful, stately, tightly organized campaign.

I am most grateful that William Earl Smith left us another of those terribly personal records we chance upon from time to time, for history is not a dull recitation of historical facts. Instead, history is the record of *human* events. Not merely the when and where of conflict, but more so the *how* and *why* of those clashes. If for no other reason, I want my novels to stand apart from all others for bringing the breath of life and the pain of a human soul to this crucial period in American history. How unfortunate that all too few of us were ever taught a *biographical* history.

So I am in Sherry Smith's debt, for she did in her *Sagebrush Soldier* what more historians should be doing for the reading public, what I attempt to do as I knit together many different accounts of every campaign, every battle, in hopes that through those different points of view we will more closely arrive at what really took place. Unlike what most of the academic historians do in their work—striving to support and defend one point of view—Smith herself says:

> Rather than present participants' accounts separately, this approach aims for greater integration of perspectives. It rests on the belief that such a method lends itself to a closer approximation of the truth.

I'm grateful too for the brief, terse diary left us by Sergeant James McClellan, from whose words I have gleaned some rare nuggets of daily life for the cavalry trooper serving in Crook's cavalry. He served out his five-year enlistment, receiving his discharge in June of 1877—the back of his certificate noting that he was credited with killing the warrior known as Bull Head.

Over half a century later *Motor Travel* magazine (published by the American Automobile Club) began running a two-year series of articles on the Powder River Campaign of 1876. Survivors of the battle were contacted to participate, and McClellan himself wrote seven of the articles. Perhaps most interesting to me was that during those two years of renewed interest in the campaign, an era when the motion picture was flickering into its golden age, McClellan publicly stated the time had come to produce a film of the attack on the village. He believed it should be done sooner than later as there were still a few survivors left who could serve as consultants "about the essential details."

Needless to say, nothing ever came of his personal campaign, and he died soon thereafter in 1936. An interesting footnote to those of you who have been reading the Plainsmen Series from its beginning six years ago is that McClellan served in H Troop, Third Cavalry, under Captain Henry W. Wessels, son of the Henry W. Wessels who marched north to Fort Phil Kearny to relieve Colonel Henry B. Carrington following the disastrous Fetterman Massacre almost a decade before the army defeated the Cheyenne in the valley of the Red Fork.

It comes as no surprise to me, therefore, that history is indeed often a study of converging, diverging, then reconverging currents.

Another interesting footnote to our story is that Red Shirt—one of the seven Lakota scouts who located the Cheyenne village, and one of the two who remained behind to watch for signs of discovery—later joined Buffalo Bill Cody's wild west show when it sailed across the ocean to England, performing before her Majesty, Queen Victoria.

Because of the cold gloom of that night, because of the cold fog settling in the valley, Red Shirt and the other scouts never got a count of lodges to report so that Mackenzie would know just exactly what he was facing at the moment of attack. Indeed, there has persisted a minor dispute as to the number of lodges in the village. A few accounts state 175 lodges. Lieutenant John Bourke himself states there were 205 lodges, while later in his own account he states there were 200. Another contemporary account, this time by Lieutenant Homer Wheeler, states there were 205 lodges. In *Son of the Morning Star* Evan Connell's arduous research states there were "more than two hundred lodges." But in the end I have chosen to go with the number given by Luther North in his record, since Mackenzie himself sent the North brothers to get him an official count: 173.

So now we have the village in place, and they know the soldiers are coming (despite the erroneous statement Cyrus Townsend Brady makes in *Indian Fights and Fighters*, when he writes: "The sleeping Indians in the camp had not the slightest suspicion that the enemy was within a hundred miles[!]").

Why didn't the Cheyenne move? Or if they had determined they were going to fight, why not prepare to withstand the assault, as some of the chiefs suggested before they were bullied and shouted down by Last Bull and his Kit Fox Society?

Likely those will remain unanswered questions until the end of time.

It is almost certain that if Last Bull and the other war chief's had worked together to prepare for the attack, the outcome might well have been dramatically different. Why did they choose not to set up an ambush somewhere near the narrow east gap where the weary, cold soldiers were most vulnerable on their played-out horses that terribly cold night? Another question for which I have no answer.

For the longest time the army believed that they had surprised the Dull Knife village—but the testimony of the Cheyenne participants in later years bring ruin to that myth. Young Two Moon and the others knew not only that the soldiers were coming, but knew they were being led by their friends from the Red Cloud Agency—Lakota and Cheyenne both!

How was it that Last Bull was able to cow the chiefs in that village, as well as the protectors and priests of the Cheyenne peoples' two great medicines: the Sacred Hat and the Sacred Arrows? How could those chiefs ignore the power of Box Elder's prophetic vision, when the man had been right time after time before?

Perhaps some clue comes to us in the interclan relationships within the *Ohmeseheso* in that year of 1876. Clearly, sometime in that spring Last Bull's Kit Fox Society had gained the ascendancy over all other warrior societies among the Northern Cheyenne. Sherry Smith calls them "not only arrogant but even overbearing." They were known among their own people as "Wife Steal-ers," often called the "Beating-Up Soldiers." They plainly had most everyone else afraid.

Everyone, except the rival Elk Scrapers Society.

During the previous February the rivalry between the two warrior groups had reached a peak when Last Bull had warned of the proximity of soldiers, but was ignored, even scorned by the Elk Scrapers. Days later when a group of Elk Scraper hunters came in with news of soldiers in the area, their reports were believed. This wound to his pride would fester for nine moons until the new emergency in the Big Freezing Moon allowed him to seize control from those less ruthless than he.

Among the Northern Cheyenne, Last Bull is still strongly blamed for the disaster. He was later deposed as leader of his society. In those years to come during his final days on the reservations, Last Bull chose instead to live with the nearby Crow. Some say the Northern Cheyenne military societies "ran him off." As a result, his son, Fred Last Bull, grew up speaking Crow in Montana.

Needless to say, Last Bull's adolescent bravado in the Big Freezing Moon of 1876 cost his people everything.

So when it came time for the cavalry to gallop across the broken ground of the valley, the Northern Cheyenne weren't ready. Yet some thirty or forty warriors valiantly hurried into the deep ravine and waited for Lieutenant John A. McKinney's troopers to come charging into point-blank range. But here is where I run up against one of those historical inconsistencies in a trifling detail that just nettles the hell out of me!

There's a problem in the campaign literature in regard to what company McKinney led in his fateful charge that cold day.

In his carefully researched biography on Mackenzie, Charles M. Robinson states that McKinney rode at the head of A Troop.

But the confusion deepens. Second Lieutenant Harrison G. Otis, who was there to assist with holding McKinney's men when they were being shot to pieces (and who would later take over command of McKinney's company) is listed on the military rosters as being in K Troop. In my list of characters, I've arbitrarily placed Otis as second in command in McKinney's M.

Next we have another esteemed biography of Mackenzie in which the author, Michael D. Pierce, relates that McKinney did in fact lead M Troop into action that day.

No less than John Bourke himself states for the record that

McKinney led *M* Troop toward its fateful encounter at the deep ravine.

So, like Pierce and author Fred Werner, I'll throw my weight behind the contemporary source, an army officer and adjutant who is accustomed to paying attention to such details.

A most fitting memorial to this fallen officer was the establishment of Fort McKinney in 1877 near the present-day town of Buffalo, Wyoming, after the army abandoned Reno Cantonment.

It never fails. In every battle I have written about in this dramatic and tragic struggle so far, there are Indian and soldier combatants who rise above the rest in the heat of conflict, throwing their bodies into the line of fire, heedless of personal danger as they pull a dead or wounded comrade out of harm's way, or stand over a fallen comrade as the enemy charges in. And such action never fails to bring tears to my eyes, or my heart to my throat.

Time and again in this battle Cheyenne warriors rode out alone to draw soldier fire that would allow women and children to escape up the narrow canyon and on to the breastworks. Men like Yellow Eagle, who escorted the old and the infirm to safety. Men like Little Wolf, who was wounded six times that day guarding the mouth of the escape ravine. Men like Long Jaw, who repeatedly drew bullets to himself so that the shamans would be better protected. The powerful mystics: Black Hairy Dog; Coal Bear; Box Elder.

And then there was Sergeant Thomas M. Forsyth who, although wounded, stayed with the body of his company commander, the dying John A. McKinney. More than any other officer, noncoms such as he were the "bone and the sinew" of the frontier army.

Forsyth's bravery in the face of overwhelming odds and almost sure defeat did not go unnoticed. Five days after the battle Lieutenant Harrison Otis, now in command of M Troop, went to Mackenzie to personally recommend Forsyth (along with Sergeant Frank Murray and Corporal William J. Linn) for honorable mention. Private Thomas Ryan, who of his own volition stood at Forsyth's side over McKinney's bullet-riddled body, was eventually awarded a Certificate of Merit, an honor reserved for privates who had distinguished themselves in combat.

While Mackenzie did approve Forsyth's promotion to regimental sergeant major the following summer, it was not until the end of the great Indian wars that the old, white-headed sergeant finally received what he had been long deserving.

Nearing the end of his career, Forsyth wrote to Captain J. H. Dorst, former adjutant to the deceased Mackenzie, discussing the propriety of his applying for a Certificate of Merit himself at that late date after going a decade and a half without any sort of recognition. Congress had just recently passed a law that would allow noncommissioned officers to receive the award previously reserved for privates. Ever a modest, but highly sentimental, man, the sergeant wrote Dorst:

> I would like to leave my children something besides my name when I answer the last roll-call and anything that could bear testimony to bravery and gallantry on the part of their father in action, would be the best and noblest remembrance, that a soldier's children could have.

It should go without saying that Dorst was extremely moved. So moved that the captain went one step further: he began the laborious process of approving the old sergeant for the Congressional Medal of Honor.

Only months before that day when Forsyth stood ramrod straight on the parade at Fort Leavenworth, Kansas, Sitting Bull had been killed by his own police. Within two weeks of that murder Big Foot's Miniconjou had been slaughtered by the remnants of Custer's Seventh Cavalry at Wounded Knee. Finally, late in 1891, the Medal of Honor was approved for his heroic, selfless action that horribly cold day in the valley of the Red Fork Canyon some fifteen years before.

Sergeant Thomas H. Forsyth stood in the last rays of sunset before the assembled troops and officers, there among his wife Lizzie and what they called their "tribe" of five children, as this nation's highest award for bravery was placed around his neck.

He had offered his life to protect a fellow soldier, and now in the final days of his long army career, Thomas H. Forsyth had finally given his children an intangible inheritance no soldier's pension could ever match.

There are other small glimpses of bravery that history has penciled in the margins from this tragic campaign. The lone Indian scout wounded in the fight, that Shoshone named Anzi, sought to ride like a warrior as long as he could, although suffering greatly (having been shot through the abdomen). He remained in the post hospital at Reno Cantonment for nearly three weeks, then with two companions rode back home to Chief

Washakie's Wind River Reservation—more than two hundred miles away. John Bourke saw Anzi the following year at the time of the Nez Perce war.

"[Anzi] was still living," Bourke wrote, "although by no means, so his friends told me, the man he had been before being so terribly wounded."

A year or so after that, other Shoshone reported that Anzi was shot on a horse-stealing raid.

Captain John M. Hamilton led his troops in to rescue the remnants of McKinney's butchered men. An extremely courageous soldier, he himself would not fall in battle until July 1, 1898, when as the lieutenant colonel of the First Cavalry, a bullet found him as he was leading his men in a charge up the side of San Juan Hill.

In our story we have mentioned that Sergeant James H. McClellan was credited with having killed the warrior named Bull Head in close-quarters combat in that struggle Wessels's company had of it near the head of the deep ravine where McKinney's men were ambushed. In our story of the battle, we also recount the tale of McClellan taking from the body a cartridge belt bearing a buckle engraved with the name Little Wolf. Because Bull Head for some reason had grabbed up Little Wolf's pistol and cartridge belt at the moment of attack, it was long believed by the soldiers that they had indeed killed the Sweet Medicine Chief of the Cheyenne. Just another piece of circumstantial evidence that history allows us to chuckle over after the fact.

As you have learned in our story, there were many items pulled from the lodges that caused a great deal of anger among Mackenzie's troops, just as there had been when souvenirs from the Custer battle dead were found among the lodges of American Horse's Miniconjou after the day-long fight at Slim Buttes, a tale we told you in Volume Ten, *Trumpet on the Land*. But perhaps no better than here in the Cheyenne village was the severity of the Custer disaster brought home as both the number and variety of personal items began to mount on the blankets where the soldiers piled those ghostly relics.

Clearly one of the most interesting of these is the roster book, the sort taken into the field, this one carried by First Sergeant Alexander Brown, G Troop, Seventh Cavalry, commanded by Lieutenant Donald McIntosh, into the valley of the Little Bighorn. The roster was started on 19 April 1876 at which time the troop was leaving Louisiana, ordered back to Fort Abraham Lincoln for the summer campaign.

Its next-to-last entry is quite prophetic:

McEgan lost his carbine on the march while on duty
with pack train, June 24, 1876.

From summer into fall, across the next five months, the
pages in that roster book were filled with pictures by High Bear,
its new owner, a warrior who was himself killed in the Dull Knife
battle. One of the pages shows High Bear lancing a soldier clearly
wearing the chevrons of a sergeant major. In the months and
years to come, the officers who examined the warrior's crude
drawing, and its chronological placement among his career of
those coups depicted within the book, later came to believe High
Bear was the one who killed Sergeant Major Walter Kennedy, the
man who attempted to ride for help once Major Joel H. Elliott's
company was completely surrounded during the Seventh Cavalry's attack on Black Kettle's camp along the Washita in 1868.*
   I am in hopes of receiving permission to reproduce in this
novel a page from Lieutenant Donald McIntosh's memoranda
book so that the reader can see where the lieutenant has listed
the "best shots" in his company, starting with Sergeant Brown
himself. Unlike the Brown roster book, which is in private custody, McIntosh's was for a long time displayed at the little Bighorn Battlefield Visitor Center, complete with its single bullet
hole perforating the entire book. Then some two years ago it was
stolen, its protective case ripped from the wall. Only recently has
the thief admitted that he burned this priceless, dramatic relic.
What a senseless tragedy! At times I would like to believe the
thief merely told federal prosecutors that it was destroyed, and
that it has really been sold to some wealthy collector who, like far
too many others, hasn't the slightest desire to share his or her
precious relics with the rest of us.
   Unlike the stingy, niggardly kind, Lieutenant John Bourke
gave to posterity those grisly trophies he collected in the Cheyenne village. Pictured in his book on Mackenzie's last fight are
the two relics not meant for the faint of heart. First, there is a
beaded necklace from which is suspended at least eight complete
human fingers; between their array are sections of other human
fingers, as well as teeth and iron arrow points. The second necklace appears to be made of trade wool sewn to a long strip of
leather, much in the fashion of a soldier's cartridge belt, con-

*Long Winter Gone, Vol. 1, Son of the Plains Trilogy.

structed in such a way as to be worn around the neck with a narrow thong. But instead of the leather loops to hold the bullets, there are beaded loops holding twenty short fingers, from the fingertips down to the first joint.

These, the amateur ethnologist Bourke reported, in addition to a bag made from a human scrotum, were once the property of High Wolf, whom the lieutenant mistakenly called "the chief medicine man" of the Cheyenne. In 1877 he presented these war trophies to the Smithsonian Institution in Washington, D.C., as specimens of "aboriginal religious art."

While such relics might appear ghoulish and offend white sensibilities, Sherry Smith explains:

> To be sure, the Northern Cheyenne did not see matters the same way. The saddles and canteens branded with Seventh Cavalry insignia, the scalps, the necklace of fingers—all represented Cheyenne victories over constant enemies who had, on other occasions, done the same to them.

It is with no small regret that we now bid Lieutenant John Bourke farewell for some time to come in this continuing narrative. The defeat of Morning Star's Cheyenne marks the end of the *fighting* stage of his military career. But we will see him again in the years and stories yet to come: not as a warrior, but as an observer of the Northern Cheyenne flight from Indian Territory in 1878; again during the Ute War in Colorado, 1879; and finally among the Apache campaigns of the 1880s.

But—sadly—when he rode away from the Red Fork Valley, he had fought his last fight against Indians.

He, among many others both civilian and military with George C. Crook, had been in the field constantly since the previous winter's campaign that began with the Reynolds's fight on, and flight from, the Powder River.* Time and again the privations, the cold, the rain and snow, the hunger, and the interminable marches between battles took their toll on lesser men—breaking the health and sanity of their fragile human bodies and psyches. This is something I cannot stress enough—how these warriors on both sides suffered, even when they weren't wounded . . . but *endured*.

Twice John G. Bourke had narrowly escaped death: once at

Blood Song, Vol. 8, The Plainsmen Series.

the Reynolds's fight, when he barely made the retreat, and again at the Rosebud fight, when he found himself alone during that horse charge and had to wheel and gallop back to safety just ahead of the enemy's bullets—bullets that struck the soldier racing beside him.*

— Perhaps we should slow down our twentieth-century rush and pay heed to such an experienced soldier when, after all that he had been through, John Bourke began in 1877 to question the struggle of which he had been such an integral part, the mindless machinery that had cost so many lives, both red and white.

From here on out, the lieutenant will lay down his carbine and pistol and pick up a far mightier weapon: his pen.

And while we're on the subject of plunder, I often found among the literature much made of the Pawnee scouts' abilities as talented plunderers. Luther North was quick to point out that his battalion of scouts ended up with less from the lodges than did the soldiers themselves. What the Pawnee did ride away with it seems they paid for in one way or another. What about those saddles they left behind at the East Gap that morning just moments before the attack? Perfectly natural for the North brothers to assume that the Sioux and Cheyenne scouts cut the cinches and straps—making the saddles all but unusable—if for no other reason than the Sioux and Cheyenne scouts had followed the Pawnee into the valley that morning.

But doesn't it somehow seem just as reasonable to consider that one or more of Morning Star's warriors took some revenge on that property they happened upon in wandering southeast across the difficult terrain—perhaps searching for an ideal sniping position? No one was ever charged with the crime, nor has any person or band ever claimed responsibility for the act. It simply remains one of those nagging mysteries with which the Indian wars are so rife.

Before we leave the Pawnee, it might be interesting to note that Luther North very nearly missed that dawn charge!

So weary was he by the time they reached the point where Mackenzie had his men wait and form up for the charge, that North ordered one of the Pawnee to switch his saddle over to the strong Sioux pony he had captured in Red Cloud's village. While that was being done, he trudged over to some nearby rocks where he could get out of the cold wind and sat down, immediately falling asleep.

*Reap the Whirlwind, Vol. 9, The Plainsmen Series.

When Mackenzie began to call for the men to mount up, Frank went looking for his brother, sending out some Pawnee, who returned unsuccessful. Lucky for Luther that he awoke himself with the growing clamor and happened to stumble out just in time to leap aboard his Sioux war pony at the very moment his brother Frank ordered the Pawnee to charge—the first horsemen into the valley.

After all the trouble Major Frank North was caused about his own captured Sioux pony by an indignant Three Bears and his Sioux scouts at Fort Fetterman, as well as on the march north—he finally elected to sell the horse to "a white scout who took him to the Shoshoni agency in the Wind River mountains, where he soon won the reputation of being the fastest runner in that section of the country." Unfortunately, history does not tell us if that white scout was Tom Cosgrove or Yancy Eckles.

As had been the fate of the Sioux ponies, the captured Cheyenne ponies were later divided among the scouts, as I've told you, with the remainder being sold at auction. But the loss to the Cheyenne people cannot solely be measured in terms of ponies captured and lodges destroyed. The toll in human life was, as always, hardest to bear. Their casualties were never fully known until the tribe came in to surrender at Red Cloud Agency over the next year, when they ultimately submitted a list of forty warriors killed in the Dull Knife fight, but refused to speak of how many were wounded. Even sadder still, Cheyenne etiquette did not allow them to utter a word of the children and old people who froze to death escaping winter's grip on the Big Horns. Only from what knowledgeable old soldiers and frontiersmen saw of the many gashed arms and legs of those mourning and grieving widows and orphan girls could they tell that the Cheyenne had paid a terrible price in Mackenzie's victory. Especially in the cruel, hand-to-hand fighting at the deep ravine where the members of the tribe said at least twenty Cheyenne fell, the majority of the warrior dead.

What seems most significant to me about this campaign is that rather than merely pitting soldier against Indian—even more than pitting those longtime white allies like Shoshone and Crow and Pawnee against the Sioux and Cheyenne—this battle hurled Sioux and Cheyenne scouts from the Red Cloud Agency against the Cheyenne of Morning Star and Little Wolf. This Powder River Expedition therefore becomes as much an Indian tragedy as it is an Indian-wars tragedy.

Why would some men be induced to scout against their own people?

First of all, we might consider that these were men totally steeped in a warrior tradition. They were trained for battle, taught to regard ponies and rifles as the only legitimate displays of one's manhood. When offered the chance to go riding off to war, even against the members of one's own band, such a venture would likely seem much more preferable to endless days of boredom and confinement on the reservation.

Certainly there were others, especially among the Sioux scouts, who used the army's need for their services as a wedge or lever to extract what they in turn wanted from the white man—in the way of pay, ponies, weapons, and so on.

But in the end, we must remember that while the white man saw the Sioux as Sioux, and the Cheyenne as Cheyenne, there were not only separate bands among each tribe, but separate kin-based clans and extended-family groupings as well. Loyalties went first to those family clans rather than some loose confederation of the *Ohmeseheso*, or the Oglalla, or the Hunkpapa. In addition, the record shows that some of the army scouts believed they were doing what they considered to be right by their people in going to help the soldiers drive their nomadic cousins back to their reservations. Such a life would be better for them in the end, they rationalized, better than being chased and harried, shot and impoverished, after all.

So the presence of those Sioux and Cheyenne scouts was vital not only to demoralize the Morning Star warriors, but the scouts had already played an important role in knowing how and where to locate the village. They were the ones who stayed behind among the rocks while the rest scampered down the backtrail to inform Mackenzie to hurry up. They were the ones who made possible the long-night march through the rugged mountain terrain. And they were the ones who played a prominent role in the day's fighting: showing themselves to the Morning Star Cheyenne, thereby exacting a demoralizing effect hour after hour as the destruction of the village began.

For generations afterward there was bad blood between many of the Sioux and Cheyenne groups. Like Wooden Leg, many of the Cheyenne were highly critical of those who would come with the soldiers "to kill their friends." For years many of the tribe did not allow stories to be told by those who had served as scouts for Crook and Mackenzie. Wooden Leg had himself lost a brother in the battle, and for years he often wondered if one of the Cheyenne scouts who had come with the *ve-ho-e* had killed him.

Forgiveness would come hard. Very, very hard.

Without a doubt, that winter campaign signaled the end of the great Sioux-Cheyenne coalition that had crushed Custer, twice held Crook at bay, and given Phil Sheridan one hell of an ulcer. No more would the warrior bands so readily trust one another.

The first of the Cheyenne limped into the Red Cloud Agency by January 1877. Dull Knife himself would surrender in April of that year, saying to Mackenzie, "You are the one I was afraid of when you came here [to Camp Robinson] last summer."

So it was that years later Cyrus Townsend Brady made a glaring mistake in his story of the battle in *Indian Fights and Fighters* when he wrote: "Dull Knife, their leader, was found in the village with half a dozen bullets in him. He had fought gallantly in the open until he died."

After they were beaten by the soldiers, after suffering the loss of everything they owned, but especially after being rebuffed by no less than Crazy Horse himself, some of the *Ohmeseheso* decided to go into the reservation. Other small bands began to send in runners to the agency, saying they would come in when they were able to—impoverished of weapons and horses, lodges, and clothing—so poor were they. And many of those runners mentioned the inhospitable reception they got from the Crazy Horse people, sending word to the reservation agents that they would be willing to go out with the army and hunt down the Oglalla leader.

In fact, more than one of the Northern Cheyenne war chiefs specifically stated as a condition of his surrender that he be "allowed to send his warriors with the white soldiers to fight Crazy Horse."

To this day, this is a continuing controversy between the former allies once considered so close as to be "cousins." While the Crazy Horse faction among the Oglalla Lakota deny the war chief's rejection of the Morning Star people at worst, and play it down as inconsequential at best—the Northern Cheyenne still harbor a resentment against the man, a resentment against the Lakota band who refused them help in that awful winter.

Once Crazy Horse turned his back on the *Ohmeseheso*, there was no other hope for them. No other choice for many a man but to take his family in to be fed at the agency, and there to offer his services to the army desperately seeking to capture the elusive Oglalla war chief.

Unlike their former allies, the Northern Arapaho were able to establish a good relationship with their longtime enemies—the Shoshone. Beginning from that council Crook held with his allies at Reno Cantonment in the days prior to the Dull Knife Battle, the Arapaho fostered good relations with the Shoshone, who eventually invited the Arapaho to settle on the Wind River Reservation—thereby avoiding exile to Indian Territory—what would be the final humiliation and punishment for the Northern Cheyenne ... but that is another story for us to tell through the eyes of Seamus Donegan in the years to come.

In those weeks leading up to the battle, we see the beginning of the erosion of those traditional powers of the Cheyenne chiefs. Last Bull's success in blunting the orders of Old-Man Chiefs first to pick up and flee, then to build defensive breastworks, would be paid out in a heavy cost for many years to come. At the beginning of the reservation period more and more of the Cheyenne saw that nothing remained for them in practicing their traditional ways, so adopted the white culture. As well, Indian Bureau officials were quick to play upon this weakening of the traditional Cheyenne way of governing, acerbating the intratribal, intrasocietal frictions for their own benefit and to keep matters on the "civilizing pathway."

Through the next few winters there were some traditionalists among the *Ohmeseheso* who watched from the wings and found good reason to believe in the old ways.

You will recall how Black Hairy Dog performed his ritual curse against the soldiers and those scouts who led the *ve-ho-e* against the Morning Star village. Even Old Crow, one of those scouts, recognized the gravity of what was going on and went to offer cartridges to the warriors and priests in the rocks.

"I must fight against you, but I am leaving a lot of ammunition on this hill," he shouted to the priest, hoping to mollify the spirits.

Despite finding the bullets where Old Crow said he would leave them, for many years afterward the Cheyenne scorned their chief, Old Crow—openly declaring that he had betrayed his own.

In his research while writing *Sweet Medicine*, Father Peter Powell states, "Many of the Old Ones, alive during the 1950's and 1960's, declared that all the Cheyennes who scouted for the soldiers died not long after this fighting [at the Dull Knife Battle]. They were killed by the power of *Maahotse*, when the Sacred Arrow points were turned against them."

And tribal historian John Stands in Timber agrees in his

book compiled by Margot Liberty, saying that all of Mackenzie's Cheyenne scouts were dead by 1885 because the Sacred Arrows were turned against them that day in the Red Fork valley.

The Sacred Buffalo Hat remains not only a spiritual object, but a pawn in the struggles between warring factions in the Northern Cheyenne here on their Montana reservation. As recently as November 11, 1994, the traditionalists "kidnapped" the Hat from its Sacred Lodge near Lame Deer. For nearly three months the lines were clearly drawn between those who are traditional and those who are more willing to accommodate white culture on the reservation. And then, even after Cheyenne U.S. Senator Ben Nighthorse Campbell came west to mediate unsuccessfully, the two sides agreed at least to talk.

Eventually, as one would turn over a hostage, the Sacred Hat Bundle was peacefully turned over to the Sun Dance Priest, Francis Kills Night, although Bureau of Indian Affairs police were on hand in the event matters got out of hand. It was agreed that the tribe's traditional warrior societies would now discuss and decide upon who would become the new Keeper of the Hat. They stated it was far better to solve their religious differences among themselves than allow the interference of outside forces including the Indian Bureau and the FBI.

So it was that at three minutes till noon on Friday, January 27, 1995—Sun Dance Priest Kills Night trudged through the mud and a misting rain with the sacred bundle on his back. He entered its Sacred Lodge. *Esevone* had come home to her people.

On the Northern Cheyenne Reservation there are three people I have called upon to help in explaining culture and religion to this *ve-ho-e* writer, hoping that I would get it right, praying I would capture the spirit of those people, the true spirit of that time. First of all, I want to thank Josephine Sootkis and her daughter Ruby, of the Dull Knife Memorial College, both of whom are direct descendants of Morning Star. And I appreciate the help of Ted Rising Sun, another direct descendant of the chief known to the white man as Dull Knife. Their stories and heartfelt scholarship have proved invaluable to me in expressing the horror of this tragic conflict. Ruby herself is busy at work on a screenplay dealing with the 1879 outbreak of the Dull Knife forces from Fort Robinson. In addition, Bill Tall Bull, tribal historian, always makes himself available to answer questions, however minute, no matter how ignorant those questions may sound coming from the mouth of a white man.

Disappointed and cold, Crook and Mackenzie sat on the

banks of the Belle Fourche as long as they could in that December. Then on the twentieth they received a terse telegram from Phil Sheridan with the information that their transportation bill for the campaign was sixty thousand dollars per month, while the allowance was a mere twenty-eight thousand dollars. "Those few words," John Bourke noted in his diary, "mean that this campaign must terminate speedily."

The commanders were forced at last to turn the expedition back to Fort Fetterman, where within weeks the campaign was disbanded.

Headquarters Powder River
Expedition
Cheyenne, W.T., January 8, 1877

General Orders
No. 10

The Brigadier General Commanding announces the close of the Powder River Expedition, and avails himself of the opportunity to thank the officers and men composing it, for the ability, courage, endurance and zeal exhibited by them during its progress.

With the mercury indicating such extreme degrees of cold as to make life well nigh unbearable, even when surrounded by the comforts of civilization, you have endured, with uncomplaining fortitude, the rigors of the weather from which you had less to protect you than an Indian is usually provided with.

The disintegration of many of the hostile bands of savages against whom you have been operating attests the success of the brilliant fight made by the Cavalry with the Cheyennes on the North Fork, and your toilsome marches along the Powder River and Belle Fourche.

It is a matter for solemn regret that you have to mourn the loss of the distinguished and brilliant young Cavalry officer, First Lieutenant John A. McKinney, 4th Cavalry, and the gallant enlisted men who fell with him in the lonely gorges of the Big Horn Mountains ...

By Command of Brigadier-General Crook
(signed) John G. Bourke

As Crook disbanded the expedition, he ordered Mackenzie's Fourth Cavalry back to Camp Robinson. Not only were many of the animals broken down and almost out of forage in those final weeks, but the endless and severe cold, coupled with that intensely contested battle and their brutal march to the Belle Fourche, had all taken its toll on not just the soldiers but Crook's officer corps as well.

Most dramatic was the deteriorating mental condition of Ranald Mackenzie himself.

In those weeks leading up to the battle and the days that followed, the colonel's extreme sensitivity to the most minor slight was exhibited with increasing degrees of paranoia. To the soldiers who had served under him for some time, it seemed they were now serving under a commander who was becoming inconsistent at best, capricious at worst. But in the emotional wake following the Dull Knife Battle, Mackenzie's fellow officers and his troopers simply believed their leader was suffering from nothing more than self-doubts about his actions during the fight.

Most of those closest to Mackenzie at that time, including Crook and Dodge, merely believed the colonel's mental state was a result of Mackenzie's so severely chastising himself for not bringing the battle to a more concrete conclusion, for not pursuing the Cheyenne into the mountains and capturing (if not killing) more of the enemy. Clearly, a supreme opportunity had been laid in his lap, so that over the days following the battle he criticized himself more and more for not fully seizing that opportunity.

There existed such an intense rivalry among the officers serving the frontier army—especially among those few colonels who had their gaze firmly set on the stars: *general's* stars. In fact, one of those very human pieces to the puzzle that is the Mackenzie legend has it that one night in bivouac, while campaigning against the Kwahadi Comanche on the Staked Plain of the Texas-panhandle country, the colonel walked some distance from his campfire and stood staring up at the brilliant, crystal-clear night sky dusted with a resplendent display of heaven's brightest lights twinkling overhead.

The legend goes on to tell us that Mackenzie's adjutant came up in the dark to stand beside his commander, then said, "Sir, there's someone between you and that star."

"Whatever do you mean?" Mackenzie turned to ask.

"His name is Miles, sir."

Indeed, from the days of that campaign on the southern plains when Miles and his Fifth Infantry were whittling away at the Indians every bit as effectively as was Mackenzie and his Fourth Cavalry—it had become clear to everyone in the army that the three rising stars were Custer, Miles, and Mackenzie. As in any endeavor when the reward is so rich, so great as a general's star, the feelings of competition had to be extremely keen ... the chance for messing up and making a mistake so precarious.

Perhaps his self-doubts about how he could have done better in the Dull Knife fight began to aggravate what had heretofore been nothing but an imbalanced mental state.

Yet here I stand more than a century later, with the benefit of twenty-twenty hindsight knowing what despair Mackenzie was to exhibit in the months and years left him, knowing that his would be a premature death exacerbated by the severe depression he was wallowing in, and from which he could not save himself.

While he was on the return trip to Camp Robinson, Mackenzie received orders to report to Washington, where he was to place himself under no less than the secretary of war. By that time back east the disputed returns from three southern states meant that the outcome of the presidential election was still in question—a situation that with every day was raising more and more passion among the parties on both sides. Many of the more extreme Democrats were threatening to raise their own private armies to force the seating of their candidate, Tilden.

Determined to preserve order, a worried President Grant began to call in troops from the western frontier in the event of a revolt or civil insurrection. He personally selected Ranald Mackenzie to take command of those troops who would be protecting Washington City itself—a remarkable testament of faith in the abilities of this commander who continued to suffer so many self-doubts.

Over the years many of you have written to say just how much you appreciate having me list a bibliography for you to use when you go in search of further sources on each particular campaign. So for those of you who want to do some more digging into Crook's and Mackenzie's Powder River Campaign and the Dull Knife Battle, you've got some winter reading to do:

Across the Continent with the Fifth Cavalry, by George F. Price.

"A Day With the 'Fighting Cheyennes': Stirring Scenes in the Old Northwest, Recalled for Motor Tourists," *Motor Travel Magazine* (December 1930, January 1931, February 1931).

Bad Hand—A Biography of General Randal S. Mackenzie, by Charles M. Robinson III.

Bad Hand: The Military Career of Ranald Slidell Mackenzie, 1871–1889, by Lessing H. Noel, Jr. (Ph.D. dissertation), Department of History, University of New Mexico, 1962.

Battles and Skirmishes of the Great Sioux War, 1876–1877—The Military View, edited by Jerome A. Greene.

Bury My Heart at Wounded Knee—An Indian History of the American West, by Dee Brown.

By Cheyenne Campfires, by George Bird Grinnell.

Campaigning with Crook and Stories of Army Life, by Charles King.

"Campaigning with the 5th Cavalry: Private James B. Frew's Diary and Letters from the Great Sioux War of 1876," by Paul L. Hedren. *Nebraska History* 65 (Winter 1984).

Campaigning with King—Charles King, Chronicler of the Old Army, edited by Paul L. Hedren.

Centennial Campaign—The Sioux War of 1876, by John S. Gray.

Cheyenne (Wyoming) *Daily Leader* (Aug., Oct., Nov., Dec., 1876).

Cheyenne Memories, by John Stands in Timber and Margot Liberty.

Chronological List of Engagements Between the Regular Army of the United States and Various Tribes of Hostile Indians Which Occurred During the Years 1790 to 1898, Inclusive, by George W. Webb.

Crazy Horse and Custer—The Parallel Lives of Two American Warriors, by Stephen E. Ambrose.

Crazy Horse—The Strange Man of the Oglalas, by Mari Sandoz.

Crimsoned Prairie—The Wars Between the United States and the

Plains Indians During the Winning of the West, by S. L. A. Marshall, Brigadier General (Ret.).

"The Death of Lt. McKinney in the Dull Knife Fight," by L. A. LaGarde (Address at the Order of the Indian Wars Assembly, March 6, 1915).

Death on the Prairie—The Thirty Years Struggle for the Western Plains, by Paul I. Wellman.

Death Song—The Last of the Indian Wars, by John Edward Weems.

The Dull Knife Battle—"Doomsday for the Northern Cheyennes," by Fred H. Werner.

"The Dull Knife Symposium," presented by the Fort Phil Kearny/ Bozeman Trail Association, funded by the Wyoming Council for the Humanities—August 1989 (papers delivered by John D. McDermott, moderator; Margot P. Liberty; Jerome A. Greene; Ted Risingsun; Sherry L. Smith; and Douglas C. McChristian).

The Fighting Cheyennes, by George Bird Grinnell.

The Fighting Norths and Pawnee Scouts, by Robert Bruce.

"Fighting the Cheyennes: A Hot Little Battle on the Red Fork of the Powder River, Nov. 23, 1876, with Renegades," by S. Millison, *National Tribune*, May 17, 1928.

Following the Indian Wars: The Story of the Newspaper Correspondents Among the Indian Campaigners, by Oliver Knight.

Fort Laramie—"Visions of a Grand Post," by Robert A. Murray.

Fort Robinson—Outpost on the Plains, by Roger T. Grange, Jr.

Forty Miles a Day on Beans and Hay—The Enlisted Soldier Fighting the Indian Wars, by Don Rickey, Jr.

Frank Grouard, Army Scout, edited by Margaret Brock Hanson.

Frontier Regulars—The United States Army and the Indian, 1866–1891, by Robert M. Utley.

The Frontier Trail, by Colonel Homer W. Wheeler (Ret.).

General George Crook—His Autobiography, edited by Martin F. Schmitt.

"General Philip Sheridan's Legacy: The Sioux Pony Campaign of 1876," by Richmond L. Clow. *Nebraska History* 57 (Winter 1976).

"Getting Into Uniform: Northern Cheyenne Scouts in the United States Army, 1876–81," by Karen Easton (master's thesis, University of Wyoming), 1985.

"Historical Address of Brig. Gen'l. W. C. Brown, U.S. Army Retired" (Read at Unveiling of Monument to Lieut. Frank D. Baldwin Near Olanda, Montana; June, 11, 1932), *Winners of the West*, August 30, 1932.

Indian-Fighting Army, by Fairfax Downey.

Indian Fights and Fighters, by Cyrus Townsend Brady.

"The Indian Situation: Mackenzie's Fight with the Cheyennes," *Army Navy Journal*, December 19, 1876.

Indian Wars, by Robert M. Utley and Wilcomb E. Washburn.

The Indian Wars of the West, by Paul I. Wellman.

"The Journals of James S. McClellan, 1st Sgt., Company H., 3rd Cavalry," edited by Thomas R. Buecker, *Annals of Wyoming* 57 (Spring 1985).

The Lance and the Shield—The Life and Times of Sitting Bull, by Robert M. Utley.

Life and Adventures of Frank Grouard, by Joe DeBarthe.

Life and Manners in the Frontier Army, by Oliver Knight.

"Mackenzie Against Dull Knife: Breaking the Northern Cheyennes in 1876," by Lessing H. Nohl. In *Probing the American West: Papers from the Santa Fe Conference*, edited by K. Ross Toole, et al.

Mackenzie's Last Fight with the Cheyennes: A Winter Campaign in Wyoming and Montana, by Captain John G. Bourke.

Man of the Plains—Recollections of Luther North, 1856–1882, edited by Donald F. Danker.

Military Posts in the Powder River Country of Wyoming, 1865–1894, by Robert A. Murray.

Military Posts of Wyoming, by Robert A. Murray.

The Most Promising Young Officer—A Life of Ranald Slidell Mackenzie, by Michael D. Pierce.

Motor Travel Magazine, articles by Lieutenant John G. Bourke, May 1930, July 1930, August 1930.

"Mounted Riflemen: The Real Role of the Cavalry in the Indian Wars," by James S. Hutchins. In *Probing the American West: Papers from the Sante Fe Conference,* edited by K. Ross Toole, et al.

Nelson A. Miles—A Documentary Biography of His Military Career, 1861–1903, edited by Brian C. Pohanka.

Nelson A. Miles and The Twilight of the Frontier Army, by Robert Wooster.

On the Border with Crook, by John G. Bourke.

Paper Medicine Man—John Gregory Bourke and His American West, by Joseph C. Porter.

"Pawnee Trails and Trailers," by Captain Luther H. North, *Motor Travel Magazine,* March 1929, April 1929, May 1929, June 1929, July 1929, August 1929, September 1929, October 1929, December 1929, January 1930, February 1930, March 1930, June 1930, July 1930, May 1931, June 1931, August 1931.

People of the Sacred Mountain: A History of the Northern Cheyenne Chiefs and Warrior Societies, 1830–1879, by Peter J. Powell.

Personal Diary, by John G. Bourke, on microfilm, in possession of the Denver Public Library, Western History Section.

Personal Recollections of General Nelson A. Miles, by Nelson A. Miles.

The Plainsmen of the Yellowstone—A History of the Yellowstone Basin, by Mark H. Brown.

Sagebrush Soldier, by Sherry L. Smith.

The Shoshonis—Sentinels of the Rockies, by Virginia Cole Trenholm and Maurine Carley.

"Sitting Bull Strikes the Glendive Supply Trains," *Westerners Brand Book,* (Chicago) Vol. 28, (June, 1971).

Soldiers West—Biographies from the Military Frontier, edited by Paul Andrew Hutton.

Son of the Morning Star, by Evan S. Connell.

Spotted Tail's Folk—A History of the Brule Sioux, by George E. Hyde.

Sweet Medicine: The Continuing Role of the Sacred Arrows, the Sun Dance, and the Sacred Buffalo Hat in Northern Cheyenne History, by Peter J. Powell.

Two Great Scouts and Their Pawnee Battalion—The Experiences of Frank J. North and Luther H. North, by George Bird Grinnell.

The View from Officers' Row—Army Perceptions of Western Indians, by Sherry L. Smith.

Warpath—The True Story of the Fighting Sioux (The Biography of White Bull), by Stanley Vestal.

Warpath and Council Fire—The Plains Indians' Struggle for Survival in War and in Diplomacy, 1851–1891, by Stanley Vestal.

War-Path and Bivouac—The Big Horn and Yellowstone Expedition, by John F. Finerty.

William Jackson, Indian Scout, by James Willard Schultz.

Wolves for the Blue Soldiers—Indian Scouts and Auxiliaries with the United States Army, 1860–1890, by Thomas W. Dunlay.

Wooden Leg—A Warrior Who Fought Custer, interpreted by Thomas B. Marquis.

Yellowstone Command—Colonel Nelson A. Miles and the Great Sioux War, 1876–1877, by Jerome A. Greene.

The Dull Knife Battlefield exists today much as it did over a hundred years ago—with the exception of the simple stone marker erected near the village site, the single dirt road that hugs the foot of Mackenzie Mountain, and the fact that in the last century the leafy cottonwoods have taken hold along the stream bottom and down in the bogs once infested with ten-foot-high willow at the time soldiers and warriors clashed here.

Only a year after the fight Harmon Fraker came in to homestead the valley. The mountain that forms the north rim of the site is named Fraker Mountain for that first settler. Then in

1901 a rancher by the name of Charles N. Graves came to Wyoming out of Nebraska, gaining title to the valley five years later. Through the twenties and into the thirties, both he and his son, Frank O. Graves, witnessed numerous visits to the battle site by many of the old soldiers and aging Indians who had taken part in the tragic struggle. Next to take over operations was Norris Graves, and now his son and daughter-in-law, Ken and Cheri, run cattle and sheep in that ruggedly secluded corner of the Big Horns.

This is the famous "Hole in the Wall" country of Butch Cassidy and the Sundance Kid.

Climbing close to five thousand feet above sea level, you reach the valley by a long, twisting stretch of dirt road that winds through some stunning blood-red mountains dotted with one variety or another of emerald evergreen. As you draw closer, the walls begin to rise dramatically to a height of a thousand feet or more above you. And then, before you're really prepared, you are suddenly thrust around a bend and down the slope into the valley itself, which measures some two miles long and from a quarter of a mile to about a mile wide in places.

The Morning Star camp was pitched for the most part along some flat ground on the south bank of a gentle, trickling stream running from west to east all year long because it was fed by a warm spring that prevented the stream from freezing (a fact heretofore neglected by the historians). Here, where the village stood, the valley is its widest. Downstream to the east, where Mackenzie's cavalry burst through the gap, the valley is at its most narrow.

This is truly a dramatically spectacular symbol of some of God's finest sculpturin's!

And there was no finer way to see such sculpturin's than on horseback, accompanied by the two most knowledgeable guides I could have wanted. Ken Graves saddled us up just before sunrise on this anniversary date as I trudged over to the corral and got to know his part-time ranch hand, Mike Freidel—a historian in his own right and athletic coach over at the University of South Dakota in Vermillion. Mike's been coming over to the place for better than fifteen years now, and—believe me—Ken and Mike know every square foot of that valley, from far out of the east gap where the cavalry came in, formed up, and began their charge, to the breastworks and the narrow escape canyon at the other end of the valley, and on up the mountainsides where the Cheyenne fled into the winter night toward Fraker Pass.

More important, for all those years the two of them have traveled the ground by horseback, in and out of that maze of rocky walls, trackless ravines, and well-used game trails, coming to know exactly where Mackenzie's scouts led the soldiers into the valley, just where Cosgrove and Schuyler led their Shoshone single file up the steep and precarious mountain path to reach the top of what is today called Mackenzie Mountain. So if I was forced to choose in a disagreement between an academic historian and these rancher-horsemen on how an army was going to march into the east gap and on into the valley, you can bet your last twenty-dollar gold piece I'd lay everything I had on Ken Graves and Mike Freidel showing me just where Mackenzie's horse planted its hooves back in 1876.

And those fellas did just that. They led me all the way east to that flat area the Sioux scouts called the race ground, where Mackenzie stopped his scouts and troopers and sent ahead his small band of spies while they listened to the Cheyenne drum echo down the canyon. From there we rode into the valley as the charging cavalry would have, picking our way across the narrow feeder creeks and down into the willow bogs, just as those cavalrymen would have done. Finally onto the flat where we hugged the long, low plateau at the base of Fraker Mountain until we stopped, getting our first magnificent view of the valley itself.

Just as Mackenzie would have seen his first view. The village is arrayed on our left in a crude horseshoe. Ahead of us, as the Shoshone open fire and the Pawnee hurl themselves against the fringe of lodges, the enemy is already bolting out of the upper end of the village, some of the warriors sprinting into a deep ravine—a large band of them hurrying across the open ground to seize some of their ponies before the herd can be captured.

These are the ponies Mackenzie does not want to lose.

"Would you like to ride it the way McKinney's men charged that morning?" Ken asked.

Already my eyes were misting, and I had one hell of a lump in my throat. "You damn bet I would!" I croaked.

Without another word, those two horsemen suddenly spurred themselves away, leaving room between them for me as we rolled those three eager horses into a full, windblown gallop that whipped the cold breeze across my cheeks, the tears from my eyes. On and on over the gently rolling ground we raced, heading for the knoll where the Cheyenne riflemen were setting up shop. Then suddenly—

Ken and Mike reined up just ahead of me, shouting for me to do the same. If I hadn't stopped when I had, your author would have been faced with choosing to jump his horse across an impossibly wide ravine, or slam into the far side, where I would have eaten a few yards of the Wyoming landscape for breakfast.

I came to see firsthand how Lieutenant John A. McKinney and the men of his M Troop failed to see the ravine until they were all but on top of it—at the moment the Cheyenne warriors rose out of the bowels of the earth like screaming demons and fired point-blank into those blue ranks.

Believe me, the more I travel these battlefields, I become all the more a believer that there is no substitute for being *there*. Going to the place myself, so that I can factually, accurately translate the countryside, the very *feel* of a piece of sacred ground like this for the millions of readers who will never get a chance to be there themselves.

Ken and Mike showed it all to me from horseback, around the Red Butte behind which the surgeons set up their field hospital and near which private Baird was buried by the willows in an unmarked, unknown grave. We rode halfway up the precipitous slope of the rocky outcrop Mackenzie used as his command post during the hottest of the fighting. With them I circled around toward the twin buttes, which stood near the final northernmost end of the soldier line. Then we climbed the horses up the front of the ridge where the sharpshooters sat in the snow, the very top of which was occupied by the women and others singing the strong-heart songs to their warriors.

What a thrill it was for me to dismount, moving carefully among the piles of rocks frozen hands placed one on top of another more than a century ago! To stand there where the *Ohmeseheso* stood, watching their greatness spiral into the cold blue sky overhead with the oily black curl of smoke rising from every burning lodge. Then finally to mount up and ride on to the far upper end of the valley, there to get a feel of the steepness of the slope as the survivors scurried hand and foot, scrambling ever higher toward Fraker Pass, hoping for safety from the soldiers.

By the time we returned to the corrals near the ranch house, the three of us had been out in the saddle for more than five and a half hours. Unlike those two saddle-hardened veterans, this ol' boy doesn't get much of a chance to do that kind of *real* riding: almost straight up or straight down in places! So you better believe that the following day, my ol' bones were cussing me but good!

We had lunch with Cheri and the Graves daughters, then spent part of the afternoon sharing more stories of that battle, tales of Custer and the Indian wars in general, and with me just wanting to get a feel for what winter was like in that beautiful, silent valley. For, you see, the only problem with our ride this anniversary day was that I looked out of the Graves's ranch-house window, but I didn't see any snow.

That afternoon on the way back to Buffalo, Wyoming for the night, the local radio weatherman said there was a major winter storm expected late tomorrow. Ain't that the luck? But it's something I've come to expect in this country. Here I came down on the battle's anniversary: sunny, almost shirtsleeve weather . . . and tomorrow there's going to be at least a fifty-degree drop in the temperature, and a major amount of snow blowing in! Just what the old frontiersmen came to know about this country—you better be prepared for anything, because you're bound to get it in the way of fickle weather.

In the months to follow, Ken and Cheri Graves, as well as Mike Freidel, kindly answered my numerous questions, all three of them putting up with me until I could finally send them both big "overnight" packages filled with the appropriate chapters on the battle—asking for their corrections and suggestions. I can't thank them enough for allowing me to impose upon them at a particularly busy time of the year as I finish this afterword March is, after all, recruiting season for Mike, and it's when the lambs and calves are dropping for Ken and Cheri.

I especially want to express my gratitude to Mike Freidel for his repeated work with me on the battlefield map. From those first days of the four of us going over the maps done for previous works on the Dull Knife fight—when Ken, Cheri, and Mike pointed out errors and discrepancies—to coming up with our own crude pencil sketches, and finally to working over a dining-room-table-sized USGS topographic map . . . all that labor just so we could give the reader as much a feeling of being right there as we could. Ken and Cheri and Mike all had a big hand in helping me make this battle come to life for you.

Long will I be in their debt.

Being on private land, where this fourth generation of a ranching family works at making a living the same way as those who came here in the years immediately following the battle, I get an immense amount of pride just from knowing folks like these. Hardworking, straight-talking, God-fearing, and life-loving people who possess what all too few today don't—a genuine love for the land, and a love for what that land has always meant to those who passed this way to share in God's bounty.

So again to Ken, Cheri, and Mike, I say thanks for welcoming me into your hearts and your homes, and for teaching me all that I needed to know so I could write the book that would tell not only an accurate story, but the *authentic* story of what happened here among these tall red mountains that terribly cold day in hell, 25 November, 1876.

> TERRY C. JOHNSTON
> *Dull Knife Battlefield*
> *Red Fork Ranch, Wyoming*
> *25 November 1994*

ABOUT THE AUTHOR

TERRY C. JOHNSTON was born in 1947 on the plains of Kansas, and has lived all his life in the American West. His first novel, *Carry the Wind*, won the Medicine Pipe Bearer's Award from the Western Writers of America, and his subsequent books have appeared on bestseller lists throughout the country. He lives and writes in Big Sky country near Billings, Montana. For two weeks every summer, the author takes readers on his very own "Terry C. Johnston's West: A Novelist's Journey into the Indian Wars"—a HistoryAmerica tour to the famous battlesites and landmarks of the historical West. All those desiring information on taking part in the author's summer tours can write to him at:

TERRY C. JOHNSTON
P. O. Box 50594
Billings, MT 59105

SON OF THE PLAINS

TERRY C. JOHNSTON

Few names of the American frontier resonate like that of George Armstrong Custer, whose fiery temperament and grand vision led him to triumph and tragedy. Now bestselling chronicler Terry C. Johnston brings to life the Custer legacy as never before in this masterful trilogy.

Long Winter Gone ___28621-8 $5.99/$6.99 in Canada

In 1868, George Custer captured a raven haired firebrand of only seventeen. He risked his reputation and career for her—for in love, as on any other battlefield, Custer would never know retreat.

Seize the Sky ___28910-1 $6.50/$8.99 in Canada

What should have been Custer's greatest triumph, a march on the Sioux in June 1876, became an utterly devastating defeat that would ring through the ages.

Whisper of the Wolf ___29179-3 $6.50/$8.99 in Canada

Yellow Bird, George Custer's son, grew to manhood with the Cheyennes, bound to his father by their warrior's spirit, preparing to fight for his home, his life, and his own son.

*Don't miss any of Terry C. Johnston's thrilling novels
of the American frontier*

___29974-3	**Reap the Whirlwind**	$6.50/$8.50 in Canada
___56240-1	**Cry of the Hawk**	$5.99/$6.99 in Canada
___56770-5	**Winter Rain**	$6.50/$8.99 in Canada
___57257-1	**Dream Catcher**	$5.99/$7.99 in Canada
___29975-1	**Trumpet on the Land**	$6.50/$8.50 in Canada
___09071-2	**Dance on the Wind**	$21.95/$29.95 in Canada

Ask for these books at your local bookstore or use this page to order.

Please send me the books I have checked above. I am enclosing $_____ (add $2.50 to cover postage and handling). Send check or money order, no cash or C.O.D.'s, please.

Name _____

Address _____

City/State/Zip _____

Send order to: Bantam Books, Dept. TJ, 2451 S. Wolf Rd., Des Plaines, IL 60018
Allow four to six weeks for delivery.
Prices and availability subject to change without notice. TJ 1/96

Don't miss **TERRY C. JOHNSTON**'s award-winning saga
of the making of a nation, a drama of blood and courage
played out in the great American West.

CARRY THE WIND

Pure luck brought young Josiah Paddock, on the run from his past,
into the old trapper's camp high up in the Rockies. But it was skill with
a gun and a knife that kept them both alive as they rode deep into the
majestic land of Blackfeet and Crow.

_____ 25572-X $6.50/$8.99 in Canada

BORDERLORDS

A misunderstanding over a beautiful Crow woman drives Josiah
Paddock and Ol' Scratch apart, sending Scratch into the unforgiving
wilderness on a lonely, dangerous quest. But they were destined to meet
again and to reaffirm a bond deeper than blood.

_____ 26224-6 $6.50/$8.99

ONE-EYED DREAM

Pursued by a vengeful Arapaho raiding party, Scratch and Josiah lead
their small band on a trail of blood all the way to St. Louis. Scratch
and Josiah will defy the wilderness to bury the past and settle a
ten-year-old score.

_____ 28139-9 $6.50/$8.99